From the Pages of
Paradise Lost

Of man's first disobedience, and the fruit
Of that forbidden tree, whose mortal taste
Brought death into the world, and all our woe,
With loss of Eden, till one greater Man
Restore us, and regain the blissful seat,
Sing heavenly Muse.
(p. 10)

      What in me is dark,
Illumine; what is low, raise and support!
That to the height of this great argument
I may assert eternal Providence,
And justify the ways of God to men.
(p. 11)

Th'infernal serpent, he it was, whose guile
Stirr'd up with envy and revenge, deceiv'd
The mother of mankind.
(p. 11)

The mind is its own place, and in itself
Can make a heaven of hell, a hell of heaven.
(p. 19)

      Who overcomes
By force, hath overcome but half his foe.
(p. 32)

From morn
To noon he fell, from noon to dewy eve,
A summer's day; and with the setting sun
Dropp'd from the zenith like a falling star.
(p. 36)

Long is the way
And hard, that out of hell leads up to light.
(p. 54)

So farewell hope, and with hope farewell fear,
Farewell remorse: all good to me is lost;
Evil be thou my good.
(p. 110)

What if earth
Be but the shadow of heaven, and things therein,
Each to other like, more than on earth is thought?
(pp. 164–165)

Her rash hand in evil hour
Forth reaching to the fruit, she pluck'd, she ate;
Earth felt the wound, and Nature from her seat,
Sighing through all her works, gave signs of woe
That all was lost.
(p. 290)

The world was all before them, where to choose
Their place of rest, and Providence their guide.
They, hand in hand, with wand'ring steps and slow
Through Eden took their solitary way.
(p. 403)

PARADISE LOST
JOHN MILTON

EDITED WITH AN INTRODUCTION AND NOTES
by David Hawkes

ENGRAVINGS
by William Blake

George Stade
Consulting Editorial Director

BARNES & NOBLE CLASSICS
NEW YORK

℔

BARNES & NOBLE CLASSICS
NEW YORK

Published by Barnes & Noble Books
122 Fifth Avenue
New York, NY 10011

www.barnesandnoble.com/classics

Paradise Lost was first published in ten books in 1667. The present text is based on the second edition (1674), which was split into twelve books.

Published in 2004 by Barnes & Noble Classics with new Introduction, Notes, Biography, Chronology, Appendix, Comments & Questions, and For Further Reading.

Paradise Lost
ISBN-13: 978-1-59308-095-2
ISBN-10: 1-59308-095-6
LC Control Number 2004101081

Produced and published in conjunction with:
Fine Creative Media, Inc.
322 Eighth Avenue
New York, NY 10001

Michael J. Fine, President and Publisher

Printed in the United States of America
QM
12 14 16 18 20 19 17 15 13

John Milton

John Milton was born in London on December 9, 1608, to John and Sara Milton. The elder Milton was a well-to-do scrivener—a profession that combined the functions of solicitor, public notary, and moneylender—and was able to provide his son with a first-rate education and financial independence. Milton was educated at home and at St. Paul's School, then entered Christ's College, Cambridge. He quickly earned the respect of his fellow students and tutors, and completed a Master of Arts degree in 1632; then, living with his father outside London, he undertook an intense six-year reading program in history, philosophy, and literature. In 1638 and 1639 Milton made the Grand Tour of Europe, where he and his early verse were well received and where he met with such accomplished intellectuals as the great astronomer Galileo.

When Milton returned to England in 1639, the country was on the brink of civil war, in which Oliver Cromwell would lead parliamentary forces in a struggle that would culminate in the execution of King Charles I in 1649 and that abolished Anglicanism as the state church. Milton threw himself into the fray in 1641 by publishing pamphlets on ecclesiastical reform. Civil war was declared in 1642, and that year Milton, then thirty-three, married seventeen-year-old Mary Powell, an uneducated girl from a staunchly royalist family. Mary went back to live with her parents soon after the wedding but returned in 1645 and bore four children, dying in childbirth with the fourth in 1652. Milton would marry twice again.

Mary's desertion had prompted Milton to write a pamphlet, *The Doctrine and Discipline of Divorce* (1643), which earned him a place among the radical elements of the revolution. In 1644 he published *Areopagitica*, a defense of free expression, and *Of Education*, which promotes the study of the classics rather than of the Bible and Christian thought. In 1645 his first collection of poetry appeared, including "L'Allegro," "Il Penseroso," and "Lycidas." From 1648 to 1658, Milton served the new government of Oliver Cromwell as secretary for foreign languages to the Council of State, a position that required him to justify to the public in England and abroad the execution of Charles I. Milton's vision had been weakening for years, and in 1652 he became completely blind.

The restoration of the monarchy in 1660 put Milton in grave danger, but he was allowed to retreat from public life into retirement. In 1667 he produced his greatest work, *Paradise Lost* (which he had been composing, in one form or another, since he was a young man), followed by *The History of Britain* (1670), and *Paradise Regained* and *Samson Agonistes* (published together in 1671). John Milton died of gout on November 8, 1674.

Table of Contents

List of Engravings • VIII

The World of John Milton and *Paradise Lost* • IX

Introduction by David Hawkes • XIII

Paradise Lost • 1

Endnotes • 405

Inspired by *Paradise Lost* • 429

Comments & Questions • 433

For Further Reading • 439

List of Engravings

Christ Offers to Redeem Mankind • 86

Satan with Adam and Eve • 118

Raphael with Adam and Eve • 159

The Downfall of the Rebel Angels • 208

The Creation of Eve • 252

The Temptation of Eve • 289

The Prophecy of the Crucifixion • 393

The Expulsion from Eden • 401

The World of John Milton and *Paradise Lost*

1590–
1596   *The Faerie Queene*, by Edmund Spenser, is published.

1603   King James VI of Scotland becomes James I of England, succeeding Elizabeth I.

1608   John Milton is born on December 9 in London to John and Sara Milton. During the next several years William Shakespeare's last plays appear, as do many works of poet and dramatist Ben Jonson.

1611   The King James Version of the Bible is published.

1616   William Shakespeare dies.

1618–
1620   Milton is tutored by Presbyterian cleric Thomas Young.

1620–
1625   Milton attends St. Paul's School in London, where he receives instruction in classical languages and literature and in Christian doctrine. He reads and is greatly influenced by the works of Edmund Spenser and sixteenth-century French Huguenot poet Guillaume du Bartas. Milton befriends Charles Diodati, for whom he writes some of his first poems. In 1623 the first folio of Shakespeare's works is published.

1625   Milton enters Christ's College, Cambridge, intending to study religion. He leaves briefly during his first year due to disagreements with a tutor, but returns. The death of James I places his son on the throne of England as Charles I.

1629   Milton receives his B.A. and composes "On the Morning of Christ's Nativity," his first major poem. The authoritarian Charles I discontinues parliament.

1631   Poet John Donne dies, and poet, dramatist, and critic John Dryden is born.

1632   Milton's "On Shakespeare," his first published poem, appears anonymously in the second folio of Shakespeare's works. Milton receives his M.A.; living with his father near London, he begins a six-year reading program in history, philosophy, and literature.

1634   *Comus*, a masque Milton has written at the request of composer Henry Lawes, is presented at Ludlow Castle in Shropshire.

1637   Milton's mother dies, as does Ben Jonson.

1638   Milton writes "Lycidas" in memory of a former Cambridge classmate who has drowned. He embarks on a Grand Tour of Europe and spends most of the next fifteen months in Italy, where he finds a warm reception and praise for his work. Among the prominent intellectual figures he meets is the aged astronomer Galileo, under house arrest in Florence. Milton's longtime friend Charles Diodati dies.

1639   Returning to England, Milton settles in London and begins tutoring his nephews.

1640   Milton completes "Epitaphium Damonis," an elegy to Charles Diodati. Parliament is reconvened.

1641   Milton begins publishing tracts calling for the reform of the Church of England.

1642   The First Civil War begins, with parliament opposing the monarchy. Milton marries seventeen-year-old Mary Powell, but she soon goes back to live with her parents, who are staunch royalists and therefore politically at odds with Milton and his Puritan allegiances.

1643   Milton's difficulties with Mary prompt him to write *The Doctrine and Discipline of Divorce*, the first of several tracts on that theme; the publication incites considerable controversy. The government puts into effect a licensing act that allows censorship before publication.

1644   Milton publishes *Areopagitica*, his defense of free expression, and *Of Education*, which promotes the study of the classics rather than of the Bible and Christian thought.

1645   Mary returns to Milton. His first collection of poetry appears; it includes "L'Allegro," "Il Penseroso," and "Lycidas."

1646   Mary gives birth to a daughter, Anne. The First Civil War ends with the defeat of the royalists. Mary's relations join the Milton household.

1647   Milton's father dies.

1648   Mary gives birth to the couple's second daughter, Mary.

1649   Charles I is executed and the Commonwealth is established. Oliver Cromwell, as the new ruler of England, appoints Milton secretary for foreign languages to the Council of State. Milton publishes *The Tenure of Kings and Magistrates*, which defends the execution of Charles I and argues that power resides in the people, and *Eikonoklastes*, which makes a case against monarchy.

1651   Mary gives birth to Milton's only son, John. Milton publishes *The Defence of the English People*, another argument in support of the execution of Charles I.

1652   Milton's eyesight has been failing for years; now blindness overtakes him. Mary Milton dies of complications from the birth of their daughter Deborah. The couple's son, John, also dies.

1654   *The Second Defence of the English People* appears in celebration of Cromwell and the Commonwealth he has established.

1656   Milton marries Katherine Woodcock. He begins *Of Christian Doctrine*, which will not be published until 1825.

1657   Katherine gives birth to a daughter, Katherine.

1658   Katherine Woodcock and her daughter die. In response, Milton composes one of his most touching sonnets, "Methought I Saw My Late Espousèd Saint." Cromwell dies and is succeeded by his son Richard.

1660   Milton's *A Ready and Easy Way to Establish a Free Commonwealth* appears. The Restoration reinstates the monarchy and the Church of England and puts Charles II on the throne. Parliament burns Milton's works and orders his arrest. The influence of the poet Andrew Marvell and others secures Milton's life and his freedom.

1663   Milton marries Elizabeth Minshull.

1665   Milton flees the plague that is overtaking London; he stays in the town of Chalfont St. Giles, in Buckinghamshire.

1666   The Great Fire destroys much of London, including Milton's home.

1667   *Paradise Lost*, Milton's masterpiece, is published.

1670   Milton's *The History of Britain* is published.

1671   *Paradise Regained*, a sequel to *Paradise Lost*, and *Samson Agonistes*, a tragedy based on the end of Samson's life as told in the Old Testament, appear in the same volume.

1674   John Milton dies of gout November 8 and is buried at the church of St. Giles Cripplegate in London, next to his father.

Introduction

Many new readers of *Paradise Lost* may be tempted to agree with Victorian critic Sir Walter Raleigh's notorious description of the poem as a "monument to dead ideas." It took Milton's reputation most of the twentieth century to recover from this dubious accolade, but Raleigh's verdict was monstrously unjust. Milton himself would have recoiled from the suggestion that a book, any book, could be "a monument to dead ideas." Almost four decades before the publication of *Paradise Lost*, his poem in memory of William Shakespeare scorned as idolatry the very notion of external monuments. Shakespeare did not need "the labour of an age in piled stones," because he had constructed a "live-long monument" in the hearts of his admirers. A true monument could never be dead but must be living, animate. That is how Milton imagined the afterlife of his own work. In *Areopagitica* (1644), he declared:

> Books are not absolutely dead things, but doe contain a
> potencie of life in them to be as active as that soule whose
> progeny they are; nay they do preserve as in a violl the purest
> efficacie and extraction of the living intellect that bred them. I
> know they are as lively, and as vigorously productive, as those
> fabulous Dragon's teeth; and being sown up and down, may
> chance to spring up armed men.

Milton thought of himself as a prophet, doomed by Providence to speak truths that his age was not yet capable of understanding and to sow seeds of revolutionary upheaval that only posterity could bring to fruition. The most hardened skeptic must concede that on points ranging from freedom of the press to divorce, Milton's ideas have indeed proved prophetic. With regard to *Paradise Lost*, however, Raleigh's criticism might seem more plausible. Did Milton miscalculate when he composed his main legacy to the ages in a theological vocabulary that would be obsolescent within a century?

Modern readers often question the relevance of the biblical creation myth to our scientific age, in which the historical veracity of Genesis has been disproved. The first task facing newcomers to the poem is to overcome the prejudice, shared today by religious fundamentalists and secular atheists alike, that the Bible story must be either literally true or utterly false. We must understand that for Milton and his contemporaries, scripture was to be interpreted on many different levels, of which the literal was by no means the most significant. Similarly, we need to move beyond the naive question of whether one "believes in" beings such as God, his Son, or Satan. These are not entities comparable to the Yeti or the Loch Ness monster, which either do or do not exist. They designate, rather, aspects of human experience that, today, we usually think of in other terms. We tend to debate the matters on which Milton meditates through the abstract concepts of philosophy or psychology, but those disciplines employ figures, metaphors, and symbols just as surely as Milton's poem does, with its devils, angels, and talking snakes. To suggest that *Paradise Lost* presents "dead ideas" is like denying the relevance of the Oedipus complex on the grounds that King Oedipus never existed.

Milton believed that truth was historical, that it changed and developed along with human society. He viewed history as a narrative, a continuously evolving revelation of truth. As he puts it in *Areopagitica*: "The light which we have gain'd was giv'n us, not to be ever staring on, but by it to discover onward things more remote from our knowledge." Truth is a journey, not a destination, and we are driven along this pilgrimage by a series of clashes between logically opposed forces: "Let [Truth] and Falshood grapple; who ever knew Truth put to the wors, in a free and open encounter." In *Paradise Lost*, the character who rebels against this historical and dialectical view of truth, boasting of his "mind not to be chang'd by place or time" (1.253), is Satan. Satan also denies the fact that he was created by a power beyond himself, instigates the idolatrous worship of signs, transmits his materialist approach to the world to human beings, and inculcates in them an empty, self-destructive hedonism. There is a good case to be made that the power Milton calls "Satan" has, in the twenty-first century, finally conquered the world. *Paradise Lost* is the prophetic story of how he has achieved his triumph. There could be no idea less "dead" than that.

II

Critics like Raleigh assume that the mark of genius is universality. They believe that a truly great artist must transcend their particular cultural and historical environment and be, as Ben Jonson remarked about Shakespeare, "not of an age but for all time." By this standard, Milton is indeed sorely deficient. His ideas, and the means by which he expresses them, are deeply rooted in the local circumstances of seventeenth-century England, and we must have some knowledge of this background before we can understand his work. But if we believe that human thought is a process, in which any era's events and beliefs are necessarily the consequences of their predecessors, then Milton's historical specificity is no bar to his continuing pertinence. We can learn much about early modern England by reading *Paradise Lost*, but we can learn even more about our own time, because we live among the consequences of the events it describes.

The most portentous process taking place in early modern England was the rapid expansion, and globalization, of a money-based, market economy. Such an economy demands two essential prerequisites: the recognition of money as an independent, self-generating force—an efficacious sign—and the commodification of human activity as "labor." During the sixteenth and seventeenth centuries, England was moving painfully, often violently, through both of these processes. Millions of subsistence farmers were robbed of their land, and thus of their livelihood, by the practice euphemistically known to history as "enclosing." The means of enclosure varied greatly with time and place, but at bottom it involved large landowners stealing the property of the peasantry. The dispossessed peasants were forced to become wage laborers, who exchanged their labor-power for money. This gradually brought about an epochal shift in the way human beings regarded themselves. People came to view their productive activity as a *thing*, which could be bought and sold on the market like any other commodity. They began, in other words, to "objectify" themselves. Furthermore, they learned to conceive of an equivalence between their lives, which they parceled out and sold piecemeal as "labor," and the money for which they exchanged them. People learned, in other words, to translate themselves into a system of signs—for money, like language, is a medium of symbols through which human beings impose an artificial, man-made significance upon the world.

In Milton's day, the financial medium of signs was beginning the process of becoming autonomous and self-generating, as customary and legal restrictions on "usury" were gradually relaxed and a system of wage-labor was introduced. This independent power of signs struck many contemporaries as idolatrous, as did the concomitant necessity for people to conceive of their labor as a thing, a commodity. In the terms of modern philosophy, early modern England was experiencing a growing "autonomy of representation" and witnessing the "objectification of the human subject." The effects of these processes are so universal today that people often forget that they are quite recent developments. Their psychological consequences have become part of our identities, and it is therefore tempting to assume that they are natural and immutable. *Paradise Lost* tells us otherwise. Milton lived at a time when these tendencies were new enough to be clearly visible, and his work describes them in minute detail. He did not, of course, consider them to be "economic" phenomena: The concept of the "economy" was invented decades after his death, precisely in order to conceal the impact of "economic" practices throughout other areas of human life and thought. But the materialism, literalism, cynicism, and above all the idolatry with which Satan infects humanity are impossible to sustain without the simultaneous alienation of human life into symbolic form, and the progressive exaltation of symbols to the position of complete predominance that they enjoy over modern society.

The Protestant reformation began a century before Milton's birth, but the course of his entire life and thought was determined by its repercussions. Although it expressed itself in terms that we narrowly cordon off as "religious," the reformation was a general, visceral reaction against the objectification of the subject and the autonomous power of representation. The spark that lit the fuse was Martin Luther's protest against the papal sale of "indulgences," which were fetishistic financial symbols of penitential human activity, but this critique was immediately extrapolated into an attack on the whole sacramental structure of the Catholic Church. The reformers felt themselves surrounded by image-worshipers, and they set out to destroy idolatry in its political, economic, and religious aspects, as well as within their own minds.

In England, Henry VIII inadvertently introduced the Reformation when he obtained the divorce that the Pope had refused to grant him by simply usurping the Pope's position as head of the church. The reformation provided him with a rationale and offered a protection against reprisals, but Henry was less than enthusiastic about Protestant doctrine, and this produced a set of ideological contradictions that permanently divided the Anglican faith. The official church retained a hierarchical disciplinary structure whereby the consciences of its members were compelled to follow the dictates of the monarch. In liturgical practice, the church continued to follow the logic of pre-Reformation theology, using set forms of prayer and copious iconic imagery as tools of devotion. From the moment of its foundation, the church was therefore plagued by "Puritans," who sought to purify it of these residual Catholic influences. Since the head of the state was also the head of the church, moreover, protests against the official religion inevitably acquired dangerous political overtones.

There was little organized political opposition to the English monarchy until the eve of the civil war. But during the reigns of James I (1603–1625) and Charles I (1625–1649), relations between king and parliament deteriorated to the point where armed conflict became unavoidable. The monarch had traditionally summoned representatives of his noble and wealthy subjects for regular consultations, and by custom he had required their assent before introducing many legal measures, including the raising of new taxes. However, the growing power of the market economy, to which the expropriation of the peasantry and its conversion into a force of wage-laborers were necessary precursors, was bringing a new form of power into being: the power of money. Money, which could be acquired by trade, offered an alternative to the inheritance of land as a means to influence, and it proved a profoundly subversive social force. The logic of money, and of the market in goods and labor that generated it, was in many ways inimical to the traditional social order, and the possessors of money saw less and less reason to bow to tradition. The system of mutual bonds, relations, and ideas that we call "feudalism" was being inexorably undermined by money, and England's customary system of government was among the first edifices to topple.

From 1629 until 1640, after calling a series of acrimonious parliaments that either refused to grant new taxes or insisted on political and religious reform as their precondition, Charles I ruled without parliament's advice or consent. He developed methods of "personal rule" that tended toward absolutism and, as his opponents claimed, tyranny. The consequent resentment of many of his subjects, especially those whose wealth took the form of money rather than land, coalesced neatly with the Puritans' frustration with the state church. Despite the reservations of "revisionist" historians, it is not simplistic to say that the English revolution was brought about by an alliance of radical Protestant theology with the mercantile economic interest.

The king's opponents looked for precedent and inspiration to the "classical republicanism" of Athens and Rome, and especially to the Roman civil war between Julius Caesar and such republicans as Cato and Cicero. These latter figures became the heroes of the parliamentarians, and, combined with the more recent revolutionary examples of continental Protestantism, their work provided a potent rationale for civil disobedience and, eventually, insurrection. By 1642, when the king desperately needed to raise an army to quell a rebellion in Ireland, parliament was in no mood to trust him with its command. Understandably unwilling to relinquish control over so fundamental a power, Charles left London and raised his battle standard at Oxford, thus initiating the civil war. It is at this crucial juncture that John Milton emerges from studious obscurity onto the stage of English history.

III

The entire tenor of Milton's family history and early life had prepared him for the role he was about to play. The roots of *Paradise Lost* lie in a small Oxfordshire village in the mid-sixteenth century, when Richard Milton, the poet's grandfather, discovered his son John in possession of an improper book: an English Bible. Richard Milton was a Roman Catholic, one of many Englishmen who saw the vernacular Bible as a direct threat to the authority of their church, which rested on patristic and ecclesiastical tradition, rather than on scripture. He expelled his unrepentant son from the family home and disinherited him, forcing him to seek his own fortune among the sharp-elbowed merchants of London. John Milton senior prospered in the commercial metropolis, becoming a scrivener—a profession that combined the functions of solicitor, realtor, public notary, and money-lender.

Insufficient critical attention has been paid to the fact that the two towering geniuses of early modern English literature, Milton and Shakespeare, were both the sons of moneylenders. This profession was very controversial, and the late sixteenth and early seventeenth centuries saw a series of debates in pulpit, press, and parliament about its legal and moral status. John Milton senior seems to have avoided criminal prosecution, but Shakespeare's father was twice convicted of usury by the Royal Exchequer. Many people felt that taking interest on a loan ipso facto constituted the sin, and the crime, of usury, which was regarded as an unnatural vice akin to sodomy and as an antisocial practice demonstrating a rapacious avarice utterly at odds with Christian charity. Milton must have been aware that his father's money, on which he lived well into adulthood, had been acquired by means that were widely considered disreputable.

Over the course of the poet's lifetime, usury was defined in progressively narrower ways, and moneylending incrementally acquired legitimacy. This is generally acknowledged as a momentous process in the history of economics, since it prepared the ground for the system of capitalist global exchange that currently holds the world in its grip. But modern economists often neglect the ethical implications of this process, and it is here that the "Dragon's teeth" sown by *Paradise Lost* may yet bear the fruit that Milton prophesied. The fact that money was not somehow incarnated in precious metals, but was rather a sign with a purely figurative existence, was revealed to early modern Europeans by the sudden influx of American gold and silver into Europe and the consequent fluctuations in value of the coinage. The debate over whether money can or should be allowed to reproduce, as in usury, was at root a discussion about the ethical status of representation: Were signs properly referential, or did they enjoy an autonomous and self-generating existence—were they efficacious? The legitimization of usury was thus part of a wider movement whereby signs, whether financial, religious, or linguistic, floated free from the world to which they referred, attaining a degree of autonomous power that many people, including Milton, considered to be Satanic.

Paradise Lost is a broadly extended, but minutely detailed, diagnosis of idolatry. It embodies the source of idolatry in Satan, and it describes Satan's imposition of an idolatrous consciousness on humanity. A naive reader might say that since we know that Satan does not exist, Milton has indeed erected a "monument to dead ideas." But this would be to make precisely the error the poem indicts. It would be to commit idolatry, by taking the *sign* of Satan for the *referent*. Milton does not ask us to believe in the existence of a ruddy, cloven-hoofed fellow with a widow's peak and goatee—this creature is the traditional symbol of Satan, not the reality. Instead, *Paradise Lost* demands that we consider the reality of Satan, which it identifies as the tendency to bestow subjective agency upon mere symbols. Milton would have conceived of the tyrannical power accorded to signs today as clear evidence of the earthly triumph of Satan, and in *Paradise Lost* he has left us one of the most perspicacious accounts of this process.

The poet's background situated him solidly in the economic, political, and religious vanguards of his age—capitalism, republicanism, and Puritanism—and his temperament rendered him uniquely suited to reflect on their implications. He was born in 1608, in a mercantile neighborhood at the heart of the city of London, and soon revealed himself to be a preternaturally intellectual child. By the age of ten he was regularly substituting study for sleep, initiating a lifelong regimen that gives him a reasonable claim to be among the most learned men who have ever lived. He took lessons at home from the well-known Presbyterian cleric Thomas Young, while simultaneously astonishing his instructors at St. Paul's School with his precocity. At the age of sixteen he moved on to Christ's College, Cambridge, where he earned the soubriquet "the Lady" by means that are sadly lost to history. His surviving undergraduate work demonstrates a degree of learning that would be considered utterly beyond the reach of any modern teenager, and which also seems to have distanced him from his contemporaries.

In one of his "Prolusions," written for an audience of his fellow un-
dergraduates, he claims that most of them bear "malice" toward him,
and a painful altercation with his tutor led to a brief suspension from
the university. Such conflicts were, however, resolved sufficiently for
Milton to earn his B.A. in 1629, and his M.A. three years later.

The natural career for the academically inclined was then the
church, and Milton at first planned to enter the Anglican priesthood.
Over the course of his twenties, however, he became disillusioned with
England's official faith. Like many "Puritans," Milton resented the re-
maining Catholic influences, or "rags of Rome," within the Anglican
confession. He particularly blanched at the church's hierarchical or-
ganization, which gave inordinate authority to the bishops, and to its
union with the state, which bestowed ultimate religious power on the
king. Both these aspects of Anglican discipline appeared intolerably
repressive of free individual inquiry, a liberty that Milton prized
above all others. By his thirtieth birthday, his conscience had devel-
oped to the point that, as he later put it, he felt himself "church-outed
by the prelates," and unable to fulfill the functions of an Anglican
minister.

At this stage of his life, in fact, it was by no means clear what func-
tions Milton *was* able to fulfill. After leaving Cambridge he effectively
retired, living at his father's houses near London and spending the re-
mainder of his twenties engaged in a spectacularly arduous program
of study. By the time he emerged from his retreat at the age of thirty,
he had fashioned himself into a veritable freak of erudition. There
was little practical to show for it, however. The poems Milton com-
posed during these years were occasional works, written for specific
events, and usually at the request of others. They are remarkably ac-
complished and strikingly idiosyncratic, but by themselves they would
not have won their author a seat among the immortals. For our pur-
poses, their most notable characteristic is their anticipation of the the-
matic concerns that would come to fruition in *Paradise Lost*. Milton's
basic preoccupations remain remarkably consistent throughout the vi-
cissitudes of his life and career.

His earliest juvenilia includes several formal, elegiac verse letters to
friends, and even these contain polished rehearsals of themes he
would never abandon. The first elegy, composed at the age of eighteen

during Milton's suspension from the university, juxtaposes the competing attractions of the flesh and the spirit. The adolescent poet describes his pleasure in girl-watching, but pointedly rejects such trivia in favor of the cultivation of the mind. The paired poems "L'Allegro" and "Il Penseroso" ("The Cheerful Man" and "The Melancholy Man") explore this dichotomy in greater depth, and they evince a finely tuned awareness of the interpenetration of opposites. Although the two lifestyles are sharply contrasted, Milton subtly introduces elements of melancholy into "L'Allegro" and hints of mirth into "Il Penseroso." He was never to lose this understanding that all binary oppositions are mutually definitive, that the terms of such polarities depend upon each other for their existence.

Milton wrote the hymn "On the Morning of Christ's Nativity" within weeks of his twenty-first birthday. It treats the opposition between pagan idolatry and monotheism as the driving force of human history, and the lengthy description of the banishment of the pagan gods suggests that the destruction of the idols was the most significant result of the birth of Christ. These stanzas look forward to *Paradise Lost*'s careful identification of pagan gods with the fallen angels, and Milton's thought always centered around the conflict between idolatry and true religion. He explored it further in 1634, when he composed the libretto to a masque celebrating the investiture of the Lord President of Wales. *Comus*, as this work is known to posterity, features an eponymous tempter, who uses magic and sensuality in a vain attempt to seduce a "Lady." The sorcerer's scheme involves arguments that we would call "economic"—he makes a protocapitalist case for the reproductive power of money in his effort to persuade the Lady to circulate her sexual favors—but Milton presents these as part of the more general phenomenon of magic, which he understands as the manipulation of representation for practical ends. Magic is the science of the efficacious sign; it is the practical, secular application of idolatry. The villainous figure of Comus, whose carnal temptations and magical arts feed off and blend into each other, provides a convincing rough draft for the Satan of *Paradise Lost*.

"Lycidas," the last significant work of Milton's early period, was written in 1638 for a volume in memory of one of his Cambridge classmates who had recently met an untimely death. The poem is egregiously inappropriate to this context. Milton was evidently unable to stem the stream of thought that drew him far away from his ostensible subject into an intricate meditation on the human condition and topical politics. His epigraph disingenuously describes "Lycidas" as a "monody"—a song in one voice. In fact, however, the poem presents the reflections of various characters, ranging from Apollo to Saint Peter, who speak to and through Milton. It thus prefigures the method of *Paradise Lost*, which was originally conceived as a drama and presents a conversation taking place within the poet's mind, as well as an external metaphysical conflict between supernatural beings.

Magnificent as they are, it is hard to avoid the impression that works like *Comus* and "Lycidas" are addressed to posterity, rather than designed to win fame in Milton's lifetime. Many of his early works announce his intention to write a great epic poem at some future date, and he frequently suggests that his shorter poems are merely place markers, preparing the way for this impending *magnum opus*. His juvenilia won him some local acclaim, but as Milton approached his thirtieth birthday, he had neither a career nor any obvious desire for one.

In 1638 Milton belatedly began the conventional final phase of an upper-class seventeenth-century education, setting off to visit the sites of classical antiquity in Italy and Greece. After a brief passage through France, he arrived in Italy, where his budding talent definitively bloomed. He attended the symposia of literary academies in Florence and was delighted to find that his Latin poetry won the praise he knew it deserved, and he visited Galileo, who was under house arrest following his persecution by the Inquisition. Milton's strong faith in his own literary abilities was thus confirmed, as was his equally strong aversion to ecclesiastical tyranny. But as he was on the point of departing for Greece, he received news of serious civil strife in England. This struck him as a vocation, and he felt compelled to abandon his journey and return home to share, and if possible participate in, his country's tribulation.

IV

We can divide the causes of the English revolution into "religious," "political," and "economic" spheres for our convenience, as long as we remember that the people of the seventeenth century did not view these as discrete areas of experience, but rather as elements within a unified, overarching totality. The sullen hostility between King Charles I and parliament blazed into conflict over the question of who should control the army, which we would consider a political matter. But the parliament could draw on the support of those who resented the liturgical practices of the Anglican Church, and it could also exploit the dissatisfaction of the mercantile classes at being taxed to fund the aristocratic extravagance of the court. For Milton, these various grounds for opposition to the monarch coalesced to form the earthly manifestation of a greater, metaphysical conflict between the forces of good and evil.

The intricate connections between the different issues at stake are immediately apparent in Milton's writings from the 1640s. On his return to London, Milton hurled himself into the maelstrom of controversy raging in the revolutionary capital. Parliament had lifted the government censorship in 1640, unleashing an unprecedented torrent of radical opinion, and Milton eagerly joined the fray. His first pamphlets, such as *Of Reformation* and *The Reason of Church Government*, advocate the Presbyterian case for ecclesiastical reform, but they range wildly beyond these bounds, alluding to aesthetic, political, economic, and, above all, personal concerns. In fact, the most striking characteristic of Milton's early tracts is their assumption of an intimate and indissoluble connection between the psychological and the political arenas. He considered the argument ad hominem to be perfectly legitimate, because he believed that only those in a condition of interior servitude to their own appetites and desires could argue for the subjection of free men to a tyrannous ruler. Milton's political writings help us to understand why the political dispute between republicans and royalists was simultaneously a conflict between "puritan" and "cavalier" lifestyles. For Milton, the personal is always political, and the prevalence of this notion in our own time is sufficient demonstration that his ideas are by no means superseded.

This connection is evident throughout the "antiprelatical" tracts. Milton believed, correctly though immodestly, that a church not broad enough to accommodate him must be irrationally narrow, and his first prose works are acts of revenge on the bishops who had "church-outed" him. Similarly, such later works as *The Tenure of Kings and Magistrates* and *The Defence of the English People* argue for the identity of personal virtue and political liberty. Milton's domestic circumstances during the 1640s predisposed him to perceive the intimacy between these spheres, for the crisis in the English state coincided with an equally profound crisis in his personal life. The convergence of these events was painful, but it spurred his thought into regions where it might not otherwise have ventured. In 1642, as the nation descended into civil war, the thirty-three-year-old Milton married a seventeen-year-old girl, Mary Powell. It was by any standards an inauspicious match. The Powell family was royalist, so Milton soon found himself quite literally at war with his in-laws. Stranger still, Mary's father, Richard Powell, had been heavily in debt to Milton's family for more than fifteen years, and in 1640 Milton had repossessed some of his lands for nonpayment. It is hard to escape the conclusion that Powell was, formally or informally, giving away his daughter in order to ameliorate his financial obligations. Milton acquired his bride through usury.

The sin of usury was fraught with sexual implications. It was constantly compared to sodomy, because it perverted the properly barren nature of money, artificially making it "breed," just as sodomy perverts the properly generative nature of sex, making it sterile. If, as seems likely, both Milton and Mary were aware that she was in some sense an interest payment on a loan, this can only have introduced further distractions to an erotic relationship in which—we must presume—both parties were complete novices. Such speculation is consistent with the fact that three weeks after the wedding, Mary ran away, taking refuge with her family and refusing to acknowledge Milton's messages. When war broke out two months later, the couple was separated by physical as well as emotional battle lines, and reconciliation must have seemed impossible.

Milton's reaction tells us a great deal about his intellectual orientation, and also about the spirit of the times. He immediately, and as it were instinctively, turned his personal disappointment into a public issue. In 1643, a year after his wife's desertion, he published *The Doctrine and Discipline of Divorce*, the first-ever argument for what we would call "no fault" divorce, or divorce on the sole grounds of psychological incompatibility. He rested his case on the analogy between divorce and political revolution. Both events involve the abnegation of a contract that has been invalidated because of its failure to meet the end for which it was devised. In the case of marriage, that end is spiritual companionship; in the case of politics it is government for the good of the country as a whole. Where those ends are not achieved, claimed Milton, both contracts are automatically void.

As in sixteenth-century Germany, eighteenth-century France, and twentieth-century Russia, in England revolution was accompanied by the startling emergence of "antinomian" sects who sought to radicalize personal morality along with the political state. Groups such as the Ranters believed themselves above the moral law, and thus free to practice communism, free love, and various forms of hedonistic debauchery. To his horror, Milton's divorce pamphlet earned him a place among such company in the public mind. He was accused of advocating "divorce at pleasure," a man's right to cast his wife aside on a whim and take another, or even to practice polygamy. These charges were not entirely groundless; Milton did explicitly permit polygamy in *Of Christian Doctrine*, he did consider a bigamous marriage, and *The Doctrine and Discipline of Divorce* conspicuously failed to explain how a genuine, objective incompatibility could be distinguished from a merely whimsical or lustful desire for a new or more attractive mate. Knowing his own motives to be pure, however, Milton was outraged by charges that he was a libertine, and he spent two years in bitter controversy with his accusers.

He also faced a more practical threat. The Presbyterian party, which controlled parliament following the departure of the royalists, had been taken aback by the seething cauldron of radical opinion revealed by the lifting of the censorship, and Milton's divorce tract was singled out in parliament as an especially egregious example of such dangerous views. Milton felt personally insulted by the proposal to reimpose censorship that came before parliament in 1644, and his chagrin drove him yet further in advance of contemporary public opinion. In *Areopagitica*, published in the same year, Milton's opposition to the Presbyterians overflows into a general justification of freedom of the press. It was the first theoretical statement of a position that became a fundamental tenet of liberal democracy centuries after Milton's death, and it testifies to the quantum leaps made by his intelligence in these revolutionary years.

Not all the attention Milton generated was unwelcome. His innovative mind won him friends on what we would now call the "left wing" of the revolution, and as these more radical elements gained ascendancy, Milton's star rose. The leaders of the Independent Party, who soon displaced the Presbyterians as the guiding lights of parliament and its army, saw the potential in his indisputable brilliance, and they determined to harness it. By 1648 Milton was close to the centers of political power. For the next decade he served the government of Oliver Cromwell, as secretary for foreign tongues—a more important post than it may sound, roughly approximate to a modern foreign secretary—and as its chief propagandist, responsible for justifying the ways and means of England's new rulers to the European public.

By this time Milton's wife had returned. In 1645, facing the prospect of a royalist defeat and the confiscation of their property, and perceiving that Milton was poised for prominence in the new regime, the entire Powell family threw itself on his mercy. Although he had been courting a woman named Mary Davis, Milton accepted his wife's plea, even allowing her family to share his house. This was an act of great magnanimity and unselfishness, which belies his mother-in-law's ungrateful characterization of the poet as a "harsh and choleric man." The marriage was sufficiently harmonious for Mary to give birth to three daughters, and to a son who died in infancy. Mary herself died shortly following the birth of her third daughter, whom Milton named Deborah, after the prophetess who liberated the Israelites from their heathen oppressors. He married again in 1656, but his beloved wife Katherine Woodcock died two years later, along with a stillborn daughter. Milton married a third time in 1663, to Elizabeth Minshull, who survived him.

His most important and difficult professional task was to justify the execution of Charles I, which took place in 1649. This act, which horrified most English people and terrified the crowned heads of continental Europe, was completely without precedent. Never before had a reigning monarch been tried, convicted, and executed by his subjects. The idea, so familiar to us today, that political power ultimately and rightfully resides with the people, had few adherents, and Milton has as good a claim as anyone to have invented its modern form. His regicidal tracts, such as *Eikonoklastes* and *The Tenure of Kings and Magistrates* (both published in 1649), mingle religious, political, and economic arguments, but they rest their case, once again, on personal morality. The problem with the hereditary principle, according to Milton, was its inability to guarantee the rule of the most virtuous men. Unfortunately, neither Milton nor anyone else was able to devise a system that would guarantee such rule. His recourse was to extol the surpassing virtue of Oliver Cromwell, but this could only be temporary; after Cromwell's death in 1658 the Restoration of the monarchy was only a matter of time.

When it came, in 1660, Milton had good reason to fear for his life. Charles II was wisely merciful to most of his opponents, but he did exact vengeance on those directly responsible for his father's decapitation, and several regicides were executed. Fearing such a fate, Milton went into hiding, but in the event he suffered only a brief imprisonment before being released on condition that he play no further part in public affairs. He may have been saved by the fact that, since 1652, he had been completely blind. His enemies found it convenient to interpret this affliction as divine retribution for his faulty political vision; they were content to let him live on as an example to other heretics until his peaceful death in 1674.

Here, the royalists made a mistake that was to prove fatal to their successors. Milton used the enforced retirement of his old age, as he had used the voluntary retirement of his youth, to undertake a course of study and meditation that issued in his three greatest works, *Paradise Lost*, *Paradise Regained*, and *Samson Agonistes*. All three are protests against tyranny that would inspire future generations of revolutionaries, but *Paradise Lost* is much more than this. Milton had been working on it, in one form or another, for his entire life. The verse letters he wrote as a teenager allude to a work in progress dealing with spiritual conflict in Heaven and Hell, and he showed a completed section of the poem to his nephew in 1642, twenty-five years before the publication of the first edition. It would appear that Milton consciously assimilated his whole life's experience, with its bold intellectual insights, its personal triumphs and misfortunes, and its righteous but failed political enterprises, into the architectonic framework of his literary legacy.

V

As we have seen, Milton's earliest work reveals an interest in the mutual determination of such binary oppositions as mirth and melancholy, or the flesh and the spirit. This relational view of identity informs the staggeringly complex morality of *Paradise Lost*, where the conflicts between good and evil, and between God and Satan, are presented as at once real and illusory. The monotheist belief in an omnipotent God requires that apparent evil must be seen as part of the divine plan and thus, finally and paradoxically, as good (the opposing, Manichaean, view that evil is an independent force is espoused, in *Paradise Lost*, by Satan). To grasp the implications of Milton's epic, we must take seriously his contention in *Areopagitica* that:

> It was from out the rind of one apple tasted, that the
> knowledge of good and evil, as two twins cleaving together,
> leaped forth into the world. And perhaps this is that doom
> that Adam fell into of knowing good and evil, that is to say,
> of knowing good by evil.

This does not, however, imply moral relativism. On the contrary, his awareness of their mutually determining nature sharpened the intensity of Milton's distinction between good and evil. He was an extremist by nature, to whom the middle ground was foreign territory, and his writings are notable for their radicalism of opinion and vehemence of expression. How can Milton's fiercely partisan approach to every issue that he considered—from whether day is preferable to night in his student exercises, to whether God is more admirable than Satan in *Paradise Lost*—be reconciled with his constant conviction that every concept, and every thing, is defined by its other?

The answer lies in the distinction between "concept" and "thing." Milton believed that the kind of knowledge that can be attained by the human mind was necessarily contingent, or limited. It was limited by cultural and historical context: The ancient Greeks, for example, had been culturally unable to arrive at monotheism. But it was also *inherently* limited by its internal properties. The human mind is designed, or has developed, in such a way as to live in time and space. To exist outside time and space, the human mind would have to become something different than what it currently is. The same goes for such ideas as causality or extension; without the capacity to think according to these categories it would be simply impossible to have any kind of recognizably human experience. We do not, therefore, experience the world as it really is, we experience the world as it appears to human beings. And we know that this experience is contingent upon—limited by—the inherent nature of the human mind.

It follows that the concepts we form of things, the way they appear to us, do not correspond to the things in themselves. There are thus two kinds of truth: the truth "for us," in what modern philosophers call the world of "phenomena," and the truth "in itself," in what is known as the world of "noumena." In John Keats's "Ode on a Grecian Urn," for example, the poet laments that he can never experience the urn in its noumenal state, as it is in itself. Keats comes to this realization by considering the difference between the significance it possesses for him, as a modern Englishman, and the meanings it conveyed to its creator, an ancient Greek. The "phenomenal" appearance of the urn has changed, although the urn "in itself" has not. In a sense the noumenal is more true, because it is more absolute, than the phenomenal, but the truth "in itself" is by definition beyond the grasp of human thought. We are stuck with a consciousness that we know to be incomplete. This is philosophical terminology, but Milton expresses the same ideas in quasi-mythological, religious terms. *Paradise Lost* hinges upon the fundamental, unbridgeable, qualitative distinction between the world of earthly phenomena as experienced by Adam and Eve (and also by the poem's all-too-human narrator), and the world of spiritual noumena as it is represented to them (and us) through the intricate system of characters, figures, and images that make up the Western mythological and religious traditions.

Above all, Milton insists on the disparity in nature between the Creator and His creation. *Paradise Lost* describes the alienation of labor in a cosmic context; it tells of how the universe that God made came to be alien to Him, and how it came to seem autonomous and self-generating to its inhabitants. The disjunction between the Maker and the made involves a contradiction between two different kinds of value, of significance. It follows that any knowledge we can have of

God or His Providential designs must always be "mediated," translated into the contingent terms and concepts to which the human mind has access.

Almost half of *Paradise Lost* consists of stories told to Adam and/or Eve through the voices of the archangels Raphael and Michael. These characters incessantly remind their auditors that they are attempting the impossible task of representing noumena in terms of phenomena. Asked to describe the fall of Satan to the human couple, Raphael falls into a quandary: "how shall I relate / To human sense th'invisible exploits / Of warring spirits" (5.564–566). He decides that he must tell his story in the form of an extended metaphor, using images that Adam and Eve are equipped to understand: "what surmounts the reach / Of human sense, I shall delineate so, / By likening spiritual to corporal forms, / As may express them best" (5.571–574). We are thus warned not to take the action of the "war in Heaven" that the angel describes literally, but to remain conscious that we are receiving figural representations of spiritual (we might call them psychological or philosophical) events. We can only understand those events if we take account of the fact that they are mediated for us through contingent human discourse:

> Immediate are the acts of God, more swift
> Than time or motion; but to human ears
> Cannot without process of speech be told,
> So told as earthly notion can receive (7.176–179).

The action of *Paradise Lost* takes place, then, in many different registers simultaneously. The ability to read a text as both literal and symbolic, and also at infinite gradations between these poles, came more naturally to educated people in Milton's time than it does to us, trained as they were in the intricate hermeneutics of biblical exegesis. Furthermore, their facility with textual interpretation was matched by a happy disregard for the boundaries between what we regard as mutually exclusive intellectual fields. *Paradise Lost* is certainly a work of theology, representing the spiritual conflict between metaphysical beings, but this conflict is also the determining factor in world history, as well as within the human psyche. Although more than twenty characters address us in the course of the poem, such figures also represent disputing forces within Milton's mind and, by implication, within the mind of the reader.

The poem describes the attempted conquest of Heaven, the world, and the mind by the forces of evil. It personifies evil in the figure of "Satan," which, as Milton repeatedly reminds us, is the Hebrew word for "enemy." The sixteenth and seventeenth centuries witnessed a pan-European (and even transatlantic) panic over what was perceived as Satan's vastly increased practical power in the world. Tens of thousands of people were executed as "witches," on the grounds that they had entered into a pact with Satan that enabled them to use magical signs and rituals to achieve pragmatic ends. Ritual magic works on the assumption that signs are efficacious, so that, for example, harming the image of a man can bring harm to the man himself. The "witch hunt" may have been vicious and misogynist, but it was by no means irrational. It seemed extremely important to establish the point that the use of efficacious signs was not, as the magicians argued, an ethically neutral practice, but the work of the devil. This produced the necessity of forcing, by torture if necessary, witches to confess that they had signed a formal contract with Satan. *Paradise Lost* is replete with references to magic, and to such associated concepts as sorcery, witches, charms, wonders, prodigies, and other forms of Satanic "art." We are left in no doubt that Milton considers the power of the devil to be genuinely, literally, active in the real world.

The power of autonomous signification was not the exclusive preserve of magicians. Protestants of Milton's stripe saw the same Satanic influence in Catholic and Anglican religious practices, which implied that icons and rituals could be magically efficacious for salvation. Republicans like Milton believed that monarchy was the secular arm of religious idolatry, since it evoked an analogous fetishistic awe in its adherents. And many people identified the burgeoning autonomous power of money, a purely abstract sign, as a further example of diabolical influence. Milton is not generally regarded as having been interested in the "economic" debates of his day, but this is only because modern critics often impose their anachronistically narrow understanding of the term "economic" onto the seventeenth century. *Paradise Lost* is an extended protest against the fetishizing, or making an icon of, the sign, and this fact is the key to its continued relevance. Our own "postmodern condition" is characterized by the virtually complete dominance of representation over reality, but few twenty-first-century thinkers are capable of constructing an ethical critique of this situation. *Paradise Lost* offers such a critique, and that is why Milton's poem is more pertinent today than ever before. In our time, *Paradise Lost* is revealing itself as what Milton thought it was: a prophecy.

Far from representing "dead ideas," *Paradise Lost* reinterprets and revivifies the entire Western cultural tradition. It blends Judeo-Christian monotheism with Platonic idealism, Homeric mythology, Italian humanism, recent English literature, personal biography, and topical politics, to produce a wholly original, syncretic account of the universe and humanity's place within it. The opening lines of book I stake Milton's claim to be writing a third testament, directly inspired by both the Holy Spirit and the classical muses, and thus empowered to surpass both Hebraic and Hellenic wisdom. The poet invokes the Gods of Sinai, Sion, and the human heart (by which he means, respectively, the Father, Son, and Holy Spirit), to guide him beyond the insights of classical literature, represented by Mount Helicon, the "Aonian mount" (1.15) above which Milton "intends to soar" (1.14). But his ambitions do not stop there. When Milton informs his readers that he will pursue "things unattempted yet in prose or rhyme" (1.16), he announces his intention to surpass not just pagan poetry, but the Bible itself.

VI

It often comes as a surprise to new readers of Milton to discover that he was not, in any orthodox sense, a Christian. Among many other heresies, Milton denied the Trinity, and he did not believe that Jesus of Nazareth was the only incarnation of Jehovah. He took from Christianity, as from classical polytheism, only those elements that he found congenial to his own system of thought. That system was heavily influenced by the political and personal events of his life, and his historical view of truth suggested that the ideas expressed in ancient texts were inevitably subjected to a process of constant revision.

For example, Milton often alludes to the war of the Titans

against the Olympian gods, as it is described in Hesiod's *Theogony*. He suggests that this pagan myth is primitive and inexact, but he also treats it as an alternative expression of the same conflict that monotheism represents as taking place between angels and demons. In the prefatory poem published in the second edition of *Paradise Lost* (1674), Andrew Marvell recalls his worry that Milton would "ruin," or reduce, "the sacred truths to fable." But that was not Milton's intention. Instead, he elevates classical mythology to a prefiguration of the sacred biblical truths, and he sees his own work as a further updating of these truths in the light of recent events. Like such later philosophical works as Immanuel Kant's three *Critiques* (1781, 1788, 1790), Georg Hegel's *Phenomenology of Mind* (1807), and Karl Marx's *Capital* (1867), *Paradise Lost* announces itself as the accumulation and transcendence of all previous human wisdom. If *Paradise Lost* is indeed a "monument to dead ideas," however magnificent, it is according to its own terms a failure. It was intended to be a prophecy, addressed to posterity, to us, and it is as a prophecy that it must be evaluated.

What the poem prophesies is the degeneration of human consciousness from monotheism into idolatry. The curtain rises on the fallen angels weltering in Hell, and we are informed that they will persuade mankind "to forsake / God their Creator, and th'invisible / Glory of him that made them, to transform / Oft to the image of a brute, adorn'd / With gay religions full of pomp and gold, / And devils to adore for deities" (1.368–373). The devils will become "various idols through the heathen world" (1.375), and Milton identifies them with the gods worshiped by the Israelites' neighbors in the Old Testament. Their significance is more than local, however. Dagon, Astoreth, and their colleagues are not dead; they are more powerful today than ever before. Mammon, for example, is merely the Hebrew word for "money," but Milton's personification tells us in detail of money's psychological effects, and also predicts the spread of those effects over the course of history:

> . . . Mammon led them on,
> Mammon, the least erected spirit that fell
> From heaven: for even in heaven his looks and thoughts

Were always downward bent; admiring more
The riches of heaven's pavement, trodden gold,
Than aught divine or holy else, enjoy'd
In vision beatific: by him first
Men also, and by his suggestion taught,
Ransack'd the centre, and with impious hands
Rifled the bowels of their mother earth
For treasures better hid. Soon had his crew
Open'd into the hill a spacious wound,
And digg'd out ribs of gold. (Let none admire
That riches grow in hell; that soil may best
Deserve the precious bane.) (1.678–692).

Money is at once a fictional character in the poem and a real historical force. Its effect is to distract us from the contemplation of God, thus involving us in a hostile and rapacious attitude toward the nature He has created. Financial value constitutes an artificial "second nature" that human beings impose upon the first, and the impious violence of such imposition is marked by the "wound" that the devils open. Mammon's advice to his colleagues is that they should "seek / Our own good from ourselves, and from our own / Live to ourselves" (2.252–254). The power of money makes possible a demonic recreation, as Martin Luther had understood when he remarked that "Money is the word of the Devil, by which he creates everything in the world, just as God creates through the true Word." Mammon suggests that the devils can construct an image of Heaven that will surpass the reality: "This desert soil / Wants not her hidden lustre, gems, and gold; / Nor want we skill or art, from whence to raise / Magnificence; and what can heaven show more?" (2.270–273) The entire Satanic enterprise aims at this perverse, artificial distortion of God's creation, allowing the devils to imagine a second nature "in emulation opposite to heaven" (2.298). The Satanic sin is to deny the distinction between phenomena and noumena; to imagine that the contingent world the devils construct in Hell is equivalent to the disposition of the divine Creator.

This gulf between noumena and phenomena, which Milton represents as "Chaos"—a "wild abyss" (2.917), the "nethermost abyss"

(2.969), a "dark abyss" (2.1027), and "the vast immeasurable abyss" (7.211)—introduces a paradoxical, or ironic, dual perspective into *Paradise Lost*. For example, the poem's pivotal event, the Fall of Man, is unequivocally a bad thing "for us," and Satan, as the being who brings it about, is thus unequivocally evil from a human perspective. On the monotheistic assumption of an omnipotent God, however, we must inevitably conclude that God intended the Fall to occur, and that it and its author, Satan, are therefore, in a sense that is by definition beyond human comprehension, good.

This irony informs many of the poem's exquisite ambiguities, which have produced the most heated critical debates in Milton criticism, such as whether Milton sympathized with Satan, and whether he subscribed to the doctrine of *felix culpa* (the fortunate fall), which suggests that since God intended it, the fall must be good. From a consideration of such issues alone, it would be easy to get the impression that the poem's morality is somehow ambivalent, but of course this is very far from being the case. This is because, for Milton, sin consists in the refusal to recognize, and thus in the attempt to bridge, the abyss between the world of experience and the world beyond experience. This is the sin of Satan, whose basic mistake is the failure to understand that the difference between himself and God is qualitative, rather than quantitative. In one of his soliloquies he recalls how, in Heaven:

> I s'dain'd subjection, and thought one step higher
> Would set me highest, and in a moment quit
> The debt immense of endless gratitude,
> So burdensome still paying, still to owe;
> Forgetful what from him I still receiv'd,
> And understood not that a grateful mind
> By owing owes not, but still pays, at once
> Indebted and discharg'd (4.50–57).

Because he does not understand the absolute nature of the distinction between Creator and creation, Satan imagines that it is possible to usurp the place of God. He thinks of his relationship to God in numerical, financial terms, whereby a quantitative increase in his strength might make him stronger than the Deity. This is the revolt of the clay against the potter, the work against the worker, that forms the biblical definition of idolatry: "Their land also is full of idols; they worship the work of their own hands, that which their own fingers have made" (Isaiah 2:8; King James Version). Satan rebels against the power that, as he admits at one point, "created what I was" (4.43), and *Paradise Lost* often reminds us of the basic absurdity of Satan's daring to "defy th'Omnipotent to arms" (1.49). All of Satan's apparently heroic exhortations must be viewed in the light of the madness of trying to be the equal of an omnipotent God. This false equivalence is identified as the root of idolatry both in *Paradise Lost*, as when king Jeroboam is mocked for "Lik'ning his Maker to the grazed ox" (1.486), and in the Bible, where God mockingly asks, "To whom will ye liken me, and make me equal, and compare me, that we may be like?" (Isaiah 46:5).

Satan's aim is to replace the worship of the Creator with the idolatrous worship of created things, and he must therefore deny that he was created by a force outside himself. He believes himself to be autonomous and self-sufficient, and thus "trusted to have equall'd the Most High" (1.40). In this sense, "Satan" is what happens to created beings when they refuse to refer their existence to an end beyond themselves, and thus "fall off / From their Creator" (1.30–31). Milton repeatedly identifies this mistake as the basic component of Satanic consciousness. When Satan manages to raise himself from the fiery lake, we are reminded that the power that allows him to do so is not his own:

> . . . nor ever thence
> Had risen, or heav'd his head, but that the will
> And high permission of all-ruling Heaven,
> Left him at large to his own dark designs (1.210–213).

The devils, however, remain under the illusion that their power is autonomous; a little later we find them "glorying to have 'scap'd the Stygian flood, / As gods, and by their own recover'd strength; / Not by the suff'rance of supernal power" (1.239–241). This leads them to worship Satan, "and as a god / Extol him equal to the highest in heaven" (2.478–479). More reliable sources also inform us that equality with God is Satan's purpose; the Father tells the Son that Satan "intends to erect his throne / Equal to ours" (5.725–726), and Raphael describes him as "affecting all equality with God" (5.763).

What this means in historical terms is that Satan obtrudes the world of appearances, of phenomena—the sphere that early modern people referred to as "custom"—in front of the world of essences, of noumena—of "nature," in Milton's term. He claims, in other words, that the contingent appearances of things constitutes their true reality. Idolatry involves the worship, and magic the manipulation, of appearances, of signs. In "economic" terms, the Satanic claim is that the significance, the value of the world lies in its financial representation rather than in its natural qualities—in "exchange value" rather than in "use value." In "scientific" terms, it involves the Baconian substitution of the empirical, material causes of things for their teleological, final causes, as the proper end of human reason. The serpent, or rather Satan in the serpent, aptly summarizes the empiricist approach to the world in his temptation of Eve:

> The gods are first, and that advantage use
> On our belief, that all from them proceeds:
> I question it; for this fair earth I see,
> Warm'd by the sun, producing every kind,
> Them nothing . . . (9.718–722).

Eve's first actions after her fall are to worship the tree itself, and to extol "experience" as her "best guide" (9.807–808). The two impulses are intimately connected. Empiricism takes the surface appearance of the world—the way it *seems*, to use *Paradise Lost*'s most important word—for its reality. It ignores the fact that the world as it appears *to* us has been constructed *by* us, mediated through our systems of understanding and representation. It treats the sign as though it were the referent. This is, in fact, the very definition of Sin in *Paradise Lost*. When the allegorical figure of "Sin" recounts her birth to her "father" Satan, she recalls how the witnessing angels were initially startled at her appearance:

> . . . back they recoil'd, afraid
> At first, and call'd me Sin; and for a sign
> Portenteous held me: but familiar grown,
> I pleas'd, and with attractive graces won
> The most averse, thee chiefly, who full oft
> (Thyself in me thy perfect image viewing)
> Becam'st enamour'd (2.759–765).

Satan becomes "enamour'd" of Sin when he forgets that she is a sign, and instead perceives her as his own "perfect image." The distinction between a "sign" of an Other and an "image" of the Self may seem trivial from the perspective of our unsophisticated semiotic capacities, but it was of fundamental importance to Milton. The ability to make this distinction is the first lesson Eve must learn after her creation. At first, in a recapitulation of the Narcissus myth, she mistakes her own image, reflected in a pool, for reality:

> A shape within the wat'ry gleam appear'd,
> Bending to look on me: I started back;
> It started back: but pleas'd I soon return'd;
> Pleas'd it return'd as soon; with answering looks
> Of sympathy and love: there had I fixt
> Mine eyes till now, and pin'd with vain desire,
> Had not a voice thus warn'd me: What thou seest,
> What there thou seest, fair creature, is thyself;
> With thee it came and goes: but follow me,
> And I will bring thee where no shadow stays
> Thy coming, and thy soft embraces, he
> Whose image thou art: him thou shalt enjoy,
> Inseparably thine . . . (4.461–473).

Eve's tendency to make a spectacle of herself later provides Satan with his successful means of tempting her: "one man except, / Who sees thee? (and what is one?) who shouldst be seen / A goddess among gods" (9.545–547). To idolize an image is to forget that it is an image, and thus neglect to refer images to their source in an ultimate *logos*. *Logos* is the original Greek term for the "Word" of God, which is identified with His Son in John 1.1–14. In philosophical terms it refers to the origin and final cause of all meaning. Consider, for example, the relation between Satan and the serpent, into which he enters in order to deceive Eve. The Genesis account does not mention Satan, but ascribes the temptation of Eve to "the serpent [which] was more subtil than any beast of the field" (Genesis 3:1), while New Testament glosses like the one in Revelation interpret the serpent as a material symbol for a spiritual being, referring to "that old serpent, which is the Devil, and Satan" (Revelation 20:2).

Milton emphasizes the centrality of this distinction in the Argument to book I of *Paradise Lost*, which ascribes the Fall to "the serpent, or rather Satan in the serpent." This qualification preempts any confusion when the verse itself names "th'infernal serpent" (1.34) as humanity's seducer, immediately before reporting "his" expulsion from Heaven "with all his host / Of rebel angels" (1.37–38). Right at the beginning of his epic, Milton directs his readers' attention to the fact that he is dealing simultaneously with the material symbols of phenomenological experience (the serpent) and with their imperceptible, noumenal referents (Satan in the serpent). The serpent is merely a sign; if we are to understand the nature of the Fall we must learn to read the concealed significance within such appearances.

The snake is not, however, an arbitrary sign: It could not mean just anything. There are qualities inherent in the serpent's nature that make it a "fit vessel" (9.89) for Satan. Before the Fall, Milton describes how "the serpent sly / Insinuating, wove with Gordian twine / His braided train, and of his fatal guile / Gave proof unheeded" (4.347–350), and he creates the acrostic "SATAN" with the initial letters of five lines that describe the snake's initial approach to Eve (9.510–514). Human beings are not free to interpret signs as they please, but must learn to distinguish natural, God-given significances from customary, humanly imposed meanings. As in Genesis, therefore, Milton stresses that the Son of God curses the serpent *qua* serpent:

> To judgment he proceeded on th'accurs'd
> Serpent, though brute, unable to transfer
> The guilt on him who made him instrument
> Of mischief, and polluted from the end

> Of his creation; justly then accurs'd,
> As vitiated in nature . . . (10.164–169).

The sign, as well as the referent, is cursed, because it has ceased to be a sign. The serpent's "nature" has been "vitiated;" it is a serpent in appearance and physical manifestation, but this natural aspect of the animal has attained an unnatural significance. Milton's assertion that the Son of God is "unable" to curse Satan at this point is provocative and startling. It clearly cannot mean what it appears to mean, since the Son shares with the Father the quality of omnipotence. The following lines explain that the Son is "unable" to do this only because His purpose is to instruct the human couple, and Adam and Eve would be unable to understand a curse on a purely spiritual entity. Like Raphael, the Son accommodates his speech to human understanding, "measuring things in heaven by things on earth" (6.893). Human knowledge must always proceed through the mediation of symbols like the serpent:

> . . . more to know
> Concern'd not man (since he no further knew)
> Not alter'd his offence; yet God at last
> To Satan, first in sin, his doom applied,
> Though in mysterous terms, judg'd as then best
> And on the serpent thus his curse let fall . . . (10.169–174).

Satan is the being who denies the mediating function of signs. In other words, he is a literalist, who does not understand that the phenomenal world is a set of signs that designate noumenal referents. As a result, he is confident that the Son has cursed the sign alone, and that he himself has escaped judgment. As he reports to his colleagues in Hell:

> True is, me also he hath judg'd, or rather
> Me not, but the brute serpent, in whose shape
> Man I deceiv'd: that which to me belongs
> Is enmity, which he will put between
> Me and mankind; I am to bruise his heel;
> His seed, when is not set, shall bruise my head.
> A world who would not purchase with a bruise . . . (10.494–500).

The devil imagines that he is to receive a literal "bruise," and he makes a canny, financial evaluation of the exchange. His error is immediately and ironically revealed by his literal, physical transformation into a serpent. As Raphael does with Adam, God accommodates his message to Satan's understanding—the literalist who takes appearance for reality is instructed by the forcible union of the form in which he appeared with his essential nature—and the devil finds himself "punish'd in the shape he sinn'd" (10.516).

VII

This inability to perceive the mediating functions of signs is not merely the effect, but also the cause of Satan's alienation from God. As he flies toward the earth, for instance, the devil catches sight of a stairway leading to Heaven. He instinctively assumes that it is a literal means by which he could, in theory, reascend to the presence of God. This leads him to interpret the vision as a cruel mockery, intended by God to "aggravate / His sad exclusion from the doors of bliss" (3.524–525). In fact, however, the stairs are supposed to be read not as a physical entity, but as a sign: "Each stair mysteriously was meant, nor stood / There always, but drawn up to heaven sometimes / Viewless" (3.516–518). But Satan is a materialist, and does not believe in things that are "viewless." It is on these grounds that he denies the fact of his creation, as his scornful rhetoric in the debate with the virtuous Abdiel reveals. The zealous angel asks whether Satan can truly believe himself to be "equal to him, begotten Son? by whom, / As by his Word, the mighty Father made / All things, even thee . . . (5.835–837). At this point Satan reveals his basic misconception:

> That we were form'd then say'st thou? and the work
> Of secondary hands, by task transferr'd
> From Father to his Son? Strange point and new;
> Doctrine which we would know whence learn'd, who saw
> When this creation was? remember'st thou
> Thy making, while the Maker gave thee being?
> We know no time when we were not as now;

> Know none before us, self-begot, self-rais'd
> By our own quick'ning power . . . (5.853–861).

Satan's reasoning is in sharp contrast to the unfallen Adam's reaction to his creation. From the fact of his existence, Adam immediately and logically deduces both the existence of a Creator and the need for communion with Him: ". . . how came I thus, how here? / Not of myself; by some great Maker then, / In goodness and in power pre-eminent; / Tell me how may I know him, how adore . . ." (8.277–280). The answer to his question is that the Creator can be known through his "Son," and Adam's awareness of this fact constitutes the difference between his perspective and Satan's. It is, in fact, the exaltation, or "begetting," of the Son that provokes Satan to revolt. Modern readers tend simply to identify the "Son" of God with the historical figure of Jesus of Nazareth, but the concept is far more complex than that. Milton's interest in *Paradise Lost* is not in the Galilean, but in the *logos*. The term *logos* can be translated as "word," but also as "mind," "act," and "thought," and Milton clearly includes all these senses, and more, in his conception of the Son, whom the Father calls "My word, my wisdom, and effectual might" (3.170).

Paradise Lost's most significant departure from orthodox Christianity is its declaration that the Son was created by the Father in time. This heresy is known as Arianism, and it has been anathema to the church since the fourth-century Council of Nicea. Milton finds it vitally important to distinguish between the Creator (the "Father") and His power of creation (the "Son"): "So spake th'Almighty, and to what he spake / His Word, the filial Godhead, gave effect" (7.174–175). The Son is the *logos* that guarantees an ultimate meaning in the world, and thus the mediator between creation and the Creator:

> . . . of all Creation first,
> Begotten Son, divine similitude,
> In whose conspicuous count'nance, without cloud
> Made visible, th'almighty Father shines,
> Whom else no creature can behold: on thee
> Impressed, th'effulgence of his glory abides,
> Transfus'd on thee his ample Spirit rests (3.383–389).

Theologically speaking, the "begetting" of God's "Son" involves the declaration that the universe is God's creation, that He is immanent within it, and that He is the meaning of which it is the sign. The "Son" of God, in short, is the guarantee that life is significant, that it means something, rather than nothing. It is this proposition against which Satan reacts. Thus Raphael tells Adam that Satan was:

. . . fraught
With envy against the Son of God, that day
Honour'd by his great Father, and proclaim'd
Messiah, King anointed, could not bear,
Through pride that sight, and thought himself impair'd (5.661–665).

It is the notion that the created world is an image of something beyond itself, a sign pointing to a referent, that Satan cannot stand. As he says himself, he finds it intolerable to be asked to give worship "to one, and to his image now proclaim'd" (5.784). The recognition of the "Son" logically implies the existence of a "Father," and for Milton, the "Son" is essentially the referral of creation to a Creator. The Son describes Himself to the Father as "Image of thee in all things" (6.736), and this renders His "dearest mediation" (3.226) genuinely efficacious, in contrast to Satan's artificial, magical efficacy. The Son, in short, is what Satan aspires to be: "Equal to God, and equally enjoying / Godlike fruition" (3.306–307). In "begetting" the Son, God announces his immanent presence throughout creation; he declares the world to be his handiwork. His exaltation immediately induces the birth of Sin from Satan's head, as the possibility of regarding creation with reference to the Creator simultaneously produces the antithetical possibility of denying the Creator and regarding creation as autonomous. It is this latter tendency of thought that Milton presents under the figure of "Satan."

Satan's conception of himself as autonomous and self-created has several important consequences. Being now "alienate from God" (5.877), he ceases to perceive an ultimate cause or significance—a *logos*—behind appearances, and he becomes unable to distinguish representation from reality. This produces an idolatrous attitude to creation, with which he infects first his fellow devils—who regard him as an "idol of majesty divine" (6.101)—and then the human couple. In serpentine guise he assures Eve that "ye shall be as gods" (9.708), that the fruit is itself "divine" (5.67) and thus "able to make gods of men" (5.70), and he urges her to "Take this, and be henceforth among the gods, / Thyself a goddess" (5.77–78). He also adopts an empirical approach to knowledge, assuming that the world of experience, the world of appearances, is the real world. His address to the tree of knowledge contains one of the poem's many connections between Baconian science and idolatry:

> O sacred, wise, and wisdom-giving plant,
> Mother of science, now I feel thy power
> Within me clear, not only to discern
> Things in their causes, but to trace the ways
> Of highest agents, deem'd however wise (9.679–683).

The "causes" after which Satan will seek are the "material," empirically perceptible causes, rather than the "final," teleological, and thus invisible cause. The newly fallen Eve's reaction to the plant is similar; she displays signs of worship and

> . . . low reverence done, as to the power
> That dwelt within, whose presence had infus'd
> Into the plant sciential sap, deriv'd
> From nectar, drink of gods . . . (9.835–838).

In these lines Milton skillfully indicts both primitive animism, which perceives a spirit within the plant, and classical mythology, which evolves a complicated pantheon of nectar-swilling gods.

But if we are tempted to relegate such idolatry to the superstitious civilizations of the past, we have paid insufficient attention to the message of *Paradise Lost*. The idea that what the Bible calls the "work of men's hands" (Psalm 135.15) can enter into an alien, hostile relationship to their producers should not be foreign to our world, which is ruled by the autonomous representation of human activity known as "money," and which systematically instills in its denizens the illusion that the domain of appearances is real. It is often remarked today that we live in a "society of the spectacle," in a condition of "alien-ation"; in some circles the biblical figure of "Babylon" still functions, as it did for Milton, as an appropriate trope for our situation. Generally speaking, however, the secularized Western mind eschews the vocabulary of scripture as representing what Raleigh called "dead ideas." Milton's historical understanding of truth as continuous revelation would have predisposed him to accept our abandonment of religious terminology with equanimity. He would not, however, have accepted the concomitant abandonment of the concepts to which that terminology refers. Nor should we. *Paradise Lost* teaches us that the inseparable companion—the "son"—of Sin and Satan is Death. If we choose to adopt the modes of thought and behavior that the poem describes as sinful and Satanic, we must confront the possibility that it is not Milton's ideas that are "dead," but our own.

———

DAVID HAWKES is Associate Professor of English at Lehigh University. He is the author of *Idols of the Marketplace* (Palgrave, 2001) and *Ideology* (Routledge, second edition, 2003). His work has appeared in *Milton Studies*, *The Nation*, *Times Literary Supplement*, *Journal of the History of Ideas*, *Huntingdon Library Quarterly*, and *Studies in English Literature*. Professor Hawkes recently received a long-term fellowship from the National Endowment for the Humanities to work on a book-length history and analysis of the Faust myth.

PARADISE LOST

A POEM

In Twelve Books

ON
PARADISE LOST

When I beheld the Poet blind, yet bold,
In slender book his vast design unfold;
Messiah crown'd, God's reconcil'd decree,
Rebelling angels, the forbidden tree,
Heaven, hell, earth, chaos, all! the argument
Held me a while misdoubting his intent,
That he would ruin (for I saw him strong)
The sacred truths to fable, and old song;
So Samson grop'd the temple's post in spite,
The world o'erwhelming, to revenge his sight.

Yet, as I read, soon growing less severe,
I lik'd his project, the success did fear;
Through that wide field how he his way should find,
O'er which lame faith leads understanding blind
Lest he perplex'd the things he would explain,
And what was easy he should render vain.

Or, if a work so infinite he spann'd,
Jealous I was that some less skilful hand
(Such as disquiet always what is well,
And by ill imitating would excel)
Might hence presume the whole creation's day
To change in scenes, and show it in a play.

Pardon me, mighty Poet, nor despise,
My causeless, yet not impious surmise.
But I am now convinc'd, and none will dare
Within thy labours to pretend a share.
Thou hast not miss'd one thought that could be fit,
And all that was improper dost omit;
So that no room is here for writers left,
But to detect their ignorance, or theft.

That majesty which through thy work doth reign,
Draws the devout, deterring the profane:
And things divine thou treat'st of in such state,
As them preserves, and thee, inviolate.
At once delight and horror on us seize,
Thou sing'st with so much gravity and ease;
And above human flight dost soar aloft,
With plume so strong, so equal and so soft;
The bird nam'd from that Paradise you sing
So never flags, but always keeps on wing.

Where couldst thou words of such a compass find?
Whence furnish such a vast expanse of mind?
Just heaven thee, like Tiresias, to requite,
Rewards with prophecy thy loss of sight.

Well might'st thou scorn thy readers to allure
With tinkling rhyme, of thy own sense secure;
While the Town-bays writes all the while and spells,
And, like a pack-horse, tires without his bells:
Their fancies like our bushy points appear,
The poets tag them, we for fashion wear.
I, too, transported by the mode, commend,
And while I mean to praise thee must offend.
Thy verse created like thy theme sublime,
In number, weight, and measure, needs not rhyme.

ANDREW MARVELL

The Verse

The measure is English heroic verse without rhyme, as that of Homer in Greek and of Virgil in Latin; rhyme being no necessary adjunct or true ornament of poem or good verse, in longer works especially, but the invention of a barbarous age, to set off wretched matter and lame meter; graced indeed since by the use of some famous modern poets, carried away by custom, but much to their own vexation, hindrance, and constraint to express many things otherwise, and for the most part worse than else they would have expressed them. Not without cause therefore some both Italian and Spanish poets of prime note have rejected rhyme both in longer and shorter works, as have also long since our best English tragedies, as a thing of itself, to all judicious ears, trivial and of no true musical delight; which consists only in apt numbers, fit quantity of syllables, and the sense variously drawn out from one verse into another, not in the jingling sound of like endings, a fault avoided by the learned ancients both in poetry and all good oratory. This neglect then of rhyme so little is to be taken for a defect, though it may seem so perhaps to vulgar readers, that it rather is to be esteemed an example set, the first in English, of ancient liberty recovered to heroic poem from the troublesome and modern bondage of rhyming.   [1668]

Contents

Book I • 9

Book II • 39

Book III • 77

Book IV • 105

Book V • 143

Book VI • 177

Book VII • 211

Book VIII • 235

Book IX • 261

Book X • 305

Book XI • 345

Book XII • 377

BOOK I

THE ARGUMENT

This first book proposes first, in brief, the whole subject, man's disobedience, and the loss thereupon of Paradise, wherein he was placed. Then touches the prime cause of his fall, the serpent, or rather Satan in the serpent;[1] who revolting from God, and drawing to his side many legions of angels, was, by the command of God, driven out of heaven with all his crew into the great deep. Which action passed over, the poem hastes into the midst of things, presenting Satan with his angels now fallen into hell, described here, not in the centre (for heaven and earth may be supposed as yet not made, certainly not yet accursed)* but in a place of utter darkness fitliest called Chaos:† Here Satan, with his angels, lying on the burning lake, thunder-struck and astonished, after a certain space recovers, as from confusion, calls up him who next in order and dignity lay by him; they confer of their miserable fall. Satan awakens all his legions, who lay till then in the same manner confounded; they rise; their numbers, array of battle, their chief leaders named according to the idols known afterwards in Canaan, and the countries adjoining. To these Satan directs his speech, comforts them with hope yet of regaining heaven; but tells them lastly of a new world, and new kind of creature to be created, according to an ancient prophecy or report in heaven; (for that angels were long before

---

* The fall of Satan must precede the fall of man, for he will be its cause.
† "Chaos" will be the allegorical character who both represents and rules the "abyss," where there is no meaning.

*this visible creation, was the opinion of many ancient
fathers.)* To find out the truth of this prophecy, and what to
determine thereon, he refers to a full council. What his
associates thence attempt. Pandemonium,† the palace of Satan,
rises, suddenly built out of the deep: the infernal peers there sit
in council.*

1   OF man's first disobedience, and the fruit
2   Of that forbidden tree, whose mortal taste
     Brought death into the world, and all our woe,
4   With loss of Eden, till one greater Man
5   Restore us, and regain the blissful seat,
6   Sing heavenly Muse; that on the secret top
7   Of Oreb, or of Sinai, didst inspire
8   That shepherd, who first taught the chosen seed,
     In the beginning how the heavens and earth
10   Rose out of Chaos: Or if Sion hill
11   Delight thee more, and Siloa's brook that flow'd
12   Fast by the oracle of God; I thence
     Invoke thy aid to my advent'rous song,
     That with no middle flight intends to soar

---

*An uncharacteristic reliance on patristic tradition, of which Milton is generally quite
skeptical.
†Literally, "place of all the demons."

1 *fruit* Also "result," the first of many usages that will condense literal and logical significances.   2 *mortal* Deadly.   4 *one greater Man* Jesus of Nazareth, known as the "second
Adam."   5 *seat* Dwelling place: The direct reference is to Eden, but metaphorically the
term also refers to heaven, to the "paradise within thee," and arguably to a new earthly
utopia.   6 *heavenly Muse* Like Homer and Virgil, Milton begins his epic with an invocation of the Muse; but the word "heavenly" suggests the Holy Spirit, and Milton's muse
is a composite source of inspiration, alluding to both monotheist and pagan concepts.
Fowler (p. 58) associates it with "the divine logos."   7 *Of Oreb, or of Sinai* Oreb is a spur
of Mt. Sinai, where Moses received the Ten Commandments.   8.1 *shepherd* Moses; 8.2
chosen seed The Israelites.   11 *Siloa's brook* Where Jesus restores the sight of a blind man
in John 9:7.   12 *the oracle of God* The temple in Jerusalem; Milton's use of the pagan term
"oracle" indicates that he is synthesizing Greek and Judaic traditions.

Above th'Aonian mount, while it pursues   15
Things unattempted yet in prose or rhyme.   16

And chiefly thou O spirit, that dost prefer
Before all temples th'upright heart and pure,   18
Instruct me, for thou know'st: thou from the first
Wast present, and, with mighty wings outspread,   20
Dove-like sat'st brooding on the vast abyss,   21
And mad'st it pregnant:² what in me is dark,   22
Illumine; what is low, raise and support;
That to the height of this great argument   24
I may assert eternal Providence,   25
And justify the ways of God to men.   26

Say first, for heaven hides nothing from thy view,
Nor the deep tract of hell, say first what cause
Mov'd our grand parents, in that happy state   29
Favour'd of Heaven so highly, to fall off   30
From their Creator, and transgress his will,
For one restraint, lords of the world besides?   32
Who first seduc'd them to that foul revolt?
Th'infernal serpent, he it was, whose guile
Stirr'd up with envy and revenge, deceiv'd   35
The mother of mankind, what time his pride   36
Had cast him out from heaven, with all his host
Of rebel angels; by whose aid aspiring
To set himself in glory above his peers,   39
He trusted to have equall'd the Most High,   40

---

15 *th'Aonian mount* Helicon, haunt of the classical Muses.   16 *Things . . . in prose or rhyme*
Paraphrasing *Orlando Furioso* 1.2 (1516), by the Italian poet Ludovico Ariosto, Milton
promises to surpass all previous authors.   18 *heart* The internal, figurative temple.   21.1
Dove-like In Luke 3:22 and John 1:32, the Holy Spirit descends in the form of a dove at the
baptism of Jesus.   21.2 *abyss* Chaos, the place of nonmeaning.   22 *pregnant* With meaning,
but anticipating the Holy Spirit's impregnation of Mary.   24 *argument* Subject.   26 *jus-
tify the ways of God to men* The technical term for this endeavor is "theodicy."   29 *our
grand parents* Adam and Eve.   32 *For* Because of.   36 *what time* At the time when.   39
peers Equals.

If he opposed: and with ambitious aim
Against the throne and monarchy of God,
Rais'd impious war in heaven and battle proud
44 With vain attempt. Him the Almighty power
45 Hurl'd headlong flaming from th'ethereal sky,
46 With hideous ruin and combustion down
To bottomless perdition, there to dwell
48 In adamantine chains and penal fire,
49 Who durst defy th'Omnipotent to arms.
50 Nine times the space that measures day and night
To mortal men, he with his horrid crew
Lay vanquish'd rolling in the fiery gulf
53 Confounded though immortal; but his doom
54 Reserv'd him to more wrath: for now the thought
55 Both of lost happiness and lasting pain
Torments him. Round he throws his baleful eyes
57 That witness'd huge affliction and dismay,
Mix'd with obdurate pride and steadfast hate
59 At once, as far as angels' ken, he views
60 The dismal situation waste and wild:
A dungeon horrible, on all sides round,
As one great furnace, flam'd: yet from those flames
No light, but rather darkness visible,
64 Serv'd only to discover sights of woe,
65 Regions of sorrow, doleful shades, where peace
66 And rest can never dwell; hope never comes
67 That comes to all: but torture without end

44–45 *Him . . . sky* Compare Isaiah 14:12: "How art thou fallen from heaven, O Lucifer, son of the morning!" (Throughout, quotations from the Bible are from the King James Version.) **46** *combustion* Conflagration. **48** *adamantine* Strong, but anticipates "Adam." **50–51** *Nine times the space . . . men* In *Theogeny* 664–735, the ninth-century B.C. Greek poet Hesiod says the Titans fell for nine days after their defeat by the Olympians. **53** *Confounded* Both "frustrated" and "damned." **54** *Reserved* Destined. **57** *witness'd huge affliction and dismay* Satan perceives abstract qualities as physically palpable. **59** *ken* Both "knowledge" and "physical sight." **60** *dismal situation waste and wild* The infernal landscape is at once literal and figural. **64** *discover* Reveal. **66–67** *hope never comes that comes to all* In Dante's *Inferno* (1321) the gates of Hell are inscribed with the words "Abandon all hope, ye who enter here" (3.9).

Still urges, and a fiery deluge, fed   68
With ever-burning sulphur unconsum'd,
Such place eternal justice had prepar'd   70
For those rebellious; here their prison ordain'd,
In utter darkness; and their portion set   72
As far removed from God and light of heaven
As from the centre thrice to th'utmost pole.   74
O how unlike the place from which they fell!   75
There the companions of his fall, o'erwhelm'd
With floods and whirlwinds of tempestuous fire,
He soon discerns: and welt'ring by his side   78
One next himself in power, and next in crime,
Long after known in Palestine, and nam'd   80
Beelzebub. To whom the arch-enemy,[3]   81
And thence in heaven called Satan, with bold words,   82
Breaking the horrid silence thus began:

If thou beest he—But O how fall'n! how chang'd
From him, who in the happy realms of light   85
Cloth'd with transcendent brightness, didst outshine
Myriads though bright; if he, whom mutual league,
United thoughts and counsels, equal hope,
And hazard in the glorious enterprise,
Join'd with me once, now misery hath join'd   90
In equal ruin; into what pit thou seest,
From what height fallen; so much the stronger prov'd
He with his thunder; and till then who knew   93
The force of those dire arms? Yet not for those,
Nor what the potent Victor in his rage   95
Can else inflict, do I repent or change,
Though chang'd in outward lustre, that fixt mind,   97
And high disdain from sense of injur'd merit,

---

68 *Still urges* Constantly torments. 72 *utter* Outer. 74 *the centre* Earth. 78 *welt'ring*
Tossing. 81 *Beelzebub* In Hebrew, "Lord of the Flies"; a Philistine sun-god. 82 *thence* Be-
cause of this. 93.1 *He* God; 93.2 *who knew* Satan is unwilling to alter his opinions ac-
cording to his external circumstances. 97 *fixt mind* Satan is unwilling to alter his
opinions according to his external circumstances.

That with the Mightiest rais'd me to contend:
100 And to the fierce contention brought along
Innumerable force of spirits arm'd,
That durst dislike his reign: and me preferring
His utmost power with adverse power oppos'd,
104 In dubious battle on the plains of heaven,
105 And shook his throne. What though the field be lost?
All is not lost; the unconquerable will,
And study of revenge, immortal hate,
And courage never to submit or yield;
(And what is else not to be overcome?)
110 That glory never shall his wrath or might
Extort from me, to bow and sue for grace
112 With suppliant knee and deify his power,
Who from the terror of his arm so late
Doubted his empire. That were low indeed;
115 That were an ignominy and shame beneath
116 This downfall; since by fate the strength of gods,
117 And this empyreal substance cannot fail;
Since through experience of this great event,
In arms not worse, in foresight much advanc'd,
120 We may with more successful hope resolve
To wage by force or guile eternal war,
Irreconcilable to our grand foe,
Who now triumphs, and in th'excess of joy
124 Sole reigning, holds the tyranny of heaven.

125 So spake the apostate angel, though in pain;
126 Vaunting aloud, but rack'd with deep despair:
127 And him thus answer'd soon his bold compeer:

104.1 *dubious* Refers to the ethics of the battle, but also suggests that the outcome was in doubt; 104.2 *plains of heaven* Satan describes Heaven as a physical place. 112 *deify his power* Make a god out of God's manifest qualities. 116 *by fate* Satan ascribes his nature to a force other than God; compare 7.173, where God declares, "What I will is fate." 117 *empyreal* Heavenly; recalls "imperial." 124 *Sole reigning . . . heaven* Contains an echo of the "personal rule" practiced by Charles I from 1629 to 1640, when he refused to call parliament, thus earning him the title of "tyrant" in Milton's eyes. 125 *apostate* Fallen, alienated. 126 *Vaunting* Boasting. 127 *compeer* Peer, companion.

O Prince; O chief of many throned powers,
That led th'embattled seraphim to war   129
Under thy conduct; and in dreadful deeds   130
Fearless, endanger'd heaven's perpetual King   131
And put to proof his high supremacy;
Whether upheld by strength, or chance, or fate,   133
Too well I see and rue the dire event,
That with sad overthrow and foul defeat,   135
Hath lost us heaven, and all this mighty host
In horrible destruction laid thus low,
As far as gods, and heavenly essences,   138
Can perish: for the mind and spirit remains
Invincible, and vigor soon returns,   140
Though all our glory extinct, and happy state,
Here swallow'd up in endless misery;
But what if he our conqueror (whom I now
Of force believe Almighty, since no less   144
Than such could have o'erpower'd such force as ours)   145
Have left us this our spirit and strength entire,
Strongly to suffer and support our pains;
That we may so suffice his vengeful ire,   148
Or do him mightier service, as his thralls
By right of war, whate'er his business be,   150
Here in the heart of hell to work in fire,
Or do his errands in the gloomy deep;
What can it then avail, though yet we feel
Strength undiminish'd, or eternal being,
To undergo eternal punishment?   155
Whereto with speedy words th'arch-fiend replied: 156

---

129 *seraphim* The highest order of angels. 131 *endanger'd* An implausible claim. 133 *Whether . . . fate* The possible reasons for God's triumph omit the true one: He is omnipotent. 138.1 *gods* Angels, but alluding to the classical pantheon; 138.2 *essences* Spirits. 144 *Of force* Both "by necessity" and "as a result of force"; in book VI God explains that force is the only language Satan understands. 148 *suffice* Satisfy. 156 *fiend* In Old English, "enemy."

Fallen Cherub, to be weak is miserable,
Doing or suffering: but of this be sure,
To do aught good never will be our task;
160   But ever to do ill our sole delight:
As being the contrary to his high will
Whom we resist. If then his providence
Out of our evil seek to bring forth good,
164   Our labour must be to pervert that end,
165   And out of good still to find means of evil:
Which oft-times may succeed, so as perhaps
167   Shall grieve him, if I fail not, and disturb
His inmost counsels from their destin'd aim.
But see! the angry Victor hath recall'd
170   His ministers of vengeance and pursuit
Back to the gates of heaven: the sulph'rous hail
Shot after us in storm, o'er-blown, hath laid
The fiery surge, that from the precipice
Of heaven receiv'd us falling, and the thunder,
175   Wing'd with red lightning and impetuous rage,
Perhaps hath spent his shafts, and ceases now
To bellow through the vast and boundless deep.
178   Let us not slip th'occasion, whether scorn,
Or satiate fury, yield it from our foe.
180   Seest thou yon dreary plain, forlorn and wild,
The seat of desolation, void of light,
Save what the glimmering of these livid flames
Casts pale and dreadful? thither let us tend
From off the tossing of these fiery waves;
185   There rest, if any rest can harbour there:
And re-assembling our afflicted powers,
Consult how we may henceforth most offend
Our enemy; our own loss how repair;
How overcome this dire calamity;

---

164 *to pervert that end* Satan's function will be to steer creation away from its proper purpose, or *telos.*   **167** *if I fail not* If I am not mistaken.   **178** *slip th'occasion* Miss the chance.

What reinforcement we may gain from hope;   190
If not, what resolution from despair.

Thus Satan talking to his nearest mate,
With head uplift above the wave, and eyes
That sparkling blaz'd; his other parts besides
Prone on the flood, extended long and large,   195
Lay floating many a rood: in bulk as huge,   196
As whom the fables name, of monstrous size,
Titanian, or Earth-born, that warr'd on Jove,   198
Briareus, or Typhon, whom the den   199
By ancient Tarsus held; or that sea-beast   200
Leviathan, which God of all his works   201
Created hugest that swim th'ocean stream:
(Him, haply slumb'ring on the Norway foam,
The pilot of some small night-founder'd skiff,
Deeming some island, oft, as seamen tell,   205
With fixed anchor in his scaly rind,
Moors by his side under the lee, while night   207
Invests the sea, and wished morn delays.)
So stretch'd out huge in length the arch-fiend lay,
Chain'd on the burning lake: nor ever thence   210
Had risen, or heav'd his head, but that the will   211
And high permission of all-ruling Heaven,   212
Left him at large to his own dark designs: 213
That with reiterated crimes he might   214
Heap on himself damnation, while he sought   215
Evil to others; and enrag'd might see,   216
How all his malice serv'd but to bring forth   217
Infinite goodness, grace, and mercy shown   218

---

196 *rood* Measure of land, approximately a quarter-acre. **198–200** *Titanian . . . held* In Hesiod's *Theogony*, the Titans, or Giants, warred against Jove, providing a Greek parallel to Satan's rebellion against God. Briareus was a Titan dwelling near Tarsus, in modern Syria. **201** *Leviathan* Sea monster, referred to as a serpent in Isaiah 27:1; used by English philosopher Thomas Hobbes to symbolize the state in his eponymous book (1651). **207** *lee* Shelter.

219 On man by him seduc'd; but on himself
220 Treble confusion, wrath, and vengeance poured.
Forthwith upright he rears from off the pool
His mighty stature; on each hand the flames
Driven backward slope their pointing spires, and roll'd
224 In billows, leave i' th'midst a horrid vale.
225 Then with expanded wings he steers his flight
Aloft, incumbent on the dusky air,
That felt unusual weight: till on dry land
He lights, if it were land that ever burn'd
With solid, as the lake with liquid fire:
230 And such appear'd in hue, as when the force
231 Of subterranean wind transports a hill
232 Torn from Pelorus, or the shatter'd side
233 Of thund'ring Ætna, whose combustible
234 And fuel'd entrails thence conceiving fire,
235 Sublim'd with mineral fury, aid the winds,
236 And leave a singed bottom all involv'd
237 With stench and smoke; such resting found the sole
Of unbless'd feet; him follow'd his next mate,
239 Both glorying to have 'scap'd the Stygian flood,
240 As gods, and by their own recover'd strength;
241 Not by the suff'rance of supernal power.

Is this the region, this the soil, the clime,
Said then the lost archangel, this the seat,
That we must change for heaven? this mournful gloom
245 For that celestial light? be it so; since he
Who now is sovereign can dispose, and bid
What shall be right: farthest from him is best,
Whom reason hath equall'd, force hath made supreme
Above his equals. Farewell, happy fields,

210–220 *nor ever thence . . . vengeance poured* An explicit assertion that Satan continues to serve God's purposes. 224 *horrid* Bristling. 230–237 Note the scatological imagery. 233 *Aetna* Live volcano on the island of Sicily. 239 *Stygian* Reminiscent of the infernal River Styx. 241 *supernal* Higher.

Where joy for ever dwells; hail, horrors; hail, 250
Infernal world; and thou profoundest hell
Receive thy new possessor! One, who brings
A mind not to be chang'd by place or time.
The mind is its own place, and in itself 254
Can make a heaven of hell, a hell of heaven.[4] 255
What matter where, if I be still the same,
And what I should be, all but less than he
Whom thunder hath made greater? Here at least
We shall be free; th'Almighty hath not built
Here for his envy; will not drive us hence: 260
Here we may reign secure; and in my choice
To reign is worth ambition, though in hell;
Better to reign in hell, than serve in heaven;
But wherefore let we then our faithful friends,
Th'associates and copartners of our loss, 265
Lie thus astonish'd on th'oblivious pool, 266
And call them not to share with us their part
In this unhappy mansion: or once more 268
With rallied arms to try, what may be yet
Regain'd in heaven, or what more lost in hell? 270

So Satan spake, and him Beelzebub
Thus answer'd: Leader of those armies bright,
Which but th'Omnipotent none could have foil'd;
If once they hear that voice, their liveliest pledge
Of hope in fears and dangers, heard so oft 275
In worst extremes, and on the perilous edge 276
Of battle when it rag'd, in all assaults
Their surest signal, they will soon resume
New courage, and revive, though now they lie
Grov'ling and prostrate on yon lake of fire, 280

---

254 *its* Milton uses "its" only three times in his poetry: here, at 4.813, and in l. 106 of his early poem "On the Morning of Christ's Nativity," also known as the "Nativity Ode" (1630); he generally personifies abstract qualities and forces of nature by using "his" or "hers." **266.1** *astonish'd* Thunder-struck; **266.2** *oblivious* Causing oblivion. **268** *mansion* Dwelling place. **276** *edge* Front line.

(As we erewhile,) astounded and amaz'd;

282   No wonder, fallen such a pernicious height.

He scarce had ceas'd, when the superior fiend
Was moving toward the shore; his pond'rous shield,

285   Etherial temper, massy, large, and round,
Behind him cast; the broad circumference
Hung on his shoulders like the moon, whose orb

288   Through optic glass the Tuscan artist views
At ev'ning from the top of Fesole,

290   Or in Valdarno, to descry new lands,
Rivers, or mountains, on her spotty globe.
His spear, (to equal which the tallest pine
Hewn on Norwegian hills, to be the mast

294   Of some great ammiral, were but a wand,)

295   He walk'd with, to support uneasy steps

296   Over the burning marle (not like those steps
On heaven's azure!) and the torrid clime
Smote on him sore besides, vaulted with fire.

299   Nathless he so endur'd, till on the beach

300   Of that inflamed sea he stood and call'd
His legions, angel-forms, who lay entranc'd,
Thick as autumnal leaves that strew the brooks

303   In Vallombrosa, where th'Etrurian shades,

304   High over-arch'd imbower; or scattered sedge

305   Afloat, when with fierce winds Orion arm'd

306   Hath vex'd the Red-Sea coast, whose waves o'erthrew

307   Busiris, and his Memphian chivalry,

308   While with perfidious hatred they pursu'd

309   The sojourners of Goshen, who beheld

---

282 *pernicious* Destructive. **285.1** *Etherial temper* Made in heaven; **285.2** *massy* Massive, heavy. **288.1** *optic glass* Telescope; **288.2** *the Tuscan artist* The astronomer Galileo, whom Milton visited in 1638–1639. Leonard (p. 297) notes that he "is the only one of Milton's contemporaries to be named" in *Paradise Lost*. **294** *ammiral* Flagship. **296** *marle* Soil. **299** *Nathless* Nonetheless. **303** *Vallombrosa* Near the Italian city of Florence; literally, "valley of shadows." **304** *sedge* Seaweed. **305** *Orion* Constellation supposed to bring storms.

From the safe shore their floating carcasses,   310
And broken chariot-wheels: so thick bestrown,   311
Abject and lost lay these, covering the flood,   312
Under amazement of their hideous change.
He call'd so loud, that all the hollow deep
Of hell resounded: Princes, Potentates,   315
Warriors, the flower of heaven! once yours, now lost,
If such astonishment as this can seize
Eternal spirits: or have ye chosen this place
After the toil of battle to repose
Your wearied virtue, for the ease you find   320
To slumber here, as in the vales of heaven?
Or in this abject posture have ye sworn
T'adore the Conqueror? who now beholds
Cherub and seraph rolling in the flood,
With scatter'd arms and ensigns; till anon   325
His swift pursuers from heaven-gates discern
Th'advantage, and descending tread us down
Thus drooping; or with linked thunderbolts
Transfix us to the bottom of this gulf.
Awake, arise, or be for ever fallen.   330

They heard, and were abash'd and up they sprung
Upon the wing; as when men wont to watch   332
On duty, sleeping found by whom they dread,
Rouse and bestir themselves ere well awake.
Nor did they not perceive the evil plight   335
In which they were, or the fierce pains not feel;
Yet to their general's voice they soon obey'd,
Innumerable; as when the potent rod
Of Amram's son, in Egypt's evil day,   339

306–311 *Hath . . . chariot wheels* Refers to Pharaoh's pursuit of the Israelites across the Red Sea.   312 *Abject* Cast down.   320 *virtue* Power, essence.   332 *wont* Used.   339 *Amram's son* Moses, whose miraculous power contrasts with Satan's demonic magic. Milton may have had in mind a correlation with his own life: In Ezra 10, another Amram marries a foreign woman and is ordered to separate from her.

340   Wav'd round the coast, up call'd a pitchy cloud
341   Of locusts, warping on the eastern wind,
       That o'er the realm of impious Pharaoh hung
       Like night, and darken'd all the land of Nile:
       So numberless were those bad angels, seen
345   Hov'ring on wing under the cope of hell,
       'Twixt upper, nether, and surrounding fires
       Till, as a signal given, th'uplifted spear
348   Of their great sultan waving to direct
       Their course, in even balance down they light
350   On the firm brimstone, and fill all the plain:
351   A multitude, like which the populous north
352   Pour'd never from her frozen loins, to pass
353   Rhine or the Danaw, when her barbarous sons
354   Came like a deluge on the south, and spread
355   Beneath Gibraltar to the Libyan sands.
       Forthwith from every squadron, and each band,
       The heads and leaders thither haste where stood
358   Their great commander; godlike shapes and forms
       Excelling human, princely dignities,
360   And powers! that erst in heaven sat on thrones;
       Though of their names in heavenly records now
362   Be no memorial; blotted out and raz'd,
       By their rebellion, from the books of life.
       Nor had they yet among the sons of Eve
365   Got them new names; till wand'ring o'er the earth,
366   Through God's high sufferance for the trial of man,
       By falsities and lies the greatest part
       Of mankind they corrupted, to forsake
       God their Creator, and th'invisible

---

340 *pitchy* Black.   341 *warping* Prince identifies this as a nautical term meaning "moving forward by jerks or degrees."   345 *cope* Canopy, cloak.   348 *sultan* Associated with tyrannical, arbitrary personal government, and also with Satan.   351–355 *A multitude . . . Libyan sands* Refers to the barbarian invasions of the Roman empire.   358 *godlike shapes and forms* The demons have the appearance of angels, but no longer the essence.   360 *erst* Formerly. 362 *raz'd* Erased.   366 *sufferance* Permission.

Glory of him that made them, to transform   370
Oft to the image of a brute, adorn'd
With gay religions full of pomp and gold,
And devils to adore for deities:[5]
Then were they known to men by various names,
And various idols through the heathen world.   375

Say, Muse, their names then known; who first, who last,
Rous'd from the slumber, on that fiery couch,
And their great emperor's call as next in worth   378
Came singly where he stood on the bare strand,   379
While the promiscuous crowd stood yet aloof?   380
The chief were those who, from the pit of hell
Roaming to seek their prey on earth, durst fix
Their seats long after next the seat of God,
Their altars by his altar, gods ador'd
Among the nations round, and durst abide   385
Jehovah[6] thund'ring out of Sion, thron'd
Between the cherubim; yea, often plac'd
Within his sanctuary itself their shrines,
Abominations; and with cursed things
His holy rites and solemn feasts profan'd,   390
And with their darkness durst affront his light.
First Moloch, horrid king, besmear'd with blood   392
Of human sacrifice, and parents' tears;
Though, for the noise of drums and timbrels loud
Their children's cries unheard, that pass'd through fire   395
To his grim idol. Him the Ammonite   396
Worshipp'd in Rabba, and her watery plain   397
In Argob, and in Basan, to the stream   398
Of utmost Arnon. Nor content with such   399

---

378 *emperor's call* Associates Satan with the triumph of Julius Caesar over the Republicans
in the Roman civil war, which made Rome into an empire and thus, in Milton's opinion,
causing her decadence, decline, and destruction.   379 *strand* Beach.   380 *promiscuous*
Swarming, confused.   385 *abide* Endure.   392 *Moloch* Hebrew for "king;" a heathen sun-
god worshiped with human sacrifice.   396–399 *Him . . . Arnon* Fowler (p. 85) notes that
the cities mentioned in this passage are associated in 2 Samuel 12:30 with the defeat of the
worshipers of Moloch by King David.

400	Audacious neighbourhood, the wisest heart
401	Of Solomon he led by fraud, to build
402	His temple right against the temple of God,
403	On the opprobrious hill; and made his grove
	The pleasant valley of Hinnom, Tophet thence
405	And black Gehenna called, the type of hell.[7]
406	Next Chemos, th'obscene dread of Moab's sons,
407	From Aroar to Nebo, and the wild
408	Of southmost Abarim; in Hesebon
409	And Horonaim, Seon's realm, beyond
410	The flowery dale of Sibma, clad with vines;
411	And Eleale to th'Asphaltic pool:
	Peor his other name, when he entic'd
	Israel in Sittim, on their march from Nile,
	To do him wanton rites, which cost them woe.[8]
415	Yet thence his lustful orgies he enlarg'd
	Even to that hill of scandal, by the grove
417	Of Moloch homicide; lust hard by hate;
418	Till good Josiah drove them thence to hell.
	With these came they, who from the bord'ring flood
420	Of old Euphrates, to the brook that parts
	Egypt from Syrian ground, had general names
	Of Baalim, and Ashtaroth;[9] those male,
	These feminine: For spirits when they please

---

400 *heart* Solomon's heart, the interior temple, is contrasted with his idolatrous external temples.   **401** *Solomon* Whose heathen wives induced him to build temples to idols. Fowler notes that "James I's Solomon cult provoked the charge that he was punished through his son for whoring after the strange god of Catholicism" (p. 85).   **402** *right against* Both "just next to" and "directly opposed to."   **403.1** *opprobrious hill* The Mount of Olives, called the Mount of Corruption in 2 Kings 23:13, because Solomon built his shrines to idols there; see also lines 416 and 443; **403.2** *grove* In Hebrew, *ashera*; referring to Asherah, a Canaanite goddess.   **406–411** *Next Chemos . . . pool* Chemos was the Moabite sun-god; Milton here maps out the biblical land of the Moabites; the "Asphaltic pool" is the Dead Sea.   **417.1** *homicide* Murderer, a reference to the human sacrifice Moloch demanded of his worshipers; **417.2** *lust hard by hate* One god was worshiped through the sexual act, the other through murder. Milton signals that we are to regard the characters of Peor and Moloch as symbols of lust and hate, respectively.   **418** *Josiah* Iconoclast king of Judah, who in 2 Kings 23:10–14 purged the land of Assyrian idols.

Can either sex assume, or both; so soft
And uncompounded is their essence pure;   425
Not tied or manacled with joint or limb,
Nor founded on the brittle strength of bones,
Like cumbrous flesh; but in what shape they choose
Dilated or condens'd, bright or obscure   429
Can execute their airy purposes,   430
And works of love or enmity fulfil.[10]
For those the race of Israel oft forsook
Their living strength, and unfrequented left   433
His righteous altar, bowing lowly down
To bestial gods; for which their heads as low   435
Bow'd down in battle, sunk before the spear
Of despicable foes. With these in troop
Came Astoreth, whom the Phenicians call'd
Astarte, queen of heaven, with crescent horns   439
To whose bright image nightly by the moon,   440
Sidonian virgins paid their vows and songs;   441
In Sion also not unsung, where stood
Her temple on th'offensive mountain, built   443
By that uxorious king, whose heart, though large,   444
Beguil'd by fair idolatresses, fell   445
To idols foul. Thammuz came next behind,   446
Whose annual wound in Lebanon allur'd
The Syrian damsels, to lament his fate
In am'rous ditties all a summer's day;
While smooth Adonis from his native rock   450

---

429 *Dilated* Expanded, swollen.   433 *Their living strength* Jehovah.   435 *bestial gods* Sign and
significance are in harmony here: The fact that these gods were represented as animals be-
trays their morally repugnant nature.   439 *Astarte, queen of heaven* Phoenician goddess, as-
sociated with the Greek Aphrodite and Roman Venus, possibly identical to Ashtoreth,
another Phoenician goddess.   441 *Sidonian* From Sidon, in Phoenicia.   443 *th'offensive
mountain* See note for "opprobrious hill" at line 403.   444 *uxorious king* Solomon was
ruled in matters of religion by his heathen wives.   446 *Thammuz* Phoenician god who was
a lover of Astarte; associated with the Greek Adonis; see also note for Astarte at 1.439.
450 *Adonis* Greek god, lover of Aphrodite, and also a river in Lebanon. Prince notes: "The
festival of Thammuz-Adonis was a vegetation and fertility cult based on the 'death' of the
sun in the winter solstice, and his return in spring" (p. 123).

Ran purple to the sea, suppos'd with blood
Of Thammuz yearly wounded: the love-tale
Infected Sion's daughters with like heat;
Whose wanton passions in the sacred porch
455   Ezekiel saw, when, by the vision led,
His eye survey'd the dark idolatries
457   Of alienated Judah. Next came one
458   Who mourn'd in earnest, when the captive ark
459   Maim'd his brute image, head and hands lopp'd off
460   In his own temple, on the grunsel edge,
461   Where he fell flat, and sham'd his worshippers;
462   Dagon his name; sea monster; upward man
And downward fish: yet had his temple high
464   Rear'd in Azotus, dreaded through the coast
465   Of Palestine, in Gath, and Ascalon,
466   And Accaron, and Gaza's frontier bounds.
467   Him follow'd Rimmon, whose delightful seat
Was fair Damascus, on the fertile banks
Of Abbana, and Pharphar, lucid streams;
470   He also against the house of God was bold:
471   A leper once he lost, and gain'd a king,
472   Ahaz, his sottish conqueror, whom he drew
God's altar to disparage, and displace,
474   For one of Syrian mode, whereon to burn
475   His odious off'rings, and adore the gods
Whom he had vanquish'd. After these appear'd
A crew who under names of old renown,
Osiris, Isis, Orus,[11] and their train,

---

457 *alienated* Both "exiled" and "made other." In Ezekiel 8, the prophet condemns the Israelites for falling into this cult; their idolatry is described as a kind of Fall, resulting in separation from God.   460 *grunsel edge* Threshold.   457–462 *Next . . . Dagon his name* 1 Samuel 5:1–4 tells the story of how God destroyed an icon of Dagon, the main Philistine deity.   464–466 *Azotus . . . Accaron* Major Philistine cities.   467 *Rimmon* Syrian god. 471 *A leper once he lost* Naaman, a captain in the Syrian army, renounces Rimmon after being cured of leprosy by Elisha in 2 Kings 5.   472.1 *Ahaz* Israelite king who, in 2 Kings 16, abandons God for Rimmon, sacrifices a son to him, and ignores Isaiah's prophecy of the incarnation; 472.2 *sottish* Foolish.   474 *mode* Manufacture.

With monstrous shapes and sorceries abus'd   479
Fanatic Egypt, and her priests, to seek   480
Their wand'ring gods disguis'd in brutish forms
Rather than human. Nor did Israel 'scape
The infection, when their borrow'd gold compos'd
The calf in Oreb; and the rebel king   484
Doubled that sin in Bethel, and in Dan,   485
Lik'ning his Maker to the grazed ox,
Jehovah, who in one night when he pass'd
From Egypt marching, equall'd with one stroke
Both her first-born and all her bleating gods.
Belial came last, than whom a spirit more lewd   490
Fell not from heaven, or more gross to love
Vice for itself: to him no temple stood,
Or altar smok'd; yet who more oft than he
In temples, and at altars, when the priest
Turns atheist, as did Eli's sons, who fill'd   495
With lust and violence the house of God?
In courts and palaces he also reigns,
And in luxurious cities, where the noise
Of riot ascends above their loftiest towers,
And injury and outrage: and when night   500
Darkens the streets, then wander forth the sons   501
Of Belial, flown with insolence and wine.   502
Witness the streets of Sodom, and that night
In Gibeah, when the hospitable door
Expos'd a matron, to avoid worse rape.[12]   505

These were the prime, in order and in might;
The rest were long to tell, though far renown'd.
Th'Ionian gods, of Javan's issue[13] held

---

479 *abus'd* Deceived, often used with reference to idolatry.   **484.1** *calf* Golden calf destroyed by Moses in Exodus 32;   **484.2** *rebel king* Jeroboam, who makes two calves of gold in 1 Kings 12:28–33. Leonard points out: "The oxymoron implies that kingship is a kind of rebellion" (p. 301).   **490** *Belial* Hebrew for "Worthlessness" or "Vanity."   **495** *Eli's sons* They are called "sons of Belial" in 1 Samuel 2:12.   **501–502** *the sons / Of Belial* Sensualists; **502** *flown* Flushed.

509   Gods, yet confess'd later than heaven and earth,
510   Their boasted parents. Titan, heaven's first born,
        With his enormous brood, and birthright seiz'd
        By younger Saturn:[14] he from mightier Jove,
513   (His own and Rhea's son,) like measure found
        So Jove usurping reign'd; these first in Crete
515   And Ida known; thence on the snowy top
516   Of cold Olympus rul'd the middle air,
517   Their highest heaven; or on the Delphian cliff,
518   Or in Dodona, and through all the bounds
519   Of Doric land; or who with Saturn old
520   Fled over Adria to th'Hesperian fields,
521   And o'er the Celtic roam'd the utmost isles.

        All these and more came flocking, but with looks
        Downcast and damp; yet such wherein appear'd
        Obscure some glimpse of joy to have found their chief
525   Not in despair, to have found themselves not lost
        In loss itself; which on his count'nance cast
        Like doubtful hue: but he his wonted pride
        Soon recollecting, with high words, that bore
529   Semblance of worth, not substance, gently rais'd
530   Their fainting courage, and dispell'd their fears.
        Then straight commands that at the warlike sound
        Of trumpets loud, and clarions, be uprear'd
        His mighty standard: that proud honour claim'd
534   Azazel as his right, a cherub tall;
535   Who forthwith from the glittering staff unfurl'd

---

509 *heaven and earth* Uranus and Gaea, in Greek mythology.   **509–510.1** *yet confess'd . . . parents* Milton finds it absurd that gods should be imagined as having been born after the heaven and earth; he believes that deity consists in the power of creation; **510.2** *Titan* Son of Uranus and Gaea.   **513** *Rhea* Daughter of Uranus and Gaea, wife of Saturn, mother of Zeus (also known as Jove).   **515** *Ida* Birthplace of Zeus (Jove).   **516** *Olympus* Home of the Olympian gods.   **517** *the Delphian cliff* The oracle of Apollo at Delphi.   **518** *Dodona* Site of the oracle of Zeus (Jove).   **519** *Doric* Greek.   **520.1** *Adria* The Adriatic Sea, over which Saturn fled when his son, Zeus (Jove), overthrew him; **520.2** *Hesperian fields* Italy.   **521.1** *Celtic* France; **521.2** *the utmost isles* The British Isles.   **529** *semblance of worth, not substance* Satan is a rhetorician, not a logician.   **534** *Azazel* Hebrew for "scapegoat."

Th'imperial ensign; which, full high advanc'd,
Shone like a meteor streaming to the wind,
With gems and golden lustre rich emblaz'd,
Seraphic arms and trophies; all the while
Sonorous metal blowing martial sounds: 540
At which the universal host up sent
A shout that tore hell's concave; and beyond   542
Frighted the reign of Chaos and old Night.
All in a moment through the gloom were seen
Ten thousand banners rise into the air,   545
With orient colours waving: with them rose   546
A forest huge of spears; and thronging helm   547
Appear'd, and serried shields in thick array,   548
Of depth immeasurable: anon they move   549
In perfect phalanx, to the Dorian mood   550
Of flutes, and soft recorders; such as rais'd
To height of noblest temper heroes old
Arming to battle; and instead of rage,
Deliberate valour breath'd, firm, and unmov'd
With dread of death to flight, or foul retreat;   555
Nor wanting power to mitigate and swage,   556
With solemn touches, troubled thoughts, and chase
Anguish, and doubt, and fear, and sorrow, and pain,
From mortal or immortal minds. Thus they
Breathing united force, with fixed thought   560
Mov'd on in silence to soft pipes, that charm'd   561
Their painful steps o'er the burnt soil: and now
Advanc'd in view, they stand, a horrid front
Of dreadful length, and dazzling arms, in guise
Of warriors old with order'd spear and shield,   565
Awaiting what command their mighty chief
Had to impose: he through the armed files

---

542 *concave* Vaulted ceiling. 546 *orient* Pearly. 547 *helm* Helmets. 548 *serried* Interlinked. 549 *anon* Straight away. 550 *Dorian mood* Mode of Greek music associated with martial valor. 556 *swage* Assuage. 561 *charm'd* The demons are associated with magic.

568   Darts his experienc'd eye, and soon traverse
      The whole battalion views, their order due,
570   Their visages and stature as of gods;
      Their number last he sums. And now his heart
572   Distends with pride, and hard'ning in his strength
      Glories: for never since created man
      Met such embodied force, as nam'd with these
575   Could merit more than that small infantry
576   Warr'd on by cranes; though all the giant brood
577   Of Phlegra with th'heroic race were join'd,
578   That fought at Thebes and Ilium, on each side
579   Mix'd with auxiliar gods: and what resounds
580   In fable or romance of Uther's son,
581   Begirt with British and Armoric knights;
      And all who since baptiz'd or infidel,
583   Jousted in Aspramont, or Montalban,
584   Damasco, or Morocco, or Trebisond;
585   Or whom Biserta sent from Afric shore,
      When Charlemain with all his peerage fell
587   By Fontarabbia. Thus far these beyond
      Compare of mortal prowess, yet observ'd
589   Their dread commander: he above the rest
590   In shape and gesture proudly eminent
      Stood like a tower: his form had not yet lost
      All her original brightness, nor appear'd
      Less than archangel ruin'd, and th'excess

---

568 *traverse* Across.   572 *hard'ning in* Becoming hard because of, as God "hardens" Pharaoh's heart in Exodus 10:1.   575–576 *that small . . . cranes* The story of the war between the Pygmies and the cranes is from the *Iliad* 3.3–6.   577 *Phlegra* Where the Titans battled the Olympians.   578 *Ilium* Troy.   579 *auxiliar* Auxiliary.   580 *Uther's son* King Arthur, about whom Milton had considered writing an epic. Having considered the heathen and the classical gods, he now begins a meditation on the value of human heroes.   581 *Begirt* Surrounded.   583 *Aspramont* Where Charlemagne defeated the Saracens.   584–585 *Damasco . . . Biserta* Scenes of famous chivalric tournaments.   587 *Fontarabbia* Fuenterrabía, on the border between France and Spain, near the scene of Charlemagne's famous defeat. Fowler (p. 97) points out that Charles II visited the city in 1659, to rally French and Spanish support against the Commonwealth.   589 *dread* Feared.

Of glory obscur'd: as when the sun new risen 594
Looks through the horizontal misty air, 595
Shorn of his beams; or from behind the moon, 596
In dim eclipse, disastrous twilight sheds 597
On half the nations, and with fear of change 598
Perplexes monarchs; darken'd so, yet shone 599
Above them all th'archangel: but his face 600
Deep scars of thunder had intrench'd, and care
Sat on his faded cheek, but under brows
Of dauntless courage, and considerate pride
Waiting revenge: cruel his eye, but cast
Signs of remorse and passion, to behold 605
The fellows of his crime, the followers rather,
(Far other once beheld in bliss) condemn'd
For ever now to have their lot in pain;
Millions of spirits, for his fault amerc'd 609
Of heaven, and from eternal splendours flung 610
For his revolt; yet faithful how they stood,
Their glory wither'd: as when heaven's fire
Hath scath'd the forest oaks, or mountain pines, 613
With singed top their stately growth, though bare,
Stands on the blasted heath. He now prepar'd 615
To speak, whereat their doubled ranks they bend
From wing to wing, and half enclose him round
With all his peers: attention held them mute: 618
Thrice he assay'd, and thrice in spite of scorn, 619
Tears, such as angels weep, burst forth, at last 620
Words interwove with sighs found out their way.

594–597 *as when . . . in dim eclipse* Satan is compared to the sun behind clouds, or in eclipse.
597 *disastrous* Of a malign star.   598–599 *with fear of change / Perplexes monarchs* Eclipses were supposed to presage political upheaval. Leonard reminds us that "Charles II's censor objected to these lines."   605 *Signs* Satan deals in the currency of sign, not substance.
609 *amerc'd* Held financially liable, fined.   613 *scath'd* Injured.   615 *blasted heath* In Shakespeare's *Macbeth* (act 1, scene 3), this is where the witches meet.   618 *peers* Both "nobility" and "equals."   619 *assay'd* Attempted to begin.   620 *such as angels weep* Reminding us that angels are spiritual as well as physical beings.

O myriads of immortal spirits; O powers
Matchless, but with th'Almighty, and that strife
624   Was not inglorious, though th'event was dire,
625   As this place testifies, and this dire change,
Hateful to utter: but what power of mind,
Foreseeing, or presaging, from the depth
Of knowledge past or present, could have fear'd,
How such united force of gods, how such
630   As stood like these, could ever know repulse?
631   For who can yet believe, though after loss,
632   That all these puissant legions, whose exile
Hath emptied heaven, shall fail to reascend
634   Self-rais'd, and repossess their native seat?
635   For me be witness all the host of heaven,
636   If counsels different, or danger shunn'd
By me, have lost our hopes: but he who reigns
Monarch in heaven, till then as one secure
639   Sat on his throne, upheld by old repute,
640   Consent, or custom, and his regal state
Put forth at full, but still his strength conceal'd,
642   Which tempted our attempt, and wrought our fall.
Henceforth his might we know, and know our own,
So as not either to provoke, or dread
645   New war, provok'd. Our better part remains
646   To work in close design, by fraud or guile,
What force effected not: that he no less
At length from us may find, who overcomes
By force, hath overcome but half his foe.
650   Space may produce new worlds; whereof so rife
651   There went a fame in heaven, that he, ere long,

---

624 *event* Result.   631 *loss* Defeat.   632 *puissant* Powerful.   634 *Self-rais'd* Satan's mistake
is to believe that his power is independent of God's.   636 *different* Simultaneously, "dif-
fering from what I have just said," "deferring action," and "recognizing difference." The
aim of Satan's rebellion is to erase his difference from God.   639–640 *upheld by old repute,
/ Consent, or custom* Satan gives three contradictory justifications for God's authority.
642 *Which tempted our attempt* God is absurdly described as tempting Satan to rebel.
646 *close* Secret.   651 *fame* Rumor.

Intended to create; and therein plant
A generation, whom his choice regard
Should favour equal to the sons of heaven:
Thither, if but to pry, shall be perhaps   655
Our first eruption, thither or elsewhere:
For this infernal pit shall never hold
Celestial spirits in bondage, nor th'abyss
Long under darkness cover. But these thoughts
Full counsel must mature: Peace is despair'd,   660
For who can think submission? War then, war
Open or understood, must be resolv'd.

He spake: and to confirm his words out flew
Millions of flaming swords, drawn from the thighs
Of mighty cherubim: the sudden blaze   665
Far round illumin'd hell; highly they rag'd
Against the Highest, and fierce with grasped arms
Clash'd on their sounding shields the din of war,
Hurling defiance toward the vault of heaven.

There stood a hill not far, whose grisly top   670
Belch'd fire and rolling smoke; the rest entire
Shone with a glassy scurf; (undoubted sign
That in his womb was hid metallic ore,
The work of sulphur,) thither wing'd with speed   674
A numerous brigade hasten'd: as when bands   675
Of pioneers, with spade and pickaxe arm'd,
Forerun the royal camp, to trench a field,
Or cast a rampart: Mammon led them on,   678
Mammon, the least erected spirit that fell
From heaven: for even in heaven his looks and thoughts   680
Were always downward bent; admiring more

---

674 *work of sulphur* In the alchemical worldview, metals could be grown in the earth by the
agency of sulfur or mercury.   678 *Mammon* Personification of money, associated with the
Greek Plutus, god of money, and Pluto, ruler of the underworld. Jesus twice makes the un-
ambiguous assertion: "Ye cannot serve God and Mammon" (Matthew 6:24, Luke 16:13).

682 The riches of heaven's pavement, trodden gold,
   Than aught divine or holy else, enjoy'd
   In vision beatific: by him first
685 Men also, and by his suggestion taught,
   Ransack'd the centre, and with impious hands
   Rifled the bowels of their mother earth
688 For treasures better hid. Soon had his crew
   Open'd into the hill a spacious wound,
690 And digg'd out ribs of gold. (Let none admire
   That riches grow in hell; that soil may best
692 Deserve the precious bane.) And here let those
   Who boast in mortal things, and wond'ring tell
694 Of Babel, and the works of Memphian kings,
695 Learn how their greatest monuments of fame,
   And strength, and art, are easily outdone
   By spirits reprobate, and in an hour,
   What in an age they with incessant toil,
699 And hands innumerable, scarce perform.
700 Nigh on the plain in many cells prepar'd,
   That underneath had veins of liquid fire
702 Sluic'd from the lake, a second multitude
703 With wondrous art founded the massy ore
704 Severing each kind, and scumm'd the bullion dross.
705 A third as soon had form'd within the ground
   A various mould; and from the boiling cells

---

682 *gold* Mammon idolizes gold. 688 *better hid* Mammon inspires human beings to worship gold. In antiquity, the idea of mining as a rape of the earth was even more widespread than it is today, and for this reason miners were the most despised kind of slaves. 690 *ribs of gold* A demonic re-creation, ironically prefiguring God's creation of Eve. 692 *precious bane* An oxymoron, using "precious" in the financial sense and "bane" (poison) in the moral sense. 694.1 *Babel* Tower of Babel, near Babylon, destroyed by God as a warning against human hubris; 694.2 *works of Memphian kings* The Egyptian pyramids, emblems of vainly fetishized labor (see Introduction). 699 *scarce perform* The efficacy of demonic labor reveals the absurdity of fetishizing human works. 702 *Sluic'd* Drained. 703.1 *wondrous art* Connotes magic; 703.2 *founded* The 1674 edition has "found out." 704 *scumm'd the bullion dross* Note the ethical coloring Milton gives to the description. The devils are in fact purifying the ore, but the vain purpose behind their enterprise robs their activity of any beneficent associations.

By strange conveyance fill'd each hollow nook:
As in an organ, from one blast of wind,
To many a row of pipes the sound-board breathes.
Anon out of the earth a fabric huge   710
Rose like an exhalation, with the sound
Of dulcet symphonies, and voices sweet,
Built like a temple, where pilasters round   713
Were set, and Doric pillars, overlaid
With golden architrave: nor did there want   715
Cornice, or frieze, with bossy sculptures graven;
The roof was fretted gold. Not Babylon,   717
Nor great Alcairo, such magnificence   718
Equall'd in all their glories, to inshrine
Belus, or Serapis, their gods; or seat   720
Their kings, when Egypt with Assyria strove
In wealth and luxury. Th'ascending pile   722
Stood fixt her stately height: and straight the doors
Op'ning their brazen folds, discover wide   724
Within her ample spaces o'er the smooth   725
And level pavement: from the arched roof,
Pendent by subtle magic, many a row   727
Of starry lamps, and blazing cressets, fed   728
With Naphtha and Asphaltus, yielded light,   729
As from a sky. The hasty multitude   730
Admiring enter'd, and the work some praise,
And some the architect: his hand was known
In heaven by many a tow'red structure high,
Where sceptred angels held their residence,
And sat as princes; whom the supreme King   735

---

710 *Anon* At once.   713 *temple* An idolatrous parallel to the Temple of God.   715 *archi-trave* Beam.   717 *Babylon* Biblical city that has become the archetypal symbol of alien-ation.   718 *Alcairo* Cairo, Egypt, an archetypal symbol of bondage.   720 *Belus, or Serapis* Baal and Osiris, Assyrian and Egyptian fertility gods.   722 *pile* Building.   724 *discover* Re-veal.   727 *magic* The means by which demons exercise their power; 728.1 *starry lamps* Em-phasizes the artificial, unnatural character of the building;   728.2 *cressets* Lamps in baskets.   729 *Naphtha and Asphaltus* Oil and pitch.   730 *As from a sky* Again, the demons have manufactured an artificial creation.

Exalted to such power, and gave to rule,
737 Each in his hierarchy, the orders bright:
Nor was his name unheard, or unador'd,
In ancient Greece; and in Ausonian land
740 Men call'd him Mulciber: and how he fell
From heaven they fabled, thrown by angry Jove
Sheer o'er the crystal battlements; from morn
To noon he fell, from noon to dewy eve,
A summer's day; and with the setting sun
745 Dropp'd from the zenith like a falling star,
On Lemnos th'Ægean isle: thus they relate,
747 Erring; for he with this rebellious rout
Fell long before; nor aught avail'd him now
T'have built in heaven high towers; nor did he scape
750 By all his engines, but was headlong sent
With his industrious crew to build in hell.

Meanwhile the winged heralds by command
753 Of sov'reign power, with awful ceremony
And trumpet's sound, throughout the host proclaim
755 A solemn council forthwith to be held
756 At Pandemonium, the high capital
Of Satan and his peers: their summons call'd,
From every band and squared regiment,
759 By place or choice the worthiest, they anon
760 With hundreds, and with thousands, trooping came
Attended: all access was throng'd, the gates
And porches wide, but chief the spacious hall
(Though like a cover'd field, where champions bold
764 Wont ride in arm'd, and at the Soldan's chair

---

737 *hierarchy* Rank.   740 *Mulciber* The Greek Hephaestos and Roman Vulcan, blacksmith to the gods, thrown out of heaven by Zeus in Homer's *Iliad* 1.588–95.   747.1 *Erring* A typically Miltonic deflation.   747.2 *rout* Rabble.   753 *awful* Awesome.   756.1 *Pandemonium* In Greek, "place of all the demons"; the word is Milton's coinage;   756.2 *capital* The 1667 edition has "capitol."   759 *by place or choice* The question of what qualifies the demons as "worthiest" is left significantly vague.   764 *Soldan's* Sultan's.

Defied the best of Panim chivalry   765
To mortal combat, or career with lance)   766
Thick swarm'd, both on the ground, and in the air,
Brush'd with the hiss of rustling wings. As bees
In spring time, when the sun with Taurus rides,
Pour forth their populous youth about the hive   770
In clusters; they among fresh dews and flowers
Fly to and fro, or on the smoothed plank,
(The suburb of their straw-built citadel,)
New rubb'd with balm, expatiate and confer   774
Their state affairs: so thick the airy crowd   775
Swarm'd and were straiten'd; till the signal given: 776
Behold a wonder; they but now who seem'd   777
In bigness to surpass earth's giant sons,
Now less than smallest dwarf's, in narrow room
Throng numberless, like that pygmean race   780
Beyond the Indian mount; or fairy elves;   781
Whose midnight revels, by a forest side,
Or fountain, some belated peasant sees,   783
Or dreams he sees; while over head the moon   784
Sits arbitress, and nearer to the earth   785
Wheels her pale course; they on their mirth and dance
Intent, with jocund music charm his ear: 787
At once with joy and fear his heart rebounds.
Thus incorporeal spirits to smallest forms
Reduc'd their shapes immense: and were at large   790
Though without number still, amidst the hall
Of that infernal court. But far within,
And in their own dimensions like themselves,   793
The great Saraphic lords, and cherubim,

---

765 *Panim* Pagan.   766 *career* Gallop.   774 *expatiate* Walk.   776 *straiten'd* Pushed together.   777 *wonder* Magical trick, mentioned in a line of numerical importance to magicians.   781 *Indian mount* The Himalayas.   783 *belated peasant* Possibly returning from the tavern, he encounters supernatural beings.   784.1 *Or dreams he sees* Milton leaves open the question of whether the elves are real; 784.2 *moon* Diana, patroness of witches.   787 *charm* Bewitch.   793 *like themselves* The members of Satan's inner conclave have undemocratically retained their original stature.

795   In close recess and secret conclave sat;
      A thousand demi-gods on golden seats,
      Frequent and full. After short silence then,
      And summons read, the great consult began.

END OF BOOK FIRST

---

795 *conclave* Council; used for the meeting in which cardinals of the Catholic Church select a pope.

BOOK II

The consultation begun, Satan debates whether another battle is to be hazarded for the recovery of heaven: some advise it, others dissuade. A third proposal is preferred, mentioned before by Satan,* to search the truth of that prophecy or tradition in heaven concerning another world, and another kind of creature, equal, or not much inferior to themselves, about this time to be created: their doubt who shall be sent on this difficult search: Satan, their chief, undertakes alone the voyage; is honoured and applauded. The council thus ended, the rest betake them several ways, and to several employments, as their inclinations lead them, to entertain the time till Satan return. He passes on his journey to hell gates, finds them shut, and who sat there to guard them, by whom at length they are opened, and discover to him the great gulf between hell and heaven: with what difficulty he passes through, directed by Chaos,† the power of that place, to the sight of this new world which he sought.

HIGH on a throne of royal state, which far   1
Outshone the wealth of Ormus and of Ind;   2

---

*Who has prearranged the debate's course.
†An allegorical figure through which Milton will describe the consequences of a materialist worldview.

1 *royal state* Satan's monarchical qualities are emphasized. 2 *Ormus . . . Ind* Hormuz (an island in the Persia Gulf) and India, world trade centers; in Milton's lifetime, both were venues of some of England's first colonial wars. Satan is associated with trading ventures throughout *Paradise Lost*.

Or where the gorgeous east with richest hand
4   Showers on her kings barbaric pearl and gold,
5   Satan exalted sat, by merit rais'd
To that bad eminence: and from despair
7   Thus high uplifted beyond hope, aspires
Beyond thus high; insatiate to pursue
9   Vain war with heaven; and by success untaught,
10   His proud imaginations thus display'd:

11   Powers, and dominions, deities of heaven
(For since no deep within her gulf can hold
Immortal vigour, though oppress'd and fallen,
I give not heaven for lost: from this descent
15   Celestial virtues rising, will appear
16   More glorious and more dread than from no fall,
And trust themselves to fear no second fate.)
18   Me, though just right and the fixt laws of heaven
19   Did first create your leader; next free choice;
20   With what besides, in council or in fight
Hath been achiev'd of merit: yet this loss
Thus far at least recover'd, hath much more
Established in a safe unenvied throne,
24   Yielded with full consent. The happier state
25   In heaven, which follows dignity, might draw
26   Envy from each inferior: but who here
27   Will envy whom the highest place exposes

---

4 *barbaric* Uncivilized; refers to both "kings" and "pearl and gold."   5 *by merit rais'd* Here Satan's claim to authority rests on his personal qualities.   7 *aspires* Desires to become spiritual; Milton often uses this word to describe Satan's ambition to "equal" God.   9.1 *Vain* In religious discourse of the period, "vanity" refers to any kind of worldly enterprise or concern; 9.2 *success* Outcome.   10 *His proud . . . display'd* Satan does not argue rationally, but through the manipulation of empty images.   11 *Powers, and dominions* Orders of angels.   15 *virtues* An order of angels; also essences, powers.   16 *than from no fall* A rehearsal of the doctrine of *felix culpa*, the fortunate Fall, which holds that the Fall was a good thing, since our redeemed condition is preferable to our condition before the Fall.   18 *just right and the fixt laws of heaven* Two new justifications for Satan's rule.   19 *free choice* Yet another rationalization of Satan's authority.

Foremost to stand against the Thunderer's aim,   28
Your bulwark; and condemns to greatest share   29
Of endless pain? Where there is then no good   30
For which to strive, no strife can grow up there
From faction: for none sure will claim in hell
Precedence; none, whose portion is so small   33
Of present pain, that with ambitious mind
Will covet more; with this advantage then   35
To union, and firm faith, and firm accord,
More than can be in heaven, we now return
To claim our just inheritance of old,
Surer to prosper than prosperity
Could have assur'd us; and by what best way,   40
Whether of open war, or covert guile,
We now debate: who can advise may speak.

He ceas'd; and next him Moloch, sceptred king,
Stood up, the strongest and the fiercest spirit
That fought in heaven, now fiercer by despair: 45
His trust was with th'Eternal to be deem'd
Equal in strength, and rather than be less,
Cared not to be at all; with that care lost
Went all his fear: of God, or hell, or worse,
He reck'd not; and these words thereafter spake.   50

My sentence is for open war; of wiles,   51
More unexpert, I boast not: them let those
Contrive who need; or when they need, not now.
For while they sit contriving, shall the rest,
Millions that stand in arms, and longing wait   55
The signal to ascend, sit ling'ring here
Heaven's fugitives, and for their dwelling-place

24–30 *The . . . pain* Satan's disingenuous argument marks him as a tyrant, rebelling against reason for his personal ends.   33 *Precedence* A performative contradiction: Satan is claiming precedence in the act of renouncing it.   50 *reck'd* Both "cared" and "calculated."   51 *sentence* Verdict.

Accept this dark opprobrious den of shame,
The prison of his tyranny[1] who reigns
60 By our delay? No, let us rather choose,
Arm'd with hell-flames and fury, all at once
62 O'er heaven's high towers to force resistless way,
63 Turning our tortures into horrid arms
64 Against the Torturer: when to meet the noise
65 Of his Almighty engine he shall hear
66 Infernal thunder; and, for lightning, see
67 Black fire and horror shot with equal rage
Among his angels: and his throne itself
69 Mix'd with Tartarean sulphur, and strange fire,
70 His own invented torments. But, perhaps,
The way seems difficult and steep, to scale
With upright wing against a higher foe.
73 Let such bethink them, (if the sleepy drench
Of that forgetful lake benumb not still,)
75 That in our proper motion we ascend
76 Up to our native seat: descent and fall
77 To us is adverse. Who but felt of late,
When the fierce foe hung on our broken rear
Insulating, and pursu'd us through the deep,
80 With what compulsion, and laborious flight
We sunk thus low? Th'ascent is easy then;
Th'event is fear'd; should we again provoke
Our stronger, some worse way his wrath may find
To our destruction: (if there be in hell
85 Fear to be worse destroy'd,) What can be worse
Than to dwell here, driven out from bliss, condemn'd
In this abhorred deep to utter woe?

---

62 *resistless* Irresistible. 63 *horrid* Bristling. 64 *Torturer* The devils' experience of God as
sadist. 66–67 *see . . . rage* The mingling of abstract and material indicates Moloch's epis-
temological confusion. 69 *Tartarean* Hellish; in Virgil's *Aeneid* (6) Tartarus is the area of
the underworld where the wicked are confined. 73 *sleepy drench* Narcotic drink. 75–77
That . . . adverse Moloch assumes that, being originally angelic, the devils will naturally
tend to develop upward; he does not understand how completely their fall has inverted
their nature.

Where pain of unextinguishable fire
Must exercise us, without hope of end,
The vassals of his anger, when the scourge   90
Inexorably, and the torturing hour,
Calls us to penance? more destroy'd than thus,   92
We should be quite abolished, and expire.
What fear we then? what doubt we to incense
His utmost ire? which to the height enrag'd,   95
Will either quite consume us, and reduce
To nothing this essential; happier far,   97
Than miserable to have eternal being;
Or if our substance be indeed divine,
And cannot cease to be, we are at worst   100
On this side nothing: and by proof we feel
Our power sufficient to disturb his heaven,
And with perpetual inroads to alarm,
Though inaccessible, his fatal throne: 104
Which, if not victory, is yet revenge.   105

He ended frowning, and his look denounc'd   106
Desperate revenge, and battle dangerous   107
To less than gods. On th'other side uprose
Belial, in act more graceful and humane:
A fairer person lost not heaven; he seem'd   110
For dignity compos'd, and high exploit:
But all was false and hollow: though his tongue
Dropp'd manna, and could make the worse appear   113
The better reason, to perplex and dash
Maturest counsels; for his thoughts were low: 115
To vice industrious, but to nobler deeds   116

---

90 *vassals* Moloch can conceive of no other relation to God than that of slave to master.
92 *penance* A dig at the Catholic view of penance as a sacrament.   97 *essential* Essence.
104 *fatal* Moloch repeats Satan's erroneous assumption that God's throne is upheld by fate.
105 *revenge* Moloch's awareness of his proposal's irrationality does not prevent him from advocating it.   106 *denounc'd* Announced.   107 *Desperate* Hopeless.   113 *manna* The actions of the devils mirror those of God, who showers manna on the wandering Israelites in Numbers 11:9.   116 *To vice industrious* Milton believed that sensualists were incapable of reason.

Timorous and slothful: yet he pleas'd the ear
And with persuasive accents thus began:

I should be much for open war, O peers,
120 As not behind in hate, if what was urg'd
Main reason to persuade immediate war,
Did not dissuade me most; and seem to cast
Ominous conjecture on the whole success;
When he who most excels in fact of arms,
125 In what he counsels, and in what excels,
Mistrustful, grounds his courage on despair,
And utter dissolution, as the scope
Of all his aim, after some dire revenge.
First, what revenge? The towers of heaven are fill'd
130 With armed watch, that render all access
Impregnable: oft on the bordering deep
Encamp their legions; or with obscure wing,
Scout far and wide into the realm of night,
Scorning surprise. Or could we break our way
135 By force, and at our heels all hell should rise
With blackest insurrection, to confound
Heaven's purest light; yet our great enemy,
All incorruptible, would on his throne
Sit unpolluted; and th'ethereal mould
140 Incapable of stain, would soon expel
Her mischief, and purge off the baser fire,
Victorious. Thus repuls'd, our final hope
Is flat despair: we must exasperate
Th'Almighty Victor to spend all his rage,
145 And that must end us; that must be our cure
To be no more.—Sad cure; for who would lose,
Though full of pain, this intellectual being;
Those thoughts, that wander through eternity
To perish rather, swallow'd up and lost

---

130 *watch* Guards.

In the wide womb of uncreated night, 150
Devoid of sense and motion? And who knows,
Let this be good, whether our angry foe
Can give it, or will ever? how he can, 153
Is doubtful; that he never will, is sure. 154
Will he, so wise, let loose at once his ire, 155
Belike through impotence, or unaware, 156
To give his enemies their wish, and end
Them in his anger, whom his anger saves
To punish endless?—Wherefore cease we then?
Say they who counsel war; we are decreed, 160
Reserv'd, and destin'd to eternal woe: 161
Whatever doing, what can we suffer more;
What can we suffer worse?—Is this then worst,
Thus sitting, thus consulting, thus in arms?
What! when we fled amain, pursu'd, and struck 165
With heaven's afflicting thunder, and besought
The deep to shelter us? This hell then seem'd
A refuge from those wounds. Or, when we lay
Chain'd on the burning lake? That sure was worse.
What if the breath that kindled those grim fires, 170
Awak'd, should blow them into sevenfold rage,
And plunge us in the flames? Or, from above,
Should intermitted vengeance arm again 173
His red right hand[2] to plague us? What if all
Her stores were open'd, and this firmament 175
Of hell should spout her cataracts of fire?
Impendent horrors; threat'ning hideous fall 177
One day upon our heads: while we perhaps
Designing or exhorting glorious war,
Caught in a fiery tempest shall be hurl'd 180

---

150 *uncreated night* Chaos.   153–154 *how . . . doubtful* Like the other devils, Belial fails to grasp the concept of omnipotence.   156 *Belike* Probably.   161 *woe* Belial expresses the doctrine of predestination from the perspective of the reprobate.   173 *intermitted* Interrupted.
177 *Impendent* Hanging over us.

181   Each on his rock transfix'd, the sport and prey
        Of racking whirlwinds: or for ever sunk
        Under yon boiling ocean, wrapp'd in chains;
        There to converse with everlasting groans,
185   Unrespited, unpitied, unrepriev'd,
        Ages of hopeless end? This would be worse.
        War therefore, open or conceal'd, alike
        My voice dissuades: for what can force or guile
        With him, or who deceive his mind, whose eye
190   Views all things at one view? He from heaven's height
191   All these our motions vain sees and derides:
        Not more almighty to resist our might,
        Than wise to frustrate all our plots and wiles.
        Shall we then live thus vile, the race of heaven
195   Thus trampled, thus expell'd, to suffer here
        Chains and these torments? Better these than worse,
197   By my advice; since fate inevitable
198   Subdues us, and omnipotent decree;
199   The victor's will. To suffer, as to do,
200   Our strength is equal, nor the law unjust
201   That so ordains: this was at first resolv'd
        If we were wise, against so great a foe
        Contending, and so doubtful what might fall.
        I laugh, when those who at the spear are bold
205   And vent'rous, if that fail them, shrink, and fear
        What yet they know must follow, to endure
        Exile or ignominy, or bonds, or pain,
        The sentence of their conqueror: This is now
        Our doom; which if we can sustain and bear,
210   Our supreme foe, in time, may such remit
        His anger: and, perhaps, thus far remov'd,
        Not mind us, not offending, satisfied

---

181 *transfix'd* Alludes to *Prometheus,* by Greek playwright Aeschylus (c.525–455 B.C.)   191 *motions* Proposals.   197–199 *since fate . . . victor's will* Belial gives three contradictory explanations for the devils' subjection: fate, God's omnipotence, and the right of conquest.   200–201 *nor . . . ordains* According to the justice of the law, all human beings are damned eternally.

With what is punished: whence these raging fires
Will slacken, if his breath stir not their flames.
Our purer essence then will overcome   215
Their noxious vapour; or inur'd, not feel;
Or chang'd at length, and to the place conform'd
In temper, and in nature, will receive
Familiar the fierce heat, and void of pain,
This horror will grow mild, this darkness, light: 220
Besides what hope the never-ending flight
Of future days may bring, what chance, what change
Worth waiting, since our present lot appears
For happy, though but ill; for ill, not worst;
If we procure not to ourselves more woe.   225

Thus Belial with words cloth'd in reason's garb   226
Counsell'd ignoble ease, and peaceful sloth,
Not peace: and after him thus Mammon spake.

Either to disenthrone the King of heaven
We war, if war be best, or to regain   230
Our own right lost: Him to unthrone we then
May hope, when everlasting Fate shall yield   232
To fickle Chance, and Chaos judge the strife: 233
The former vain to hope, argues as vain
The latter: for what place can be for us   235
Within heaven's bound, unless heaven's Lord supreme
We overpower? Suppose he should relent
And publish grace to all, on promise made
Of new subjection; with what eyes could we   239
Stand in his presence humble, and receive   240
Strict laws imposed to celebrate his throne
With warbled hymns, and to his Godhead sing   242

---

226 *reason's garb* Belial's rhetoric disguises itself as reason.   232–233 *Fate . . . Chance . . .
Chaos* Mammon ascribes causality to arbitrary, irrational forces.   239 *subjection* Subordi-
nation.   242 *Godhead* Godhood; the three persons of the Trinity.

243 Forc'd hallelujahs? while he lordly sits
244 Our envied Sovereign, and his altar breathes
245 Ambrosial odours and ambrosial flowers,
246 Our servile offerings; this must be our task
    In heaven, this our delight; how wearisome
    Eternity so spent, in worship paid
    To whom we hate. Let us not then pursue
250 By force impossible, by leave obtain'd
    Unacceptable, though in heaven, our state
252 Of splendid vassalage: but rather seek
253 Our own good from ourselves, and from our own
    Live to ourselves; though in this vast recess,
255 Free, and to none accountable; preferring
    Hard liberty before the easy yoke
257 Of servile pomp. Our greatness will appear
258 Then most conspicuous, when great things of small,
259 Useful of hurtful, prosperous of adverse
260 We can create; and in what place soe'er
    Thrive under evil, and work ease out of pain,
262 Through labour and endurance. This deep world
    Of darkness do we dread? How oft amidst
    Thick clouds and dark, doth heaven's all-ruling Sire
265 Choose to reside, his glory unobscur'd
    And with the majesty of darkness round
    Covers his throne; from whence deep thunders roar
268 Mustering their rage, and heaven resembles hell?
    As he our darkness, cannot we his light
270 Imitate when we please? This desert soil

---

243 *hallelujahs* Hebrew for "praise Jah (Yahweh)." 244–245 *his altar . . . flowers* Mammon's portrayal of God's altar recalls Catholic liturgy and decoration. 246 *servile* Slavish.
252 *vassalage* Slavery. 252–253 *but . . . ourselves* Mammon refuses to locate his *summum bonum* (supreme good) in anything outside himself; an example of vanity. 257 *servile pomp*
An oxymoron suggesting that excessive ceremony is degrading. 257–260 *Our . . . create*
Mammon hopes to reverse the essential qualities of creation through a fiendish re-creation;
his reasoning anticipates the notion of *felix culpa*, the fortunate fall. 262 *labour* Mammon
fetishizes his own activity, an example of works of righteousness. 268 *heaven resembles hell*
From the alienated perspective proper relations are reversed.

Wants not her hidden lustre, gems, and gold; 271
Nor want we skill or art, from whence to raise 272
Magnificence; and what can heaven show more? 273
Our torments also may, in length of time,
Become our elements; these piercing fires 275
As soft as now severe, our temper chang'd
Into their temper; which must needs remove
The sensible of pain. All things invite 278
To peaceful counsels, and the settled state
Of order, how in safety best we may 280
Compose our present evils, with regard
Of what we are, and were; dismissing quite
All thought of war.—Ye have what I advise.

He scarce had finish'd, when such murmur fill'd
Th'assembly, as when hollow rocks retain 285
The sound of blustering winds, which all night long
Had rous'd the sea, now with hoarse cadence lull
Sea-faring men o'erwatch'd, whose bark by chance, 288
Or pinnace, anchors in a craggy bay 289
After the tempest: such applause was heard 290
As Mammon ended, and his sentence pleas'd,
Advising peace. For, such another field 292
They dreaded worse than hell: so much the fear
Of thunder, and the sword of Michael, 294
Wrought still within them; and no less desire 295
To found this nether empire, which might rise,
By policy, and long process of time, 297
In emulation opposite to heaven. 298
Which when Beelzebub perceiv'd (than whom,

270–273 *This . . . more?* Fetishizing both financial value and labor. 278 *sensible* Sensation; Mammon conceives of pain only as physical. 288 *bark* Ship. 289 *pinnace* Small ship. 292 *field* Battlefield. 294 *Michael* In Hebrew, "Who is like God." Michael, the angel associated with the warlike power of God, as in Revelation 12:7, was often conceived as the Son of God prior to the birth of Jesus. 297 *policy* Cunning planning and politics. 298 *in emulation opposite to* The antithesis of.

300 Satan except, none higher sat) with grave
Aspect he rose, and in his rising seem'd
302 A pillar of state: deep on his front engraven,
303 Deliberation sat, and public care;
And princely counsel in his face yet shone,
305 Majestic though in ruin; sage he stood,
306 With Atlantean shoulders fit to bear
The weight of mightiest monarchies; his look
Drew audience and attention still as night,
Or summer's noon-tide air; while thus he spake:

310 Thrones and imperial powers, offspring of heaven,
Ethereal virtues, or these titles now
Must we renounce, and, changing style, be call'd
Princes of hell? For, so the popular vote
Inclines, here to continue, and build up here
315 A growing empire: doubtless; while we dream,
And know that the King of heaven hath doom'd
This place our dungeon; not our safe retreat
Beyond his potent arm, to live exempt
From Heaven's high jurisdiction, in new league
320 Banded against his throne: but to remain
321 In strictest bondage, though thus far remov'd,
322 Under th'inevitable curb, reserv'd
323 His captive multitude: for he, be sure,
324 In height, or depth, still first and last will reign
325 Sole king, and of his kingdom lose no part
326 By our revolt; but over hell extend
327 His empire, and with iron sceptre rule
328 Us here, as with his golden those in heaven.
329 What sit we then projecting peace and war?

---

302 *engraven* Like a graven image, a manufactured idol. 303 *public care* Both "care for the public" and "care for public consumption." 306 *Atlantean* The Titan Atlas bore the world on his shoulders, as a punishment for his part in the war against the Olympians. 320–329 *but to remain . . . peace and war* Beelzebub finally draws the logical conclusion from God's omnipotence: The demonic role is to oppose His will.

War hath determin'd us, and foil'd with loss 330
Irreparable; terms of peace yet none
Vouchsaf'd, or sought: for what peace will be given 332
To us enslav'd, but custody severe,
And stripes, and arbitrary punishment 334
Inflicted? and what peace can we return? 335
But to our power hostility and hate, 336
Untam'd reluctance, and revenge; though slow,
Yet ever plotting how the Conqueror least
May reap his conquest, and may least rejoice
In doing what we most in suffering feel? 340
Nor will occasion want, nor shall we need 341
With dangerous expedition, to invade
Heaven, whose high walls fear no assault or siege,
Or ambush from the deep: what if we find
Some easier enterprize? There is a place, 345
(If ancient and prophetic fame in heaven
Err not,) another world, the happy seat
Of some new race call'd Man; about this time 348
To be created like to us, though less
In power and excellence, but favour'd more 350
Of him who rules above: so was his will
Pronounc'd among the gods, and by an oath, 352
That shook heaven's whole circumference, confirm'd.
Thither let us bend all our thoughts, to learn
What creatures there inhabit, of what mould, 355
Or substance, how endued, and what their power,
And where their weakness, how attempted best,
By force, or subtilty. Though heaven be shut,
And heaven's high arbitrator sit secure 359

---

332 *Vouchsaf'd* Granted.   334 *arbitrary* Irrational and tyrannical, as in republican denunci-
ations of Charles I's "arbitrary government."   336 *to our power* As far as lie within our
power.   341 *occasion* Opportunity.   348 *Man* The human mind is the destined ground for
the battle between Heaven and Hell.   352 *gods* The description of angels as "gods" implies
that the gods of the classical pantheon were prefigurations of the angels of the Judeo-
Christian tradition.   355 *mould* Shape, form, and substance.   359 *arbitrator* Judge.

360 In his own strength, this place may lie expos'd
361 The utmost border of his kingdom, left
    To their defence who hold it: here perhaps
    Some advantageous act may be achiev'd
    By sudden onset, either with hell fire
365 To waste his whole creation; or possess
    All as our own, and drive, as we were driven,
367 The puny habitants; or, if not drive,
    Seduce them to our party, that their God
    May prove their foe, and with repenting hand
370 Abolish his own works. This would surpass
    Common revenge, and interrupt his joy
    In our confusion, and our joy upraise
373 In his disturbance; when his darling sons,
    Hurl'd headlong to partake with us, shall curse
375 Their frail original, and faded bliss:
    Faded so soon. Advise if this be worth
    Attempting, or to sit in darkness here
378 Hatching vain empires. Thus Beelzebub
    Pleaded his devilish counsel, first devis'd
380 By Satan, and in part propos'd: for whence,
    But from the author of all ill, could spring
382 So deep a malice to confound the race
    Of mankind in one root, and earth with hell
    To mingle and involve, done all to spite
385 The great Creator? But their spite still serves
386 His glory to augment. The bold design
387 Pleas'd highly those infernal states, and joy
    Sparkled in all their eyes; with full assent
    They vote: whereat his speech he thus renews.

---

361 *utmost* Outer. 367 *puny* From the French *puis ne* ("born later"). 373 *darling* Used sarcastically to indicate Satan's jealousy of God's love for man. 375 *original* Ancestor—that is, Adam; the 1667 edition has "originals." 378 *Beelzebub* Satan's front man. 382 *confound* Mix together and destroy. 385–386 *But . . . argument* The narrator repeats the doctrine of *felix culpa*. 387 *states* Estates, an archaic term for parliaments.

Well have ye judg'd, well ended long debate,   390
Synod of gods, and, like to what ye are,   391
Great things resolv'd; which from the lowest deep
Will once more lift us up, in spite of fate,
Nearer our ancient seat; perhaps in view
Of those bright confines, whence with neighbouring arms,   395
And opportune excursion, we may chance
Re-enter heaven: or else, in some mild zone
Dwell not unvisited of heaven's fair light,
Secure, and at the bright'ning orient beam
Purge off this gloom: the soft delicious air,   400
To heal the scar of these corrosive fires,
Shall breathe her balm.——But first whom shall we send
In search of this new world? whom shall we find
Sufficient? Who shall tempt with wandering feet   404
The dark, unbottom'd, infinite abyss,   405
And through the palpable obscure find out   406
His uncouth way; or spread his airy flight,   407
Upborne with indefatigable wings,
Over the vast abrupt, ere he arrive   409
The happy isle? What strength, what art can then   410
Suffice, or what evasion bear him safe
Through the strict sentries, and stations thick
Of angels watching round? Here he had need
All circumspection; and we now no less
Choice in our suffrage; for, on whom we send,   415
The weight of all, and our last hope, relies.

This said, he sat; and expectation held
His look suspense, awaiting who appear'd
To second or oppose, or undertake
The perilous attempt: but all sat mute,   420

---

391 *Synod* Usually an ecclesiastical term for an assembly of prelates.   **395** *confines* Frontiers.
404.1 *Sufficient* Capable;   **404.2** *tempt* Satan's very presence brings temptation.   **405** *abyss*
Chaos.   **406** *palpable obscure* Satan conceives of abstract concepts as physical things.
407 *uncouth* Unknown.   **409** *abrupt* Abyss.   **415** *suffrage* Vote.   **420** *but all sat mute* Compare the Father's request for a volunteer in heaven, described in 3.217.

Pondering the danger with deep thoughts; and each
In other's countenance read his own dismay,
423 Astonish'd; none, among the choice and prime
424 Of those heaven-warring champions, could be found
425 So hardy, as to proffer, or accept
Alone the dreadful voyage: till at last
Satan, whom now transcendent glory rais'd
428 Above his fellows, with monarchal pride
(Conscious of highest worth) unmov'd thus spake:

430 O progeny of heaven, empyreal thrones;
With reason hath deep silence, and demur,
Seiz'd us, though undismay'd: long is the way
And hard, that out of hell leads up to light:
Our prison strong; this huge convex of fire,
435 Outrageous to devour, immures us round
Ninefold: and gates of burning adamant
Barr'd over us, prohibit all egress.
These pass'd (if any pass) the void profound
439 Of unessential night receives him next
440 Wide gaping; and with utter loss of being
441 Threatens him, plung'd in that abortive gulf.
If thence he 'scape into whatever world,
Or unknown region, what remains him less
Than unknown dangers, and as hard escape?
445 But I should ill become this throne, O peers!
And this imperial sovereignty, adorn'd
With splendour, arm'd with power, if aught propos'd
448 And judg'd of public moment, in the shape
Of difficulty, or danger, could deter

---

423 *Astonish'd* Turned to stone.   424 *champions* Milton associates the devils with the aristocratic virtue of chivalry.   428 *monarchal pride* Milton associates the devils with monarchy.   435.1 *Outrageous* Desperate; 435.2 *immures* Walls.   439 *unessential night* Night has no essence, no being, of its own; it consists merely of the absence of its opposite. This was a common theological account for the existence of evil: It was merely the absence of good, and so a beneficent God could be acquitted of creating it.   441 *abortive* Bringing to nothing.   448 *moment* Importance.

Me from attempting. Wherefore do I assume   450
These royalties, and not refuse to reign,
Refusing to accept as great a share
Of hazard, as of honour due alike   453
To him who reigns, and so much to him due
Of hazard more, as he above the rest   455
High honour'd sits? Go, therefore, mighty powers,   456
Terror of heaven, though fallen; intend at home,
(While here shall be our home,) what best may ease
The present misery, and render hell
More tolerable; if there be cure, or charm,   460
To respite, or deceive, or slack the pain
Of this ill mansion. Intermit no watch   462
Against a wakeful foe, while I abroad,
Through all the coasts of dark destruction, seek
Deliverance for us all: this enterprise   465
None shall partake with me. Thus saying, rose
The monarch, and prevented all reply: 467
Prudent, lest, from his resolution rais'd,   468
Others among the chiefs might offer now   469
(Certain to be refused) what erst they fear'd;   470
And so refus'd, might in opinion stand   471
His rivals; winning cheap the high repute,   472
Which he through hazard huge must earn. But they
Dreaded not more th'adventure, than his voice
Forbidding; and at once with him they rose: 475
Their rising all at once was as the sound
Of thunder heard remote. Towards him they bend
With awful reverence prone; and as a god   478

---

453 *hazard* Danger, chance.   455–456 *as . . . sits* Satan uses his willingness to undertake the mission as an ex post facto rationalization of his power.   460 *charm* The automatic demonic recourse to magic.   462 *mansion* Dwelling place.   470 *erst* Earlier.   471 *opinion* Reputation.   467–472 *and prevented . . . rivals* The narrator reveals the self-aggrandizement behind Satan's hollow heroism, as well as the tyrannical will behind his show of democracy.   475 *Forbidding* Satan rules by fear.   478 *awful* awestruck.

479   Extol him equal to the highest in heaven;
480   Nor fail'd they to express how much they prais'd,
        That for the general safety he despis'd
482   His own, (for neither do the spirits damn'd
        Lose all their virtue; lest bad men should boast
484   Their specious deeds on earth, which glory excites;
485   Or close ambition varnish'd o'er with zeal.)
        Thus they their doubtful consultations dark
        Ended, rejoicing in their matchless chief:
        As when from mountain-tops the dusky clouds
        Ascending, while the north-wind sleeps, o'er-spread
490   Heaven's cheerful face, the louring element
        Scowls o'er the darken'd landscape snow, or shower;
        If chance the radiant sun with farewell sweet
        Extends his evening beam, the fields revive,
        The birds their notes renew, and bleating herds
495   Attest their joy, that hill and valley rings.
        O shame to men! Devil with devil damn'd
497   Firm concord holds, men only disagree
498   Of creatures rational, though under hope
        Of heavenly grace: and, God proclaiming peace,
500   Yet live in hatred, enmity, and strife
        Among themselves, and levy cruel wars,
        Wasting the earth, each other to destroy:
        As if (which might induce us to accord)
        Man had not hellish foes enow besides,
505   That day and night, for his destruction wait.

---

479 *equal . . . heaven* The absurd, false equivalence between creature and Creator is the source of idolatry, which the early Christian writer Tertullian and others identify as the root of all sin; see St. Paul on money as "the root of all evil" (1 Timothy 6:10).   **482** *His own* The true situation is the reverse: It is Satan who has acted like a tyrant, in pursuing his own ends rather than those of his subjects.   **484** *excites* Motivates; the "deeds" are "specious" because they are undertaken for a vain, earthly end.   **485.1** *close* Hidden; **485.2** *zeal* Possibly a reference to insincere members of the Puritan factions, who often boasted of their "zeal."   **497–498** *men . . . rational* Man's possession of reason should make it possible for all to arrive at the same truth; the fact that we do not bespeaks our tendency to be influenced by passion, pleasure, and self-interest, rather than by reason.

The Stygian council thus dissolv'd; and forth
In order came the grand infernal peers: 507
'Midst came their mighty paramount, and seem'd
Alone th'antagonist of heaven, nor less
Than hell's dread emperor, with pomp supreme,   510
And godlike imitated state. Him round   511
A globe of fiery seraphim inclos'd,
With bright emblazonry, and horrent arms.   513
Then, of their session ended, they bid cry
With trumpets' regal sound the great result: 515
Towards the four winds four speedy cherubim
Put to their mouths the sounding alchymy,   517
By heralds' voice explain'd: the hollow abyss
Heard far and wide, and all the host of hell
With deaf'ning shout return'd them loud acclaim.   520

Thence more at ease their minds, and somewhat rais'd
By false presumptuous hope, the ranged powers
Disband, and wand'ring, each his several way
Pursues, as inclination or sad choice
Leads him perplex'd, where he may likeliest find   525
Truce to his restless thoughts, and entertain
The irksome hours, till his great chief return.
Part on the plain, or in the air sublime
Upon the wing; or in swift race contend,
As at th'Olympian games; or Pythian fields: 530
Part curb their fiery steeds, or shun the goal
With rapid wheels, or fronted brigades form.
As when, to warn proud cities, war appears
Wag'd in the troubled sky, and armies rush
To battle in the clouds; before each van   535

---

507 *peers* The term has now shed its meaning of "equals," but retains the connotation of "lords." Leonard notes that Pandemonium has a monarch and a House of Lords, but no House of Commons.   510 *pomp* Pretentious grandeur.   511 *godlike imitated state* Satan imitates his perverted idea of God as an ostentatious despot.   513 *horrent* Spiked; the word is Milton's coinage.   517 *sounding alchymy* Golden trumpets.   530 *Olympian . . . Pythian fields* The Olympic and Pythian games were Greek athletic competitions.

536   Prick forth the airy knights and couch their spears
        Till thickest legions close; with feats of arms
538   From either end of heaven the welkin burns.
539   Others, with vast Typhoean rage, more fell!
540   Rend up both rocks and hills, and ride the air
541   In whirlwind: hell scarce holds the wild uproar.
542   As when Alcides from Œchalia crown'd
543   With conquest, felt th'envenom'd robe, and tore
544   Through pain up by the roots Thessalian pines,
545   And Lichas from the top of Œta threw
546   Into th'Euboic Sea. Others, more mild,
        Retreated in a silent valley, sing
        With notes angelical to many a harp
549   Their own heroic deeds and hapless fall
550   By doom of battle; and complain that fate
551   Free virtue should enthrall to force or chance.
552   Their song was partial; but the harmony
        (What could it less when spirits immortal sing!)
554   Suspended hell, and took with ravishment
555   The thronging audience. In discourse more sweet,
556   (For eloquence the soul, song charms the sense,)
557   Others apart sat on a hill retir'd,
558   In thoughts more elevate, and reason'd high,
559   Of providence, foreknowledge, will, and fate,
560   Fixt fate, free will, foreknowledge absolute;
561   And found no end, in wand'ring mazes lost.
        Of good and evil much they argued then,

---

536 *Prick* Spur.   538 *welkin* Sky.   539 *Typhoean* Pertaining to Typhon, one of the Titans who fought against Zeus.   541 *whirlwind* Flannagan notes: "Witches in Milton's era were generally supposed to 'ride the whirlwind'" (p. 396).   542–546 *Alcides . . . Sea* Hercules (Alcides), maddened by pain from a poisoned robe, hurled his servant Lichas into the Euboic Sea.   549 *deeds* The devils fetishize their works.   550–551 *and complain . . . chance* This school of demonic philosophy resembles the Stoics.   552 *partial* Biased and polyphonic.   554 *Suspended hell* Allusion to the persuasive effect of Orpheus' music on Pluto, the king of the underworld. Compare "L'Allegro," ll. 145–150, and "Il Penseroso," ll. 105–108.   556 *For . . . sense* Rhetorical "eloquence" like Satan's acts as a magical "charm," analogous to sensual music.   557–561 *Others . . . lost* The concerns and methods of the infernal thinkers seem not dissimilar to those of *Paradise Lost* itself.

Of happiness, and final misery,
Passion, and apathy, and glory, and shame,   564
Vain wisdom all, and false philosophy;   565
Yet with a pleasing sorcery, could charm   566
Pain for a while, or anguish; and excite
Fallacious hope, or arm th'obdurate breast
With stubborn patience, as with triple steel.
Another part, in squadrons and gross bands,   570
On bold adventure to discover wide
That dismal world (if any clime perhaps
Might yield them easier habitation) bend
Four ways their flying march, along the banks
Of four infernal rivers, that disgorge   575
Into the burning lake their baleful streams;
Abhorred Styx, the flood of deadly hate;
Sad Acheron, of sorrow; black and deep;
Cocytus, nam'd of lamentation loud
Heard on the rueful stream: fierce Phlegethon   580
Whose waves of torrent fire inflame with rage.
Far off from these, a slow and silent stream,
Lethe, the river of oblivion, rolls   583
Her wat'ry labyrinth? whereof who drinks,
Forthwith his former state and being forgets;   585
Forgets both joy and grief, pleasure and pain.
Beyond this flood a frozen continent
Lies dark and wild: beat with perpetual storms
Of whirlwind, and dire hail; which on firm land
Thaws not but gathers heap, and ruin seems   590
Of ancient pile: all else deep snow and ice:
A gulf profound; as that Serbonian bog   592

---

564 *apathy* For the Stoics, a commendable freedom from emotion. 566 *sorcery . . . charm* The devil's philosophy is compared to magic, which instantly discredits it. Magic works by the manipulation of images, not by reason. 570 *gross* Thick. 575 *four infernal rivers* Drawing attention to the process of figuration, Milton gives the names of the rivers, then renders them in English as the emotion they represent: "Styx" is "hate," and so on. 583 *Lethe* A drink from this river, in the underworld of Greek mythology, would bring forgetfulness. 592 *Serbonian bog* Serbonis, a region of quicksand on the Egyptian coast.

Betwixt Damiata, and mount Casius old,
Where armies whole have sunk: the parching air
595 Burns frore, and cold performs the effect of fire.
596 Thither by harpy-footed furies hal'd,
At certain revolutions, all the damn'd
Are brought; and feel by turns the bitter change
Of fierce extremes, extremes by change more fierce;
600 From beds of raging fire to starve in ice
Their soft ethereal warmth, and there to pine
Immoveable, infixed, and frozen round,
Periods of time; thence hurried back to fire.
They ferry over this Lethean sound
605 Both to and fro, their sorrow to augment,
And wish, and struggle as they pass to reach
The tempting stream, with one small drop to lose
In sweet forgetfulness all pain and woe,
All in one moment, and so near the brink:
610 But fate withstands, and to oppose th'attempt
611 Medusa, with Gorgonian terror, guards
The ford, and of itself the water flies
All taste of living wight; as once it fled
614 The lip of Tantalus. Thus roving on,
615 In confus'd march forlorn, th'advent'rous bands,
With shudd'ring horror pale, and eyes aghast.
View'd first their lamentable lot and found
No rest: through many a dark and dreary vale
They pass'd, and many a region dolorous;
620 O'er many a frozen, many a fiery Alp;
621 Rocks, caves, lakes, fens, bogs, dens, and shades of death;
A universe of death; which God by curse

---

595 *frore* Frozen. **596** *furies* The monstrous harpies, half-bird, half-woman, feature in Virgil's *Aeneid* 3.211–218. **611** *Medusa* One of the Gorgons, flying female monsters, whose hair was made up of serpents and whose gaze turned men to stone. **614** *Tantalus* His punishment for revealing the secrets of the gods was to be tormented in Hades by food and drink that is forever just out of his reach; see Homer's *Odyssey* 5.582–592. **620** *fiery Alp* Volcanic mountain. **621** *Rocks . . . death* As usual, the landscape is both literal and symbolic.

Created evil; for evil only good,
Where all life dies, death lives, and nature breeds
Perverse, all monstrous, all prodigious things,   625
Abominable, unutterable; and worse
Than fables yet have feign'd, or fear conceiv'd,   627
Gorgons, and Hydras, and Chimeras dire.   628

Meanwhile the adversary of God and man,
Satan, with thoughts inflam'd of highest design,   630
Puts on swift wings, and towards the gates of hell
Explores his solitary flight: sometimes
He scours the right-hand coast, sometimes the left:
Now shaves with level wing the deep; then soars
Up to the fiery concave tow'ring high.   635
As when far off at sea a fleet descry'd,   636
Hangs in the clouds, by equinoctial winds
Close sailing from Bengala, or the isles   638
Of Ternate and Tidore, whence merchants bring   639
Their spicy drugs: they on the trading flood   640
Through the wide Ethiopian to the Cape   641
Ply, stemming nightly toward the Pole: so seem'd
Far off the flying fiend. At last appear
Hell bounds, high-reaching to the horrid roof;
And thrice threefold the gates: three folds were brass,   645
Three iron, three of adamantine rock;
Impenetrable, impal'd with circling fire,

---

625 *Perverse . . . things* Evil is a perversion of nature.   627 *Than fables . . . feign'd* Than were
expressed in figurative form by classical mythology. The fact that such monsters are prod-
ucts of the human mind makes them more, rather than less, frightening for Milton.   628.1
Hydras Many-headed serpents; slain by Hercules as one of his labors; 628.2 *Chimeras* Part
serpent, goat, and lion. A Chimera appears in Homer's *Iliad* 6.181. The term came to mean
any illusory image.   636 *descry'd* Sighted.   639 *Ternate and Tidore* Two of the so-called
Spice Islands in modern Malaya. Flannagan notes that these were ports of call for the East
India Company.   640 *trading flood* Both "sea route for traders" and "flood of trade."
638–640 *Bengala . . . drugs* Bengal, India, was already home to many English merchants.
Milton associates Satan's flight with the globalization of trade.   641 *Through the . . . Cape*
Route, from the coast of Ethiopia to the Cape of Good Hope, for English ships return-
ing from India or the Spice Islands.

Yet unconsum'd. Before the gates there sat
649 On either side a formidable shape;
650 The one seem'd woman to the waist, and fair:
But ended foul in many a scaly fold,
Voluminous and vast; a serpent arm'd
With mortal sting; about her middle round
A cry of hell-hounds never ceasing bark'd
655 With wide Cerberian mouths full loud, and rung
A hideous peal: yet, when they list, would creep,
If aught disturb'd their noise, into her womb,
And kennel there; yet there still bark'd, and howl'd
Within, unseen.³ Far less abhorr'd than these
660 Vex'd Scylla, bathing in the sea that parts
661 Calabria from the hoarse Trinacrian shore;
662 Nor uglier follow the night-hag, when call'd
In secret, riding through the air she comes,
Lur'd with the smell of infant-blood, to dance
665 With Lapland witches, while the lab'ring moon
666 Eclipses at their charms.⁴ The other shape
667 (If shape it might be call'd, that shape had none
Distinguishable in member, joint, or limb;
669 Or substances might be call'd that shadow seem'd,
670 For each seem'd either:) black it stood as night,
Fierce as ten furies, terrible as hell,
And shook a dreadful dart: what seem'd his head.
The likeness of a kingly crown had on.
Satan was now at hand, and from his seat

---

649 *shape* Image. **655** *Cerberian* Reminiscent of Cerebus, three-headed watchdog of Hades. **660** *Scylla* Whose lower body the sorceress Circe transformed into a pack of barking dogs in Ovid's *Metamorphoses* 14.40–74. **660–661** *sea . . . shore* The Straits of Messina, between the Italian mainland and Sicily. **662** *night-hag* Hecate, queen of witches. **665** *Lapland* In the seventeenth century, northern Scandinavia was still the frontier between Christianity and paganism. Shakespeare refers to "Lapland sorcerers" in *Comedy of Errors* (act 4, scene 3). **666–667** *The other . . . none* Death is the disunion of soul and body; it thus simultaneously renders the body a merely physical "shape" and deprives the body of what gave it "shape" in the sense of "form." **669** *Or . . . seem'd* Milton leaves us in doubt as to whether Death is to be taken as a symbol (a "shadow") or in a literal, substantial sense.

The monster moving, onward came as fast   675
With horrid strides: hell trembled as he strode.
Th'undaunted fiend what this might be admir'd;   677
Admir'd, not fear'd; God and his Son except,
Created thing nought valued he, nor shunn'd;
And with disdainful look thus first began: 680

Whence, and what art thou, execrable shape,
That dar'st, though grim and terrible, advance
Thy miscreated front athwart my way   683
To yonder gates? through them I mean to pass,
That be assur'd, without leave or ask of thee.   685
Retire, or taste thy folly, and learn by proof,
Hell-born, not to contend with spirits of heaven.

To whom the goblin full of wrath reply'd: 688
Art thou that traitor-angel, art thou he,
Who first broke peace in heaven, and faith, till then   690
Unbroken; and in proud rebellious arms
Drew after him the third part of heaven's sons,
Conjured against the Highest; for which both thou   693
And they, outcast from God, are here condem'd
To waste eternal days in woe and pain?   695
And reckon'st thou thyself with spirits of heaven,
Hell-doom'd, and breath'st defiance here and scorn,
Where I reign king, and to enrage thee more,
Thy king, and lord? Back to thy punishment,
False fugitive; and to thy speed add wings;   700
Lest with a whip of scorpions I pursue   701
Thy ling'ring; or with one stroke of this dart
Strange horror seize thee, and pangs unfelt before.

---

677 *admire'd* Wondered.   683 *miscreated* Satan recognizes Death's perverted nature.   688
goblin Evil spirit.   693 *Conjured* Tricked by magic, joined together by an oath. The word
referred to witches' pacts with the devil.   701 *whip of scorpions* From King Rehoboam's
threat in 1 Kings 12:11: "My father hath chastised you with whips, but I will chastise you
with scorpions."

So spake the grisly terror, and in shape
705 (So speaking, and so threat'ning) grew tenfold
More dreadful and deform. On th'other side,
Incens'd with indignation, Satan stood
Unterrify'd; and like a comet burn'd,
709 That fires the length of Ophiucus huge
710 In th'arctic sky, and from his horrid hair
Shakes pestilence and war. Each at the head
Levell'd his deadly aim; their fatal hands
No second stroke intend: and such a frown
Each cast at th'other, as when two black clouds
715 With heaven's artil'ry fraught, come rattling on
716 Over the Caspian; then stand front to front,
Hov'ring a space, till winds the signal blow
To join their dark encounter in mid-air:
So frown'd the mighty combatants, that hell
720 Grew darker at their frown: so match'd they stood:
721 For never but once more was either like
To meet so great a foe. And now great deeds
Had been achiev'd, whereof all hell had rung,
724 Had not the snaky sorceress that sat
725 Fast by hell-gate, and kept the fatal key,
Risen, and with hideous outcry rush'd between.

O father, what intends thy hand, she cry'd,
Against thy only son? What fury, O son,
Possesses thee to bend that mortal dart
730 Against thy father's head? and knowest for whom;
For him who sits above, and laughs the while
732 At thee, ordain'd his drudge, to execute
Whate'er his wrath, which he calls justice, bids;
His wrath, which one day will destroy ye both.

---

709 *Ophiucus* The constellation of the Serpent Bearer.   **716** *Caspian* The Caspian Sea was proverbially stormy.   **721** *never . . . like* Foreshadows God's final victory over both Death and Satan.   **724** *sorceress* Witch.   **732** *drudge* Slave; Death is the servant of God.

She spake, and at her words the hellish pest   735
Forbore: then these to her Satan return'd:

So strange thy outcry, and thy words so strange
Thou interposest, that my sudden hand   738
Prevented, spares to tell thee yet by deeds
What it intends; till first I know of thee,   740
What thing thou art, thus double-form'd; and why
In this infernal vale first met, thou call'st
Me father, and that phantom call'st my son:
I know thee not, nor ever saw till now
Sight more detestable than him and thee.   745

T'whom thus the portress of hell-gate reply'd;   746
Hast thou forgot me then, and do I seem
Now in thine eye so foul? once deem'd so fair   748
In heaven; when at th'assembly, and in sight
Of all the seraphim, with thee combin'd   750
In bold conspiracy against heaven's King,
All on a sudden miserable pain
Surpris'd thee, dim thine eyes, and dizzy swam
In darkness; while thy head flames thick and fast
Threw forth; till on the left side op'ning wide,   755
Likest to thee in shape, and count'nance bright,
Then shining heavenly fair, a goddess arm'd,
Out of thy head I sprung: amazement seiz'd   758
All th'host of heaven; back they recoil'd, afraid

---

735 *pest* Plague—that is, Death.   738 *interposest* Interject, put between.   745 *thee* The first indication that Satan's memory of events in heaven is distorted. Fowler observes, "Allegorically, [Satan] denies his own sin" (p. 147).   746 *portress of hell-gate* See Shakespeare's *Macbeth* (act 2, scene 3): "If a man were porter of hell-gate." Milton often alludes to this play in *Paradise Lost.*   748 *foul . . . fair* An opposition used by Shakespeare throughout *Macbeth* to indicate the confusion of natural values brought about by intercourse with witches. It is the witches themselves who declare that "fair is foul and foul is fair" (act 1, scene 1).   758 *Out of thy head I sprung* Alluding to the birth of Athena (Wisdom) from the head of Zeus.

760 At first; and call'd me Sin; and for a sign
761 Portenteous held me: but familiar grown,
    I pleas'd, and with attractive graces won
    The most averse, thee chiefly, who full oft
764 (Thyself in me thy perfect image viewing)
765 Becam'st enamour'd, and such joy thou took'st
    With me in secret, that my womb conceiv'd
    A growing burden. Meanwhile war arose,
    And fields were fought in heaven; wherein remain'd
    (For what could else?) to our almighty foe
770 Clear victory; to our part loss, and rout,
    Through all the empyrean: down they fell,
    Driven headlong from the pitch of heaven, down
    Into this deep; and in the general fall
    I also: at which time this powerful key
775 Into my hand was given, with charge to keep
    These gates for ever shut, which none can pass
    Without my opening. Pensive here I sat
    Alone, but long I sat not, till my womb
    Pregnant by thee, and now excessive grown,
780 Prodigious motion felt, and rueful throes.
    At last this odious offspring whom thou seest,
    Thine own begotten, breaking violent way
    Tore through my entrails; that with fear and pain
784 Distorted, all my nether shape thus grew
785 Transform'd. But he, my inbred enemy
    Forth-issu'd, brandishing his fatal dart
    Made to destroy: I fled, and cry'd out, *Death!*
    Hell trembled at the hideous name, and sigh'd
    From all her caves, and back resounded, Death!
790 I fled, but he pursu'd (though more, it seems,

760–761 *a sign / Portenteous* "Sin" and "sign" share a common etymology. Milton had the iconoclast's mistrust of efficacious signs, or "idols." Here, Sin is an autonomous, powerful, and ominous sign.   764 *thy perfect image* Again, sin is described as a sign. Satan recognizes himself in the autonomous power of significance; his response anticipates that of Eve to her reflection.   780 *Prodigious* Enormous, monstrous, ominous.   784 *nether* Lower.

Inflam'd with lust than rage) and, swifter far,
Me overtook, his mother, all dismay'd:
And in embraces forcible, and foul,
Engendering with me, of that rape begot
These yelling monsters; that with ceaseless cry   795
Surround me, as thou saw'st; hourly conceiv'd,
And hourly born, with sorrow infinite
To me. For, when they list, into the womb
That bred them they return; and howl, and gnaw
My bowels, their repast: then bursting forth,   800
Afresh with conscious terrors vex me round,   801
That rest or intermission none I find.   802
Before mine eyes in opposition sits
Grim Death, my son and foe: who sets them on,
And me his parent would full soon devour   805
For want of other prey, but that he knows
His end with mine involv'd: and knows that I
Should prove a bitter morsel, and his bane,
Whenever that shall be; so Fate pronounc'd.   809
But thou, O father, I forewarn thee, shun   810
His deadly arrow; neither vainly hope
To be invulnerable in those bright arms,
Though temper'd heavenly; for that mortal dint,
Save he who reigns above, none can resist.

She finish'd, and the subtle fiend his lore   815
Soon learn'd, now milder, and thus answer'd smooth:

Dear daughter, since thou claim'st me for thy sire,
And my fair son here show'st me (the dear pledge   818

---

801 *conscious terrors* Both "terrors of which I am conscious" and "terrors to my conscience."
802 *none I find* The viciously cyclical relation between sin and guilt was an axiom of
Protestant theology.   809 *so Fate pronounc'd* Both sin and death will ultimately die; like
Satan in book I, Sin ascribes their destiny to "Fate," not to God.   815 *his lore* His story.
Note that Sin's account diagnoses Death with an Oedipus complex: He desires to kill his
father and rape his mother.

819   Of dalliance had with thee in heaven, and joys

820   Then sweet, now sad to mention, through dire change

        Befallen us, unforeseen, unthought of) know

        I come no enemy, but to set free

        From out this dark and dismal house of pain,

        Both him and thee, and all the heavenly host

825   Of spirits that (in our just pretences arm'd,)

        Fell with us from on high: from them I go

827   This uncouth errand sole; and one for all

        Myself expose, with lonely steps to tread

        Th'unsounded deep, and through the void immense

830   To search with wand'ring quest a place foretold

831   Should be, and, by concurring signs, ere now

        Created, vast and round; a place of bliss

833   In the purlieus of heaven, and therein plac'd

        A race of upstart creatures, to supply

835   Perhaps our vacant room; though more remov'd,

        Lest heaven surcharg'd with potent multitude

        Might hap to move new broils. Be this, or aught

        Than this more secret, now design'd, I haste

        To know; and this once known, shall soon return,

840   And bring ye to the place where thou, and Death,

        Shall dwell at ease, and up and down unseen

842   Wing silently the buxom air, embalm'd

        With odours: there ye shall be fed, and fill'd

        Immeasurably, all things shall be your prey.

845   He ceas'd, for both seem'd highly pleas'd, and Death

        Grinn'd horrible a ghastly smile, to hear

847   His famine should be fill'd; and bless'd his maw

818–819 *the dear pledge / Of dalliance* Satan slips into a hideously inappropriate courtly mode.   825 *pretences* Satan has been a "pretender" to the throne of heaven.   827.1 *uncouth* Strange; 827.2 *sole* Pun on "soul."   830 *a place foretold* An ironic inversion of the Israelites' quest for the promised land.   831 *concurring signs* Signs confirming the prophecy.   833 *purlieus* Surroundings.   842 *buxom* Yielding.   847 *maw* Jaw.

Destin'd to that good hour: no less rejoic'd
His mother bad, and thus bespake her sire:

The key of this infernal pit by due,   850
And by command of heaven's all-powerful King,
I keep; by him forbidden to unlock
These adamantine gates; against all force
Death ready stands to interpose his dart,
Fearless to be o'ermatched by living might.   855
But what I owe to his commands above
Who hates me, and hath hither thrust me down
Into this gloom of Tartarus profound,
To sit in hateful office here confin'd,
Inhabitant of heaven, and heavenly-born,   860
Here in perpetual agony and pain,
With terrors, and with clamours compass'd round,
Of mine own brood, that on my bowels feed:
Thou art my father, thou my author, thou   864
My being gav'st me; whom should I obey   865
But thee? whom follow? thou wilt bring me soon   866
To that new world of light and bliss, among
The gods who live at ease, where I shall reign
At thy right hand voluptuous, as beseems
Thy daughter, and thy darling, without end.   870

Thus saying, from her side the fatal key,
Sad instrument of all our woe, she took;
And towards the gate rolling her bestial train,
Forthwith the huge portcullis high up-drew;
Which but herself, not all the Stygian powers   875
Could once have mov'd; then in the key-hole turns
Th'intricate wards, and every bolt and bar
Of massy iron, or solid rock, with ease

864–866 *Thou . . . But thee* Sin owes obedience to Satan because he created her; of course, the same logic applies to Satan's relation to God.

Unfastens: on a sudden open fly,
880 With impetuous recoil, and jarring sound
Th'infernal doors, and on their hinges grate
Harsh thunder, that the lowest bottom shook
883 Of Erebus. She open'd, but to shut
Excell'd her power; the gates wide open stood,
885 That with extended wings a banner'd host
Under spread ensigns marching, might pass through
With horse, and chariots, rank'd in loose array,
So wide they stood; and like a furnace mouth,
889 Cast forth redounding smoke, and ruddy flame.
890 Before their eyes in sudden view appear
The secrets of the hoary deep; a dark
Illimitable ocean, without bound,
Without dimension; where length, breadth, and height,
894 And time, and place are lost; where eldest Night
895 And Chaos,⁵ ancestor's of Nature, hold
896 Eternal anarchy, amidst the noise
Of endless wars, and by confusion stand:
898 For hot, cold, moist, and dry, four champions fierce,
899 Strive here for mast'ry, and to battle bring
900 Their embryon atoms; they around the flag
Of each his faction, in their several clans,
Light arm'd, or heavy, sharp, smooth, swift, or slow,
Swarm populous, unnumber'd as the sands
904 Of Barca, or Cyrene's torrid soil,
905 Levied to side with warring winds and poise
Their lighter wings. To whom these most adhere,
He rules a moment: Chaos umpire sits,
And by decision more embroils the fray,

---

883 *Erebus* In Hesiod's *Theogony*, Erebus is the first child of Chaos.   889 *redounding* Billowing.   894 *Night* In Hesiod, the second child of Chaos.   896 *anarchy* Not a political concept for Milton, but a condition of nonmeaning, of insignificance.   898–899 *For hot . . . mast'ry* The combination of the four elements believed to make up matter is described as a Darwinian struggle.   900 *embryon atoms* The Greek philosopher Democritus and the Roman Lucretius held that matter consisted of invisible atoms.   904 *Barca, or Cyrene* Cities in northern Africa.   905 *Levied* Raised, both as in air and as in an army.

By which he reigns: next him high arbiter   909
Chance governs all. Into this wild abyss,[6]   910
(The womb of nature, and perhaps her grave,)   911
Of neither sea, nor shore, nor air, nor fire,
But all these in their pregnant causes mix'd
Confus'dly, and which thus must ever fight,
(Unless th'Almighty Maker them ordain   915
His dark materials to create more worlds,)
Into this wild abyss the wary fiend
Stood on the brink of hell, and look'd awhile,
Pond'ring his voyage; (for no narrow frith   919
He had to cross:) nor was his ear less peal'd   920
With noises loud, and ruinous, (to compare   921
Great things with small,) than when Bellona storms   922
With all her batt'ring engines bent to raze
Some capital city; or less than if this frame
Of heaven were falling, and these elements   925
In mutiny had from her axle torn
The steadfast earth. At last his sail-broad vans   927
He spreads for flight, and in the surging smoke
Uplifted spurns the ground: thence many a league,
As in a cloudy chair, ascending rides   930
Audacious; but that seat soon failing, meets
A vast vacuity: all unawares,
Fluttering his pennons vain, plumb down he drops   933
Ten thousand fathom deep: and to this hour
Down had been falling, had not by ill chance   935
The strong rebuff of some tumultuous cloud,
Instinct with fire and nitre, hurried him   937

---

909 *arbiter* Judge; the word is used ironically of Chance.   911 *The womb . . . grave* A trans-
lation of Lucretius's *De Rerum Natura* 5.259. Leonard notes: "Lucretius is speaking of the
earth, not chaos" (p. 742). Milton again emphasizes that Lucretian materialism produces
a view of the universe as meaningless chaos.   919 *frith* Inlet.   921–922 *to compare . . . small*
A phrase used by first-century B.C. Roman poet Virgil in *Eclogues* 1.24 and *Georgics* 4.176.
922 *Bellona* Roman goddess of war.   927 *vans* Wings.   933 *pennons* Wings.   935 *ill chance*
The narrator appears to echo Satan's error by ascribing his rescue to chance, not Provi-
dence.   937 *Instinct* Filled.

As many miles aloft: that fury stay'd,
939 Quench'd in a boggy Syrtis, neither sea,
940 Nor good dry land, nigh founder'd on he fares,
941 Treading the crude consistence, half on foot,
942 Half flying; behooves him now both oar and sail.
943 As when a griffon, through the wilderness
With winged course o'er hill, or moory dale,
945 Pursues the Arimaspian, who by stealth
Had from his wakeful custody purloin'd
947 The guarded gold: so eagerly the fiend
948 O'er bog or steep, through strait, rough, dense or rare,
949 With head, hands, wings, or feet, pursues his way;
950 And swims, or sinks, or wades, or creeps, or flies.
At length a universal hubbub wild
Of stunning sounds, and voices all confus'd,
Borne through the hollow dark assaults his ear
With loudest vehemence: thither he plies,
955 Undaunted to meet there whatever power,
Or spirit, of the nethermost abyss,
Might in that noise reside, of whom to ask
Which way the nearest coast of darkness lies,
Bordering on light: when strait behold the throne
960 Of Chaos, and his dark pavilion spread
Wide on the wasteful deep: with him enthron'd
962 Sat sable-vested Night, eldest of things,
The consort of his reign: and by them stood
964 Orcus and Ades, and the dreaded name
965 Of Demogorgon: Rumour next, and Chance,

---

939 *Syrtis* A sandbank off the coast of northern Africa. 941 *crude consistence* Raw mixture.
942 *behooves him* He could do with. 943 *griffon* In *The Histories* 3.116, by fifth-century B.C
Greek historian Herodotus, this monster was half eagle and half lion and guarded the gold
of Scythia. 945 *Arimaspian* One-eyed tribe aspiring to steal the gold. 948 *strait* Narrow.
947–950 *so eagerly . . . or flies* Satan's entire journey is confused and chaotic; the lines frame
the destructive effect of his influence in literal terms. 960 *pavilion* Canopy. 962 *sable-
vested* Black-clothed. 964 *Orcus and Ades* Pluto and Hades, kings respectively of the
Roman and Greek underworlds. 965 *Demogorgon* Associated with Plato's Demiurge, by
whom the universe is created. In Percy Bysshe Shelley's poem *Prometheus Unbound* (1820),
Demogorgon, asked who created Hell, replies ambiguously, "He reigns" (2.4.28).

And Tumult, and Confusion all embroil'd,   966
And Discord with a thousand various mouths.   967
T'whom Satan turning boldly, thus: Ye powers,
And spirits of this nethermost abyss,
Chaos and ancient Night, I come no spy   970
With purpose to explore, or to disturb
The secrets of your realm; but by constraint
Wand'ring this darksome desert, as my way
Lies through your spacious empire up to light,
Alone and without guide, half lost, I seek   975
What readiest path leads where your gloomy bounds
Confine with heaven: or if some other place   977
From your dominion won, th'ethereal king
Possesses lately, thither to arrive
I travel this profound: direct my course;   980
Directed, no mean recompense it brings
To your behoof: if I that region lost,   982
All usurpation thence expell'd, reduce
To her original darkness, and your sway,
(Which is my present journey,) and once more   985
Erect the standard there of ancient Night;
Yours be th'advantage all, mine the revenge.

Thus Satan; and him thus the anarch[7] old,
With fault'ring speech, and visage incompos'd,
Answer'd: I know thee stranger, who thou art,   990
That mighty leading angel, who of late
Made head against heaven's King, tho' overthrown.
I saw, and heard; for such a num'rous host
Fled not in silence through the frighted deep,   994
With ruin upon ruin, rout on rout,   995
Confusion worse confounded: and heaven-gates
Pour'd out by millions her victorious bands

965–967 *Rumour . . . Discord* The inhabitants of the abyss personify the consequences of life without *logos*, or meanings   977 *Confine* Border.   982 *behoof* Benefit.   994 *frighted deep* Ascribes emotion to a physical place.

Pursuing. I upon my frontiers here
Keep residence; if all I can will serve,
1000 That little which is left so to defend,
1001 Encroach'd on still through our intestine broils,
Weak'ning the sceptre of old Night: first hell,
Your dungeon, stretching far and wide beneath:
Now lately heaven and earth, another world
1005 Hung o'er my realm, link'd in a golden chain,
To that side heaven from whence your legions fell:
If that way be your walk, you have not far;
So much the nearer danger; go, and speed;
Havoc, and spoil, and ruin are my gain.

1010 He ceas'd, and Satan staid not to reply,
But glad that now the sea should find a shore,
With fresh alacrity, and force renew'd,
1013 Springs upward, like a pyramid of fire,
Into the wild expanse; and through the shock
1015 Of fighting elements, on all sides round
Environ'd, wins his way: harder beset,
And more endanger'd, than when Argo pass'd
1018 Through Bosphorus, betwist the justling rocks:
Or when Ulysses on the larboard shunn'd
1020 Charybdis, and by th'other whirlpool steer'd.
1021 So he with difficulty, and labour hard
1022 Moved on; with difficulty and labour he:

1001 *intestine broils* Civil wars.   1005 *golden chain* A now-common image that first appeared in Homer's *Iliad* 8.18–27, indicating heaven's unity with and control over earth.   1013 *pyramid* Archetypal symbol of vain and alienated labor.   1018 *justling rocks* In Greek legend, Jason navigated the Argo through the lashing rocks of the Bosphorus by following the flight of a dove; the Genesis story of Noah's ark contains a similar motif. Both myths have been read as anticipations of Christian redemption. 1020 *Charybdis . . . steer'd* In Homer's *Odyssey* 12.234–259, Odysseus must navigate between the reef Scylla and the whirlpool Charybdis.   1021–1022 *difficulty, and labour . . . difficulty and labour* Milton's repetitions are always significant; here Satan's "labour" is "difficult" because it is in vain, since he is alienated from God.

But he once pass'd, soon after, when man fell,
Strange alteration; Sin, and Death, amain,   1024
Following his tract (such was the will of heaven)   1025
Pav'd after him a broad and beaten way   1026
Over the dark abyss, whose boiling gulf
Tamely endur'd a bridge of wondrous length,
From hell continued, reaching th'utmost orb   1029
Of this frail world; by which the spirits perverse   1030
With easy intercourse pass to and fro,
To tempt or punish mortals, except whom
God and good angels guard by special grace.   1033

But now at last the sacred influence
Of light appears, and from the walls of heaven   1035
Shoots far into the bosom of dim night
A glimmering dawn: here Nature first begins
Her farthest verge, and Chaos to retire,
As from her outmost works a broken foe,
With tumult less, and with less hostile din;   1040
That Satan with less toil, and now with ease,
Wafts on the calmer wave by dubious light;
And like a weather-beaten vessel holds
Gladly the port, though shrouds and tackle torn:
Or in the emptier waste, resembling air,   1045
Weighs his spread wings, at leisure to behold
Far off th'empyreal heaven, extended wide
In circuit undetermin'd square or round:
With opal towers and battlements adorn'd
Of living saphire, (once his native seat)   1050
And fast by, hanging in a golden chain,   1051
This pendent world, in bigness as a star   1052

1024 *amain* As closely as they could.   1026 *broad and beaten way* The way to Hell is easy and, paradoxically, already well traveled.   1029 *utmost orb* Outer sphere.   1033 *specal grace* Seems to assume a body of "elect" human beings, but does not necessarily imply predestination.   1051 *golden chain* Homer's *Iliad* 8.18–27 describes Zeus dangling the world on a golden chain.   1052 *world* Universe.

Of smallest magnitude, close by the moon.
Thither full fraught with mischievous revenge,
1055 Accurs'd and in a cursed hour, he hies.

END OF BOOK SECOND

1055 *hies* Hurries.

BOOK III

God sitting on his throne sees Satan flying towards this world, then newly created; shows him to the Son who sat at his right hand;* foretells the success of Satan in perverting† mankind: clears his own justice and wisdom from all imputation,‡ having created man free, and able enough to have withstood his tempter; yet declares his purpose of grace towards him, in regard he fell not of his own malice, as did Satan, but by him seduced. The Son of God renders praises to his Father for the manifestation of his gracious purpose towards Man; but God again declares, that grace cannot be extended towards Man without the satisfaction of divine justice; Man hath offended the majesty of God by aspiring to Godhead,§ and, therefore, with all his progeny devoted to death, must die, unless some one can be found sufficient to answer for his offence, and undergo his punishment. The Son of God freely offers himself a ransom for Man; the Father accepts him, ordains his incarnation, pronounces his exaltation above all names in heaven and earth; commands all the angels to adore him; they obey, and hymning to their harps in full choir, celebrate the Father and the Son. Meanwhile Satan alights upon the bare convex of this world's

---

*See 2.174 and endnote 2 for book II.

†Since Satan cannot create anything, his only power is to distort God's creation away from its proper ends.

‡Blame.

§Refers to a composite conception of a single deity, as in the Christian Trinity or the Hebrew *Elohim*.

*outermost orb; where wandering he first finds a place, since
called the Limbo of Vanity; what persons and things fly up
thither; thence comes to the gate of heaven, described ascending by
stairs, and the waters above the firmament that flow about it:
his passage thence to the orb of the sun: he finds there Uriel, the
regent of that orb; but first changes himself into the shape of a
meaner angel; and pretending a zealous desire to behold the new
creation and Man whom God had placed there, inquires of him
the place of his habitation, and is directed; alights first on
mount Niphates.*

1	*H*AIL holy Light, offspring of heaven first-born,[1]
	Or of th'eternal co-eternal beam.
3	May I express thee unblam'd? since God is light,
	And never but in an unapproached light
5	Dwelt from eternity; dwelt then in thee,
	Bright effluence of bright essence increate;[2]
7	Or hearest thou rather pure ethereal stream,
8	Whose fountain who shall tell? Before the sun,
	Before the heavens thou wert, and at the voice
10	Of God, as with a mantle, didst invest
	The rising world of waters dark and deep,
	Won from the void and formless infinite.
13	Thee I revisit now with bolder wing,
14	Escap'd the Stygian pool, though long detain'd
15	In that obscure sojourn; while in my flight
	Through utter and through middle darkness borne,

---

1 *Hail holy Light* Either physical light, or the Son of God, or both.   3.1 *unblam'd* Without
blasphemy; 3.2 *God is light* Reference to John 1:4–9; God also *creates* light in Genesis 1:3, and
Jesus is frequently called "the light of the world," as in John 3:19.   7.1 *hearest thou rather*
Would you rather be called; 7.2 *stream* The Father is the fountain, the Son the stream.   8
Whose . . . tell The Father transcends human thought; we know Him only through the Son.
10 *invest* Enter into.   13 *I* Modern literary theory warns us against an easy identification
of a text's narrator with its author, but in this case the biographical parallels with Milton
are impossible to ignore.   14 *Stygian pool* "Stygian" refers to Styx, one of the rivers of
Hades, but "pool" suggests chaos, the "abyss" or the "deep."

With other notes than to th'Orphean lyre,[3]
I sung of Chaos, and eternal Night;
Taught by the heavenly Muse to venture down   19
The dark descent, and up to reascend,   20
Though hard, and rare. Thee I revisit safe,
And feel thy sovereign vital lamp: but thou
Revisit'st not these eyes, that roll in vain
To find thy piercing ray, and find no dawn;[4]
So thick a drop serene hath quench'd their orbs,   25
Or dim suffusion veil'd. Yet not the more   26
Cease I to wander, where the Muses haunt   27
Clear spring, or shady grove, or sunny hill,
Smit with the love of sacred song: but chief   29
Thee, Sion, and the flowery brooks beneath,   30
That wash thy hallow'd feet, and warbling flow,
Nightly I visit: nor sometimes forget
Those other two equall'd with me in fate,
(So were I equall'd with them in renown,)
Blind Thamyris, and blind Mæonides: 35
And Tiresias and Phineus, prophets old.   36
Then feed on thoughts, that voluntary move
Harmonious numbers; as the wakeful bird   38
Sings darkling, and in shadiest covert hid
Tunes her nocturnal note. Thus with the year   40
Seasons return; but not to me returns
Day, or the sweet approach of even or morn,

---

19 *heavenly Muse* The Holy Spirit, but also Urania, Greek muse of astronomy.   25–26 *drop serene . . . suffusion* These terms translate technical, medical terms for diseases of the eye. 27 *Muses* i.e. Classical literature.   29 *sacred song* Milton seems willing to attribute holiness to the classical canon.   30 *Sion* Milton ultimately prefers the Bible to pagan literature. 35.1 *Thamyris* Milton begins a catalogue of blind "seers." Thamyris was blinded for aspiring to out-sing the Muses in Homer's *Iliad* 2.594–600. Hughes reminds us that Plutarch "made him the author of a poem about the war between the Titans against the gods" (p. 258); 35.2 *Mæonides* Homer, who was blind, according to legend.   36.1 *Tiresias* Blind Theban prophet who appears in *Oedipus Rex* and *Antigone*, by fifth-century B.C. Greek playwright Sophocles. He is revived in T. S. Eliot's "The Wasteland" (1922); 36.2 *Phineus* Blind Thracian prophet.   38 *wakeful bird* The nightingale, which sings beautiful songs in darkness, and is therefore an important symbol for the blind Milton.

Or sight of vernal bloom, or summer's rose,
44 Or flocks, or herds, or human face divine:
45 But cloud instead, and ever-during dark
Surrounds me; from the cheerful ways of men
Cut off; and for the book of knowledge fair,
Presented with a universal blank
Of nature's works, to me expung'd and raz'd,
50 And wisdom at one entrance quite shut out.
So much the rather thou, celestial Light,
Shine inward, and the mind through all her powers
Irradiate; there plant eyes; all mist from thence
Purge and disperse; that I may see and tell
55 Of things invisible to mortal sight.

Now had the Almighty Father from above,
(From the pure empyrean where he sits
High thron'd above all height,) bent down his eye,
59 His own works and their works at once to view:
60 About him all the sanctities of heaven
Stood thick as stars, and from his sight receiv'd
Beatitude past utterance: on his right
The radiant image of his glory[5] sat,
His only Son. On earth he first beheld
65 Our two first parents (yet the only two
Of mankind) in the happy garden plac'd,
Reaping immortal fruits of joy and love;
Uninterrupted joy, unrivall'd love,
In blissful solitude. He then survey'd
70 Hell, and the gulf between, and Satan there
Coasting the wall of heaven on this side night,
72 In the dun air sublime; and ready now
To stoop with wearied wings, and willing feet,

---

44 *human face divine* Because made in the image of God.   55 *to mortal sight* Not "the sight of mortals" but "sight, which is mortal." Milton is not claiming immortality.   59 *His . . . works* Note the distinction between divine creature (nature) and human recreation (culture). Idolatry consists in taking the latter for the former.   72 *dun* Dark.

On the bare outside of this world, that seem'd
Firm land imbosom'd without firmament;   75
Uncertain which, in ocean, or in air.
Him God beholding from his prospect high,
Wherein past, present, future he beholds,
Thus to his only Son foreseeing spake:

Only begotten Son, seest thou what rage   80
Transports our adversary, whom no bounds   81
Prescrib'd, no bars of hell, nor all the chains
Heap'd on him there, nor yet the main abyss
Wide interrupt, can hold? So bent he seems   84
On desperate revenge, that shall redound   85
Upon his own rebellious head. And now
Through all restraint broke loose, he wings his way
Not far off heaven, in the precincts of light,
Directly towards the new created world.
And man there plac'd; with purpose to assay   90
If him by force he can destroy, or worse,
By some false guile pervert: and shall pervert;
For man will hearken to his glozing lies,   93
And easily transgress the sole command,
Sole pledge of his obedience: so will fall,   95
He, and his faithless progeny. Whose fault?   96
Whose but his own? Ingrate, he had of me   97
All he could have; I made him just and right;
Sufficient to have stood, though free to fall.   99

75.1 *imbosom'd* Enclosed; 75.2 *firmament* Shell, roof.   81 *Transports* Carries away, both phys-
ically and emotionally; a signal that Satan's voyage is internal as well as literal.   84 *inter-
rupt* Torn apart.   85 *desperate* Hopeless.   90 *assay* Attempt.   93 *glozing* Flattering;
compare Christopher Marlowe's *Edward II* (1584): "The glozing head of thy base minion"
(act 1, scene 1). But Flannagan also points to the synonym with "glossing" or "interpret-
ing." Satan will induce a false mode of interpretation in Eve.   95 *pledge* Token, sign, evi-
dence, symptom.   96 *progeny* Both the literal descendants of Adam and the psychological
consequences of disobeying God's will.   96–97 *Whose fault . . . but his own?* The Father's
rhetorical question is unsatisfying, since an omnipresent deity is logically responsible for
everything that occurs in His creation.   99 *Sufficient to have stood* Capable of standing.

100 Such I created all th'ethereal powers,
And spirits, both them who stood, and them who fail'd;
Freely they stood who stood, and fell who fell.
Not free, what proof could they have given sincere
Of true allegiance, constant faith, or love,
105 Where only what they needs must do, appear'd;
Not, what they would? What praise could they receive?
What pleasure I from such obedience paid,
108 When will and reason (reason also is choice)
Useless and vain, of freedom both despoil'd,
110 Made passive both, had serv'd necessity,
Not me? They therefore, as to right belong'd,
So were created, nor can justly accuse
Their Maker, or their making, or their fate;
114 As if predestination over-rul'd
115 Their will, dispos'd by absolute decree,
116 Or high foreknowledge. They themselves decreed
Their own revolt, not I: if I foreknew,
Foreknowledge had no influence on their fault,
Which had no less prov'd certain unforeknown.
120 So without least impulse, or shadow of fate,
Or aught by me immutably foreseen,
122 They trespass; authors to themselves in all,
Both what they judge, and what they choose; for me
I form'd them free, and free they must remain,
125 Till they enthrall themselves: I also must change
Their nature, and revoke the high decree
Unchangeable, eternal, which ordain'd
Their freedom; they themselves ordain'd their fall.
129 The first sort by their own suggestion fell,
130 Self-tempted, self-deprav'd: man falls, deceiv'd,

---

108 *reason also is choice* Alludes to Aristotle's concept of *proairesis* ("right reason").   114–116
As if . . . foreknowledge The fact that God knew the Fall would occur and chose not to pre-
vent it, does not mean that He caused it. Once again, the reasoning seems disingenuous.
122 *authors to themselves in all* This is just what Satan claims of himself; a signal that we are
here experiencing God from a fallen perspective.

By th'other first: man, therefore, shall find grace,   131
The other none. In mercy, and justice both,   132
Through heaven and earth, so shall my glory excel;
But mercy, first and last, shall brightest shine.

Thus while God spake, ambrosial fragrance fill'd   135
All heaven, and in the blessed spirits elect
Sense of new joy ineffable diffus'd.
Beyond compare the Son of God was seen
Most glorious; in him all his Father shone
Substantially express'd; and in his face   140
Divine compassion visibly appear'd,   141
Love without end, and without measure grace;
Which uttering, thus he to his father spake:

O Father, gracious was that word which clos'd
Thy sovereign sentence, that man should find grace   145
For which both heaven and earth shall high extol
Thy praises, with th'innumerable sound
Of hymns and sacred songs, wherewith thy throne
Encompass'd shall resound thee ever bless'd.
For should man finally be lost, should man   150
Thy creature late so lov'd, thy youngest son,   151
Fall circumvented thus by fraud, though join'd
With his own folly? That be from thee far,   153
That far be from thee, Father, who art judge   154
Of all things made, and judgest only right.   155
Or shall the adversary thus obtain
His end, and frustrate thine? shall he fulfil
His malice, and thy goodness bring to nought;
Or proud return, though to his heavier doom,

129–132 *The first sort . . . none* The fact that man is seduced into sin entitles him to redemption and, by the same token, disqualifies the seducer.   140 *Substantially express'd* The Son is of the same substance as the Father, but not of the same essence; the Son is the sign, the Father is the referent.   141 *visibly appear'd* The Son is the manifestation of the Father.   151 *thy youngest son* Man.   153–154 *That be . . . thee* Echoes Abraham's plea for the Sodomites in Genesis 18:25.

160   Yet, with revenge accomplish'd, and to hell
       Draw after him the whole race of mankind,
       By him corrupted? Or wilt thou thyself
       Abolish thy creation, and unmake,
164   For him, what for thy glory thou hast made?
165   So should thy goodness and thy greatness, both
       Be questioned, and blasphem'd without defence.

       To whom the great Creator thus replied:
       O Son, in whom my soul hath chief delight,
       Son of my bosom, Son who art alone
170   My word, my wisdom, and effectual might.
       All hast thou spoken as my thoughts are, all
       As my eternal purpose hath decreed.
       Man shall not quite be lost, but sav'd who will
       Yet not of will in him, but grace in me
175   Freely vouchsaf'd: once more I will renew
       His lapsed powers, though forfeit, and inthrall'd
       By sin to foul exorbitant desires:
       Upheld by me, yet once more he shall stand
       On even ground against his mortal foe:
180   By me upheld, that he may know how frail
       His fallen condition is, and to me owe
       All his deliverance, and to none but me.
       Some I have chosen of peculiar grace
184   Elect above the rest: so is my will.
185   The rest shall hear me call, and oft be warn'd
186   Their sinful state, and to appease betimes
187   Th'incensed Deity, while offer'd grace
       Invites: for I will clear their senses dark,
       What may suffice, and soften stony hearts[6]

---

164 *For him* Because of him.   170 *My . . . might* The Son is the Father in effect, in action, in practice.   184 *Elect above the rest* Implies predestination in the sense of divine prescience, but, as the father goes on to explain, this does not preclude human free will.   186–187 *to appease . . . Deity* Ricks (p. 104) observes that this suggests the idolatrous view that God can be appeased by the ritualistic burning of incense.

To pray, repent, and bring obedience due.   190
To prayer, repentance, and obedience due,
Though but endeavour'd with sincere intent,
Mine ear shall not be slow, mine eye not shut;
And I will place within them as a guide
My umpire Conscience;[7] whom if they will hear,   195
Light after light well us'd they shall attain,
And to the end persisting, safe arrive.   197
This my long sufferance, and my day of grace,   198
They who neglect and scorn shall never taste;
But hard he harden'd, blind he blinded more,   -   200
That they may stumble on, and deeper fall;
And none but such from mercy I exclude.
But yet all is not done: Man disobeying,
Disloyal breaks his fealty, and sins   204
Against the high supremacy of heaven,   205
Affecting Godhead, and so losing all,
To expiate his treason hath nought left,
But to destruction, sacred and devote,
He with his whole posterity must die;
Die he or justice must; unless for him   210
Some other able, and as willing, pay
The rigid satisfaction, death for death.[8]
Say, heavenly powers, where shall we find such love?
Which of ye will be mortal to redeem
Man's mortal crime, and just th'unjust to save?   215
Dwells in all heaven charity so dear?   216

He ask'd, but all the heavenly choir stood mute,   217
And silence was in heaven: on man's behalf

---

197 *end* The Aristotelian "end," in the sense of "purpose," is here applied to chronological
history.   198 *sufference* Forbearance.   204 *fealty* Faith, usually used in the sense of loyalty
to a feudal lord.   215 *th'unjust* See 1 Peter 3:18: "the just for the unjust."   216 *charity* Love.
217 *stood mute* Compare the scene in Hell at 2.418–429. Fowler notes that, in contrast to
Satan's manipulation of the devils, heaven is "meritocratic . . . any angel has an opportu-
nity to be mankind's redeemer" (p. 180).

Christ Offers to Redeem Mankind

Patron or intercessor none appear'd;
Much less that durst upon his own head draw   220
The deadly forfeiture, and ransom set.   221
And now, without redemption, all mankind   222
Must have been lost, adjudg'd to death and hell
By doom severe, had not the Son of God,
In whom the fulness dwells of love divine,   225
His dearest mediation thus renew'd: 226

Father, thy word is pass'd; man shall find grace,
And shall grace not find means, that finds her way,
The speediest of thy winged messengers,
To visit all thy creatures, and to all   230
Comes unprevented, unimplor'd, unsought?
Happy for man, so coming; he her aid
Can never seek, once dead in sins and lost;
Atonement for himself, or offering meet,   234
(Indebted,[9] and undone,) hath none to bring.   235
Behold me then, me for him, life for life
I offer; on me let thine anger fall;
Account me man: I for his sake will leave   238
Thy bosom, and this glory next to thee
Freely put off, and for him lastly die   240
Well pleas'd: on me let death wreak all his rage;
Under his gloomy power I shall not long
Lie vanquish'd; thou hast given me to possess
Life in myself for ever; by thee I live,
Though now to death I yield, and am his due   245
All that of me can die; yet that debt paid,
Thou wilt not leave me in the loathsome grave
His prey, nor suffer my unspotted soul
For ever with corruption there to dwell;   249
But I shall rise victorious, and subdue   250

---

221 *forfeiture* The loss of the principal for failure to repay a debt.   **222** *redemption* Payment
of a debt.   **226** *dearest mediation* The Son is the "mediator" who relates the individual to
the totality.   **234** *Atonement* Being "at one" with God.   **238** *Account me* Treat me as.   **249**
corruption In both the physical and the moral sense.

My vanquisher, spoiled of his vaunted spoil;
252 Death his death's wound shall then receive, and stoop
253 Inglorious, of his mortal sting disarm'd.
254 I through the ample air in triumph high
255 Shall lead hell captive maugre hell; and show
The powers of darkness bound. Thou at the sight
Pleas'd, out of heaven shalt look down and smile;
While by thee rais'd I ruin all my foes,
259 Death last, and with his carcass glut the graves:
260 Then, with the multitude of my redeem'd,
261 Shall enter heaven, long absent, and return,
262 Father, to see thy face, wherein no cloud
263 Of anger shall remain; but peace assured
264 And reconcilement: wrath shall be no more
265 Thenceforth, but in thy presence joy entire.

His words here ended, but his meek aspect
Silent yet spake, and breath'd immortal love
To mortal men, above which only shone
269 Filial obedience: as a sacrifice
270 Glad to be offer'd, he attends the will
Of his great Father. Admiration seiz'd
All heaven, what this might mean, and whither tend,
Wond'ring; but soon th'Almighty thus replied:

O thou, in heaven and earth the only peace
275 Found out for mankind under wrath; O thou,
276 My sole complacence; well thou know'st how dear
To me are all my works, nor man the least,
278 Though last created; that for him I spare
Thee from my bosom and right hand, to save,

---

252 *Death . . . receive* Compare John Donne's Holy Sonnet 10, also known as "Death Be Not Proud" (1633): "death thou shalt die" (l.14). 253 *sting* Compare 1 Corinthians 15:55, "O Death, where is thy sting?" 254 *ample* Spacious. 255 *maugre* In spite of. 259 *glut* Satisfy. 260–265 *Then . . . entire* Redemption consists in the creature's overcoming its alienation from the Creator. 269 *sacrifice* The sacrifice of Christ obviates the need for all other sacrifices. 276 *complacence* Comfort. 278 *Though last created* By this logic, the fact that Eve is created after Adam does not imply she is less favored of God.

By losing thee a while, the whole race lost.   280
Thou, therefore, whom thou only canst redeem,
Their nature also to thy nature join,
And be thyself man among men on earth,
Made flesh, when time shall be, of virgin seed,
By wondrous birth: be thou in Adam's room,   285
The head of all mankind, though Adam's son,
As in him perish all men, so in thee,
As from a second root, shall be restor'd   288
As many as are restor'd, without thee none.
His crime makes guilty all his sons; thy merit   290
Imputed shall absolve them who renounce
Their own both righteous and unrighteous deeds   292
And live in thee transplanted, and from thee
Receive new life. So man, as is most just,
Shall satisfy for man, be judg'd, and die,   295
And dying rise, and rising with him raise
His brethren, ransom'd with his own dear life.   297
So heavenly love shall outdo hellish hate,
Giving to death, and dying to redeem,
So dearly to redeem what hellish hate   300
So easily destroy'd, and still destroys,
In those who, when they may, accept not grace.
Nor shalt thou, by descending to assume   303
Man's nature, lessen or degrade thine own.   304
Because thou hast, though thron'd in highest bliss   305
Equal to God, and equally enjoying   306
Godlike fruition, quitted all to save   307
A world from utter loss, and hast been found

---

285 *Adam's room* Adam's place, his body.   288 *a second root* The Son's figurative "progeny" in the human mind negates Adam's "progeny" at 3.96.   292 *Their . . . deeds* Human beings must renounce *all* their works, since no human deeds, however admirable, can be efficacious in bringing about salvation.   295 *satisfy* Atone.   297 *ransom'd* See Matthew 20-28: "The Son of Man came . . . to give his life a ransom for many."   303-304 *Nor . . . own* Christ will remain fully divine, even while He becomes fully human.   306 *Equal to God* The Son is "equal" to God, while simultaneously being created by Him; this is what Satan cannot understand.   307 *Godlike fruition* Full realization of your divine nature.

309 By merit more than birthright Son of God,
310 Found worthiest to be so by being good,
311 Far more than great or high; because in thee
Love hath abounded more than glory abounds;
Therefore thy humiliation shall exalt
With thee thy manhood also to this throne,
315 Here shalt thou sit incarnate, here shalt reign
Both God and Man, Son both of God and Man,
Anointed Universal King; all power
I give thee; reign for ever, and assume
Thy merits: under thee, as head supreme,
320 Thrones, princedoms, powers, dominions, I reduce;
All knees to thee shall bow, of them that bide
In heaven, or earth, or under earth in hell.
When thou, attended gloriously from heaven,
Shalt in the sky appear, and from thee send
325 The summoning archangels to proclaim
Thy dread tribunal: forthwith from all winds
327 The living, and forthwith the cited dead
328 Of all past ages to the general doom
Shall hasten, such a peal shall rouse their sleep:
330 Then, all thy saints assembled, thou shalt judge
Bad men and angels; they arraign'd shall sink
Beneath thy sentence; hell, her numbers full,
333 Thenceforth shall be for ever shut. Meanwhile
334 The world shall burn, and from her ashes spring
335 New heaven and earth, wherein the just shall dwell;
And, after all their tribulations long,
See golden days, fruitful of golden deeds,
With joy and love triumphing, and fair truth.
Then thou thy regal sceptre shalt lay by,

309–311 *By merit . . . high* Compare 2.5, where Satan is alo raised "by merit."   327 *cited* Chosen.   328 *the general doom* The day of judgment.   333–335 *Meanwhile . . . earth* Milton alludes to the Phoenix, the mythical bird that is reborn from its own funeral pyre, as a prefiguration of the destruction and the rebirth of the world in the fire of the apocalypse.

For regal sceptre then no more shall need;   340
God shall be all in all. But all ye gods,
Adore him, who to compass all this dies;   342
Adore the Son, and honour him as me.

No sooner had th'Almighty ceas'd, but all
The multitude of angels, with a shout   345
Loud as from numbers without number, sweet,
As from bless'd voices uttering joy, heaven rung
With jubilee, and loud hosannas fill'd   348
Th'eternal regions. Lowly reverent
Towards either throne they bow, and to the ground   350
With solemn adoration down they cast
Their crowns, inwove with amaranth and gold;
Immortal amaranth, a flower which once   353
In Paradise, fast by the tree of life,
Began to bloom; but soon for man's offence   355
To heaven remov'd, where first it grew, there grows,
And flowers aloft, shading the fount of life;
And where the river of bliss through midst of heaven
Rolls o'er Elysian flowers her amber stream:[10]
With these, that never fade, the spirits elect   360
Bind their resplendent locks, inwreath'd with beams;
Now in loose garlands thick thrown off; the bright
Pavement, that like a sea of jasper shone,
Impurpled with celestial roses smil'd.
Then crown'd again, their golden harps they took,   365
Harps ever tun'd, that, glittering by their side,
Like quivers hung, and with preamble sweet
Of charming symphony they introduce
Their sacred song, and waken raptures high;
No voice exempt; no voice but well could join   370
Melodious part, such concord is in heaven.

---

340 *need* Be necessary.   342 *compass* Accomplish.   348 *jubilee* Every fifty years the Israelites
held a "Jubilee" festival, at which slaves were freed, as a symbol of liberation from sin and
death.   353 *amaranth* Legendary immortal plant.

372 Thee, Father, first they sung, omnipotent,
373 Immutable, immortal, infinite,
374 Eternal King; thee, Author of all being,
375 Fountain of light, thyself invisible
376 Amidst the glorious brightness where thou sitt'st
377 Thron'd inaccessible, but when thou shad'st
378 The full blaze of thy beams, and through a cloud,
279 Drawn round about thee like a radiant shrine,
380 Dark with excessive bright, thy skirts appear,
381 Yet dazzle heaven, that brightest seraphim
382 Approach not, but with both wings veil their eyes.
     Thee, next they sang, of all creation first,
384 Begotten Son, divine similitude,
385 In whose conspicuous count'nance, without cloud
386 Made visible, th'almighty Father shines,
387 Whom else no creature can behold: on thee
388 Impress'd, th'effulgence of his glory abides,
389 Transfus'd on thee his ample Spirit rests.
390 He heaven of heavens, and all the powers therein,
391 By thee created, and by thee threw down
392 Th'aspiring dominations: thou that day
     Thy Father's dreadful thunder did not spare,
     Nor stop the flaming chariot-wheels, that shook
395 Heaven's everlasting frame, while o'er the necks
     Thou drov'st warring angels disarray'd.
     Back from pursuit thy powers with loud acclaim
     Thee only extol'd, Son of thy Father's might,
     To execute fierce vengeance on his foes.
400 Not so on man: him through their malice fallen,
     Father of mercy and grace, thou didst not doom
     So strictly, but much more to pity incline:

372–382 *Thee . . . eyes* These lines emphasize the inaccessibility of the Father, in contrast to His perceptible manifestation in the Son.   384 *similitude* Likeness, metaphor.   385–387 *In whose . . . behold* The Son makes the Father visible.   388 *Impress'd* Stamped, like a coin, with God's image.   389 *Transfus'd on* Infused into, transmitted to.   391 *By thee created* The Son is the power by which the Father has created the universe.   392 *dominations* An order of angels, but with the implication of "aspiring to dominion," or supremacy.

No sooner did thy dear and only Son
Perceive thee purpos'd not to doom frail man
So strictly, but much more to pity incline,   405
He, to appease thy wrath, and end the strife
Of mercy and justice in thy face discern'd,
Regardless of the bliss wherein he sat
Second to thee, offer'd himself to die
For man's offence. O unexampled love,   410
Love no where to be found less than divine!
Hail, Son of God, Saviour of men! Thy name
Shall be the copious matter of my song
Henceforth, and never shall my harp thy praise
Forget, nor from thy Father's praise disjoin.   415

Thus they in heaven, above the starry sphere,
Their happy hours in joy and hymning spent.
Meanwhile upon the firm opacous globe
Of this round world, whose first convex divides
The luminous inferior orbs, enclos'd   420
From Chaos, and th'inroad of darkness old,
Satan alighted walks. A globe far off
It seem'd, now seems a boundless continent,   423
Dark, waste, and wild, under the frown of nigh
Starless expos'd, and ever-threat'ning storms   425
Of Chaos blust'ring round, inclement sky;
Save on that side from which the wall of heaven,
Though distant far, some small reflection gains
Of glimmering air, less vex'd with tempest loud:
Here walk'd the fiend at large in spacious field.   430
As when a vulture, on Imaus bred,   431
Whose snowy ridge the roving Tartar bounds,
Dislodging from a region scarce of prey,
To gorge the flesh of lambs, or yeanling kids
On hills where flocks are fed, flies tow'rds the springs   435

---

405 *incline* Tend.   423 *seem'd . . . seems* The repetition of this vital word indicates that Satan's perspective is limited and partial.   431 *Imaus* Range in the Himalayas.

Of Ganges, or Hydaspes, Indian streams;
But in his way lights on the barren plains
438 Of Sericana, where Chineses drive
With sails of wind their cany wagons light:
440 So on this windy sea of land, the fiend
441 Walk'd up and down alone, bent on his prey;
Alone, for other creature in this place,
Living or lifeless, to be found was none;
None yet; but store hereafter from the earth
445 Up hither like aerial vapours flew,
Of all things transitory and vain, when sin
447 With vanity had fill'd the works of men:
Both all things vain, and all who in vain things
Built their fond hopes of glory or lasting fame,
450 Or happiness in this or th'other life:
All who have their reward on earth, the fruits
Of painful superstition and blind zeal,
Nought seeking but the praise of men, here find
454 Fit retribution, empty as their deeds:
455 All th'unaccomplish'd works of nature's hand,
Abortive, monstrous, or unkindly mix'd,
Dissolv'd on earth,[11] fleet hither, and in vain,
Till final dissolution, wander here:
Not in the neighb'ring moon, as some have dream'd;
460 Those argent fields more likely habitants,
461 Translated saints or middle spirits hold,
Betwixt the angelical and human kind.
Hither, of ill-join'd sons and daughters born,
First from the ancient world those giants came,
465 With many a vain exploit, though then renown'd:
The builders next of Babel on the plain
467 Of Sennaar, and still with vain design

---

438 *Sericana* China.   441 *up and down* Compare Job 1:7.   447 *vanity* Pointlessness (as used in Ecclesiastes 1:2), but the Hebrew is often translated as "idolatry."   454 *deeds* The belief that humans can gain salvation through deeds is the ultimate "vanity."   460 *argent* Silver. 461 *Translated* Taken from the earth without dying, like Enoch and Elijah.   467 *Sennaar* Shinar, from Genesis 11:2: "They found a plain in the land of Shinar"; compare 12:41.

New Babels, had they wherewithal, would build:
Others came single; he who to be deem'd
A god, leap'd fondly into Ætna's flames,   470
Empedocles; and he who, to enjoy   471
Plato's Elysium, leap'd into the sea,
Cleombrotus; and many more too long,   473
Embryos, and idiots, eremites, and friars,   474
White, black, and grey, with all their trumpetry.   475
Here pilgrims roam, that stray'd so far to seek
In Golgotha him dead, who lives in heaven;   477
And they who, to be sure of Paradise,
Dying put on the weeds of Dominic,   479
Or in Franciscan think to pass disguis'd,   480
They pass the planets seven, and pass the fixt,
And that chrystalline sphere whose balance weighs   482
The trepidation talk'd, and that first-mov'd:
And now Saint Peter at heaven's wicket seems   484
To wait them with his keys, and now at foot   485
Of heaven's ascent they lift their feet, when lo
A violent cross wind from either coast
Blows them transverse, ten thousand leagues awry   488
Into the devious air; then might ye see
Cowls, hoods, and habits, with their wearers, tost   490
And flutter'd into rags; then reliques, beads,   491
Indulgences, dispenses, pardons, bulls,   492
The sport of winds: all these, up-whirl'd aloft,

---

471 *Empedocles* In *Art of Poetry* 464–466, by first-century B.C. Roman poet Horace, he throws himself into the volcano Aetna in a vain attempt to disguise his mortality.   473 *Cleombrotus* A Platonist who tried to achieve immortality by suicide.   474 *Embryos, and idiots, eremites* Aborted fetuses, the mentally handicapped, and an order of Augustinian hermits. Milton mocks the Catholic doctrine that assigned the first two to "limbo" by locating some of its propagators in the same place.   475 *White, black, and grey* The Carmelite, Dominican, and Franciscan orders of friars.   477 *Golgotha* Literally, "the place of the skull"; the hill of Calvary outside Jerusalem, where Jesus was crucified.   479 *weeds* Clothes.   482 *that chrystalline sphere* The ninth sphere of the Ptolemaic universe.   484 *Saint Peter . . . seems* The final word reveals that heaven is being described from the Catholic perspective, in which Peter's role as keeper of heaven's gate ("wicket") is connected to his rank as the first "Pope."   488 *transverse* Sideways.   490–492 *Cowls . . . bulls* Representative Catholic fetishes.

494 Fly o'er the backside of the world far off,
495 Into a Limbo large and broad, since call'd
496 The Paradise of Fools, to few unknown
Long after: now unpeopled, and untrod.
All this dark globe the fiend found as he pass'd,
And long he wander'd, till at last a gleam
500 Of dawning light turn'd thither-ward in haste
His travell'd steps: far distant he descries,
Ascending by degrees magnificent
Up to the wall of heaven, a structure high,
At top whereof, but far more rich, appear'd
505 The work as of a kingly palace gate,
With frontispiece of diamond, and gold
Embellish'd; thick with sparkling orient gems
The portal shone, inimitable on earth,
By model, or by shading pencil drawn.
510 The stairs were such as whereon Jacob saw
Angels ascending and descending, bands
Of guardians bright, when he from Esau fled
To Padan-aram, in the field of Luz,
Dreaming by night under the open sky,
515 And waking cried, This is the gate of heaven.
516 Each stair mysteriously was meant, nor stood
517 There always, but drawn up to heaven sometimes
518 Viewless; and underneath a bright sea flow'd
Of jasper, or of liquid pearl, whereon
520 Who after came from earth, sailing arriv'd,
Wafted by angels, or flew o'er the lake
Wrapp'd in a chariot drawn by fiery steeds.
The stairs were then let down, whether to dare
The fiend by easy ascent, or aggravate
525 His sad exclusion from the doors of bliss:[12]

---

494 *backside* Anus.   495 *Limbo* Compare the Limbo of Vanity in Ludovico Ariosto's *Orlando Furioso* 24 (1516), and Alexander Pope's "The Rape of the Lock," canto 5 (1712).   496 *The Paradise of Fools* A proverbial term.   510 *Jacob* See Genesis 28:12.   516–518 *Each . . . Viewless* The stairs are not literal but allegorical.

Direct against which open'd from beneath,
Just o'er the blissful seat of Paradise,
A passage down to th'earth, a passage wide,
Wider by far than that of after-times
Over mount Sion, and, though that were large,   530
Over the promis'd Land to God so dear,
By which, to visit oft those happy tribes,
On high behests his angels to an fro
Pass'd frequent, and his eye with choice regard,
From Paneas, the fount of Jordan's flood,   535
To Beersaba, where the Holy Land   536
Borders on Egypt and th'Arabian shore;   537
So wide the opening seem'd, where bounds were set
To darkness, such as bound the ocean wave.
Satan from hence, now on the lower stair,   540
That scal'd by steps of gold to heaven gate,
Looks down with wonder at the sudden view
Of all this world at once. As when a scout,
Through dark and desert ways with peril gone
All night, at last, by break of cheerful dawn,   545
Obtains the brow of some high-climbing hill,   546
Which to his eye discovers unaware   547
The goodly prospect of some foreign land
First seen, or some renown'd metropolis,
With glist'ring spires and pinnacles adorn'd,   550
Which now the rising sun gilds with his beams.
Such wonder seiz'd, though after heaven seen,
The spirit malign; but much more envy seiz'd
At sight of all this world beheld so fair.
Round he surveys and well might where he stood   555
So high above the circling canopy
Of night's extended shade from eastern point
Of Libra, to the fleecy star, that bears   558

535–537 *From Paneas . . . shore* Paneas and Beersaba (Beersheba) are regions of ancient Israel; this phrase is commonly used in the Bible to indicate the whole of the country.   546 *Obtains* Attains, takes possession of.   547 *discovers* Reveals.   558.1 *Libra* The scales, as of justice; 558.2 *fleecy star* Aries, the ram.

Andromeda far off Atlantic seas,
560   Beyond th'horizon: then from pole to pole
He views in breadth; and without longer pause
Down right into the world's first region throws
His flight precipitant, and winds with ease,
564   Through the pure marble air his oblique way,
565   Amongst innumerable stars, that shone,
Stars distant, but nigh hand seem'd other world's:
Or other worlds they seem'd, or happy isles,
568   Like those Hesperian gardens fam'd of old,
Fortunate fields, and groves, and flowery vales,
570   Thrice happy isles! But who dwelt happy there
He stay'd not to inquire. Above them all
The golden sun, in splendour likest heaven,
573   Allur'd his eye; thither his course he bends
Through the calm firmament, (but, up or down
575   By centre or eccentric, hard to tell;[13]
576   Or longitude,) where the great luminary,
577   Aloof the vulgar constellations thick,
That from his lordly eye keep distance due,
Dispenses light from far; they as they move
580   Their starry dance in numbers that compute
Days, months, and years, tow'rds his all-cheering lamp
Turn swift their various motions, or are turn'd
583   By his magnetic beam, that gently warms
The universe, and to each inward part,
585   With gentle penetration, though unseen,
586   Shoots invisible virtue even to the deep;
So wondrously was set his station bright.
There lands the fiend, a spot like which perhaps

---

564 *oblique* Refers both to Satan's journey itself and the means by which Milton expresses it.   568 *Hesperian gardens* Where the Hesperides, daughters of Venus in Greek mythology, tended apples.   573 *Allur'd his eye* Satan is tempted by intense sensory stimulation.   576 *luminary* Shining one, the sun.   577 *vulgar* Common, from the snobbish perspective of Satan's "lordly" eye.   580 *numbers* Both musical and mathematical.   583 *his magnetic beam* The magnetic force of the sun supposedly dictated the motions of the planets.   586 *Shoots . . . deep* A sexualized image.

Astronomer in the sun's lucent orb,
Through his glaz'd optic tube, yet never saw.   590
The place he found beyond expression bright,
Compar'd with aught on earth, metal, or stone:
Not all parts alike, but all alike inform'd
With radiant light, as glowing iron with fire;
If metal, part seem'd gold, part silver clear;   595
If stone, carbuncle most or chrysolite,
Ruby or topaz, or the twelve that shone
In Aaron's breast-plate, and a stone besides
Imagin'd rather oft than elsewhere seen,
That stone, or like to that which here below   600
Philosophers in vain so long have sought,
In vain, though by their powerful art they bind
Volatile Hermes, and call up unbound
In various shapes old Proteus from the sea,
Drain'd through a limbec to his native form.[14]   605
What wonder then if fields and regions here
Breathe forth elixir pure, and rivers run
Potable gold, when with one virtuous touch   608
Th'arch-chemic sun, so far from us remote,   609
Produces, with terrestrial humour mix'd,   610
Here in the dark so many precious things
Of colour glorious, and effect so rare?
Here matter new to gaze the Devil met
Undazzled; far and wide his eye commands
For sight no obstacle found here, nor shade,   615
But all sunshine, as when his beams at noon
Culminate from th'equator, as they now
Shot upward still direct, whence no way round
Shadow from body opaque can fall; and th'air,
No where so clear, sharpen'd his visual ray   620
To objects distant far, whereby he soon
Saw within ken a glorious angel stand,

---

590 *glaz'd optic tube* Telescope.   608 *Potable* Drinkable.   609 *arch-chemic* Chief alchemist.

623 The same whom John saw also in the sun:
His back was turn'd, but not his brightness hid:
625 Of beaming sunny rays a golden tiar
Circled his head, nor less his locks behind
Illustrious on his shoulders, fledged with wings,
Lay waving round; on some great charge employ'd
He seem'd, or fixt in cogitation deep.
630 Glad was the spirit impure, as now in hope
To find who might direct his wand'ring flight
To Paradise, the happy seat of man,
His journey's end, and our beginning woe.
But first he casts to change his proper shape,
635 Which else might work him danger or delay:
And now a stripling cherub he appears,
Not of the prime, yet such as in his face
Youth smil'd celestial, and to every limb
639 Suitable grace diffus'd, so well he feign'd:
640 Under a coronet his flowing hair
In curls on either cheek play'd; wings he wore
Of many a colour'd plume, sprinkled with gold
643 His habit fit for speed succinct, and held
Before his decent steps a silver wand.
645 He drew not nigh unheard; the angel bright,
Ere he drew nigh, his radiant visage turn'd,
Admonish'd by his ear; and strait was known
648 Th'archangel Uriel, one of the seven
Who in God's presence, nearest to his throne,
650 Stand ready at command, and are his eyes
That run through all the heavens, or down to th'earth
652 Bear his swift errands over moist and dry,
653 O'er sea and land: him Satan thus accosts:

---

623 *whom John saw* See Revelation 19:17: "I saw an angel standing in the sun."   625 *tiar*
Crown.   639 *feign'd* Acted.   643 *succinct* Ready.   648 *Uriel* Hebrew for "fire, or light of
God"; one of the four archangels in Jewish tradition—the others are Michael, Raphael,
and Gabriel.   652–653 *Bear his . . . land* Compare Milton's Sonnet 19 (c. 1652): "Thou-
sands at his bidding speed, / And post o'er land and ocean without rest; / They also serve
who only stand and wait."

Uriel, for thou of those seven spirits that stand   654
In sight of God's high throne, gloriously bright,   655
The first art wont his great authentic will
Interpreter through highest heaven to bring,
Where all his sons thy embassy attend;
And here art likeliest by supreme decree
Like honour to obtain, and as his eye   660
To visit oft this new creation round;
Unspeakable desire to see, and know   662
All these his wondrous works, but chiefly man,
His chief delight and favour; him, for whom
All these his works so wondrous he ordain'd,   665
Hath brought me from the choirs of cherubim
Alone thus wand'ring. Brightest seraph, tell
In which of all these shining orbs hath man
His fixed seat, or fixed seat hath none,
But all these shining orbs his choice to dwell;   670
That I may find him, and with secret gaze,
Or open admiration, him behold,
On whom the great Creator hath bestow'd
Worlds, and on whom hath all these graces pour'd;
That both in him and all things, as is meet,   675
The universal Maker we may praise;
Who justly hath driven out his rebel foes
To deepest hell; and, to repair that loss,
Created this new happy race of men
To serve him better: wise are all his ways.   680

So speak the false dissembler unperceiv'd;
For neither man nor angel can discern
Hypocrisy, the only evil that walks   683
Invisible, except to God alone,
By his permissive will, through heaven and earth: 685

---

654 *seven spirits* In Revelation 1:4, seen by John guarding the throne of God.   **662** *Un-
speakable* Inexpressible, but with a telltale undertone of "hideous."   **683** *Hypocrisy* Liter-
ally, "acting."

And oft though wisdom wake, suspicion sleeps
At wisdom's gate, and to simplicity
Resigns her charge, while goodness thinks no ill
Where no ill seems; which now for once beguil'd
690 Uriel, though regent of the sun, and held
The sharpest sighted spirit of all in heaven;
Who to the fraudulent imposter foul,
In his uprightness, answer thus return'd:
Fair angel, thy desire which tends to know
695 The works of God, thereby to glorify
The great Work-Master, leads to no excess
That reaches blame, but rather merits praise
The more it seems excess, that led thee hither
From thy empyreal mansion thus alone,
700 To witness with thine eyes what some perhaps,
Contented with report, hear only in heaven:
For wonderful indeed are all his works,
Pleasant to know, and worthiest to be all
Had in remembrance always with delight:
705 But what created mind can comprehend
Their number, or the wisdom infinite
That brought them forth, but hid their causes deep?
I saw when at his word the formless mass,
This world's material mould, came to a heap:
710 Confusion heard his voice, and wild uproar
711 Stood rul'd, stood vast infinitude confin'd;
Till at his second bidding darkness fled,
Light shone, and order from disorder sprung.
Swift to their several quarters hasted then
715 The cumbrous elements, earth, flood, air, fire,
716 And this ethereal quintessence of heaven
Flew upward, spirited with various forms,
That roll'd orbicular, and turned to stars
Numberless, as thou seest, and how they move;

710–711 *Confusion . . . rul'd* Milton again personifies chaotic qualities.   716 *ethereal quintessence* The fifth element of ether.

Each had his place appointed, each his course;   720
The rest in circuit walls this universe.
Look downward on that globe, whose hither side   722
With light from hence, though but reflected, shines;
That place is Earth, the seat of man; that light
His day, which else, as th'other hemisphere,   725
Night would invade; but there the neighb'ring moon
(So call that opposite fair star) her aid
Timely interposes, and her monthly round,
Still ending, still renewing, through mid heaven,
With borrow'd light her countenance triform   730
Hence fills and empties to enlighten th'earth,
And in her pale dominion checks the night.
That spot to which I point is Paradise,
Adam's abode, these lofty shades his bower:
Thy way thou canst not miss, me mine requires.   735
Thus said, he turn'd; and Satan bowing low,
As to superior spirits is wont in heaven,
Where honour due and reverence none neglects,
Took leave, and tow'rd the coast of earth beneath,
Down from th'ecliptic, sped with hop'd success,   740
Throws his steep flight in many an airy wheel,
Nor staid, till on Niphates' top he lights.   742

END OF BOOK THIRD

---

722 *hither* Nearer.   730 *With . . . triform* Classical tradition divided the moon into three:
Luna ruled in heaven; Diana, on earth; and Hecate, in Hades. The moon's light is "bor-
row'd" because it is a reflection of the sun.   735 *me mine requires* I must be on my way.
740 *ecliptic* The orbit of the sun.   742 *Niphates* In Armenia, near Syria.

BOOK IV

THE ARGUMENT

Satan, now in prospect of Eden, and nigh the place where he
must now attempt the bold enterprise which he undertook alone
against God and Man, falls into many doubts with himself, and
many passions,† fear, envy, and despair; but at length confirms
himself in evil, journeys on to Paradise, whose outward prospect
and situation is described, overleaps the bounds,‡ sits in the shape
of a cormorant on the tree of life,§ as highest in the garden, to
look about him. The garden described; Satan's first sight of
Adam and Eve; his wonder at their excellent form and happy
state, but with resolution to work their fall; overhears their
discourse, thence gathers that the tree of knowledge was forbidden
them to eat of, under penalty of death; and thereon intends to
found his temptation, by seducing them to transgress: then leaves
them a while, to know further of their state by some other
means. Meanwhile Uriel, descending on a sun-beam, warns
Gabriel, who had in charge the gate of Paradise, that some evil
spirit had escaped the deep, and passed at noon by his sphere, in
the shape of a good angel, down to Paradise, discovered‖ after by
his furious gestures in the mount. Gabriel promises to find him
ere morning. Night coming on, Adam and Eve discourse of going*

---

*Sight.
†Satan's consciousness has become internally conflicted and a prey to passion, rather than
being ruled by reason.
‡In both literal and metaphorical senses.
§The fruit of this tree conferred immortality; in Revelation 2:7 and 22:2 it is reserved for
the righteous after the Day of Judgment.
‖Revealed.

to their rest: their bower described; their evening worship.
Gabriel, drawing forth his bands of night-watch to walk the
round of Paradise, appoints two strong angels to Adam's bower,
lest the evil spirit should be there doing some harm to Adam or
Eve sleeping; there they find him at the ear of Eve tempting her
in a dream, and bring him, though unwilling, to Gabriel; by
whom questioned, he scornfully answers, prepares resistance, but
hindered by a sign from heaven, flies out of Paradise.

1	O for that warning voice, which he who saw
2	Th'Apocalypse heard cry in heaven aloud,
3	Then when the Dragon, put to second rout,
	Came furious down to be reveng'd on men
5	Woe to th'inhabitants on earth, that now,
6	While time was, our first parents had been warn'd
	The coming of their secret foe, and scap'd,
	Haply so scap'd his mortal snare: for now
	Satan, now first inflam'd with rage, came down,
10	The tempter, ere th'accuser of mankind,
	To wreak on innocent frail man his loss
	Of that first battle, and his flight to hell.
	Yet not rejoicing in his speed, though bold,
	Far off and fearless, nor with cause to boast,
15	Begins his dire attempt; which nigh the birth
16	Now rolling, boils in his tumultuous breast,
17	And like a devilish engine back recoils
18	Upon himself: horror and doubt distract

---

1 *O for that warning voice* A negative invocation, in contrast to the invocations that open books I, III, and IX.   1–2 *he who saw / Th' Apocalypse* The apostle John, who saw and recorded the visions that make up the book of Revelation (in Greek "Apocalypse") during his exile on the Greek island of Patmos.   3 *Dragon* A trope for Satan.   5 *Woe . . . earth* From Revelation 12:12: "Woe to the inhabiters of the earth and of the sea! for the devil is come down unto you, having great wrath, because he knoweth that he hath but a short time."   6 *While time was* While there was time.   10 *accuser* In Greek, "accuser" is *diabolus*.   15–18 *which . . . himself* Compare the birth of the hell-hounds from Sin in book II.

His troubled thoughts, and from the bottom stir
The hell within him; for within him hell   20
He brings, and round about him, nor from hell   21
One step, no more than from himself, can fly   22
By change of place: now conscience wakes despair   23
That slumber'd; wakes the bitter memory
Of what he was, what is, and what must be   25
Worse; of worse deeds worse sufferings must ensue.
Sometimes tow'rds Eden, which now in his view   27
Lay pleasant, his griev'd look he fixes sad;
Sometimes tow'rds heaven, and the full blazing sun,   29
Which now sat high in his meridian tower: 30
Then, much revolving, thus in sighs began.

O thou, that with surpassing glory crown'd,   32
Look'st from thy sole dominion like the god   33
Of this new world; at whose sight all the stars   34
Hide their diminish'd heads; to thee I call,   35
But with no friendly voice, and add thy name,   36
O sun, to tell thee how I hate thy beams,[1]   37
That bring to my remembrance from what state   38
I fell; how glorious once above thy sphere;   39
Till pride and worse ambition threw me down,   40
Warring in heaven against heaven's matchless King.   41
Ah, wherefore, he deserv'd no such return
From me, whom he created what I was   43
In that bright eminence, and with his good

20–23 *For within him . . . place* Compare Marlowe's *Doctor Faustus* (1604), where Mephistopheles declares, "Why, this is hell, nor am I out of it" (act 1, scene 3).   27 *Eden* Hebrew for "delight."   29 *sun* Satan mistakes the sun for the Son.   33 *Look'st . . . like the god* The sun resembles, but is not, a god.   32–41 *O thou . . . King* According to Edward Phillips, Milton's nephew and biographer, these lines were completed more than twenty years before *Paradise Lost*'s publication. Fowler describes this passage as "dramatic interior duologue between better and worse selves, like those between good and evil in Marlowe's *Doctor Faustus*" (p. 217).   43 *whom he created what I was* If we assume that God created Satan's prelapsarian (pre-Fall) condition, while Satan himself created what he became after his fall, there is no contradiction with his later claim to be "self-begot" (5.860).

45 Upbraided none; nor was his service hard,
46 What could be less than to afford him praise,
   The easiest recompense, and pay him thanks,
   How due; yet all his good prov'd ill in me,
   And wrought but malice; lifted up so high
50 I 'sdain'd subjection, and thought one step higher
51 Would set me highest, and in a moment quit
   The debt immense of endless gratitude,
   So burdensome still paying, still to owe;
   Forgetful what from him I still receiv'd,
55 And understood not that a grateful mind
56 By owing owes not, but still pays, at once
   Indebted and discharg'd: what burden then?
   O had his powerful destiny ordain'd
   Me some inferior angel, I had stood
60 Then happy; no unbounded hope had rais'd
   Ambition. Yet why not? some other power
   As great might have aspir'd, and me, though mean,
   Drawn to his part; but other powers as great
   Fell not, but stand unshaken, from within
65 Or from without, to all temptations arm'd.
66 Hadst thou the same free will and power to stand?
   Thou hadst: whom hast thou then or what to accuse,
68 But heaven's free love dealt equally to all?
   Be then his love accurs'd, since love or hate,
70 To me alike, it deals eternal woe.
   Nay curs'd be thou; since against his thy will
   Chose freely, what it now so justly rues.
   Me miserable, which way shall I fly
   Infinite wrath, and infinite despair?

---

46 *afford* pay.   **50** *I 'sdain'd subjection* I disdained to be made a subject.   **50–51** *and thought . . . highest* Satan was under the misconception that his difference from God was quantitative, rather than qualitative.   **51** *quit* Pay.   **55–56** *a grateful mind . . . owes not* Acknowledgment of a debt cancels it; a dictum that Milton did not follow in his own financial dealings.   **66** *thou* Satan addresses himself in the third person, as though alienated from himself.   **68** *But . . . all* Satan's reasoning about free will recalls God's; he does not blame himself for the alienation, however, but absurdly resents God's love.   **70** *eternal woe* A creature who aspires to equality with the Creator can never be happy.

Which way I fly is hell; myself am hell;   75
And in the lowest deep a lower deep,
Still threat'ning to devour me, opens wide,
To which the hell I suffer seems a heaven.
O then at last relent: is there no place
Left for repentance, none for pardon left?   80
None left but by submission; and that word   81
Disdain forbids me, and my dread of shame
Among the spirits beneath, whom I seduc'd
With other promises and other vaunts
Than to submit, boasting I could subdue   85
Th' Omnipotent. Ay me, they little know
How dearly I abide that boast so vain,   87
Under what torments inwardly I groan,
While they adore me on the throne of hell.
With diadem and sceptre high advanc'd,   90
The lower still I fall, only supreme
In misery; such joy ambition finds.
But say I could repent and could obtain
By act of grace my former state; how soon
Would height recall high thoughts, how soon unsay   95
What feign'd submission swore; ease would recant
Vows made in pain, as violent and void.
For never can true reconcilement grow,
Where wounds of deadly hate have pierc'd so deep;
Which would but lead me to a worse relapse   100
And heavier fall: so should I purchase dear
Short intermission bought with double smart.   102
This knows my punisher; therefore as far
From granting he, as I from begging peace:
All hope excluded thus, behold, instead   105
Of us, outcast, exil'd, his new delight,

---

75 *Which way . . . hell* In striking contrast to 1.254–255, Satan now understands that he is himself the personification of Hell.   81 *that word* Operating as usual at the level of signs, Satan is repelled by the word, not the concept, of submission.   87 *abide* Pay for.   102 *smart* Pain.

Mankind, created, and for him this world.
So farewell hope, and with hope farewell fear,
Farewell remorse: all good to me is lost;
110 Evil be thou my good; [2] by thee at least
111 Divided empire with heaven's King I hold,
By thee, and more than half perhaps will reign;
As man ere long, and this new world shall know.

Thus while he spake each passion dimm'd his face,
115 Thrice chang'd with pale ire, envy, and despair;
Which marr'd his borrow'd visage, and betray'd
117 Him counterfeit, if any eye beheld:
For heavenly minds from such distempers foul
Are ever clear. Whereof he soon aware,
120 Each perturbation smooth'd with outward calm,
121 Artificer of fraud; and was the first
That practis'd falsehood, under saintly show
123 Deep malice to conceal, couch'd with revenge.
Yet not enough had practis'd to deceive
125 Uriel once warn'd; whose eye pursued him down
The way he went, and on th'Assyrian mount
Saw him disfigur'd, more than could befall
Spirit of happy sort: his gestures fierce
He mark'd, and mad demeanour, then alone,
130 As he suppos'd, all unobserv'd, unseen.
So, on he fares; and to the border comes
Of Eden, where delicious Paradise,
Now nearer, crowns with her inclosure green,
134 As with a rural mound, the champaign head
135 Of a steep wilderness; whose hairy sides
With thicket overgrown, grotesque and wild,
Access denied: and over head up-grew

---

111 *Divided . . . hold* Satan endorses the Manichean heresy that God and the devil compete for rule over creation.   115 *ire* Anger.   117 *counterfeit* A counterfeit coin is an empty sign that does not refer to true value.   121 *Artificer* Manufacturer.   123 *couch'd with* Intimate with.   134 *champaign head* Cleared plain.   135 *hairy* Tangled.

Insuperable height of loftiest shade,
Cedar, and pine, and fir, and branching palm,
A sylvan scene. And, as the ranks ascend,   140
Shade above shade, a woody theatre   141
Of stateliest view. Yet higher than their tops
The verdurous wall of Paradise up-sprung: 143
Which to our general sire gave prospect large
Into his nether empire, neighb'ring round.   145
And higher than that wall a circling row
Of goodliest trees, loaden with fairest fruit,
Blossoms, and fruits at once of golden hue,
Appear'd, with gay enamel'd colours mix'd: 149
On which the sun more glad impress'd his beams,   150
Than in fair evening cloud, or humid bow,   151
When God has shower'd the earth; so lovely seem'd
That landscape. And of pure now purer air
Meets his approach; and to the heart inspires
Vernal delight and joy, able to drive   155
All sadness but despair: now gentle gales,
Fanning their odoriferous wings, dispense
Native perfumes, and whisper whence they stole
Those balmy spoils. As when to them who sail
Beyond the Cape of Hope, and now are past   160
Mozambic, off at sea north-east winds blow
Sabean odours, from the spicy shore   162
Of Araby the bless'd, with such delay
Well pleas'd they slack their course, and many a league
Cheer'd with the grateful smell old Ocean smiles: 165
So entertain'd those odorous sweets the fiend,
Who came their bane; though with them better pleased
Than Asmodeus with the fishy fume
That drove him, though enamour'd, from the spouse
Of Tobit's son, and with a vengeance sent   170
From Media post to Egypt, there fast bound.[3]

---

140 *sylvan* Wooded.   140–141 *scene . . . theatre* Satan considers Paradise as a theatrical spectacle.   143 *verdurous* Green.   149 *enamel'd* Bright.   151 *humid bow* Rainbow.   162 *Sabean* From Saba, or Sheba, an ancient country on the Arabian Peninsula.

Now to th'ascent of that steep savage hill
Satan had journey'd on, pensive and slow;
But further way found none, so thick intwin'd,
175 As one continued brake, the undergrowth
Of shrubs and tangling bushes had perplex'd
All path of man or beast that pass'd that way.
One gate there only was and that look'd east
On th'other side; which when th'arch-felon saw,
180 Due entrance he disdain'd, and in contempt
At one slight bound high overleap'd all bound
Of hill, or highest wall, and sheer within
183 Lights on his feet. As when a prowling wolf,
Whom hunger drives to seek new haunt for prey,
185 Watching where shepherds pen their flocks at eve,
In hurdled cotes amid the field secure,
Leaps o'er the fence with ease into the fold:
Or as a thief, bent to unhoard the cash
Of some rich burgher, whose substantial doors,
190 Cross-barr'd and bolted fast, fear no assault,
In at the window climbs, or o'er the tiles:
So clomb this first grand thief into God's fold;
So since into his church lewd hirelings[4] climb;
Thence up he flew and on the tree of life,
195 (The middle tree, and highest there that grew,)
Sat like a cormorant; yet not true life
Thereby regain'd, but sat devising death
To them who liv'd: nor on the virtue thought
199 Of that life-giving plant, but only us'd
200 For prospect, what well us'd had been the pledge
201 Of immortality. So little knows
Any, but God alone, to value right
The good before him, but perverts best things

---

175 *brake* Thicket.   183 *wolf* A frequent figure for enemies of the church, who desired to devour the "sheep" of the congregation.   199–201 *but only . . . immortality* Satan is only interested in the physical view ("prospect") the tree affords him, he does not understand that it is a sign.

To worst abuse, or to their meanest use.[5]
Beneath him, with new wonder, now he views,   205
To all delight of human sense expos'd
In narrow room, nature's whole wealth, yea more,
A heaven on earth; for blissful Paradise
Of God the garden was, by him in th'east
Of Eden planted; Eden stretch'd her line   210
From Auran eastward to the royal towers   211
Of great Seleucia, built by Grecian kings,   212
Or where the sons of Eden long before
Dwelt in Telassar. In this pleasant soil   214
His far more pleasant garden God ordain'd.   215
Out of the fertile ground he caus'd to grow
All trees of noblest kind, for sight, smell, taste;
And all amid them stood the tree of life,
High eminent, blooming ambrosial fruit
Of vegetable gold: and next to life,   220
Our death, the tree of knowledge, grew fast by;
Knowledge of good bought dear by knowing ill.
Southward through Eden went a river large,
Nor chang'd his course, but through the shaggy hill
Pass'd underneath ingulf'd; for God had thrown   225
That mountain as his garden mould, high rais'd
Upon the rapid current, which through veins
Of porous earth, with kindly thirst updrawn,   228
Rose a fresh fountain, and with many a rill   229
Watered the garden; thence united fell   230
Down the steep glade, and met the nether flood,
Which from his darksome passage now appears:
And now divided into four main streams,
Runs diverse, wand'ring many a famous realm

---

211 *Auran* Town on the east bank of the Jordan River.   212 *Grecian kings* Seleucus Nicator, one of Alexander the Great's generals, established the Seleucid empire after Alexander's death.   214 *Telassar* City in Mesopotamia (modern Iraq) near Eden.   220 *vegetable gold* In alchemy, gold was supposed to grow in the earth like a vegetable; the implied contrast is between this natural gold of Eden and the unnatural use of gold as the incarnation of financial value.   228 *kindly* Natural.   229 *rill* Brook.

235 And country, whereof he needs no account:
236 But rather to tell, if art could tell
237 How from sapphire fount the crisped brooks
    Rolling on orient pearls, and sands of gold,
239 With mazy error under pendent shades
240 Ran nectar, visiting each plant, and fed
241 Flowers worthy of Paradise, which not nice art
242 In beds and curious knots, but nature boon
    Pour'd forth profuse on hill, and dale, and plain,
    Both where the morning sun first warmly smote
245 The open field, and where the unpierc'd shade
    Imbrown'd the noon-tide bowers. Thus was this place,
    A happy rural seat of various views:
    Groves where rich trees wept odorous gums and balm;
    Others whose fruit, burnish'd with golden rind,
250 Hung amiable; Hesperian fables true,
    If true, here only, and of delicious taste.
    Betwixt them lawns, or level downs, and flocks
    Grazing the tender herb, were interpos'd:
    Or palmy hillock, or the flowery lap
255 Of some irriguous valley spread her store;
    Flowers of all hue, and without thorn the rose.
257 Another side, umbrageous grots, and caves
    Of cool recess, o'er which the mantling vine
    Lays forth her purple grape, and gently creeps
260 Luxuriant: meanwhile murm'ring waters fall
    Down the slope hills, dispers'd, or in a lake,
    That to the fringed bank with myrtle crown'd
    Her crystal mirror holds, unite their streams.
    The birds their choir apply: airs, vernal airs,
265 Breathing the smell of field and grove, attune

---

236 *if art could tell* A reminder that the scene described is mediated through "art," since it is inaccessible to the fallen human imagination.   237 *crisped* Rippled.   239 *mazy error* Trance-like wandering.   241 *nice* Overly elaborate.   242.1 *curious knots* Intricate bunches; 242.2 *boon* Bountiful.   245 *unpierc'd* That is, by sunlight.   255 *irriguous* Irrigating.   257 *umbrageous grots* Shadowy grottoes.

The trembling leaves, while universal Pan,   266
Knit with the Graces, and the Hours, in dance,   267
Led on th'eternal spring. Not that fair field
Of Enna, where Proserpine gathering flowers,
Herself a fairer flower, by gloomy Dis   270
Was gather'd; which cost Ceres all that pain
To seek her through the world;⁶ nor that sweet grove   272
Of Daphne by Orontes, and th'inspir'd   273
Castalian spring, might with this Paradise   274
Of Eden strive; nor that Nyseian isle   275
Girt with the river Triton, where old Cham,
Whom Gentiles Ammon call, and Libyan Jove,
Hid Amalthea, and her florid son,
Young Bacchus, from his stepdame Rhea's eye;⁷
Nor where Abassin kings their issue guard,   280
Mount Amara, though this be some suppos'd   281
True Paradise, under the Ethiop line   282
By Nilus' head, enclos'd with shining rock,   283
A whole day's journey high, but wide remote   284
From this Assyrian garden, where the fiend   285
Saw undelighted all delight, all kind   286
Of living creatures new to sight and strange.

Two of far nobler shape, erect and tall,
Godlike erect, with native honour clad,
In naked majesty seem'd lords of all,   290
And worthy seem'd; for in their looks divine   291

---

266 *universal Pan* Because the word "pan" means universal, the Greek god Pan was some-
times associated with Christ, as in Milton's "Nativity Ode" (89).   267 *the Graces, and the
Hours* Personified qualities of natural beauty; compare *Comus* (l. 986): "The Graces and
the rosy-bosom'd Hours."   272–274 *nor that . . . Castalian spring* The grove of Daphne
contained a shrine to Apollo.   280–284 *Nor where . . . high* The kings of Abyssinia (mod-
ern Ethiopia) sent their sons to be raised in seclusion on Mt. Amara; this story and the
ones that precede it concern attempts to preserve innocence through seclusion.   286 *Saw
undelighted all delight* Satan's viewpoint is completely at odds with objective reality.
290–291 *seem'd . . . seem'd* The verb "to seem" is always significant in *Paradise Lost*; here it
implies that the hierarchical relations of Eden are viewed from Satan's perspective.

292   The image of their glorious Maker shone,
        Truth, wisdom, sanctitude severe and pure,
        Severe, but in true filial freedom plac'd,
295   Whence true authority in men; though both
296   Not equal, as their sex not equal seem'd;
        For contemplation he and valour form'd,
        For softness she and sweet attractive grace,
299   He for God only, she for God in him.
300   His fair large front and eye sublime declar'd
301   Absolute rule; and hyacinthine locks
        Round from his parted forelock manly hung
        Clust'ring, but not beneath his shoulders broad:
        She, as a veil, down to the slender waist
305   Her unadorned golden tresses wore
306   Dishevell'd, but in wanton ringlets wav'd
307   As the vine curls her tendrils, which implie
308   Subjection, but requir'd with gentle sway
        And by her yielded, by him best receiv'd,
310   Yielded with coy submission, modest pride,
        And sweet reluctant amorous delay.
312   Nor those mysterious parts were then conceal'd;
        Then was not guilty shame, dishonest shame
        Of nature's works, honour dishonourable:
315   Sin-bred, how have ye troubled all mankind
316   With shows instead, mere shows of seeming pure,
        And banish'd from man's life his happiest life,

---

292 *The image of their glorious Maker* Adam and Eve represent an authentic "image" of God, since He created them, but an image is distinct from its referent. In contrast, Satan will tempt the human couple with the promise of an equivalence to God, thus idolatrously collapsing this distinction.   296 *Not equal . . . seem'd* Wittreich (p. 86) argues that the human couple only "seem" unequal from Satan's perspective, and that Satan is noted for his obsession with hierarchy.   299 *He for . . . in him* This does not indicate that Eve is inferior to Adam; the relation of the Son to the Father is simultaneously subordinate and equal. 300 *front* Brow.   301 *Absolute rule* Milton spent his life fighting against absolute rule.   306 *wanton* Sexy.   307–308 *which implie / Subjection* Satan has projected his own obsession with precedence onto Eve: There is nothing inherent in her hairstyle that implies she is subjected to Adam.   312 *mysterious parts* Sexual organs.   316 *seeming* The uncertainty of mere seeming is now made clear.

Simplicity and spotless innocence
So pass'd they naked on, nor shunn'd the sight
Of God or angel, for they thought no ill: 320
So hand in hand they pass'd, the loveliest pair
That ever since in love's embraces met;
Adam, the goodliest man of men since born
His sons; the fairest of her daughters, Eve.
Under a tuft of shade, that on a green   325
Stood whisp'ring soft, by a fresh fountain side,
They sat them down: and, after no more toil
Of their sweet gard'ning labour than suffic'd
To recommend cool Zephyr, and make ease   329
More easy, wholesome thirst and appetite   330
More grateful, to their supper fruits they fell,
Nectarine fruits which the compliant boughs
Yielded them, sidelong as they sat recline
On the soft downy bank damask'd with flowers: 334
The savoury pulp they chew, and in the rind   335
Still as they thirsted scoop the brimming stream;
Nor gentle purpose nor endearing smiles
Wanted, nor youthful dalliance, as beseems   338
Fair couple, link'd in happy nuptial league,
Alone as they. About them frisking play'd   340
All beasts of th'earth, since wild, and of all chase
In wood or wilderness, forest or den;
Sporting the lion ramp'd, and in his paw
Dandled the kid; bears, tigers, ounces, pards,   344
Gambol'd before them; the unwieldy elephant,   345
To make them mirth, us'd all his might, and wreath'd
His lithe proboscis; close the serpent sly   347
Insinuating, wove with Gordian twine   348
His braided train, and of his fatal guile

---

329 *Zephyr* The west wind.   334 *damask'd* Embroidered.   338 *dalliance* Sex.   344 *ounces*
Panthers.   347 *proboscis* Trunk.   348 *Gordian* Alexander the Great established his claim to
dominion by severing the Gordian knot, which had allegedly been tied by Gordius, king of
the Phrygians, and was thought to be impossible to untie.

Satan with Adam and Eve

Gave proof unheeded; others on the grass   350
Couch'd, and, now fill'd with pasture, gazing sat,
Or bedward ruminating; for the sun
Declin'd was hasting now with prone career
To th'ocean isles, and in th'ascending scale   354
Of heaven the stars that usher evening rose: 355
When Satan, still in gaze as first he stood,
Scarce thus at length fail'd speech recover'd sad:

O hell, what do mine eyes with grief behold?
Into our room of bliss thus high advanc'd
Creatures of other mould; earth-born perhaps,   360
Not spirits; yet to heavenly spirits bright
Little inferior; whom my thoughts pursue
With wonder, and could love, so lively shines
In them divine resemblance, and such grace
The hand that form'd them on their shape hath pour'd.   365
Ah, gentle pair, ye little think how nigh
Your change approaches; when all these delights
Will vanish, and deliver ye to woe;
More woe, the more your taste is now of joy:
Happy, but for so happy ill secur'd   370
Long to continue; and this high seat your heaven,   371
Ill-fenc'd for heaven, to keep out such a foe   372
As now is enter'd: yet no purpos'd foe   373
To you, whom I could pity thus forlorn,   374
Though I unpitied. League with you I seek,   375
And mutual amity, so strait, so close,
That I with you must dwell, or you with me
Henceforth: my dwelling haply may not please,
Like this fair Paradise, your sense; yet such

---

350 *proof unheeded* It is unclear how the serpent's physical appearance could prove its guile, especially before Satan has possessed it. The narrator appears to share Satan's tendency to impose arbitrary significances on appearances.   354 *th' ocean isles* The Azores.   370–375 *Happy . . . unpitied . . .* Note Satan's repetitions: "Happy . . . happy . . . heaven . . . heaven . . . pity . . . unpitied."

380 Accept your Maker's work; He gave it me,
Which I as freely give: hell shall unfold,
To entertain you two, her widest gates,
And send forth all her kings: there will be room,
Not like these narrow limits, to receive

385 Your numerous offspring: if no better place,
Thank him who puts me loath to this revenge
On you, who wrong'd me not, for him who wrong'd.
And should I at your harmless innocence

389 Melt, as I do, yet public reason just,

390 Honour and empire with revenge enlarg'd,
By conqu'ring this new world, compels me now
To do, what else (though damn'd) I should abhor.

So spake the fiend, and with necessity,

394 (The tyrant's plea,) excus'd his devilish deeds.

395 Then from his lofty stand on that high tree,
Down he alights among the sportful herd
Of those four-footed kinds; himself now one,
Now other, as their shape serv'd best his end
Nearer to view his prey, and unespied

400 To mark what of their state he more might learn

401 By word or action mark'd: about them round
A lion now he stalks with fiery glare;
Then as a tiger, who by chance hath spied,

404 In some purlieu, two gentle fawns at play,

405 Strait couches close, then rising changes oft

406 His couchant watch, as one who chose his ground,
Whence rushing he might surest seize them both,
Grip'd in each paw: when Adam, first of men,
To first of women, Eve, thus moving speech,

410 Turn'd him, all ear, to hear new utterance flow:

---

389 *public reason just* The imperatives of political expediency.   394 *the tyrant's plea* The excuse for tyrannical behavior.   401 *By word or action mark'd* The devil was believed to be unable to enter into the minds of human beings; he had to rely on external signs for his knowledge of human thoughts.   404 *purlieu* Clearing.   405 *couches* Lies.   406 *couchant* Lying.

Sole partner, and sole part of all these joys.
Dearer thyself than all: needs must the power   412
That made us, and for us this ample world,   413
Be infinitely good, and of his good   414
As liberal, and free as infinite;   415
That rais'd us from the dust, and plac'd us here
In all this happiness, who at his hand
Have nothing merited, nor can perform
Aught whereof he hath need: he who requires
From us no other service than to keep   420
This one, this easy charge, of all the trees
In Paradise that bear delicious fruit
So various, not to taste that only tree
Of knowledge, planted by the tree of life.
So near grows death to life, whate'er death is;   425
Some dreadful thing no doubt: for well thou know'st
God hath pronounc'd it death to taste that tree,
The only sign of our obedience left,   428
Among so many signs of power and rule,   429
Confer'd upon us; and dominion given   430
Over all other creatures that possess
Earth, air, and sea. Then let us not think hard
One easy prohibition, who enjoy
Free leave so large to all things else, and choice
Unlimited of manifold delights: 435
But let us ever praise him, and extol
His bounty, following our delightful task,
To prune these growing plants, and tend these flowers;
Which were it toilsome, yet with thee were sweet.

To whom thus Eve replied: O thou for whom,   440
And from whom, I was form'd; flesh of thy flesh;
And without whom am to no end; my guide   442

412–415 *needs must . . . infinite* The rational response to creation is to deduce the existence of a Creator.   428–429 *The only sign . . . signs of power and rule* Before the Fall, Adam understands the significant nature of his surroundings.   442 *to no end* To no purpose.

And head, what thou hast said is just and right.
For we to him indeed all praises owe,
445 And daily thanks; I chiefly, who enjoy
446 So far the happier lot, enjoying thee
Pre-eminent by so much odds; while thou
Like consort to thyself canst no where find.
That day I oft remember, when from sleep
450 I first awak'd, and found myself repos'd
451 Under a shade on flowers; much wond'ring where
452 And what I was, whence thither brought, and how.
Not distant far from thence a murmuring sound
Of waters issued from a cave, and spread
455 Into a liquid plain, then stood unmov'd,
Pure as th'expanse of heaven: I thither went,
With unexperienc'd thought, and laid me down
On the green bank, to look into the clear
Smooth lake, that to me seem'd another sky.
460 As I bent down to look, just opposite
461 A shape within the wat'ry gleam appear'd,
Bending to look on me: I started back;
It started back: but pleas'd I soon return'd;
Pleas'd it return'd as soon; with answering looks
465 Of sympathy and love: there I had fixt
466 Mine eyes till now, and pin'd with vain desire,
Had not a voice thus warn'd me: What thou seest,
468 What there thou seest, fair creature, is thyself;
With thee it came and goes: but follow me,
470 And I will bring thee where no shadow stays
Thy coming, and thy soft embraces; he

---

446 *the happier lot* Eve assumes that the fact that she finds her "end," or fulfillment, in Adam renders her more fortunate than him.   451–452 *much wond'ring . . . and how* These are the questions Satan neglects to ask.   461 *A shape* Eve's reflection; Milton uses the common term for unreal appearances or idols.   466 *vain desire* Milton has described the essence of idolatry: fascination with surface appearances.   468.1 *creature* The voice is careful to remind Eve that she was created; 468.2 *thyself* Eve has made the idolatrous error of taking the image for reality. She is now informed that the image in the water stands for something beyond itself.   470 *shadow* Image.

Whose image thou art:[8] him thou shalt enjoy,
Inseparably thine, to him shalt bear
Multitudes like thyself, and thence be call'd
Mother of human race. What could I do   475
But follow straight, invisibly thus led
Till I espied thee, fair indeed, and tall,
Under a platain; yet, methought, less fair,   478
Less winning soft, less amiably mild
Than that smooth wat'ry image: back I turn'd;   480
Thou following cried'st aloud, Return, fair Eve,
Whom fliest thou? Whom thou fliest, of him thou art,   482
His flesh, his bone; to give thee being I lent
Out of my side to thee, nearest my heart,
Substantial life, to have thee by my side   485
Henceforth an individual solace dear: 486
Part of my soul I seek thee; and thee claim,
My other half.—With that, thy gentle hand
Seiz'd mine; I yielded; and from that time see   489
How beauty is excell'd by manly grace,   490
And wisdom, which alone is truly fair.   491

So spake our general mother; and with eyes
Of conjugal attraction unreprov'd,   493
And meek surrender, half embracing lean'd
On our first father: half her swelling breast   495
Naked met his, under the flowing gold
Of her loose tresses hid: he in delight
Both of her beauty and submissive charms,   498
Smil'd with superior love; as Jupiter
On Juno smiles, when he impregns the clouds,   500
That shed May flowers; and press'd her matron lip

---

478 *platain* Plane tree.   482 *of him thou art* It is absurd to flee the source of one's creation.
486 *individual* Undivided.   489–491 *and from that time . . . truly fair* Not necessarily a
misogynist statement: Eve refers to masculine and feminine characteristics, rather than to
male and female genders.   493 *unreprov'd* Sexual desire is blameless.   498 *charms* Hints at
the fetishistic, magical effect that Eve's beauty will have on Adam after the fall.

With kisses pure; aside the Devil turn'd
503   For envy, yet with jealous leer malign
Eyed them askance; and to himself thus plain'd:

505   Sight hateful, sight tormenting. Thus these two
Imparadis'd in one another's arms,
507   (The happier Eden,) shall enjoy their fill
Of bliss on bliss: while I to hell am thrust,
Where neither joy nor love, but fierce desire,
510   Amongst our other torments not the least,
Still unfulfill'd with pain of longing, pines.
Yet let me not forget what I have gain'd
From their own mouths: all is not theirs it seems:
One fatal tree there stands of knowledge call'd,
515   Forbidden them to taste. Knowledge forbidden?
Suspicious, reasonless. Why should their Lord
517   Envy them that? Can it be sin to know?
Can it be death? And do they only stand
By ignorance? Is that their happy state,
520   The proof of their obedience and their faith?
O fair foundation laid whereon to build
Their ruin! Hence I will excite their minds
With more desire to know, and to reject
Envious commands, invented with design
525   To keep them low whom knowledge might exalt
526   Equal with gods: aspiring to be such,
They taste and die: what likelier can ensue?
528   But first, with narrow search I must walk round
This garden, and no corner leave unspied;
530   A chance but chance may lead where I may meet
Some wand'ring spirit of heaven by fountain side
Or in thick shade retir'd, from him to draw

---

503 *leer* Satan is salacious, as opposed to loving.   507 *The happier Eden* A signal that the poem's action is psychological as well as mythological.   517 *Envy* Satan projects his envy onto God.   526 *Equal with gods* Satan projects his own aspiration onto the human couple. 528 *narrow* Thorough.

What further would be learn'd. Live while ye may,
Yet happy pair; enjoy, till I return,
Short pleasures; for long woes are to succeed.   535

So saying, his proud step he scornful turn'd,
But with sly circumspection, and began,
Through wood, through waste, o'er hill, o'er dale, his roam,
Meanwhile in utmost longitude, where heaven
With earth and ocean meets, the setting sun   540
Slowly descended; and with right aspect
Against the eastern gate of Paradise
Levell'd his evening rays: it was a rock
Of alabaster, pil'd up to the clouds,
Conspicuous far; winding with one ascent   545
Accessible from earth, one entrance high:
The rest was craggy cliff, that overhung
Still as it rose, impossible to climb.
Betwixt these rocky pillars Gabriel sat,   549
Chief of th'angelic guards, awaiting night: 550
About him exercis'd heroic games
Th'unarm'd youth of heaven; but nigh at hand
Celestial armoury, shields, helms, and spears,
Hung high with diamond flaming, and with gold.
Thither came Uriel, gliding through the even   555
On a sun-beam, swift as a shooting star
In autumn thwarts the night, when vapours fir'd   557
Impress the air, and shows the mariner   558
From what point of his compass to beware
Impetuous winds: he thus began in haste: 560

Gabriel, to thee thy course by lot hath given
Charge, and strict watch, that to this happy place
No evil thing approach, or enter in.

---

549 *Gabriel* In Hebrew, the name means "strength of God." He interprets symbols in
Daniel 8:16–27, and prophesies the births of John the Baptist (Luke 1:11–22) and Christ
(Luke 1:26–38). 555 *even* Evening. 557 *thwarts* Moves across. 558 *Impress* Imprint.

This day, at height of noon, came to my sphere
565   A spirit; zealous, as he seem'd, to know
More of th'Almighty's work; and chiefly man,
God's latest image: I describ'd his way,
Bent all on speed, and mark'd his airy gait:
But, in the mount that lies from Eden north,
570   Where he first lighted, soon discern'd his looks
571   Alien from heaven, with passions foul obscur'd:
Mine eye pursued him still, but under shade
Lost sight of him. One of the banish'd crew,
I fear, hath ventur'd from the deep, to raise
575   New troubles; him thy care must be to find.

To whom the winged warrior thus return'd:
Uriel, no wonder if thy perfect sight,
Amid the sun's bright circle, where thou sitt'st,
See far and wide: in at this gate none pass
580   The vigilance here plac'd, but such as come
581   Well known from heaven; and since meridian hour
No creature thence: if spirit of other sort,
So minded, have o'erleap'd these earthy bounds
584   On purpose, hard thou know'st it to exclude
585   Spiritual substance with corporeal bar.
But, if within the circuit of these walks,
In whatsoever shape he lurk, of whom
Thou tell'st, by morrow dawning I shall know.

So promis'd he: and Uriel to his charge
590   Return'd, on that bright beam, whose point now raised
Bore him slope downward to the sun, now fallen
592   Beneath th'Azores: whether the prime orb,
593   Incredible how swift, had thither roll'd
594   Diurnal; or this less voluble earth,

---

571 *Alien* Alienated.   581 *meridian hour* Noon.   584 *hard thou know'st it* You know it is difficult.   592 *Azores* Islands off the west coast of Africa.

By shorter flight to th'east, had left him there,   595
Arraying with reflected purple and gold   596
The clouds that on his western throne attend.

Now came still evening on, and twilight grey
Had in her sober livery all things clad: 599
Silence accompanied; for beast, and bird,   600
They to their grassy couch, these to their nests,
Were slunk; all but the wakeful nightingale;
She all night long her amorous descant sung;
Silence was pleas'd: now glow'd the firmament
With living sapphires; Hesperus, that led   605
The starry host, rode brightest; till the moon
Rising in clouded majesty, at length,
Apparent queen, unveil'd her peerless light,   608
And o'er the dark her silver mantle threw.

When Adam thus to Eve: Fair consort, th'hour   610
Of night, and all things now retir'd to rest,
Mind us of like repose; since God hath set   612
Labour and rest, as day and night, to men   613
Successive; and the timely dew of sleep,   614
Now falling with soft slumb'rous weight, inclines   615
Our eyelids; other creatures all day long   616
Rove idle, unemploy'd, and less need rest: 617
Man hath his daily work of body, or mind,   618
Appointed, which declares his dignity,   619
And the regard of heaven on all his ways: 620

592–595 *the prime orb . . . there* Milton considers the possibility that the sun ("the prime orb") moves, and also that the earth moves, concluding that it makes no difference to the subject under discussion: The physical structure of the universe is less significant than its spiritual design.   596 *Arraying* Decorating.   599 *livery* Uniform.   605 *Hesperus* Venus, also associated with Lucifer.   608 *Apparent* Obvious, appearing.   612 *Mind* Remind.   613 *Labour and rest* The division of human activity into these categories precedes the Fall; but the prelapsarian activities of Adam and Eve are not onerous and are carried out joyfully, in contrast to the hard labor with which Adam is cursed after the Fall.   614 *Successive* In turn.

621　While other animals unactive range;
622　And of their doings God takes no account.
　　　To-morrow, ere fresh morning streak the east
　　　With first approach of light, we must be risen,
625　And at our pleasant labour, to reform
　　　Yon flowery arbours; yonder alleys green,
　　　Our walk at noon, with branches overgrown:
　　　That mock our scant manuring, and require
629　More hands than ours to lop their wanton growth:
630　Those blossoms also, and those dropping gums,
　　　That lie bestrown, unsightly and unsmooth,
　　　Ask riddance, if we mean to tread with ease:
　　　Meanwhile, as nature wills, night bids us rest.

　　　To whom thus Eve, with perfect beauty adorn'd:
635　My author, and disposer, what thou bid'st
　　　Unargued I obey; so God ordains:
637　God is thy law, thou mine; to know no more
638　Is woman's happiest knowledge and her praise.
　　　With thee conversing I forget all time;
640　All seasons and their change, all please alike:
641　Sweet is the breath of morn, her rising sweet,
642　With charm of earliest birds: pleasant the sun,
643　When first on this delightful land he spreads
644　His orient beams, on herb, tree, fruit, and flower,
645　Glist'ring with dew: fragrant the fertile earth
646　After soft showers: and sweet the coming on
647　Of grateful evening mild: then silent night,
648　With this her solemn bird, and this fair moon,
　　　And these the gems of heaven, her starry train:
650　But neither breath of morn, when she ascends

616–622 *other creatures . . . no account* Labor, in the general sense of purposeful subjective activity, is the definitive characteristic of humanity.　625 *reform* An allusion to the Protestant reformation.　629 *wanton* Directionless.　635 *My author* Eve derives from Adam. 637–638 *God is . . . her praise* Eve is to Adam as Adam is to God. Again, this does not imply her inferiority, since the Son stands in the same relation to the Father.　648 *solemn bird* Nightingale.

With charm of earliest birds: nor rising sun   651
On this delightful land: nor herb, fruit, flower,   652
Glist'ring with dew: nor fragrance after showers: 653
Nor grateful evening mild: nor silent night,   654
With this her solemn bird: nor walk by moon,   655
Or glitt'ring starlight, without thee is sweet.   656
But wherefore all night long shine these? For whom
This glorious sight, when sleep hath shut all eyes?

To whom our general ancestor replied:
Daughter of God and man, accomplish'd Eve,   660
These have their course to finish round the earth
By morrow evening, and from land to land
In order, though to nations yet unborn,
Minist'ring light prepar'd, they set and rise;
Lest total darkness should by night regain   665
Her old possession, and extinguish life
In nature and all things, which these soft fires
Not only enlighten, but with kindly heat
Of various influence foment and warm,
Temper or nourish, or in part shed down   670
Their stellar virtue on all kinds that grow
On earth, made hereby apter to receive
Perfection from the sun's more potent ray.
These then, though unbeheld in deep of night,
Shine not in vain; nor think, though men were none,   675
That heaven would want spectators, God want praise,
Millions of spiritual creatures walk the earth
Unseen, both when we wake and when we sleep:
All these with ceaseless praise his works behold
Both day and night. How often, from the steep   680
Of echoing hill, or thicket, have we heard
Celestial voices, to the midnight air,
Sole, or responsive each to others note,
Singing the great Creator? oft in bands

650–656 *But . . . sweet* The passage is deliberately repetitious, for rhetorical emphasis.   660
accomplish'd Completed.

685 While they keep watch, or nightly rounding walk,
With heavenly touch of instrumental sounds,
In full harmonic number join'd, their songs
Divide the night, and lift our thoughts to heaven.

Thus talking, hand in hand alone they pass'd
690 On to their blissful bower: it was a place
691 Chosen by the sov'reign Planter, when he fram'd
All things to man's delightful use: the roof
Of thickest covert, was inwoven shade,
Laurel and myrtle; and what higher grew,
695 Of firm and fragrant leaf: on either side
Acanthus, and each odorous bushy shrub,
Fenc'd up the verdant wall: each beauteous flower,
Iris all hues, roses and jessamine,
Rear'd high their flourish'd heads between, and wrought
700 Mosaic: underfoot the violet,
Crocus, and hyacinth, with rich inlay
Broider'd the ground; more colour'd than with stone
703 Of costliest emblem: other creature here,
Beast, bird, insect, or worm, durst enter none;
705 Such was their awe of man. In shadier bower
706 More sacred, and sequester'd, though but feign'd,
707 Pan, or Sylvanus, never slept; nor nymph,
708 Nor Faunus, haunted. Here, in close recess,
With flowers, garlands, and sweet smelling herbs,
710 Espoused Eve deck'd first her nuptial bed:
711 And heavenly choirs the hymenean sung,
712 What day the genial angel to our sire

---

691 *the sov'reign Planter* God is likened to a colonist, and Eden is his plantation.   **703** *emblem* Badge, crest.   **706** *feign'd* Mythological.   **707–708.1** *Pan . . . Faunus* Flannagan notes: "Pan, Sylvanus and Faunus were Greek and Roman satyr gods often identified with one another because all had goat bodies from the waist down" (p. 464); **708.2** *haunted* With a derogatory comparison to ghosts.   **710** *Espoused* Married. Milton's application of the term to Eve reflects his belief that marriage was not a sacrament, dependent on the performance of external rituals, but was a purely internal, spiritual occurrence: Adam and Eve are married because they are in love.   **711** *hymenean* Marriage hymn.   **712** *What* Which.

Brought her, in naked beauty more adorn'd,
More lovely than Pandora; whom the gods   714
Endow'd with all their gifts, and O, too like   715
In sad event, when to th'unwiser son
Of Japhet brought by Hermes, she insnar'd
Mankind with her fair looks, to be aveng'd
On him who had stole Jove's authentic fire.[9]

Thus, at their shady lodge arriv'd, both stood,   720
Both turn'd, and under open sky ador'd
The God that made sky, air, earth, and heaven,
Which they beheld; the moon's resplendent globe,
And starry pole; Thou also mad'st the night,
Maker Omnipotent, and thou the day,   725
Which we in our appointed work employ'd
Have finish'd, happy in our mutual help,
And mutual love, the crown of all our bliss
Ordain'd by thee; and this delicious place,
For us too large; where thy abundance wants   730
Partakers, and uncropp'd falls to the ground.
But thou hast promis'd from us two a race
To fill the earth, who shall with us extol
Thy goodness infinite, both when we wake,
And when we seek, as now, thy gift of sleep.   735

This said unanimous, and other rites   736
Observing none, but adoration pure,
Which God likes best, into their inmost bower   738
Handed they went; and eas'd the putting off   739
These troublesome disguises which we wear,   740
Straight side by side were laid: nor turn'd, I ween,   741
Adam from his fair spouse; nor Eve the rites

---

714 *Pandora* In Hesiod's *Theogony*, Pandora is the first woman; she opens a box, letting free all the ills of the world and was therefore regarded as a pagan prototype of Eve.   736 *unanimous* With one voice.   738 *Which God likes best* Milton goes beyond the typical Puritan advocacy of plain, unostentatious devotion suggesting that any kind of liturgy is superfluous. 739 *Handed* Hand-in-hand.   740 *troublesome disguises* Clothes.   741 *ween* Believe.

743 Mysterious of connubial love refus'd:

744 Whatever hypocrites austerely talk

745 Of purity, and place, and innocence:
Defaming as impure what God declares
Pure; and commands to some, leaves free to all.

748 Our Maker bids increase; who bids abstain,
But our destroyer, foe to God and man?

750 Hail, wedded love,[10] mysterious law, true source
Of human offspring, sole propriety
In Paradise; of all things common else.

753 By thee adulterous lust was driven from men,
Among the bestial herds to range; by thee,

755 Founded in reason, loyal, just, and pure,

756 Relations dear, and all the charities
Of father, son, and brother, first were known.
Far be it, that I should write thee sin, or blame,
Or think thee unbefitting holiest place;

760 Perpetual fountain of domestic sweets
Whose bed is undefil'd, and chaste, pronounc'd,
Present, or past; as saints and patriarchs us'd.

763 Here Love his golden shafts employs, here lights
His constant lamp; and waves his purple wings;

765 Reigns here, and revels: not in the bought smile

766 Of harlots, loveless, joyless, unendear'd;

767 Casual fruition;[11] nor in court amours,

768 Mix'd dance, or wanton mask, or midnight ball,

---

743 *connubial* Conjugal.　744 *hypocrites* Catholic priests, who are forbidden to have sex.
748 *Our Maker bids increase* See Genesis 1:28: "Be fruitful, and multiply.　753 *adulterous lust*
For Milton, adultery did not consist in sexual intercourse between unmarried partners, but
in sexual intercourse motivated by lust, rather than by love.　756 *charities* Loves.　763 *Love*
Cupid, whose "golden shafts" infused love into their victim.　765–766.1 *the bought smile /
Of harots* The logical end of lust is prostitution, a process in which the sexual act is openly
commodified; 766.2 *unendear'd* Leonard notes that the term means both "devoid of affec-
tion" and "lacking value." Since we have just been told that the harlot's smile does possess
financial value, Milton is pointing to the distinction between "exchange value" and "use
value"—that is, between financial and utilitarian significance.　767 *court amours* A dig at
the sexual promiscuity of the royalist "cavaliers."　768 *Mix'd dance* A favorite target of
Puritan strictures.

Or serenade, which the starv'd lover sings   769
To his proud fair; best quitted with disdain.   770
These, lull'd by nightingales, embracing slept;
And on their naked limbs the flowery roof
Shower'd roses, which the morn repaired. Sleep on
Bless'd pair; and O yet happiest, if ye seek
No happier state, and know to know no more.   775

Now had night measur'd with her shadowy cone   776
Half-way up hill this vast sublunar vault:
And from their ivory port the cherubim   778
Forth issuing at th'accustom'd hour, stood arm'd
To their night watches in warlike parade,   780
When Gabriel to his next in power thus spake:

Uzziel, half these draw off, and coast the south   782
With strictest watch: these other wheel the north;
Our circuit meets full west. As flame they part,
Half wheeling to the shield, half to the spear.   785
From these, two strong and subtle spirits he call'd,
That near him stood, and gave them thus in charge:

Ithuriel and Zephon, with wing'd speed   788
Search through this garden, leave unsearch'd no nook
But chiefly where those two fair creatures lodge,   790
Now laid perhaps asleep, secure of harm.
This evening from the sun's decline arriv'd,
Who tells of some infernal spirit, seen
Hitherward bent, (who could have thought?) escap'd
The bars of hell; on errand bad, no doubt: 795
Such, where ye find, seize fast, and hither bring.

---

769 *starv'd* Sexually frustrated. 769–770 *Or serenade . . . disdain* Milton mocks the Pe-
trarchan conception of love as a form of idolatry that masochistically fetishizes the "proud
fair." 776 *cone* Shadow. 778 *ivory port* The source of false dreams in Homer's *Odyssey*
(19.592) and Virgil's *Aeneid* (6.893). 782 *Uzziel* In Hebrew, "strength of God." 785
Half . . . spear Half to the left, half to the right. 788 *Ithuriel and Zephon* In Hebrew, "dis-
covery of God" and "lookout."

797   So saying, on he led his radiant files,
        Dazzling the moon: these to the bower direct,
        In search of whom they sought: him there they found,
800   Squat like a toad, close at the ear of Eve;
        Assaying, by his devilish art, to reach
802   The organs of her fancy, and with them forge
803   Illusions, as he list, phantoms, and dreams:
804   Or if, inspiring venom, he might taint
805   Th'animal spirits, that from pure blood arise,
        Like gentle breaths from rivers pure; thence raise
        At least distemper'd, discontented thoughts;
808   Vain hopes, vain aims, inordinate desires,
        Blown up with high conceits engend'ring pride.
810   Him thus intent Ithuriel with his spear
        Touch'd lightly; for no falsehood can endure
        Touch of celestial temper, but returns
        Of force to its own likeness; up he starts,
        Discover'd and surpris'd. As when a spark
815   Lights on a heap of nitrous powder, laid
816   Fit for the tun, some magazine to store
        Against a rumour'd war, the smutty grain
        With sudden blaze diffus'd, inflames the air:
        So started up in his own shape the fiend.
820   Back stepp'd those two fair angels, half amazed,
821   So sudden to behold the grisly king;
        Yet thus, unmov'd with fear, accost him soon:

        Which of those rebel spirits, adjudg'd to hell,
        Com'st thou, escap'd thy prison? and transform'd,

---

797 *files* Ranks.   800 *Squat like a toad* Note the striking difference from Satan's heroic aspect in books I and II.   802 *The organs of her fancy* What psychoanalysts would call her "unconscious," in which thoughts take the form of irrational images.   803 *Illusions . . . dreams* Satan cannot create anything real; he is the source of delusion.   804 *inspiring venom* The image ascribes a spiritual influence to a physical substance.   805 *animal spirits* The faculty that converts sense impressions into reason. Satan cannot appeal to reason, so he tries to influence the pre-rational faculties.   808 *Vain* Worldly, hence pointless.   816 *tun* Barrel.   821 *grisly king* Compare the "Navity Ode" (l. 209), where this term describes the heathen sun-god, Moloch.

Why sat'st thou, like an enemy in wait,   825
Here watching at the head of these that sleep?

Know ye not then, said Satan, fill'd with scorn.
Know ye not me? ye knew me once no mate   828
For you; there sitting where ye durst not soar: 829
Not to know me argues yourselves unknown,   830
The lowest of your throng: or if ye know,
Why ask ye, and superfluous begin
Your message, like to end as much in vain?

To whom thus Zephon, answering scorn with scorn:
Think not revolted spirit, thy shape the same,   835
Or undiminish'd brightness, to be known
As when thou stood'st in heaven, upright and pure
That glory then, when thou no more wast good,
Departed from thee; and thou resemblest now   839
Thy sin, and place of doom, obscure and foul.   840
But come; for thou, be sure, shalt give account
To him who sent us, whose charge is to keep
This place inviolable, and these from harm.

So spake the cherub; and his grave rebuke,
Severe in youthful beauty, added grace   845
Invincible: abash'd the Devil stood,
And felt how awful goodness is, and saw
Virtue in her shape how lovely; saw, and pin'd
His loss: but chiefly to find here observ'd
His lustre visibly impair'd: yet seem'd   850
Undaunted. If I must contend, said he,   851

828–829 *no mate / For you* Satan instinctively "pulls rank"; his recourse is always to hierarchy.   839–840 *thou resemblest now / Thy sin* Compare 10.516, where Satan is "punish'd in the shape he sinn'd."   850 *visibly impair'd* In his ridiculous vanity, Satan is primarily concerned with his physical appearance.   850–851 *yet seem'd / Undaunted* Satan can only "seem" thus to the reader, for we have already been told that the angels perceive him as he really is.

852 Best with the best, the sender not the sent,
Or all at once; more glory will be won,
Or less be lost. Thy fear, said Zephon bold,
855 Will save us trial what the least can do
856 Single against thee wicked, and thence weak.

The fiend replied not, overcome with rage;
But like a proud steed rein'd, went haughty on,
Champing his iron curb: to strive or fly
860 He held it vain; awe from above had quell'd
His heart, not else dismay'd. Now drew they nigh
The western point, where those half-rounding guards
Just met, and closing stood in squadron join'd,
Awaiting next command. To whom their chief,
865 Gabriel, from the front thus call'd aloud:

O friends, I hear the tread of nimble feet
Hasting this way, and now by glimpse discern
Ithuriel and Zephon through the shade,
And with them comes a third of regal port,
870 But faded splendour wan; who, by his gait
And fierce demeanour, seems the prince of hell,
Not likely to part hence without contest;
Stand firm, for in his look defiance lowers.

He scarce had ended, when those two approach'd,
875 And brief related whom they brought, where found,
How busied, in what form and posture couch'd.

To whom with stern regard thus Gabriel spake:
Why hast thou, Satan, broke the bounds prescrib'd
879 To thy transgressions, and disturb'd the charge
880 Of others, who approve not to transgress

---

852 *the sender not the sent* Another instance of Satan's urge to conquer his Creator, the Absolute Subject.   856 *wicked, and thence weak* Compare Milton's *Samson Agonistes* (1671): "All wickedness is weakness" (l. 834).   879 *transgressions* Sins of excess, which involve going beyond proper bounds.

By thy example, but have power and right
To question thy bold entrance on this place;
Employ'd it seems to violate sleep, and those
Whose dwelling God hath planted here in bliss?

To whom thus Satan with contemptuous brow: 885
Gabriel, thou hadst in heaven th'esteem of wise,
And such I held thee; but this question ask'd
Puts me in doubt. Lives there who loves his pain?
Who would not, finding way, break loose from hell,
Though thither doom'd? Thou wouldst thyself, no doubt,   890
And boldly venture to whatever place
Farthest from pain, where thou might'st hope to change
Torment with ease, and soonest recompense
Dole with delight, which in this place I sought;
To thee no reason, who know'st only good,   895
But evil hast not tried; and wilt object   896
His will who bound us? let him surer bar   897
His iron gates, if he intends our stay   898
In that dark durance: thus much what was ask'd,   899
The rest is true, they found me where they say;   900
But that implies not violence or harm.

Thus he in scorn. The warlike angel mov'd,
Disdainfully, half-smiling, thus replied:
O loss of one in heaven to judge of wise,
Since Satan fell, whom folly overthrew,   905
And now returns him from his prison scap'd,
Gravely in doubt whether to hold them wise
Or not, who ask what boldness brought him hither
Unlicens'd, from his bounds in hell prescrib'd;   909

---

896 *object* Make objective, give objective form to.   897–899 *let him . . . durance* Satan's
point is insolent but sound: Clearly God did not intend to keep Satan in Hell, since He
permitted his escape.   909 *Unlicens'd* In *Areopagitica* (1644), his pamphlet on freedom of
expression, and elsewhere, Milton points out that only those who are not free require per-
mission, or "license," for their actions; licentiousness thus does not indicate freedom from
the law, but subjection to it.

910 So wise he judges it to fly from pain
However, and to scape his punishment.
So judge thou still, presumptuous, till the wrath,
Which thou incurr'st by flying, meet thy flight
Sevenfold, and scourge that wisdom back to hell,
915 Which taught thee yet no better, that no pain
Can equal anger infinite provok'd.
But wherefore thou alone? wherefore with thee
Came not all hell broke loose? is pain to them
Less pain, less to be fled? or thou than they
920 Less hardy to endure? Courageous chief,
The first in flight from pain, hadst thou alleg'd
To thy deserted host this cause of flight,
Thou surely hadst not come sole fugitive.

To which the fiend thus answer'd, frowning stern:
925 Not that I less endure, or shrink from pain,
Insulting angel: well thou know'st I stood
Thy fiercest, when in battle to thy aid
The blasting vollied thunder made all speed,
And seconded thy else not dreaded spear:
930 But still thy words at random, as before,
931 Argue thy inexperience what behoves,
932 From hard assays and ill successes past,
A faithful leader, not to hazard all
Through ways of danger by himself untried.
935 I, therefore, I alone first undertook
936 To wing the desolate abyss, and spy
This new created world, whereof in hell
Fame is not silent, here in hope to find
Better abode, and my afflicted powers
940 To settle here on earth, or in mid air;
Though for possession put to try once more
What thou and thy gay legions dare against;

---

931 *behoves* Befits.   932 *assays* Attempts.   936 *abyss* Chaos.

Whose easier business were to serve their Lord
High up in heaven, with songs to hymn his throne,
And practis'd distances to cringe, not fight.   945

To whom the warrior angel soon replied:
To say and straight unsay, pretending first
Wise to fly pain, professing next the spy,
Argues no leader but a liar trac'd,
Satan, and couldst thou faithful add? O name,   950
O sacred name of faithfulness profan'd!
Faithful to whom? to thy rebellious crew?
Army of fiends, fit body to fit head.
Was this your discipline and faith engag'd,
Your military obedience, to dissolve   955
Allegiance to th'acknowledg'd power supreme?
And thou, sly hypocrite, who now wouldst seem
Patron of liberty, who more than thou
Once fawn'd and cring'd, and servilely ador'd
Heaven's awful monarch? wherefore, but in hope   960
To dispossess him, and thyself to reign?
But mark what I areed thee now—Avaunt: 962
Fly thither whence thou fledst: if from this hour
Within these hallow'd limits thou appear,
Back to th'infernal pit I drag thee chain'd,   965
And seal thee so, as henceforth not to scorn
The facile gates of hell too slightly barr'd.   967

So threaten'd he; but Satan to no threats
Gave heed, but waxing more in rage, replied:

Then when I am thy captive talk of chains,   970
Proud limitary cherub, but ere then   971

---

950 *couldst thou faithful add?* Are you capable of calling yourself faithful, too?   962.1 *areed* Advise; 962.2 *Avaunt* Begone.   967 *too slightly barr'd* Gabriel appears to echo Satan's criticisms of God's skill as a jailer; see footnote for 4.897–899.   971 *limitary* Limiting, guarding the limit.

Far heavier load thyself expect to feel
From my prevailing arm; though heaven's King
Ride on thy wings, and thou with thy compeers,
975 Us'd to the yoke, draw'st His triumphant wheels
976 In progress through the road of heaven star-pav'd.

While thus he spake, th'angelic squadron bright
978 Turn'd fiery red, sharp'ning in mooned horns
Their phalanx, and began to hem him round
980 With ported spears, as thick as when a field
981 Of Ceres ripe for harvest waving bends
Her bearded groves of ears, which way the wind
Sways them; the careful ploughman doubting stands,
984 Lest on the threshing-floor his hopeful sheaves
985 Prove chaff. On th'other side, Satan, alarm'd,
986 Collecting all his might, dilated stood,
987 Like Teneriff or Atlas unremov'd:
His stature reach'd the sky, and on his crest
989 Sat horror plum'd; nor wanted in his grasp
990 What seem'd both spear and shield. Now dreadful deeds
Might have ensu'd; nor only Paradise
992 In this commotion, but the starry cope
Of heaven perhaps, or all the elements,
994 At least had gone to wrack, disturb'd, and torn
995 With violence of this conflict, had not soon
Th'Eternal, to prevent such horrid fray,
997 Hung forth in heaven his golden scales, yet seen
998 Betwixt Astrea and the Scorpion sign,

---

976 *progress* Procession.   978 *mooned horns* Crescent.   980 *ported* Carried.   981 *Ceres* Goddess of grain.   984–985 *Lest . . . chaff* See Matthew 3:12.   986 *dilated* Swollen.   987 *Teneriff or Atlas* The mountainous island of Teneriffe, off the coast of west Africa, and Mt. Atlas, in modern Morocco; the latter bears an association with Atlas the Titan.   989 *plum'd* Feathered.   990 *What seem'd both spear and shield* An explicit acknowledgment of the metaphorical nature of the action.   992 *cope* Cloak.   994 *wrack* Wreck, ruin.   997–998 *his golden scales . . . sign* In the *Iliad* (22.209), Zeus weighs the destinies of Hector and Achilles in a pair of golden scales; Milton identifies God's scales with the zodiac sign Libra; "Astraea" is Virgo.

Wherein all things created first he weigh'd,
The pendulous round earth with balanc'd air   1000
In counterpoise, now ponders all events,   1001
Battles and realms: in these he put two weights,   1002
The sequel each of parting and of fight;   1003
The latter quick up flew, and kick'd the beam;   1004
Which Gabriel spying, thus bespake the fiend: 1005

Satan, I know thy strength, and thou know'st mine,
Neither our own, but given; what folly then   1007
To boast what arms can do? since thine no more
Than heaven permits, nor mine, tho' doubled now
To trample thee as mire: for proof look up,   1010
And read thy lot in yon celestial sign,   1011
Where thou art weigh'd, and shown how light, how weak,
If thou resist. The fiend look'd up, and knew
His mounted scale aloft: nor more; but fled
Murm'ring, and with him fled the shades of night.   1015

END OF BOOK FOURTH

1001 *ponders* Weighs.   1001–1002 *all events, / Battles and realms* The conflict between Satan
and Gabriel is replicated in all earthly conflict.   1003 *sequel* Result.   1004 *kick'd the beam*
One side of the scales shoots up and hits the balance beam.   1007 *Neither . . . given* A re-
minder that the action is figurative; any literal fight would be absurd in light of the fact
that the outcome is preordained.   1011 *And read . . . sign* Gabriel tells Satan that his for-
tune ("lot") is already inscribed in the "sign" of Libra, the scales, but reading signs is pre-
cisely what Satan is unable to do.

BOOK V

THE ARGUMENT

Morning approached, Eve relates to Adam her troublesome dream; he likes it not, yet comforts her. They come forth to their day-labours: * *their morning hymn at the door of their bower. God, to render man inexcusable,*† *sends Raphael*‡ *to admonish him of his obedience; of his free estate; of his enemy near at hand, who he is, and why his enemy; and whatever else may avail Adam to know. Raphael comes down to Paradise: his appearance described; his coming discerned by Adam afar off sitting at the door of his bower; he goes out to meet him, brings him to his lodge, entertains him with the choicest fruits of Paradise got together by Eve; their discourse at table. Raphael performs his message, minds Adam of his state and of his enemy; relates, at Adam's request, who that enemy is, and how he came to be so, beginning from his first revolt in heaven, and the occasion thereof; how he drew his legions after him to the parts of the north,*§ *and there incited them to rebel with him, persuading all but only Abdiel,*|| *a seraph, who in argument dissuades and opposes him, then forsakes him.*

---

*The work of a laborer hired by the day; wage-labor. See Milton's Sonnet 19, "doth God exact day-labour, light denied?" (l. 7).
†Without excuse. Raphael's purpose in warning Adam and Eve about the Fall is not to prevent it, but to deprive the human couple of the excuse that they had not been warned.
‡In Hebrew, "Medicine of God." In Judaism, Raphael, Gabriel, Uriel, and Michael are the "Angels of the Presence," one of four classes of angels mentioned in the apocryphal biblical Books of Jubilees.
§Traditionally associated with the power of evil.
|| See 5.805

1   Now Morn, her rosy steps in th'eastern clime
    Advancing, sow'd the earth with orient pearl,
    When Adam wak'd, so custom'd, for his sleep
    Was airy-light, from pure digestion bred,
5   And temp'rate vapours bland, which th'only sound
6   Of leaves and fuming rills, Aurora's fan,
7   Lightly dispers'd, and the shrill matin song
    Of birds on every bough: so much the more
    His wonder was to find unwaken'd Eve
10 With tresses discompos'd, and glowing cheek,
    As through unquiet rest: he, on his side
12 Leaning half rais'd, with looks of cordial love,
    Hung over her enamour'd; and beheld
    Beauty, which, whether waking or asleep,
15 Shot forth peculiar graces; then, with voice
16 Mild as when Zephyrus on Flora breathes,
    Her hand soft touching, whisper'd thus: Awake,
18 My fairest, my espous'd, my latest found,
    Heaven's last best gift, my ever new delight,
20 Awake; the morning shines and the fresh field
21 Calls us; we lose the prime, to mark how spring
22 Our tended plants, how blows the citron grove,
23 What drops the myrrh, and what the balmy reed,
24 How nature paints her colours, how the bee
25 Sits on the bloom extracting liquid sweet.

    Such whisp'ring wak'd her, but with startled eye
    On Adam, whom embracing, thus she spake:

28 O sole, in whom my thoughts find all repose,
    My glory, my perfection, glad I see

---

1 *rosy steps* Recalling the stock Homeric image of "rosy-fingered dawn."   6 *Aurora* God-
dess of the dawn.   7 *matin* Morning.   12 *cordial* Medicinal.   16.1 *Zephyrus* The west wind;
16.2 *Flora* Goddess of flowers.   18 *espous'd* Wife.   21 *prime* The first hour of sunlight.   22
blows Blooms.   23 *myrrh* A healing ointment.   24 *nature paints her colours* A paradoxical
image of nature using artificial makeup.   28 *sole* Only one, with a pun on "soul": The soul
is the purpose, or end, of the human being, as Adam is Eve's purpose and end.

Thy face and morn return'd; for I this night   30
(Such night till this, I never pass'd) have dream'd,
If dream'd, not, as I oft am wont, of thee,
Works of day past, or morrow's next design,
But of offence and trouble, which my mind
Knew never till this irksome night. Methought   35
Close at mine ear one call'd me forth to walk
With gentle voice; I thought it thine; it said,   37
Why sleep'st thou, Eve? now is the pleasant time,   38
The cool, the silent, save where silence yields
To the night-warbling bird, that now awake   40
Tunes sweetest his love-labour'd song; now reigns   41
Full orb'd the moon, and with more pleasing light   42
Shadowy sets off the face of things;[1] in vain,   43
If none regard; heaven wakes with all his eyes,   44
Whom to behold but thee, nature's desire?   45
In whose sight all things joy, with ravishment   46
Attracted by the beauty still to gaze.   47
I rose as at thy call, but found thee not: 48
To find thee I directed then my walk;
And on, methought, alone I pass'd through ways   50
That brought me on a sudden to the tree
Of interdicted knowledge: fair it seem'd,   52
Much fairer to my fancy than by day;   53
And, as I wond'ring look'd, beside it stood

---

37 *I thought it thine* The serpent sounds like Adam.   38 *Why . . . time* Compare *Comus:* "What hath night to do with sleep?" (122).   40 *night-warbling bird* Nightingale.   41 *love-labour'd* A labor of love, but Flannagan (p. 476) notes the implication of illegitimate conception. "Labor" was a common euphemism for the sexual act, as in John Donne's Elegy XIX, "To His Mistress Going to Bed" (1633): "Until I labor, I in labor lie."   41–42 *now reigns / Full orb'd the moon* The moon is full, a phase especially connected with witchcraft.   43–44 *in vain, / If none regard* Compare 9.546–547. In both temptation scenes, Satan tells Eve that her only value is to be a spectacle, an object for the eyes of others.   45 *nature's desire* Eve is the object of desire.   46–47 *with ravishment . . . gaze* Satan claims that Eve provokes an irrational fascination in those who see her.   48 *as at thy call* Satan falsely implies that Eve has invited him into her boudoir.   52 *interdicted* Forbidden.   52–53 *fair it seem'd . . . day* Eve's unconscious "fancy" is to her conscious reason what night is to day; both distort the true nature of things.

55 One shap'd and wing'd like one of those from heaven
    By us oft seen: his dewy locks distill'd
57 Ambrosia; on that tree he also gaz'd;
    And, O fair plant, said he, with fruit surcharg'd,
    Deigns none to ease thy load and taste thy sweet?
60 Nor God, nor man? is knowledge so despis'd?
    Or envy, or what reserve, forbids to taste?
    Forbid who will, none shall from me withhold
    Longer thy offer'd good; why else set here?
    This said he paus'd not, but with vent'rous arm
65 He pluck'd, he tasted; me damp horror chill'd
66 At such bold words, vouch'd with a deed so bold:
67 But he thus, overjoy'd: O fruit divine,
    Sweet of thyself, but much more sweet thus cropt,
    Forbidden here, it seems as only fit
70 For gods, yet able to make gods of men:
    And why not gods of men, since good, the more
72 Communicated, more abundant grows,
    The author not impair'd, but honour'd more?
74 Here, happy creature, fair angelic Eve,
75 Partake thou also; happy though thou art,
    Happier thou may'st be, worthier canst not be:
    Take this, and be henceforth among the gods,
78 Thyself a goddess, not to earth confin'd,
    But sometimes in the air, as we, sometimes
80 Ascend to heaven, by merit thine, and see
    What life the gods live there, and such live thou.
    So saying, he drew nigh, and to me held,
    Even to my mouth of that same fruit held part
    Which he had pluck'd; the pleasant savoury smell

---

55 *One . . . heaven* Satan claims to have been tempted to eat the fruit by an angel. 57 *gaz'd*
Satan inculcates into Eve his own fascination with visual spectacles. 66 *vouch'd* Backed up;
a financial metaphor, as in "voucher." 67 *O fruit divine* Satan's sensuality has prepared us
for his idolatry. 72 *Communicated* As the grace of God is automatically communicated
in Holy Communion. 74 *angelic* Satan's flattery promotes Eve up the chain of being. 78
Thyself a goddess Satan projects his own ambition onto Eve. 80 *by merit thine* Satan claims
that, having eaten the fruit, Eve will have the power within herself to ascend to Heaven.

So quicken'd appetite, that I, methought,   85
Could not but taste. Forthwith up to the clouds   86
With him I flew, and underneath beheld   87
The earth outstretch'd immense, a prospect wide
And various: wond'ring at my flight and change
To this high exaltation; suddenly   90
My guide was gone, and I, methought, sunk down,
And fell asleep; but O how glad I wak'd
To find this but a dream. Thus Eve her night
Related, and thus Adam answer'd sad:

Best image of myself and dearer half,   95
The trouble of thy thoughts this night in sleep
Affects me equally; nor can I like
This uncouth dream, of evil sprung I fear;   98
Yet evil whence? in thee can harbour none,
Created pure. But know, that in the soul   100
Are many lesser faculties, that serve
Reason as chief; among these Fancy next
Her office holds; of all external things,
Which the five watchful senses represent,
She forms imaginations, airy shapes,   105
Which Reason, joining or disjoining, frames
All what we affirm or what deny, and call
Our knowledge or opinion; then retires
Into her private cell when nature rests.   109
Oft in her absence mimic Fancy wakes   110
To imitate her; but misjoining shapes,   111
Wild work produces oft, and most in dreams,   112

---

85 *appetite* Compare Christopher Marlowe's *Doctor Faustus* (1604): "The god thou servest is thine own appetite" (act 2, scene 1).   86–87 *up to the clouds / With him I flew* Echoes commonplace descriptions from contemporary confessions of witches, which usually included claims to have attained the power of flight with the devil's aid.   95 *Best image* In the legitimate sense that Eve is derived from Adam, as opposed to the illicit sense of a fascinating appearance. See note to 4:292.   98 *uncouth* Strange.   105 *imaginations, airy shapes* The data of sense impressions, which are merely empty images before they are ordered by reason.   109 *when nature rests* During sleep.   111–112 *misjoining shapes / Wild work produces oft* Fancy operates through the medium of appearances ("shapes") that, unmoored from reason, combine to form disordered impressions in the imagination.

Ill matching words and deeds long past or late.
114   Some such resemblances methinks I find
115   Of our last evening's talk in this thy dream,
But with addition strange: yet be not sad:
117   Evil into the mind of God or man
118   May come and go, so unapprov'd, and leave
No spot or blame behind: which gives me hope,
120   That what in sleep thou didst abhor to dream,
Waking thou never wilt consent to do.
Be not dishearten'd then, nor cloud those looks,
That wont to be more cheerful and serene,
Than when fair morning first smiles on the world;
125   And let us to our fresh employments rise,
Among the groves, the fountains, and the flowers,
That open now their choicest bosom'd smells,
Reserv'd from night, and kept for thee in store.

129   So cheer'd he his fair spouse, and she was cheer'd;
130   But silently a gentle tear let fall
From either eye, and wip'd them with her hair;
Two other precious drops that ready stood,
Each in their crystal sluice, he ere they fell
Kiss'd, as the gracious signs of sweet remorse
135   And pious awe, that fear'd to have offended.

So all was clear'd, and to the field they haste.
But first, from under shady arborous roof,
Soon as they forth were come to open sight
Of day-spring, and the sun, who scarce up-risen,
140   With wheels yet hov'ring o'er the ocean brim,
Shot parallel to th'earth his dewy ray,
Discov'ring in wide landscape all the east

---

114 *resemblances* Duplicated images.   117–118 *Evil . . . unapprov'd* Satan can only be admitted to the conscious mind by a deliberate act of will, or "approval"; since none has been granted here, his infection of Eve's dream imputes no sin to her.   129 *So . . . cheer'd* Adam is the subject, Eve the object.

Of Paradise and Eden's happy plains,
Lowly they bow'd adoring, and began
Their orisons, each morning duly paid   145
In various style; for neither various style   146
Nor holy rapture wanted they to praise
Their Maker, in fit strains pronounc'd or sung
Unmeditated, such prompt eloquence
Flow'd from their lips, in prose or numerous verse;   150
More tunable than needed lute or harp
To add more sweetness; and they thus began;

These are thy glorious works, Parent of Good,   153
Almighty, thine this universal frame,
Thus wondrous fair; thyself how wondrous then;   155
Unspeakable, who sitt'st above these heavens   156
To us invisible, or dimly seen
In these thy lowest works; yet these declare
Thy goodness beyond thought, and power divine.
Speak, ye who best can tell, ye sons of light,   160
Angels; for ye behold him, and with songs
And choral symphonies, day without night,
Circle his throne rejoicing; ye in heaven:
On earth join all ye creatures, to extol
Him first, him last, him midst, and without end.   165
Fairest of stars, last in the train of night,   166
If better thou belong not to the dawn,
Sure pledge of day, that crown'st the smiling morn
With thy bright circlet, praise him in thy sphere,
While day arises, that sweet hour of prime.   170
Thou sun, of this great world both eye and soul,
Acknowledge him thy greater, sound his praise

---

145 *orisons* Prayers.   146 *various style* Their prayers do not follow "set forms" but vary with
their minds.   153 *thy glorious works* Praise of God begins by acknowledging him as Cre-
ator.   155 *thyself how wondrous then* God's nature is deduced from his works.   156 *Un-
speakable* Incommunicable.   166 *Fairest of stars* Venus, the morning star, also known as
"Lucifer."

In thy eternal course, both when thou climb'st,
And when high noon hast gain'd, and when thou fall'st.
175 Moon that now meet'st the orient sun, now fliest
With the fixt stars, fixt in their orb that flies;
177 And ye five other wand'ring fires, that move
178 In mystic dance, not without song, resound
His praise, who out of darkness call'd up light,
180 Air, and ye elements, the eldest birth
181 Of Nature's womb, that in quaternion run
182 Perpetual circle, multiform; and mix,
And nourish all things; let your ceaseless change
184 Vary to our great Maker still new praise.
185 Ye mists and exhalations, that now rise
From hill or steaming lake, dusky or grey,
Till the sun paint your fleecy skirts with gold,
In honour to the world's great Author rise;
Whether to deck with clouds th'uncolour'd sky,
190 Or wet the thirsty earth with falling showers,
Rising or falling still advance his praise.
192 His praise, ye winds, that from four quarters blow,
Breathe soft or loud; and wave your tops ye pines,
194 With every plant, in sign of worship wave.
195 Fountains, and ye that warble, as ye flow,
Melodious murmurs, warbling tune his praise.
Join voices all ye living souls; ye birds,
That singing up to heaven-gate ascend,
Bear on your wings and in your notes his praise.
200 Ye that in waters glide, and ye that walk
The earth, and stately tread, or lowly creep,
Witness if I be silent, morn or even,
To hill or valley, fountain or fresh shade,

---

177 *five other wand'ring fires* Mars, Venus, Mercury, Jupiter, and Saturn; note that Venus is mentioned here and just above, in line 166.   178.1 *mystic* Symbolic; 178.2 *not without song* The planets emit the music of the spheres.   181 *quaternion* Group of four.   182 *multiform* Multifarious.   184 *Vary . . . praise* The various appearances all point to the same *logos*. 192 *four quarters* Four points of the compass.   194 *sign of worship* Properly interpreted, all nature refers to its Creator.

Made vocal by my song, and taught his praise.
Hail, universal Lord, be bounteous still   205
To give us only good; and, if the night
Have gather'd aught of evil, or conceal'd,
Disperse it, as now light dispels the dark.

So pray'd they, innocent; and to their thoughts
Firm peace recover'd soon, and wonted calm.   210
On to their morning's rural work they haste,
Among sweet dews and flowers; where any row
Of fruit-trees over-woody reach'd too far
Their pamper'd boughs, and needed hands to check
Fruitless embraces: or they led the vine   215
To wed her elm; she spous'd about him twines   216
Her marriageable arms, and with her brings
Her dower, th'adopted clusters, to adorn
His barren leaves. Them thus employ'd beheld
With pity heaven's high King, and to him call'd   220
Raphael, the sociable spirit, that deign'd
To travel with Tobias, and secur'd
His marriage with the seventimes-wedded maid.

Raphael, said he, thou hear'st what stir on earth
Satan, from hell scap'd through the darksome gulf   225
Hath rais'd in Paradise, and how disturb'd
This night the human pair; how he designs
In them at once to ruin all mankind.   228
Go, therefore, half this day as friend with friend
Converse with Adam, in what bower or shade   230
Thou find'st him, from the heat of noon retir'd,
To respite his day-labour with repast,
Or with repose; and such discourse bring on,

---

210 *wonted* Former.   215 *Fruitless embraces* The proper end of "embraces" is to bear fruit
in the form of offspring; sexual intercourse for its own sake constituted the sin of "con-
cupiscence," or desire, which Adam and Eve seek to prevent even in the vegetable world.
216 *spous'd* Married.   228 *In them . . . mankind* A reference to the doctrine of original sin,
whereby the disobedience of Adam and Eve stamps its image on their posterity.

As may advise him of his happy state,
235 Happiness in his power left free to will,
Left to his own free will; his will, though free,
Yet mutable; whence warn him to beware
238 He swerve not, too secure: tell him withal,
His danger, and from whom; what enemy,
240 Late fallen himself from heaven, is plotting now
The fall of others from like state of bliss;
By violence? no, for that shall be withstood;
But by deceit and lies: this let him know,
244 Lest wilfully transgressing he pretend
245 Surprisal, unadmonish'd, unforewarn'd.

246 So spake th'eternal Father, and fulfill'd
247 All justice: nor delay'd the wing'd saint
After his charge receiv'd; but from among
Thousand celestial ardours, where he stood
250 Veil'd with gorgeous wings, up springing light,
Flew through the midst of heaven; th'angelic choirs
On each hand parting, to his speed gave way
253 Through all the empyreal road; till at the gate
Of heaven arriv'd, the gate self-open'd wide,
255 On golden hinges turning, as by work
Divine the sov'reign Architect had fram'd.
From hence, no cloud, or, to obstruct his sight,
Star interpos'd, however small, he sees,
259 Not unconform to other shining globes,
260 Earth, and the garden of God, with cedars crown'd
Above all hills. As when by night the glass
262 Of Galileo, less assur'd, observes
263 Imagin'd lands and regions in the moon;

---

238 *swerve* Depart from the proper road.   244 *pretend* Claim.   246–247 *fulfill'd / All justice* Did all that was necessary for Him to be just.   253 *empyreal* Heavenly, but with overtones of "imperial."   259 *Not unconform* Not dissimilar.   262 *Galileo, less assur'd* No denigration of the astronomer is intended; his steadfast insistence on the truth in the face of persecution by the Inquisition made him one of the poet's most important role models.   263 *Imagin'd* Made into a visible image.

Or pilot, from amidst the Cyclades,   264
Delos or Samos first appearing, kens   265
A cloudy spot. Down thither prone in flight
He speeds, and through the vast ethereal sky
Sails between worlds and worlds; with steady wing
Now on the polar winds, then with quick fan
Winnows the buxom air; till, within soar   270
Of tow'ring eagles, to all the fowls he seems
A phœnix, gaz'd by all, as that sole bird,
When to inshrine his reliques in the sun's
Bright temple, to Egyptian Thebes he flies.[2]
At once on th'eastern cliff of Paradise   275
He lights, and to his proper shape returns,
A seraph wing'd; six wings he wore to shade
His lineaments divine; the pair that clad   278
Each shoulder broad, came mantling o'er his breast   279
With regal ornament; the middle pair   280
Girt like a starry zone his waist, and round   281
Skirted his loins and thighs with downy gold
And colours dipp'd in heaven; the third his feet   283
Shadow'd from either heel with feather'd mail,   284
Sky-tinctur'd grain. Like Maia's son he stood,   285
And shook his plumes, that heavenly fragrance fill'd
The circuit wide. Straight knew him all the bands
Of angels under watch; and to his state,
And to his message high, in honour rise;
For on some message high they guess'd him bound.   290
Their glittering tents he pass'd, and now is come
Into the blissful field, through groves of myrrh,
And flowering odours, cassia, nard, and balm;   293

---

264 *Cyclades* Aegean islands. Fowler (p. 297) notes that Raphael is compared to a naviga-
tor and Satan to a trader.   265 *kens* Sees.   278 *lineaments* Outlines, shapes.   279 *mantling*
Wrapping, like a cloak.   281 *zone* Belt.   283 *dipp'd* Dipped in dye, but with a suggestion
of "baptized": The Baptists were satirically known as the "dippers."   284 *feather'd mail*
Raphael wears a combination of armor and plumage.   285.1 *Sky-tinctur'd grain* Dye mixed
by the sky; 285.2 *Maia's son* Mercury, messenger of the gods, and god of trade.   293.1 *cas-
sia* Used in Exodus 30:24 to anoint the Tabernacle; 293.2 *nard* Used in Mark 14:3 to anoint
Jesus' head before his execution.

A wildness of sweets; for Nature here
295   Wanton'd as in her prime,³ and play'd at will
Her virgin fancies, pouring forth more sweet,
297   Wild above rule or art; enormous bliss.
Him through the spicy forest onward come,
Adam discern'd, as in the door he sat
300   Of his cool bower, while now the mounted sun
301   Shot down direct his fervid rays to warm
Earth's inmost womb, more warmth than Adam needs:
And Eve within, due at her hour, prepar'd
For dinner savoury fruits, of taste to please
305   True appetite, and not disrelish thirst
Of nect'rous draughts between, from milky stream,
Berry or grape; to whom thus Adam call'd:

Haste hither, Eve, and, worth thy sight, behold,
Eastward among those trees, what glorious shape,
310   Comes this way moving; seems another morn
311   Risen on mid-noon: some great behest from heaven
312   To us perhaps he brings, and will vouchsafe
This day to be our guest. But go with speed,
And what thy stores contain bring forth, and pour
315   Abundance, fit to honour and receive
316   Our heavenly stranger: well we may afford
317   Our givers their own gifts, and large bestow
From large bestow'd, where nature multiplies
Her fertile growth, and by disburd'ning grows
320   More fruitful, which instructs us not to spare.

321   To whom thus Eve: Adam, earth's hallow'd mould,
322   Of God inspir'd, small store will serve, where store

---

297 *enormous* Outside of rules.   301 *fervid* Boiling.   305 *True appetite* Honest, not excessive, desire for food, for the purpose of nutrition, not sensual pleasure.   311 *behest* Mission. 312 *vouchsafe* Agree.   316–317 *well . . . gifts* Note the harmonious relationship Adam assumes between subject and object.   321 *hallow'd mould* Holy shape.   322 *inspir'd* Given the breath of life.

All seasons, ripe for use hangs on the stalk;
Save what by frugal storing firmness gains
To nourish, and superfluous moist consumes: 325
But I will haste, and from each bough and brake,   326
Each plant and juiciest gourd, will pluck such choice
To entertain our angel guest, as he
Beholding shall confess, that here on earth
God hath dispens'd his bounties as in heaven.   330

So saying, with despatchful looks in haste   331
She turns, on hospitable thoughts intent
What choice to choose for delicacy best;
What order, so contriv'd as not to mix
Tastes, not well join'd, inelegant, but bring   335
Taste after taste, upheld with kindliest change: 336
Bestirs her then, and from each tender stalk
Whatever earth, all bearing mother, yields
In India East or West, or middle shore
In Pontus, or the Punic coast, or where   340
Alcinous reign'd, fruit of all kinds in coat   341
Rough or smooth rind, or bearded husk, or shell
She gathers, tribute large, and on the board
Heaps with unsparing hand; for drink the grape
She crushes, inoffensive must, and meathes   345
From many a berry; and from sweet kernels press'd
She tempers dulcet creams; nor these to hold   347
Wants her fit vessels pure; then strews the ground
With rose and odours from the shrub unfum'd.   349

Meanwhile our primitive great sire, to meet   350
His godlike guest, walks forth, without more train

---

326 *brake* Thicket.   331 *despatchful* Eager.   336 *kindliest* Most natural.   340.1 *Pontus* Southern shore of the Black Sea, in modern Turkey; 340.2 *Punic* Carthaginian; Carthage was in what today is Tunisia.   341 *Alcinous* King of the Phaeacians, he ruled over a mythical land of constant fertility in Homer's *Odyssey* (7.112–132).   345.1 *must* Unfermented wine; 345.2 *meathes* Mead.   347 *dulcet* Sweet.   349 *unfum'd* Without artificial odor.

Accompanied than with his own complete

353   Perfections: in himself was all his state,

354   More solemn than the tedious pomp that waits

355   On princes, when their rich retinue long

356   Of horses led, and grooms besmear'd with gold,

357   Dazzles the crowd, and sets them all agape.

358   Nearer his presence Adam, though not awed,

Yet with submiss approach, and reverence meek,

360   As to a superior nature, bowing low

Thus said: Native of heaven, for other place

None can than heaven such glorious shape contain;

Since, by descending from the thrones above,

Those happy places thou hast deign'd awhile

365   To want, and honour these, vouchsafe with us

Two only, who yet by sov'reign gift possess

This spacious ground, in yonder shady bower

To rest, and what the garden choicest bears

369   To sit and taste, till this meridian heat

370   Be over, and the sun more cool decline.

371   Whom thus th'angelic virtue answer'd mild:

Adam, I therefore came; nor art thou such

Created, or such place hast here to dwell,

As may not oft invite, though spirits of heaven,

375   To visit thee: lead on then where thy bower

O'ershades; for these midhours, till evening rise,

I have at will. So to the sylvan lodge

378   They came, that like Pomona's arbour smil'd

379   With flowerets deck'd and fragrant smells; but Eve,

380   Undeck'd save with herself, more lovely fair

---

353 *in himself was all his state* He was naked.   354–357 *More solemn . . . agape* As Leonard (p. 779) notes, this may be a topical allusion to the spectacular procession that accompanied Charles II's entry into London on May 29, 1660.   358 *not awed* Adam's attitude is properly respectful, not irrationally or slavishly adoring.   365 *want* Be absent from, deprive oneself of.   369 *meridian* Noontime.   371 *virtue* Power.   378 *Pomona* Goddess of orchards in Roman mythology.   379 *flowerets* Ornaments made from flowers.   380 *Undeck'd save with herself* Naked.

Than wood-nymph, or the fairest goddess feign'd   381
Of three that in mount Ida naked strove,   382
Stood to entertain her guest from heaven: no veil
She needed, virtue proof; no thought infirm   384
Alter'd her cheek. On whom the angel Hail   385
Bestow'd, the holy salutation us'd
Long after to bless'd Mary, second Eve.   387

Hail, mother of mankind, whose fruitful womb
Shall fill the world more numerous with thy sons,
Than with these various fruits the trees of God   390
Have heap'd this table. Rais'd of grassy turf
Their table was, and mossy seats had round;
And on her ample square from side to side
All autumn pil'd, though spring and autumn here   394
Danc'd hand in hand. A while discourse they hold,   395
No fear lest dinner cool; when thus began   396
Our author: Heavenly stranger, pleas'd to taste   397
These bounties, which our nourisher, from whom
All perfect good, unmeasur'd out, descends
To us for food and for delight, hath caus'd   400
Th'earth to yield; unsavoury food perhaps
To spiritual natures; only this I know,
That one celestial Father gives to all.

To whom the angel: Therefore what he gives
(Whose praise be ever sung;) to man in part   405
Spiritual, may of purest spirits be found   406
No ingrateful food: and food alike those pure   407

---

381 *feign'd* Mythological.   382 *three . . . strove* The Greek goddesses Hera, Athena, and Aphrodite; Zeus asked Paris to choose which of them was the fairest.   384.1 *virtue proof* Impregnable because of virtue; 384.2 *infirm* Both "inconstant" and "sick."   387 *second Eve* Who was not the wife, but the mother, of the second Adam.   394–395 *though spring . . . hand* The rebirth of spring and the fruition of autumn are both constantly present in Eden.   396 *No fear lest dinner cool* The meal is to be eaten raw.   397 *Our author* Our progenitor, Adam.   405–406 *man in part / Spiritual* Man is part spirit, part flesh; the former dominates before the Fall, the latter afterward.   407 *ingrateful* Unpleasant.

408 Intelligential substances require,
409 As doth your rational; and both contain
410 Within them every lower faculty
411 Of sense, whereby they hear, see, smell, touch, taste.
412 Tasting concoct, digest, assimilate,
413 And corporeal to incorporeal turn.
414 For know, whatever was created, needs
415 To be sustain'd and fed; of elements,
416 The grosser feeds the purer, earth the sea,
Earth and the sea feed air, the air those fires
Ethereal, and, as lowest, first the moon;
419 Whence in her visage round, those spots unpurg'd
420 Vapours not yet into her substance turn'd.
Nor doth the moon no nourishment exhale
From her moist continent to higher orbs.
The sun, that light imparts to all, receives
424 From all his alimental recompense
425 In humid exhalations; and at even
Sups with the ocean. Though in heaven the trees
Of life ambrosial fruitage bear, and vines
Yield nectar; though from off the boughs each morn
429 We brush mellifluous dews, and find the ground
430 Cover'd with pearly grain: yet God hath here
Varied his bounty so with new delights,
As may compare with heaven; and to taste
433 Think not I shall be nice. So down they sat,
434 And to their viands fell; nor seemingly

---

408 *Intelligential substances* Angels are substantial, and thus they engage in such bodily functions as eating and sexual intercourse, but their substance is not fleshly, consisting instead of pure intellect.   409 *rational* Reason is the human equivalent of angelic intelligence. 409–413 *both contain . . . turn* Milton scrupulously assigns all the definitive characteristics of earthly life to angels, including excretion.   414–415 *whatever was created . . . fed* This presumably includes the Son of God.   416 *grosser* More fleshly.   419–420 *those spots . . . turn'd* Unlike Galileo, who discovered that the "spots" visible on the sun were caused by mountains on the moon, Raphael identifies them as insubstantial exhalations of the planets.   424 *alimental recompense* Nourishing reward.   425 *even* Evening.   429 *mellifluous* Honey-dripping.   430 *pearly grain* Manna.   433 *nice* Fussy.   434.1 *viands* Food; 434.2 *nor seemingly* Leonard calls Milton's view that angels really need food "materialist" (p. 360).

Raphael with Adam and Eve

435 The angel, nor in mist, the common gloss
436 Of theologians, but with keen despatch
437 Of real hunger, and concoctive heat
438 To transubstantiate; what redounds, transpires
   Through spirits with ease; nor wonder, if by fire
440 Of sooty coal, th'empiric alchemist[4]
   Can turn, or holds it possible to turn,
   Metals of drossiest ore to perfect gold,[5]
   As from the mine. Meanwhile at table Eve
   Minister'd naked, and their flowing cups
445 With pleasant liquors crown'd. O innocence
   Deserving Paradise; if ever, then,
   Then had the sons of God excuse to have been
448 Enamour'd at that sight; but in those hearts
449 Love unlibidinous reign'd, nor jealousy
450 Was understood, the injur'd lover's hell.

   Thus when with meats and drinks they had suffic'd
452 Not burden'd nature, sudden mind arose
   In Adam, not to let th'occasion pass,
   Given him by this great conference, to know
455 Of things above this world, and of their being
   Who dwell in heaven, whose excellence he saw
   Transcend his own so far, whose radiant forms
458 Divine effulgence, whose high power so far

435–436 *the common gloss / Of theologians* The early church fathers and scholastics could not accept that angels needed physical nutrition. Milton views their opinion as reflecting a blasphemous distaste for the divinely designed body.   437 *concoctive* Productive.   438.1 *transubstantiate* Transform into a different substance, with an ironic glance at the Catholic doctrine (which Milton regarded as magical) that during the Mass bread and wine are transubstantiated into the body and blood of Christ; 438.2 *redounds* Remains; 438.3 *transpires* Passes through a spirit.   448 *Enamour'd at that sight* The narrator hints at the possibility of regarding Eve with physical lust; in Genesis 6:2 the "sons of God" have sex with human women.   449 *unlibidinous* The narrator quickly exonerates Adam and Raphael from lustful thoughts; his own feeling toward Eve, like that of Satan, is implicitly differentiated from that of these unfallen beings.   452 *Not burden'd nature* Adam and Eve observe the rule of moderation, eating in accordance with their natural appetites, not with superfluous desire.   458 *effulgence* Emission.

Exceeded human, and his wary speech
Thus to th'empyreal minister he fram'd;   460

Inhabitant with God, now know I well
Thy favour, in this honour done to man,
Under whose lowly roof thou hast vouchsaf'd
To enter, and these earthly fruits to taste,
Food not of angels, yet accepted so,   465
As that more willingly thou couldst not seem
At heaven's high feasts to have fed: yet what compare?   467

To whom the winged hierarch replied:
O Adam, one almighty is, from whom   469
All things proceed, and up to him return,   470
If not deprav'd from good, created all   471
Such to perfection, one first matter all,   472
Endued with various forms various degrees,
Of substance, and in things that live, of life;
But more refin'd, more spiritous, and pure,   475
As nearer to him plac'd, or nearer tending,
Each in their several active spheres assign'd
Till body up to spirit work, in bounds   478
Proportion'd to each kind. So from the root
Springs lighter the green stalk, from thence the leaves   480
More airy, last the bright consummate flower
Spirits odorous breathes: flowers and their fruit,
Man's nourishment, by gradual scale sublim'd,   483
The vital spirits aspire, to animal,   484

460.1 *minister* Servant (that is, of God); 460.2 *fram'd* That is, his question. 467 *yet what compare?* Adam asks about the degree to which heaven and earth are comparable, or analogous. 469 *one almighty is* God is the ultimate source of all creation. 471 *deprav'd* Perverted. 472 *one first matter* The *prima materia*, out of which the various elements were supposed to have been formed. 478 *work* Develop, evolve. 480 *lighter* More airy, less fleshly. 483 *sublim'd* Turned from solid matter into vapor; the term carries ethical implications drawn from alchemy. 484.1 *vital* Living, from the heart; 484.2 *aspire* Desire to become spiritual. The natural aspiration appropriate to all creatures in the great chain of being is contrasted with Satan's "aspiring" to escape from creation altogether and become "equal" with the Creator; 484.3 *animal* Endowed with soul.

485 To intellectual; give both life and sense,
486 Fancy and understanding; whence the soul
487 Reason receives, and reason is her being,
488 Discursive, or intuitive; discourse
     Is oftest yours, the latter most is ours,
490 Differing but in degree, of kind the same.
     Wonder not, then, what God for you saw good
     If I refuse not, but convert, as you,
     To proper substance: time may come, when men
     With angels may participate, and find
495 No inconvenient diet, nor too light fare;
     And from these corporal nutriments perhaps
497 Your bodies may at last turn all to spirit,
     Improv'd by tract of time, and wing'd ascend
     Ethereal, as we, or may at choice
500 Here or in heavenly Paradises dwell;
     If ye be found obedient, and retain
     Unalterably firm his love entire,
     Whose progeny you are. Meanwhile enjoy
     Your fill what happiness this happy state
505 Can comprehend, incapable of more.

     To whom the patriarch of mankind replied:
     O favourable spirit, propitious guest,
     Well hast thou taught the way that might direct
     Our knowledge, and the scale of nature set
510 From centre to circumference, whereon,
     In contemplation of created things,
     By steps we may ascend to God.[6] But say,
     What meant that caution join'd, If ye be found

---

485 *intellectual* Endowed with thought.   486 *Fancy and understanding* Imagination and rationality.   487 *reason is her being* Reason is the end, or purpose, of the soul.   488.1 *Discursive* Rational deduction of truth; 488.2 *intuitive* Immediate apprehension of truth. 490 *of kind the same* The difference between men and angels is quantitative, not qualitative; again, the implicit contrast is with Satan's misconception that the same applies to the distinction between creatures and the Creator.   497 *turn all to spirit* Raphael envisages this as a gradual, incremental process, whereas Satan convinces Eve that she can become completely spiritual by the magical, material act of eating the fruit.

Obedient? can we want obedience then
To him, or possibly his love desert,   515
Who form'd us from the dust, and plac'd us here,
Full to the utmost measure of what bliss
Human desires can seek or apprehend?

To whom the angel: Son of heaven and earth,
Attend: That thou art happy, owe to God;   520
That thou continuest such, owe to thyself,
That is, to thy obedience; therein stand.
This was that caution given thee; be advis'd.
God made thee perfect, not immutable;
And good he made thee, but to persevere   525
He left it in thy power; ordain'd thy will
By nature free, not overrul'd by fate   527
Inextricable, or strict necessity: 528
Our voluntary service he requires,
Not our necessitated; such with him   530
Finds no acceptance, nor can find; for how
Can hearts not free be tried whether they serve
Willing or no, who will but what they must
By destiny, and can no other choose?[7]
Myself, and all th'angelic host that stand   535
In sight of God enthron'd, our happy state
Hold, as you yours, while our obedience holds;
On other surety none; freely we serve,   538
Because we freely love, as in our will
To love or not; in this we stand or fall: 540
And some are fallen, to disobedience fallen,
And so from heaven to deepest hell; O fall
From what high state of bliss into what woe.

To whom our great progenitor: Thy words
Attentive, and with more delighted ear   545

527–528 *fate / Inextricable* Human beings have free will, which is not subject to fate. Milton shows the influence of the Stoic idea that *virtu* (virtue) can conquer *fortuna* (chance).
538 *surety* Guarantee, as of a loan.

Divine instructor, I have heard, than when
Cherubic songs by night from neighboring hills
548 Aerial music send: nor knew I not
To be both will and deed created free;
550 Yet that we never shall forget to love
Our Maker, and obey him, whose command
552 Single is yet so just, my constant thoughts
Assur'd me, and still assure: though what thou tell'st
554 Hath pass'd in heaven, some doubt within me move,
555 But more desire to hear, if thou consent,
The full relation, which must needs be strange,
Worthy of sacred silence to be heard;
And we have yet large day, for scarce the sun
Hath finish'd half his journey, and scarce begins
560 His other half in the great zone of heaven.

Thus Adam made request; and Raphael,
After short pause assenting, thus began:

High matter thou enjoin'st me, O prime of men,
564 Sad task and hard; for how shall I relate
565 To human sense th'invisible exploits
566 Of warring spirits? how, without remorse,
The ruin of so many, glorious once,
And perfect while they stood? how, last, unfold
The secrets of another world, perhaps
570 Not lawful to reveal? yet for thy good
571 This is dispens'd; and what surmounts the reach
572 Of human sense, I shall delineate so,
573 By likening spiritual to corporal forms,
574 As may express them best; though what if earth

---

548 *Aerial* Airy.   552 *Single* Sole.   554 *some doubt within me move* It is Raphael's instruc-
tion, not Satan's temptation, that first causes Adam to "doubt" God.   564–566 *for how . . .
spirits* Raphael faces the problem of how to convey *invisibilia* in terms that Adam can un-
derstand.   571–574 *what surmounts . . . best* Refers to the doctrine of "accommodated
speech," whereby God does not reveal Himself as He "really" is but communicates His na-
ture through a series of tropes and figures.

Be but the shadow of heaven, and things therein,   575
Each to other like, more than on earth is thought?   576

As yet this world was not, and Chaos wild
Reign'd where these heavens now roll, where earth now rests
Upon her centre pois'd; when, on a day,
(For time, though in eternity, applied   580
To motion, measures all things durable
By present, past, and future,) on such day
As heaven's great year brings forth, th'empyreal host   583
Of angels, by imperial summons call'd,
Innumerable, before th'Almighty's throne   585
Forthwith from all the ends of heaven appear'd
Under their hierarchs in orders bright:
Ten thousand thousand ensigns high advanc'd,
Standards and gonfalons 'twixt van and rear,   589
Stream in the air, and for distinction serve   590
Of hierarchies, of orders, and degrees;
Or in their glittering tissues bear emblaz'd   592
Holy memorials, acts of zeal and love
Recorded eminent. Thus, when in orbs
Of circuit inexpressible they stood,   595
Orb within orb, the Father infinite,
By whom in bliss imbosom'd sat the Son,
Amidst, as from a flaming mount, whose top
Brightness had made invisible, thus spake:

Hear, all ye angels, progeny of light,   600
Thrones, dominations, princedoms, virtues, powers;

574–576 *though what . . . thought* Heaven and earth exist in a relation of analogy, not re-
semblance. Raphael asks what would follow if earth were an image ("shadow") of heaven:
What would this imply about his decision to describe heavenly events by means of earthly
metaphors? Note that he anticipates the didactic method of Jesus' parables.   583 *heaven's
great year* In Plato's *Timaeus* (c.360 B.C.), this is a duration of 36,000 earthly years.   589.1
gonfalons Standards; 589.2 *van* Vanguard.   592 *tissues* Banners; in accordance with his man-
date, Raphael is describing the angels allegorically, in terms that Adam can understand, by
comparing them to a human army.   595 *inexpressible* One of many reminders that the
things Raphael discusses cannot be expressed except through metaphorical mediation.

Hear my decree, which unrevok'd shall stand.
603 This day I have begot whom I declare
My only Son, and on this holy hill
605 Him have anointed, whom ye now behold
At my right hand; your head I him appoint;
And by myself have sworn, to him shall bow
All knees in heaven, and shall confess him Lord.
Under his great vicegerent reign abide
610 United as one individual soul,
For ever happy. Him who disobeys,
Me disobeys, breaks union, and that day,
Cast out from God and blessed vision, falls
Into utter darkness, deep ingulf'd, his place
615 Ordain'd, without redemption, without end.

So spake th'Omnipotent, and with his words
All seem'd well pleas'd; all seem'd, but were not all.
That day, as other solemn days, they spent
In song and dance about the sacred hill;
620 Mystical dance, which yonder starry sphere
Of planets and of fixt in all her wheels
Resembles nearest, mazes intricate,
623 Eccentric, intervolv'd, yet regular
624 Then most, when most, irregular they seem
625 And in their motions harmony divine
So smooths her charming tones, that God's own ear
Listens delighted. Evening now approach'd
(For we have also our evening and our morn,
We ours for change delectable, not need;)
630 Forthwith from dance to sweet repast they turn
Desirous; all in circles as they stood,

---

603 *This day I have begot* Implies the Son is not eternal, so Milton heretically denies the orthodox Christian doctrine of the Trinity.   620 *Mystical* Symbolic or allegorical, rather than literal.   623–624 *yet regular . . . seem* A hint at the doctrine of *felix culpa*, the fortunate fall; just as heaven's motions have purpose especially when they appear to be random, so the fall is part of God's purpose although it seems to be a disaster.

Tables are set, and on a sudden pil'd
With angel's food, and rubied nectar flows
In pearl, in diamond, and massy gold,
Fruit of delicious vines, the growth of heaven.   635
On flowers repos'd, and with fresh flowerets crown'd,
They eat, they drink, and in communion sweet
Quaff immortality and joy, secure
Of surfeit, where full measure only bounds
Excess, before the all bounteous King, who shower'd   640
With copious hand, rejoicing in their joy.
Now, when ambrosial night with clouds exhal'd
From that high mount of God, whence light and shade
Spring both, the face of brightest heaven had chang'd
To grateful twilight, (for night comes not there   645
In darker veil,) and roseate dews dispos'd
All but th'unsleeping eyes of God to rest;
Wide over all the plain, and wider far
Than all this globous earth in plain outspread,   649
(Such are the courts of God,) th'angelic throng,   650
Dispers'd in bands and files, their camp extend
By living streams among the trees of life,
Pavilions numberless, and sudden rear'd,
Celestial tabernacles, where they slept
Fann'd with cool winds, save those who in their course   655
Melodious hymns about the sov'reign throne
Alternate all night long: but not so wak'd
Satan (so call him now, his former name
Is heard no more in heaven;) he of the first,
If not the first archangel, great in power,   660
In favour and pre-eminence, yet fraught
With envy against the Son of God, that day
Honour'd by his great Father, and proclaim'd
Messiah, King anointed, could not bear,   664
Through pride that sight, and thought himself impair'd.[8]   665

---

649 *globous* Globular.   664 *Messiah* Anointed one, chosen savior.

Deep malice thence conceiving, and disdain,
Soon as midnight brought on the dusky hour
Friendliest to sleep and silence, he resolv'd
With all his legions to dislodge, and leave
670   Unworshipp'd, unobey'd the throne supreme,
Contemptuous, and his next subordinate
Awak'ning, thus to him in secret spake:

673   Sleep'st thou, companion dear; what sleep can close
Thy eye-lids? and remember'st what decree
675   Of yesterday, so late hath pass'd the lips
Of heaven's Almighty. Thou to me thy thoughts
Wast wont, I mine to thee was wont t'impart;
Both waking we were one; how then can now
Thy sleep dissent? New laws thou seest impos'd;
680   New laws from him who reigns, new minds may raise
In us who serve, new counsels, to debate
What doubtful may ensue: more in this place
To utter is not safe. Assemble thou
Of all those myriads which we lead the chief;
685   Tell them that, by command, ere yet dim night
Her shadowy cloud withdraws, I am to haste,
And all who under me their banners wave,
Homeward with flying march where we possess
The quarters of the north: there to prepare
690   Fit entertainment to receive our King,
The great Messiah, and his new commands,
Who speedily through all the hierarchies
Intends to pass triumphant, and give laws.

So spake the false archangel, and infus'd
695   Bad influence into th'unweary breast
Of his associate: he together calls,

---

673 *Sleep'st thou, companion dear* Note the similarities with Satan's attempted seduction of
the dreaming Eve (5.38) and with his wakening of Beelzebub in (1.84–124).

Or several one by one, the regent powers,
Under him regent; tells, as he was taught,
That, the Most High commanding, now ere night,
Now ere dim night had disencumbered heaven,   700
The great hierarchal standard was to move;
Tells the suggested cause, and casts between
Ambiguous words and jealousies, to sound
Or taint integrity. But all obey'd
The wonted signal, and superior voice   705
Of their great potentate; for great indeed
His name, and high was his degree in heaven:
His count'nance, as the morning star that guides   708
The starry flock, allur'd them, and with lies   709
Drew after him the third part of heaven's host.   710
Meanwhile th'eternal eye, whose sight discerns
Abstrusest thoughts, from forth his holy mount,
And from within the golden lamps that burn
Nightly before him, saw, without their light,
Rebellion rising; saw, in whom, how spread   715
Among the sons of morn, what multitudes
Were banded to oppose his high decree;
And, smiling, to his only Son thus said:

Son, thou in whom my glory I behold
In full resplendence, Heir of all my might,   720
Nearly it now concerns us to be sure
Of our omnipotence, and with what arms
We mean to hold what anciently we claim
Of deity or empire; such a foe
Is rising, who intends to erect his throne   725
Equal to ours, throughout the spacious north;   726
Nor so content, hath in his thought to try,

708–709 *the morning star . . . flock* The "morning star" is Lucifer, soon to be known as Satan, who leads the "flock" of angels astray.   720 *resplendence* The Son is the perceptible manifestation of the Father.   726 *Equal to ours* Lucifer aspires to equate himself with his Creator.

In battle, what our power is, or our right.
Let us advise, and to this hazard draw
730   With speed what force is left, and all employ
In our defence, lest unawares we lose
This our high place, our sanctuary, our hill.

To whom the Son, with calm aspect and clear,
Lightning divine, ineffable, serene,
735   Made answer: Mighty Father, thou thy foes
Justly hast in derision, and, secure,
Laugh'st at their vain designs and tumults vain;
Matter to me of glory, whom their hate
739   Illustrates, when they see all regal power
740   Given me to quell their pride, and in event
741   Know whether I be dext'rous to subdue
Thy rebels, or be found the worst in heaven.

So spake the Son; but Satan with his powers
Far was advanc'd on winged speed, an host
745   Innumerable as the stars of night,
Or stars of morning, dew-drops, which the sun
Impearls on every leaf, and every flower.
748   Regions they pass'd, the mighty regencies
Of seraphim, and potentates, and thrones,
750   In their triple degrees; regions to which
751   All thy dominion, Adam, is no more
752   Than what this garden is to all the earth,
And all the sea, from one entire globose
Stretch'd into longitude; which, having pass'd,
755   At length into the limits of the north
They came; and Satan to his royal seat
757   High on a hill, far blazing, as a mount

---

739 *Illustrates* Makes brighter.   741 *dext'rous* Handy.   748 *regencies* Domains.   750–752 *regions . . . earth* Like Milton, Raphael frequently indulges in similes, to instruct Adam by comparing unfamiliar concepts with familiar things.   757 *mount* Satan is attempting to imitate God's throne, which is also on a "mount" (5.598); see also lines 764–765.

Rais'd on a mount, with pyramids and towers   758
From diamond quarries hewn, and rocks of gold;   759
The palace of great Lucifer, (so call   760
That structure in the dialect of men
Interpreted,) which not long after he,   762
Affecting all equality with God,
In imitation of that mount whereon
Messiah was declar'd in sight of heaven,   765
The Mountain of the Congregation call'd;
For thither he assembled all his train,
Pretending so commanded, to consult
About the great reception of their King
Thither to come, and with calumnious art   770
Of counterfeited truth thus held their ears: 771

Thrones, dominations, princedoms, virtues,
If these magnific titles yet remain powers;
Not merely titular, since by decree
Another now hath to himself engross'd   775
All power, and us eclips'd, under the name
Of King Anointed; for whom all this haste
Of midnight march, and hurried meeting here;
This only to consult how we may best,
With what may be devis'd of honours new,   780
Receive him, coming to receive from us
Knee-tribute, yet unpaid; prostration vile,
Too much to one, but double how endur'd,
To one, and to his image now proclaim'd?⁹
But what if better counsels might erect   785
Our minds, and teach us to cast off this yoke?
Will ye submit your neck; and choose to bend

---

758 *pyramids* The pyramids were proverbial symbols of worldly vanity, monuments to alien-
ated, idolatrous human activity.   759 *rocks of gold* Satan's palace is artificially constructed.
762 *Interpreted* Satan did not literally build a "palace," but this is the visual image most
closely corresponding to the invisible heavenly structure.   771 *counterfeited* False, not en-
dorsed by the ruler; a financial term.   775 *engross'd* Usurped.

The supple knee? Ye will not, if I trust
To know ye right, or if ye know yourselves
790   Natives and sons of heaven, possess'd before
By none, and if not equal all, yet free,
Equally free; for orders and degrees
Jar not with liberty, but well consist.
Who can in reason then, or right, assume
795   Monarchy over such as live by right
His equals, if in power and splendour less,
In freedom equal? Or can introduce
Law and edict on us, who without law
Err not? much less for this to be our Lord,
800   And look for adoration, to th'abuse
Of those imperial titles, which assert
Our being ordain'd to govern, not to serve.

Thus far his bold discourse without control
Had audience; when among the seraphim
805   Abdiel, than whom none with more zeal ador'd[10]
The Deity, and divine commands obey'd,
Stood up, and in a flame of zeal severe,
The current of his fury thus oppos'd:

O argument blasphemous, false and proud;
810   Words which no ear ever to hear in heaven
Expected, least of all from thee, ingrate,
In place thyself so high above thy peers.
813   Canst thou with impious obloquy condemn
The just decree of God, pronounc'd and sworn,
815   That to his only Son, by right endu'd
With regal sceptre, every soul in heaven
Shall bend the knee, and in that honour due
Confess him rightful King? Unjust, thou say'st,
Flatly unjust, to bind with laws the free,

---

800 *abuse* Misuse.   **813** *obloquy* Abuse.

And equal over equals to let reign,   820
One over all with unsucceeded power.
Shalt thou give law to God? Shalt thou dispute
With him the points of liberty, who made   823
Thee what thou art, and form'd the powers of heaven   824
Such as he pleas'd and circumscrib'd their being?   825
Yet, by experience taught, we know how good,
And of our good, and of our dignity
How provident he is; how far from thought
To make us less, bent rather to exalt
Our happy state, under one head more near   830
United. But to grant it thee unjust,
That equal over equals monarch reign:
Thyself, though great and glorious, dost thou count,
Or all angelic nature join'd in one,
Equal to him, begotten Son? by whom,   835
As by his Word, the mighty Father made   836
All things, even thee; and all the spirits of heaven   837
By him created in their bright degrees,
Crown'd them with glory, and to their glory nam'd
Thrones, dominations, princedoms, virtues, powers,   840
Essential powers, nor by his reign obscur'd,
But more illustrious made; since he, the head,
One of our number thus reduc'd becomes;   843
His laws our laws; all honour to him done
Returns our own. Cease then this impious rage,   845
And tempt not these; but hasten to appease
Th'incensed Father, and th'incensed Son,
While pardon may be found, in time besought.

823–824 *who made / Thee what thou art* Abdiel points out the perversity of the product revolting against the producer; Satan is the alienated labor of God. 835–837 *by whom . . . even thee* The Son is the power by which the Father created the universe, so it is ridiculous for Satan to consider himself impaired by the Son's exaltation. Satan is the being who cannot refer his identity to any force beyond himself. 843 *One of . . . becomes* The begetting of the Son, properly understood, signifies a union of Creator and creation, not a further separation, as Satan wrongly assumes.

So spake the fervent angel; but his zeal
850 None seconded, as out of season judg'd,
Or singular and rash; whereat rejoic'd
Th'apostate, and more haughty thus replied:
853 That we were form'd then say'st thou? and the work
854 Of secondary hands, by task transferr'd
855 From Father to his Son? Strange point and new;
Doctrine which we would know whence learn'd, who saw
When this creation was? remember'st thou
858 Thy making, while the Maker gave thee being?
We know no time when we were not as now;
860 Know none before us, self-begot, self-rais'd
861 By our own quick'ning power, when fatal course
Had circled his full orb, the birth mature
Of this our native heaven, ethereal sons.
Our puissance is our own; our own right hand
865 Shall teach us highest deeds, by proof to try
Who is our equal: then thou shalt behold
Whether by supplication we intend
Address, and to begirt th'Almighty throne
Beseeching or besieging. This report,
870 These tidings carry to th'anointed King;
And fly, ere evil intercept thy flight.

He said, and, as the sound of waters deep,
Hoarse murmur echoed to his words applause
Through the infinite host; nor less for that
875 The flaming seraph, fearless, though alone
876 Encompass'd round with foes, thus answer'd bold:

---

850 *out of season* Untimely. The theme of the "one just man," who continues to speak the truth when everyone else is in error, was important to Milton. It is prefigured in the person of Abdiel, and reinforced with copious biblical examples in books XI and XII. **853–855** *That we . . . Son* Satan believes himself to be autonomous and self-generating. **858** *being* Satan takes an empiricist approach to knowledge; he refuses to believe in what he has not experienced. **861** *quick'ning* Life-giving. **876** *Encompass'd round with foes* It is hard to escape the parallel with Milton's own position following the Restoration.

O alienate from God, O spirit accurs'd,   877
Forsaken of all good; I see thy fall
Determin'd, and thy hapless crew involv'd   879
In this perfidious fraud, contagion spread   880
Both of thy crime and punishment: henceforth
No more be troubled how to quit the yoke
Of God's Messiah; those indulgent laws
Will not be now vouchsaf'd: other decrees
Against thee are gone forth without recall;   885
That golden sceptre, which thou didst reject,
Is now an iron rod to bruise and break
Thy disobedience. Well thou didst advise;
Yet not for thy advice or threats I fly
These wicked tents devoted, lest the wrath   890
Impendent, raging into sudden flame,   891
Distinguish not: for soon expect to feel
His thunder on thy head, devouring fire.
Then who created thee lamenting learn,
When who can uncreate thee thou shalt know.   895

So spake the seraph Abdiel, faithful found
Among the faithless, faithful only he
Among innumerable false, unmov'd,
Unshaken, unseduc'd, unterrified,
His loyalty he kept, his love, his zeal;   900
Nor number, nor example, with him wrought
To swerve from truth, or change his constant mind,
Though single. From amidst them forth he pass'd,
Long way through hostile scorn, which he sustain'd
Superior, nor of violence fear'd aught;   905
And with retorted scorn his back he turn'd
On those proud towers to swift destruction doom'd.   907

END OF BOOK FIFTH

---

877 *alienate* Other. 879 *Determin'd* Preordained. 891 *Impendent* Hanging over. 907
doom'd Suggests the tower of Babel in Genesis 11:1–9.

BOOK VI

THE ARGUMENT

Raphael continues to relate how Michael and Gabriel were sent forth to battle against Satan and his angels. The first fight described. Satan and his powers retire under night. He calls a council, invents devilish engines,* which in the second day's fight put Michael and his angels to some disorder: but they at length pulling up mountains, overwhelmed both the force and machines of Satan. Yet the tumult not so ending, God on the third day sends Messiah his Son, for whom he had reserved the glory of that victory: He, in the power of his Father,† coming to the place, and causing all his legions to stand still on either side, with his chariot and thunder driving into the midst of his enemies, pursues them, unable to resist, towards the wall of heaven: which opening, they leap down with horror and confusion into the place of punishment prepared for them in the deep. Messiah returns with triumph to his Father.

ALL night the dreadless angel, unpursued,   1
Through heaven's wide champaign held his way; till morn, 2
Wak'd by the circling hours, with rosy hand
Unbarr'd the gates of light. There is a cave   4
Within the mount of God, fast by his throne,   5

---

*Machines.
†The Son is the Father's power in practical effect.

1 *dreadless* Fearless; the reference is to Abdiel.   2 *champaign* Field.   4 *a cave* The image is from Hesiod's *Theogony* 736–757.

Where light and darkness in perpetual round
Lodge and dislodge by turns, which makes through heaven
Grateful vicissitude, like day and night;
Light issues forth, and at the other door
10 Obsequious darkness enters, till her hour
To veil the heaven, though darkness there might well
Seem twilight here: and now went forth the morn,
Such as in highest heaven, array'd in gold
Empyreal; from before her vanish'd night,
15 Shot through with orient beams; when all the plain,
16 Cover'd with thick embattled squadrons bright,
Chariots, and flaming arms, and fiery steeds,
Reflecting blaze on blaze, first met his view.
19 War he perceiv'd, war in procinct, and found
20 Already known, what he for news had thought
To have reported: gladly then he mix'd
Among those friendly powers, who him receiv'd
With joy and acclamations loud, that one,
That of so many myriads fallen, yet one
25 Return'd not lost. On to the sacred hill
They led him high applauded, and present
Before the seat supreme; from whence a voice,
From midst a golden cloud, thus mild was heard:

Servant of God, well done, well hast thou fought
30 The better fight, who single hast maintain'd
Against revolted multitudes the cause
Of truth, in word mightier than they in arms,
And for the testimony of truth hast borne
Universal reproach, far worse to bear
35 Than violence; for this was all thy care
To stand approv'd in sight of God, though worlds
Judg'd thee perverse: the easier conquest now
Remains thee, aided by this host of friends,

---

10 *Obsequious* Following.　16 *embattled* Prepared for battle.　19 *in procinct* Immanent.　35 *care* Concern.

Back to thy foes more glorious to return,
Than scorn'd thou didst depart, and to subdue   40
By force, who reason for their law refuse,
Right reason for their law, and for their king   42
Messiah, who by right of merit reigns.
Go, Michael, of celestial armies prince,   44
And thou, in military prowess next,   45
Gabriel, lead forth to battle these my sons
Invincible; lead forth my armed saints,
By thousands and by millions rang'd for fight,
Equal in number to that godless crew
Rebellious; then with fire and hostile arms   50
Fearless assault, and to the brow of heaven
Pursuing, drive them out from God and bliss
Into their place of punishment, the gulf
Of Tartarus, which ready opens wide   54
His fiery Chaos to receive their fall.   55

So spake the Sovereign voice, and clouds began
To darken all the hill, and smoke to roll
In dusky wreaths, reluctant flames, the sign   58
Of wrath awak'd; nor with less dread the loud
Ethereal trumpet from on high 'gan blow: 60
At which command the powers militant,
That stood for heaven, in mighty quadrate join'd   62
Of union irresistible, mov'd on
In silence their bright legions, to the sound
Of instrumental harmony, that breath'd   65
Heroic ardour to advent'rous deeds,

---

42 *Right reason for their law* For Milton, right reason—in Greek *proairesis*, in Latin *recto ratio*—supersedes all external law.   44 *Michael* In Hebrew, "Who is equal to God." Michael is the warrior angel in Daniel 12 and Revelation 12.   54 *Tartarus* In Virgil's *Aeneid* 6.577–581, the lowest region of Hades.   55 *His fiery Chaos* Chaos belongs to Hell because, while it is a distinct place, it lacks the benign order that God has imposed on the created universe.   58.1 *reluctant* Struggling; 58.2 *sign* God communicates with the angels through signs, just as He does with man.   60 *'gan* Began to.   62 *quadrate* Square.   65 *instrumental* Both "pertaining to musical instruments" and "efficacious."

Under their godlike leaders, in the cause
Of God and his Messiah. On they move
69 Indissolubly firm; nor obvious hill,
70 Nor strait'ning vale, nor wood, nor stream divides
Their perfect ranks; for high above the ground
Their march was, and the passive air upbore
73 Their nimble tread; as when the total kind
74 Of birds, in orderly array, on wing,
75 Came, summon'd over Eden, to receive
76 Their names of thee; so over many a tract
Of heaven they march'd, and many a province wide
78 Tenfold the length of this terrene. At last,
Far in th'horizon, to the north, appear'd
80 From skirt to skirt a fiery region, stretch'd
81 In battailous aspect, and nearer view
Bristled with upright beams innumerable
Of rigid spears, and helmets throng'd, and shields
84 Various, with boastful argument portray'd
85 The banded powers of Satan, hasting on
86 With furious expedition; for they ween'd
That self-same day, by fight, or by surprise,
To win the mount of God, and on his throne
To set the envier of his state, the proud
90 Aspirer; but their thoughts prov'd fond and vain
91 In the midway: though strange to us it seem'd
At first, that angel should with angel war,
93 And in fierce hosting meet, who wont to meet
So oft in festival of joy and love
95 Unanimous, as sons of one great sire,
Hymning th'eternal Father. But the shout
Of battle now began, and rushing sound

---

69 *obvious* In the way.   70 *strait'ning* Confining.   73–76 *as when . . . thee* Raphael contin-
ues to use "accommodated" speech, describing spiritual affairs in terms familiar to Adam's
experience.   78 *terrene* The earth.   81 *battailous* Warlike.   84 *argument* Significance.
86 *ween'd* Hoped.   90 *fond* Foolish.   91 *though strange to us it seem'd* Like human beings,
the angels must work to interpret God's signs.   93 *hosting* Encounter.

Of onset ended soon each milder thought.
High in the midst, exalted as a god,
Th'apostate in his sun-bright chariot sat.   100
Idol of majesty divine,[1] enclos'd
With flaming cherubim and golden shields;
Then lighted from his gorgeous throne, for now
'Twixt host and host but narrow space was left,
A dreadful interval, and front to front   105
Presented stood in terrible array
Of hideous length; before the cloudy van,   107
On the rough edge of battle ere it join'd,
Satan, with vast and haughty strides, advanc'd,
Came tow'ring, arm'd in adamant and gold.   110
Abdiel that sight endur'd not, where he stood
Among the mightiest, bent on highest deeds,
And thus his own undaunted heart explores: 113

O heaven, that such resemblance of the highest   114
Should yet remain, where faith and reality   115
Remain not: wherefore should not strength and might   116
There fail where virtue fails, or weakest prove
Where boldest, though to sight unconquerable?
His puissance, trusting in th'Almighty's aid,   119
I mean to try, whose reason I have tried   120
Unsound and false; nor is it aught but just,
That he who in debate of truth hath won,
Should win in arms, in both disputes alike
Victor; though brutish that contest and foul,
When reason hath to deal with force, yet so   125
Most reason is that reason overcome.   126

---

107 *van* Vanguard.   113 *And thus . . . explores* A translation of Homer's description of Hector's ruminations before facing Achilles in the *Iliad* 22.98.   114–116 *that such resemblance . . . not* Abdiel is distressed by the realization that appearances do not conform to essences.   119 *puissance* Power.   126 *Most reason . . . overcome* Milton emphasizes that reason is more powerful than brute force.

So pondering, and from his arm'd peers
Forth stepping opposite, half way he met
129   His daring foe, at this prevention more
130   Incens'd, and thus securely him defied:

131   Proud, art thou met? thy hope was to have reach'd
The height of thy aspiring unoppos'd,
The throne of God unguarded, and his side
Abandon'd at the terror of thy power
135   Or potent tongue: fool, not to think how vain
136   Against th'Omnipotent to rise in arms;
Who out of smallest things could without end
Have rais'd incessant armies to defeat
Thy folly; or with solitary hand,
140   Reaching beyond all limit, at one blow
141   Unaided could have finish'd thee, and whelm'd
Thy legions under darkness. But thou seest
All are not of thy train; there be who faith
Prefer, and piety to God, though then
145   To thee not visible, when I alone
146   Seem'd in thy world erroneous to dissent
147   From all; my sect thou seest; now learn too late
How few sometimes may know, when thousands err.

149   Whom the grand foe, with scornful eye askance,
150   Thus answer'd: Ill for thee, but in wish'd hour
Of my revenge, first sought for, thou return'st
152   From flight, seditious angel, to receive

---

129 *prevention* Confrontation.   130 *securely* Confidently.   131 *Proud* Proud one.   136 *Against . . . arms* A reminder that, despite Raphael's extended metaphor comparing the conflict in heaven to an earthly battle, Satan's enterprise is logically impossible and absurd. 141 *whelm'd* Overwhelmed.   145 *To thee not visible* Satan's vision has been impaired by his renunciation of faith in God.   146 *Seem'd in thy world* Satan now inhabits his own "world," separated from God's creation.   147 *my sect* The word "sect" was frequently used to denigrate Puritan "sectaries."   149 *askance* Both "sidelong" and "hostile."   152 *seditious* In Satan's distorted perception, it is Abdiel who is the rebel. The line implies an analogy with Charles I's depiction of the parliamentarians as seditious; but Milton regarded the king as the true rebel, since he was in revolt against God.

Thy merited reward, the first assay
Of this right hand provok'd, since first that tongue,
Inspir'd with contradiction, durst oppose   155
A third part of the gods, in synod met   156
Their deities to assert, who while they feel
Vigour divine within them, can allow
Omnipotence to none. But well thou com'st
Before thy fellows, ambitious to win   160
From me some plume, that thy success may show   161
Destruction to the rest: this pause between,
Unanswer'd lest thou boast, to let thee know;   163
At first I thought that liberty and heaven
To heavenly souls had been all one; but now   165
I see that most through sloth had rather serve,
Minist'ring spirits, train'd up in feast and song;
Such hast thou arm'd, the minstrelsy of heaven,
Servility with freedom to contend,
As both their deeds compared this day shall prove.   170

To whom in brief thus Abdiel stern replied:
Apostate, still thou err'st, nor end wilt find
Of erring, from the path of truth remote:
Unjustly thou deprav'st it with the name   174
Of servitude, to serve whom God ordains,   175
Or Nature; God and Nature bid the same,   176
When he who rules worthiest, and excels
Them whom he governs. This is servitude,   178
To serve th'unwise, or him who hath rebell'd   179
Against his worthier, as thine now serve thee,   180
Thyself not free, but to thyself enthrall'd;²

---

155 *contradiction* Satan does not refer to logical contradiction, but to Abdiel's stubborn de-
termination to contradict him.   156 *synod* Ecclesiastical conference.   161 *plume* Badge of
honor.   163 *Unanswer'd . . . boast* Lest you boast that your protests went unanswered.
174–176 *Unjustly . . . same* Milton remained constant in his conviction that the most vir-
tuous were naturally entitled to dominion.   178–180 *This is servitude . . . thee* Any other
form of rule than that of the most virtuous constitutes irrational slavery.

182 Yet lewdly dar'st our minist'ring upbraid.
183 Reign thou in hell, thy kingdom; let me serve
     In heaven God ever bless'd and his divine
185 Behests obey, worthiest to be obey'd;
     Yet chains in hell, not realms expect; meanwhile
187 From me return'd, as erst thou saidst, from flight,
     This greeting on thy impious crest receive.

     So saying, a noble stroke he lifted high,
190 Which hung not, but so swift with tempest fell
     On the proud crest of Satan, that no sight,
     Nor motion of swift thought, less could his shield,
     Such ruin intercept: ten paces huge
     He back recoil'd: the tenth on bended knee
195 His massy spear upstay'd; as if on earth
     Winds under ground, or waters forcing way,
     Sidelong had push'd a mountain from his seat,
     Half sunk with all his pines. Amazement seiz'd
199 The rebel thrones, but greater rage to see
200 Thus foil'd their mightiest; ours joy fill'd, and shout,
     Presage of victory, and fierce desire
     Of battle: whereat Michael bid sound
     Th'archangel trumpet: through the vast of heaven
     It sounded, and the faithful armies rung
205 Hosannah to th'Highest; nor stood at gaze
     The adverse legions, nor less hideous join'd
207 The horrid shock. Now storming fury rose,
     And clamour such as heard in heaven till now
     Was never; arms on armour clashing bray'd
210 Horrible discord, and the madding wheels
     Of brazen chariots rag'd; dire was the noise
     Of conflict; over head the dismal hiss
     Of fiery darts in flaming vollies flew,

---

182 *lewdly* Ignorantly. 183 *Reign . . . serve* Compare 1.263. 187 *erst* Before. 199 *rebel thrones* An oxymoron, again suggesting Milton's opinion that Charles I was the true rebel. 200 *ours* A reminder that we hear the story from one of the participants. 207 *shock* Clash.

And flying, vaulted either host with fire.   214
So under fiery cope together rush'd   215
Both battles main, with ruinous assault
And inextinguishable rage; all heaven
Resounded, and had earth been then, all earth
Had to her centre shook. What wonder? when
Millions of fierce encount'ring angels fought   220
On either side, the least of whom could wield
These elements, and arm him with the force
Of all their regions: how much more of power
Army against army numberless to raise
Dreadful combustion warring, and disturb,   225
Though not destroy, their happy native seat:
Had not th'eternal King omnipotent
From his strong hold of heaven high overrul'd   228
And limited their might; though number'd such
As each divided legion might have seem'd   230
A numerous host, in strength each arm'd hand
A legion, led in fight, yet leader seem'd,
Each warrior single as in chief, expert
When to advance, or stand, or turn the sway
Of battle, open when, and when to close   235
The ridges of grim war: no thought of flight,
None of retreat, no unbecoming deed
That argued fear; each on himself relied,   238
As only in his arm the moment lay
Of victory. Deeds of eternal fame   240
Were done, but infinite; for wide was spread
That war and various, sometimes on firm ground
A standing fight, then, soaring on main wing,
Tormented all the air; all air seem'd then

---

214 *vaulted* Covered.   **225** *combustion* Explosion, conflagration.   **228** *overrul'd* Ruled over. Raphael assures Adam that the "battle" is orchestrated by God.   **230** *might have seem'd* A further reminder that the angel speaks in similitudes.   **238** *each on himself relied* In his political writings, Milton suggested that victory in the internal battle against sin was a necessary prerequisite for success in external affairs.

245   Conflicting fire. Long time in even scale
     The battle hung; till Satan, who that day
247   Prodigious power had shown, and met in arms
     No equal, ranging through the dire attack
     Of fighting seraphim confus'd, at length
250   Saw where the sword of Michael smote and fell'd
251   Squadrons at once: with huge two-handed sway,
     Brandish'd aloft, the horrid edge came down
     Wide wasting; such destruction to withstand
     He hasted, and oppos'd the rocky orb
255   Of tenfold adamant, his ample shield,
     A vast circumference. At his approach
     The great archangel from his warlike toil
258   Surceas'd, and glad, as hoping here to end
259   Intestine war in heaven, th'arch-foe subdu'd,
260   Or captive dragg'd in chains, with hostile frown,
     And visage all inflam'd, first thus began:

     Author of evil, unknown till thy revolt,
     Unnam'd in heaven, now plenteous, as thou seest,
     These acts of hateful strife, hateful to all,
265   Though heaviest by just measure on thyself
     And thy adherents: how hast thou disturb'd
     Heaven's blessed peace, and into nature brought
     Misery, uncreated till the crime
     Of thy rebellion? how hast thou instill'd
270   Thy malice into thousands, once upright
     And faithful, now prov'd false? But think not here
     To trouble holy rest; heaven casts thee out
     From all her confines. Heaven the seat of bliss,
     Brooks not the works of violence and war:

---

247 *Prodigious* Enormous, but also monstrous.   251 *two-handed* Compare the prophecy in "Lycidas" of "the ruin of our corrupted clergy": "But that two-handed engine at the door, / Stands ready to smite once, and smite no more" (ll. 130–131).   255 *shield* The implied comparison is with the famous shield of Achilles, hero of Homer's *Iliad*; Milton associates Satan with vain pagan pride in martial valor.   258 *Surceas'd* Ceased.   259 *Intestine war* Civil war.

Hence then, and evil go with thee along,   275
Thy offspring, to the place of evil, hell,
Thou and thy wicked crew; there mingle broils,   277
Ere this avenging sword begin thy doom,
Or some more sudden vengeance, wing'd from God,
Precipitate thee with augmented pain.   280

So spake the prince of angels; to whom thus
The adversary: Nor think thou with wind   282
Of airy threats to awe whom yet with deeds
Thou canst not. Hast thou turn'd the least of these
To flight, or if to fall, but that they rise   285
Unvanquish'd, easier to transact with me
That thou shouldst hope, imperious, and with threats
To chase me hence? err not that so shall end
The strife which thou call'st evil, but we style   289
The strife of glory; which we mean to win,   290
Or turn this heaven itself into the hell
Thou fablest,³ here however to dwell free,
If not to reign: meanwhile thy utmost force,
And join him nam'd Almighty to thy aid,
I fly not, but have sought thee far and nigh.   295

They ended parle, and both address'd for fight   296
Unspeakable; for who, though with the tongue   297
Of angels, can relate, or to what things
Liken on earth conspicuous, that may lift
Human imagination to such height   300
Of godlike power?⁴ for likest gods they seem'd,
Stood they or mov'd, in stature, motion, arms,
Fit to decide the empire of great heaven.
Now wav'd their fiery swords, and in the air

---

277 *mingle broils* Stir up trouble.   282 *The adversary* Flannagan points out that Satan "now has not just one name but many generic titles, all standing for the being who defines himself as alien from God" (p. 515).   289 *style* Call.   296 *parle* Parley; discussion of disputed points.   297 *Unspeakable* "Hideous," but also "inexpressible."

305 Made horrid circles; two broad suns their shields
    Blaz'd opposite, while expectation stood
    In horror; from each hand with speed retir'd,
308 Where erst was thickest fight, th'angelic throng,
    And left large fields unsafe within the wind
310 Of such commotion: such as, to set forth
311 Great things by small, if Nature's concord broke
    Among the constellations war were sprung,
    Two planets rushing from aspect malign
    Of fiercest opposition in mid-sky
315 Should combat, and their jarring spheres confound,[5]
    Together both with next to Almighty arm
    Uplifted eminent, one stroke they aim'd
    That might determine, and not need repeat,
319 As not of power at once; nor odds appear'd
320 In might or swift prevention: but the sword
    Of Michael, from the armoury of God,
322 Was given him temper'd so, that neither keen
323 Nor solid might resist that edge: it met
324 The sword of Satan with steep force to smite
325 Descending, and in half cut sheer; nor stay'd,
326 But with swift wheel reverse, deep ent'ring shar'd
    All his right side: then Satan first knew pain,
    And writh'd him to and fro convolv'd; so sore
329 The griding sword with discontinuous wound
330 Pass'd through him; but th'ethereal substance clos'd
    Not long divisible; and from the gash
    A stream of nect'rous humour issuing flow'd
333 Sanguine, such as celestial spirits may bleed,
334 And all his armour stain'd erewhile so bright.
335 Forthwith on all sides to his aid was run

---

308 *erst* Before.   **310–311** *to set forth / Great things by small* Common Homeric qualification, used here as another reminder that Raphael's story is accommodated to the human imagination.   **319** *odds* Difference.   **322–323** *neither keen / Nor solid* Neither sword nor shield.   **324** *steep* Both "strong" and "vertical."   **326** *shar'd* Sheared.   **329.1** *griding* Sawing; **329.2** *discontinuous* Gaping.   **333** *Sanguine* Blood-like.   **334** *erewhile* Before.

By angels many and strong, who interpos'd
Defence, while others bore him on their shields
Back to his chariot, where it stood retir'd
From off the files of war; there they him laid
Gnashing for anguish, and despite, and shame,　　　　340
To find himself not matchless, and his pride　　　　341
Humbled by such rebuke, so far beneath
His confidence to equal God in power.　　　　343
Yet soon he heal'd; for spirits that live throughout
Vital in every part, not as frail man　　　　345
In entrails, heart or head, liver or reins,　　　　346
Cannot but by annihilating die;
Nor in their liquid texture mortal wound
Receive, no more than can the fluid air:
All heart they live, all head, all eye, all ear,　　　　350
All intellect, all sense; and as they please,　　　　351
They limb themselves, and colour, shape, or size,　　　　352
Assume, as likes them best, condense or rare.　　　　353

Meanwhile in other parts like deeds deserv'd
Memorial, where the might of Gabriel fought,　　　　355
And with fierce ensigns pierc'd the deep array
Of Moloch, furious king; who him defied,
And at his chariot-wheels to drag him bound
Threaten'd, nor from the Holy One of heaven
Refrain'd his tongue blasphemous: but anon,　　　　360
Down cloven to the waist, with shatter'd arms
And uncouth pain, fled bellowing. On each wing
Uriel and Raphael his vaunting foe,　　　　363
Though huge, and in a rock of diamond arm'd,

---

340 *despite* Spite, resentment.　341 *not matchless* Satan's anguish springs from the realization that he is not unique.　343 *to equal God* A reminder of Satan's essential purpose.　345 *Vital in every part* The power of life lies in each part of the angels' essence, so they would have to be completely obliterated in order to die.　346 *reins* Kidneys.　351–353 *and as they please . . . rare* Both good and evil angels are able to assume material form by condensing air so it coalesces into solid matter.　360 *anon* Suddenly.　363 *vaunting* Boasting.

365 Vanquish'd Adramelech and Asmadai,
   Two potent thrones, that to be less than gods
367 Disdain'd, but meaner thoughts learn'd in their flight,
   Mangled with ghastly wounds through plate and mail,
   Nor stood unmindful Abdiel to annoy
370 The atheist crew, but with redoubled blow
371 Ariel and Arioch, and the violence
372 Of Ramiel, scorch'd and blasted, overthrew.
   I might relate of thousands, and their names
374 Eternize here on earth; but those elect
375 Angels, contented with their fame in heaven,
376 Seek not the praise of men: the other sort,
   In might though wondrous, and in acts of war,
   Nor of renown less eager, yet by doom
   Cancel'd from heaven and sacred memory,
380 Nameless in dark oblivion let them dwell.
   For strength, from truth divided and from just,
382 Illaudable, nought merits but dispraise
383 And ignominy, yet to glory aspires
   Vain glorious, and through infamy seeks fame:
385 Therefore eternal silence be their doom.

   And now their mightiest quell'd, the battle swerv'd,
   With many an inroad gor'd: deformed rout
   Enter'd, and foul disorder; all the ground
   With shiver'd armour strown, and on a heap
390 Chariot and charioteer lay overturn'd,

365.1 *Adramelech* Literally, "mighty king"; an Assyrian sun-god; **365.2** *Asmadai* Asmodeus, the demon opponent of Raphael in the apocryphal biblical book of Tobit. **367** *meaner* More humble. **371.1** *Ariel* In Hebrew, "lion of God," but also the name for an evil spirit, and the agent of Prospero's magic in Shakespeare's *The Tempest* (1611); **371.2** *Arioch* In Hebrew, "lion-like." **372** *Ramiel* In Hebrew, "thunder of God"; refers to a fallen angel in the apocryphal biblical book of Enoch. **374.1** *Eternize* Make eternal; **374.2** *elect* Chosen. **375–376** *contented . . . men* Compare "Lycidas": "Fame is no plant that grows on mortal soil" (l. 78). **376** *the other sort* The fallen angels. **382** *Illaudable* Not worthy of praise, possibly with a pun on Archbishop William Laud, the leading prelate of Milton's time. **383** *ignominy* Namelessness.

And fiery foaming steeds; what stood, recoil'd,
O'erwearied, through the faint Satanic host
Defensive scarce, or with pale fear surpris'd, 393
Then first with fear surpris'd and sense of pain,
Fled ignominious, to such evil brought 395
By sin of disobedience, till that hour
Not liable to fear, or flight, or pain.
Far otherwise, th'inviolable saints
In cubic phalanx firm advanc'd entire,
Invulnerable, impenetrably arm'd; 400
Such high advantages their innocence
Gave them above their foes, not to have sinn'd,
Not to have disobey'd; in fight they stood
Unwearied, unobnoxious to be pain'd 404
By wound, tho' from their place by violence mov'd.[6] 405

Now night her course began, and over heaven
Inducing darkness, grateful truce impos'd,
And silence on the odious din of war:
Under her cloudy covert both retir'd,
Victor and vanquish'd. On the foughten field 410
Michael and his angels prevalent
Encamping, plac'd in guard their watches round,
Cherubic waving fires: on th'other part
Satan with his rebellious disappear'd,
Far in the dark dislodg'd; and, void of rest, 415
His potentates to council call'd by night;
And in the midst thus undismay'd began:

O now in danger tried, now known in arms
Not to be overpower'd, companions dear, 419
Found worthy not of liberty alone, 420
Too mean pretence, but, what we more affect,

---

393 *Defensive scarce* Scarcely in defensive formation; completely disordered.   404 *unobnoxious* Impossible to harm.   410 *foughten field* Battlefield.   419 *companions dear* A financial metaphor; they will pay dearly for being Satan's companions. Compare 5.673.

Honour, dominion, glory, and renown;
Who have sustain'd one day in doubtful fight,
(And if one day, why not eternal days?)
425 What Heaven's Lord had powerfullest to send
426 Against us from about his throne, and judg'd
427 Sufficient to subdue us to his will,
428 But proves not so: then fallible, it seems,
429 Of future we may deem him, though till now
430 Omniscient thought. True is, less firmly arm'd,
Some disadvantage we endur'd and pain,
Till now not known, but known, as soon contemn'd;
Since now we find this our empyreal form
Incapable of mortal injury,
435 Imperishable, and, though pierc'd with wounds,
436 Soon closing, and by native vigour heal'd.
Of evil then so small, as easy think
438 The remedy; perhaps more valid arms,
439 Weapons more violent, when next we meet,
440 May serve to better us, and worse our foes,
Or equal what between us made the odds,
442 In nature none: if other hidden cause
Left them superior, while we can preserve
Unhurt our minds and understanding sound,
445 Due search and consultation will disclose.

He sat; and in th'assembly next upstood
447 Nisroch, of principalities the prime;
As one he stood escap'd from cruel fight,
449 Sore toil'd, his riven arms to havoc hewn,

426–430 *and judg'd . . . thought* Satan holds to this misconception in book I. He repeats his mistake of literalism, assuming that he is participating in a literal battle he could in theory win by superior physical force; this is the mode of interpretation against which Raphael has just warned Adam (6.297–301). 436 *by native vigour* Satan perceives only the material cause of his recovery, which is in the "native" qualities of his essence; he ignores the final cause, which is God's Providence. 438 *valid* Powerful. 439 *Weapons more violent* Satan proposes an arms race. 442 *hidden cause* The final cause, or *telos*, is invisible to Satan. 447 *Nisroch* Assyrian god. 449 *his riven arms to havoc hewn* His torn arms hacked to pieces.

And cloudy in aspect thus answ'ring spake: 450
Deliverer from new Lords, leader to free
Enjoyment of our right as gods; yet hard
For gods, and too unequal work we find,
Against unequal arms to fight in pain,
Against unpain'd, impassive; from which evil   455
Ruin must needs ensue; for what avails
Valour or strength, though matchless, quell'd with pain
Which all subdues, and makes remiss the hands
Of mightiest? Sense of pleasure we may well
Spare out of life perhaps, and not repine,   460
But live content, which is the calmest life
But pain is perfect misery, the worst
Of evils, and excessive, overturns
All patience. He who, therefore, can invent   464
With what more forcible we may offend   465
Our yet unwounded enemies, or arm   466
Ourselves with like defence, to me deserves
No less than for deliverance what we owe.

Whereto with look compos'd Satan replied:
Not uninvented that, which thou aright   470
Believ'st so main to our success, I bring.   471
Which of us who beholds the bright surface
Of this ethereous mould whereon we stand,   473
This continent of spacious heaven, adorn'd
With plant, fruit, flower ambrosial, gems, and gold;   475
Whose eye so superficially surveys   476
These things, as not to mind from whence they grow   477
Deep under ground, materials dark and crude,   478

464–466 *He who . . . enemies* Nisroch believes that the difference between the armies is one of degree, not one of kind; although the unfallen angels are "unwounded," Nisroch does not conclude that they cannot be wounded. **471** *main* Important. **473.1** *ethereous* Made of ether; **473.2** *mould* Material. **475** *plant . . . gold* Note the glib elision between living and dead matter. **476–478** *Whose eye . . . crude* It is Satan himself who is being superficial, since he once again sees only the material cause of natural phenomena. He makes the mistake that George Herbert, in his religious poem "The Pulley" (1633), calls to "rest / In Nature, not the God of Nature."

479 Of spiritous and fiery spume, till touch'd
480 With heaven's ray, and temper'd, they shoot forth
481 So beauteous, opening to the ambient light?
482 These in their dark nativity the deep
    Shall yield us pregnant with infernal flame;
484 Which into hollow engines long and round
485 Thick-ramm'd, at th'other bore with touch of fire
    Dilated and infuriate, shall send forth
    From far, with thund'ring noise, among our foes
    Such implements of mischief, as shall dash
    To pieces, and o'erwhelm whatever stands
490 Adverse, that they shall fear we have disarm'd
    The Thund'rer of his only dreaded bolt.
    Nor long shall be our labour; yet ere dawn
493 Effect shall end our wish. Meanwhile revive;
    Abandon fear; to strength and counsel join'd
495 Think nothing hard, much less to be despair'd.

    He ended, and his words their drooping cheer
    Enlighten'd, and their languish'd hope reviv'd.
    Th'invention all admir'd, and each how he
    To be th'inventor miss'd; so easy it seem'd
500 Once found, which yet unfound, most would have thought
501 Impossible: yet haply of thy race,
502 In future days, if malice should abound,
503 Some one, intent on mischief, or inspir'd
504 With devilish machination, might devise
505 Like instrument to plague the sons of men
506 For sin, on war and mutual slaughter bent.
    Forthwith from council to the work they flew;
    None arguing stood; innumerable hands

---

479 *spume* Foam, brine.　481 *ambient* Atmospheric.　482 *nativity* Birth.　484 *engines* Machines; Satan will describe his inventions of gunpowder and cannons.　485 *bore* Hole.
493 *Effect shall end our wish* Satan wishes only for materially efficacious ends; his reason is purely instrumental.　501–506 *yet haply . . . bent* Raphael suggests to Adam and Eve that his narrative is simultaneously history and prophecy.

Were ready; in a moment up they turn'd
Wide the celestial soil, and saw beneath   510
Th'originals of nature in their crude   511
Conception; sulphurous and nitrous foam
They found, they mingled, and with subtle art,
Concocted and adjusted, they reduc'd   514
To blackest grain, and into store convey'd: 515
Part hidden veins digged up (nor hath this earth
Entrails unlike) of mineral and stone,
Whereof to found their engines and their balls
Of missive ruin; part incentive reed   519
Provide, pernicious with one touch to fire.   520
So all ere day-spring, under conscious night,   521
Secret they finish'd and in order set,
With silent circumspection unespied.   523

Now when fair morn orient in heaven appear'd,
Up rose the victor angels, and to arms   525
The matin trumpet sung: in arms they stood   526
Of golden panoply, refulgent host,   527
Soon banded; others from the dawning hills
Look'd round, and scouts each coast light-arm'd scour
Each quarter, to descry the distant foe,   530
Where lodg'd, or whither fled, or if for fight,
In motion or in halt: him soon they met
Under spread ensigns moving nigh, in slow
But firm battalion; back with speediest sail
Zophiel, of cherubim the swiftest wing,   535
Came flying, and in mid air aloud thus cried:

511.1 *Th'originals of nature* The original matter of which the physical universe is constructed; 511.2 *crude* Raw.   514.1 *adjusted* Reduced to dust, an alchemical term; 514.2 *reduc'd* In alchemy, such terms had ethical, as well as chemical, implications.   519.1 *missive* Missile; 519.2 *incentive* Kindling.   520 *pernicious* Swift.   521 *day-spring* Dawn.   523 *With silent circumspection* Furtively looking around them.   526 *matin* Morning.   527.1 *panoply* Full armor; 527.2 *refulgent* Shining.   535 *Zophiel* In Hebrew, "spy of God."

Arm warriors, arm for fight; the foe at hand,
Whom fled we thought, will save us long pursuit
This day; fear not his flight; so thick a cloud
540   He comes, and settled in his face I see
541   Sad resolution and secure; let each
His adamantine coat gird well, and each
543   Fit well his helm, gripe fast his orbed shield,
Borne even or high; for this day will pour down,
545   If I conjecture aught, no drizzling shower,
But rattling storm of arrows barb'd with fire.

So warn'd he them, aware themselves, and soon
548   In order, quit of all impediment;
549   Instant without disturb they took alarm,
550   And onward move embattled: when behold
Not distant far with heavy pace the foe
Approaching, gross and huge, in hollow cube
553   Training his devilish enginry, impal'd
On every side with shadowing squadrons deep,
555   To hide the fraud. At interview both stood
Awhile; but suddenly at head appear'd
Satan, and thus was heard commanding loud:

Vanguard, to right and left the front unfold;
That all may see who hate us, how we seek
560   Peace and composure, and with open breast
Stand ready to receive them, if they like
562   Our overture, and turn not back perverse:
But that I doubt; however, witness heaven,
Heaven witness thou anon, while we discharge
565   Freely our part; ye who appointed stand,

---

541 *Sad* Serious.   543 *gripe* Grip.   548 *quit* Rid.   549 *Instant without disturb* Immediately and without becoming disturbed.   550 *embattled* In battle array.   553.1 *Training* Trailing; 553.2 *impal'd* Surrounded by pikes.   555 *At interview* Looking each other in the eye.   560 *composure* Settlement.   562 *overture* Opening, with a musical pun; Satan begins using words with ironic double meanings.

Do as you have in charge, and briefly touch
What we propound, and loud that all may hear.   567

So scoffing in ambiguous words,[7] he scarce
Had ended, when to right and left the front
Divided, and to either flank retir'd;   570
Which to our eyes discover'd, new and strange,
A triple mounted row of pillars laid
On wheels (for like to pillars most they seem'd
Or hollow'd bodies made of oak or fir,
With branches lopt, in wood or mountain fell'd)   575
Brass, iron, stony mould, had not their mouths   576
With hideous orifice gap'd on us wide,
Portending hollow truce: at each behind
A seraph stood, and in his hand a reed
Stood waving tipt with fire; while we suspense   580
Collected stood within our thoughts amus'd;   581
Not long, for sudden all at once their reeds
Put forth, and to a narrow vent applied   583
With nicest touch. Immediate in a flame,   584
But soon obscur'd with smoke, all heaven appear'd,   585
From those deep-throated engines belch'd, whose roar
Embowel'd with outrageous noise the air,   587
And all her entrails tore, disgorging foul
Their devilish glut, chain'd thunderbolts and hail   589
Of iron globes; which on the victor host   590
Levell'd, with such impetuous fury smote,   591
That whom they hit, none on their feet might stand,
Though standing else as rocks, but down they fell
By thousands, angel on archangel roll'd;
The sooner for their arms; unarm'd they might   595
Have easily as spirits evaded swift
By quick contraction or remove; but now
Foul dissipation follow'd and forc'd rout;   598

---

567 *propound* Put forward.   576 *mould* Material.   581 *amus'd* Puzzled.   583 *vent* Hole.
584 *nicest* Most skillful.   587 *Embowel'd* Packed.   589 *glut* Load.   591 *Levell'd* Aimed.
598 *dissipation* Dispersal, retreat.

599 Nor serv'd it to relax their serried files.
600 What should they do? if on they rush'd, repulse
Repeated, and indecent overthrow
Doubled, would render them yet more despis'd,
And to their foes a laughter; for in view
Stood rank'd of seraphim another row,
605 In posture to displode their second tire
Of thunder: back defeated to return
They worse abhorr'd. Satan beheld their plight.
And to his mates thus in derision call'd:

O friends, why come not on these victors proud?
610 Erewhile they fierce were coming; and when we
611 To entertain them fair with open front
And breast, (what could we more?) propounded terms
613 Of composition, straight they chang'd their minds,
614 Flew off, and into strange vagaries fell,
615 As they would dance; yet for a dance they seem'd
Somewhat extravagant and wild, perhaps
For joy of offer'd peace: but I suppose,
If our proposals once again were heard,
We should compel them to a quick result.

620 To whom thus Belial in like gamesome mood:
621 Leader, the terms we sent were terms of weight,
622 Of hard contents, and full of force urg'd home,
Such as we might perceive amus'd them all,
And stumbled many; who receives them right,
625 Had need from head to foot well understand;
Not understood, this gift they have besides,
They show us when our foes walk not upright.

---

599 *serried* Ranked.   605 *In posture . . . tire* Ready to fire their second volley.   611 *To entertain . . . front* Satan puns on "front," meaning both "front line" and "face"; his conceit portrays his army as a seductress.   613 *composition* Truce.   614 *vagaries* Random movements.   620 *gamesome* Playful.   621–622 *the terms . . . home* Belial uses rhetorical terms to describe the battle, indicating the devils' commitment to victory rather than to truth.

So they among themselves in pleasant vein
Stood scoffing, heighten'd in their thoughts beyond
All doubt of victory; eternal might   630
To match with their inventions they presum'd   631
So easy, and of his thunder made a scorn,
And all his host derided, while they stood
Awhile in trouble: but they stood not long;
Rage prompted them at length, and found them arms   635
Against such hellish mischief fit to oppose.
Forthwith (behold the excellence, the power,
Which God hath in his mighty angels plac'd)
Their arms away they threw, and to the hills
(For earth hath this variety from heaven   640
Of pleasure situate in hill and dale)
Light as the lightning glimpse they ran, they flew;
From their foundations loos'ning to and fro
They pluck'd the seated hills with all their load,   644
Rocks, waters, woods, and by the shaggy tops   645
Uplifting bore them in their hands. Amaze,   646
Be sure, and terror seiz'd the rebel host,
When coming towards them so dread they saw
The bottom of the mountains upward turn'd;
Till on those cursed engines triple-row   650
They saw them whelm'd, and all their confidence   651
Under the weight of mountains buried deep;
Themselves invaded next, and on their heads
Main promontories flung, which in the air   654
Came shadowing, and oppress'd whole legions arm'd;   655
Their armour help'd their harm, crush'd in and bruis'd
Into their substance pent, which wrought them pain   657

630–631 *eternal might . . . presum'd* The devils assume that the works of their hands are more powerful than those of the Creator.   644–645 *pluck'd . . . tops* A tactic pioneered by the forces of Zeus fighting against the Titans in Hesiod's *Theogony* 713–720. Whereas the fallen angels invent their own weapons, the unfallen use natural materials.   645 *shaggy* Wooded; compare "Lycidas," "the shaggy top of Mona high" (l. 54).   646 *Amaze* Confusion.   651 *whelm'd* Buried.   654 *Main* Entire.   657 *pent* Confined.

658   Implacable, and many a dolorous groan,

659   Long struggling underneath, ere they could wind

660   Out of such prison, though spirits of purest light,

Purest at first, now gross by sinning grown.

The rest, in imitation, to like arms

Betook them, and the neighb'ring hills uptore;

So hills amid the air encounter'd hills,

665   Hurl'd to and fro with jaculation dire,

That under ground they fought in dismal shade;

Infernal noise; war seem'd a civil game

To this uproar; horrid confusion heap'd

Upon confusion rose. And now all heaven

670   Had gone to wrack, with ruin overspread,

Had not th'almighty Father, where he sits

Shrin'd in his sanctuary of heaven secure,

673   Consulting on the sum of things, foreseen

674   This tumult, and permitted all, advis'd;

675   That his great purpose he might so fulfil,

676   To honour his anointed Son aveng'd

677   Upon his enemies, and to declare

678   All power on him transferr'd; whence to his Son

679   Th'assessor of his throne, he thus began:

680   Effulgence of my glory, Son belov'd,

681   Son, in whose face invisible is beheld,

682   Visibly, what by deity I am,

And in whose hand what by decree I do,

Second Omnipotence; two days are past,

685   Two days, as we compute the days of heaven,

Since Michael and his powers went forth to tame

These disobedient: sore hath been their fight,

---

658 *Implacable* Inconsolable, irremediable.   659 *wind* Wriggle.   665 *jaculation* Hurling. 673 *Consulting on the sum of things* God considers things from the perspective of the total- ity.   673–675 *foreseen . . . fulfil* The rebellion and war are necessary elements in God's providential plan.   676–678 *To honour . . . transferr'd* God allows the battle to continue in order to manifest the power of the Son.   679 *assessor* One sitting beside.   680 *Effulgence* Beam, ray.   681–682 *Son . . . I am* The Son reveals the nature of the Father.

As likeliest was, when two such foes met arm'd;
For to themselves I left them, and thou know'st,
Equal in their creation they were form'd,   690
Save what sin hath impair'd, which yet hath wrought
Insensibly, for I suspend their doom;   692
Whence in perpetual fight they needs must last
Endless, and no solution will be found.
War wearied hath perform'd what war can do,   695
And to disorder'd rage let loose the reins,
With mountains as with weapons arm'd, which makes
Wild work in heaven, and dangerous to the main.   698
Two days are therefore pass'd, the third is thine;
For thee I have ordain'd it, and thus far   700
Have suffer'd, that the glory may be thine   701
Of ending this great war, since none but Thou
Can end it. Into thee such virtue and grace
Immense I have transfus'd, that all may know
In heaven and hell thy power above compare;   705
And this perverse commotion govern'd thus,
To manifest thee worthiest to be Heir
Of all things, to be Heir, and to be King   708
By sacred unction, thy deserv'd right.
Go then, thou Mightiest, in thy Father's might,   710
Ascend my chariot, guide the rapid wheels
That shake heaven's basis, bring forth all my war,   712
My bow and thunder, my almighty arms
Gird on, and sword upon thy puissant thigh;   714
Pursue these sons of darkness, drive them out   715
From all heaven's bounds into the utter deep:
There let them learn, as likes them, to despise   717
God, and Messiah his anointed King.

---

692 *Insensibly* Imperceptibly.   698 *main* Totality.   701 *suffer'd* Permitted.   708 *to be Heir, and to be King* The Son will succeed the Father, as the New Testament supersedes the Old. 712 *basis* Foundation.   714 *puissant* Potent.   717 *as likes them* As they like.

He said, and on his Son with rays direct
720 Shone full; he all his Father full express'd
721 Ineffably into his face receiv'd;
And thus the filial Godhead answ'ring spake:

O Father, O supreme of heav'nly thrones,
First, highest, holiest, best; thou always seek'st
725 To glorify thy Son, I always Thee,
As is most just; this I my glory account,
My exaltation, and my whole delight,
That thou in me, well pleas'd, declar'st thy will
Fulfill'd, which to fulfil is all my bliss.
730 Sceptre and power, thy giving, I assume,
731 And gladlier shall resign, when in the end
732 Thou shalt be all in all, and I in thee
733 For ever, and in me all whom thou lov'st:
But whom thou hatest I hate, and can put on
735 Thy terrors, as I put thy mildness on,
736 Image of thee in all things; and shall soon,
Arm'd with thy might, rid heaven of these rebell'd,
To their prepar'd ill mansion driven down,
739 To chains of darkness, and th'undying worm,
740 That from thy just obedience could revolt,
Whom to obey is happiness entire.
742 Then shall thy saints unmix'd, and from th'impure
Far separate, circling thy holy mount,
Unfeigned hallelujahs to thee sing,
745 Hymns of high praise, and I among them chief.

---

720 *he all his Father full express'd* The Son is the Word of the Father.   **721** *Ineffably* Inexpressibly.   **730** *thy giving* As opposed to Satan, who tried to take God's scepter by force. **731–733** *And gladlier . . . lov'st* At the end of time, the Son will unite with the Father; compare 1 Corinthians 15:24–28.   **736** *Image of thee in all things* The Son consists in the ability to perceive the signs of divine Providence in creation.   **739** *undying worm* See Mark 9:48: "Where their worm dieth not, and the fire is not quenched."   **742** *unmix'd* Separated from their polluting elements.

So said, he, o'er his sceptre bowing, rose
From the right hand of glory where he sat;
And the third sacred morn began to shine,   748
Dawning through heaven: forth rush'd with whirlwind round   749
The chariot of paternal Deity,   750
Flashing thick flames, wheel within wheel undrawn,   751
Itself instinct with spirit, but convey'd   752
By four cherubic shapes; four faces each   753
Had wondrous; as with stars their bodies all
And wings were set with eyes, with eyes the wheels   755
Of beryl, and careering fires between;   756
Over their heads a crystal firmament
Whereon a sapphire throne inlaid with pure
Amber, and colours of the showery arch.   759
He in celestial panoply all arm'd   760
Of radiant Urim, work divinely wrought,   761
Ascended, at his right hand victory   762
Sat eagle-wing'd; beside him hung his bow
And quiver with three-bolted thunder stor'd,
And from about him fierce effusion roll'd   765
Of smoke and bickering flames and sparkles dire   766
Attended with ten thousand thousand saints
He onward came, far off his coming shone;
And twenty thousand (I their number heard)   769
Chariots of God, half on each hand were seen: 770
He on the wings of cherub rode sublime

---

748 *third sacred morn* Prefigures Christ's ascension on the third day after his crucifixion.
748–749 *began to shine, / Dawning* Milton puns by using "sun" imagery in relation to the
Son.   **751** *wheel within wheel undrawn* The image of the chariot is from Ezekiel 1:16.
752–753 *Itself . . . shapes* Although the "chariot" is spiritual, its significance can be "con-
vey'd" by the image, or "shapes," of the cherubs.   **752** *instinct* Infused.   **756** *beryl* A pre-
cious stone.   **759** *showery arch* The rainbow.   **761.1** *Urim* Jewels used to decorate Aaron's
armor in Exodus 28:30; **761.2** *work divinely wrought* In contrast to the idolized "works of
men's hands."   **762** *Ascended* In the original edition of 1667 this word comes exactly
halfway through the poem.   **766** *bickering* Flickering.   **769** *I their number heard* A reminder
that Raphael himself has been instructed in the story he imparts to the human couple; a
caution against assuming his speech is unmediated.

772 On the christalline sky, in sapphire thron'd,
773 Illustrious far and wide, but by his own
       First seen; them unexpected joy surpris'd
775 When the great ensign of Messiah blaz'd
776 Aloft by angels borne, his sign in heaven;
777 Under whose conduct Michael soon reduc'd
778 His army, circumfus'd on either wing,
       Under their head embodied all in one.
780 Before him power divine his way prepar'd:
       At his command th'uprooted hills retir'd
       Each to his place; they heard his voice and went
783 Obsequious; heaven his wonted face renew'd,
784 And with fresh flowerets hill and valley smil'd.
785 This saw his hapless foes, but stood obdur'd,
       And to rebellious fight rallied their powers
787 Insensate, hope conceiving from despair.
788 In heavenly spirits could such perverseness dwell,
789 But to convince the proud what signs avail,
790 Or wonders move, th'obdurate to relent?
791 They, harden'd more by what might most reclaim,
       Grieving to see his glory, at the sight
       Took envy;[8] and, aspiring to his height,
       Stood re-embattled fierce, by force or fraud
795 Weening to prosper and at length prevail
       Against God and Messiah, or to fall
       In universal ruin last; and now

---

772 *christalline* Saving, with a pun on "Christ," or "savior." 773 *Illustrious* Both "shining" and "famous." 776 *his sign in heaven* Matthew 24:30 promises that at the apocalypse, there "shall appear the sign of the Son of man in heaven." 777 *reduc'd* Led back. 778 *circumfus'd* Spread around. 783.1 *Obsequious* Obedient; 783.2 *wonted* Former. 784 *flowerets* Bunches of flowers. 785 *obdur'd* Hardened, as when God hardens Pharaoh's heart, rendering him incapable of reading the signs of God's wrath, in Exodus 14:4–8. The connection between hardness of heart and literalist interpretation is deeply rooted in Christian typology. Compare 1:572. 787.1 *Insensate* Insensible; 787.2 *hope conceiving from despair* Since "despair" literally means "absence of hope," the fallen angels have reversed logic. 788–790 *In heavenly spirits . . . relent?* Raphael's rhetorical question indicates that his story is a "sign" designed to teach a lesson for earthly consumption. Hughes (p. 343) points out that line 788 translates Virgil's *Aeneid* 1.11. 791 *reclaim* Redeem. 795 *Weening* Thinking.

To final battle drew, disdaining flight,
Or faint retreat; when the great Son of God
To all his host on either hand thus spake: 800

Stand still in bright array, ye saints; here stand,   801
Ye angels arm'd, this day from battle rest;
Faithful hath been your warfare, and of God   803
Accepted, fearless in his righteous cause;   804
And as ye have receiv'd, so have ye done   805
Invincibly; but of this cursed crew
The punishment to other hand belongs;
Vengeance is his, or whose he sole appoints;   808
Number to this day's work is not ordain'd,   809
Nor multitude; stand only and behold   810
God's indignation on these godless pour'd
By me; not you, but me, they have despis'd   812
Yet envied; against me is all their rage,   813
Because the Father, to whom in heaven supreme
Kingdom, and power, and glory appertains,   815
Hath honour'd me according to his will.
Therefore to me their doom he hath assign'd;   817
That they may have their wish, to try with me
In battle which the stronger proves; they all,
Or I alone against them, since by strength   820
They measure all, of other excellence   821

---

801 *saints* One of several hints that the righteous angels represent elect human beings.
803–804 *of God / Accepted* Both "accepted from God" and "acceptable to God." 808.1
Vengeance is his See Romans 12:19: "Vengeance is mine." 808.2 *or whose he sole appoints* A
suspiciously capacious description of those who have the right to administer God's
vengeance. 809–810 *Number . . . multitude* This battle will not be decided by quantitative
factors, such as the relative strength of the armies, but because of the qualitative difference
between the Son and the angels. 812 *By me; not you, but me* The real object of Satan's
wrath is the Son, who embodies the fact that creation is God's handiwork. 813 *against me
is all their rage* The fallen angels have been infuriated by the suggestion that creation refers
to a Creator. 817 *Therefore . . . assign'd* Therefore God has made the Son a sign of divine
judgment. 820–821 *by strength / They measure all* As Flannagan notes, "The implication
is that Messiah is using force only because the materialistic values of Satan's troops de-
mand a show of force" (p. 533).

822 Not emulous, nor care who them excels;
Nor other strife with them do I vouchsafe.

So spake the Son, and into terror chang'd
825 His count'nance too severe to be beheld,
And full of wrath bent on his enemies.
827 At once the Four spread out their starry wings,
828 With dreadful shade contiguous, and the orbs
Of his fierce chariot roll'd, as with the sound
830 Of torrent floods, or of a numerous host.
He on his impious foes right onward drove,
Gloomy as night; under his burning wheels
833 The steadfast empyrean shook throughout,
834 All but the throne itself of God. Full soon
835 Among them he arriv'd, in his right hand
Grasping ten thousand thunders, which he sent
Before him, such as in their souls infix'd
838 Plagues; they astonish'd, all resistance lost,
839 All courage; down their idle weapons dropp'd;
840 O'er shields, and helms, and helmed heads he rode
Of thrones, and mighty seraphim prostrate,
842 That wish'd the mountains now might be again
843 Thrown on them as a shelter from his ire.
Nor less on either side tempestuous fell
845 His arrows, from the fourfold-visag'd Four
846 Distinct with eyes, and from the living wheels
Distinct alike with multitude of eyes;
One spirit in them rul'd, and every eye
849 Glar'd lightning, and shot forth pernicious fire
850 Among th'accurs'd, that wither'd all their strength,

---

822 *emulous* Desiring to emulate.   827 *the Four* The cherubim accompanying the Son.
828.1 *contiguous* Joined together; 828.2 *orbs* Wheels, but the word often referred to heavenly
bodies.   833 *empyrean* Heavenly sphere.   834 *All . . . God* Refutes Satan's claim, in book
I, to have shaken God's throne.   838 *Plagues* Anticipating the plagues visited on Pharaoh
in the book of Exodus.   839 *idle* With a pun on "idol."   840 *helms* Helmets.   842–843
That wish'd . . . ire Compare Revelation 6:16, where the kings of the earth "said to the
mountains and rocks, 'Fall on us.'"   846 *Distinct* Adorned.   849 *pernicious* Destructive.

And of their wonted vigour left them drain'd,
Exhausted, spiritless, afflicted, fall'n.
Yet half his strength he put not forth, but check'd
His thunder in mid volley: for he meant
Not to destroy, but root them out of heaven: 855
The overthrown he rais'd, and, as a herd
Of goats or timorous flock together throng'd,   857
Drove them before him thunder-struck, pursu'd,
With terrors and with furies, to the bounds
And crystal wall of heaven, which opening wide   860
Roll'd inward, and a spacious gap disclos'd   861
Into the wasteful deep; the monstrous sight
Struck them with horror backward, but far worse
Urg'd them behind; headlong themselves they threw
Down from the verge of heaven; eternal wrath   865
Burn'd after them to the bottomless pit.

Hell heard th'unsufferable noise, hell saw   867
Heaven ruining from heaven, and would have fled
Affrighted; but strict Fate had cast too deep   869
Her dark foundations, and too fast had bound.   870
Nine days they fell; confounded Chaos roar'd,
And felt tenfold confusion in their fall
Through his wild anarchy, so huge a rout
Encumber'd him with ruin: hell at last
Yawning receiv'd them whole, and on them clos'd: 875
Hell, their fit habitation, fraught with fire
Unquenchable, the house of woe and pain.
Disburden'd heaven rejoic'd, and soon repair'd
Her mural breach, returning whence it roll'd.   879

---

857 *throng'd* Alludes to Mark 5:13, where Jesus exorcises the devils from men, transferring them into swine who immediately plunge to their destruction in the sea. Fyodor Dostoevsky's *Devils* (1872) gives this story a political significance that is foreshadowed here. 861 *disclos'd* Opened. 867–869 *Hell . . . Affrighted* Hell is personified here. 869 *strict Fate* Used here to refer to God, as in the "Nativity Ode": "But wisest Fate says no / This must not yet be so" (ll. 149–150). 879.1 *mural* In the wall; 879.2 *breach* With a pun on "breeches," adding to the scatological associations of heaven's expulsion of the devils.

The Downfall of the Rebel Angels

Sole victor, from th'expulsion of his foes,   880
Messiah his triumphal chariot turn'd:
To meet him all his saints, who silent stood
Eye-witnesses of his almighty acts,
With jubilee advanc'd; and as they went,   884
Shaded with branching palm, each order bright,   885
Sung triumph, and him sung victorious King,
Son, Heir, and Lord; to him dominion given,
Worthiest to reign: he celebrated rode
Triumphant through mid heaven, into the courts
And temple of his mighty Father thron'd   890
On high; who into glory him receiv'd,
Where now he sits at the right hand of bliss.

Thus, measuring things in heaven by things on earth,   893
At thy request, and that thou may'st beware
By what is past, to thee I have reveal'd   895
What might have else to human race been hid;   896
The discord which befell, and war in heaven
Among the angelic powers, and the deep fall
Of those too high aspiring, who rebell'd
With Satan; he who envies now thy state,   900
Who now is plotting how he may seduce
Thee also from obedience, that with him,
Bereav'd of happiness, thou may'st partake
His punishment, eternal misery;
Which would be all his solace and revenge,   905
As a despite done against the Most High,   906
Thee once to gain companion of his woe.
But listen not to his temptations; warn
Thy weaker; let it profit thee to have heard,   909

---

884 *jubilee* Festive celebration.   885 *palm* Jesus is greeted with palms on his entry into Jerusalem; see also Revelation 7:9.   893 *measuring . . . earth* Another reminder of Raphael's accommodated speech.   896 *hid* The exploits of the angels would be invisible to human beings unless expressed in physical, figural images such as Raphael has used.   906 *despite* Spiteful act.   909 *Thy weaker* Eve.

910 By terrible example, the reward
    Of disobedience; firm they might have stood,
    Yet fell. Remember, and fear to transgress.

END OF BOOK SIXTH

BOOK VII

THE ARGUMENT

Raphael, at the request of Adam, relates how and wherefore*
this world was first created; that God, after the expelling of
Satan and his angels out of heaven, declared his pleasure to
create another world, and other creatures to dwell therein; sends
his Son with glory and attendance of angels to perform the
work of creation in six days: the angels celebrate with hymns
the performance thereof, and his re-ascension into heaven.

DESCEND from heaven, Urania, by that name   1
If rightly thou art call'd whose voice divine   2
Following, above th'Olympian hill I soar,   3
Above the flight of Pegasean wing.   4
The meaning not the name I call: for thou   5
Nor of the Muses nine, nor on the top
Of old Olympus dwell'st; but heavenly born,   7
Before the hills appear'd, or fountain flow'd,
Thou with eternal Wisdom didst converse,
Wisdom thy sister, and with her didst play   10

---

*Why.

1.1 *Descend from heaven* Horace addresses these words to the Muse Calliope in *Odes* 3.4.1;
1.2 *Urania* The Muse of astronomy, thus "heavenly." Guillaume du Bartas's "Urania" had
converted her into the Muse of Christian poetry; 1–3 *by that name . . . soar* Milton makes
an unequivocal claim to divine inspiration.   4 *Above . . . wing* Milton claims to surpass the
classical poets; the winged horse Pegasus was a symbol of poetic inspiration.   5 *The mean-
ing not the name* This phrase is the key to Milton's syncretic approach to theology and
mythology. It does not matter whether the power he invokes is called Urania or the Holy
Spirit, since these are different ways of expressing the same significance.   7 *heavenly born*
Implying that "Urania" can be identified with the Holy Spirit.

11   In presence of th'almighty Father, pleas'd
      With thy celestial song. Up led by thee
      Into the heaven of heavens I have presum'd,
      An earthly guest, and drawn empyreal air,
15   Thy temp'ring; with like safety guided down
16   Return me to my native element:
17   Lest from this flying steed unrein'd, (as once
18   Bellerophon, though from a lower clime,)
19   Dismounted, on th'Aleian field I fall,
20   Erroneous there to wander, and forlorn.
21   Half yet remains unsung, but narrow bound
22   Within the visible diurnal sphere;
      Standing on earth, not rapt above the pole,
      More safe I sing with mortal voice, unchang'd
25   To hoarse or mute, though fallen on evil days,
26   On evil days though fallen, and evil tongues;
27   In darkness, and with dangers compass'd round,
      And solitude; yet not alone, while thou
      Visit'st my slumbers nightly, or when morn
30   Purples the east. Still govern thou my song,
31   Urania; and fit audience find though few.
32   But drive far off the barbarous dissonance
33   Of Bacchus and his revellers, the race
34   Of that wild rout that tore the Thracian bard

10–11 *Wisdom thy sister . . . Father* "Wisdom" translates the Greek *sophia*, beloved of Socrates and Plato, but was also associated with the deity, often identified with the Holy Spirit, that in Proverbs 8:22–30 claims to have been present at creation. 15 *Thy temp'ring* Made suitable by Urania. 16 *my native element* The earth. 17–18 *as once . . . clime* In the *Iliad* 6.200–202, Bellerophon was thrown from the winged horse Pegasus when he tried to fly to heaven. Pegasus was a conventional symbol for poetic inspiration. 19 *th'Aleian field* Where Bellerophon wandered after his fall, having been blinded, according to Natale Conti's *Mythologiae* (1567), 9.4. 20 *Erroneous* Straying. 21 *Half* The poem is halfway through. 22 *diurnal* Earthly. 25 *evil days* A biographical allusion to what Milton found to be the inhospitable climate of Restoration England. 26 *evil tongues* Milton was always very sensitive to criticism. 27 *In darkness . . . round* Evokes a parallel between the literal, interior darkness of the blind poet and the external, figurative darkness of the Restoration milieu. 31 *fit audience find though few* A famous phrase expressing Milton's conviction that it is preferable to address even one just man than a world of false men. 32–33 *But drive far off . . . revellers* Compare *Comus* 550.

In Rhodope, where woods and rocks had ears   35
To rapture, till the savage clamour drown'd   36
Both harp and voice; nor could the Muse defend   37
Her son. So fall not thou, who thee implores;   38
For thou art heavenly, she an empty dream.   39

Say, goddess, what ensued when Raphael,   40
The affable archangel, had forewarn'd
Adam by dire example to beware
Apostasy, by what befell in heaven   43
To those apostates, lest the like befall
In Paradise to Adam or his race,   45
Charg'd not to touch the interdicted tree,   46
If they transgress, and slight that sole command,
So easily obey'd, amid the choice
Of all tastes else to please their appetite,   49
Though wand'ring. He with his consorted Eve   50
The story heard attentive, and was fill'd
With admiration and deep muse, to hear   52
Of things so high and strange, things to their thought
So unimaginable as hate in heaven,
And war so near the peace of God in bliss   55
With such confusion: but the evil soon
Driven back; redounded as a flood on those   57
From whom it sprung, impossible to mix
With blessedness. Whence Adam soon repeal'd   59
The doubts that in his heart arose: and now   60
Led on, yet sinless, with desire to know
What nearer might concern him; how this world

33–38 *the race . . . son* See Ovid's *Metamorphoses* 11.1–60 and "Lycidas" 58–63. Orpheus' mother was Calliope, the Muse of epic poetry.   39 *heavenly . . . dream* "Urania" literally means "heavenly."   43 *Apostasy* Alienation from God.   46 *interdicted* Forbidden.   49–50 *their appetite, / Though wand'ring* Adam and Eve's appetite seems naturally inclined to wander, and Adam's appetite for knowledge is implicitly criticized at 7.66–68 and elsewhere in book VII.   50 *consorted Eve* Eve has been present throughout Raphael's discourse.   52 *muse* Thought.   57 *redounded* Rebounded.   59 *repeal'd* Ambiguous: "recalled" and "took back."

63 Of heaven and earth conspicuous first began,
    When, and whereof created, for what cause,
65 What within Eden, or without was done
66 Before his memory; as one whose drought,
67 Yet scarce allay'd, still eyes the current stream,
68 Whose liquid murmur heard new thirst excites,
    Proceeded thus to ask his heavenly guest:

70 Great things, and full of wonder in our ears,
    Far differing from this world, thou hast reveal'd,
72 Divine interpreter, by favour sent
73 Down from the empyrean to forewarn
    Us timely of what might else have been our loss,
75 Unknown, which human knowledge could not reach:
    For which to th'infinitely Good we owe
    Immortal thanks, and his admonishment
    Receive, with solemn purpose to observe
79 Immutably his sov'reign will, the end
80 Of what we are. But since thou hast vouchsaf'd
    Gently for our instruction to impart
    Things above earthly thought, which yet concern'd
    Our knowing, as to highest wisdom seem'd,
    Deign to descend now lower, and relate
85 What may no less perhaps avail us known;
    How first began this heaven, which we behold
    Distant so high, with moving fires adorn'd
    Innumerable, and this which yields or fills
    All space, the ambient air wide interfus'd
90 Embracing round this florid earth; what cause
    Mov'd the Creator, in his holy rest

---

63 *conspicuous* Perceptible to the senses.   66–68 *as one . . . excites* Adam's thirst ("drought")
for knowledge is not wholly laudable, since it is compared to a physical appetite.   72 *Divine interpreter* This is Virgil's term for Mercury, messenger of the gods, in the *Aeneid* 4.378.
72–73 *by favour . . . to forewarn* Adam has too generous an interpretation of God's motive,
which was "to render man inexcusable."   79–80 *the end / Of what we are* The purpose of
human existence is to fulfill God's will.   90 *florid* Blooming.

Through all eternity, so late to build
In Chaos, and, the work begun, how soon
Absolv'd, if unforbid thou may'st unfold   94
What we, not to explore the secrets, ask   95
Of his eternal empire, but the more   96
To magnify his works the more we know.   97
And the great light of day yet wants to run   98
Much of his race tho' steep; suspense in heaven,   99
Held by thy voice, thy potent voice, he hears,   100
And longer will delay to hear thee tell
His generation, and the rising birth   102
Of Nature from the unapparent deep: 103
Or if the star of evening and the moon   104
Haste to thy audience, night with her will bring   105
Silence, and sleep, list'ning to thee, will watch,
Or we can bid his absence, till thy song
End, dismiss thee ere the morning shine.

Thus Adam his illustrious guest besought;
And thus the godlike angel answer'd mild: 110

This also thy request, with caution ask'd,
Obtain: though to recount almighty works   112
What words or tongue of seraph can suffice,   113
Or heart of man suffice to comprehend?   114
Yet what thou can'st attain, which best may serve   115
To glorify the Maker, and infer   116
Thee also happier, shall not be withheld

94.1 *Absolv'd* Accomplished; 94.2 *if unforbid* Adam senses that the knowledge Raphael imparts may be dangerous.   95–97 *not to explore . . . works* Adam does not seek after knowledge for its own sake, as in a Baconian, instrumental model of scientific inquiry; rather, he seeks knowledge of the empirical world for the higher purpose of glorifying its creator.   98 *yet wants to run* Has yet to run.   99 *suspense* Both "suspended" and "in suspense."   102 *His generation* How he was generated.   103 *unapparent* Invisible, in the theological sense of *res non apparens* ("things that do not appear").   104 *the star of evening and the moon* Venus and Diana, among the more dubious pagan deities.   112–114 *though to recount . . . comprehend* Raphael understands that immediate comprehension of noumenal concepts is impossible for phenomenal beings (see Introduction).   116 *infer* Bring about as a logical consequence.

Thy hearing; such commission from above.
I have receiv'd, to answer thy desire
120 Of knowledge within bounds; beyond abstain
To ask, nor let thine own inventions hope
Things not reveal'd, which th'invisible King,
Only omniscient, hath suppress'd in night,
To none communicable in earth or heaven:
125 Enough is left besides to search and know.
126 But knowledge is as food, and needs no less
127 Her temp'rance over appetite, to know
128 In measure what the mind may well contain;
Oppresses else with surfeit, and soon turns
130 Wisdom to folly, as nourishment to wind.

131 Know then, that after Lucifer from heaven
132 (So call him, brighter once amidst the host
Of angels than that star the stars among)
Fell with his flaming legions through the deep
135 Into his place, and the great Son return'd
Victorious with his saints, th'omnipotent
Eternal Father from his throne beheld
Their multitude, and to his Son thus spake:

At least our envious foe hath fail'd, who thought
140 All like himself rebellious, by whose aid
This inaccessible high strength, the seat
Of Deity supreme, us dispossess'd,
He trusted to have seiz'd, and into fraud
Drew many, whom their place knows here no more;
145 Yet far the greater part have kept, I see,
Their station; heaven yet populous retains

---

120 *knowledge within bounds* Another hint that Adam is aspiring to know too much.
126–128 *But knowledge . . . contain* The desire for too much knowledge in quantitative terms
brings about a qualitative change in the nature of knowledge.   131 *Lucifer* The morning
star; literally, "Light-bearer."   132 *So call him* Satan's name, as well as his nature, has been
changed by his rebellion.

Number sufficient to possess her realms
Though wide, and this high temple to frequent
With ministeries due and solemn rites:
But lest his heart exalt him in the harm   150
Already done, to have dispeopled heaven,
My damage fondly deem'd, I can repair   152
That detriment, if such it be to lose
Self-lost, and in a moment will create
Another world, out of one man a race   155
Of men innumerable, there to dwell,
Not here, till by degrees of merit rais'd   157
They open to themselves at length the way   158
Up hither, under long obedience tried,   159
And earth be chang'd to heaven, and heaven to earth,   160
One kingdom, joy and union without end.   161
Meanwhile inhabit lax, ye powers of heaven,   162
And thou my Word, begotten Son, by thee   163
This I perform; speak thou, and be it done: 164
My overshadowing Spirit and might with thee   165
I send along; ride forth, and bid the deep
Within appointed bounds be heaven and earth,
Boundless the deep, because I am who fill
Infinitude, nor vacuous the space.
Though I uncircumscrib'd myself retire,   170
And put not forth my goodness, which is free
To or not, necessity and chance   172
Approach not me, and what I will is fate.   173

---

152 *My damage fondly deem'd* Which he foolishly imagines to have damaged me.   157–161
till by degrees . . . end This account works both at the level of the individual, who can work
his way to heaven by faith, and of human history, which will culminate in the apocalyptic
union of heaven and earth.   162 *lax* Relaxed.   163 *Word* In Greek, *Logos*, an alternative
metaphor for the "son," as in John 1:1: "In the beginning was the Word, and the Word was
with God, and the Word was God."   163–164 *by thee / This I perform* The Son is the Fa-
ther in action, in effect.   165 *My overshadowing Spirit* The Holy Spirit.   170 *Though I . . .
retire* Allusion to the doctrine of *deus absconditus*, the departed God.   172–173 *Necessity . . .
fate* The lines can be paraphrased as: "The concepts of 'necessity'and 'chance' do not even
come close to describing me (and do not affect me); what people call 'fate' is in fact my
will."

So spake th'Almighty, and to what he spake
175   His Word, the filial Godhead, gave effect.
176   Immediate are the acts of God, more swift
177   Than time or motion; but to human ears
178   Cannot without process of speech be told,
179   So told as earthly notion can receive.
180   Great triumph and rejoicing was in heaven,
     When such was heard declar'd th'Almighty's will;
     Glory they sung to the Most High, good-will
     To future men, and in their dwellings peace:
     Glory to him, whose just avenging ire
185   Had driven out th'ungodly from his sight,
     And th'habitations of the just; to him
     Glory and praise, whose wisdom had ordain'd
188   Good out of evil to create, instead
     Of spirits malign, a better race to bring
190   Into their vacant room, and thence diffuse
     His good to worlds and ages infinite.

So sang the hierarchies: meanwhile the Son
     On his great expedition now appear'd,
194   Girt with omnipotence, with radiance crown'd
195   Of majesty divine; sapience and love
     Immense, and all his Father in him shone.
     About his chariot numberless were pour'd
     Cherub and seraph, potentates and thrones,
199   And virtues, winged spirits, and chariots wing'd
200   From th'armoury of God, where stand of old
201   Myriads between two brazen mountains lodg'd
202   Against a solemn day, harness'd at hand,
203   Celestial equipage; and now came forth

176–179 *Immediate . . . receive* Human knowledge of God is inevitably mediated through history and language.   188 *Good out of evil to create* What appears to us as mutually exclusive binary opposition will be revealed as mutually determining.   194 *Girt* Wrapped.   195 *sapience* Wisdom.   199–201 *chariots . . . lodg'd* The image is from Zechariah 6:1.   202.1 *Against* Ready for; 202.2 *harness'd at hand* Kept ready in harness.   203 *equipage* Equipment.

Spontaneous, for within them spirit liv'd,
Attendant on their Lord: heaven open'd wide   205
Her ever-during gates, harmonious sound,
On golden hinges moving, to let forth
The King of glory, in his powerful Word
And Spirit coming to create new worlds.
On heavenly ground they stood, and from the shore   210
They view'd the vast immeasurable abyss   211
Outrageous as a sea, dark, wasteful, wild,
Up from the bottom turn'd by furious winds
And surging waves, as mountains to assault
Heaven's height, and with the centre mix the pole.   215

Silence, ye troubled waves, and thou deep, peace.
Said then th'omnific Word, your discord end: 217
Nor stay'd but, on the wings of cherubim
Uplifted, in paternal glory rode   219
Far into Chaos, and the world unborn;   220
For Chaos heard his voice. Him all his train
Follow'd in bright procession to behold
Creation, and the wonders of his might.
Then stay'd the fervid wheels, and in his hand   224
He took the golden compasses, prepar'd   225
In God's eternal store, to circumscribe
This universe, and all created things:
One foot he centred, and the other turn'd,
Round through the vast profundity obscure,
And said, Thus far extend, thus far thy bounds,   230
This be thy just circumference, O world.

Thus God the heaven created, thus the earth,
Matter unform'd and void: darkness profound   233

---

211 *the vast immeasurable abyss* Chaos.   217 *omnific* All-creating.   219 *in paternal glory* The
Son represents the Father.   224 *fervid* Burning.   225 *the golden compasses* From Proverbs
8:27.   233 *Matter unform'd* In *Timaeus*, Plato describes the demiurge's creation of the world
out of formless matter.

Cover'd th'abyss; but on the wat'ry calm
235   His brooding wings the Spirit of God outspread,
236   And vital virtue infus'd, and vital warmth
237   Throughout the fluid mass; but downward purg'd
238   The black, tartareous, cold, infernal dregs,
239   Adverse to life; then founded, then conglob'd
240   Like things to like, the rest to several place
241   Disparted, and between spun out the air,
And earth self-balanc'd on her centre hung.

Let there be light; said God, and forthwith light
244   Ethereal, first of things, quintessence pure,
245   Sprung from the deep, and from her native east
To journey through the airy gloom began,
247   Spher'd in a radiant cloud, for yet the sun
248   Was not; she in a cloudy tabernacle
249   Sojourn'd the while. God saw the light was good;
250   And light from darkness by the hemisphere
Divided: light the day, and darkness night
He nam'd. Thus was the first day even and morn.
Nor pass'd uncelebrated, nor unsung
By the celestial choirs, when orient light
255   Exhaling first from darkness they beheld;
Birth-day of heaven and earth, with joy and shout
The hollow universal orb they fill'd,
And touch'd their golden harps, and hymning prais'd
God and his works, Creator him they sung,
260   Both when first evening was, and when first morn.

---

235 *brooding* Compare 1.21.   236 *vital virtue* Power of life.   237–239 *but downward . . . life*
As Flannagan notes, the imagery is scatological: "The Spirit seems to excrete the regions
of Hell" (p. 545).   239 *conglob'd* Compacted.   241 *Disparted* Divided.   244 *first . . . pure*
As Milton emphasizes below, this light does not emanate from the sun, which has not yet
been created. Light was not one of the four elements, but Milton makes it into the fifth
essence, or "quintessence," which was also identified with the "philosophers' stone," a
chemical elixir alchemists believed would act as a catalyst to bring the world to a state of
perfection.   247 *Spher'd* Contained.   248 *tabernacle* Connects the primal light with the
ark of the covenant, which was also kept in a tabernacle.   249 *Sojourn'd* Spent the day.
255 *Exhaling* Evaporating.

Again, God said, Let there be firmament   261
Amid the waters, and let it divide
The waters from the waters; And God made
The firmament, expanse of liquid, pure,
Transparent, elemental air, diffus'd   265
In circuit to the uttermost convex
Of this great round; partition firm and sure,   267
The waters underneath from those above
Dividing; for as earth, so he the world   269
Built on circumfluous waters calm, in wide   270
Crystalline ocean, and the loud misrule
Of Chaos far remov'd, lest fierce extremes
Contiguous might distemper the whole frame.   273
And heaven he nam'd the firmament: so even
And morning chorus sung the second day.   275

The earth was form'd; but in the womb as yet   276
Of waters, embryon immature involv'd,   277
Appear'd not: over all the face of earth
Main ocean flow'd, not idle, but with warm
Prolific humour soft'ning all her globe,   280
Fermented the great mother to conceive,
Satiate with genial moisture: when God said,   282
Be gather'd now ye waters under heaven
Into one place, and let dry land appear;
Immediately the mountains huge appear   285
Emergent, and their broad bare backs upheave
Into the clouds, their tops ascend the sky;
So high as heav'd the tumid hills, so low   288
Down sunk a hollow bottom broad and deep,
Capacious bed of waters: thither they   290
Hasted with glad precipitance, uproll'd   291

---

261 *firmament* The universe's ceiling, or roof.   267 *round* Universe.   269 *world* Universe.
270 *circumfluous* Flowing around.   273 *distemper* Put into disorder.   276–277 *in the womb . . . involv'd* Hints at the evolution of species, an ancient idea espoused by the Greek philosophers Empedocles and Aristotle.   280 *Prolific humour* Life-giving substance.   282 *genial* Generative.   288 *tumid* Swollen.   291 *precipitance* Both "hurry" and "precipitation."

As drops on dust conglobing from the dry;
Part rise in crystal wall, or ridge direct,
For haste; such flight the great command impress'd
295 On the swift floods. As armies at the call
296 Of trumpet (for of armies thou hast heard)
Troop to their standard, so the wat'ry throng,
Wave rolling after wave, where way they found;
If steep, with torrent rapture; if through plain,
300 Soft-ebbing; nor withstood them rock or hill;
301 But they, or under ground, or circuit wide
302 With serpent-error wand'ring, found their way,
And on the washy ooze deep channels wore;
Easy, ere God had bid the ground be dry,
305 All but within those banks, where rivers now
306 Stream, and perpetual draw their humid train.
The dry land, earth, and the great receptacle
Of congregated waters, he call'd seas:
And saw that it was good, and said, Let the earth
310 Put forth the verdant grass, herb yielding seed,
311 And fruit-tree yielding fruit after her kind,
Whose seed is in herself upon the earth
He scarce had said, when the bare earth, till then
Desert and bare, unsightly, unadorn'd,
315 Brought forth the tender grass, whose verdure clad
Her universal face with pleasant green;
Then herbs of every leaf, that sudden flower'd
Opening their various colours, and made gay
319 Her bosom smelling sweet; and these scarce blown,
320 Forth flourish'd thick the clustering vine, forth crept
321 The smelling gourd, up stood the corny reed

---

296 *(for of armies thou hast heard)* Raphael finds it appropriate to continue using the images with which Adam is now familiar. 301 *or . . . or* Either . . . or. 302 *serpent-error wand'ring* Raphael already reads a moral significance into the snake. 306 *humid* Wet. 311 *kind* Nature. 319 *blown* Bloomed. 321 *smelling* Most modern editors substitute "swelling," but both editions published in Milton's lifetime have "smelling."

Embattled in her field, and th'humble shrub,   322

And bush with frizzled hair implicit: last   323

Rose as in dance the stately trees, and spread

Their branches hung with copious fruit, or gemm'd   325

Their blossoms; with high woods the hills were crown'd,

With tufts the valleys, and each fountain side,

With borders long the rivers; that earth now

Seem'd like to heaven, a seat where gods might dwell,   329

Or wander with delight, and love to haunt   330

Her sacred shades: though God had yet not rain'd

Upon the earth, and man to till the ground

None was; but from the earth a dewy mist

Went up, and water'd all the ground, and each

Plant of the field, which ere it was in th'earth   335

God made, and every herb, before it grew   336

On the green stem. God saw that it was good:

So even and morn recorded the third day.   338

Again the Almighty spake: Let there be lights

High in th'expanse of heaven, to divide   340

The day from night; and let them be for signs,   341

For seasons, and for days, and circling years;

And let them be for lights, as I ordain

Their office in the firmament of heaven,

To give light on the earth and it was so.   345

And God made two great lights, great for their use

To man, the greater to have rule by day,

The less by night altern; and made the stars,   348

And set them in the firmament of heaven

To illuminate the earth, and rule the day   350

322.1 *Embattled in her field* Raphael continues to press the martial metaphor; 322.2 *humble* Literally, "low-growing"; another instance of Raphael's blending literal and ethical usages. 323 *implicit* Entwined.   325 *gemm'd* Budded.   329 *Seem'd . . . dwell* Raphael's implication that the human couple live in an environment fit for gods will be exploited by Satan, who tempts Eve with the desire to be divine.   336 *before it grew* Milton follows Genesis 2:5, suggesting that the idea of each plant was created before its physical manifestation.   338 *recorded* Witnessed.   341 *let them be for signs* From Genesis 1:14.   348 *altern* Alternately.

In their vicissitude, and rule the night,
And light from darkness to divide. God saw
Surveying his great work, that it was good:
For of celestial bodies first the sun,

355   A mighty sphere, he fram'd; unlightsome first,
Though of ethereal mould; then form'd the moon

357   Globose, and every magnitude of stars,
And sow'd with stars the heaven thick as a field.
Of light by far the greater part he took,

360   Transplanted from her cloudy shrine, and plac'd
In the sun's orb, made porous to receive

362   And drink the liquid light, firm to retain
Her gather'd beams, great palace now of light.
Hither, as to their fountain, other stars

365   Repairing, in their golden urns draw light,
And hence the morning planet gilds her horns;
By tincture or reflection they augment
Their small peculiar,¹ though from human sight
So far remote, with diminution seen.

370   First in his east the glorious lamp was seen,
371   Regent of day, and all th'horizon round
372   Invested with bright rays, jocund to run
His longitude through heaven's high road; the gray
374   Dawn and the Pleiades before him danc'd
375   Shedding sweet influence. Less bright the moon,
But opposite in levell'd west was set,
377   His mirror, with full face borrowing her light
378   From him, for other light she needed none
In that aspect, and still that distance keeps
380   Till night, then in the east her turn she shines,

---

355 *unlightsome* Dark.   357 *Globose* Globular.   362 *liquid light* Milton follows first-century
B.C. Roman poet Lucretius (*De rerum natura* 5.281) and first-century A.D. Roman scholar
Pliny (*Natural History* 2.4.6) in speculating that the sun is hollow and filled with liquid
light, which it pours out like a fountain.   371 *Regent* Ruler.   372 *jocund* Jolly.   374 *Pleiades*
A constellation.   377–378 *His mirror . . . none* The moon reflects the sun in the same way
that Eve reflects Adam, Adam reflects God, and the Son reflects the Father.

Revolv'd on heaven's great axle, and her reign
With thousand lesser lights dividual holds,   382
With thousand thousand stars, that then appear'd
Spangling the hemisphere: then first adorn'd   384
With her bright luminaries that set and rose,   385
Glad evening and glad morn crown'd the fourth day.

And God said, Let the waters generate
Reptile with spawn abundant, living soul: 388
And let fowl fly above the earth, with wings
Display'd on the open firmament of heaven.   390
And God created the great whales, and each
Soul living, each that crept, which plenteously
The waters generated by their kinds;
And every bird of wing after his kind:
And saw that it was good, and bless'd them, saying,   395
Be fruitful, multiply, and in the seas,
And lakes, and running streams, the waters fill;
And let the fowl be multiplied on th'earth.
Forthwith the sounds and seas, each creek and bay
With fry innumerable swarm, and shoals   400
Of fish, that with their fins and shining scales
Glide under the green wave, in sculls that oft   402
Bank the mid-sea: part single or with mate,
Graze the sea-weed, their pasture, and through groves
Of coral stray, or, sporting, with quick glance,   405
Show to the sun their wav'd coats dropp'd with gold,
Or, in their pearly shells at ease, attend
Moist nutriment, or under rocks their food   408
In jointed armour watch: on smooth the seal,   409
And bended dolphins play; part huge of bulk   410
Wallowing unwieldy, enormous in their gait,

---

382 *dividual* Divided.   384 *Spangling* Sparkling in.   388.1 *Reptile* Creeping animal; 388.2 *living soul* The souls of animals differ from those of human beings insofar as they are not rational.   400 *fry* Minnows.   402 *sculls* Schools.   408 *nutriment* Nutrition.   409 *watch* Wait for.

412

412	Tempest the ocean. There the leviathan,
	Hugest of living creatures, on the deep,
	Stretch'd like a promontory, sleeps or swims,
415	And seems a moving land, and at his gills
	Draws in, and at his trunk spouts out, a sea.
417	Meanwhile the tepid caves, and fens, and shores,
	Their brood as numerous hatch, from th'egg that soon
419	Bursting with kindly rupture, forth disclos'd
420	Their callow young, but feather'd soon and fledge,
421	They summ'd their pens, and soaring th'air sublime,
422	With clang despis'd the ground, under a cloud
	In prospect; there the eagle and the stork
	On cliffs and cedar tops their eyries build:
425	Part loosely wing the region, part more wise
426	In common, rang'd in figure, wedge their way,
427	Intelligent of seasons, and set forth
	Their airy caravan, high over seas
	Flying, and over lands with mutual wing
430	Easing their flight: so steers the prudent crane
	Her annual voyage, borne on winds; the air
	Floats, as they pass, fann'd with unnumber'd plumes.
	From branch to branch the smaller birds with song
434	Solac'd the woods, and spread their painted wings
435	Till even; nor then the solemn nightingale
436	Ceas'd warbling, but all night tun'd her soft lays:
	Others on silver lakes and rivers bath'd
	Their downy breast; the swan, with arched neck
439	Between her white wings mantling proudly, rows
440	Her state with oary feet; yet oft they quit
441	The dank, and, rising on stiff pennons, tower
	The mid aerial sky. Others on ground

---

412 *leviathan* Compare the "sea-beast" at 1.200–208. 417 *tepid* Lukewarm. 419 *kindly* Both "natural" and "beneficent." 421 *summ'd their pens* Completed their plumage. 422.1 *clang* Cry; 422.2 *despis'd* Looked down on. 425 *loosely wing the region* Fly in the sky alone. 426.1 *rang'd* Arranged, ordered; 426.2 *wedge* Fly in a wedge formation, another image drawn from the battlefield. 427 *Intelligent* Understanding. 434 *Solac'd* Comforted. 436 *lays* Songs. 439 *mantling* Cloaking. 441.1 *dank* Pool; 441.2 *pennons* Wings.

Walk'd firm; the crested cock, whose clarion sounds   443
The silent hours, and the other whose gay train   444
Adorns him, coloured with the florid hue   445
Of rainbows and starry eyes. The waters thus
With fish replenish'd, and the air with fowl,
Evening and morn solemniz'd the fifth day.

The sixth, and of creation last, arose
With evening harps and matin, when God said,   450
Let th'earth bring forth soul living in her kind,   451
Cattle, and creeping things, and beast of th'earth,
Each in their kind. The earth obey'd, and straight,
Opening her fertile womb, teem'd at a birth
Innumerous living creatures, perfect forms,   455
Limb'd and full grown: out of the ground uprose,
As from his lair, the wild beast, where he wons   457
In forest wild, in thicket, brake, or den;   458
Among the trees in pairs they rose, they walk'd.
The cattle in the fields and meadows green: 460
Those rare and solitary, these in flocks
Pasturing at once, and in broad herds upsprung.
The grassy clods now calv'd, now half appear'd   463
The tawny lion, pawing to get free
His hinder parts, then springs as broke from bonds,   465
And rampant shakes his brinded mane; the ounce,   466
The libbard, and the tiger, as the mole   467
Rising, the crumbled earth above them threw
In hillocks; the swift stag from under ground

---

443 *sounds* Both "fills with sound" and "searches." 444 *the other* The peacock. 450 *matin* Morning. 451 *soul* The editions published in Milton's lifetime have "fowl." 457 *wons* Dwells. 458 *brake* Thicket. 463 *The grassy . . . calv'd* The earth gives birth to living animals, an image taken from *De rerum natura* (2.991–998), by first-century B.C. Roman poet Lucretius. In Lucretius the image serves the purposes of materialism, but Milton gives both this material cause and the Providential final cause of animal life. 466.1 *rampant* Rearing, a heraldic term; the lion is described in overtly symbolic terms; 466.2 *brinded* Tortoiseshell; 466.3 *ounce* Lynx. 467 *libbard* Leopard.

470 Bore up his branching head; scarce from his mould
471 Behemoth, biggest born of earth, upheav'd
    His vastness; fleec'd the flocks and bleating rose.
473 As plants; ambiguous between sea and land
474 The river horse and scaly crocodile.
475 At once came forth whatever creeps the ground,
476 Insect or worm: those wav'd their limber fans
    For wings, and smallest lineaments exact,
478 In all the liveries deck'd of summer's pride,
    With spots of gold and purple, azure and green,
480 These as a line their long dimension drew,
    Streaking the ground with sinuous trace; not all
482 Minims of nature; some of serpent kind,
483 Wondrous in length and corpulence, involv'd
    Their snaky folds, and added wings. First crept
485 The parsimonious emmet, provident
    Of future, in small room large heart enclos'd
487 Pattern of just equality perhaps
488 Hereafter, join'd in her popular tribes
489 Of commonalty; swarming next appear'd
490 The female bee, that feeds her husband drone
    Deliciously, and builds her waxen cells
    With honey stor'd. The rest are numberless,
493 And thou their natures know'st, and gav'st them names,
    Needless to thee repeated; nor unknown
495 The serpent, subtlest beast of all the field,
496 Of huge extent sometimes, with brazen eyes

---

470 *branching* Antlered.   471 *Behemoth* The word had monstrous connotations; Hughes (p. 358) reminds us that in the marginalia of the Geneva Bible it signifies the devil.   473 *ambiguous* Amphibious.   474 *river horse* Hippopotamus.   476 *limber fans* Light wings.   478 *liveries* Uniforms.   482 *Minims* Smallest forms.   483 *involv'd* Coiled.   485 *The parsimonious emmet* The thrifty ant.   487–488 *Pattern . . . Hereafter* A hint that Milton viewed social inequality as the inevitable, but nevertheless regrettable, result of the Fall.   489 *commonalty* Commonwealth.   493 *and gav'st them names* Anticipates 8.349–354.   495 *The serpent . . . field* Follows Genesis 3:1: "The serpent was more subtil than any beast of the field."   496 *brazen* Brassy, in both the literal and the figurative sense.

And hairy mane terrific, though to thee 497
Not noxious, but obedient at thy call. 498

Now heaven in all her glory shone, and roll'd
Her motions, as the great first Mover's hand 500
First wheel'd their course; earth, in her rich attire,
Consummate lovely smil'd; air, water, earth,
By fowl, fish, beast, was flown, was swam, was walk'd
Frequent: and of the sixth day yet remain'd; 504
There wanted yet the master work, the end 505
Of all yet done; a creature who, not prone
And brute as other creatures, but endued
With sanctity of reason, might erect 508
His stature, and upright, with front serene, 509
Govern the rest, self-knowing, and from thence 510
Magnanimous to correspond with heaven; 511
But grateful to acknowledge whence his good
Descends, thither with heart and voice and eyes
Directed in devotion, to adore
And worship God supreme, who made him chief 515
Of all his works: therefore th'Omnipotent
Eternal Father (for where is not he
Present) thus to his Son audibly spake:

Let us make now Man in our image, Man
In our similitude, and let them rule 520

497.1 *hairy mane* The prelapsarian serpent appears less abject than the version known to us.
In Virgil's *Aeneid* (2.203–207), maned sea serpents devour Laocoon and his sons; 497.2 *ter-rific* Terrifying. Raphael tells Adam and Eve to fear snakes, but he seems to do so only on
the grounds of their appearance. In fact, however, we learn below that he believes the snake
holds no terrors for them. So he instructs them to draw a conclusion from sensual data—
one that he believes to be false but that is in fact true. 497–498 *though to thee . . . call*
Raphael is evidently unaware that the serpent will provide Satan with his vehicle. 500 *first
Mover's* Refers to Aristotle's proto-monotheist doctrine that the universe has an ultimate
cause, or "prime mover." 504 *Frequent* In throngs. 505 *end* Purpose. 508 *sanctity of rea-son* Milton regarded reason as holy. 509 *front* Face. 510 *self-knowing* Conscious of exis-tence as a self. 511.1 *Magnanimous* Having a sufficiently large soul; 511.2 *correspond* Both
"parallel" and "communicate with." 515 *who made him* Raphael emphasizes that God de-serves man's worship because of his role as Creator.

Over the fish and fowl of sea and air,
Beast of the field, and over all the earth,
And every creeping thing that creeps the ground.
This said, he form'd thee, Adam, thee, O Man;
525 Dust of the ground, and in thy nostrils breath'd
526 The breath of life; in his own image he
527 Created thee, in the image of God
528 Express, and thou becam'st a living soul.
Male he created thee, but thy consort
530 Female, for race; then bless'd mankind, and said,
Be fruitful, multiply, and fill the earth,
532 Subdue it, and throughout dominion hold,
Over fish of the sea, and fowl of th'air,
And every living thing that moves on th'earth.
535 Wherever thus created, for no place
Is yet distinct by name. Thence, as thou know'st,
He brought thee into this delicious grove,
This garden, planted with the trees of God,
Delectable both to behold and taste;
540 And freely all their pleasant fruit for food
Gave thee; all sorts are here that all the earth yields,
Variety without end; but of the tree
Which tasted works knowledge of good and evil,
544 Thou may'st not; in the day thou eat'st, thou diest;
545 Death is the penalty impos'd: beware,
And govern well thy appetite, lest Sin
Surprise thee, and her black attendant Death.

Here finish'd he, and all that he had made
View'd, and behold, all was entirely good;
550 So even and morn accomplish'd the sixth day:

---

525 *Dust of the ground* From Genesis 2:7: "God formed man of the dust of the ground."
526–528 *in his own . . . Express* In Hebrews 1:3 the Son is said to be "the express image" of
the Father. 530 *for race* For the propagation of the species. 532 *Subdue it* Genesis 1:28:
"Replenish the earth, and subdue it." 544 *Thou may'st not* Leonard comments: " 'Taste'
is understood, the abrupt omission being mimetic of restraint" (p. 390).

Yet not till the Creator from his work
Desisting, though unwearied, up return'd,
Up to the heaven of heavens, his high abode,
Thence to behold this new-created world,
Th'addition of his empire, how it show'd   555
In prospect from his throne, how good, how fair,
Answering his great Idea. Up he rode,   557
Follow'd with acclamation, and the sound
Symphonious of ten thousand harps that tun'd
Angelic harmonies: the earth, the air   560
Resounded, (thou remember'st, for thou heard'st)
The heavens, and all the constellations rung,
The planets in their stations list'ning stood,
While the bright pomp ascended jubilant.   564
Open, ye everlasting gates, they sung,   565
Open, ye heavens, your living doors; let in
The great Creator from his work return'd
Magnificent, his six days work, a world;
Open, and henceforth oft; for God will deign   569
To visit oft the dwellings of just men   570
Delighted, and with frequent intercourse   571
Thither will send his winged messengers   572
On errands of supernal grace. So sung   573
The glorious train ascending: He through heaven,
That open'd wide her blazing portals, led   575
To God's eternal house direct the way,
A broad and ample road, whose dust is gold   577
And pavement stars, as stars to thee appear,
Seen in the galaxy, that milky way
Which nightly as a circling zone thou seest   580
Powder'd with stars. And now on earth the seventh

---

557 *Answering his great Idea* Alluding to Plato's *Timaeus* 37c–d, Milton uses "Idea" in the
sense of Platonic form. Leonard (p. 390) notes that this is the only time Milton uses this
word in his English poetry.   564 *pomp* Triumphal procession.   569–573 *for God will . . .
grace* Another indication that Raphael is unaware of the consequences of the fall.   577
broad and ample road See Ovid's description of the Milky Way in *Metamorphoses* 1.166–169.

Evening arose in Eden, for the sun
Was set, and twilight from the east came on,
584 Forerunning night; when at the holy mount
585 Of heaven's high seated top, th'imperial throne
Of Godhead, fixt for ever firm and sure,
587 The Filial Power arriv'd, and sat him down
With his great Father, for he also went
Invisible, yet stay'd, (such privilege
590 Hath Omnipresence,) and the work ordain'd
Author and end of all things, and from work
Now resting, bless'd and hallow'd the seventh day,
As resting on that day from all his work,
But not in silence holy kept; the harp
595 Had work and rested not, the solemn pipe,
596 And dulcimer, all organs of sweet stop,
All sounds on fret by string or golden wire,
Temper'd soft tunings intermix'd with voice
Choral or unison: of incense clouds
600 Fuming from golden censers hid the mount.[2]
Creation and the six days acts they sung:
Great are thy works, Jehovah; infinite
Thy power; what thought can measure thee, or tongue
Relate thee greater now in thy return
605 Than from the giant angels;[3] thee that day
606 Thy thunders magnified; but to create
607 Is greater than, created, to destroy.
Who can impair, thee, mighty King, or bound
Thy empire? easily the proud attempt
610 Of spirits apostate and their counsels vain
Thou hast repell'd, while impiously they thought
Thee to diminish, and from thee withdraw
613 The number of thy worshippers. Who seeks
614 To lessen thee, against his purpose serves

---

584 *Forerunning* Heralding. 587 *The Filial Power* The Son. 596.1 *dulcimer* A stringed musical instrument; 596.2 *stop* Hole. 606–607 *to create . . . destroy* In contrast, Satan does not create anything, but only destroys or perverts what already exists.

To manifest the more thy might: his evil   615
Thou usest, and from thence creat'st more good.   616
Witness this new-made world, another heaven
From heaven-gate not far, founded in view
On the clear hyaline, the glassy sea;   619
Of amplitude almost immense, with stars   620
Numerous, and every star perhaps a world   621
Of destin'd habitation; but thou know'st   622
Their seasons: among these the seat of men,
Earth with her nether ocean circumfus'd,   624
Their pleasant dwelling-place. Thrice happy men,   625
And sons of men, whom God hath thus advanc'd,
Created in his image, there to dwell
And worship him, and in reward to rule
Over his works, on earth, in sea, or air,
And multiply a race of worshippers   630
Holy and just: thrice happy, if they know
Their happiness, and persevere upright!

So sung they, and the empyrean rung
With hallelujahs: thus was Sabbath kept.
And thy request think now fulfill'd, that ask'd   635
How first this world and face of things began,   636
And what before thy memory was done
From the beginning, that posterity
Inform'd by thee might know; if else thou seek'st
Aught, not surpassing human measure, say.   640

END OF BOOK SEVENTH

613–616 *Who seeks . . . good* God will bring about the union of apparent opposites.   **619** *hyaline* Translates the Greek word for "glassy." Revelation 4:6 describes a "sea of glass" before God's throne.   **621–622** *and every star . . . habitation* Compare 3.667–670.   **624** *her nether ocean* The waters below the firmament.   **636** *face* A reminder that Adam's perception remains empirical; he is curious about the outward appearances of things.   **640** *Aught* Anything.

BOOK VIII

THE ARGUMENT

Adam inquires concerning celestial motions; is doubtfully*
answered, and exhorted to search rather things more worthy of
knowledge. Adam assents, and, still desirous to detain Raphael,
relates to him what he remembered since his own creation, his
placing in Paradise, his talk with God concerning solitude and
fit society, his first meeting and nuptials† with Eve; his
discourse with the angel thereupon, who, after admonitions
repeated, departs.

THE angel ended, and in Adam's ear   1
So charming left his voice, that he awhile   2
Thought him still speaking, still stood fixt to hear: 3
Then, as new wak'd, thus gratefully replied: 4

What thanks sufficient, or what recompense   5
Equal have I to render thee, divine
Historian, who thus largely hast allay'd   7
The thirst I had of knowledge, and vouchsaf'd
This friendly condescension, to relate   9

---

*Confusingly.
†Both "wedding celebration" and "sexual intercourse."

1–4 *The angel . . . replied* These lines were added to the 1674 edition. In the original edition of 1667, book VII was divided at line 640 to include the present book VIII; the original line 641 read: "To whom thus Adam gratefully replied." 4 *as new wak'd* Echoes the response to Orpheus' creation hymn in *Argonautica* (1.512–516), by third-century B.C. Greek poet Appolonius Rhodius. 7 *largely* Generously. 9 *condescension* The word carries no negative associations here.

10   Things else by me unsearchable, now heard
      With wonder, but delight, and, as is due,
      With glory attributed to the high
      Creator; Something yet of doubt remains,
      Which only thy solution can resolve.
15   When I behold this goodly frame, this world,
      Of heaven and earth consisting, and compute
      Their magnitudes, this earth a spot, a grain,
      An atom, with the firmament compar'd
      And all her number'd stars, that seem to roll
20   Spaces incomprehensible, (for such
21   Their distance argues and their swift return
22   Diurnal,) merely to officiate light
23   Round this opacous earth, this punctual spot,
      One day and night, in all their vast survey
25   Useless besides; reasoning, I oft admire
      How Nature, wise and frugal, could commit
      Such disproportions, with superfluous hand
      So many nobler bodies to create,
      Greater so manifold, to this one use,
30   For aught appears, and on their orbs impose
      Such restless revolution, day by day
32   Repeated, while the sedentary earth,
      That better might with far less compass move,
      Serv'd by more noble than herself, attains
35   Her end without least motion, and receives,
36   As tribute, such a sumless journey brought
      Of incorporeal speed, her warmth and light;
      Speed, to describe whose swiftness number fails.

---

15 *this goodly frame* This well-organized universe. Leonard (p. 392) notes the echo of Shakespeare's *Hamlet* (act 2, scene 2). 21 *argues* Suggests. 22.1 *Diurnal* Daily; 22.2 *officiate* Administer. 23.1 *opacous* Dark; 23.2 *punctual* Both "on time" and "as small as a point." 25.1 *Useless besides* Adam has a limited, pragmatist notion of what is useful; 25.2 *admire* Wonder. 30 *For aught appears* Apparently. 32 *sedentary* Motionless; the fact that Adam assumes principles established by second-century astronomer Ptolemy does not suggest that Milton embraced these concepts as well. 36 *sumless* Both "incalculable" and "useless."

So spake our sire, and by his count'nance seem'd
Ent'ring on studious thoughts abstruse, which Eve   40
Perceiving, where she sat retir'd in sight
With lowliness majestic from her seat,   42
And grace that won who saw to wish her stay,
Rose, and went forth among her fruits and flowers,
To visit how they prosper'd, bud and bloom,   45
Her nursery; they at her coming sprung,
And, touch'd by her fair tendance, gladlier grew.   47
Yet went she not, as not with such discourse   48
Delighted, or not capable her ear   49
Of what was high: such pleasure she reserv'd   50
Adam relating, the sole auditress;   51
Her husband the relater she preferr'd   52
Before the angel, and of him to ask   53
Chose rather; he, she knew, would intermix   54
Grateful digressions, and solve high dispute   55
With conjugal caresses; from his lip
Not words alone pleas'd her. O when meet now   57
Such pairs, in love and mutual honour join'd?   58
With goddess-like demeanour forth she went,   59
Not unattended, for on her as queen   60
A pomp of winning graces waited still,   61
And from about her shot darts of desire   62
Into all eyes to wish her still in sight.   63
And Raphael now, to Adam's doubt propos'd,
Benevolent and facile thus replied: 65

---

42 *lowliness majestic* The oxymoron anticipates Raphael's reply, which will correct Adam's
assumption that what is larger or more powerful is "nobler."   47 *tendance* Nurture.
48–54 *Yet went . . . rather* See 1 Corinthians 14:35.   55 *solve* Resolve.   57–58 *O . . . join'd*
An unusually impassioned piece of editorializing by the narrator.   59 *goddess-like* The nar-
rative voice speaks from a fallen perspective, idolizing Eve and anticipating the language
Satan will use to tempt.   60–61 *as queen / A pomp* Again, the narrator announces himself
as a fallen man who, unlike Milton, is impressed by queen and pomp.   61 *still* Always.
62–63 *And from . . . sight* The narrator lusts for Eve, describing her sensual appeal to the
eyes in frankly erotic terms.   65 *facile* Fluent.

To ask or search I blame thee not, for heaven
67 Is as the book of God before thee set,
Wherein to read his wondrous works, and learn
His seasons, hours, or days, or months, or years;
70 This to attain, whether heaven move or earth,
71 Imports not if thou reckon right; the rest
From man or angel the great Architect
Did wisely to conceal, and not divulge
His secrets to be scann'd by them who aught
75 Rather admire; or if they list to try
76 Conjecture, he his fabric of the heavens
77 Hath left to their disputes, perhaps to move
78 His laughter at their quaint opinions wide
79 Hereafter, when they come to model heaven
80 And calculate the stars, how they will wield
81 The mighty frame, how build, unbuild, contrive
82 To save appearances, how gird the sphere
83 With centric and eccentric scribbled o'er,
84 Cycle and epicycle, orb in orb;
85 Already by thy reasoning this I guess
86 Who art to lead thy offspring, and supposest
That bodies bright and greater should not serve
The less not bright, nor heaven such journies run,
Earth sitting still, when she alone receives
90 The benefit. Consider first, that great
91 Or bright infers not excellence: the earth
Though, in comparison of heaven, so small,
Nor glist'ring, may of solid good contain

---

67 *book of God* The stars constitute a text, and a correct interpretation of their significance can reveal the nature of God. 70 *attain* Learn. 70–71 *whether heaven . . . right.* The question of whether the earth moves in a physical sense is irrelevant, and by asking it Adam reveals that he has missed the point. 75–84 *or if they list . . . orb* Astronomical investigations will teach human beings only that the physical universe is far beyond their comprehension; this is in fact the real lesson to be learned from contemplating it. 75 *list* Want. 85–86 *Already . . . offspring* Adam's assumption that the more physically imposing heavenly bodies are rightfully superior to the lesser leads Raphael to deduce that the human race will be subjected to tyrants who rule by physical force. 90–91 *great . . . excellence* True worth is not to be judged by externals.

More plenty than the sun that barren shines,
Whose virtue on itself works no effect, 95
But in the fruitful earth; there, first receiv'd
His beams, unactive else, their vigour find.[1]
Yet not to earth are those bright luminaries
Officious, but to thee earth's habitant. 99
And for the heaven's wide circuit, let it speak 100
The Maker's high magnificence, who built 101
So spacious, and his line stretch'd out so far; 102
That man may know he dwells not in his own; 103
An edifice too large for him to fill, 104
Lodg'd in a small partition, and the rest 105
Ordain'd for uses to his Lord best known
The swiftness of those circles attribute,
Though numberless, to his omnipotence,
That to corporeal substances could add
Speed almost spiritual: me thou think'st not slow, 110
Who since the morning hour set out from heaven
Where God resides, and ere mid-day arriv'd
In Eden; distance inexpressible
By numbers that have name. But this I urge, 114
Admitting motion in the heavens, to show 115
Invalid that which thee to doubt it mov'd;
Not that I so affirm, though so it seem
To thee who hast thy dwelling here on earth.
God, to remove his ways from human sense, 119
Plac'd heaven from earth so far, that earthly sight, 120
If it presume, might err in things too high,
And no advantage gain. What if the sun 122
Be centre to the world, and other stars,

---

99 *to thee earth's habitant* The sun is in fact the servant of man. Raphael hints at the inverted relationship that Adam's descendants will soon fall into when they worship the sun. 100–105 *let it speak . . . partition* By studying the heavens, man will be driven to the conclusion that they could only have been framed by an omnipotent power. 110 *Speed almost spiritual* Almost the speed of thought. 114 *urge* Argue. 119 *God . . . sense* God does not wish to be apprehended through the senses. 122 *What if* Both "what does it matter if" and "what would follow if."

124 By his attractive virtue and their own
125 Incited, dance about him various rounds?
Their wand'ring course now high, now low, then hid,
Progressive, retrograde, or standing still,
128 In six thou seest; and what if seventh to these
129 The planet earth, so steadfast though she seem,
130 Insensibly three different motions move?
131 Which else to several spheres thou must ascribe,
132 Mov'd contrary with thwart obliquities,
Or save the sun his labour, and that swift
134 Nocturnal and diurnal rhomb suppos'd,
135 Invisible else above all stars, the wheel
Of day and night; which needs not thy belief,
137 If earth industrious of herself, fetch day
Travelling east, and with her part averse
From the sun's beam meet night, her other part
140 Still luminous by his ray. What if that light
141 Sent from her through the wide transpicuous air
142 To the terrestrial moon be as a star
Enlight'ning her by day, as she by night.
This earth? reciprocal, if land be there,
145 Fields and inhabitants: her spots thou seest
As clouds, and clouds may rain, and rain produce
Fruits in her soften'd soil, for some to eat
Allotted there; and other suns perhaps
149 With their attendant moons thou wilt descry
150 Communicating male and female light,

---

124 *attractive virtue* Power of attraction. 128 *six* The six then-visible "planets": Saturn, Jupiter, Mars, Venus, Mercury, and the Moon. 129 *earth* Ptolemaic cosmology held that the seventh planet was the sun, but Raphael asks Adam to consider the consequences of Copernicus's opinion that it was the earth. 130 *three different motions* Daily, yearly, and on its axis. 131 *several spheres* Leonard reminds us: "Aristotle had imagined fifty-six spheres" (p. 815). 132 *thwart obliquities* Elliptical orbits. 134 *rhomb* The sphere of the Prime Mover, the invisible force that moves all the other spheres. 137 *industrious* Because moving. 141 *transpicuous* Transparent. 142 *terrestrial moon* The earth's moon. 149 *descry* Discern. 150 *male and female* As Campbell (p. 572) notes, Milton uses the terms in the sense of "original and reflected"; the macrocosm of the universe parallels the microcosm of individual human relationships.

Which two great sexes animate the world.

Stor'd in each orb perhaps with some that live.

For such vast room in Nature unpossess'd   153

By living soul, desert and desolate,   154

Only to shine, yet scarce to contribute   155

Each orb a glimpse of light convey'd so far   156

Down to this habitable, which returns   157

Light back to them, is obvious to dispute.   158

But whether thus these things, or whether not;

Whether the sun predominant in heaven   160

Rise on the earth, or earth rise on the sun;

He from the east his flaming road begin,

Or she from the west her silent course advance,

With inoffensive pace that spinning sleeps

On her soft axle, while she paces even   165

And bears thee soft with the smooth air along   166

Solicit not thy thoughts with matters hid,   167

Leave them to God above, him serve and fear;

Of other creatures, as him pleases best,

Wherever plac'd, let him dispose: joy thou   170

In what he gives to thee, this Paradise

And thy fair Eve; heaven is for thee too high   172

To know what passes there; be lowly wise: 173

Think only what concerns thee and thy being;

Dream not of other worlds, what creatures there   175

Live, in what state, condition, or degree,

Contented that thus far hath been reveal'd,

Not of earth only, but of highest heaven.

To whom thus Adam, clear'd of doubt, replied:

How fully hast thou satisfied me, pure   180

153–158 *For . . . dispute* Raphael has repeated Adam's logic, which he earlier corrected, suggesting that the heavenly bodies must be populated, because otherwise their only function would be the apparently paltry one of supporting life on earth.   158 *obvious to dispute* Obviously open to dispute, with the implication of *too* obvious.   166 *bears thee soft* The earth is likened to a baby in its mother's arms.   167 *Solicit* Bother.   172–173 *heaven is . . . there* A statement that casts doubt on the validity of the events described in book VI.

181 Intelligence of heaven, angel serene!
And, freed from intricacies, taught to live,
The easiest way, nor with perplexing thoughts
To interrupt the sweet of life, from which
185 God hath bid dwell far off all anxious cares,
186 And not molest us, unless we ourselves
187 Seek them with wand'ring thoughts, and notions vain.
But apt the mind or fancy is to rove
189 Uncheck'd, and of her roving is no end;
190 Till warn'd, or by experience taught, she learn,
That not to know at large of things remote,
From use, obscure and subtle, but to know
That which before us lies in daily life,
194 Is the prime wisdom; what is more, is fume
195 Or emptiness, or fond impertinence,
And renders us in things that most concern
197 Unpractis'd, unprepar'd, and still to seek.
Therefore from this high pitch let us descend
A lower flight, and speak of things at hand
200 Useful, whence haply mention may arise
Of something not unseasonable to ask,
202 By sufferance, and thy wonted favour deign'd.
Thee I have heard relating what was done
Ere my remembrance; now hear me relate
205 My story, which perhaps thou hast not heard;
And day is yet not spent; till then thou seest
How subtly to detain thee I devise,
Inviting thee to hear while I relate,
209 Fond, were it not in hope of thy reply:

---

181 *Intelligence* Medieval cosmology conceived the planets as moving within "spheres" that were governed by spiritual "intelligences." Flannagan (p. 566) cites John Donne's contrast between lovers' bodies and their spirits in his poem "The Ecstasy" (1633): "We are / Th'intelligences, they the sphere" (ll. 51–52). 186–187 *And . . . vain* Adam demonstrates that he has understood Raphael's warning against superfluous knowledge. Eve has been absent for the preceding 150 lines and has not heard the angel's admonitions. 189 *no end* No purpose, no use. 194 *fume* Smoke, especially from incense. 195 *fond impertinence* Foolish irrelevance. 197 *still* Always. 200 *haply* Perhaps. 202 *sufferance* Permission. 209 *Fond* Foolish.

For while I sit with thee I seem in heaven,   210
And sweeter thy discourse is to my ear
Than fruits of palm-tree, pleasantest to thirst
And hunger both, from labour, at the hour
Of sweet repast; they satiate, and soon fill   214
Though pleasant; but thy words, with grace divine   215
Imbued, bring to their sweetness no satiety.

To whom thus Raphael answer'd heavenly meek.
Nor are thy lips ungraceful, sire of men!
Nor tongue ineloquent; for God on thee
Abundantly his gifts hath also pour'd,   220
Inward and outward both, his image fair;
Speaking or mute, all comeliness and grace
Attends thee, and each word each motion forms;
Nor less think we in heaven of thee on earth
Than of our fellow servant, and inquire   225
Gladly into the ways of God with man;
For God we see hath honour'd thee, and set
On man his equal love: say therefore on,
For I that day was absent, as befell,   229
Bound on a voyage uncouth and obscure,   230
Far on excursion toward the gates of hell;
Squar'd in full legion (such command we had)
To see that none thence issued forth a spy,
Or enemy, while God was in his work,
Lest he, incens'd at such eruption bold,   235
Destruction with creation might have mix'd.   236
Not that they durst without his leave attempt,   237

---

214 *repast* Meal. 225 *fellow servant* The angel of Revelation 22:9 forbids St. John to wor-
ship him because "I am thy fellow servant." 229 *as befell* As it happened. 230 *uncouth*
Unknown. 235–236 *Lest he . . . mix'd* As William Empson (p. 242) noticed, Raphael de-
scribes a childish and petulant deity, who might have become enraged at Satan's escape that
he would ruin his own creation. 237 *Not . . . attempt* Raphael immediately undercuts his
preceding statement by indicating that any such escape would have been planned by God
in the first place.

238   But us he sends upon his high behests
239   For state, as Sov'reign King, and to inure
240   Our prompt obedience. Fast we found, fast shut
       The dismal gates and barricado'd strong;
       But, long ere our approaching, heard within
243   Noise, other than the sound of dance or song,
244   Torment, and loud lament, and furious rage.
245   Glad we return'd up to the coasts of light
       Ere sabbath evening: so we had in charge.
       But thy relation now; for I attend,
       Pleas'd with thy words, no less than thou with mine.

       So spake the godlike power, and thus our sire.
250   For man to tell how human life began
251   Is hard; for who himself beginning knew?
       Desire with thee still longer to converse
       Induc'd me. As new wak'd from soundest sleep,
       Soft on the flowery herb I found me laid
255   In balmy sweat, which with his beams the sun
256   Soon dried, and on the reeking moisture fed.
257   Straight toward heaven my wond'ring eyes I turn'd,
258   And gaz'd awhile the ample sky; till rais'd
259   By quick instinctive motion up I sprung,
260   As thitherward endeavouring, and upright
       Stood on my feet; about me round I saw
       Hill, dale, and shady woods, and sunny plains,
263   And liquid lapse of murm'ring streams; by these,
       Creatures that liv'd and mov'd, and walk'd, or flew,

237–240 *Not that . . . obedience* Now Raphael suggests that God sends the angels on errands simply to establish and reinforce their master/servant relationship.   239 *inure* Get us used to.   243–244 *Noise . . . Torment* Alludes to Aeneas' listening outside the gates of Tartarus in Virgil's *Aeneid* 6.557–559.   251 *who himself beginning knew?* As Leonard (p. 816) observes, referring to 5.859–863: "Like Satan, Adam cannot remember his origins, but where Satan takes this as a proof that he was not created, Adam infers the existence of a 'Maker.'"   256 *reeking* Steaming.   257 *Straight . . . turn'd* Adam instinctively looks toward heaven.   258–260 *till rais'd . . . endeavouring* Adam instinctively moves toward heaven.   263.1 *lapse* Fall; 263.2 *murm'ring* Complaining.

Birds on the branches warbling; all things smil'd;   265
With fragrance, and with joy my heart o'erflow'd.
Myself I then perus'd, and limb by limb
Survey'd, and sometimes went, and sometimes ran   268
With supple joints, as lively vigour led:
But who I was, or where, or from what cause,   270
Knew not: to speak I tried, and forthwith spake
My tongue obey'd, and readily could name
Whate'er I saw.[2] Thou sun, said I, fair light,
And thou enlighten'd earth, so fresh and gay,
Ye hills, and dales, ye rivers, woods, and plains,   275
And ye that live and move, fair creatures, tell,
Tell, if ye saw, how came I thus, how here?
Not of myself; by some great Maker then,   278
In goodness and in power pre-eminent;
Tell me how may I know him, how adore,   280
From whom I have that thus I move and live,   281
And feel that I am happier than I know.
While thus I call'd, and stray'd I knew not whither,
From where I first drew air, and first beheld
This happy light, when answer none return'd,   285
On a green shady bank, profuse of flowers,
Pensive I sat me down; there gentle sleep
First found me, and with soft oppression seiz'd   288
My drowsed sense, untroubled, though I thought   289
I then was passing to my former state   290
Insensible, and forthwith to dissolve;   291
When suddenly stood at my head a dream,
Whose inward apparition gently mov'd   293
My fancy to believe I yet had being,   294

---

268 *went* Walked.   278 *Not . . . then* Adam logically deduces the existence of God from the fact of his own existence.   281 *From whom I have that thus* From whom I have the ability to.
288 *oppression* Weighing down.   289–291 *untroubled . . . dissolve* In his unfallen condition Adam has no fear of death.   293 *inward apparition* Internal image.   294 *My fancy . . . being* Of course, Adam *does* still have being, so his "fancy" is true; on the other hand, "fancy" is the faculty through which Satan entered the mind of the sleeping Eve. In the *Iliad* 2.20, Zeus sends a "lying dream" into the mind of Agamemnon in order to precipitate conflict.

295 And liv'd. One came, methought, of shape divine,
296 And said, Thy mansion wants thee, Adam, rise
First man, of men innumerable ordain'd
First father; call'd by thee I come thy guide
To the garden of bliss, thy seat prepar'd.
300 So saying, by the hand he took me rais'd,
301 And over fields and waters, as in air
302 Smooth sliding without step, last led me up
303 A woody mountain; whose high top was plain,
304 A circuit wide enclos'd; with goodliest trees
305 Planted, with walks and bowers, that what I saw
306 Of earth before scarce pleasant seem'd. Each tree
Loaden with fairest fruit, that hung to th'eye
Tempting, stirr'd in me sudden appetite
To pluck and eat; whereat I wak'd, and found
310 Before mine eyes all real, as the dream
311 Had lively shadow'd. Here had new begun
My wand'ring, had not he, who was my guide
Up hither, from among the trees appear'd,
314 Presence divine. Rejoicing, but with awe,
315 In adoration at his feet I fell
316 Submiss: he rear'd me, and, Whom thou sought'st I am,
Said mildly, Author of all this thou seest[3]
Above, or round about thee, or beneath.
This Paradise I give thee, count it thine
320 To till, and keep, and of the fruit to eat:
321 Of every tree that in the garden grows
322 Eat freely with glad heart; fear here no dearth:

---

295 *methought* Satan can disguise himself as an "angel of light." 296 *mansion* Dwelling place. 301 *as in air* Supernatural flight was usually enabled by the devil. 302 *Smooth sliding without step* Serpentine. 303 *mountain* Where Satan flies with Jesus, the "second Adam." 303 *plain* Bare. 304 *trees* As Satan led Eve to a tree. 305 *that* So that. 306 *scarce pleasant seem'd* Adam becomes weary of the rest of creation. 310–311 *all real . . . shadow'd* Unlike Eve, Adam assumes that what has been represented to him is reality. 314 *Presence divine* The identity of this "presence" must be a matter of serious doubt. Adam identifies it with the "guide" who appeared in his dream, but this figure has acted in the same manner as Satan did toward Eve. 315–316 *In adoration . . . Submiss* Adam attempts to idolize the apparition. "Submiss" literally means "cast down." 320–322 *of the fruit to eat . . . Eat freely* The "guide" twice emphasizes the permission before the prohibition. 322 *dearth* Famine.

But of the tree whose operation brings   323
Knowledge of good and ill, which I have set   324
The pledge of thy obedience and thy faith,   325
Amid the garden by the tree of life,   326
Remember what I warn thee, shun to taste,   327
And shun the bitter consequence: for know
The day thou eatest thereof, my sole command
Transgress'd, inevitably thou shalt die,   330
From that day mortal, and this happy state
Shalt lose, expell'd from hence into a world
Of woe and sorrow. Sternly he pronounc'd
The rigid interdiction, which resounds   334
Yet dreadful in mine ear, though in my choice   335
Not to incur; but soon his clear aspect   336
Return'd, and gracious purpose thus renew'd: 337
Not only these fair bounds, but all the earth
To thee and to thy race I give; as lords
Possess it, and all things that therein live,   340
Or live in sea, or air, beast, fish, and fowl.
In sign whereof each bird and beast behold
After their kinds; I bring them to receive   343
From thee their names, and pay thee fealty   344
With low subjection; understand the same   345
Of fish within their wat'ry residence,
Not hither summon'd, since they cannot change
Their element, to draw the thinner air.
As thus he spake, each bird and beast behold
Approaching two and two, these cow'ring low   350
With blandishment, each bird stoop'd on his wing.
I nam'd them, as they pass'd, and understood

323–327 *But . . . taste* In several of his prose tracts, Milton argues that rigid, legalistic prohibition—as of divorce or unlicensed publication—actually produces the violations it seems designed to prohibit.   334 *rigid interdiction* Strict prohibition.   335–336 *though . . . incur* Both "though I can choose not to violate the interdiction" and "though I'd rather the interdiction had not been imposed."   337 *purpose* Discourse.   343 *kinds* Natures. 344–345 *fealty / With low subjection* The animals are ascribed a feudal, servile relationship with Adam, which seems incongruous in prelapsarian Eden.

Their nature, with such knowledge God endued
My sudden apprehension; but in these
355 I found not what methought I wanted still;
And to the heavenly vision thus presum'd:

O by what name, for thou above all these,
Above mankind, or ought than mankind higher,
Surpassest far my naming, how may I
360 Adore thee, Author of this universe,
And all this good to man? for whose well-being
So amply, and with hands so liberal,
Thou hast provided all things: but with me
I see not who partakes. In solitude
365 What happiness, who can enjoy alone,
Or all enjoying, what contentment find?
Thus I presumptuous; and the vision bright,
As with a smile more brighten'd, thus replied:

What call'st thou solitude? is not the earth
370 With various living creatures, and the air
Replenish'd, and all these at thy command
To come and play before thee? knowest thou not
Their language and their ways? they also know,
And reason not contemptibly; with these
375 Find pastime and bear rule; thy realm is large.
So spake the universal Lord, and seem'd
So ord'ring. I with leave of speech implor'd,
378 And humble deprecation, thus replied:

Let not my words offend thee, heavenly Power,
380 My Maker, be propitious while I speak.
381 Hast thou not made me here thy substitute,
And these inferior far beneath me set?
383 Among unequals what society

---

378 *deprecation* Request.   381 *substitute* Deputy.

Can sort, what harmony or true delight? 384

Which must be mutual, in proportion due 385

Given and receiv'd; but in disparity,

The one intense, the other still remiss, 387

Cannot well suit with either, but soon prove

Tedious alike: of fellowship I speak 389

Such as I seek, fit to participate 390

All rational delight, wherein the brute 391

Cannot be human consort; they rejoice

Each with their kind, lion with lioness;

So fitly them in pairs thou hast combin'd;

Much less can bird with beast, or fish with fowl 395

So well converse, nor with the ox the ape;

Worse then can man with beast, and least of all.

Whereto th'Almighty answer'd, not displeas'd

A nice and subtle happiness I see

Thou to thyself proposest, in the choice 400

Of thy associates, Adam, and wilt taste

No pleasure, though in pleasure, solitary.

What think'st thou then of me, and this my state?

Seem I to thee sufficiently possess'd

Of happiness, or not? who am alone 405

From all eternity, for none I know

Second to me[4] or like, equal much less.

How have I then with whom to hold converse,

Save with the creatures which I made, and, those

To me inferior, infinite descents 410

Beneath what other creatures are to thee?

He ceas'd; I lowly answer'd: To attain 412

The height and depth of thy eternal ways

383–384 *Among unequals . . . sort* Adam's request is for an *equal.*   387 *intense . . . remiss* Musical terms, meaning high-pitched and low-pitched, respectively.   389–391 *of fellowship . . . rational delight* A rational being cannot enjoy true fellowship with irrational creatures.   412 *lowly* Humbly.

All human thoughts come short, Supreme of things
415 Thou in thyself art perfect, and in thee
Is no deficience found; not so is man,
417 But in degree, the cause of his desire,
By conversation with his like, to help
Or solace his defects. No need that thou
420 Shouldst propagate, already infinite,
421 And through all numbers absolute, though one;
But man by number is to manifest
His simple imperfection, and beget
Like of his like, his image multiplied,
425 In unity defective, which requires
426 Collateral love, and dearest amity.
Thou in thy secrecy, although alone,
Best with thyself accompanied, seek'st not
429 Social communication, yet, so pleas'd,
430 Canst raise thy creatures to what heighth thou wilt
Of union or communion, deified;
I by conversing cannot these erect
433 From prone, nor in their ways complacence find.
Thus I embolden'd spake, and freedom us'd
435 Permissive, and acceptance found, which gain'd
This answer from the gracious voice divine:

437 Thus far to try thee, Adam, I was pleas'd,
And find thee knowing, not of beasts alone,
Which thou hast rightly nam'd, but of thyself,
440 Expressing well the spirit within thee free,
441 My image, not imparted to the brute,
Whose fellowship therefore unmeet for thee

---

417 *But . . . desire* Desire is produced by the recognition of difference. 421 *And through . . . one* Fowler observes: "The divine monad contains all other numbers" (p. 451). 426 *Collateral* Corresponding; a financial term. 429 *so pleas'd* If you please. 433 *complacence* Satisfaction. Fowler notes that the Son is the Father's "complacence" in 3.276. 437 *try* Test. 440–441 *the spirit . . . image* Man is God's image in a spiritual, rather than a physical, sense.

Good reason was thou freely shouldst dislike,
And be so minded still; I, ere thou spak'st,
Knew it not good for man to be alone,   445
And no such company as then thou saw'st
Intended thee, for trial only brought,
To see how thou couldst judge of fit and meet.
What next I bring shall please thee, be assur'd,
Thy likeness, thy fit help, thy other self,   450
Thy wish exactly to thy heart's desire.

He ended, or I heard no more, for now
My earthly by his heavenly overpower'd   453
Which it had long stood under, strain'd to the heighth
In that celestial colloquy sublime,   455
As with an object that excels the sense,   456
Dazzled and spent, sunk down, and sought repair   457
Of sleep, which instantly fell on me, call'd
By Nature as in aid, and clos'd mine eyes.
Mine eyes he clos'd, but open left the cell   460
Of Fancy, my internal sight, by which   461
Abstract as in a trance methought I saw,   462
Though sleeping, where I lay, and saw the shape   463
Still glorious before whom awake I stood;
Who, stooping, open'd my left side, and took   465
From thence a rib, with cordial spirits warm,   466

---

445 *alone* Echoes Genesis 2:18: "It is not good that the man should be alone." **450.1** *likeness* Image; **450.2** *fit help . . . self* As Hughes puts it: "Against the biblical term for wife, 'help-meet' (fit help) Milton puts the classical term for an ideal friend, an *other self*" (p. 373). **453** *My . . . overpower'd* My earthly nature overpowered by his heavenly nature. **455** *colloquy* Conversation. **456** *an object that excels the sense* A paradox, since objects are by definition sensual. **457** *spent* The term frequently referred to orgasm. **460–461** *the cell . . . sight* Flannagan comments: " 'the cell / Of Fancy' is a precise term describing what was thought to be a storage space in the brain for images gathered by the senses during waking time and then recombined by the fancy in sleep" (p. 575). **462** *Abstract* Abstracted, made other than the self. **463** *shape* Image. **465** *my left side* This detail is not in the Bible, but Sin is born from the left side of Satan's head at 2.755. **466** *cordial* Vital, from the heart.

The Creation of Eve

And life-blood streaming fresh; wide was the wound,
But suddenly with flesh fill'd up and heal'd:
The rib he form'd and fashion'd with his hands;
Under his forming hands a creature grew,   470
Manlike, but different sex, so lovely fair,
That what seem'd fair in all the world, seem'd now
Mean, or in her summ'd up, in her contain'd,
And in her looks, which from that time infus'd
Sweetness into my heart, unfelt before,   475
And into all things from her air inspir'd
The spirit of love and amorous delight.   477
She disappear'd, and left me dark; I wak'd   478
To find her, or for ever to deplore   479
Her loss, and other pleasures all abjure: 480
When out of hope, behold her, not far off,
Such as I saw her in my dream, adorn'd
With what all earth or heaven could bestow
To make her amiable. On she came,
Led by her heavenly Maker, though unseen,   485
And guided by his voice, nor uninform'd
Of nuptial sanctity and marriage rites:
Grace was in all her steps, heaven in her eye,
In every gesture dignity and love;
I, overjoy'd, could not forbear aloud.   490

This turn hath made amends; thou hast fulfill'd
Thy words, Creator bounteous and benign,
Giver of all things fair, but fairest this
Of all thy gifts, nor enviest. I now see   494
Bone of my bone, flesh of my flesh, myself   495
Before me; Woman is her name, of man
Extracted: for this cause he shall forego   497

---

477 *amorous delight* Sexual desire.   478 *She disappear'd . . . wak'd* Compare Milton's Sonnet
23 (c.1658): "I wak'd, she fled, and day brought back my night."   479 *deplore* Mourn.   490
forbear aloud Refrain from saying.   494 *nor enviest* Nor given grudgingly.

498   Father and mother, to his wife adhere;

499   And they shall be one flesh, one heart, one soul.

500   She heard me thus, and though divinely brought,

        Yet innocence and virgin modesty,

502   Her virtue and the conscience of her worth,

503   That would be woo'd, and not unsought be won

504   Not obvious, not obtrusive, but retir'd

505   The more desirable, or to say all,

506   Nature herself, though pure of sinful thought,

        Wrought in her so, that seeing me, she turn'd:

        I follow'd her; she what was honour knew,

509   And with obsequious majesty approv'd

510   My pleaded reason. To the nuptial bower

        I led her, blushing like the morn: all heaven,

        And happy constellations, on that hour

        Shed their selectest influence; the earth

514   Gave sign of gratulation, and each hill;

515   Joyous the birds; fresh gales and gentle airs

        Whisper'd it to the woods, and from their wings

        Flung rose, flung odours from the spicy shrub,

518   Disporting till the amorous bird of night

519   Sung spousal, and bid haste the evening star

520   On his hill top, to light the bridal lamp.

        Thus have I told thee all my state, and brought

        My story to the sum of earthly bliss

        Which I enjoy, and must confess to find

        In all things else delight indeed, but such

525   As, us'd or not, works in the mind no change,

497–499 *for this cause . . . soul* Paraphrases Genesis 2:23–24.   **502** *conscience* Consciousness, but a suggestion of guilt may also be projected onto Eve by the narrator, who seems, like Adam, to regard Eve as provocative.   **503** *not unsought be won* Adam sees Eve as a coquette. **504–505** *retir'd / The more desirable* Like the forbidden fruit.   **506** *sinful* Raises the question of how Adam can conceptualize sin before the Fall.   **509** *obsequious* Lowly.   **514** *gratulation* Celebration.   **518** *amorous bird of night* Nightingale.   **519** *evening star* Venus, or Hesperus.

Nor vehement desire, these delicacies 526
I mean of taste, sight, smell, herbs, fruits, and flowers,
Walks, and the melody of birds; but here
Far otherwise! transported I behold, 529
Transported touch; here passion first I felt, 530
Commotion strange, in all enjoyments else 531
Superior and unmov'd; here only weak
Against the charm of beauty's powerful glance. 533
Or nature fail'd in me, and left some part
Not proof enough such object to sustain, 535
Or from my side subducting, took perhaps 536
More than enough; at least on her bestow'd
Too much of ornament, in outward show 538
Elaborate, of inward less exact. 539
For well I understand in the prime end 540
Of nature her th'inferior, in the mind
And inward faculties, which most excel,
In outward also her resembling less
His image who made both, and less expressing
The character of that dominion given 545
O'er other creatures; yet when I approach
Her loveliness, so absolute she seems, 547
And in herself complete, so well to know
Her own, that what she wills to do or say
Seems wisest, virtuousest, discreetest, best; 550
All higher knowledge in her presence falls
Degraded, wisdom in discourse with her 552
Loses discount'nanc'd, and like folly shows; 553
Authority and reason on her wait,
As one intended first, not after made 555

---

526 *vehement* Mindless. 529.1 *Far otherwise* That is, Eve *does* provoke "vehement desire.";
529.2 *transported* Carried beyond oneself; often used to describe the flights of witches.
531 *Commotion* Excitement. 533 *charm* Magical spell; compare 9.999. 535 *object* Adam has
already objectified Eve. 536 *subducting* Removing. 538 *Too much of ornament* Adam
blames God's design for his own intemperate lust. 539 *exact* Perfect. 545 *dominion* Rule.
547 *absolute* Indissoluble. 552–553 *wisdom . . . shows* Adam's fascination with Eve's body
reverses his rational and ethical judgment.

556   Occasionally; and, to consummate all,
        Greatness of mind and nobleness their seat
        Build in her loveliest, and create an awe
        About her, as a guard angelic plac'd.

560   To whom the angel with contracted brow:
561   Accuse not nature, she hath done her part;
562   Do thou but thine, and be not diffident
        Of wisdom; she deserts thee not, if thou
        Dismiss not her, when most thou need'st her nigh,
565   By attributing overmuch to things
        Less excellent, as thou thyself perceiv'st.
        For what admir'st thou, what transports thee so?
568   An outside? fair no doubt, and worthy well
        Thy cherishing, thy honouring, and thy love,
570   Not thy subjection: weigh with her thyself;
571   Then value. Oft-times nothing profits more
572   Than self-esteem, grounded on just and right
        Well manag'd; of that skill the more thou know'st,
        The more she will acknowledge thee her head,
575   And to realities yield all her shows:
576   Made to adorn for thy delight the more,
577   So awful, that with honour thou may'st love
        Thy mate, what sees when thou art seen least wise.
579   But if the sense of touch, whereby mankind
580   Is propagated, seem such dear delight
581   Beyond all other, think the same vouchsaf'd
582   To cattle and each beast; which would not be

---

556 *Occasionally* Incidentally.   561 *Accuse not nature* Adam has projected his faulty subjective reaction to Eve onto her objective, natural qualities.   562 *diffident* Suspicious.   568 *outside* Body.   570–571 *weigh . . . value* In other words, "Compare your rational capacities with the physical desire evoked in you by Eve, and then say which is more valuable."   572 *self-esteem* According to Leonard (p. 821), Milton coined this term in *An Apology for Smectymnuus* (1642).   576 *adorn* According to Flannagan, "Milton coined this adjectival form of what is usually a noun . . . The Italian *adorno*, from which he may have derived his usage, means 'naturally beautiful' " (p. 579).   577 *awful* Awe-inspiring.   579–582 *But if . . . beast* Animals, like men, feel sexual lust; it follows that sexual pleasure cannot be the proper end of human love.

To them made common and divulg'd, if aught
Therein enjoy'd were worthy to subdue
The soul of man, or passion in him move.   585
What higher in her society thou find'st
Attractive, human, rational, love still;
In loving thou dost well, in passion not,
Wherein true love consists not; love refines   589
The thoughts, and heart enlarges, hath his seat   590
In reason, and is judicious, is the scale
By which to heavenly love thou may'st ascend;
Not sunk in carnal pleasure, for which cause
Among the beasts no mate for thee was found.   594

To whom thus half abash'd, Adam replied: 595
Neither her outside form'd so fair, nor aught
In procreation common to all kinds,
(Though higher of the genial bed by far   598
And with mysterious reverence I deem,)   599
So much delights me, as those graceful acts,   600
Those thousand decencies that daily flow
From all her words and actions, mix'd with love
And sweet compliance, which declare unfeign'd
Union of mind, or in us both one soul;
Harmony to behold in wedded pair   605
More grateful than harmonious sound to th'ear.
Yet these subject not; I to thee disclose
What inward thence I feel, not therefore foil'd,
Who meet with various objects, from the sense
Variously representing; yet still free,   610
Approve the best, and follow what I approve.
To love thou blam'st me not, for love thou say'st

---

589 *refines* Purifies.   594 *Among . . . found* Raphael points out that Adam's sensual and passionate reaction to Eve contradicts his original request for a rational "equal."   595 *half abash'd* By no means completely abashed.   598 *genial* Fertile.   599 *mysterious reverence* The word "mystery" was often applied to the sacraments. Unlike Adam, Milton did not view marriage as a sacrament.   605 *wedded* In a spiritual, not a sacramental, sense.

Leads up to heaven, is both the way and guide;
Bear with me then, if lawful what I ask;
615   Love not the heavenly spirits, and how their love
Express they, by looks only, or do they mix
617   Irradiance, virtual or immediate touch?

To whom the angel, with a smile that glow'd
619   Celestial rosy red, love's proper hue,
620   Answer'd: Let it suffice thee that thou know'st
Us happy, and without love no happiness.
Whatever pure thou in the body enjoy'st
(And pure thou wert created) we enjoy
In eminence, and obstacle find none
625   Of membrane, joint or limb, exclusive bars;
Easier than air with air, if spirits embrace,
Total they mix, union of pure with pure
Desiring; nor restrain'd conveyance need,
As flesh to mix with flesh, or soul with soul.
630   But I can now no more; the parting sun
631   Beyond the earth's green Cape and verdant Isles
632   Hesperian sets, my signal to depart.
Be strong, live happy, and love; but first of all,
Him whom love is to obey, and keep
635   His great command; take heed lest passion sway
Thy judgment to do aught, which else free will
Would not admit: thine and of all thy sons
638   The weal or woe in thee is plac'd; beware.
I in thy persevering shall rejoice,
640   And all the bless'd: stand fast; to stand or fall
Free in thine own arbitrament it lies.
Perfect within no outward aid require;
And all temptation to transgress repel.

---

617 *virtual* Essential, real.   619 *rosy red* Raphael is blushing.   625 *exclusive* Shutting out.
630 *can* Can say.   631 *green Cape and verdant Isles* The Cape Verde Isles, off western Africa.
632 *Hesperian* Venusian.   638 *weal* Welfare.

So saying, he arose; whom Adam thus
Follow'd with benediction: Since to part,   645
Go, heavenly guest, ethereal messenger,
Sent from whose sov'reign goodness I adore.
Gentle to me and affable hath been
Thy condescension, and shall be honour'd ever
With grateful memory: thou to mankind   650
Be good and friendly still, and oft return.

So parted they; the angel up to heaven
From the thick shade, and Adam to his bower.

END OF BOOK EIGHTH

645.1 *benediction* Thanksgiving, but the word was associated with Catholic liturgy; 645.2
Since to part Since you must go.

BOOK IX

ARGUMENT

Satan having compassed the earth, with mediated guile returns as
a mist by night into Paradise, and enters into the serpent sleeping.
Adam and Eve in the morning go forth to their labours, which
Eve proposes to divide in several† places, each labouring apart.
Adam consents not, alleging the danger, lest that enemy, of whom
they were forewarned, should attempt her found alone. Eve, loth to
be thought not circumspect or firm enough, urges her going apart,
the rather desirous to make trial of her strength: Adam at last
yields. The Serpent finds her alone; his subtle approach, first
gazing, then speaking, with much flattery extolling Eve above all
other creatures. Eve, wondering to hear the Serpent speak, asks
how he attained to human speech and such understanding not till
now; the Serpent answers, that by tasting of a certain tree in the
garden he attained both to speech and reason, till then void of both.
Eve requires‡ him to bring her to that tree, and finds it to be the
tree of knowledge forbidden. The Serpent, now grown bolder, with
many wiles and arguments induces her at length to eat: she,
pleased with the taste, deliberates awhile whether to impart thereof
to Adam or not; at last brings him of the fruit, relates what
persuaded her to eat thereof. Adam, at first amazed, but perceiving
her lost, resolves, through vehemence of love,§ to perish with her;*

---

*Circumnavigated.
†Different.
‡Asks.
§As Fowler points out, "vehemence" literally means "mindlessness"; compare 8.526.

*and, extenuating the trespass, eats also of the fruit. The effects
thereof in them both; they seek to cover their nakedness; then fall to
variance* and accusation of one another.*

1   No more of talk, where God or angel guest
2   With man, as with his friend familiar us'd
     To sit indulgent, and with him partake
     Rural repast, permitting him the while
5   Venial discourse unblam'd: I now must change
     Those notes to tragic; foul distrust, and breach
     Disloyal on the part of man, revolt
     And disobedience; on the part of heaven,
9   Now alienated, distance and distaste,
10   Anger and just rebuke, and judgment given,
     That brought into this world a world of woe,
     Sin, and her shadow Death, and Misery
13   Death's harbinger. Sad task; yet argument
     Not less but more heroic than the wrath
15   Of stern Achilles on his foe pursu'd,
16   Thrice fugitive, about Troy wall; or rage
     Of Turnus for Lavinia disespous'd:[1]
18   Or Neptune's ire or Juno's, that so long
     Perplex'd the Greek and Cytherea's son[2]
20   If answerable style I can obtain
21   Of my celestial patroness, who deigns
     Her nightly visitation unimplor'd,
     And dictates to me slumb'ring, or inspires

---

*Disagreement.

1 *No more of talk* A negative invocation; compare the openings of books I, III, and VII.   2
familiar Like a member of the family; but the term was often used of the animal owned
by a witch, through whom she communicated with the devil.   5 *Venial* Blameless.   9 *alien-
ated* Made other.   13 *harbinger* Forerunner.   15–16 *Achilles . . . wall* Achilles chased Hector
three times around the walls of Troy. Milton asserts that the martial heroism celebrated in
classical epics is less heroic than the interior struggle against temptation.   18 *Or . . . or* Ei-
ther . . . or.   20 *answerable* Corresponding.   21 *celestial patroness* Divine inspiration.

Easy my unpremeditated verse:[3]
Since first this subject for heroic song   25
Pleas'd me, long choosing, and beginning late;[4]
Not sedulous by nature to indite   27
Wars, hitherto the only argument.
Heroic deem'd, chief mast'ry to dissect   29
With long and tedious havoc, fabled knights   30
In battles feign'd; the better fortitude
Of patience and heroic martyrdom
Unsung;[5] or to describe races and games,
Or tilting furniture, emblazon'd shields,   34
Impresses quaint, caparisons, and steeds;   35
Bases and tinsel trappings, gorgeous knights   36
At joust and tournament; then marshall'd feast
Serv'd up in hall with sewers, and seneschals;   38
The skill of artifice or office mean,
Not that which justly gives heroic name   40
To person or to poem. Me, of these
Nor skill'd nor studious, higher argument
Remains, sufficient of itself to raise
That name, unless an age too late, or cold   44
Climate, or years, damp my intended wing   45
Depress'd, and much they may, if all be mine,   46
Not hers who brings it nightly to my ear.   47

The sun was sunk, and after him the star
Of Hesperus, whose office is to bring

27.1 *sedulous* Industrious; 27.2 *indite* Write down.   29 *dissect* "Analyze," but also "chop up." 30 *havoc* Chaos, butchery.   34 *tilting furniture* Jousting equipment. Milton now turns to the denigration of chivalric Romance.   36 *tinsel trappings* Leonard (p. 823) notes that this term is twice applied to horses in Edmund Spenser's *Faerie Queene* (1.2.13 and 3.1.15).   38 *sewers, and seneschals* Stewards and servants.   44.1 *That name* John Milton; 44.2 *age too late* The post-Christian era heralded by the Restoration.   44–45 *cold / Climate* The English climate was far colder in the seventeenth century than it is today; Milton had enjoyed the sun and warmth of Italy.   45 *years* Milton's own years; he was fifty-eight when *Paradise Lost* was published.   46–47 *if all be mine . . . ear* Milton points out that age and circumstances should make it impossible for him to complete a work on the scale of *Paradise Lost*, and deduces that there must be some force or spirit that is speaking through him.

50 Twilight upon the earth, short arbiter
    'Twixt day and night; and now from end to end
    Night's hemisphere had veil'd the horizon round:
    When Satan, who late fled before the threats
    Of Gabriel out of Eden, now improv'd
55 In meditated fraud and malice, bent
56 On man's destruction, maugre what might hap
    Of heavier on himself, fearless return'd.
    By night he fled, and at midnight return'd
    From compassing the earth, cautious of day,
60 Since Uriel, regent of the sun, descried
    His entrance, and forewarn'd the cherubim
    That kept their watch; thence, full of anguish driven,
    The space of seven continued nights he rode
    With darkness, thrice the equinoctial line
65 He circled, four times cross'd the car of night
    From pole to pole, traversing each colure;
67 On th'eighth return'd, and on the coast, averse
    From entrance or cherubic watch, by stealth
    Found unsuspected way. There was a place,
70 Now not, though sin, not time, first wrought the change,
71 Where Tigris at the foot of Paradise
    Into a gulf shot under ground, till part
    Rose up a fountain by the tree of life;
    In with the river sunk, and with it rose
75 Satan involv'd in rising mist, then sought
    Where to lie hid; sea he had search'd, and land
77 From Eden over Pontus, and the pool
78 Mæotis, up beyond the river Ob;
    Downward as far antarctic; and in length
80 West from Orontes to the ocean barr'd
81 At Darien, thence to the land where flows

---

56 *maugre what might hap* Despite what might happen. 60 *descried* Discerned. 67 *averse*
On the other side. 71 *Tigris* River in modern Iraq. 77 *Pontus* Black Sea. 78.1 *Mæotis*
The Sea of Azov, in Russia; 78.2 *river Ob* In Siberia. 80 *Orontes* River in Syria.
81 *Darien* Panama.

Ganges and Indus. Thus the orb he roam'd 82
With narrow search, and with inspection deep
Consider'd every creature which of all
Most opportune might serve his wiles, and found 85
The serpent subtlest beast of all the field.
Him, after long debate, irresolute
Of thoughts revolv'd, his final sentence chose
Fit vessel, fittest imp of fraud, in whom 89
To enter, and his dark suggestions hide 90
From sharpest sight: for in the wily snake,
Whatever sleights, none would suspicious mark,
As from his wit and native subtlety
Proceeding, which in other beasts observ'd
Doubt might beget of diabolic power, 95
Active within beyond the sense of brute.
Thus he resolv'd; but first from inward grief
His bursting passion into plaints thus pour'd; 98

O earth, how like to heaven, if not preferr'd
More justly, seat worthier of gods, as built 100
With second thoughts, reforming what was old![6] 101
For what God after better worse would build?
Terrestrial heaven, danc'd round by other heavens
That shine, yet bear their bright officious lamps,
Light above light, for thee alone, as seems, 105
In thee concentring all their precious beams 106
Of sacred influence! As God in heaven 107
Is centre, yet extends to all, so thou
Centring receiv'st from all those orbs; in thee, 109

82.1 *Ganges and Indus* Rivers in India; 82.2 *roam'd* Compare Job 1:7.   89 *imp* "Evil spirit,"
but also "to graft," as onto a tree.   95 *Doubt* Suspicion.   98.1 *His bursting passion* Satan's
emotional nature endeared him to the Romantics, but for Milton the fact that he acts on
passion rather than on reason is evidence of his lack of faith; 98.2 *plaints* Complaints.   101
reforming what was old Allusion to the Protestant Reformation, and more generally to Mil-
ton's conviction that redemption is preferable to innocence.   105–107 *for thee alone . . . in-
fluence* Satan echoes Adam's puzzlement that seemingly superior heavenly bodies appear to
serve the ends of the earth.

110 Not in themselves, all their known virtue appears
Productive in herb, plant, and nobler birth
112 Of creatures animate with gradual life
Of growth, sense, reason, all summ'd up in man.
With what delight could I have walk'd thee round,
115 If I could joy in aught, sweet interchange
Of hill and valley, rivers, woods, and plains,
Now land, now sea, and shores with forest crown'd,
Rocks, dens, and caves; but I in none of these
119 Find place of refuge; and the more I see
120 Pleasures about me, so much more I feel
121 Torment within me, as from the hateful siege
122 Of contraries; all good to me becomes
123 Bane, and in heaven much worse would be my state.
But neither here seek I, no nor in heaven,
125 To dwell, unless by mast'ring heaven's Supreme;
126 Nor hope to be myself less miserable
127 By what I seek, but others to make such
128 As I, though thereby worse to me redound:
129 For only in destroying I find ease
130 To my relentless thoughts; and him destroy'd,
Or won to what may work his utter loss,
For whom all this was made, all this will soon
133 Follow, as to him link'd in weal or woe;
In woe then; that destruction wide may range.
135 To me shall be the glory sole among
136 The infernal powers, in one day to have marr'd
137 What he, Almighty styl'd, six nights and days
Continued making, and who knows how long

109–110 *in thee . . . appears* The heavenly bodies do not exist for themselves; their purpose is to serve earth's purposes. **112** *gradual* Gradated. **119–121** *the more I see . . . within me* A concise statement of Satan's alienation from his surroundings. **121–122** *the hateful siege / Of contraries* Satan's alienation means that he cannot conceive of difference without opposition. **122–123** *all good . . . Bane* Alienation produces contradiction. **126–128** *Nor hope . . . As I* Misery loves company. **129** *destroying* Satan is the principle of destruction, as God is the principle of creation. **130** *him* Adam. **133** *weal* Wellness. **136** *marr'd* Destroyed. **137** *styl'd* Called.

Before had been contriving, though perhaps
Not longer than since I in one night freed   140
From servitude inglorious well nigh half
Th'angelic name, and thinner left the throng
Of his adorers: he to be aveng'd,
And to repair his numbers thus impair'd,
Whether such virtue spent of old now fail'd   145
More angels to create, if they at least   146
Are his created, or to spite us more,
Determin'd to advance into our room
A creature form'd of earth, and him endow,
Exalted from so base original,   150
With heavenly spoils, our spoils. What he decreed
He effected; man he made, and for him built
Magnificent this world, and earth his seat,
Him lord pronounc'd, and, O indignity;
Subjected to his service angel wings,   155
And flaming ministers, to watch and tend
Their earthly charge. Of these the vigilance
I dread, and to elude; thus wrapp'd in mist
Of midnight vapour glide obscure, and pry
In every bush and brake, where hap may find   160
The serpent sleeping, in whose mazy folds
To hide me, and the dark intent I bring.
O foul descent! that I, who erst contended   163
With gods to sit the highest, am now constrain'd   164
Into a beast, and mix'd with bestial slime,   165
This essence to incarnate and imbrute,   166
That to the height of Deity aspir'd;
But what will not ambition and revenge

---

145 *virtue spent* Exhausted power. Satan speculates that God may have used up all his potency. The phrase carries blasphemous sexual connotations.   146 *if* Satan's opinion on God's creative power is hopelessly vacillatory. Here he is uncertain whether the angels were created by God; earlier he claimed to be certain that he was "self-begot," but he also admits that God created him.   163 *O foul descent* Satan's disgust at having to take fleshly form contrasts with the Son's happy willingness to become man.   164 *constrain'd* Both "compressed" and "forced."   166 *imbrute* Make into an animal.

Descend to? who aspires, must down as low
170 As high he soar'd, obnoxious first or last,
To basest things. Revenge, at first though sweet,
Bitter ere long, back on itself recoils;
173 Let it; I reck not, so it light well aim'd,
174 Since higher I fall short, on him who next
175 Provokes my envy, this new favorite
Of heaven, this man of clay, son of despite,
Whom us the more to spite his Maker rais'd
From dust. Spite then with spite is best repaid.

So saying, through each thicket, dank or dry,
180 Like a black mist low creeping, he held on
His midnight search, where soonest he might find
The serpent: him fast sleeping soon he found
183 In labyrinth of many a round self roll'd,
His head the midst, well stor'd with subtle wiles.
185 Not yet in horrid shade or dismal den,
186 Nor nocent yet, but on the grassy herb,
Fearless unfear'd he slept: in at his mouth
188 The Devil enter'd, and his brutal sense,
In heart, or head, possessing, soon inspir'd
190 With act intelligential; but his sleep
Disturb'd not, waiting close th'approach of morn.

Now, when the sacred light began to dawn
In Eden on the humid flowers, that breath'd
Their morning incense, when all things that breathe
195 From the earth's great altar send up silent praise
196 To the Creator, and his nostrils fill
With grateful smell, forth came the human pair,

---

170 *obnoxious* Exposed.   173 *reck* Care.   174 *Since . . . short* Since my weapons cannot hit any being higher than man.   175.1 *Provokes* Satan sees Eve as lust-provoking; 175.2 *favorite* Satan thinks of man as the favored minion of a king.   180 *held* Continued.   183 *labyrinth* In Greek mythology, it contained the Minotaur: half man, half bull.   186 *nocent* Guilty. 188 *brutal* Animal.   196 *nostrils* The image draws attention to its own artificiality, and so to the impossibility of accurately representing God.

And join'd their vocal worship to the choir
Of creatures wanting voice; that done, partake   199
The season, prime for sweetest scents and airs: 200
Then commune how that day they best may ply
Their growing work; for much their work outgrew
The hands despatch the two gard'ning so wide,
And Eve first to her husband thus began:

Adam; well may we labour still to dress   205
This garden, still we tend plant, herb, and flower,
Our pleasant task enjoin'd, but till more hands
Aid us, the work under our labour grows,
Luxurious by restraint; what we by day
Lop overgrown, or prune, or prop, or bind,   210
One night or two with wanton growth derides,
Tending to wild. Thou therefore now advise
Or hear what to my mind first thoughts present,
Let us divide our labours,[7] thou where choice
Leads thee, or where most needs, whether to wind   215
The woodbine round this arbour, or direct
The clasping ivy where to climb, while I
In yonder spring of roses intermix'd   218
With myrtle, find what to redress till noon:
For while so near each other thus all day   220
Our task we choose, what wonder if so near
Looks intervene, and smiles, or object new
Casual discourse draw on, which intermits   223
Our day's work brought to little, though begun
Early, and th'hour of supper comes unearn'd.   225

To whom mild answer Adam thus return'd:
Sole Eve, associate sole, to me beyond   227

---

199 *wanting* Lacking.   218 *spring of roses* Milton may be thinking of George Herbert's poem "Virtue" (1633): "Sweet spring, full of sweet days and roses."   223 *intermits* Interrupts.   227 *associate sole* In three senses: "only associate," "associated soul," and "associate of my soul."

Compare above all living creatures dear,
Well hast thou motion'd, well thy thoughts employ'd,
230 How we might well fulfil the work which here
God hath assign'd us, nor of me shalt pass
Unprais'd; for nothing lovelier can be found
In woman, than to study household good,
234 And good works in her husband to promote.
235 Yet not so strictly hath our Lord impos'd
Labour, as to debar us when we need
Refreshment, whether food, or talk between,
Food of the mind, or this sweet intercourse
Of looks and smiles; for smiles from reason flow,
240 To brute denied, and are of love the food,
Love not the lowest end of human life.
242 For not to irksome toil, but to delight
243 He made us, and delight to reason join'd.
These paths and bowers, doubt not but our joint hands
245 Will keep from wilderness with ease, as wide
246 As we need walk, till younger hands ere long
Assist us: but if much converse perhaps
Thee satiate, to short absence I could yield;
For solitude sometimes is best society,
250 And short retirement urges sweet return.
But other doubt. possesses me, lest harm
Befall thee sever'd from me; for thou know'st
What hath been warn'd us, what malicious foe,
Envying our happiness, and of his own
255 Despairing, seeks to work us woe and shame
By sly assault; and somewhere nigh at hand
Watches, no doubt, with greedy hope to find,
His wish and best advantage, us asunder,
Hopeless to circumvent us join'd, where each

---

234 *And good . . . promote* The woman's goodness is reflected in the man.   242 *to . . . to*
For . . . for.   243 *delight to reason join'd* Milton alludes to Aristotle's doctrine that the high-
est end and chief delight of man is a life of intellectual speculation.   246 *younger hands*
The hands of their future offspring.

To other speedy aid might lend at need;   260
Whether his first, design be to withdraw   261
Our fealty from God, or to disturb   262
Conjugal love, than which perhaps no bliss   263
Enjoy'd by us excites his envy more;   264
Or this, or worse, leave not the faithful side   265
That gave thee being, still shades thee and protects   266
The wife, where danger or dishonour lurks,
Safest and seemliest by her husband stays,
Who guards her, or with her the worst endures.

To whom the virgin majesty of Eve,   270
As one who loves, and some unkindness meets,
With sweet austere composure thus replied:

Offspring of heaven and earth, and all earth's lord
That such an enemy we have, who seeks
Our ruin, both by thee inform'd I learn,   275
And from the parting angel overheard,
As in a shady nook I stood behind,
Just then return'd at shut of evening flowers.
But that thou shouldst my firmness therefore doubt
To God or thee, because we have a foe   280
May tempt it, I expected not to hear.
His violence thou fear'st not, being such
As we, not capable of death or pam,
Can either not receive, or can repel.
His fraud is then thy fear, which plain infers   285
Thy equal fear, that my firm faith and love
Can by his fraud be shaken or seduc'd;
Thoughts, which how found they harbour in thy breast,
Adam, misthought of her to thee so dear?   289

261–262 *to withdraw / Our fealty* To draw away our loyalty.   263–264 *Conjugal love . . . more* Adam correctly infers that sexual jealousy is a large part of Satan's motive.   265–266 *leave not . . . being* Emphasizing that Eve is to Adam as Adam is to God.   270 *virgin majesty* Alludes to Elizabeth I, the "virgin queen."   289 *misthought of her* Both "badly thought of her" and "badly thought of by her."

290 To whom with healing words Adam replied.
    Daughter of God and man, immortal Eve!
292 For such thou art, from sin and blame entire;
293 Not diffident of thee do I dissuade
    Thy absence from my sight; but to avoid
295 Th'attempt itself, intended by our foe.
296 For he who tempts, though in vain, at least asperses
297 The tempted with dishonour foul, suppos'd
298 Not incorruptible of faith, not proof
299 Against temptation: thou thyself with scorn
300 And anger wouldst resent the offer'd wrong,
301 Though ineffectual found; misdeem not then,
    If such affront I labour to aver:
    From thee alone, which on us both at once
    The enemy, though bold, will hardly dare,
305 Or daring, first on me th'assault shall light.
306 Nor thou his malice and false guile contemn;
    Subtle he needs must be, who could seduce
    Angels, nor think superfluous others aid.
    I from the influence of thy looks receive
310 Access in every virtue, in thy sight
    More wise, more watchful, stronger, if need were
    Of outward strength; while shame, thou looking on,
    Shame to be overcome or over-reach'd,
    Would utmost vigour raise, and rais'd unite.
315 Why shouldst not thou like sense within thee feel
    When I am present, and thy trial choose
    With me, best witness of thy virtue tried?

318 So spake domestic Adam in his care
    And matrimonial love; but Eve, who thought

---

292 *entire* Entirely free. 293 *diffident* Distrustful. 296 *asperses* Casts aspersions on.
296–299 *For he . . . temptation* This reasoning contradicts Milton's message in *Comus* and
Areopagitica, where he argues that virtue is impervious to temptation. 299–300 *scorn /
And anger* Adam wrongly believes that Eve would fall, and thus experience sinful emotions,
simply by being tempted. 301 *misdeem* Misunderstand. 306 *contemn* Underestimate.
310 *Access in* Access to. 318 *domestic* Having responsibility for the home.

Less attributed to her faith sincere,   320
Thus her reply with accent sweet renew'd: 321

If this be our condition, thus to dwell
In narrow circuit straiten'd by a foe,   323
Subtle or violent, we not endued   324
Single with like defence, wherever met,   325
How are we happy, still in fear of harm?   326
But harm precedes not sin; only our foe
Tempting affronts us with his foul esteem
Of our integrity; his foul esteem
Sticks no dishonour on our front, but turns   330
Foul on himself: then wherefore shunn'd or fear'd
By us? who rather double honour gain   332
From his surmise prov'd false, find peace within,
Favour from heaven, our witness from th'event.
And what is faith, love, virtue, unassay'd.   335
Alone, without exterior help sustain'd?
Let us not then suspect our happy state
Left so imperfect by the Maker wise,
As not secure to single or combin'd.
Frail is our happiness, if this be so,   340
And Eden were no Eden thus expos'd.

To whom thus Adam fervently replied:
O Woman, best are all things as the will
Of God ordain'd them; his creating hand
Nothing imperfect or deficient left   345
Of all that he created, much less man,

---

321 *sweet* The pejorative connotations of "sweet" gradually become more pronounced; compare 9.272.   323 *straiten'd* Confined.   324 *endued* Endowed.   325 *Single* Alone.   326 *still* Always.   330 *Sticks . . . front* As horns were proverbially stuck on the forehead ("front") of a cuckold.   332 *double honour* As Flannagan notes: "The quantification of honor, as if double honor could be gained by brute force, is associated more with Satan in *Paradise Lost* than with any other character" (p. 594).   335 *And what . . . unassay'd* Milton expressed an identical sentiment in *Areopagitica* (1644): "I cannot praise a fugitive and cloistered virtue, unexercised and unbreathed, that never sallies out and sees her adversary."

Or aught that might his happy state secure,
Secure from outward force; within himself
The danger lies, yet lies within his power:
350 Against his will he can receive no harm.
But God left free the will; for what obeys
Reason is free, and reason he made right,
353 But bid her well beware, and still erect,
354 Lest by some fair appearing good surpris'd,
355 She dictate false, and misinform the will
To do what God expressly hath forbid.
Not then mistrust, but tender love enjoins,
358 That I should mind thee oft, and mind thou me.
359 Firm we subsist, yet possible to swerve,
360 Since reason not impossibly may meet
Some specious object by the foe suborn'd,
And fall into deception unaware,
363 Not keeping strictest watch, as she was warn'd.
Seek not temptation then, which to avoid
365 Were better, and most likely if from me
Thou sever not: trial will come unsought.
367 Wouldst thou approve thy constancy, approve
First thy obedience; th'other who can know,
Not seeing thee attempted, who attest?
370 But if thou think trial unsought may find
Us both securer than thus warn'd thou seem'st,
372 Go; for thy stay, not free, absents thee more;
Go in thy native innocence, rely
On what thou hast of virtue, summon all,
375 For God tow'rds thee hath done his part, do thine.

---

350 *Against . . . harm* The Stoic doctrine that one could become impervious to fortune by an act of will was always attractive to Milton.   353 *still erect* Always alert, but with phallic overtones: Milton is identifying reason with masculinity; compare John Donne's reference to "my words' masculine persuasive force" (Elegy 16, "On His Mistress").   354 *fair appearing good* Temptation is feminized.   358 *mind* Remind.   359 *swerve* Err.   363 *she* Reason, which, in erring mode, is referred to as feminine.   367 *approve* Prove.   372 *thy stay . . . more* Like God, Adam values only voluntary obedience.

So spake the patriarch of mankind; but Eve
Persisted, yet submiss, though last, replied:

With thy permission then, and thus forewarn'd,
Chiefly by what thy own last reasoning words
Touch'd only, that our trial, when least sought,   380
May find us both perhaps far less prepar'd,
The willinger I go; nor much expect,
A foe so proud will first the weaker seek;
So bent, the more shall shame him his repulse.

Thus saying, from her husband's hand her hand   385
Soft she withdrew, and like a wood-nymph light
Oread or Dryad, or of Delia's train,   387
Betook her to the groves, but Delia's self   388
In gait surpass'd, and goddess-like deport;   389
Though not as she, with bow and quiver arm'd,   390
But with such gard'ning tools as Art yet rude,   391
Guiltless of fire had form'd, or angels brought.   392
To Pales, or Pomona, thus adorn'd,   393
Likest she seem'd Pomona when she fled
Vertumnus, or to Ceres in her prime,   395
Yet virgin of Proserpina from Jove.   396
Her long with ardent look his eye pursu'd
Delighted, but desiring more her stay.

---

380 *Touch'd only* Only touched upon. 387.1 *Oread or Dryad* Mountain- or wood-nymph;
387.2 *Delia's train* In Milton's time, "Delia"—Diana, goddess of the moon—was associ-
ated with witchcraft; her "train," or followers, were thus a dubious crew. 388 *groves* As-
sociated with idolatry throughout the Old Testament. 389.1 *gait* Deportment; 389.2
goddess-like deport The narrator is also tempted to make an idol of Eve, fetishizing her be-
cause of the lust she evokes in him. 390 *arm'd* Diana was also the goddess of hunting.
391 *rude* Rudimentary. 392 *Guiltless* Ignorant, innocent. 393.1 *Pales* Goddess of pastures
in Roman mythology; 393.2 *Pomona* Goddess of orchards. 395 *Vertumnus* God of gar-
dens. Flannagan points out that Milton often uses him as "the epitome of shifty think-
ing" (p. 596), because of the various disguises he used to woo Pomona in Ovid's
Metamorphoses 14.622–699. 395–396 *Ceres . . . Jove* In Roman mythology, Ceres, goddess
of grain, was impregnated by Jove with "Prosperine" (Persephone), who was carried away
by Pluto and forced to spend half the year with him in Hades.

399 Oft he to her his charge of quick return
400 Repeated, she to him as oft engag'd
     To be return'd by noon amid the bower,
     And all things in best order to invite
403 Noontide repast, or afternoon's repose.
     O much deceiv'd, much failing, hapless Eve,
405 Of thy presum'd return! event perverse!
     Thou never from that hour in Paradise
     Found'st either sweet repast, or sound repose;
     Such ambush hid among sweet flowers and shades
     Waited with hellish rancour imminent
410 To intercept thy way, or send thee back
     Despoil'd of innocence, of faith, of bliss.
     For now, and since first break of dawn, the fiend,
413 Mere serpent in appearance, forth was come,
     And on his quest where likeliest he might find
415 The only two of mankind, but in them
     The whole included race, his purpos'd prey.
     In bower and field he sought, where any tuft
     Of grove or garden-plot more pleasant lay,
419 Their tendance or plantation for delight;
420 By fountain or by shady rivulet
421 He sought them both, but wish'd his hap might find
     Eve separate; he wish'd, but not with hope
     Of what so seldom chanc'd, when to his wish,
     Beyond his hope, Eve separate he spies,
425 Veil'd in a cloud of fragrance, where she stood,
     Half spied, so thick the roses bushing round
     About her glow'd; oft stooping to support
     Each flower of slender stalk, whose head tho' gay
429 Carnation, purple, azure, or speck'd with gold,
430 Hung drooping unsustain'd; them she upstays

---

399 *charge* Instruction. 400 *engag'd* Promised. 403 *repast* Meal. 413 *Mere serpent in appearance* Looking just like a serpent. 419 *tendance or plantation* Tending or planting. 421 *hap* Luck. 429 *azure* Blue.

Gently with myrtle band, mindless the while
Herself, though fairest unsupported flower,
From her best prop so far, and storms so nigh.
Nearer he drew, and many a walk travers'd
Of stateliest covert, cedar, pine, or palm;   435
Then voluble and bold, now hid, now seen,   436
Among thick-woven arborets and flowers   437
Imborder'd on each bank, the hand of Eve:
Spot more delicious than those gardens feign'd   439
Or of reviv'd Adonis,[8] or renown'd   440
Alcinous, host of old Laertes' son,   441
Or that, not mystic, where the sapient king   442
Held dalliance with his fair Egyptian spouse.   443
Much he the place admir'd, the person more.
As one who long in populous city pent,   445
Where houses thick and sewers annoy the air,   446
Forth issuing on a summer's morn, to breathe
Among the pleasant villages and farms
Adjoin'd, from each thing met conceives delight,   449
The smell of grain, or tedded grass, or kine,   450
Or dairy, each rural sight, each rural sound;
If chance with nymph-like step fair virgin pass,   452
What pleasing seem'd, for her now pleases more,   453
She most, and in her look sums all delight;   454
Such pleasure took the serpent to behold   455
This flowery plat, the sweet recess of Eve   456
Thus early, thus alone; her heavenly form
Angelic, but more soft and feminine,

---

436 *voluble* Rolling.   **437** *arborets* Shrubs.   **439** *feign'd* False; Milton again declares the superiority of biblical over classical myth.   **441** *Alcinous . . . son* Laertes' son Odysseus visits the famous gardens of Alcinous in Homer's *Odyssey* 7.112–135.   **442** *not mystic* Not mythical or allegorical.   **442–443** *the sapient king . . . spouse* King Solomon kept beautiful gardens (Song of Solomon 6:2) and married Pharaoh's daughter (1 Kings 3:1).   **445** *pent* Shut up.   **446** *annoy* Make noisome.   **449** *Adjoin'd* Adjoining.   **450.1** *tedded* Spread out to dry; **450.2** *kine* Cattle.   **452–454** *If chance . . . delight* The eighteen-year-old Milton had extolled the pleasures of watching girls in a verse letter to his friend, Charles Diodati; here, however, the blind Milton attributes visually inspired lust to Satan.   **456.1** *plat* Plot; **456.2** *sweet recess of Eve* With heavily sexual overtones.

Her graceful innocence, her every air
460 Of gesture, or least action, overaw'd
461 His malice, and with rapine sweet bereav'd
462 His fierceness of the fierce intent it brought:
463 That space the evil one abstracted stood
464 From his own evil, and for the time remain'd
465 Stupidly good, of enmity disarm'd,
Of guile, of hate, of envy, of revenge;
But the hot hell that always in him burns,
Though in mid heaven, soon ended his delight,
And tortures him now more, the more he sees
470 Of pleasure not for him ordain'd: then soon
Fierce hate he recollects, and all his thoughts
472 Of mischief, gratulating, thus excites.

473 Thoughts, whither have ye led me, with what sweet
474 Compulsion thus transported to forget
475 What hither brought us; hate, not love, nor hope
476 Of Paradise for hell, hope here to taste
Of pleasure, but all pleasure to destroy,
Save what is in destroying; other joy
To me is lost. Then let me not let pass
480 Occasion which now smiles; behold alone
The woman, opportune to all attempts,
Her husband, for I view far round, not nigh,
483 Whose higher intellectual more I shun,
And strength, of courage haughty, and of limb
485 Heroic built, though of terrestrial mould,
Foe not informidable, exempt from wound,
I not; so much hath hell debas'd, and pain
Enfeebled me, to what I was in heaven.

---

461 *rapine* Rape.   461–464 *bereav'd . . . evil* Eve transforms Satan's nature, "abstracting," or alienating, him from evil, which is his essence.   470 *pleasure* Both Satan and the narrator objectify Eve, identifying her with "pleasure."   472 *gratulating* Rejoicing.   473 *Thoughts* Satan addresses his "thoughts" as though they were alien to him.   474 *transported* Carried away.   476 *for* In exchange for.   480 *Occasion* Opportunity.   483 *intellectual* Intellect.

She fair, divinely fair, fit love for gods,
Not terrible, though terror be in love   490
And beauty, not approach'd by stronger hate,
Hate stronger, under show of love well feign'd,
The way which to her ruin now I tend.

So spake the enemy of mankind, enclos'd
In serpent, inmate bad, and toward Eve   495
Address'd his way, not with indented wave,
Prone on the ground, as since; but on his rear,
Circular base of rising folds, that tower'd
Fold above fold, a surging maze, his head
Crested aloft, and carbuncle his eyes;   500
With burnish'd neck of verdant gold, erect   501
Amidst his circling spires, that on the grass
Floated redundant: pleasing was his shape,
And lovely; never since of serpent kind
Lovelier, not those that in Illyria chang'd   505
Hermione and Cadmus, or the god   506
In Epidaurus; nor to which transform'd   507
Ammonian Jove, or Capitoline was seen,   508
He with Olympias, this with her who bore   509
Scipio, the height of Rome. With tract oblique   510
At first, as one who sought access, but fear'd   511
To interrupt, side-long he works his way.   512
As when a ship, by skilful steersman wrought,   513

---

490 *terrible* Terrifying.   **500** *carbuncle* Mythical red jewel.   **501** *erect* With heavily sexual overtones; Fowler notes that some biblical exegetes believed that the serpent "assumed an upright posture only while being used as an instrument by Satan" (p. 499).   **505–506** *not those . . . Cadmus* In Ovid's *Metamorphoses* 4, Cadmus, the founder of Thebes, and his wife, Hermione, were turned into serpents in Ilyria (modern Albania).   **506–507** *the god / In Epidaurus* Aesculapius, god of medicine, took the form of a serpent in his temple at Epidaurus.   **508** *Ammonian Jove* In his *Parallel Lives*, Greek biographer Plutarch (c.46–119) writes that Phillip of Macedon discovered his wife Olympias in bed with a serpent, which the Delphic oracle identified as Zeus-Ammon ("Ammonian Jove"), and which was allegedly the true father of Alexander the Great.   **508–510** *Capitoline . . . Rome* The Roman general Scipio Africanus (236–184 B.C.) was reportedly fathered by Jupiter Capitolinus in serpent form.   **510** *tract oblique* Circuitous route.

514 Nigh river's mouth or foreland, where the wind
515 Veers oft, as oft so steers, and shifts her sail:
So varied he, and of his tortuous train
Curl'd many a wanton wreath in sight of Eve,
To lure her eye; she busied heard the sound
Of rustling leaves, but minded not, as us'd
520 To such disport before her through the field,
From every beast, more duteous at her call
522 Than at Circean call the herd disguis'd,
523 He bolder now, uncall'd before her stood,
But as in gaze admiring: oft he bow'd
525 His turret crest, and sleek enamell'd neck,
Fawning, and lick'd the ground whereon she trod.
His gentle dumb expression turn'd at length
The eye of Eve to mark his play; he glad
Of her attention gain'd, with serpent tongue
530 Organic, or impulse of vocal air,
His fraudulent temptation thus began:[9]

Wonder not, sov'reign mistress, if perhaps
Thou canst, who art sole wonder; much less arm
Thy looks, the heaven of mildness, with disdain,
535 Displeas'd that I approach thee thus, and gaze
536 Insatiate, I thus single, nor have fear'd
537 Thy awful brow, more awful thus retir'd.
Fairest resemblance of thy Maker fair,
Thee all things living gaze on, all things thine
540 By gift, and thy celestial beauty adore
With ravishment beheld, there best beheld
Where universally admir'd; but here
In this enclosure wild, these beasts among,

510–514 *Scipio . . . Nigh* Paul J. Klemp (*Milton Quarterly* 11 [1977], pp. 91–92) notes the acrostic: The first letters of these five lines spell "Satan"; Milton indicates the presence of the devil within the external image.   522 *Than at Circean . . . disguis'd* In Homer's *Odyssey* 10.212–219, the witch Circe transforms men into animals; she is also the mother of Milton's Comus.   536 *Insatiate* Unsatisfied, with overtones of "lustful."   537 *awful* Awe-inspiring.

Beholders rude, and shallow to discern
Half what in thee is fair, one man except, 545
Who sees thee? (and what is one?) who shouldst be seen 546
A goddess among gods, ador'd and serv'd
By angels numberless, thy daily train.

So gloz'd the tempter, and his proem tun'd; 549
Into the heart of Eve his words made way, 550
Though at the voice much marvelling: at length
Not unamaz'd she thus in answer spake:

What may this mean? language of man pronounc'd
By tongue of brute, and human sense express'd?
The first at least of these I thought denied 555
To beasts, whom God on their cretion day
Created mute to all articulate sound;
The latter I demur, for in their looks 558
Much reason, and in their actions, oft appears
Thee, Serpent, subtlest beast of all the field 560
I knew, but not with human voice endued; 561
Redouble then this miracle, and say,
How cam'st thou speakable of mute, and how 563
To me so friendly grown above the rest
Of brutal kind, that daily are in sight? 565
Say, for such wonder claims attention due.

To whom the guileful tempter thus replied:
Empress of this fair world, resplendent Eve
Easy to me it is to tell thee all
What thou command'st, and right thou shouldst be obey'd: 570
I was at first as other beasts that graze
The trodden herb, of abject thoughts and low,
As was my food; nor aught but food discern'd

---

546 *seen* Satan makes a spectacle of Eve.   549.1 *gloz'd* Both "interpreted" and "flattered";
549.2 *proem* Introduction.   558 *demur* Doubt.   561 *endued* Endowed.   563 *speakable* Able
to speak.   565 *brutal* Animal.

574 Or sex, and apprehended nothing high;

575 Till on a day, roving the field, I chanc'd

A goodly tree far distant to behold,

Loaden with fruit of fairest colours mix'd,

578 Ruddy and gold: I nearer drew to gaze;

When from the boughs a savoury odour blown,

580 Grateful to appetite, more pleas'd my sense

581 Than smell of sweetest fennel, or the teats

582 Of ewe or goat drooping with milk at even,

Unsuck'd of lamb or kid, that tend their play.

To satisfy the sharp desire I had

585 Of tasting those fair apples, I resolv'd

Not to defer; hunger and thirst at once,

587 Powerful persuaders, quicken'd at the scent

Of that alluring fruit, urg'd me so keen.

About the mossy trunk I wound me soon,

590 For high from ground the branches would require

Thy utmost reach, or Adam's: round the tree

All other beasts that saw, with like desire

Longing and envying stood, but could not reach.

Amid the tree now got, where plenty hung

595 Tempting so nigh, to pluck and eat my fill

I spar'd not, for such pleasure till that hour

At feed or fountain never had I found.

598 Sated at length, ere long I might perceive

Strange alteration in me, to degree

600 Of reason in my inward powers, and speech

Wanted not long, though to this shape retain'd.

Thenceforth to speculations high or deep

I turn'd my thoughts, and with capacious mind

Consider'd all things visible in heaven,

---

574 *apprehended* Understood. 578 *Ruddy* Red. 581 *fennel* According to Campbell, "a common emblem of pride" (p. 350). 581–582 *teats . . . even* Serpents were supposed to suck milk from the teat of cattle. "Even" is evening, but with a pun on "Eve." 585 *apples* Leonard points out: "Satan alone speaks of 'apples' in *Paradise Lost*. The good characters always refer to 'fruit,' which includes 'consequences'" (p. 411). 587 *quicken'd* Came alive. 598.1 *Sated* Satisfied; 598.2 *might* Could.

Or earth, or middle, all things fair and good; 605
But all that fair and good in thy divine 606
Semblance, and in thy beauty's heavenly ray, 607
United I beheld; no fair to thine 608
Equivalent or second, which compell'd
Me thus, though importune perhaps, to come 610
And gaze, and worship thee of right declar'd 611
Sov'reign of creatures, universal dame. 612

So talk'd the spirited sly snake; and Eve, 613
Yet more amaz'd, unwary thus replied:
Serpent, thy overpraising leaves in doubt 615
The virtue of that fruit, in thee first prov'd:
But say, where grows the tree, from hence how far?
For many are the trees of God that grow
In Paradise, and various, yet unknown
To us; in such abundance lies our choice, 620
As leaves a greater store of fruit untouch'd,
Still hanging incorruptible, till men 622
Grow up to their provision, and more hands 623
Help to disburden Nature of her bearth. 624

To whom the wily adder, blithe and glad: 625
Empress, the way is ready, and not long;
Beyond a row of myrtles, on a flat, 627
Fast by a fountain, one small thicket past 628
Of blowing myrrh and balm; if thou accept 629
My conduct, I can bring thee thither soon. 630

---

605 *middle* Air. 606–607 *thy divine / Semblance* Satan does not use the word "image," which emphasizes the difference between sign and referent, but "semblance," which stresses their likeness, or even their seeming identity. 608 *fair* Fairness. 611 *gaze, and worship* Idolatry is connected to a fascination with the visual, a capacity that the blind Milton lacked. 612 *universal dame* Mistress of the universe. 613 *spirited* Possessed. 622 *incorruptible* In both the physical and the moral sense. 622–623 *till men . . . provision* Until there are enough men to provide for them. 624 *bearth* What she bears. 627 *myrtles* Fowler claims that myrtles were conventional symbols for the female genitalia, but Flannagan disagrees. 628 *Fast by* Close by. 629 *blowing* Blooming. 630 *conduct* Guidance.

Lead then, said Eve. He leading, swiftly roll'd
632 In tangles, and made intricate seem straight,
To mischief swift. Hope elevates, and joy
Brightens his crest; as when a wand'ring fire,
635 Compact of unctuous vapour, which the night
Condenses, and the cold environs round,
Kindled through agitation to a flame,
638 Which oft, they say, some evil spirit attends,
Hovering and blazing with delusive light,
640 Misleads th'amaz'd night-wand'rer from his way,
Through bogs and mires, and oft through pond or pool,
There swallow'd up and lost, from succour far.
So glister'd the dire snake, and into fraud
Led Eve, our credulous mother, to the tree
645 Of prohibition, root of all our woe;
Which when she saw, thus to her guide she spake:

647 Serpent, we might have spar'd our coming hither,
Fruitless to me, though fruit be here to excess,
The credit of whose virtue rest with thee,
650 Wondrous indeed, if cause of such effects.
But of this tree we may not taste nor touch;
God so commanded, and left that command
Sole daughter of his voice; the rest, we live
654 Law to ourselves, our reason is our law.

655 To whom the tempter guilefully replied:
Indeed; hath God then said that of the fruit
Of all these garden trees ye shall not eat,
658 Yet lords declar'd of all in earth or air?

---

632 *made intricate seem straight* In both physical and logical terms. 635 *Compact . . . vapour*
Made up of condensed gas. 638 *Which oft . . . attends* The will-o'-the-wisp, or *ignis fatuus*,
was popularly believed to contain a demon. 647 *spar'd* Spared ourselves the trouble of.
654 *Law to ourselves* In Romans 2:14, St. Paul declares that virtuous Gentiles—and by ex-
tension Christians—are free from the Judaic law because they are "a law unto themselves."
658 *Yet lords . . . air?* Satan believes dominion must always be unlimited; he can conceive
of no kind of power except the absolute.

To whom thus Eve, yet sinless: Of the fruit
Of each tree in the garden we may eat,   660
But of the fruit of this fair tree, amidst   661
The garden, God hath said, Ye shall not eat
Thereof, nor shall ye touch it, lest ye die.

She scarce had said, though brief, when now more bold
The tempter, but with show of zeal and love   665
To man, and indignation at his wrong,   666
New part puts on, and as to passion mov'd,   667
Fluctuates disturb'd, yet comely and in act
Rais'd, as some great matter to begin.
As when of old some orator renown'd,[10]   670
In Athens, or free Rome, where eloquence   671
Flourish'd, since mute, to some great cause address'd,
Stood in himself collected, while each part,
Motion, each act, won audience ere the tongue,[11]
Sometimes in height began, as no delay   675
Or preface brooking through his zeal of right;   676
So standing, moving, or to height up-grown,
The tempter, all impassion'd, thus began:

O sacred, wise, and wisdom-giving plant,
Mother of science, now I feel thy power   680
Within me clear, not only to discern   681
Things in their causes, but to trace the ways   682
Of highest agents, deem'd however wise.   683
Queen of this universe, do not believe   684
Those rigid threats of death; ye shall not die;   685

---

661 *amidst* In the middle of.   **666** *indignation* Offended dignity.   **667** *part* Satan is an actor, playing a role.   **671** *free Rome* Republican, as opposed to imperial, Rome.   **676** *zeal* Satan's rhetorical trick is to appear overcome by sincere conviction.   **681–682** *to discern . . . causes* To explain things by their causes. Satan speaks of the Baconian pursuit of the material cause, rather than the Aristotelian pursuit of the final cause. He speaks, in other words, from the perspective of modern science.   **682–683** *to trace . . . agents* Satan claims that the fruit enables him not only to explain material phenomena but also to understand the ways of God.   **684** *Queen* Milton consistently connects royalty with idolatry.

How should ye? by the fruit? it gives you life
687   To knowledge; by the threat'ner? look on me,
Me who have touch'd and tasted, yet both live,
689   And life more perfect have attain'd than fate
690   Meant me, by vent'ring higher than my lot.
691   Shall that be shut to man, which to the beast
Is open? or will God incense his ire
For such a petty trespass, and not praise
Rather your dauntless virtue, whom the pain
695   Of death denounc'd, whatever thing death be,
Deterr'd not from achieving what might lead
To happier life, knowledge of good and evil;
698   Of good, how just? of evil, if what is evil
699   Be real, why not known, since easier shunn'd?
700   God, therefore cannot hurt ye and be just;
Not just, not God; not fear'd then, nor obey'd:
Your fear itself of death removes the fear.
703   Why then was this forbid? Why but to awe;
704   Why but to keep you low and ignorant,
705   His worshippers; he knows that in the day
Ye eat thereof, your eyes that seem so clear,
Yet are but dim, shall perfectly be then
Open'd and clear'd, and ye shall be as gods.
Knowing both good and evil as they know.
710   That ye shall be as gods, since I as man,
Internal man, is but proportion meet;
I of brute human, ye of human gods.
So ye shall die perhaps, by putting off
Human, to put on gods; death to be wish'd,

---

687 *threat'ner* God, though Satan does not say so.   **689** *fate* Satan pretends that fate, not God, controls the world.   **690** *vent'ring . . . lot* Rising above my allotted station. Such phrases were often used to denigrate the burgeoning social mobility in seventeenth-century England, particularly the rise of the merchant class.   **691** *beast* Satan unwittingly reveals his true identity.   **698–699** *if what . . . real* As Leonard notes: "Many theologians had argued that evil is a privation of good, and so has no real existence. Satan perverts this doctrine into the easy inference that evil is nothing to worry about" (p. 833).   **703–704** *Why but . . . ignorant* Satan argues that religion is the opium of the people.

Though threaten'd, which no worse than this can bring.   715
And what are gods that man may not become
As they, participating godlike food?   717
The gods are first, and that advantage use
On our belief, that all from them proceeds:
I question it; for this fair earth I see,   720
Warm'd by the sun, producing every kind,
Them nothing: if they all things, who inclos'd
Knowledge of good and evil in this tree
That whoso eats thereof, forthwith attains
Wisdom without their leave? and wherein lies   725
Th'offence, that man should thus attain to know?
What can your knowledge hurt him, or this tree
Impart against his will, if all be his?
Or is it envy, and can envy dwell
In heavenly breasts? These, these, and many more   730
Causes import your need of this fair fruit.   731
Goddess humane, reach then, and freely taste.   732

He ended, and his words replete with guile,
Into her heart too easy entrance won.
Fixt on the fruit she gaz'd, which to behold   735
Might tempt alone, and in her ears the sound
Yet rung of his persuasive words, impregn'd   737
With reason, to her seeming, and with truth.   738
Meanwhile the hour of noon drew on, and wak'd   739
An eager appetite, rais'd by the smell   740
So savoury of that fruit, which with desire,
Inclinable now grown to touch or taste,

---

717 *participating* Partaking of, with an allusion to the sacramental doctrine of "participation" in the Catholic Mass, which Milton viewed as claiming that the physical act of eating was spiritually efficacious.   731 *import your need* Satan sounds like a salesman.   732 *Goddess humane* As Fowler observes, Satan's use of "so wild an oxymoron" indicates his growing confidence that this form of flattery is having an effect (p. 513).   735 *gaz'd* As Satan gazes on Eve.   737 *impregn'd* Impregnated, adding to the underlying portrayal of the Fall as a sexual seduction.   738 *to her seeming* Both "as it seemed to her" and "to the faculty within her that deals with appearances."   739–740 *wak'd . . . appetite* Appetite is personified, adding to its threatening nature.

Solicited her longing eye; yet first,
Pausing awhile, thus to herself she mus'd:

745 Great are thy virtues, doubtless, best of fruits,
Though kept from man, and worthy to be admir'd,
747 Whose taste, too long forborne, at first essay
Gave elocution to the mute, and taught
The tongue not made for speech to speak thy praise:
750 Thy praise he also, who forbids thy use,
Conceals not from us, naming thee the tree
Of knowledge, knowledge both of good and evil;
Forbids us then to taste, but his forbidding
Commends thee more, while it infers the good
755 By thee communicated, and our want:
For good unknown, sure is not had, or had
And yet unknown, is as not had at all.
758 In plain, then, what forbids he but to know,
Forbids us good, forbids us to be wise?
760 Such prohibitions bind not. But if death
Bind us with after-bands, what profits then
Our inward freedom? In the day we eat
763 Of this fair fruit, our doom is, we shall die.
How dies the serpent? he hath eaten and lives,
765 And knows, and speaks, and reasons, and discerns,
Irrational till then. For us alone
Was death invented? or to us denied
This intellectual food, for beasts reserv'd?
For beasts it seems: yet that one beast which first
770 Hath tasted, envies not, but brings with joy
771 The good befallen him, author unsuspect,
Friendly to man, far from deceit or guile.
773 What fear I then, rather what know to fear

---

747 *essay* Trial   755 *want* Both "need" and "desire." Led by Satan, Eve now equates the
two.   758 *In plain* In plain language.   763 *doom* Both "judgment" and "fate." Eve now
elides the distinction.   771 *unsuspect* Simultaneously "unsuspected," "unsuspecting," and
"above suspicion."   773 *rather what know to fear* Rather, how can I even know what fear is?

The Temptation of Eve

Under this ignorance of good and evil,
775 Of God or death, of law or penalty?
Here grows the cure of all, this fruit divine.
Fair to the eye, inviting to the taste,
Of virtue to make wise: what hinders then
To reach, and feed at once both body and mind?

780 So saying, her rash hand in evil hour
Forth reaching to the fruit, she pluck'd, she ate;
Earth felt the wound, and Nature from her seat,
Sighing through all her works, gave signs of woe
That all was lost. Back to the thicket slunk
785 The guilty serpent, and well might; for Eve,
Intent now wholly on her taste, nought else
Regarded, such delight till then, as seem'd,
In fruit she never tasted, whether true
Or fancied so, through expectation high
790 Of knowledge, nor was Godhead from her thought.
Greedily she ingorg'd without restraint,
792 And knew not eating death. Satiate at length,
793 And heighten'd as with wine, jocund and boon,
Thus to herself she pleasingly began.

795 O sov'reign, virtuous, precious of all trees
796 In Paradise, of operation bless'd
797 To sapience, hitherto obscur'd, infam'd,
798 And thy fair fruit let hang, as to no end
Created; but henceforth my early care,
800 Not without song, each morning and due praise,
Shall tend thee, and the fertile burden ease

---

792 *knew not eating death* Leonard gives the following glosses: "she did not experience death while she ate," "she did not know that she was eating death," "she did not acquire knowledge while she ate death," and "she did not know death, which devours" (p. 834).   **793** *jocund and boon* Jolly and convivial.   **795** *O sov'reign, virtuous, precious* Eve idolizes the tree. **796** *operation* Effect.   **797.1** *sapience* Both "knowledge" and "taste"; **797.2** *infam'd* Slandered. **798** *as to no end* Eve has made the same mistake as Adam does with regard to the planets [see 5.85–96].   **800** *due praise* Eve plans to make a cult of the tree.

Of thy full branches, offer'd free to all;
Till dieted by thee I grow mature   803
In knowledge, as the gods who all things know;
Though others envy what they cannot give;   805
For had the gift been theirs, it had not here
Thus grown. Experience, next to thee I owe,   807
Best guide; not following thee I had remain'd   808
In ignorance; thou open'st wisdom's way,
And givest access, though secret she retire.   810
And I perhaps am secret; heaven is high,
High and remote to see from thence distinct   812
Each thing on earth; and other care perhaps   813
May have diverted from continual watch
Our great forbidder, safe with all his spies   815
About him. But to Adam in what sort   816
Shall I appear? shall I to him make known
As yet my change, and give him to partake
Full happiness with me, or rather not,
But keep the odds of knowledge in my power   820
Without copartner? so to add what wants
In female sex, the more to draw his love,
And render me more equal, and perhaps,   823
A thing not undesirable, sometime   824
Superior; for inferior who is free?   825
This may be well: but what if God have seen,
And death ensue? then I shall be no more,
And Adam, wedded to another Eve,   828
Shall live with her enjoying, I extinct;   829
A death to think. Confirm'd then I resolve,   830

---

803 *dieted by thee* Eve refers to herself as passive, the tree as active. 807–808 *Experience . . . guide* Eve acquires an empiricist view of knowledge. 810 *secret* Hidden. 812–813 *remote . . . earth* Eve believes that God's sight is physical. 816 *sort* Disguise. 823 *more equal* It is, of course, impossible to be more or less equal. 824 *A thing not undesirable* At first, "thing" seems to refer to Eve, but the syntax later reveals that it denotes her putative superiority to Adam. 825 *inferior who is free?* Satan's question. 828–830 *And Adam . . . think* Sexual jealously, which also motivates Satan, makes Eve determined to bring about Adam's fall.

Adam shall share with me in bliss or woe:
832 So dear I love him, that with him all deaths
I could endure, without him live no life.

So saying, from the tree her step she turn'd,
835 But first low reverence done, as to the power
836 That dwelt within, whose presence had infus'd
837 Into the plant sciential sap, deriv'd
838 From nectar, drink of gods. Adam the while
Waiting desirous her return, had wove
840 Of choicest flowers a garland to adorn
841 Her tresses, and her rural labours crown,
As reapers oft are wont their harvest queen.
Great joy he promis'd to his thoughts, and new
Solace in her return, so long delay'd;
845 Yet oft his heart, divine of something ill,
846 Misgave him; he the falt'ring measure felt;
And forth to meet her went, the way she took
That morn when first they parted; by the tree
Of knowledge he must pass, there he her met,
850 Scarce from the tree returning; in her hand
A bough of fairest fruit, that downy smil'd,
New gather'd, and ambrosial smell diffus'd.
853 To him she hasted; in her face excuse
854 Came prologue, and apology to prompt,
855 Which with bland words at will she thus address'd:

---

832 *dear* Eve's love will cost Adam dearly. Compare Satan to Beelzebub at 5.673.   835–836 *low reverence . . . within* Eve has conceived an animist view of the world; she perceives living "powers" within inanimate objects.   837 *sciential* Both "containing knowledge within it" and "giving empirical knowledge."   837–838 *deriv'd . . . gods* Milton connects Eve's animism with classical mythology.   841 *tresses* Hair.   845 *divine* Diviner, presager.   846 *the falt'ring measure* The irregular heartbeat. Adam feels Eve's fall within his breast.   853–854 *in her face . . . prompt* Like Satan, Eve's physical, facial gestures form part of her rhetoric; she reads her lines like an actor, moving through the "prologue," and receiving a "prompt;" the personifications of "excuse" and "apology" reveal her insincerity.   855 *at will* Following her will.

Hast thou not wonder'd, Adam, at my stay?
Thee I have miss'd, and thought it long, depriv'd
Thy presence, agony of love till now   858
Not felt, nor shall be twice, for never more
Mean I to try, what rash untried I sought,   860
The pain of absence from thy sight. But strange
Hath been the cause, and wonderful to hear.
This tree is not, as we are told, a tree
Of danger tasted, nor to evil unknown
Opening the way, but of divine effect   865
To open eyes, and make them gods who taste;
And hath been tasted such: the serpent wise,
Or not restrain'd as we, or not obeying,
Hath eaten of the fruit, and is become,
Not dead, as we are threaten'd, but henceforth   870
Endued with human voice and human sense,
Reasoning to admiration, and with me   872
Persuasively hath so prevail'd, that I
Have also tasted, and have also found
Th'effects to correspond; opener mine eyes,   875
Dim erst, dilated spirits, ampler heart,   876
And growing up to Godhead; which for thee
Chiefly I sought, without thee can despise.
For bliss, as thou hast part, to me is bliss;
Tedious unshar'd with thee, and odious soon.   880
Thou therefore also taste, that equal lot   881
May join us, equal joy, as equal love;   882
Lest thou not tasting, different degree
Disjoin us, and I then too late renounce
Deity for thee, when fate will not permit.   885

---

858 *agony of love* In the English-speaking islands of the Caribbean, which have preserved many seventeenth-century usages, "agony" still denotes the sexual act. 872 *Reasoning to admiration* Both "reasoning admirably" and "reasoning me into admiration." 876.1 *erst* Before; 876.2 *dilated* Compare. 881–882 *equal . . . equal . . . equal* Aspiration to equality with the Creator is the ultimate cause of original sin. 885.1 *Deity* Of course, Eve has already renounced the true deity; here she refers to her own, new, illusory Godhead; 885.2 *fate* Satan's word for "God"; but compare the "Nativity Ode" (l. 149).

Thus Eve with count'nance blithe her story told
887 But in her cheek distemper flushing glow'd.
On th'other side, Adam, soon as he heard
The fatal trespass done by Eve, amaz'd,
890 Astonished stood and blank, while horror chill
Ran through his veins, and all his joints relax'd;
From his slack hand the garland wreath'd for Eve
Down dropp'd, and all the faded roses shed:
Speechless he stood and pale, till thus at length
895 First to himself he inward silence broke:

O fairest of creation, last and best
Of all God's works, creature in whom excell'd
Whatever can to sight or thought be form'd
Holy, divine, good, amiable, or sweet.
900 How art thou lost, how on a sudden lost,
901 Defac'd, deflower'd, and now to death devote?
Rather how hast thou yielded to transgress
The strict forbiddance, how to violate
The sacred fruit forbidden? some curs'd fraud
905 Of enemy hath beguil'd thee, yet unknown,
And me with thee hath ruin'd, for with thee
Certain my resolution is to die.
How can I live without thee, how forego
Thy sweet converse, and love so dearly join'd,
910 To live again in these wild woods forlorn?
Should God create another Eve, and I
Another rib afford, yet loss of thee
Would never from my heart; no, no, I feel
914 The link of nature draw me: flesh of flesh,

---

887 *distemper flushing glow'd* The postcoital appearance is surely intended. 895 *broke* Flannagan observes that the following soliloquy "comments negatively on the need after the Fall for private conversations with oneself expressing internal contradictions" (p. 612). The ability to hold an internal conversation implies a divided psyche. 901 *deflower'd* Robbed of her spiritual virginity.

Bone of my bone thou art, and from thy state   915
Mine never shall be parted, bliss or woe.   916

So having said, as one from sad dismay
Recomforted, and after thoughts disturb'd,
Submitting to what seem'd remediless,
Thus in calm mood his words to Eve he turn'd: 920

Bold deed thou hast presum'd, advent'rous Eve,
And peril great provok'd, who thus hath dar'd,
Had it been only coveting to eye
That sacred fruit, sacred to abstinence,[12]
Much more to taste it under ban to touch.   925
But past who can recall, or done undo?
Not God omnipotent, nor Fate; yet so
Perhaps thou shalt not die, perhaps the fact   928
Is not so heinous now, foretasted fruit,
Profan'd first by the serpent, by him first   930
Made common and unhallow'd ere our taste;   931
Nor yet on him found deadly, he yet lives,
Lives as thou said'st, and gains to live as man,
Higher degree of life; inducement strong
To us, as likely tasting to attain   935
Proportional ascent, which cannot be
But to be gods, or angels demi-gods.
Nor can I think that God, Creator wise,
Though threat'ning, will in earnest so destroy
Us his prime creatures, dignified so high,   940
Set over all his works, which in our fall,
For us created, needs with us must fail,
Dependent made; so God shall uncreate,
Be frustrate, do, undo, and labour lose,   944

914–916 *The link of nature . . . woe* Fowler (p. 523) notes that in his divorce tracts, Milton claims that the view of marriage as being indissoluble is a form of idolatry. **928** *fact* Deed, crime. **931** *unhallow'd* Unholy. **940** *prime . . . dignified* Adam already shows signs of sinful pride. **944** *labour lose* Adam thinks of God's "labour" as something that could become alienated from Him; in fact, God's "labour," or creative power, is the Son.

945　Not well conceiv'd of God, who, though his power
　　　Creation could repeat, yet would be loath
　　　Us to abolish, lest the adversary
　　　Triumph, and say, Fickle their state whom God
　　　Most favours; who can please him long? Me first
950　He ruin'd, now mankind; whom will he next?
　　　Matter of scorn, not to be given the foe.
　　　However I with thee have fixt my lot,
　　　Certain to undergo like doom; if death
　　　Consort with thee, death is to me as life,
955　So forcible within my heart I feel
956　The bond of nature draw me to my own,
957　My own in thee, for what thou art is mine;
958　Our state cannot be sever'd, we are one,
　　　One flesh; to lose thee were to lose myself.

960　So Adam, and thus Eve to him replied:
　　　O glorious trial of exceeding love,
　　　Illustrious evidence, example high!
　　　Engaging me to emulate, but short
　　　Of thy perfection, how shall I attain,
965　Adam? from whose dear side I boast me sprung,
　　　And gladly of our union hear thee speak,
　　　One heart, one soul in both; whereof good proof
　　　This day affords, declaring thee resolv'd,
　　　Rather than death, or aught than death more dread,
970　Shall separate us, link'd in love so dear,
　　　To undergo with me one guilt, one crime,
　　　If any be, of tasting this fair fruit,
　　　Whose virtue for of good still good proceeds,
　　　Direct, or by occasion hath presented
975　This happy trial of thy love, which else
　　　So eminently never had been known.
　　　Were it I thought death menac'd would ensue

---

955 *I feel* Whereas Eve falls because of the rational desire for knowledge, Adam falls because of passionate desire for Eve—a less pure motive.　956–957 *my own . . . mine* Adam asserts his ownership of Eve.　958 *state* Condition.

This my attempt, I would sustain alone
The worst, and not persuade thee, rather die
Deserted, than oblige thee with a fact   980
Pernicious to thy peace, chiefly assur'd   981
Remarkably so late of thy so true,   982
So faithful love unequall'd: but I feel
Far otherwise th'event, not death but life   984
Augmented, open'd eyes, new hopes, new joys,   985
Taste so divine, that what of sweet before
Hath touch'd my sense, flat seems to this, and harsh.
On my experience, Adam, freely taste,   988
And fear of death deliver to the winds.

So saying, she embrac'd him, and for joy   990
Tenderly wept, much won that he his love   991
Had so ennobled, as of choice to incur
Divine displeasure for her sake, or death.
In recompense (for such compliance bad   994
Such recompense best merits) from the bough   995
She gave him of that fair enticing fruit
With liberal hand: he scrupled not to eat
Against his better knowledge, not deceiv'd,   998
But fondly overcome with female charm.   999
Earth trembled from her entrails, as again   1000
In pangs, and Nature gave a second groan;
Sky loured, and, muttering thunder, some sad drops   1002
Wept at completing of the mortal sin   1003
Original; while Adam took no thought,   1004

980.1 *oblige* Make liable; 980.2 *fact* Deed. 981–982 *assur'd / Remarkably so late* Both "recently and impressively assured" and "assured at a strangely late date." 984 *event* Outcome. 988 *On my experience* Reflecting the newly empirical approach to knowledge. 991 *won* Won over. 994–995 *recompense . . . recompense* Leonard's gloss is convincing: "compensation for a loss . . . retribution for an offence" (p. 837). 998–999 *Against . . . charm* From 1 Timothy 2:14: "Adam was not deceived, but the woman being deceived was in the transgression." 1002 *loured* Glowered. 1003–1004 *mortal sin / Original* According to the doctrine of "original sin," Adam acted as an efficacious prototype of humanity in general; his sin stamped its pattern on the image of his descendants. Flannagan points out that this is the only time in *Paradise Lost* that Milton uses "original" in conjunction with "sin" (p. 616).

1005 Eating his fill, nor Eve to iterate
Her former trespass fear'd, the more to sooth
Him with her lov'd society, that now,
As with new wine intoxicated both,
They swim in mirth, and fancy that they feel
1010 Divinity within them breeding wings
Wherewith to scorn the earth: but that false fruit
1012 Far other operation first display'd,
1013 Carnal desire inflaming; he on Eve
Began to cast lascivious eye; she him
1015 As wantonly repaid; in lust they burn:
1016 Till Adam thus 'gan Eve to dalliance move:

Eve, now I see thou art exact of taste,
1018 And elegant, of sapience no small part,
Since to each meaning savour we apply,
1020 And palate call judicious; I the praise
Yield thee, so well this day thou hast purvey'd.
Much pleasure we have lost, while we abstain'd
From this delightful fruit, nor known till now
True relish, tasting; if such pleasure be
1025 In things to us forbidden, it might be wish'd,
1026 For this one tree had been forbidden ten.
But come, so well refresh'd, now let us play,
1028 As meet is after such delicious fare:
For never did thy beauty, since the day
1030 I saw thee first, and wedded thee, adorn'd
With all perfections, so inflame my sense
1032 With ardour to enjoy thee, fairer now
Than ever, bounty of this virtuous tree.

1012 *operation* Effect.   1013 *Carnal* Fleshly, physical.   1016.1 *'gan* Began; 1016.2 *dalliance* Sex.
1018 *sapience* Both "wisdom" and "taste," with the implication that Adam has forgotten the
distinction.   1026 *For this . . . ten* Flannagan observes: "Adam is counting again, in alliance
with Satan's materialism and quantification" (p. 616).   1028 *meet* Appropriate, but Leonard
notes the *Oxford English Dictionary*'s citation of the early modern meaning of "meat" as
"human body regarded as instrument of sexual pleasure" (p. 837).   1032 *ardour* Lustful
burning.

So said he, and forbore not glance or toy
Of amorous intent, well understood   1035
Of Eve, whose eye darted contagious fire.
Her hand he seiz'd, and to a shady bank,
Thick over head with verdant roof imbower'd,
He led her nothing loath; flowers were the couch,   1039
Pansies, and violets, and asphodel,   1040
And hyacinth, earth's freshest, softest lap.
There they their fill of love and love's disport
Took largely, of their mutual guilt the seal,
The solace of their sin, till dewy sleep   1044
Oppress'd them, wearied with their amorous play.   1045

Soon as the force of that fallacious fruit,
That with exhilarating vapour bland   1047
About their spirits had play'd, and inmost powers
Made err, was now exhal'd; and grosser sleep,   1049
Bred of unkindly fumes, with conscious dreams   1050
Encumber'd, now had left them; up they rose   1051
As from unrest, and each the other viewing,
Soon found their eyes how open'd, and their minds
How darken'd; innocence, that as a veil
Had shadow'd them from knowing ill, was gone,   1055
Just confidence, and native righteousness,
And honour from about them naked left
To guilty shame; he cover'd, but his robe   1058
Uncover'd more. So rose the Danite strong,   1059
Herculean Samson, from the harlot-lap   1060
Of Philistean Dalilah, and wak'd
Shorn of his strength. They destitute and bare   1062
Of all their virtue: silent, and in face

1039 *nothing loath* By no means reluctant.   1040 *asphodel* With a pun on "asp," snake.   1044
solace of Consolation for.   1047 *bland* Both "sensual" and "seemingly harmless."   1049
grosser Heavier.   1050 *unkindly* Unnatural.   1051 *Encumber'd* Weighed down.   1058–1059
he cover'd . . . more Suggests both that Adam tries to conceal his nakedness but his cloak re-
veals more of his body, and that his wrapping himself in a cloak reveals the fact that he
knows he is naked.   1062 *bare* Both "naked" and "bereft."

Confounded, long they sat, as strucken mute,
1065   Till Adam, though not less than Eve abash'd,
At length gave utterance to these words constrain'd.

O Eve, in evil hour thou didst give ear
To that false worm, of whomsoever taught
To counterfeit man's voice, true in our fall,
1070   False in our promis'd rising; since our eyes
Open'd we find indeed, and find we know
Both good and evil, good lost, and evil got;
Bad fruit of knowledge, if this be to know,
Which leaves us naked thus, of honour void,
1075   Of innocence, of faith, of purity,
1076   Our wonted ornaments now soil'd and stain'd,
And in our faces evident the signs
1078   Of foul concupiscence; whence evil store;
1079   Even shame, the last of evils: of the first
1080   Be sure then. How shall I behold the face
1081   Henceforth of God or angel, erst with joy
And rapture so oft beheld? those heavenly shapes
Will dazzle now this earthly with their blaze
Insufferably bright. O might I here
1085   In solitude live savage, in some glade
Obscur'd, where highest woods, impenetrable
1087   To star or sun light, spread their umbrage broad
1088   And brown as evening. Cover me, ye pines,
Ye cedars, with innumerable boughs
1090   Hide me, where I may never see them more.
1091   But let us now as in bad plight, devise
What best may for the present serve to hide
The parts of each from other, that seem most
To shame obnoxious, and unseemliest seen;[13]

1076 *wonted* Former.   **1078** *concupiscence* Sexual desire viewed as an end in itself, rather than as a means to the higher end of spiritual love.   **1079** *Even* Note the reproachful pun on Eve's name.   **1081** *erst* Formerly.   **1087** *umbrage* Shadows.   **1088** *evening* Another pun on "Eve."   **1091** *as in bad plight* As we're in such a bad predicament.

Some tree, whose broad smooth leaves together sew'd,   1095
And girded on our loins, may cover round
Those middle parts, that this new comer, shame,   1097
There sit not, and reproach us as unclean.   1098

So counsell'd he, and both together went
Into the thickest wood; there soon they chose   1100
The fig-tree, not that kind for fruit renown'd,   1101
But such as at this day to Indians known
In Malabar or Decan spreads her arms   1103
Branching so broad and long, that in the ground
The bended twigs take root, and daughters grow   1105
About the mother tree, a pillar'd shade
High overarch'd, and echoing walks between;
There oft the Indian herdsman, shunning heat,
Shelters in cool, and tends his pasturing herds
At loop-holes cut through thickest shade. Those leaves   1110
They gather'd, broad as Amazonian targe,   1111
And with what skill they had, together sew'd,
To gird their waist, vain covering if to hide
Their guilt and dreaded shame; O how unlike   1114
To that first naked glory! Such of late   1115
Columbus found th'American; so girt
With feather'd cincture, naked else and wild   1117
Among the trees on isles and woody shores.
Thus fenc'd, and as they thought, their shame in part
Cover'd, but not at rest or ease of mind,   1120
They sat them down to weep; nor only tears   1121
Rain'd at their eyes, but high winds worse within
Began to rise, high passions, anger, hate,
Mistrust, suspicion, discord, and shook sore

1097–1098 *this new comer . . . unclean* Like Sin and Death, shame is personified.   1101 *fig-tree* Banyan tree.   1103 *Malabar or Decan* Regions of southern India.   1111 *Amazonian targe* An Amazon's shield.   1114 *O how unlike* Compare 1.75.   1117 *cincture* Belt.   1121 *They sat . . . weep* Compare the Israelites exiled in Babylon in Psalms 137:1: "By the rivers of Babylon, there we sat down, yea, we wept, when we remembered Zion."

1125   Their inward state of mind, calm region once
         And full of peace, now toss'd and turbulent:
         For understanding rul'd not, and the will
         Heard not her lore, both in subjection now
         To sensual appetite, who from beneath,
1130   Usurping over sov'reign reason, claim'd
         Superior sway: from this distemper'd breast,
1132   Adam, estrang'd in look and alter'd style,
1133   Speech intermitted thus to Eve renew'd:

         Would thou hadst hearken'd to my words, and stay'd
1135   With me, as I besought thee, when that strange
         Desire of wand'ring this unhappy morn,
         I know not whence possess'd thee; we had then
         Remain'd still happy, not as now, despoil'd
         Of all our good, sham'd, naked, miserable.
1140   Let none henceforth seek needless cause to approve
1141   The faith they owe; when earnestly they seek
1142   Such proof, conclude, they then begin to fail.

         To whom, soon mov'd with touch of blame, thus Eve:
         What words have pass'd thy lips, Adam severe;
1145   Imput'st thou that to my default, or will
         Of wand'ring, as thou call'st it, which who knows
         But might as ill have happen'd thou being by,
         Or to thyself perhaps? Hadst thou been there,
         Or here th'attempt, thou couldst not have discern'd
1150   Fraud in the serpent, speaking as he spake;
         No ground of enmity between us known,
         Why he should mean me ill, or seek to harm.
1153   Was I to have never parted from thy side?
1154   As good have grown there still a lifeless rib.

1132 *estrang'd* Alienated.   1133 *intermitted* Interrupted.   1140–1142 *Let none . . . fail* That is, "lead us not into temptation."   1140 *approve* Prove.   1153 *Was I . . . side?* Both "Was I never to leave you?" and "Should I never have been created?"   1154 *As good . . . rib* A growing rib is not lifeless. Eve equates life with independence from Adam.

Being as I am, why didst not thou the head 1155
Command me absolutely not to go, 1156
Going into such danger as thou saidst?
Too facile then thou didst not much gainsay, 1158
Nay didst permit, approve, and fair dismiss. 1159
Hadst thou been firm and fixt in thy dissent, 1160
Neither had I transgress'd, nor thou with me.

To whom then first incens'd, Adam replied:
Is this the love, is this the recompense
Of mine to thee, ingrateful Eve, express'd 1164
Immutable, when thou wert lost, not I; 1165
Who might have liv'd and joy'd immortal bliss, 1166
Yet willingly chose rather death with thee?
And am I now upbraided as the cause
Of thy transgresslng? not enough severe,
It seems in my restraint: what could I more? 1170
I warn'd thee, I admonish'd thee, foretold
The danger, and the lurking enemy
That lay in wait; beyond this had been force, 1173
And force upon free will hath here no place. 1174
But confidence then bore thee on, secure 1175
Either to meet no danger, or to find
Matter of glorious trial; and perhaps
I also err'd in overmuch admiring 1178
What seem'd in thee so perfect, that I thought
No evil durst attempt thee, but I rue 1180
That error now, which is become my crime,
And thou th'accuser. Thus it shall befall 1182

1156 *Command me absolutely* The answer, given at line 1173–1174, is that "absolute," or enforced, commands are not esteemed by God, who demands that true obedience is offered of our own free will. 1158 *facile* Easily persuaded. 1159 *fair dismiss* "Completely dismiss," "dismiss fairly," "dismiss fairness," or "dismiss the fair one." 1164–1165 *express'd / Immutable* The love between Adam and Eve had been manifested as if it were unchangeable. 1166 *joy'd* Enjoyed. 1173–1174 *beyond this . . . place* See line 1156. 1178 *admiring* Wondering. 1180.1 *durst* Would dare; 1180.2 *rue* Regret. 1182 *accuser* Adam accuses Eve of accusing him. "Accuser" is one of the literal meanings of "satan."

Him who to worth in woman overtrusting
Lets her will rule; restraint she will not brook,
1185 And left to herself, if evil thence ensue,
She first his weak indulgence will accuse.

Thus they in mutual accusation spent
The fruitless hours, but neither self-condemning
1189 And of their vain contest appear'd no end.

END OF BOOK NINTH

1189 *end* Both "finish" and "purpose."

BOOK X

THE ARGUMENT

*Man's transgression known, the guardian angels forsake Paradise,
and return up to heaven to approve* their vigilance; and are
approved;† God declaring that the entrance of Satan could not be
by them prevented. He sends his Son to judge the transgressors,
who descends and gives sentence accordingly; then in pity clothes
them both, and reascends. Sin and Death, sitting till then at the
gates of hell, by wondrous sympathy, feeling the success of Satan
in this new world,‡ and the sin by man there committed, resolve
to sit no longer confined in hell, but to follow Satan their sire up
to the place of man. To make the way easier from hell to this
world to and fro, they pave a broad highway or bridge over
Chaos, according to the track that Satan first made; then
preparing for earth, they meet him, proud of his success, returning
to hell; their mutual gratulation.§ Satan arrives at
Pandemonium; in full assembly relates, with boasting, his success
against man; instead of applause is entertained with a general hiss
by all his audience, transformed with himself also suddenly into
serpents, according to his doom given in Paradise: then, deluded
with a show‖ of the forbidden tree springing up before them, they,
greedily reaching to take of the fruit, chew dust and bitter ashes.
The proceedings of Sin and Death. God foretells the final victory*

---

*Attest.

†Vindicated.

‡As Flannagan notes (p. 623), this phrase "begins the image of perverse exploration" that runs through book X.

§Celebration.

‖The devils are in thrall to the illusory power of images.

of his Son over them, and the renewing of all things; but, for the present commands his angels to make several alterations in the heavens and elements. Adam, more and more perceiving his fallen condition, heavily bewails; rejects the condolement* of Eve; she persists, and at length appeases him: then, to evade the curse likely to fall on their offspring, proposes to Adam violent ways which he approves not, but conceiving better hope, puts her in mind of the late promise made them, that her seed should be revenged on the Serpent, and exhorts her with him to seek peace with the offended Deity by repentance and supplication.

1   MEANWHILE the heinous and despiteful act
      Of Satan done in Paradise, and how
      He in the serpent had perverted Eve,
      Her husband she, to taste the fatal fruit,
5   Was known in heaven; for what can scape the eye
      Of God all-seeing, or deceive his heart
      Omniscient? who, in all things wise and just,
      Hinder'd not Satan to attempt the mind
      Of man, with strength entire, and free-will arm'd
10   Complete to have discover'd and repuls'd
      Whatever wiles of foe or seeming friend.
      For still they knew, and aught to have still remember'd,
      The high injunction not to taste that fruit,
      Whoever tempted; which they not obeying,
15   Incurr'd (what could they less?) the penalty,
16   And, manifold in sin, deserv'd to fall.

      Up into heaven from Paradise in haste
      Th'angelic guards ascended, mute and sad

---

*Condolences.

1 *despiteful* Spiteful.   5 *scape* Escape.   10 *Complete* Completely sufficient.   16 *manifold in sin* Hughes (p. 406) cites Milton's *Of Christian Doctrine* (written 1656), which argues that the sin of eating the fruit represents sin in general.

For man, for of his state by this they knew,   19
Much wond'ring how the subtle fiend had stol'n   20
Entrance unseen. Soon as th'unwelcome news
From earth arriv'd at heaven-gate, displeas'd
All were who heard; dim sadness did not spare
That time celestial visages, yet mix'd   24
With pity, violated not their bliss.   25
About the new-arriv'd in multitudes
The ethereal people ran, to hear and know   27
How all befell: they towards the throne supreme
Accountable made haste to make appear
With righteous plea their utmost vigilance,   30
And easily approv'd; when the Most High   31
Eternal Father, from his secret cloud,
Amidst in thunder utter'd thus his voice:

Assembled angels, and ye powers return'd
From unsuccessful charge, be not dismay'd,   35
Nor troubled at these tidings from the earth,
Which your sincerest care could not prevent;
Foretold so lately what would come to pass
When first this tempter cross'd the gulf from hell.
I told ye then he should prevail and speed   40
On his bad errand, man should be seduc'd
And flatter'd out of all, believing lies
Against his Maker; no decree of mine
Concurring to necessitate his fall,
Or touch with lightest moment of impulse   45
His free-will, to her own inclining left
In even scale. But fallen he is; and now

---

19 *by this* By now.   24–25 *yet mix'd . . . bliss* The angels' sadness is produced by pity for man, but they are themselves not in any less of a blissful condition.   27 *The ethereal people* The angels resemble people in having material bodies, though theirs are made of ether, a heavenly substance that is lighter than air; see John Donne's poem "Air and Angels" (1633): "an angel, face and wings / Of air" (ll. 23–24).   31 *And easily approv'd* Both "they easily proved their vigilance" and "their vigilance was easily approved by God."   40 *speed* Succeed.   45 *moment* Weight.

48   What rests, but that the mortal sentence pass
49   On his transgression, death denounc'd that day,
50   Which he presumes already vain and void,
     Because not yet inflicted, as he fear'd,
     By some immediate stroke; but soon shall find
53   Forbearance no acquittance ere day end.
54   Justice shall not return as bounty scorn'd.
55   But whom send I to judge them? Whom but thee,
56   Vicegerent Son? to thee I have transferr'd
     All judgment, whether in heaven, or earth, or hell.
58   Easy it may be seen that I intend
     Mercy colleague with justice, sending thee
60   Man's friend, his mediator, his design'd
61   Both ransom and redeemer voluntary,
     And destin'd man himself to judge man fallen.

     So spake the Father, and unfolding bright
     Toward the right hand his glory, on the Son
65   Blaz'd forth unclouded Deity; he full
     Resplendent all his Father manifest
67   Express'd, and thus divinely answer'd mild:

     Father Eternal, thine is to decree,
     Mine both in heaven and earth to do thy will[1]
70   Supreme, that thou in me thy Son belov'd
71   May'st ever rest well pleas'd. I go to judge
     On earth these thy transgressors, but thou know'st,
73   Whoever judg'd, the worst on me must light,

48.1 *rests* Remains; 48.2 *mortal sentence* Sentence of death.   49 *denounc'd* Announced.   53 *acquittance* Settling of a debt.   54 *Justice . . . scorn'd* Flannagan points out, "The image is financial, following 'acquittance'" (p. 625).   56 *Vicegerent* One who rules in the place of the monarch.   58 *may* The 1674 edition has "might."   60 *mediator* Christ mediates, or represents, man to God, and God to man.   61 *ransom and redeemer* Both the one who pays the debt and the debt itself.   67 *Express'd* In Hebrews 1:3 St. Paul calls the Son "the express image" of the Father.   71 *well pleas'd* In Matthew 3:17, after the baptism of Christ, a voice from heaven declares, "This is my beloved Son, in whom I am well pleased."   73.1 *the worst* The crucifixion; 73.2 *light* Fall.

When time shall be, for so I undertook   74
Before thee; and not repenting, this obtain   75
Of right, that I may mitigate their doom
On me deriv'd; yet I shall temper so   77
Justice with mercy, as may illustrate most
Them fully satisfied, and thee appease.
Attendance none shall need, nor train, where none   80
Are to behold the judgment but the judged,
Those two; the third best absent is condemn'd,
Convict by flight, and rebel to all law:
Conviction to the serpent none belongs.[2]

Thus saying, from his radiant seat he rose   85
Of high collateral glory: him, thrones and powers,
Princedoms and dominations, ministrant,   87
Accompanied to heaven-gate, from whence
Eden and all the coast in prospect lay.   89
Down he descended straight; the speed of gods   90
Time counts not, tho' with swiftest minutes wing'd.[3]
Now was the sun in western cadence low   92
From noon, and gentle airs, due at their hour   93
To fan the earth now wak'd, and usher in
The evening cool when he from wrath more cool   95
Came the mild judge and intercessor both
To sentence man: the voice of God they heard,
Now walking in the garden, by soft winds
Brought to their ears, while day declin'd; they heard,
And from his presence hid themselves among   100
The thickest trees, both man and wife, till God   101
Approaching, thus to Adam call'd aloud:

Where art thou, Adam, wont with joy to meet
My coming seen far off? I miss thee here,

---

74 *When time shall be* In the fullness of time; from Galatians 4:4. 77.1 *deriv'd* Diverted;
77.2 *temper* Mix. 80 *Attendance . . . need* Simultaneously "I will need no attendants," "no
one will have to wait," and "no one will lack my attention." 87 *ministrant* Ministering.
89 *prospect* View. 92 *cadence* Falling. 93 *airs* Breezes. 101 *God* The Son.

105 Not pleased, thus entertain'd with solitude,
106 Where obvious duty erewhile appear'd unsought:
Or come I less conspicuous, or what change
108 Absents thee, or what chance detains? Come forth.

He came, and with him Eve, more loath, tho' first
110 To offend, discount' nanc'd both, and discompos'd;
Love was not in their looks, either to God
112 Or to each other, but apparent guilt,
And shame, and perturbation, and despair,
Anger, and obstinacy, and hate, and guile.
115 Whence Adam falt'ring long, thus answer'd brief.
I heard thee in the garden, and of thy voice
Afraid, being naked, hid myself. To whom
118 The gracious Judge without revile replied:
My voice thou oft hast heard, and hast not fear'd,
120 But still rejoic'd: how is it now become
121 So dreadful to thee? that thou art naked, who
122 Hath told thee? hast thou eaten of the tree,
123 Whereof I gave thee charge thou shouldst not eat?

To whom thus Adam, sore beset, replied:
125 O heaven! in evil strait this day I stand
Before my Judge, either to undergo
Myself the total crime, or to accuse
128 My other self, the partner of my life;
Whose failing, while her faith to me remains,
130 I should conceal, and not expose to blame
By my complaint; but strict necessity
Subdues me,[4] and calamitous constraint,
Lest on my head both sin and punishment,
However insupportable, be all

106.1 *obvious duty* Duty revealing itself in your physical presence; 106.2 *erewhile* Previously.
108 *Absents* Refers to a psychological alienation rather than to a physical absence, as in
9.372. 112 *apparent* Obvious. 118 *revile* Reproach. 120 *still* Always. 121–123 *that
thou . . . eat?* Paraphrases Genesis 3:11. 128 *other self* See 8.450.

Devolv'd; though should I hold my peace, yet thou 135
Wouldst easily detect what I conceal.
This woman, whom thou mad'st to be my help 137
And gav'st me as thy perfect gift, so good,
So fit, so acceptable, so divine,
That from her hand I could suspect no ill, 140
And what she did, whatever in itself,
Her doing seem'd to justify the deed;
She gave me of the tree, and I did eat.

To whom the sov'reign Presence thus replied:
Was she thy God, that her thou didst obey 145
Before his voice, or was she made thy guide, 146
Superior, or but equal, that to her 147
Thou didst resign thy manhood, and the place 148
Wherein God set thee above her, made of thee, 149
And for thee, whose perfection far excell'd 150
Hers in all real dignity? Adorn'd 151
She was indeed, and lovely to attract 152
Thy love, not thy subjection; and her gifts 153
Were such as under government well seem'd, 154
Unseemly to bear rule, which was thy part 155
And person, hadst thou known thyself aright.
So having said, he thus to Eve in few:
Say, Woman, what is this which thou hast done?

To whom sad Eve, with shame nigh overwhelm'd,
Confessing soon, yet not before her Judge 160
Bold or loquacious, thus abash'd, replied: 161
The serpent me beguil'd, and I did eat. 162

---

137 *whom thou mad'st* Like Satan, Adam blames God for his fall. 145 *Was she thy God* Idolatry is the origin and essence of all sin. 145–153 *that her . . . subjection* By succumbing to Eve's temptation, Adam has preferred his passion for her physical appearance to his rational faculties, which in Milton's view constitutes an internal form of slavery, or "subjection." 154–155 *seem'd* / *Unseemly* Milton's use of "seem'd" usually suggests an illusion. 155–156 *part* / *And person* Both words suggest a dramatic role. 161 *abash'd* Flannagan reminds us that 8.595 describes Adam as "half-abash'd." 162 *The serpent . . . eat* Echoes Genesis 3:13 precisely, unlike Adam, who adds his own reproaches to the biblical account.

Which when the Lord God heard, without delay
To judgment he proceeded on th'accurs'd
165 Serpent, though brute, unable to transfer
The guilt on him who made him instrument
Of mischief, and polluted from the end
Of his creation; justly then accurs'd,
As vitiated in nature:[5] more to know
170 Concern'd not man (since he no further knew)
Nor alter'd his offence; yet God at last
To Satan, first in sin, his doom applied,
173 Though in mysterous terms, judg'd as then best
And on the serpent thus his curse let fall:
175 Because thou hast done this, thou art accurs'd
176 Above all cattle, each beast of the field;
177 Upon thy belly grov'ling thou shalt go,
178 And dust shalt eat all the days of thy life.
179 Between thee and the woman I will put
180 Enmity, and between thine and her seed;
181 Her seed shall bruise thy head, thou bruise his heel.

182 So spake this oracle, then verified
183 When Jesus, son of Mary, second Eve,
184 Saw Satan fall like lightning down from heaven,
185 Prince of the air; then rising from his grave
Spoil'd principalities and powers, triumph'd
In open show, and with ascension bright,
188 Captivity led captive through the air,
The realm itself of Satan long usurp'd,
190 Whom he shall tread at last under our feet;
Even he who now foretold his fatal bruise,
And to the woman thus his sentence turn'd

---

173 *mysterious* Allegorical. 175–181 *Because . . . heel* Closely paraphrases Genesis 3:14–15.
182 *oracle* God is speaking symbolically, like the oracles of ancient Greece. 183–184 *When Jesus . . . heaven* In Luke 10:18–19, Jesus says, "I beheld Satan as lightning fall from heaven. Behold, I give you power to tread on serpents and scorpions." 185 *Prince of the air* The description is applied to Satan in Ephesians 2:2. 188 *Captivity led captive* Echoes Psalms 68:18 and Ephesians 4:8.

Thy sorrow I will greatly multiply
By thy conception; children thou shalt bring
In sorrow forth; and to thy husband's will   195
Thine shall submit; he over thee shall rule: 196

On Adam last thus judgment he pronounc'd.
Because thou hast hearken'd to the voice of thy wife   198
And eaten of the tree, concerning which   199
I charg'd thee, saying, Thou shalt not eat thereof: 200
Curs'd is the ground for thy sake; thou in sorrow   201
Shalt eat thereof all the days of thy life,   202
Thorns also and thistles it shall bring thee forth   203
Unbid; and thou shalt eat th'herb of the field,   204
In the sweat of thy face shalt thou eat bread,   205
Till thou return unto the ground; for thou   206
Out of the ground was taken, know thy birth,   207
For dust thou art, and shalt to dust return.   208

So judg'd he Man, both Judge and Saviour sent,
And th'instant stroke of death denounc'd, that day   210
Remov'd far off; then pitying how they stood   211
Before him naked to the air, that now
Must suffer change, disdain'd not to begin
Thenceforth the form of servant to assume,
As when he wash'd his servants' feet, so now,   215
As father of his family, he clad
Their nakedness with skins of beasts, or slain,
Or as the snake with youthful coat repaid;[6]
And thought not much to clothe his enemies;[7]
Nor he their outward only with the skins   220
Of beasts, but inward nakedness, much more.
Opprobrious, with his robe of righteousness   222

195–196 *and to . . . rule* The "rule" of man over woman is part of the punishment for the
Fall.   198–208 *Because . . . return* Closely paraphrases Genesis 3:17–19.   210–211 *that day . . .
off* The actual day of their deaths is in the future, but the process of dying begins instantly.
215 *As when . . . feet* Refers to John 13:5.   222 *robe of righteousness* From Isaiah 61:10.

Arraying, cover'd from his Father's sight.
To him with swift ascent he up return'd,
225 Into his blissful bosom reassum'd
In glory as of old; to him, appeas'd
All, though all-knowing, what had pass'd with man
Recounted, mixing intercession sweet.

Meanwhile, ere thus we sinn'd and judg'd on earth,
230 Within the gates of hell sat Sin and Death,
In counterview within the gates, that now
Stood open wide, belching outrageous flame
Far into Chaos, since the fiend pass'd through,
Sin opening, who thus now to Death began:

235 O son, why sit we here each other viewing
Idly, while Satan our great author thrives
In other worlds, and happier seat provides
For us his offspring dear? It cannot be
But that success attends him; if mishap,
240 Ere this he had return'd, with fury driven
By his avengers, since no place like this
Can fit his punishment or their revenge.
Methinks I feel new strength within me rise,
Wings growing, and dominion given me large
245 Beyond this deep; whatever draws me on,
246 Or sympathy, or some connatural force
Powerful at greatest distance to unite
With secret amity things of like kind
By secretest conveyance.[8] Thou my shade
250 Inseparable, must with me along:
For Death from Sin no power can separate.[9]
But lest the difficulty of passing back

246.1 *Or . . . or* Either . . . or; **246.2** *sympathy* As used in alchemy to describe the attraction of certain elements and minerals for each other; the term attributes subjective feeling to objective matter.

Stay his return perhaps over this gulf   253
Impassable, impervious, let us try
Advent'rous work, yet to thy power and mine   255
Not unagreeable, to found a path
Over this main from hell to that new world   257
Where Satan now prevails, a monument
Of merit high to all th'infernal host,
Easing their passage hence, for intercourse   260
Or transmigration, as their lot shall lead.
Nor can I miss the way, so strongly drawn
By this new-felt attraction and instinct.

Whom thus the meagre Shadow answer'd soon.   264
Go whither fate and inclination strong   265
Leads thee; I shall not lag behind, nor err
The way, thou leading, such a scent I draw
Of carnage, prey innumerable, and taste
The savour of death from all things there that live:
Nor shall I to the work thou enterprisest   270
Be wanting, but afford thee equal aid.

So saying, with delight he snuff'd the smell   272
Of mortal change on earth. As when a flock
Of ravenous fowl, though many a league remote   274
Against the day of battle, to a field   275
Where armies lie encamp'd, come flying, lur'd
With scent of living carcasses design'd   277
For death, the following day, in bloody fight:
So scented the grim Feature, and upturn'd
His nostril wide into the murky air,   280
Sagacious of his quarry from so far.   281

---

253 *Stay* Delay.   257 *main* The abyss of Chaos.   264 *meagre* Thin.   272 *snuff'd* Sniffed.
274 *fowl* Soothsayers often interpreted the flight formations of birds for signs of future
events.   275 *Against* In anticipation of.   277 *design'd* Destined, but with strong overtones
of God's design, which ascribe to Him the ultimate responsibility for the soldiers' death,
and perhaps for death in general.   281 *Sagacious of* Able to know by smelling.

Then both them out hell-gates into the waste
Wide anarchy of Chaos damp and dark
Flew diverse, and with power (their power was great)
285 Hovering upon the waters, what they met,
Solid or slimy, as in raging sea
Toss'd up and down, together crowded drove
From each side shoaling tow'rds the mouth of hell:
As when two polar winds, blowing adverse
290 Upon the Cronian sea, together drive
291 Mountains of ice, that stop th'imagin'd way
292 Beyond Petsora eastward, to the rich
293 Cathaian coast. The aggregated soil
294 Death, with his mace petrific, cold and dry,
295 As with a trident smote, and fixt as firm
296 As Delos floating once; the rest his look
297 Bound with Gorgonian rigour not to move
298 And with Asphaltic slime, broad as the gate,
Deep to the roots of hell, the gather'd beach
300 They fasten'd, and the mole immense wrought on
Over the foaming deep high-arch'd, a bridge
Of length prodigious, joining to the wall
303 Immoveable of this now fenceless world
304 Forfeit to death; from hence a passage broad,
305 Smooth, easy, inoffensive, down to hell.
So, if great things to small may be compar'd

---

285 *Hovering upon the waters* Compare 7:235–240 and Genesis 1:21–22.   290 *the Cronian sea*
The Arctic Ocean.   291.1 *stop* Block; 291.2 *th'imagin'd way* English explorers had for cen-
turies vainly sought a trade route to the East through the Arctic Ocean; Fowler notes Hud-
son's expedition of 1608.   292 *Petsora* A river in Siberia.   293.1 *Cathaian* North Chinese;
293.2 *aggregated* Packed together into solid form.   294.1 *mace* Ornamental staff, as the Pope
carries; 294.2 *petrific* Turning to stone. Death solidifies, or objectifies, even inanimate
things.   295–296 *As with a trident . . . once* In Greek mythology, Neptune used his trident
to form the island of Delos out of the sea.   297 *Gorgonian rigour* The look of the myth-
ical Gorgon Medusa turned men to stone; so death, which induces rigor mortis, turns
human beings into things.   298 *Asphaltic slime* Pitch.   300 *mole* Harbor.   303 *fenceless* De-
fenceless.   304–305 *a passage . . . hell* Taking the road to Hell is easy and will not offend
public opinion.

Xerxes, the liberty of Greece to yoke,
From Susa his Memnonian palace high
Came to the sea, and over Hellespont
Bridging his way, Europe with Asia join'd,[10]   310
And scourg'd with many a stroke th'indignant waves.
Now had they brought the work by wondrous art   312
Pontifical,[11] a ridge of pendent rock,   313
Over the vex'd abyss, following the track   314
Of Satan to the self-same place where he   315
First lighted from his wing, and landed safe
From out of Chaos, to the outside bare
Of this round world: with pins of adamant
And chains they made all fast, too fast they made
And durable; and now in little space   320
The confines met of empyrean heaven
And of this world, and on the left hand hell   322
With long reach interpos'd; three several ways   323
In sight, to each of these three places led.
And now their way to earth they had descried,   325
To Paradise first tending, when behold
Satan, in likeness of an angel bright,   327
Betwixt the Centaur and the Scorpion steering   328
His zenith, while the sun in Aries rose   329
Disguis'd he came, but those his children dear   330
Their parent soon discern'd, though in disguise.
He, after Eve seduc'd, unminded slunk   332
Into the wood fast by, and changing shape
To observe the sequel, saw his guileful act   334
By Eve, though all unweeting, seconded   335
Upon her husband, saw their shame that sought

---

312 *wondrous art* Flannagan reminds us that "'Art' is a word Milton often associates with witchcraft"; so is "wondrous" (p. 633).   313 *pendent* Hanging.   314 *vex'd* Both "disturbed" and "annoyed."   322 *left hand* Traditionally evil, hence "sinister."   323 *several* Separate. 325 *descried* Discerned.   327 *in likeness . . . bright* From 2 Corinthians 11:14.   328–329 *Centaur . . . rose* References to signs of the zodiac.   332 *unminded* Unnoticed.   334 *sequel* What followed.   335 *unweeting* Unwitting.

337   Vain covertures; but when he saw descend
         The Son of God to judge them, terrified
         He fled, not hoping to escape, but shun
340   The present, fearing, guilty, what his wrath
         Might suddenly inflict; that past, return'd
         By night, and list'ning where the hapless pair
343   Sat in their sad discourse, and various plaint,
344   Thence gather'd his own doom, which understood
345   Not instant, but of future time, with joy
         And tidings fraught, to hell he now return'd,
         And at the brink of Chaos, near the foot
348   Of this new wondrous pontifice, unhop'd
         Met who to meet him came, his offspring dear.
350   Great joy was at their meeting, and at sight
         Of that stupendous bridge his joy increas'd.
         Long he admiring stood, till Sin, his fair
         Enchanting daughter, thus the silence broke:

         O parent, these are thy magnific deeds,
355   Thy trophies, which thou view'st as not thine own,
         Thou art their author and prime architect:
         For I no sooner in my heart divin'd,
         My heart, which by a secret harmony
         Still moves with thine, join'd in connection sweet,
360   That thou on earth hadst prosper'd, which thy looks
361   Now also evidence, but straight I felt,
362   Though distant from thee worlds between, yet felt
         That I must after thee with this thy son,
364   Such fatal consequence unites us three:
365   Hell could no longer hold us in her bounds,
         Nor this unvoyageable gulf obscure
         Detain from following thy illustrious track.

---

337 *covertures* Coverings.   343 *plaint* Mourning.   344 *gather'd his own doom* Understood his
own judgment.   348 *pontifice* Bridge.   361 *straight* Straight away.   361–362 *felt . . . felt* Sin
thinks through intuition, feeling, and sympathy.   364 *fatal* Both "mortal" and "pertaining
to fate."

Thou hast achieved our liberty, confin'd
Within hell-gates till now, thou us impower'd
To fortify thus far, and overlay   370
With this portentous bridge the dark abyss.   · 371
Thine now is all this world; thy virtue hath won   372
What thy hands builded not, thy wisdom gain'd   373
With odds what war hath lost, and fully aveng'd
Our foil in heaven; here thou shalt monarch reign,   375
There didst not; there let him still victor sway,   376
As battle hath adjudg'd, from this new world
Retiring, by his own doom alienated,
And henceforth monarchy with thee divide
Of all things parted by th'empyreal bounds,   380
His quadrature, from thy orbicular world,   381
Or try thee now more dang'rous to his throne.

Whom thus the prince of darkness answer'd glad
Fair daughter, and thou son and grandchild both,   384
High proof ye now have given to be the race   385
Of Satan, (for I glory in the name   386
Antagonist of heaven's Almighty king,)
Amply have merited of me, of all
Th'infernal empire, that so near heaven's door
Triumphal with triumphal act have met,   390
Mine with this glorious work, and made one realm,
Hell and this world one realm, one continent
Of easy thoroughfare. Therefore while I
Descend through darkness, on your road with ease,
To my associate powers, them to acquaint   395
With these successes, and with them rejoice;

---

371 *portentous* Ominous, significant.   372–373 *thy virtue . . . not* Satan has appropriated the
products of another's labor.   375 *foil* Defeat.   375–376 *here thou . . . not* Sin repeats Satan's
observation at 1.263: "Better to reign in hell, than serve in heaven."   376 *sway* Rule.   381.1
quadrature Square; 381.2 *orbicular* Round.   384 *son and grandchild both* Satan manages to
make Death's origin in unnatural incest sound like an honorific.   386 *I glory in the name*
Leonard observes: "This is the first and only time that Satan speaks his name in *Paradise
Lost*" (p. 844).

You two this way, among these numerous orbs
All yours, right down to Paradise descend;
There dwell and reign in bliss, thence on the earth
400   Dominion exercise, and in the air.
Chiefly on man, sole lord of all declar'd,
402   Him first make sure your thrall, and lastly kill.
403   My substitutes I send ye, and create
404   Plenipotent on earth, of matchless might
405   Issuing from me: on your joint vigour now
My hold of this new kingdom all depends,
Through sin to death expos'd by my exploit.
If your joint power prevail, th'affairs of hell
No detriment need fear; go, and be strong.

410   So saying, he dismiss'd them; they with speed
Their course through thickest constellations held,
412   Spreading their bane: the blasted stars look'd wan,
413   And planets, planet-struck, real eclipse
414   Then suffer'd. Th'other way Satan went down
415   The causey to hell-gate; on either side
416   Disparted Chaos, over-built, exclaim'd,
And with rebounding Surge the bars assail'd,
That scorn'd his indigration: through the gate,
Wide open and unguarded, Satan pass'd,
420   And all about found desolate; for those
Appointed to sit there had left their charge,
Flown to the upper world; the rest were all
Far to th'inland retir'd, about the walls
Of Pandemonium, city and proud seat
425   Of Lucifer, so by allusion call'd,
Of that bright star to Satan paragon'd.

---

402 *thrall* Slave.   403 *create* Declare. Satan does not have the power of creation.
404 *Plenipotent* Full of power.   412.1 *bane* Poison; 412.2 *blasted* Infected, as in William
Blake's poem "London" (1794): "Blasts the new-born Infant's tear" (l. 15).   413–414 *planet-struck* The *Oxford English Dictionary* cites this instance as meaning "struck by the supposed
malign influence of an adverse planet."   415 *causey* Causeway.   416 *over-built, exclaim'd*
Complained at being built over.

There kept their watch the legions, while the grand
In council sat, solicitous what chance   428
Might intercept their emperor sent; so he   429
Departing gave command, and they observ'd.   430
As when the Tartar from his Russian foe
By Astracan over the snowy plains
Retires;[12] or Bactrian Sophi from the horn
Of Turkish crescent, leaves all waste beyond
The realm of Aladule, in his retreat   435
To Tauris or Casbeen:[13] so these, the late
Heaven-banish'd host, left desert utmost hell
Many a dark league, reduc'd in careful watch   438
Round their metropolis, and now expecting
Each hour their great adventurer from the search   440
Of foreign worlds. He through the midst, unmark'd   441
In show plebeian angel militant   442
Of lowest order, pass'd; and from the door
Of that Plutonian hall, invisible,   444
Ascended his high throne, which under state   445
Of richest texture spread, at th'upper end
Was plac'd in regal lustre. Down awhile
He sat, and round about him saw unseen:
At last, as from a cloud, his fulgent head
And shape star-bright appear'd, or brighter clad,   450
With what permissive glory since his fall   451
Was left him, or false glitter. All amaz'd
At that so sudden blaze, the Stygian throng   453
Bent their aspect, and whom they wish'd beheld,
Their mighty chief return'd: loud was th'acclaim;   455
Forth rush'd in haste the great consulting peers,

428–429 *solicitous . . . sent* Wondering what luck their emperor would have.   **438** *reduc'd*
Pulled back.   **441** *unmark'd* Unnoticed.   **442** *In show . . . militant* Like an ordinary fight-
ing angel; Satan will stage his return as an elaborate spectacle.   **444** *Plutonian* Alludes to
both Pluto, god of the underworld, and Plutus, god of money.   **445** *state* Canopy.   **451**
permissive With the permission of God.   **453** *Stygian* Hellish.

457   Rais'd from their dark divan, and with like joy
       Congratulant approach'd him, who with hand
       Silence, and with these words attention, won:
460   Thrones, dominations, princedoms, virtues, powers;
       For in possession such, not only of right,
       I call ye and declare ye now, return'd
       Successful beyond hope, to lead ye forth
       Triumphant out of this infernal pit
465   Abominable, accurs'd, the house of woe,
       And dungeon of our tyrant: now possess,
       As lords, a spacious world, to our native heaven
       Little inferior, by my adventure hard
       With peril great achiev'd. Long were to tell
470   What I have done, what suffer'd, with what pain
       Voyag'd the unreal, vast, unbounded deep
       Of horrible confusion, over which,
       By Sin and Death, a broad way now is pav'd
       To expedite your glorious march; but I
475   Toiled out my uncouth passage, forc'd to ride
       Th'untractable abyss, plung'd in the womb
477   Of unoriginal Night and Chaos wild,
478   That jealous of their secrets fiercely oppos'd
       My journey strange, with clamorous uproar
480   Protesting Fate supreme; thence how I found
       The new-created world, which fame in heaven
482   Long had foretold, a fabric wonderful,
       Of absolute perfection; therein man,
484   Plac'd in a Paradise, by our exile
485   Made happy. Him by fraud I have seduc'd
       From his Creator, and, the more to increase

---

457 *divan* The Ottoman state council was called the "divan." Milton would have thought of it as a passive accessory to the Sultan's tyranny.   475 *uncouth passage* Strange journey. 477 *unoriginal* Uncreated.   478 *fiercely oppos'd* As Fowler points out (pp. 565–566), Satan lies; Chaos assisted his journey.   482 *fabric* Fabrication.   484–485 *by our exile / Made happy* Satan imagines there is only a finite amount of happiness in the universe, so that in order to acquire it, one must take it from others. He thinks of happiness in quantitative, not qualitative, terms.

Your wonder, with an apple; he thereat   487
Offended, worth your laughter, hath given up
Both his beloved man, and all his world,
To Sin and Death a prey, and so to us,   490
Without our hazard, labour, or alarm,
To range in, and to dwell, and over man
To rule, as over all he should have rul'd.
True is, me also he hath judg'd, or rather
Me not, but the brute serpent, in whose shape   495
Man I deceiv'd: that which to me belongs
Is enmity, which he will put between
Me and mankind; I am to bruise his heel;
His seed, when is not set, shall bruise my head.
A world who would not purchase with a bruise,   500
Or much more grievous pain? Ye have th'account
Of my performance: what remains, ye gods,—
But up and enter now into full bliss.

So having said, awhile he stood expecting
Their universal shout and high applause   505
To fill his ear; when, contrary, he hears
On all sides, from innumerable tongues,
A dismal universal hiss, the sound   508
Of public scorn; he wonder'd, but not long
Had leisure, wond'ring at himself now more;   510
His visage drawn he felt to sharp and spare,   511
His arms clung to his ribs; his legs intwining   512
Each other, still supplanted, down he fell
A monstrous serpent on his belly prone,
Reluctant, but in vain; a greater power   515

---

487 *apple* Flannagan points out: "As always, Satan diminishes or reduces symbols to material objects" (p. 638). Only Satan refers to an "apple," the other characters speak of "fruit," which includes the sense of "consequences"; compare 9.585. **495** *Me not, but the brute serpent* Satan assumes that God has cursed the sign, not the referent. **500** *purchase* Satan imagines that he has engaged in a quasi-financial exchange with God. **508** *A dismal universal hiss* A famous onomatopoeia. **511.1** *visage* Face; **511.2** *spare* Thin. **512** *ribs* In an opposite motion to Eve's birth from Adam's rib.

Now rul'd him, punish'd in the shape he sinn'd[14]
According to his doom. He would have spoke,
But hiss for hiss return'd with forked tongue
To forked tongue, for now were all transform'd
520 Alike, to serpents all, as accessories
521 To his bold riot; dreadful was the din
Of hissing through the hail, thick swarming now
523 With complicated monsters head and tail,
524 Scorpion, and asp, and amphisbæna dire,
525 Cerastes horn'd, hydrus, and ellops drear,
526 And dipsas, (not so thick swarm'd once the soil
527 Bedropp'd with blood of Gorgon, or the isle
528 Ophiusa;) but still greatest, he the midst,
529 Now dragon grown, larger than whom the sun
530 Engender'd in the Pythian vale on slime,
531 Huge Python, and his power no less he seem'd
Above the rest still to retain. They all
Him follow'd, issuing forth to th'open field,
534 Where all yet left of that revolted rout,
535 Heaven-fallen, in station stood or just array,
536 Sublime with expectation when to see
In triumph issuing forth their glorious chief.
They saw, but other sight instead, a crowd
Of ugly serpents: horror on them fell,
540 And horrid sympathy; for what they saw
They felt themselves now changing; down their arms,
Down fell both spear and shield, down they as fast,

---

521 *riot* Revolt. 523 *complicated* Tangled. 524.1 *asp* Snake; 524.2 *amphisbæna* Hughes observes that all Milton's serpents are "understood to be real and symbolic" (p. 418). The mythical "amphisbaena" was two-headed, and thus "a symbol of adultery and inconstancy." 526 *dipsas* Snake whose venom was supposed to produce thirst; features in the epic *The Civil War* 9.737–750, by first-century A.D. Roman poet Lucan. 526–527 *the soil . . . Gorgon* In Ovid's *Metamorphoses* 4.617–620, snakes sprang from soil watered with the blood of the Gorgon Medusa. 528 *Ophiusa* In Greek, "snake-filled," the name given to a group of Balearic Islands. 529 *dragon* From Revelation 12:9: "The great dragon was cast out, that old serpent, called the Devil." 529–531 *the sun . . . Python* In Ovid's *Metamorphoses* 1.438–440, the Python is a monstrous serpent that grows out of the earth. 534 *rout* Crew, gang. 535 *in station . . . array* At their posts, in good order. 536 *Sublime* Uplifted.

And the dire hiss renew'd, and the dire form,
Catch'd by contagion, like in punishment,
As in their crime. Thus was th'applause they meant 545
Turn'd to exploding hiss, triumph to shame,
Cast on themselves from their own mouths. There stood
A grove hard by, sprung up with this their change, 548
His will who reigns above, to aggravate
Their penance, laden with fair fruit, like that 550
Which grew in Paradise, the bait of Eve
Us'd by the tempter: on that prospect strange
Their earnest eyes they fixt, imagining
For one forbidden tree a multitude
Now risen, to work them further woe or shame; 555
Yet parch'd with scalding thirst and hunger fierce,
Though to delude them sent, could not abstain,
But on they roll'd in heaps, and up the trees
Climbing, sat thicker than the snaky locks
That curl'd Magæra: greedily they pluck'd 560
The fruitage fair to sight, like that which grew
Near that bituminous lake where Sodom flam'd:[15] 562
This more delusive, not the touch, but taste
 Deceiv'd; they fondly thinking to allay 564
Their appetite with gust, instead of fruit 565
Chew'd bitter ashes, which th'offended taste
With spattering noise rejected: oft they assay'd,
Hunger and thirst constraining, drugg'd as oft,
With hatefullest disrelish writh'd their jaws
With soot and cinders fill'd; so oft they fell 570
Into the same illusion, not as man
Whom they triumph'd once laps'd. Thus were they plagu'd
And worn with famine, long and ceaseless hiss,
Till their lost shape, permitted, they resum'd,
Yearly enjoy'd, some say, to undergo 575
This annual humbling certain number'd days

548.1 *A grove* Always associated with idolatry; 548.2 *hard by* Close by.   560 *Magæra* One of
the Furies, goddesses of vengeance in mythology.   562 *bituminous lake* The Dead Sea.
564 *fondly* Foolishly.   565 *gust* Gusto.

To dash their pride, and joy for man seduc'd.
However some tradition they dispers'd
Among the heathen of their purchase got,
580   And fabled how the serpent, whom they call'd
Ophion, with Eurynome, the wide
Encroaching Eve perhaps, had first the rule
Of high Olympus, thence by Saturn driven,
And Ops, ere yet Dictæan Jove was born.[16]

585   Meanwhile in Paradise the hellish pair
586   Too soon arriv'd, Sin there in power before,
587   Once actual, now in body, and to dwell
Habitual habitant; behind her Death
Close following pace for pace, not mounted yet
590   On his pale horse: to whom Sin thus began:

Second of Satan sprung, all conqu'ring Death;
What think'st thou of our empire now, tho' earn'd
593   With travail difficult, not better far
Than still at hell's dark threshold to have sat watch,
595   Unnam'd, undreaded, and thyself half-starv'd?

Whom thus the Sin-born monster answer'd soon:
To me, who with eternal famine pine,
Alike is hell, or Paradise, or heaven,
599   There best where most with ravine I may meet;
600   Which here tho' plenteous all too little seems
601   To stuff this maw, this vast unhidebound corpse.

To whom th'incestuous mother thus replied:
Thou therefore on these herbs, and fruits, and flowers,

---

586 *in power* In effect. **587** *actual* Campbell notes: "'Actual sin' is a technical theological term for a sin which is the outcome of a free personal act of the individual will, and is therefore to be contrasted with original sin" (p. 382). **590** *pale horse* As ridden by Death in Revelation 6:8. **593** *travail* Labor. **599** *ravine* Prey. **601.1** *maw* Jaw; **601.2** *unhidebound corpse* Both "body having loose skin" (because Death is starving) and "body not enclosed by skin" (because Death is amorphous).

Feed first, on each beast next, and fish, and fowl,
No homely morsels; and whatever thing   605
The scythe of Time mows down, devour unspar'd;   606
Till I in man residing through the race,
His thoughts, his looks, words, actions, all infect,
And season him thy last and sweetest prey.

This said, they both betook them several ways,   610
Both to destroy, or unimmortal make   611
All kinds, and for destruction to mature   612
Sooner or later; which th'Almighty seeing,
From his transcendent seat the saints among,
To those bright orders utter'd thus his voice: 615

See with what heat these dogs of hell advance
To waste and havoc yonder world, which I   617
So fair and good created, and had still
Kept in that state, had not the folly of man
Let in these wasteful furies, who impute   620
Folly to me, so doth the prince of hell
And his adherents, that with so much ease
I suffer them to enter and possess   623
A place so heavenly, and conniving seem   624
To gratify my scornful enemies,   625
That laugh, as if transported with some fit
Of passion, I to them had quitted all,
At random yielded up to their misrule
And knew not that I call'd and drew them thither;   629
My hell-hounds, to lick up the draff and filth   630

---

606 *the scythe of Time* Old Father Time is often pictured carrying a scythe, as a reminder that "all flesh is grass" (Isaiah 40:6).   610 *several* Separate.   611 *unimmortal* According to Leonard, "The neologism implies that mortality is not a natural state but a privation" (p. 848).   612 *kinds* Species.   617 *havoc* Plunder.   620 *impute* Ascribe. In Protestant theology God "imputes" grace to undeserving sinners; here the devils "impute" sin to the undeserving Creator.   623 *suffer* Allow.   624 *conniving* Winking at, colluding.   629 *And knew . . . thither* The devils impute arbitrary "passion" to God; they are incapable of perceiving His providential purpose.   630 *draff* Dregs.

Which man's polluting sin with taint hath shed
On what was pure, till cramm'd and gorg'd, nigh burst
633 With suck'd and glutted offal, at one sling
Of thy victorious arm, well-pleasing Son,
635 Both sin and death and yawning grave at last,
Through Chaos hurl'd obstruct the mouth of hell
637 For ever, and seal up his ravenous jaws.
638 Then heaven and earth renew'd shall be made pure
639 To sanctity that shall receive no stain:
640 Till then the curse pronounc'd on both precedes.

He ended, and the heavenly audience loud
Sung hallelujah, as the sound of seas,
Through multitude that sung: Just are thy ways,
Righteous are thy decrees on all thy works;
645 Who can extenuate thee? Next to the Son,
Destin'd restorer of mankind, by whom
647 New heaven and earth shall to the ages rise,
648 Or down from heaven descend. Such was their song,
While the Creator, calling forth by name
650 His mighty angels, gave them several charge,
651 As sorted best with present things. The sun
Had first his precept so to move, so shine,
As might affect the earth with cold and heat
Scarce tolerable, and from the north to call
655 Decrepit winter, from the south to bring
656 Solstitial summer's heat. To the blank moon
657 Her office they prescrib'd, to th'other five
658 Their planetary motions and aspects

---

633 *sling* Recalling the sling and stone with which David kills Goliath in 1 Samuel 17:50.
637 *his* Hell's.   638–640 *Then heaven . . . precedes* The human race must remain in a state of
sin and alienation until the second coming of Christ.   645 *extenuate* Belittle, find fault
with.   647 *heaven* The universe, the physical "heavens."   648 *heaven* The abode of the
Almighty, the spiritual "heaven." The angels praise the Son as the force that will unite the
physical universe with the spiritual heaven.   651 *sorted* Suited.   656 *blank* White or pale.
657 *five* Planets.   658 *aspects* Astrological positions.

In sextile, square, and trine, and opposite.   659

Of noxious efficacy, and when to join   660

In synod unbenign; and taught the fixt   661

Their influence malignant when to shower,

Which of them rising with the sun or falling,

Should prove tempestuous: to the winds they set

Their corners, when with bluster to confound   665

Sea, air, and shore, the thunder when to roll

With terror through the dark aerial hall.

Some say he bid his angels turn askance

The poles of earth twice ten degrees and more

From the sun's axle; they with labour push'd   670

Oblique the centric globe: some say the sun

Was bid turn reins from th'equinoctial road[17]

Like distant breadth to Taurus with the seven

Atlantic Sisters, and the Spartan Twins   674

Up to the Tropic Crab; thence down amain   675

By Leo and the Virgin and the Scales,   676

As deep as Capricorn, to bring in change

Of seasons to each clime; else had the spring

Perpetual smil'd on earth with verdant flowers,

Equal in days and nights, except to those   680

Beyond the polar circles; to them day

Had unbenighted shone, with the low sun,

To recompense his distance, in their sight

Had rounded still th'horizon, and not known

Or east or west, which had forbid the snow   685

From cold Estotiland, and south as far   686

Beneath Magellan. At that tasted fruit   687

---

659 *In sextile . . . opposite* At angles of 60, 90, 120, and 180 degrees.   661.1 *synod unbenign*
Malign astrological conjunction; "synod" also means "assembly of prelates"; 661.2 *fixt*
Fixed stars.   665 *confound* Mix together.   674.1 *Atlantic Sisters* The Pleiades, a star cluster;
in the following lines Milton associates the signs of the zodiac with the consequences of
the Fall.   674.2 *Spartan Twins* Gemini.   675 *Tropic Crab* Cancer.   676 *Scales* Libra.   685
Or . . . or Either . . . or.   686 *Estotiland* In modern Labrador.   687 *Magellan* Probably the
Straits of Magellan at the southern tip of South America, but Fowler notes that what is
now Argentina was called "Magellonica" in the seventeenth century.

688   The sun, as from Thyestean banquet, turn'd
         His course intended; else how had the world
690   Inhabited, though sinless, more than now,
         Avoided pinching cold and scorching heat?
         These changes in the heavens, though slow, produc'd
693   Like change on sea and land, sideral blast,
         Vapour, and mist, and exhalation hot,
695   Corrupt and pestilent. Now from the north
696   Of Norumbega, and the Samoed shore,
697   Bursting their brazen dungeon, arm'd with ice,
698   And snow and hail, and stormy gust and flaw
699   Boreas and Cæcias, and Argestes loud,
700   And Thrasias, rend the woods and seas upturn;
         With adverse blast upturn them from the south
         Notus and Afer, black with thund'rous clouds
703   From Serraliona; thwart of these as fierce
         Forth rush the Levant and the Ponent winds,
705   Eurus and Zephyr, with their lateral noise,
         Sirocco and Libecchio. Thus began
707   Outrage from lifeless things; but Discord first.
         Daughter of Sin, among th'irrational,
         Death introduc'd through fierce antipathy:
710   Beast now with beast 'gan war, and fowl with fowl,
         And fish with fish; to graze the herb all leaving,
         Devour'd each other: nor stood much in awe
         Of man, but fled him, or with count'nance grim

---

688 *Thyestean banquest* In *Thyestes* (776–778), by first-century A.D. Roman statesman and philosopher Seneca, Thyestes seduces his brother Atreus' wife; in revenge Atreus kills one of his sons and serves the son's body to him as food; the sun shifts from its axis in revulsion at the sight.   **693** *sideral* From the stars.   **696.1** *Norumbega* As coastal northern New England and the Maritime Provinces of Canada were once known; **696.2** *Samoed* Siberian. **697** *dungeon* Like the demons, the north winds were supposed to be imprisoned when not active; the image is from Virgil's *Aeneid* 1.50–59.   **698** *flaw* Squall.   **699–700** *Boreas . . . Thrasias* A list of northern winds.   **700** *rend* Tear.   **703.1** *Serraliona* Modern Sierra Leone, in western Africa; **703.2** *thwart of* Across from.   **707** *Discord* Discord, or Eris, gave the apple marked "to the fairest" to the Olympian gods, thus sparking the rivalry among Hera, Athena, and Aphrodite that led to the judgment of Paris and the Trojan War.   **710** *'gan* Began.

Glar'd on him passing. These were from without.
The growing miseries which Adam saw   715
Already in part, though hid in gloomiest shade,
To sorrow abandon'd, but worse felt within,
And in a troubled sea of passion toss'd,
Thus to disburden sought with sad complaint:

O miserable of happy! is this the end   720
Of this new glorious world, and me so late   721
The glory of that glory, who now become
Accurs'd of blessed, hide me from the face
Of God, whom to behold was then my height
Of happiness: yet well, if here would end   725
The misery; I deserv'd it, and would bear
My own deservings; but this will not serve,   727
All that I eat or drink, or shall beget,
Is propagated curse. O voice once heard
Delightfully, Increase and multiply,   730
Now death to hear, for what can I increase
Or multiply, but curses on my head?
Who of all ages to succeed, but feeling   733
The evil on him brought by me, will curse
My head? Ill fare our ancestor impure,   735
For this we may thank Adam; but his thanks
Shall be the execration; so besides
Mine own that bide upon me, all from me
Shall with a fierce reflux on me redound,   739
On me, as on their natural centre, light   740
Heavy, though in their place. O fleeting joys
Of Paradise, dear bought with lasting woes!   742
Did I request thee, Maker, from my clay
To mould me man?[18] Did I solicit thee

---

720 *O miserable of happy* With the sense that his previous happiness has caused his present misery; Milton stresses how one condition produces its opposite.   721 *so late* So recently.
727 *serve* Suffice.   733 *all ages to succeed* All succeeding ages.   739 *redound* Rebound.   742 *dear bought* Expensively purchased.

745   From darkness to promote me, or here place
        In this delicious garden? As my will
        Concurr'd not to my being, it were but right
        And equal to reduce me to my dust,
        Desirous to resign and render back
750   All I receiv'd, unable to perform
        Thy terms too hard, by which I was to hold
        The good I sought not.[19] To the loss of that,
        Sufficient penalty, why hast thou added
        The sense of endless woes? Inexplicable
755   Thy justice seems; yet to say truth, too late
        I thus contest; then should have been refus'd
        Those terms whatever, when they were propos'd:
        Thou didst accept them; wilt thou enjoy the good,
759   Then cavil the conditions? And thou God
760   Made thee without thy leave, what if thy son
        Prove disobedient, and reprov'd, retort,
        Wherefore didst thou beget me? I sought it not:
763   Wouldst thou admit for his contempt of thee
        That proud excuse? Yet him not thy election,
765   But natural necessity begot.
        God made thee of choice his own, and of his own
        To serve him; thy reward was of his grace,
        Thy punishment that justly is at his will.
        Be it so, for I submit; his doom is fair,
770   That dust I am, and shall to dust return:
        O welcome hour whenever! Why delays
        His hand to execute what his decree
        Fixt on this day? Why do I overlive,
774   Why am I mock'd with death, and lengthen'd out
775   To deathless pain? How gladly would I meet
        Mortality my sentence, and be earth
        Insensible! How glad would lay me down

---

759 *cavil* Object to; the word "cavaliers" comes from the term "cavilers."   **763** *admit* Permit.   **774.1** *mock'd with* Tantalized with the prospect of; **774.2** *lengthen'd* Stretched out, as on a rack.

As in my mother's lap! There I should rest
And sleep secure; his dreadful voice no more
Would thunder in my ears, no fear of worse   780
To me and to my offspring would torment me   781
With cruel expectation. Yet one doubt   782
Pursues me still, lest all I cannot die,   783
Lest that pure breath of life, the spirit of man   784
Which God inspir'd, cannot together perish   785
With this corporeal clod; then in the grave,   786
Or in some other dismal place, who knows
But I shall die a living death? O thought
Horrid, if true! Yet why? It was but breath
Of life that sinn'd: what dies but what had life   790
And sin? The body properly hath neither.   791
All of me then shall die: let this appease   792
The doubt, since human reach no further knows.   793
For though the Lord of all be infinite,
Is his wrath also? Be it, man is not so,   795
But mortal doom'd. How can he exercise
Wrath without end on man whom death must end?
Can he make deathless death? That were to make
Strange contradiction, which to God himself
Impossible is held, as argument   800
Of weakness, not of power. Will he draw out
For anger's sake, finite to infinite
In punish'd man, to satisfy his rigour
Satisfied never? That were to extend
His sentence beyond dust and Nature's law,   805
By which all causes else according still

780–782 *no fear . . . expectation* The fact that religion frightens people with the prospect of
Hell would become an important argument in ethical arguments for atheism.   783 *lest all
I cannot die* Both "lest in spite of everything I cannot die" and "lest not all of me can die."
784 *spirit* Soul.   786 *corporeal clod* The body.   791 *properly* Naturally; the body is not in-
trinsically sinful, any more than was the serpent: In both cases it is the spirit that inhabits
the body that sins.   792–793 *All of me . . . knows* Adam has reasoned his way to "mortal-
ism," the belief that the soul dies with the body.   795 *Be it* Let it be so.   800 *argument*
Evidence.

To the reception of their matter act,
Not to th'extent of their own sphere. But say
That death be not one stroke, as I suppos'd,

810   Bereaving sense, but endless misery
From this day onward, which I feel begun
Both in me, and without me, and so last
To perpetuity; ay me, that fear
Comes thund'ring back with dreadful revolution

815   On my defenceless head; both Death and I
Am found eternal, and incorporate both;

817   Nor I on my part single, in me all
Posterity stands curs'd: fair patrimony
That I must leave ye, sons; O were I able

820   To waste it all myself, and leave ye none!
So disinherited how would ye bless
Me, now your curse! Ah, why should all mankind
For one man's fault thus guiltless be condemn'd,
If guiltless? But from me what can proceed,

825   But all corrupt, both mind and will deprav'd,
Not to do only, but to will the same
With me? How can they then acquitted stand
In sight of God? Him after all disputes
Forc'd I absolve: all my evasions vain,

830   And reasonings, though through mazes, lead me still

831   But to my own conviction: first and last

832   On me, me only, as the source and spring

833   Of all corruption, all the blame lights due;

834   So might the wrath. Fond wish! couldst thou support

835   That burden, heavier than the earth to bear,
Than all the world much heavier, though divided
With that bad woman? Thus what thou desir'st,
And what thou fear'st, alike destroys all hope
Of refuge, and concludes thee miserable

840   Beyond all past example and future,

---

817 *single* Alone.   831–833 *first and last . . . due* Compare 3.236 and 10.936.   834 *Fond* Foolish.

To Satan only like both crime and doom.
O conscience, into what abyss of fears
And horrors hast thou driven me; out of which
I find no way, from deep to deeper plung'd.

Thus Adam to himself lamented loud   845
Through the still night, not now, as ere man fell,
Wholesome and cool and mild, but with black air
Accompanied, with damps and dreadful gloom,
Which to his evil conscience represented
All things with double terror: on the ground   850
Outstretch'd he lay, on the cold ground, and oft
Curs'd his creation, death as oft accus'd
Of tardy execution, since denounc'd   853
The day of his offence. Why comes not death,
Said he, with one thrice-acceptable stroke   855
To end me? Shall truth fail to keep her word,
Justice divine not hasten to be just?
But death comes not at all, justice divine   858
Mends not her slowest pace for prayers or cries.   859
O woods, O fountains, hillocks, dales, and bowers,   860
With other echo late I taught your shades   861
To answer, and resound far other song.
Whom thus afflicted when sad Eve beheld,
Desolate where she sat, approaching nigh,
Soft words to his fierce passion she assay'd;   865
But her with stern regard he thus repell'd:

Out of my sight, thou serpent; that name best   867
Befits thee with him leagu'd, thyself as false   868
And hateful; nothing wants, but that thy shape,   869
Like his, and colour serpentine, may show   870
Thy inward fraud, to warn all creatures from thee

---

853 *tardy* Slow, late. 858 *at all* At once. 859 *Mends* Amends. 861 *late* Recently.
867–870 *Out of . . . serpentine* The name "Eve" was wrongly believed to be Hebrew for
"serpent."

Henceforth; lest that too heavenly form pretended
To hellish falsehood, snare them. But for thee
I had persisted happy, had not thy pride
875 And wand'ring vanity, when least was safe,
Rejected my forewarning, and disdain'd
Not to be trusted, longing to be seen,
Though by the Devil himself, him overweening
To over-reach, but with the serpent meeting
880 Fool'd and beguil'd, by him thou, I by thee,
To trust thee from my side, imagin'd wise,
Constant, mature, proof against all assaults,
And understood not all was but a show
Rather than solid virtue, all but a rib
885 Crook'd by nature, bent, as now appears,
886 More to the part sinister, from me drawn,[20]
887 Well if thrown out as supernumerary
888 To my just number found. O why did God,
Creator wise, that peopled highest heaven
890 With spirits masculine,[21] create at last
891 This novelty on earth, this fair defect
892 Of nature, and not fill the world at once
With men as angels without feminine,
Or find some other way to generate
895 Mankind? This mischief had not then befallen,
And more that shall befall, innumerable
Disturbances on earth through female snares,
And strait conjunction with this sex: for either
He never shall find out fit mate, but such
900 As some misfortune brings him, or mistake;
Or whom he wishes most shall seldom gain
Through her perverseness, but shall see her gain'd
By a far worse, or if she love, withheld

---

886 *sinister* Left.   887–888 *supernumerary . . . found* Adam continues to think of himself
and Eve in quantitative terms.   891–892 *fair defect / Of nature* Refers to the Aristotelian
theory whereby all fetuses were originally male, and the development of female character-
istics constituted a defection from this natural condition.

By parents; or his happiest choice too late
Shall meet, already link'd and wedlock-bound   905
To a fell adversary, his hate or shame: 906
Which infinite calamity shall cause
To human life, and household peace confound.

He added not, and from her turn'd: but Eve,
Not so repuls'd, with tears that ceas'd not flowing, 910
And tresses all disorder'd, at his feet   911
Fell humble, and embracing them, besought   912
His peace, and thus proceeded in her plaint: 913

Forsake me not thus, Adam; witness heaven
What love sincere, and reverence in my heart   915
I bear thee, and unweeting have offended,   916
Unhappily deceiv'd: thy suppliant
I beg, and clasp thy knees; bereave me not,
Whereon I live, thy gentle looks, thy aid,
Thy counsel in this uttermost distress,   920
My only strength and stay: forlorn of thee,   921
Whither shall I betake me, where subsist?
While yet we live, scarce one short hour perhaps,
Between us two let there be peace, both joining,
As join'd in injuries, one enmity   925
Against a foe by doom express assign'd us,
That cruel serpent. On me exercise not
Thy hatred for this misery befallen,
On me already lost, me than thyself
More miserable; both have sinn'd, but thou,   930
Against God only, I against God and thee,
And to the place of judgment will return,
There with my cries importune heaven, that all   933
The sentence from thy head remov'd may light

---

906 *fell* Dire. 911 *tresses* Hair. 911–912 *at his feet . . . humble* Recalls Mary Magdalene washing Christ's feet in Luke 7:38. 913 *plaint* Plea. 916 *unweeting* Unwittingly. 920 *counsel* Advice. 921 *stay* Support. 933 *importune* Beg; Eve vows repentance before Adam does.

935 On me, sole cause to thee of all this woe
936 Me, me only, just object of his ire.

937 She ended weeping, and her lowly plight,
    Immoveable till peace obtain'd from fault
939 Acknowledg'd and deplor'd, in Adam wrought
940 Commiseration; soon his heart relented
    Tow'rds her, his life so late and sole delight,
    Now at his feet submissive in distress,
    Creature so fair his reconcilement seeking,
    His counsel whom she had displeas'd, his aid:
945 As one disarm'd, his anger all he lost,
    And thus with peaceful words uprais'd her soon:

    Unwary, and too desirous, as before,
    So now of what thou know'st not, who desir'st
    The punishment all on thyself; alas,
950 Bear thine own first, ill able to sustain
    His full wrath, whose thou feel'st as yet least part,
    And my displeasure bear'st so ill. If prayers
    Could alter high decrees, I to that place
    Would speed before thee, and be louder heard,
955 That on my head all might be visited,
    Thy frailty and infirmer sex forgiven,
    To me committed and by me expos'd.
    But rise, let us no more contend, nor blame
    Each other, blam'd enough elsewhere, but strive,
960 In offices of love, how we may lighten
    Each other's burden, in our share of woe;
962 Since this day's death denounc'd, if aught I see
    Will prove no sudden, but a slow-pac'd evil,
    A long day's dying to augment our pain,
965 And to our seed (O hapless seed!) deriv'd.

---

936 *ire* Wrath. 937 *plight* Both "plea" and "predicament." 939–940 *in Adam wrought / Commiseration* Eve is the cause of Adam's repentance. 955 *visited* Inflicted. 962 *if aught I see* If I understand anything. 965.1 *seed* Offspring; 965.2 *hapless* Unfortunate; 965.3 *deriv'd* Passed on.

To whom thus Eve, recovering heart, replied:
Adam, by sad experiment I know 967
How little weight my words with thee can find,
Found so erroneous, thence by just event
Found so unfortunate; nevertheless, 970
Restor'd by thee, vile as I am, to place
Of new acceptance, hopeful to regain
Thy love, the sole contentment of my heart,
Living or dying, from thee I will not hide
What thoughts in my unquiet breast are risen, 975
Tending to some relief of our extremes,
Or end, though sharp and sad, yet tolerable,
As in our evils, and of easier choice.
If care of our descent perplex us most,
Which must be born to certain woe, devour'd 980
By death at last; and miserable it is
To be to others cause of misery,
Our own begotten, and of our loins to bring
Into this cursed world a woeful race,
That after wretched life must be at last 985
Food for so foul a monster; in thy power 986
It lies, yet ere conception to prevent 987
The race unbless'd, to being yet unbegot. 988
Childless thou art, childless remain: so Death
Shall be deceiv'd his glut, and with us two 990
Be forc'd to satisfy his ravenous maw.
But if thou judge it hard and difficult,
Conversing, looking, loving, to abstain
From love's due rites, nuptial embraces sweet,
And with desire to languish without hope, 995
Before the present object languishing 996
With like desire, which would be misery
And torment less than none of what we dread;

---

967 *experiment* Eve confirms her empirical view of knowledge. 980 *Which* Who.
986–988 *in thy power . . . unbegot* Eve suggests that the couple practice contraception. 990
deceiv'd Deprived of. 996 *the present object* Eve objectifies herself.

Then, both ourselves and seed at once to free
1000 From what we fear for both, let us make short,
Let us seek Death, or he not found, supply
With our own hands his office on ourselves.
Why stand we longer shivering under fears,
1004 That show no end but death, and have the power,
1005 Of many ways to die the shortest choosing,
Destruction with destruction to destroy?

She ended here, or vehement despair
Broke off the rest; so much of death her thoughts
Had entertain'd, as dy'd her cheeks with pale.
1010 But Adam, with such counsel nothing sway'd,
To better hopes his more attentive mind
Lab'ring had rais'd, and thus to Eve replied:

Eve, thy contempt of life and pleasure seems
To argue in thee something more sublime
1015 And excellent than what thy mind contemns:
But self-destruction therefore sought, refutes
That excellence thought in thee, and implies,
Not thy contempt, but anguish and regret
For loss of life and pleasure overlov'd.
1020 Or if thou covet death, as utmost end
Of misery, so thinking to evade
The penalty pronounc'd, doubt not but God
Hath wiselier arm'd his vengeful ire than so
To be forestall'd: much more I fear lest death
1025 So snatch'd will not exempt us from the pain
We are by doom to pay; rather such acts
1027 Of contumacy will provoke the Highest
To make death in us live. Then let us seek
Some safer resolution, which methinks

1000 *short* Short work.   1004 *show no end* Seem to have no purpose.   1005 *shortest* Quickest.   1010 *with . . . sway'd* Not at all convinced by such advice.   1027 *contumacy* Insolence.

I have in view, calling to mind with heed   1030
Part of our sentence, that thy seed shall bruise
The serpent's head; piteous amends, unless   1032
Be meant, whom I conjecture, our grand foe   1033
Satan, who in the serpent hath contriv'd   1034
Against us this deceit: to crush his head   1035
Would be revenge indeed; which will be lost
By death brought on ourselves, or childless days
Resolv'd as thou proposest; so our foe
Shall scape his punishment ordain'd, and we   1039
Instead shall double ours upon our heads.   1040
No more be mention'd then of violence
Against ourselves, and wilful barrenness,
That cuts us off from hope, and savours only   1043
Rancour and pride, impatience and despite,   1044
Reluctance against God and his just yoke   1045
Laid on our necks. Remember with what mild
And gracious temper he both heard and judg'd,
Without wrath or reviling; we expected
Immediate dissolution, which we thought
Was meant by death that day, when lo, to thee 1050
Pains only in child-bearing were foretold,
And bringing forth, soon recompens'd with joy,
Fruit of thy womb: on me the curse aslope
Glanc'd on the ground; with labour I must earn
My bread; what harm? Idleness had been worse; 1055
My labour will sustain me; and lest cold
Or heat should injure us, his timely care
Hath unbesought provided, and his hands
Cloth'd us unworthy, pitying while he judg'd;
How much more, if we pray him, will his ear   1060
Be open, and his heart to pity incline,

1030 *in view* In mind.   1032 *piteous* Pitiable.   1032–1034 *unless . . . Satan* Adam's ethical and hermeneutical breakthrough comes when he realizes that the serpent is merely a symbol for Satan, thus reversing Eve's error that caused the Fall.   1039 *scape* Escape.   1043 *savours* Smacks of.   1044 *despite* Spite.   1045 *Reluctance* Struggling.

And teach us further by what means to shun
Th'inclement seasons, rain, ice, hail, and snow,
Which now the sky with various face begins

1065 To show us in this mountain, while the winds
Blow moist and keen, shattering the graceful locks
Of these fair spreading trees; which bids us seek
Some better shroud, some better warmth to cherish

1069 Our limbs benumb'd, ere this diurnal star
1070 Leave cold the night, how we his gather'd beams
1071 Reflected, may with matter sere foment,
Or by collision of two bodies grind

1073 The air attrite to fire, as late the clouds
Justling or push'd with winds rude in their shock

1075 Tine the slant lightning, whose thwart flame, driven down,
Kindles the gummy bark of fir or pine,

1077 And sends a comfortable heat from far,
1078 Which might supply the sun: such fire to use,
And what may else be remedy or cure

1080 To evils which our own misdeeds have wrought,
1081 He will instruct us praying, and of grace
Beseeching him, so as we need not fear

1083 To pass commodiously this life, sustain'd
By him with many comforts, till we end

1085 In dust, our final rest and native home.
What better can we do, than to the place
Repairing where he judg'd us prostrate fall
Before him reverent, and there confess
Humbly our faults, and pardon beg, with tears

1090 Watering the ground, and with our sighs the air
1091 Frequenting, sent from hearts contrite, in sign

1069 *diurnal star* The sun.   1070–1071 *his gather'd . . . Reflected* Adam proposes using a magnifying glass to make fire. The image of the sun's "reflected" rays suggest the alienation of humanity from Heaven.   1071 *with matter sere foment* Kindle fire with dry materials.   1073.1 *attrite* Cause sparks through attrition (rubbing together); 1073.2 *late* Lately.   1075 *Tine* Ignite.   1077 *comfortable* Comforting.   1078 *supply* Make up for.   1081 *praying* While we pray.   1083 *commodiously* Usefully.   1091 *Frequenting* Filling.

Of sorrow unfeign'd, and humiliation meek?
Undoubtedly he will relent and turn
From his displeasure; in whose look serene,
When angry most he seem'd and most severe,   1095
What else but favour, grace, and mercy shone?

So spake our father penitent, nor Eve
Felt less remorse: they forthwith to the place
Repairing where he judg'd them, prostrate fell
Before him reverent, and both confess'd   1100
Humbly their faults, and pardon begg'd with tears
Watering the ground, and with their sighs the air
Frequenting, sent from hearts contrite, in sign
Of sorrow unfeign'd, and humiliation meek.

END OF BOOK TENTH

BOOK XI

THE ARGUMENT

The Son of God presents to his Father the prayers of our first
parents now repenting, and intercedes for them. God accepts
them, but declares that they must no longer abide in Paradise:
sends Michael with a band of Cherubim to dispossess them; but
first to reveal to Adam future things. Michael's coming down.
Adam shows to Eve certain ominous signs; he discerns
*Michael's approach, goes out to meet him; the Angel denounces**
their departure. Eve's lamentation. Adam pleads, but submits.
The Angel leads him up to a high hill, sets before him in vision
what shall happen till the flood.

THUS they in lowliest plight repentant stood   1
Praying, for from the mercy-seat above   2
Prevenient grace descending had remov'd   3
The stony from their hearts, and made new flesh
Regenerate grow instead, that sighs now breath'd   5
Unutterable, which the spirit of prayer
Inspir'd, and wing'd for heaven with speedier flight
Than loudest oratory: yet their port
Not of mean suitors, nor important less
Seem'd their petition, than when th'ancient pair   10
In fables old, less ancient yet than these,   11

---

*Proclaims.

1 *lowliest plight* Humblest supplication.   2 *mercy-seat* Gold covering for the ark of the
covenant in Exodus 25:18, a typological prefiguration of Christ's intercession.   3 *Prevenient*
grace Grace offered before repentance, independently of the human will.

12   Deucalion and chaste Pyrrha, to restore

13   The race of mankind drown'd, before the shrine

14   Of Themis stood devout. To heaven their prayers

15   Flew up, nor miss'd the way by envious winds,

       Blown vagabond or frustrate: in they pass'd

17   Dimensionless through heavenly doors; then clad

       With incense, where the golden altar fum'd,

19   By their great intercessor, came in sight

20   Before the Father's throne: them the glad Son

       Presenting, thus to intercede began:

22   See, Father, what first fruits on earth are sprung

23   From thy implanted grace in man, these sighs

       And prayers, which in this golden censer, mix'd

25   With incense, I thy priest before thee bring,

       Fruits of more pleasing savour from thy seed

       Sown with contrition in his heart, than those

       Which, his own hand manuring, all the trees

       Of Paradise could have produc'd, ere fallen

30   From innocence. Now therefore bend thine ear

       To supplication, hear his sighs though mute;

32   Unskilful with what words to pray, let me

       Interpret for him, me his advocate

34   And propitiation; all his works on me,

35   Good or not good, ingraft, my merit those

       Shall perfect, and for these my death shall pay.

       Accept me, and in me from these receive

       The smell of peace toward mankind; let him live

       Before thee reconcil'd, at least his days

40   Number'd, though sad, till death, his doom, (which I

10–14 *th'ancient pair . . . devout* In a classical parallel to the story of Noah, Ovid's *Metamorphoses* has Deucalian and Pyrrha, the sole survivors of a great flood, consult Themis, the goddess of justice, about how to repopulate the world.   15 *miss'd* lost.   17 *Dimensionless* The prayers have no physical form; Milton was opposed to "set forms" of prayers. 19 *intercessor* The Son.   22 *first fruits* Tithe offerings.   23 *implanted* Laid the blame for. 32 *Unskilful with* Ignorant of.   34 *propitiation* Atonement; paraphrases 1 John 2:1–2.

To mitigate thus plead, not to reverse)
To better life shall yield him, where with me
All my redeem'd may dwell in joy and bliss,
Made one with me, as I with thee am one.

To whom the Father, without cloud, serene.   45
All thy request for man, accepted Son,
Obtain; all thy request was my decree;
But longer in that Paradise to dwell,
The law I gave to nature him forbids:
Those pure immortal elements that know   50
No gross, no unharmonious mixture foul,
Eject him tainted now and purge him off
As a distemper, gross to air as gross,   53
And mortal food, as may dispose him best
For dissolution wrought by sin, that first   55
Distemper'd all things, and of incorrupt   56
Corrupted. I at first with two fair gifts
Created him endow'd, with happiness
And immortality: that fondly lost,   59
This other serv'd but to eternize woe;   60
Till I provided death; so death becomes
His final remedy, and after life
Tried in sharp tribulation, and refin'd
By faith and faithful works, to second life,   64
Wak'd in the renovation of the just,   65
Resigns him up with heaven and earth renew'd.
But let us call to synod all the bless'd
Through heaven's wide bounds; from them I will not hide
My judgments, how with mankind I proceed,
As how with peccant angels late they saw,   70
And in their state, though firm, stood more confirm'd.

---

50 *elements* Elements of Eden.   53 *distemper* Disease.   56 *Distemper'd* Disordered.   59
fondly Foolishly.   60 *eternize* Make eternal.   64 *faith and faithful works* Good works are
the result of faith.   65 *renovation* Renewal of the body at the resurrection.   70 *peccant* Sin-
ning.

He ended, and the Son gave signal high
To the bright minister that watch'd; he blew
74 His trumpet, heard in Oreb since perhaps
75 When God descended, and perhaps once more
76 To sound at general doom. Th'angelic blast
Fill'd all the regions; from their blissful bowers
78 Of amaranthine shade, fountain or spring,
By the waters of life, where'er they sat
80 In fellowships of joy, the sons of light
Hasted, resorting to the summons high,
And took their seats; till from his throne supreme
Th'Almighty thus pronounc'd his sov'reign will:

O sons, like one of us man is become
85 To know both good and evil, since his taste
86 Of that defended fruit; but let him boast
His knowledge of good lost and evil got;
Happier had it suffic'd him to have known
Good by itself, and evil not at all.[1]
90 He sorrows now, repents, and prays contrite,
91 My motions in him; longer than they move,
His heart I know how variable and vain
93 Self-left. Lest therefore his now bolder hand
94 Reach also of the tree of life, and eat,
95 And live for ever, dream at least to live
96 For ever, to remove him I decree,
97 And send him from the garden forth to till
98 The ground whence he was taken, fitter soil.

Michael, this my behest have thou in charge,
100 Take to thee from among the cherubim

---

74 *Oreb* Where Moses received the ten commandments, accompanied by the sound of a trumpet; see Exodus 20:18.   76 *general doom* The day of judgment, which is to be heralded by a trumpet; see 1 Thessalonians 4:16.   78 *amaranthine* Of the amaranth, a plant symbolizing immortality; see 3.352–357.   86 *defended* Forbidden.   91 *motions* God's working in the soul.   93 *Self-left* Left to itself.   93–98 *Lest . . . soil* Paraphrases Genesis 3:22–23.

Thy choice of flaming warriors, lest the fiend,
Or in behalf of man, or to invade   102
Vacant possession, some new trouble raise:
Haste thee, and from the Paradise of God,
Without remorse drive out the sinful pair,   105
From hallow'd ground th'unholy, and denounce
To them and to their progeny thence
Perpetual banishment. Yet, lest they faint
At the sad sentence rigorously urg'd,   109
For I behold them soften'd and with tears   110
Bewailing their excess, all terror hide.
If patiently thy bidding they obey,
Dismiss them not disconsolate; reveal   113
To Adam what shall come in future days,
As I shall thee enlighten; intermix   115
My covenant in the woman's seed renew'd;
So send them forth, tho' sorrowing, yet in peace:
And on the east side of the garden place,   118
Where entrance up from Eden easiest climbs,
Cherubic watch, and of a sword the flame   120
Wide waving, all approach far off to fright,   121
And guard all passage to the tree of life:
Lest Paradise a receptacle prove
To spirits foul, and all my trees their prey,
With whose stolen fruit man once more to delude.   125

He ceas'd; and th'archangelic power prepar'd
For swift descent, with him the cohort bright
Of watchful cherubim; four faces each
Had, like a double Janus, all their shape   129

---

102 *in behalf of man* Empson (p. 191) reads this phrase as "on man's behalf"; Campbell (p. 400) suggests "with regard to man"; Ricks (p. 301) adds "claiming to act in the name of man." 109 *urg'd* Pronounced. 113 *disconsolate* Without consolation. 118 *east side* Where Adam and Eve are driven in Genesis 3:24. 121 *fright* Frighten. 129 *double Janus* Janus, the Roman god of thresholds, had two faces but was sometimes represented with four, in the figure of Janus Quadrifons.

130 Spangled with eyes, more numerous than those
131 Of Argus, and more wakeful than to drowse,
132 Charm'd with Arcadian pipe, the pastoral reed
133 Of Hermes, or his opiate rod. Meanwhile,
     To resalute the world with sacred light,
135 Leucothea wak'd and with fresh dews embalm'd
     The earth, when Adam and first matron Eve
137 Had ended now their orisons, and found
     Strength added from above, new hope to spring
     Out of despair, joy, but with fear yet link'd;
140 Which thus to Eve his welcome words renew'd:

     Eve, easily may faith admit that all
     The good which we enjoy from heaven descends;
     But that from us aught should ascend to heaven
144 So prevalent as to concern the mind
145 Of God high-bless'd, or to incline his will
     Hard to belief may seem; yet this will prayer,
     Or one short sigh of human breath, upborne
     Even to the seat of God. For since I sought
     By prayer th'offended Deity to appease,
150 Kneel'd and before him humbled all my heart,
     Methought I saw him placable and mild,
152 Bending his ear; persuasion in me grew
     That I was heard with favour; peace return'd
     Home to my breast and to my memory
155 His promise, that thy seed shall bruise our foe;
156 Which then not minded in dismay, yet now
     Assures me that the bitterness of death
     Is past, and we shall live. Whence hail to thee,

---

130 *Spangled* Sparkling.   131 *Argus* Monster with a hundred eyes.   132–133 *pastoral . . . rod*
In Ovid's *Metamorphoses* 1.568–779, Hermes kills Argus after lulling him to sleep with his
magical pipe and rod.   135 *Leucothea* After Ino threw herself into the sea to escape her hus-
band's rage, the gods reincarnated her as the goddess Leucothea. For Milton this myth pre-
figured Christ's redemption of humanity and so he associates Leucothea with the dawn.
137 *orisons* Prayers.   140 *Which* Who; that is, Adam.   144 *prevalent* Powerful.   152 *persua-
sion* Conviction.   156 *minded* Remembered.

Eve rightly call'd, mother of all mankind,   159
Mother of all things living, since by thee   160
Man is to live, and all things live for man.

To whom thus Eve with sad demeanour meek.
Ill worthy I such title should belong
To me transgressor, who, for thee ordain'd
A help, became thy snare; to me reproach   165
Rather belongs, distrust and all dispraise:
But infinite in pardon was my Judge,
That I, who first brought death on all, am grac'd
The source of life; next favourable thou,
Who highly thus to entitle me vouchsaf'st,   170
Far other name deserving. But the field
To labour calls us now, with sweat impos'd   172
Though after sleepless night; for see the morn,   173
All unconcern'd with our unrest, begins   174
Her rosy progress smiling; let us forth,   175
I never from thy side henceforth to stray,   176
Where'er our day's work lies, though now enjoin'd   177
Laborious, till day droop; while here we dwell,   178
What can be toilsome in these pleasant walks?   179
Here let us live, though in fallen state, contest.   180

So spake, so wish'd much humbled Eve, but fate   181
Subscrib'd not; Nature first gave signs,[2] impress'd   182
On bird, beast, air, air suddenly eclips'd
After short blush of morn; nigh in her sight
The bird of Jove, stoop'd from his airy tow'r,   185
Two birds of gayest plume before him drove   186

---

159 *rightly call'd* In Hebrew, "Eve" and "life" are cognates. 165 *snare* Trap. 172–179 *labour . . . Laborious . . . toilsome* These terms look forward to the alienated condition of labor after the fall. 181–182 *fate / Subscrib'd not* Compare the "Nativity Ode:" "But wisest Fate says no, / This must not yet be so" (ll. 149–150). 182 *impress'd* Stamped. 185.1 *bird of Jove* The eagle; 185.2 *stoop'd* Swooped. 186 *Two . . . drove* The eagle is hunting two peacocks.

187 Down from a hill the beast that reigns in woods,
188 First hunter then, pursu'd a gentle brace,
189 Goodliest of all the forest, hart and hind;
190 Direct to th'eastern gate was bent their flight.
  Adam observ'd, and with his eye the chase
  Pursuing, not unmov'd, to Eve thus spake:

  O Eve, some further change awaits us nigh,
  Which heaven by these mute signs in nature shows,
195 Forerunners of his purpose, or to warn
196 Us, haply too secure, of our discharge
  From penalty, because from death releas'd
  Some days; how long, and what till then our life,
  Who knows? Or more than this, that we are dust,
200 And thither must return and be no more?
  Why else this double object in our sight
  Of flight pursu'd in th'air, and o'er the ground,
  One way the self-same hour? Why in the east
  Darkness ere day's mid-course, and morning light
205 More orient in yon western cloud, that draws
  O'er the blue firmament a radiant white,
  And slow descends, with something heavenly fraught?

208 He err'd not, for by this the heavenly bands
209 Down from a sky of jasper lighted now
210 In Paradise, and on a hill made halt;
  A glorious apparition, had not doubt
212 And carnal fear, that day dimm'd Adam's eye.
213 Not that more glorious, when the angels met
214 Jacob in Mahanaim, where he saw

---

187 *beast that reigns in woods* The lion.   188.1 *First hunter* Compare the peaceful lion of 4.343–344; 188.2 *brace* Pair.   189 *hart and hind* Male and female deer. Fowler (p. 608) notes that in each of these "signs," a figure of sovereignty—the sun, the eagle, and the lion— "displays its power grimly changed."   196 *haply too secure* Perhaps overconfident.   205 *orient* Both "eastern" and "shining."   208 *by this* By this time.   209.1 *jasper* Precious stone; 209.2 *lighted* Alighted.   212 *carnal* Fleshly, material.

The field pavilion'd with his guardians bright;   215
Nor that which on the flaming mount appear'd   216
In Dothan, cover'd with a camp of fire,   217
Against the Syrian king, who to surprise   218
One man, assassin like that levied war,   219
War unproclaim'd. The princely hierarch   220
In their bright stand, there left his powers to seize   221
Possession of the garden; he alone,   222
To find where Adam shelter'd, took his way,
Not unperceiv'd of Adam, who to Eve,
While the great visitant approach'd, thus spake: 225

Eve, now expect great tidings, which perhaps
Of us will soon determine, or impose   227
New laws to be observ'd; for I descry   228
From yonder blazing cloud that veils the hill,
One of the heavenly host, and by his gait   230
None of the meanest, some great potentate,
Or of the thrones above; such majesty
Invests him coming; yet not terrible,   233
That I should fear, nor sociably mild,
As Raphael, that I should much confide,   235
But solemn and sublime, whom not to offend,
With reverence I must meet, and thou retire.   237

He ended; and the archangel soon drew nigh,
Not in his shape celestial, but as man
Clad to meet man; over his lucid arms   240
A military vest of purple flow'd,   241

213–215 *Not that . . . bright* In Genesis 32:1–2 Jacob has a vision of an army of angels. 216–220 *Nor that . . . unproclaim'd* In 2 Kings 6, the king of Syria makes a surprise raid on the city of Dohan in an attempt to capture the prophet Elisha, but warlike angels appear to defend the righteous man.   221 *stand* Station.   222 *garden* Michael's troops occupy the garden while he alone goes in search of the human couple.   225 *visitant* Visitor.   227 *Of us* What will become of us.   228 *descry* Perceive.   233 *terrible* Terrifying.   237 *thou retire* The gender hierarchy is more firmly in place than before the Fall, when Adam and Eve entertained Raphael together; see 5.383.   240 *lucid* Bright.   241 *vest* Robe.

242 Livelier than Melibœan, or the grain
243 Of Sarra, worn by kings and heroes old
244 In time of truce; Iris had dipp'd the woof;
245 His starry helm unbuckled show'd him prime
In manhood, where youth ended; by his side,
247 As in a glist'ring zodiac, hung the sword,
248 Satan's dire dread, and in his hand the spear.
Adam bow'd low; he kingly from his state
250 Inclin'd not, but his coming thus declar'd:

Adam, heaven's high behest no preface needs:
Sufficient that thy prayers are heard, and death,
Then due by sentence when thou didst transgress,
254 Defeated of his seizure, many days
255 Given thee of grace, wherein thou may'st repent,
And one bad act with many deeds well done
May'st cover: well may then thy Lord, appeas'd,
Redeem thee quite from death's rapacious claim;
But longer in this Paradise to dwell
260 Permits not; to remove thee I am come,
And send thee from the garden forth, to till
The ground whence thou wast taken, fitter soil.

He added not, for Adam at the news
Heart-struck with chilling gripe of sorrow stood,
265 That all his senses bound; Eve, who unseen,
Yet all had heard, with audible lament
267 Discover'd soon the place of her retire.

O unexpected stroke, worse than of death!
Must I thus leave thee, Paradise? thus leave
270 Thee, native soil! these happy walks and shades,

---

242 *Melibœan* Purple dye from Thessaly.   242–243 *the grain / Of Sarra* Dye from Tyre.
244 *Iris* Goddess of the rainbow.   245 *helm* Helmet.   247 *glist'ring zodiac* Sparkling belt.
248 *Satan's dire dread* Michael wounded Satan with this sword in 6.320–327.   250 *his coming* Reason for his coming.   254 *Defeated* Deprived.   267 *Discover'd* Revealed.

Fit haunt of gods? where I had hope to spend,
Quiet, though sad, the respite of that day
That must be mortal to us both. O flowers,
That never will in other climate grow,
My early visitation, and my last   275
At even, which I bred up with tender hand   276
From the first op'ning bud, and gave ye names,   277
Who now shall rear ye to the sun, or rank   278
Your tribes, and water from th'ambrosial fount   279
Thee lastly, nuptial bower, by me adorn'd   280
With what to sight or smell was sweet, from thee   281
How shall I part, and whither wander down
Into a lower world, to this obscure   283
And wild? How shall we breathe in other air
Less pure, accustom'd to immortal fruits?   285

Whom thus the angel interrupted mild:
Lament not, Eve, but patiently resign
What justly thou hast lost; nor set thy heart,
Thus over-fond, on that which is not thine: 289
Thy going is not lonely; with thee goes   290
Thy husband; him to follow thou art bound;
Where he abides, think there thy native soil.

Adam by this from the cold sudden damp   293
Recov'ring, and his scatter'd spirits return'd,
To Michael thus his humble words address'd: 295

Celestial, whether among the thrones, or nam'd
Of them the highest, for such of shape may seem

---

276 *even* Evening.   277 *gave ye names* Leonard points out: "Milton here departs from traditional interpretations of Genesis 2:19, where Adam alone gives names" (p. 857). 278–279 *rank / Your tribes* Classify your species.   281 *what* Whatever.   283.1 *lower world* Eden is located on a mountain; 283.2 *to this* Compared to this; 283.3 *obscure* Dark.   285 *immortal fruits* Flannagan points out that these words "would provide a kind of red flag to Michael, who will interrupt Eve as soon as she uses the phrase" (p. 668).   289 *over-fond* Oversensitive.   293.1 *by this* By this time; 293.2 *cold sudden damp* Cold sweat.

Prince above princes, gently hast thou told
Thy message, which might else in telling wound,
300 And in performing end us; what besides
Of sorrow, and dejection, and despair,
Our frailty can sustain, thy tidings bring,
Departure from this happy place, our sweet
Recess, and only consolation left
305 Familiar to our eyes, all places else
Inhospitable appear, and desolate;
Nor knowing us, nor known: and if by prayer
Incessant I could hope to change the will
309 Of him who all things can, I would not cease
310 To weary him with my assiduous cries:
But prayer against his absolute decree
No more avails than breath against the wind,
Blown stifling back on him that breathes it forth:
Therefore to his great bidding I submit.
315 This most afflicts me, that departing hence,
As from his face I shall be hid, depriv'd
His blessed count'nance; here I could frequent
With worship, place by place, where he vouchsaf'd
Presence divine, and to my sons relate,
320 On this mount he appear'd, under this tree
321 Stood visible, among these pines his voice
322 I heard, here with him at this fountain talk'd:
323 So many grateful altars I would rear
Of grassy turf, and pile up every stone
325 Of lustre from the brook, in memory,
Or monument to ages, and thereon
327 Offer sweet-smelling gums, and fruits, and flowers.
328 In yonder nether world where shall I seek

---

309 *can* Can do.   320–322 *On this . . . talk'd* Adam fantasizes about setting up shrines to God, thus indicating that his understanding of the deity is already tainted with idolatry. 323 *grateful altars* Adam will seek to assuage his guilt by expressing his gratitude to God in monuments.   327 *Offer . . . flowers* Adam imagines that God can be appeased by sacrifices.   328 *nether* Lower.

His bright appearances, or footstep trace? 329
For though I fled him angry, yet recall'd 330
To life prolong'd and promis'd race, I now
Gladly behold, though but his utmost skirts
Of glory, and far off his steps adore.

To whom thus Michael with regard benign:
Adam, thou know'st heaven his, and all the earth, 335
Not this rock only; his omnipresence fills
Land, sea, and air, and every kind that lives, 337
Fomented by his virtual power and warm'd. 338
All th'earth he gave thee to possess and rule,
No despicable gift; surmise not then 340
His presence to these narrow bounds confin'd
Of Paradise or Eden: this had been
Perhaps thy capital seat, from whence had spread 343
All generations, and had hither come,
From all the ends of th'earth, to celebrate 345
And reverence thee their great progenitor.
But this pre-eminence thou hast lost, brought down,
To dwell on even ground now with thy sons:
Yet doubt not but in valley and in plain
God is as here, and will be found alike 350
Present, and of his presence many a sign
Still following thee, still compassing thee round 352
With goodness and paternal love, his face
Express, and of his steps the track divine. 354
Which that thou may'st believe, and be confirm'd, 355
Ere thou from hence depart; know I am sent 356
To show thee what shall come in future days
To thee, and to thy offspring; good with bad
Expect to hear, supernal grace contending
With sinfulness of men; thereby to learn 360

---

329 *appearances* Adam desires only visible manifestations of deity. 337 *kind* Species. 338.1 *Fomented* Nurtured. 338.2 *virtual* Full of virtue, power. 343 *seat* Residence. 352 *compassing* Encompassing. 354 *Express* Manifest. 356 *Ere* Before.

True patience, and to temper joy with fear
And pious sorrow, equally inur'd
363 By moderation either state to bear,
Prosperous or adverse: so shalt thou lead
365 Safest thy life, and best prepar'd endure
366 Thy mortal passage when it comes. Ascend
367 This hill; let Eve (for I have drench'd her eyes)
Here sleep below, while thou to foresight wak'st;
As once thou slept'st, while she to life was form'd.

370 To whom thus Adam gratefully replied:
Ascend, I follow thee, safe guide, the path
Thou lead'st me, and to the hand of heaven submit,
However chast'ning, to the evil turn
374 My obvious breast, arming to overcome
375 By suffering, and earn rest from labour won,
If so I may attain. So both ascend
377 In the visions of God. It was a hill,
Of Paradise the highest, from whose top
379 The hemisphere of earth in clearest ken
380 Stretch'd out to th'amplest reach of prospect lay.
381 Not higher that hill, or wider looking round,
382 Whereon, for diff'rent cause, the tempter set
383 Our second Adam in the wilderness,
384 To show him all earth's kingdoms and their glory.
385 His eye might there command wherever stood
386 City of old or modern fame, the seat
Of mightiest empire, from the destin'd walls
388 Of Cambalu, seat of Cathaian Can,
And Samarchand by Oxus, Temir's throne,³

---

363 *state* Condition.   366 *mortal passage* Death.   367 *drench'd* Doped.   374 *obvious* Exposed.   377 *In* Into.   379 *ken* View.   380 *th'amplest . . . prospect* Flannagan glosses this line as "the widest and deepest angles of perspective the eye might perceive" (p. 671).   381–386 *Not higher . . . fame* In Matthew 4:8 Satan brings Jesus to the top of an "exceeding high mountain" to tempt him with the possibility of ruling the world; Milton explored this incident at length in *Paradise Regained*, book III.   388 *Cambalu . . . Can* Beijing, residence of the Khan of northern China.

To Paquin, of Sinæan kings, and thence   390

To Agra, and Lahore, of great Mogul,   391

Down to the golden Chersonese, or where   392

The Persian in Ecbatan sat, or since   393

In Hispahan, or where the Russian Czar   394

In Moscow, or the Sultan in Bizance,   395

Turchestan-born; nor could his eye not ken   396

Th'empire of Negus, to his utmost port   397

Ercoco, and the less maritime kings,   398

Mombaza, and Quiloa, and Melind,   399

And Sofala, thought Ophir, to the realm   400

Of Congo, and Angola farthest south;   401

Or thence from Niger flood to Atlas mount,   402

The kingdoms of Almansor, Fez, and Sus,   403

Morocco, and Algiers, and Tremisen;   404

On Europe thence, and where Rome was to sway   405

The world: in spirit perhaps he also saw

Rich Mexico the seat of Montezume,   407

And Cusco in Peru, the richer seat   408

390.1 *Paquin* Peking, modern Beijing; **390.2** *Sinæan* Chinese.   **391** *Agra, and Lahore* Capitals of the Moguls in what are now northern India and Pakistan, respectively.   **392** *Chersonese* Mythical land of fabulous wealth in India.   **393** *Ecbatan* Summer capital of the Persian rulers.   **394** *Hispahan* Capital of Persia.   **394–395** *Russian . . . Moscow* A particular interest of Milton, who composed a *Brief History of Moscovia* (published posthumously in 1684).   **395** *Sultan in Bizance* Turkish ruler in Byzantium (modern Istanbul), the former eastern capital of the Roman empire, captured by the Ottomans in 1453.   **396.1** *Turchestan* Turkestan, original homeland of the Seljuk (Ottoman) Turks; **396.2** *ken* See.   **397** *Negus* Title of the rulers of Abyssinia, modern Ethiopia.   **398** *Ercoco* Arkiko, in modern Ethiopia. Milton begins a list of ports in east Africa.   **399.1** *Mombaza* Mombassa, city in modern Kenya; **399.2** *Quiloa* Kilwa, city in modern Tanzania; **399.3** *Melind* Malindi, city in modern Kenya.   **400** *Sofala, thought Ophir* Sofala, a city in Mozambique, was identified with the biblical Ophir, source of the gold for Solomon's temple in 1 Kings 9:28.   **401** *Congo . . . Angola* The panorama has rounded the Cape of Good Hope and now proceeds up the west coast of Africa.   **402** *Niger . . . mount* From the River Niger in western Africa to the Atlas Mountains in northern Africa.   **403.1** *Almansor* Title of north African Muslim rulers; **403.2** *Fez* City in modern Morocco; **403.3** *Sus* Sousse, city in modern Tunisia. **404** *Tremisen* City in modern Algeria. Michael has now guided Adam's sight around almost the whole of Africa.   **407** *Montezume* Montezuma II, the last Aztec ruler, conquered by Cortez's Spaniards in 1520.   **408** *Cusco in Peru* Capital of the Incas, famed as the most fertile source of gold.

409 Of Atabalipa, and yet unspoil'd
410 Guiana, whose great city Geryon's sons
411 Call El Dorado. But to nobler sights
Michael from Adam's eyes the film remov'd,
Which that false fruit that promis'd clearer sight
414 Had bred; then purg'd with euphrasy and rue
415 The visual nerve, for he had much to see;
416 And from the well of life three drops instill'd,
So deep the power of these ingredients pierc'd,
Even to the inmost seat of mental sight,
That Adam, now enforc'd to close his eyes,
420 Sunk down, and all his spirits became entranc'd;
But him the gentle angel by the hand
Soon rais'd, and his attention thus recall'd:

Adam, now ope thine eyes, and first behold
Th'effects which thy original crime hath wrought
425 In some to spring from thee, who never touch'd
426 Th'excepted tree, nor with the snake conspir'd,
Nor sinn'd thy sin, yet from that sin derive
Corruption to bring forth more violent deeds.

His eyes he open'd, and beheld a field,
430 Part arable and tilth, whereon were sheaves
New reap'd, the other part sheep-walks and folds;
432 I' the midst an altar as the land-mark stood,
433 Rustic, of grassy sward; thither anon
A sweaty reaper from his tillage brought

---

409 *Atabalipa* Last ruler of the Incas, conquered by Pizarro in 1532.   410 *Geryon's sons* In Dante's *Inferno* (1321), the monster Geryon represents fraud; in Edmund Spenser's *The Faerie Queene* (1590), Geryon is a symbol of Spain.   411 *El Dorado* Mythical land of fabulous wealth in America.   414–415 *then purg'd . . . nerve* Euphrasy and rue were herbs used to treat diseases of the eye; Milton is evidently drawing on his personal medical experience here.   416 *the well of life* Flannagan cites Proverbs 10:11: "The mouth of a righteous man is a well of life."   420 *entranc'd* Falls into a trance as Michael shows him a vision; in Daniel 10:13, the prophet is shown a vision by an angelic emissary of "Michael, one of the chief princes."   426 *excepted* Forbidden.   432 *land-mark* Boundary marker. 433 *anon* Immediately.

First fruits, the green ear, and the yellow sheaf,   435
Uncull'd, as came to hand; a shepherd next,   436
More meek, came with the firstlings of his flock
Choicest and best; then sacrificing, laid
The inwards and their fat, with incense strow'd   439
On the cleft wood, and all due rites perform'd.   440
His offering soon propitious fire from heaven
Consum'd with nimble glance, and grateful steam;   442
The other's not, for his was not sincere;
Whereat he inly rag'd, and as they talk'd,   444
Smote him into the midriff with a stone   445
That beat out life; he fell, and deadly pale
Groan'd out his soul with gushing blood effus'd.
Much at that sight was Adam in his heart
Dismay'd, and thus in haste to th'angel cried:

O teacher, some great mischief hath befall'n   450
To that meek man, who well had sacrific'd;
Is piety thus and pure devotion paid?

To whom Michael thus, he also mov'd, replied:
These two are brethren, Adam, and to come
Out of thy loins; th'unjust the just hath slain,   455
For envy that his brother's offering found
From heaven acceptance: but the bloody fact   457
Will be aveng'd, and th'other's faith approv'd   458
Lose no reward, though here thou see him die,
Rolling in dust and gore. To which our sire: 460

Alas, both for the deed and for the cause!
But have I now seen Death? Is this the way
I must return to native dust? O sight

---

435 *First fruits* Tithes.   436 *Uncull'd* Unselected, random.   439 *inwards* Innards.   442 *glance* Flash.   444 *inly* Inwardly.   457 *fact* Deed.   458 *approv'd* Vindicated.   460 *sire* Father.

Of terror, foul and ugly to behold,
465 Horrid to think, how horrible to feel!

To whom thus Michael: Death thou hast seen
In his first shape on man; but many shapes
Of death, and many are the ways that lead
469 To his grim cave, all dismal; yet to sense
470 More terrible at th'entrance than within.
Some, as thou saw'st, by violent stroke shall die,
By fire, flood, famine; by intemp'rance more
In meats and drinks, which on the earth shall bring
Diseases dire, of which a monstrous crew
475 Before thee shall appear; that thou may'st know
476 What misery th'inabstinence of Eve
Shall bring on men. Immediately a place
478 Before his eyes appear'd, sad, noisome, dark,
479 A lazar-house it seem'd, wherein were laid
480 Numbers of all diseas'd, all maladies
Of ghastly spasm, or racking torture, qualms
Of heart-sick agony, all feverous kinds,
Convulsions, epilepsies, fierce catarrhs,
Intestine stone and ulcer, cholic pangs,
485 Demoniac phrenzy, moping melancholy,
486 And moon-struck madness, pining atrophy,
487 Marasmus, and wide-wasting pestilence,
488 Dropsies, and asthmas, and joint-racking rheums.
489 Dire was the tossing, deep the groans; Despair
490 Tended the sick, busiest from couch to couch;
And over them triumphant Death his dart
Shook, but delay'd to strike, though oft invok'd
With vows, as their chief good, and final hope.

---

469 *to sense* To the sense.　**476** *inabstinence* Indulgence; the word is Milton's invention.
478 *noisome* Smelly.　**479** *lazar-house* Leper colony.　**485** *melancholy* Depression.
485–487 *Demoniac . . . pestilence* These lines were added in the 1674 edition.　**486.1** *moon-struck madness* The moon was held to cause lunacy;　**486.2** *pining atrophy* Shrinking of the
organs due to malnutrition.　**487** *Marasmus* Consumption.　**488** *rheums* Rheumatism.
489–490 *Despair . . . sick* Despair is personified as a nurse.

Sight so deform what heart of rock could long 494
Dry-eyed behold? Adam could not, but wept, 495
Though not of woman born; compassion quell'd 496
His best of man, and gave him up to tears 497
A space, till firmer thoughts restrain'd excess;
And scarce recovering words, his plaint renew'd.

O miserable mankind, to what fall 500
Degraded, to what wretched state reserv'd! 501
Better end here unborn. Why is life given
To be thus wrested from us? Rather why
Obtruded on us thus? who, if we knew 504
What we receive, would either not accept 505
Life offer'd, or soon beg to lay it down,
Glad to be so dismiss'd in peace. Can thus
Th'image of God in man, created once 508
So goodly and erect, though faulty since,
To such unsightly sufferings be debas'd 510
Under inhuman pains? Why should not man,
Retaining still divine similitude
In part, from such deformities be free,
And for his Maker's image sake exempt?

Their Maker's image, answer'd Michael, then 515
Forsook them, when themselves they vilified 516
To serve ungovern'd appetite, and took
His image whom they serv'd, a brutish vice,
Inductive mainly to the sin of Eve.
Therefore so abject is their punishment, 520
Disfiguring not God's likeness, but their own,

---

494 *deform* Milton presents physical illness as an unnatural deformation of the body's natural perfection.   496.1 *not of woman born* See Shakespeare's *Macbeth* (act 4, scene 1): "The power of man, for none of woman born shall harm Macbeth";   496.2 *quell'd* Subdued. 497 *His best of man* His reason. See Shakespeare's *Macbeth* (act 5, scene 8): "Accursed be that tongue that tells me so, / For it hath cow'd my better part of man."   501 *reserv'd* Destined.   504 *Obtruded* Forced.   508 *Th'image of God in man* Adam assumes that man is the "image" of God in a physical, rather than a spiritual, sense.   516 *vilified* Made vile.

Or if his likeness, by themselves defac'd,
While they pervert pure nature's healthful rules
To loathsome sickness; worthily, since they
525 God's image did not reverence in themselves.
526 I yield it just, said Adam, and submit.
But is there yet no other way, besides
These painful passages, how we may come
529 To death, and mix with our connatural dust?

530 There is, said Michael, if thou well observe
531 The rule of not too much, by temp'rance taught,
In what thou eat'st and drink'st, seeking from thence
Due nourishment, not gluttonous delight,
Till many years over thy head return:
535 So may'st thou live, till like ripe fruit thou drop
536 Into thy mother's lap, or be with ease
537 Gather'd, not harshly pluck'd, for death mature:
This is old age; but then thou must outlive
Thy youth, thy strength, thy beauty, which will change
540 To wither'd, weak, and gray; thy senses then
Obtuse, all taste of pleasure must forego,
542 To what thou hast; and for the air of youth,
Hopeful and cheerful, in thy blood will reign
A melancholy damp of cold and dry,
545 To weigh thy spirits down, and last consume
546 The balm of life. To whom our ancestor:

Henceforth I fly not death, nor would prolong
548 Life much; bent rather how I may be quit
549 Fairest and easiest of this cumb'rous charge,
550 Which I must keep till my appointed day

---

526 *yield* Admit.   529 *connatural* Of the same nature.   531 *The rule of not too much* A rather bland way of expressing the classical "golden rule" of "everything in moderation, nothing in excess."   536 *thy mother* The earth.   537 *for death mature* Ready for death.   542 *for* Instead of.   546 *balm of life* Vital essence, an alchemical term.   548 *quit* Rid.   549 *cumb'rous* Encumbering.

Of rend'ring up, and patiently attend 551
My dissolution. Michael replied:

Nor love thy life, nor hate; but what thou liv'st 553
Live well, how long or short permit to heaven: 554
And now prepare thee for another sight. 555

He look'd, and saw a spacious plain, whereon
Were tents of various hue; by some were herds
Of cattle grazing; others, whence the sound
Of instruments that made melodious chime
Was heard, of harp and organ; and who mov'd 560
Their stops and chords was seen; his volant touch 561
Instinct through all proportions, low and high, 562
Fled and pursu'd transverse the resonant fugue. 563
In other part stood one who at the forge, 564
Labouring, two massy clods of iron and brass 565
Had melted, (whether found where casual fire 566
Had wasted woods on mountain or in vale, 567
Down to the veins of earth, thence gliding hot
To some cave's mouth, or whether wash'd by stream
From underground,) the liquid ore he drain'd 570
Into fit moulds prepar'd; from which he form'd
First his own tools; then what might else be wrought
Fusil or grav'n in metal. After these, 573
But on the hither side, a different sort 574
From the high neighb'ring hills, which was their seat, 575
Down to the plain descended: by their guise

551.1 *rend'ring* Giving;   551.2 *attend* Wait for.   553 *Nor . . . nor* Neither . . . nor.   554 *permit* Leave.   560 *who mov'd* Jubal, "the father of all such as handle the harp and organ" in Genesis 4:21.   561.1 *stops* Holes; 561.2 *volant* Speedy.   562 *Instinct . . . proportions* Impelled through all the musical scales.   563 *Fled . . . fugue* "Fugue" derives from the Latin for "flight"; thus, as Fowler observes, "Jubal's race is the fugitive race of Cain" (p. 629).   564 *one who at the forge* Tubalcain, "an instructer of every artificer in brass and iron" in Genesis 4:22.   565.1 *Labouring* Labor was the curse laid on Adam after the fall; 565.2 *massy* Weighty.   566 *casual* Accidental.   567 *wasted* Laid waste to.   573 *Fusil or grav'n* Cast or carved; "graven" connotes "graven images," the objects of idolatry.   574.1 *hither* Nearer, thus western; 574.2 *a different sort* The descendants of Seth.   575 *seat* Residence.

Just men they seem'd, and all their study bent
To worship God aright, and know his works
Not hid, nor those things last which might preserve
580   Freedom and peace to men: they on the plain
Long had not walk'd, when from the tents behold
A bevy of fair women, richly gay
In gems and wanton dress; to th'harp they sung
584   Soft amorous ditties, and in dance came on.
585   The men, tho' grave, eyed them, and let their eyes
Rove without rein, till in the amorous net
587   Fast caught, they lik'd, and each his liking chose;
588   And now of love they treat, till th'evening star,
589   Love's harbinger, appear'd; then all in heat
590   They light the nuptial torch, and bid invoke
591   Hymen, then first to marriage-rites invok'd:
With feast and music all the tents resound.
Such happy interview and fair event
Of love and youth not lost, songs, garlands, flowers,
595   And charming symphonies, attach'd the heart
Of Adam, soon inclin'd to admit delight,
597   The bent of nature; which he thus express'd:

True opener of mine eyes, prime angel bless'd
Much better seems this vision, and more hope
600   Of peaceful days portends, than those two past;
Those were of hate and death, or pain much worse;
Here nature seems fulfill'd in all her ends.

To whom thus Michael: Judge not what is best
604   By pleasure, though to nature seeming meet,
605   Created, as thou art, to nobler end,

---

584 *came on* Approached, with overtones of sexual invitation. 587.1 *Fast* Tightly; 587.2 *his liking* The one he liked. 588.1 *treat* Deal; 588.2 *th'evening star* Venus, goddess of love. 589 *harbinger* Forerunner. 591 *Hymen* Greek god of marriage. 595.1 *charming* Flannagan notes: "The word always carries at least the faint odor of witchcraft" (p. 678); 595.2 *attach'd* Attached themselves to. 597 *bent* Inclination. 604 *meet* Appropriate.

Holy and pure, conformity divine.
Those tents thou saw'st so pleasant, were the tents
Of wickedness, wherein shall dwell his race   608
Who slew his brother; studious they appear
Of arts that polish life, inventors rare,   610
Unmindful of their Maker, though his Spirit   611
Taught them, but they his gifts acknowledg'd none.   612
Yet they a beauteous offspring shall beget;
For that fair female troop thou saw'st, that seem'd   614
Of goddesses, so blithe, so smooth, so gay,   615
Yet empty of all good, wherein consists   616
Woman's domestic honour and chief praise;   617
Bred only and completed to the taste   618
Of lustful appetence, to sing, to dance,   619
To dress, and troll the tongue, and roll the eye.   620
To these that sober race of men, whose lives
Religious titled them the sons of God,[4]
Shall yield up all their virtue, all their fame,
Ignobly, to the trains and to the smiles   624
Of these fair atheists, and now swim in joy,   625
Ere long to swim at large; and laugh, for which
The world ere long a world of tears must weep.

To whom thus Adam, of short joy bereft: 628
O pity and shame! that they who to live well
Enter'd so fair, should turn aside to tread   630
Paths indirect, or in the midway faint!

---

608 *his* Cain's, whose descendant Jubal was "the father of all such as dwell in tents" (Genesis 4:20).   610 *polish* Embellish, artificially burnish.   611–612 *Unmindful . . . none* Human inventors will be under the illusion that their art is their own, rather than a gift of God.   614–615 *that seem'd / Of goddesses* Male lust is a form of idolatry.   616 *good* The Aristotelian "good" is the proper end of any thing or person; in human beings this is the welfare of the invisible soul rather than physical beauty.   617 *domestic* Homely.   618–619 *Bred only . . . appetence* Milton deplores the fact that women's primary function will be to serve male lust, or appetence ("appetite").   620 *troll* Move in a pleasing manner.   624 *trains* Tricks.   628 *short* Short-lived.   630 *Enter'd so fair* Began so well. Adam refers not to the troop of beautiful women but to the religious men, whose way of life he now recognizes as truly "fair."

But still I see the tenor of man's woe
Holds on the same, from woman to begin.

634   From man's effeminate slackness it begins,
635   Said th'angel, who should better hold his place
     By wisdom, and superior gifts receiv'd.
637   But now prepare thee for another scene.

     He look'd, and saw wide territory spread
     Before him, towns, and rural works between,
640   Cities of men with lofty gates and towers;
     Concourse in arms, fierce faces threat'ning war,
642   Giants of mighty bone, and bold emprise;
643   Part wield their arms, part curb the foaming steed,
644   Single or in array of battle rang'd,
645   Both horse and foot, nor idly must'ring stood:
     One way a band select from forage drives
647   A herd of beeves, fair oxen, and fair kine,
     From a fat meadow-ground; or fleecy flock,
     Ewes and their bleating lambs, over the plain.
650   Their booty; scarce with life the shepherds fly,
651   But call in aid, which makes a bloody fray;
     With cruel tournament the squadrons join;
     Where cattle pastur'd late, now scatter'd lies
654   With carcasses and arms, th'ensanguin'd field
655   Deserted: others to a city strong
656   Lay siege, encamp'd; by battery, scale, and mine,
     Assaulting; others from the wall defend

---

634 *From man's . . . begins* The blame for sexual objectification is firmly placed upon men, not women; it is not femininity per se, but man's "effeminate" subjection of reason to lust that is the problem.   637 *scene* A reminder that the fallen Adam needs to be instructed through pictorial illustration.   642.1 *Giants* From Genesis 6:4: "There were giants in the earth in those days; and also after that, when the sons of God came in unto the daughters of men, and they bare children to them, the same became mighty men which were of old, men of renown"; 642.2 *emprise* Enterprise.   643 *steed* Horses.   644 *rang'd* Ranked.   645 *must'ring* Assembling.   647 *kine* Cattle.   650 *booty* Plunder.   651 *makes* The 1667 edition has "tacks," which appears to be a misprint.   654 *ensanguin'd* Made bloody.   656.1 *battery* Ordnance; 656.2 *scale* Siege ladder.

With dart and javelin, stones, and sulphurous fire
On each hand slaughter and gigantic deeds.   659
In other parts the sceptred heralds call   660
To council in the city gates; anon
Gray-headed men and grave, with warriors mix'd
Assemble, and harangues are heard, but soon
In factious opposition; till at last
Of middle age one rising, eminent   665
In wise deport, spake much of right and wrong,   666
Of justice, of religion, truth and peace,
And judgment from above: him old and young
Exploded, and had seiz'd with violent hands,   669
Had not a cloud descending snatch'd him thence   670
Unseen amid the throng; so violence
Proceeded, and oppression and sword-law,   672
Through all the plain, and refuge none was found.
Adam was all in tears, and to his guide
Lamenting turn'd full sad: O what are these,   675
Death's ministers, not men, who thus deal death
Inhumanly to men, and multiply   677
Ten thousand-fold the sin of him who slew   678
His brother; for of whom such massacre   679
Make they but of their brethren, men of men?   680
But who was that just man, whom had not heaven
Rescued, had in his righteousness been lost?

To whom thus Michael: These are the product
Of those ill-mated marriages thou saw'st;
Where good with bad were match'd, who of themselves   685
Abhor to join; and by imprudence mix'd,
Produce prodigious births of body or mind.

---

659 *gigantic* Appertaining to giants.   665 *one* Enoch; see Genesis 5:21–24.   666 *deport* Bearing.   669.1 *Exploded* Mocked; 669.2 *had* Would have.   670 *cloud descending* In the apocryphal book of Enoch (14:8–9), the eponymous prophet is translated to heaven, without dying, in a cloud.   672 *sword-law* The assumption that might is right.   677–679 *and multiply . . . brother* Like Adam's sin, the sin of Cain stamps its imprint on future generations.

Such were these giants, men of high renown;
For in those days might only shall be admir'd,
690 And valour and heroic virtue call'd;
To overcome in battle, and subdue
Nations, and bring home spoils with infinite
Manslaughter, shall be held the highest pitch
Of human glory, and for glory done
695 Of triumph, to be styl'd great conquerors,
Patrons of mankind, gods, and sons of gods,
Destroyers rightlier call'd, and plagues of men.
Thus fame shall be achiev'd, renown on earth,
And what most merits fame in silence hid.
700 But he, the seventh from thee, whom thou beheld'st
The only righteous in a world perverse,
702 And therefore hated, therefore so beset
703 With foes, for daring single to be just,
And utter odious truth, that God would come
705 To judge them with his saints: him the Most High,
706 Wrapp'd in a balmy cloud, with winged steeds
Did, as thou saw'st, receive, to walk with God
High in salvation and the climes of bliss,
Exempt from death; to show thee what reward
710 Awaits the good, the rest what punishment;
Which now direct thine eyes; and soon behold.

He look'd, and saw the face of things quite chang'd:
713 The brazen throat of war had ceas'd to roar;
All now was turn'd to jollity and game,
715 To luxury and riot, feast and dance;
Marrying or prostituting, as befell,
717 Rape or adultery, where passing fair

---

700 *seventh* Enoch, "seventh from Adam" in Jude 1:14.   **702** *hated* That is, by his contemporaries, not by Adam.   **703** *single* Alone.   **706** *cloud* Like Enoch, Elijah is "translated" to heaven without dying in 2 Kings 2:1.   **713** *brazen throat of war* Brass war-trumpets.   **715.1** *luxury* Lust; **715.2** *riot* Wild revels.   **717** *passing* Three meanings: "exceedingly," "passing by," and "temporal, transient."

Allur'd them; thence from cups to civil broils.   718

At length a reverend sire among them came,   719

And of their doings great dislike declar'd,   720

And testified against their ways; he oft

Frequented their assemblies, whereso met,   722

Triumphs or festivals, and to them preach'd

Conversion and repentance, as to souls

In prison under judgments imminent;   725

But all in vain; which when he saw, he ceas'd

Contending; and remov'd his tents far off;

Then from the mountain hewing timber tall,

Began to build a vessel of huge bulk;

Measur'd by cubit, length, and breadth, and height,   730

Smear'd round with pitch, and in the side a door

Contriv'd; and of provisions laid in large

For man and beast; when lo, a wonder strange!

Of every beast, and bird, and insect small

Came sevens, and pairs, and enter'd in, as taught   735

Their order; last the sire, and his three sons

With their four wives; and God made fast the door.   737

Meanwhile the south wind rose, and with black wings

Wide hovering, all the clouds together drove

From under heaven; the hills to their supply   740

Vapour, and exhalation dusk and moist,   741

Sent up amain; and now the thicken'd sky

Like a dark ceiling stood; down rush'd the rain

Impetuous, and continued till the earth

No more was seen; the floating vessel swam   745

Uplifted, and secure with beaked prow

Rode tilting o'er the waves; all dwellings else

Flood overwhelm'd, and them with all their pomp

718.1 *cups* Drunkenness; 718.2 *civil broils* Both "civil wars" and "domestic quarrels." These
concepts were closely linked for Milton.   719 *sire* Noah.   722 *whereso* Wheresoever.   735
sevens, and pairs From Genesis 7:2: "Of every clean beast thou shalt take to thee by sevens,
the male and his female: and of beasts that are not clean by two, the male and his female."
737 *four wives* Including Noah's own wife.   740 *supply* Assistance.   741 *exhalation dusk*
Dark vapor.

Deep under water roll'd; sea cover'd sea,
750 Sea without shore; and in their palaces,
751 Where luxury late reign'd, sea-monsters whelp'd
752 And stabled; of mankind, so numerous late,
753 All left, in one small bottom swum imbark'd.
754 How didst thou grieve then, Adam, to behold
755 The end of all thy offspring, end so sad,
Depopulation? thee another flood,
Of tears and sorrow a flood thee also drown'd,
And sunk thee as thy sons; till gently rear'd
By th'angel, on thy feet thou stood'st at last,
760 Though comfortless, as when a father mourns
761 His children, all in view destroy'd at once;
And scarce to th'angel utter'dst thus thy plaint:

O visions ill foreseen! better had I
Liv'd ignorant of future, so had borne
765 My part of evil only, each day's lot
Enough to bear; those now, that were dispens'd
The burden of many ages, on me light
At once, by my foreknowledge gaining birth
Abortive, to torment me ere their being,
770 With thought that they must be. Let do man seek
Henceforth to be foretold what shall befall
Him or his children; evil he may be sure,
773 Which neither his foreknowing can prevent,
And he the future evil shall no less
775 In apprehension than in substance feel,
Grievous to bear: but that care now is past,
777 Man is not whom to warn; those few escap'd,
Famine and anguish will at last consume,

751–752 *whelp'd / And stabled* Gave birth and lived.   753 *bottom* Hold, as of a ship.
754 *thou* The narrator, rather than Michael, addresses Adam here.   761 *in view* In front of
his eyes.   773 *Which neither . . . prevent* Adam stands in the same relation to his future off-
spring as God had stood in relation to him before the Fall.   775 *substance* Reality.
777 *Man is not whom to warn* Both "man is not the one to warn" and "there is no man left
to warn."

Wand'ring that wat'ry desert. I had hope,
When violence was ceas'd, and war on earth,   780
All would have then gone well, peace would have crown'd,
With length of happy days, the race of man:
But I was far deceiv'd; for now I see
Peace to corrupt no less than war to waste.
How comes it thus? unfold, celestial guide,   785
And whether here the race of man will end.

To whom thus Michael: Those whom last thou saw'st
In triumph and luxurious wealth, are they
First seen in acts of prowess eminent,
And great exploits, but of true virtue void;   790
Who having spilt much blood, and done much waste
Subduing nations, and achiev'd thereby
Fame in the world, high titles, and rich prey,
Shall change their course to pleasure, ease, and sloth,
Surfeit, and lust, till wantonness and pride   795
Raise out of friendship hostile deeds in peace.
The conquer'd also, and enslav'd by war,
Shall, with their freedom lost, all virtue lose,
And fear of God, from whom their piety feign'd,
In sharp contest of battle found no aid   800
Against invaders;[5] therefore cool'd in zeal,
Thenceforth shall practice how to live secure,
Worldly or dissolute, on what their lords
Shall leave them to enjoy; for th'earth shall bear
More than enough, that temp'rance may be tried: 805
So all shall turn degenerate, all deprav'd;
Justice and temp'rance, truth and faith forgot;
One man except, the only son of light
In a dark age, against example good,
Against allurement, custom, and a world   810
Offended; fearless of reproach and scorn,

785.1 *unfold* Reveal;   **785.2** *celestial* Heavenly.   **795** *Surfeit* Excess.   **805** *tried* Tested.

Or violence, he of their wicked ways
Shall them admonish, and before them set
The paths of righteousness, how much more safe,
815 And full of peace, denouncing wrath to come
On their impenitence; and shall return
Of them derided, but of God observ'd
The one just man alive; by his command
Shall build a wondrous ark, as thou beheld'st,
820 To save himself and household from amidst
821 A world devote to universal wrack.
No sooner he, with them, of man and beast
823 Select for life, shall in the ark be lodg'd,
824 And shelter'd round, but all the cataracts
825 Of heaven, set open on the earth, shall pour
Rain day and night; all fountains of the deep
Broke up, shall heave the ocean to usurp
828 Beyond all bounds, till inundation rise
Above the highest hills; then shall this mount.
830 Of Paradise by might of waves be mov'd
831 Out of his place, push'd by the horned flood,
832 With all his verdure spoil'd, and trees adrift,
833 Down the great river to the opening gulf,
834 And there take root, an island salt and bare,
835 The haunt of seals, and orcs, and sea-mews' clang:
To teach thee that God attributes to place
No sanctity, if none be thither brought
By men who there frequent, or therein dwell.
And now what further shall ensue, behold.

840 He look'd, and saw the ark hull on the flood,
Which now abated; for the clouds were fled,
Driven by a keen north wind, that blowing dry

---

821 *devote to universal wrack* Doomed to utter ruin. 823 *Select* Selected, elected. 824 *cataracts* Floodgates. 828 *inundation* Flood. 831 *horned* Leonard points out: "Greek and Roman river-gods were depicted as bull-like because of their strength" (p. 864). 832 *verdure* Greenness. 833.1 *river* The Euphrates, in modern Iraq; 833.2 *gulf* The Persian Gulf. 834 *salt* Infertile. 835.1 *orcs* Orcas; killer whales; 835.2 *sea-mews' clang* Seagulls' screech.

Wrinkled the face of deluge, as decay'd;   843
And the clear sun on his wide wat'ry glass   844
Gaz'd hot, and of the fresh wave largely drew,   845
As after thirst, which made their flowing shrink   846
From standing lake to tripping ebb, that stole   847
With soft foot tow'rds the deep, who now had stopp'd   848
His sluices, as the heaven his windows shut.

The ark no more now floats, but seems on ground   850
Fast on the top of some high mountain fixt,   851
And now the tops of hills as rocks appear,
With clamour thence the rapid currents drive
Tow'rds the retreating sea their furious tide.

Forthwith from out the ark a raven flies,   855
And after him, the surer messenger,
A dove, sent forth once and again to spy
Green tree or ground whereon his foot may light;   858
The second time returning, in his bill
An olive-leaf he brings, pacific sign: 860
Anon dry ground appears, and from his ark   861
The ancient sire descends with all his train;
Then with uplifted hands and eyes devout,
Grateful to heaven, over his head beholds
A dewy cloud, and in the cloud a bow,   865
Conspicuous with three listed colours gay,   866
Betokening peace from God, and cov'nant new.

Whereat the heart of Adam, erst so sad,   868
Greatly rejoic'd, and thus his joy broke forth:

O thou who future things canst represent   870
As present, heavenly instructor, I revive,   871
At this last sight, assur'd that man shall live

---

843 *as decay'd* As if grown old.   844 *glass* Mirror.   845 *largely drew* Deeply drank.   846 *their* The waves'.   847 *tripping* Running.   848 *deep* Sea.   850 *seems* A reminder that we are seeing events from Adam's pictorial perspective.   851 *Fast* Firm.   858 *light* Alight.   860 *pacific sign* Sign of peace.   861 *Anon* Straight away.   865 *bow* Rainbow.   866 *three listed colours* The three primary colors—red, yellow, and blue—arranged in bands.   868 *erst* Formerly.   870–871 *represent / As present* Adam now understands the nature, and the necessity, of mediated signification.   871 *revive* Come back to life.

With all the creatures, and their seed preserve.

874 Far less I now lament for one whole world
875 Of wicked sons destroy'd, than I rejoice
876 For one man found so perfect and so just,
That God vouchsafes to raise another world
From him, and all his anger to forget.
But say, what mean those colour'd streaks in heaven,
880 Distended as the brow of God appeas'd,
Or serve they as a flowery verge to bind
The fluid skirts of that same wat'ry cloud,
Lest it again dissolve and shower the earth?

884 To whom th'archangel: Dext'rously thou aim'st;
885 So willingly doth God remit his ire,
886 Though late repenting him of man deprav'd,
Griev'd at his heart, when looking down he saw
The whole earth flll'd with violence, and all flesh
Corrupting each their way; yet those remov'd,
890 Such grace shall one just man find in his sight,
That he relents, not to blot out mankind,
And makes a covenant never to destroy
893 The earth again by flood, nor let the sea
Surpass his bounds, nor rain to drown the world
895 With man therein or beast; but when he brings
Over the earth a cloud, will therein set
His triple-colour'd bow, whereon to look,
And call to mind his cov'nant: day and night,
899 Seed-time and harvest, heat and hoary frost,
900 Shall hold their course, till fire purge all things new,
Both heaven and earth, wherein the just shall dwell.

END OF BOOK ELEVENTH

874–876 *Far less . . . just* A reversal of the parable of the lost sheep in Luke 15:4, but Adam's sentiment accords with Milton's stress on the isolated, virtuous hero.   884 *Dext'rously* Accurately.   886 *Though late . . . deprav'd* Though recently repenting that He made man, who became depraved.   893 *by flood* Next time He will destroy it by fire.   899 *hoary* White.

BOOK XII

THE ARGUMENT

*The angel Michael continues from the flood to relate what shall
succeed; then, in the mention of* Abraham, comes by degrees to
explain who† that seed of the woman shall be which was
promised Adam and Eve in the fall. His incarnation, death,
resurrection, and ascension; the state of the church till his second
coming. Adam, greatly satisfied and recomforted‡ by these
relations§ and promises, ascends the hill with Michael; wakens
Eve, who all this while had slept,‖ but with gentle dreams
composed to quietness of mind and submission. Michael in either
hand leads them out of Paradise, the fiery sword waving behind
them, and the Cherubim taking their stations to guard the place.*

As one who in his journey bates at noon,   1
Tho' bent on speed; so here the archangel paus'd   2
Betwixt the world destroy'd and world restor'd,   3
If Adam ought perhaps might interpose;   4
Then with transition sweet new speech resumes.   5

*During his discussion of.
†Jesus Christ.
‡Restored to his prelapsarian condition of comfort.
§Narratives.
‖Relations between the genders become hierarchical after the Fall, so Eve is not permitted access to Michael's prophecies.

1–5 *As one . . . resumes* These lines were added to the 1674 edition, when book X of the first edition was divided into books XI and XII.   1 *bates* Abates, suspends.   3 *Betwixt* Between.   4 *interpose* Interject.   5 *new speech* Michael now conveys his message through words rather than the visual images he had previously used. As Fowler (pp. 645–646) points out, "The formal *transition* from vision to narrative is characteristic of prophecy."

Thus thou hast seen one world begin and end;

7   And man as from a second stock proceed.

Much thou hast yet to see, but I perceive

9   Thy mortal sight to fail; objects divine

10   Must needs impair and weary human sense.

11   Henceforth what is to come I will relate,

Thou therefore give due audience, and attend.

This second source of men, while yet but few,

14   And while the dread of judgment past remains

15   Fresh in their minds, fearing the Deity,

  With some regard to what is just and right,

17   Shall lead their lives, and multiply apace,

18   Lab'ring the soil and reaping plenteous crop,

Corn, wine, and oil; and, from the herd or flock,

20   Oft sacrificing bullock, lamb, or kid,

With large wine-offerings pour'd, and sacred feast,

Shall spend their days in joy unblam'd, and dwell

Long time in peace, by families and tribes,

24   Under paternal rule: till one shall rise[1]

25   Of proud ambitious heart, who not content

With fair equality, fraternal state,

27   Will arrogate dominion undeserv'd

28   Over his brethren, and quite dispossess

29   Concord and law of nature from the earth;

30   Hunting (and men not beasts shall be his game)

31   With war and hostile snare such as refuse

32   Subjection to his empire tyrannous:

---

7 *stock* Breed.   9–10 *objects divine . . . sense* Whereas before the Fall Raphael recounted the war in Heaven in rich pictorial detail, Adam is now incapable of sustaining the concentration required for the accurate interpretation of images.   11 *relate* Represent in simpler terms.   14 *dread* Fear.   17 *apace* Quickly.   18 *Lab'ring* Michael reminds Adam of the curse of labor.   20 *sacrificing* The sacrifice of animals prefigures the sacrifice of Christ.   24 *paternal* Patriarchal, benign.   27 *dominion undeserv'd* Implying that power in itself is not objectionable, but power imposed by force is.   28 *brethren* The word was associated with the radical, egalitarian wing of Puritanism.   29 *law of nature* According to which human beings are equal.   31 *snare* Trap.   32 *empire tyrannous* Milton thought of imperialism in connection with Caesar's defeat of the Roman republicans.

A mighty hunter thence he shall be styl'd   33
Before the Lord, as in despite of heaven,   34
Or from heaven claiming second sov'reignty   35
And from rebellion shall derive his name,
Though of rebellion others he accuse.
He with a crew, whom like ambition joins
With him or under him to tyrannize,
Marching from Eden towards the west, shall find   40
The plain, wherein a black bituminous gurge,   41
Boils out from under ground, the mouth of hell:
Of brick, and of that stuff they cast to build   43
A city and tower, whose top may reach to heaven;   44
And get themselves a name, lest, far dispers'd   45
In foreign lands, their memory be lost,   46
Regardless whether good or evil fame.   47
But God, who oft descends to visit men   48
Unseen, and through their habitations walks   49
To mark their doings, them beholding soon,   50
Comes down to see their city, ere the tower   51
Obstruct heaven-towers, and in derision sets   52
Upon their tongues a various spirit, to raze   53
Quite out their native language, and instead
To sow a jangling noise of words unknown;   55
Forthwith a hideous gabble rises loud   56
Among the builders; each to other calls

---

33 *styl'd* Called.   34.1 *Before* Simultaneously "in defiance of," "obtruding himself in front of," and "in typological anticipation of"; 34.2 *despite* Scorn.   35 *Or from . . . sov'reignty* Reference to the "divine right of kings," the doctrine by which the early Stuarts sought to justify their rule.   41.1 *The plain* Of Shinar; see Genesis 11:2, "they found a plain in the land of Shinar"; compare 3.467; 41.2 *gurge* Whirlpool.   43 *that stuff* Bitumen; a mineral pitch, like asphalt.   44 *tower* The tower of Babel, archetype of fetishized human works. 45–47 *And get . . . fame* The desire for earthly, as opposed to heavenly, fame does not distinguish between good and evil reputations; fame becomes an end in itself.   48–50 *But God . . . doings* The alienation of the world from God is one-sided; God is not alien to the world but present in it unperceived.   51 *ere* Before.   52 *heaven-towers* The figural magnificence of noumenal, spiritual structures is obscured by Nimrod's physical, man-made constructions.   53.1 *various* Divisive; 53.2 *raze* Erase.   56 *gabble* Gibberish.

Not understood, till hoarse, and all in rage,
As mock'd they storm: great laughter was in heaven.

60 And looking down, to see the hubbub strange
And hear the din; thus was the building left

62 Ridiculous, and the work Confusion nam'd.

63 Whereto thus Adam fatherly displeas'd:

64 O execrable son, so to aspire

65 Above his brethren, to himself assuming

66 Authority usurp'd, from God not given:
He gave us only over beast, fish, fowl,
Dominion absolute; that right we hold

69 By his donation; but man over men

70 He made not lord: such title to himself

71 Reserving, human left from human free.
But this usurper his encroachment proud

73 Stays not on man; to God his tower intends
Siege and defiance. Wretched man! what food

75 Will he convey up thither to sustain
Himself and his rash army, where thin air

77 Above the clouds will pine his entrails gross,

78 And famish him of breath, if not of bread?

To whom thus Michael: Justly thou abhorr'st

80 That son, who on the quiet state of men

81 Such trouble brought, affecting to subdue

82 Rational liberty; yet know withal,

---

62 *Confusion* The Hebrew word for "confusion" is a cognate of "Babylon." 63 *fatherly*
Flannagan points out: "The word is carefully chosen, since Michael's narrative here and
below concentrates on the proper and improper relations between fathers and sons" (p.
691). 64–65 *to aspire / Above his brethren* Adam's reaction to the story of Nimrod recalls
what he has heard about Satan. 66 *Authority . . . given* All tyranny is usurpation. 69–71
but man . . . free Again, the objection is not to power per se, but to the introduction into
human politics of "absolute" power, the kind that man exercises over the animals. 73.1
Stays not on Does not confine to; 73.2 *to* Against. 77 *pine his entrails gross* Waste his fleshly
body. 78 *famish* Starve. 81 *affecting* Pretending. 82 *Rational liberty* Freedom to reason.

Since thy original lapse, true liberty   83
Is lost, which always with right reason dwells   84
Twin'd, and from her hath no dividual being.   85
Reason in man obscur'd, or not obey'd,   86
Immediately inordinate desires   87
And upstart passions catch the government   88
From reason, and to servitude reduce   89
Man till then free. Therefore since he permits   90
Within himself unworthy powers to reign   91
Over free reason, God in judgment just   92
Subjects him from without to violent lords;   93
Who oft as undeservedly enthrall   94
His outward freedom: tyranny must be,   95
Though to the tyrant thereby no excuse.   96
Yet sometimes nations will decline so low
From virtue, which is reason, that no wrong,   98
But justice, and some fatal curse annex'd,   99
Deprives them of their outward liberty,   100
Their inward lost. Witness th'irreverent son   101
Of him who built the ark, who for the shame
Done to his father heard his heavy curse,
Servant of servants, on his vicious race.   104
Thus will this latter, as the former world,   105
Still tend from bad to worse, till God at last,
Wearied with their iniquities, withdraw   107
His presence from among them, and avert

83–85 *Since thy . . . being* The Fall has damaged man's rational capacities, impairing the free-
dom of thought that is inseparable ("hath no dividual being") from political liberty.
86–90 *Reason in man . . . free* The usurpation of reason's rightful ruling position by emo-
tion and appetite constitutes psychological slavery. 90–96 *Therefore since . . . excuse* Psy-
chological slavery inevitably results in political slavery; tyranny is unavoidable for fallen
humanity, but that does not mean that it is just. 98 *virtue, which is reason* Milton follows
Plato, proclaiming that all sin is ignorance. 99.1 *justice* God's providence; 99.2 *some fatal
curse annex'd* Added to the consequences of man's fall. 101 *son* Ham, who saw his
drunken father Noah naked, and whose descendant Canaan was consequently cursed to be
"a servant of servants" (Genesis 9:25). Ham and his kindred figure largely in book XII,
which focuses on the nature of, and reasons for, servitude. 104 *vicious* Prone to vice. 107
iniquities Perversions.

His holy eyes; resolving from thenceforth
110 To leave them to their own polluted ways;
111 And one peculiar nation to select
112 From all the rest, of whom to be invok'd,
113 A nation from one faithful man to spring:
114 Him on this side Euphrates yet residing,
115 Bred up in idol-worship. O that men
(Canst thou believe?) should be so stupid grown,
117 While yet the patriarch liv'd, who scap'd the flood,
As to forsake the living God, and fall
119 To worship their own work in wood and stone
120 For gods! Yet him God the Most High vouchsafes
To call by vision from his father's house,
His kindred and false gods, into a land
Which he will show him, and from him will raise
A mighty nation, and upon him shower
125 His benediction so, that in his seed
126 All nations shall be bless'd; he straight obeys,
Not knowing to what land, yet firm believes.
128 I see him, but thou canst not, with what faith
He leaves his gods, his friends, and native soil
130 Ur of Chaldea, passing now the ford
131 To Haran, after him a cumbrous train
132 Of herds, and flocks, and numerous servitude;
Not wand'ring poor, but trusting all his wealth
With God, who call'd him, in a land unknown.

---

111 *peculiar* Singled out, chosen.   112 *invok'd* Produced.   113 *one faithful man* Abraham.
114 *this side Euphrates* Eastern bank of this river in modern Iraq.   115 *Bred up in idol-wor-ship* Like all mankind since Noah. The name of Abraham's father, Tereh, suggests he was a priest of Ter, the moon-god of the Amorites.   117 *scap'd* Escaped.   119 *their own work* The fetishization of labor—the idolization of the "works of men's hands"—resumed imme-diately after the deluge.   125 *benediction* Blessing.   126.1 *All nations* Abraham is literally the father of the Israelites, but metaphorically the father of all believers of any nation; 126.2 *straight* Immediately.   128 *I see him, but thou canst not* Adam's fallen understanding can no longer sustain prophetic vision.   130 *Ur of Chaldea* Sumerian city in modern Iraq.   131.1 *Haran* City in modern Turkey; 131.2 *cumbrous train* Burdensome following, with the impli-cation that Abraham's servants were an encumbrance to him.   132 *servitude* Servants.

Canaan he now attains; I see his tents 135
Pitch'd about Shechem, and the neighb'ring plain 136
Of Moreh; there by promise he receives 137
Gift to his progeny of all that land, 138
From Hamath northward to the desert south, 139
(Things by their names I call, though yet unnam'd) 140
From Hermon east to the great western sea; 141
Mount Hermon, yonder sea, each place beheld
In prospect, as I point them; on the shore
Mount Carmel; here the double-founted stream 144
Jordan, true limit eastward; but his sons 145
Shall dwell to Senir, that long ridge of hills. 146
This ponder, that all nations of the earth
Shall in his seed be blessed; by that seed
Is meant the great Deliverer, who shall bruise 149
The serpent's head; whereof to thee anon 150
Plainlier shall be reveal'd. This patriarch bless'd, 151
Whom faithful Abraham due time shall call
A son, and of his son a grandchild leaves, 153
Like him in faith, in wisdom, and renown;
The grandchild with twelve sons increas'd departs 155
From Canaan, to a land hereafter call'd
Egypt, divided by the river Nile;
See where it flows, disgorging at seven mouths 158

135.1 *Canaan* Territory between the Jordan River and the Mediterranean Sea—modern Israel; 135.2 *attains* Reaches. 136 *Shechem* Where Abraham builds his first altar to God in Genesis 12:6–7. 136–137 *plain / Of Moreh* Milton follows an incorrect translation: The Hebrew refers to the "oak of Moreh," next to which Abraham constructed his altar. 137–138 *by promise . . . land* In Judaism this means that Israel was literally promised to the Jews; in Christianity it refers to the figural "kingdom" of Heaven, promised to all believers. 139–141 *From Hamath . . . east* The land promised to the Israelites extends from Hamath, in modern Syria, in the north, to the Sinai desert, in modern Egypt, in the south, and from Mt. Hermon, in modern Lebanon, to the Mediterranean ("western") Sea. 144.1 *Mount Carmel* Near Haifa, in modern Israel; 144.2 *double-founted* The River Jordan was supposed to be the conflu-ences of two separate streams, the Jor and the Dan. 146 *Senir* The Amorite name for Mt. Hermon, between modern Lebanon and Syria. 149 *Deliverer* Liberator—that is, Jesus of Nazareth. 150 *anon* Immediately. 151 *Plainlier* More plainly. 153.1 *son* Isaac; 153.2 *grandchild* Jacob. 158 *See where it flows* Adam is able to see the physical features of the landscape, but not the future events that Michael describes.

159 Into the sea: to sojourn in that land,

160 He comes invited by a younger son

161 In time of dearth; a son whose worthy deeds
   Raise him to be the second in that realm

163 Of Pharaoh: there he dies, and leaves his race

164 Growing into a nation; and now grown,

165 Suspected to a sequent king, who seeks
   To stop their overgrowth, as inmate guests

167 Too numerous; whence of guests he makes them slaves
   Inhospitably, and kills their infant males:
   Till by two brethren (those two brethren call'd

170 Moses and Aaron) sent from God to claim
   His people from enthralment, they return

172 With glory and spoil back to their promis'd land.

173 But first the lawless tyrant, who denies
   To know their God, or message to regard,

175 Must be compell'd by signs and judgments dire;
   To blood unshed the rivers must be turn'd;
   Frogs, lice, and flies, must all his palace fill
   With loath'd intrusion, and fill all the land,

179 His cattle must of rot and murrain die;

180 Botches and blains must all his flesh emboss,
   And all his people; thunder mix'd with hail,

182 Hail mix'd with fire, must rend th'Egyptian sky,
   And wheel on th'earth, devouring where it rolls,
   What it devours not, herb, or fruit, or grain;

185 A darksome cloud of locusts swarming down
   Must eat, and on the ground leave nothing green;

187 Darkness must overshadow all his bounds.

---

159 *sojourn* Live as an alien. 160 *a younger son* Joseph. 161 *dearth* Famine. 163–164 *his race / Growing into a nation* His descendants multiply and acquire a sense of collective national identity. 165.1 *Suspected to* Mistrusted by; 165.2 *sequent* Following. 167 *of* Instead of. 172 *spoil* Plunder. 173 *lawless tyrant* Tyrants were rebels for Milton, since they recognized no law above themselves. 175 *signs and judgments dire* Pharaoh is an earthly type of Satan; he is unable to interpret, or even to recognize, signs. 179.1 *rot* Infection; 179.2 *murrain* Foot-and-mouth disease. 180 *Botches . . . emboss* Sores and boils must bubble up on his body. 182 *rend* Tear. 187 *bounds* Borders, territories.

Palpable darkness, and blot out three days;   188
Last with one midnight stroke all the first born
Of Egypt must lie dead. Thus with ten wounds   190
The river-dragon tam'd at length submits   191
To let his sojourners depart, and oft
Humbles his stubborn heart, but still as ice
More harden'd after thaw, till in his rage   194
Pursuing whom he late dismiss'd, the sea   195
Swallows him with his host, but them lets pass   196
As on dry land between two crystal walls,
Awed by the rod of Moses so to stand   198
Divided, till his rescued gain their shore.   199
Such wondrous power God to his saint will lend,   200
Though present in his angel, who shall go   201
Before them in a cloud, and pillar of fire,   202
By day a cloud, by night a pillar of fire,   203
To guide them in their journey, and remove
Behind them, while th'obdurate king pursues.   205
All night he will pursue, but his approach
Darkness defends between till morning watch;   207
Then through the fiery pillar and the cloud
God, looking forth, will trouble all his host,
And craze their chariot-wheels: when by command,   210
Moses once more his potent rod extends   211
Over the sea; the sea his rod obeys;
On their embattled ranks the waves return,   213
And overwhelm their war: the race elect,   214

188.1 *Palpable* Recalls the "darkness visible" of Hell in 1.63; **188.2** *three days* Prefiguring the three days between the crucifixion and the resurrection of Christ.   **191** *The river-dragon* The croco-dile, a symbol for Pharaoh in Ezekiel 29:3.   **194** *harden'd* The "hardening" of Pharaoh's heart consists not merely in cruelty, but in the rigid literalism that prevents him from seeing the meaning behind the signs.   **196.1** *host* Army; **196.2** *them* The Israelites.   **198** *rod* A common biblical symbol for the power of God.   **199** *gain* Arrive at.   **201–203** *his angel . . . fire* Clouds and pillars are common in the Bible; here they signify both the presence and the inaccessibil-ity of God's power.   **205** *obdurate* Hardened.   **207** *defends* Forbids.   **210** *craze* Shatter.   **211** *his potent rod* The phallic imagery is more explicit than in Exodus 14:21.   **213** *embattled* Both "prepared for battle" and "beleaguered."   **214.1** *war* War equipment; **214.2** *race elect* The Is-raelites, but the word "elect" evokes the predestinarian notion that an elite group of human beings has been selected for redemption by God before the creation of the universe.

215 Safe towards Canaan from the shore advance
Through the wild desert, not the readiest way,[2]
217 Lest ent'ring on the Canaanite alarm'd
218 War terrify'd them inexpert, and fear
219 Return them back to Egypt, choosing rather
220 Inglorious life with servitude; for life
To noble and ignoble is more sweet
Untrain'd in arms, where rashness leads not on.
This also shall they gain by their delay
In the wide wilderness, there they shall found
225 Their government, and their great senate choose
Through the twelve tribes, to rule by laws ordain'd
227 God from the mount of Sinai, whose gray top
Shall tremble, he descending, will himself
In thunder, lightning, and loud trumpets sound,
230 Ordain them laws; part such as appertain
231 To civil justice, part religious rites
232 Of sacrifice, informing them, by types
233 And shadows, of that destin'd Seed to bruise
The serpent, by what means he shall achieve
235 Mankind's deliverance. But the voice of God
To mortal ear is dreadful; they beseech
That Moses might report to them his will,
And terror cease; he grants what they besought,
239 Instructed that to God is no access
240 Without mediator, whose high office now
241 Moses in figure bears, to introduce

217–220 *Lest . . . servitude* If they had proceeded straight to Canaan, the Israelites might have been defeated in battle and decided to return to Egypt, as happened to the republicans of Milton's day.   225 *senate* Parliament; Exodus does not mention this system of government among the wandering Israelites, so Milton's reference is explicitly topical.   227 *gray top* Covered with a cloud.   231 *civil justice* Secular law.   231–232 *religious rites / Of sacrifice* The religious code of the Israelites.   232–233 *by types / And shadows* Milton regarded the devotional practices of the Old Testament as symbols whose meaning is revealed in Christ; the practices themselves are thus abrogated and internalized.   235 *deliverance* Liberation.   239–240 *to God is no access / Without mediator* After the Fall, human beings can only experience deity through the mediation of human language and symbols.   241 *in figure* In symbolic form. Moses is a type of Christ, the final Mediator.   241–242 *introduce / One greater* To prefigure, or introduce us to the concept of, Christ.

One greater, of whose day he shall foretell,

And all the prophets in their age, the times   243

Of great Messiah shall sing. Thus laws and rites   244

Establish'd, such delight hath God in men   245

Obedient to his will, that he vouchsafes   246

Among them to set up his tabernacle,   247

The Holy One with mortal men to dwell:

By his prescript a sanctuary is fram'd   249

Of cedar, overlaid with gold, therein   250

An ark, and in the ark his testimony,   251

The records of his covenant, over these   252

A mercy-seat of gold between the wings   253

Of two bright cherubim; before him burn

Seven lamps, as in a zodiac representing   255

The heavenly fires; over the tent a cloud   256

Shall rest by day, a fiery gleam by night,

Save when they journey, and at length they come,   258

Conducted by his angel, to the land

Promis'd to Abraham and his seed. The rest   260

Were long to tell, how many battles fought,

How many kings destroy'd and kingdoms won,   262

Or how the sun shall in mid-heaven stand still   263

A day entire, and night's due course adjourn,   264

Man's voice commanding, Sun in Gibeon stand,   265

And thou moon in the vale of Ajalon,   266

---

243 *And . . . age* Not just Moses but all the prophets through John the Baptist tell of the coming of Christ in symbolic language. 244 *Messiah* Anointed one. 246 *vouchsafes* Promises. 247 *tabernacle* Where God dwelt among the Israelites after the Exodus. 249.1 *By his prescript* According to his instructions; 249.2 *sanctuary* From Exodus 25:8: "And let them make me a sanctuary; that I may dwell among them." 251–252 *ark . . . covenant* The ark of the covenant was a wooden chest that contained the tablets of the law and served as a symbol of the presence of God. 253 *mercy-seat* The lid of the ark, which had a cherubim at either end. 255–256 *Seven lamps . . . fires* The lamps decorating the ark symbolize the seven planets. 258 *Save* Except. 262 *kings destroy'd* The many Old Testament accounts of revolutions against kings provided seventeenth-century republicans with inspiring precedents. 263–266 *stand still . . . Ajalon* In Joshua 10:12–13 the sun stands still in order to allow the Israelites time to take vengeance on their enemies in Gibeon, in the valley of Ajalon. 264 *adjourn* Suspend for a day.

267   Till Israel overcome; so call the third
       From Abraham, son of Isaac, and from him
       His whole descent, who thus shall Canaan win.

270   Here Adam interpos'd: O sent from heaven,
271   Enlight'ner of my darkness! gracious things
       Thou hast reveal'd, those chiefly which concern
       Just Abraham and his seed: now first I find
       Mine eyes true opening, and my heart much eas'd.
275   Erewhile perplex'd with thoughts what would become
       Of me and all mankind; but now I see
       His day, in whom all nations shall be bless'd
278   Favour unmerited by me, who sought
       Forbidden knowledge by forbidden means.
280   Yet this I apprehend not, why to those
       Among whom God will deign to dwell on earth,
       So many and so various laws are given;
283   So many laws argue so many sins
       Among them; how can God with such reside?

285   To whom thus Michael: Doubt not but that sin
       Will reign among them as of thee begot;
287   And therefore was law given them to evince
288   Their natural pravity, by stirring up
289   Sin against law to fight; that when they see
290   Law can discover sin, but not remove,
291   Save by those shadowy expiations weak,

---

267 *Israel* The name given to Jacob after his wrestling with the angel in Genesis 32:28, meaning "he that fights with God." 270 *interpos'd* Interjected. 271 *gracious* Accomplished by the grace of God. 275 *Erewhile* Previously. 278 *Favour unmerited* Unwarranted grace. 280 *apprehend* Understand. 283 *argue* Suggest. 287–288 *to evince / Their natural pravity* Old Testament law, which is impossible for human beings to keep, was intended to reveal the nature of sin, as well as the fact that human beings are naturally sinful, or prone to pravity ("depravity"). 288–289 *by stirring up . . . fight* The imposition of law introduces the possibility of breaking it, thus making us conscious of sin. 290 *discover* Reveal. 291 *shadowy expiations* Symbolic acts of atonement.

The blood of bulls and goats, they may conclude   292
Some blood more precious must be paid for man,   293
Just for unjust, that in such righteousness,
To them by faith imputed, they may find   295
Justification towards God, and peace   296
Of conscience, which the law by ceremonies
Cannot appease, nor man the moral part   298
Perform, and, not performing, cannot live.   299
So law appears imperfect, and but given   300
With purpose to resign them in full time   301
Up to a better covenant, disciplin'd
From shadowy types to truth, from flesh to spirit,   303
From imposition of strict laws to free   304
Acceptance of large grace, from servile fear   305
To filial, works of law to works of faith.   306
And therefore shall not Moses, though of God
Highly belov'd, being but the minister
Of law, his people into Canaan lead;   309
But Joshua, whom the Gentiles Jesus call,   310
His name and office bearing, who shall quell
The adversary serpent, and bring back   312
Through the world's wilderness long wander'd man
Safe to eternal Paradise of rest.
Meanwhile they, in their earthly Canaan plac'd,   315

292–293 *they may conclude . . . man* The repeated, ritualistic rehearsal of symbolic sacrifices will gradually lead the human race to comprehend the nature of the true sacrifice.   295 *faith imputed* Vicariously granted faith.   295–296 *find / Justification* Not that they will become just, but that God will treat them as though they had been just.   298–299 *nor man . . . live* Since it is impossible to obey the law, the law cannot be the true means to salvation.   300 *but* Only.   301.1 *them* The Israelites; 301.2 *in full time* In the fullness of time. 303–306 *From shadowy . . . faith* A concise statement of the typological method of biblical exegesis, whereby the Old Testament is seen as a symbolic prefiguration of the New; it involves a simultaneous movement from flesh to spirit, from sign to referent, from law to grace, and from slavery to freedom.   309 *lead* Moses died the night before the Israelites crossed the River Jordan into the promised land.   310.1 *Joshua* The leader who replaced Moses and led the Israelites into Canaan; 310.2 *Jesus* "Jesus" is the Greek form of the Hebrew "Joshua," which emphasizes the latter's role as a type of Christ.   312 *adversary serpent* Combines the literal and figurative roles of the snake and Satan ("Adversary" in Hebrew).

316   Long time shall dwell and prosper; but when sins

317   National interrupt their public peace,

Provoking God to raise them enemies;

From whom as oft he saves them penitent;

320   By judges first, then under kings; of whom

321   The second, both for piety renown'd,

322   And puissant deeds, a promise shall receive

Irrevocable, that his regal throne

For ever shall endure; the like shall sing

All prophecy, that of the royal stock

Of David (so I name this king) shall rise

A Son, the woman's seed to thee foretold,

Foretold to Abraham, as in whom shall trust

329   All nations, and to kings foretold, of kings

330   The last, for of his reign shall be no end.

But first a long succession must ensue,

332   And his next son, for wealth and wisdom fam'd,

The clouded ark of God, till then in tents

334   Wand'ring, shall in a glorious temple inshrine.

335   Such follow him as shall be register'd

336   Part good, part bad; of bad the longer scroll,

Whose foul idolatries, and other faults,

338   Heap'd to the popular sum, will so incense

God, as to leave them, and expose their land,

340   Their city, his temple, and his holy ark,

With all his sacred things, a scorn and prey

To that proud city, whose high walls thou saw'st

343   Left in confusion, Babylon thence call'd.

316–317 *sins / National* Sins committed by the nation as a whole, rather than by its individual members.   320 *judges . . . kings* Foolishly, in Milton's view, the Israelites substituted a monarchy for a system of government by judges.   321 *The second* David.   322 *puissant* Powerful.   329–330 *of kings / The last* Milton follows the radical opinion that after the incarnation, Christians are obliged to acknowledge no king but Christ.   332 *son* Solomon.   334 *temple* In 1 Kings, Solomon actually builds the temple that his father David had planned.   335 *register'd* Recorded.   336 *scroll* List.   338 *Heap'd to the popular sum* Added to the total number of sins committed by the people.   343 *Babylon* Milton follows the conventional identification of Babylon with Babel.

There in captivity he lets them dwell	344
The space of seventy years, then brings them back,	345
Rememb'ring mercy, and his covenant sworn	
To David, stablish'd as the days of heaven.	347
Return'd from Babylon, by leave of kings,	348
Their lords, whom God dispos'd, the house of God	349
They first re-edify, and for a while	350
In mean estate live moderate, till grown	351
In wealth and multitude, factious they grow;	352
But first among the priests dissension springs,	353
Men who attend the altar, and should most	
Endeavour peace: their strife pollution brings	355
Upon the temple itself: at last they seize	356
The sceptre, and regard not David's sons.	357
Then lose it to a stranger, that the true	358
Anointed king Messiah might be born	359
Barr'd of his right: yet at his birth a star	360
Unseen before in heaven, proclaims him come	
And guides the eastern sages, who inquire	362
His place, to offer incense, myrrh, and gold.	363
His place of birth a solemn angel tells	
To simple shepherds, keeping watch by night;	365
They gladly thither haste, and by a choir	
Of squadron'd angels hear his carol sung.	
A Virgin is his mother, but his sire	

---

344 *captivity* Nebuchadnezzar transported the Jewish intelligentsia to Babylon, where they remained in captivity until the city's capture by Cyrus the Great of Persia. The Babylonian captivity is a figure for every kind of alienation.   347 *stablish'd* Established.   348 *by leave of kings* The Persian kings Cyrus, Artaxerxes, and Darius, under whom the Israelites were permitted to restore the temple.   349 *dispos'd* Persuaded, in contrast to Pharaoh, whose heart He hardened.   350 *re-edify* Rebuild.   351 *mean estate* Humble condition.   352 *factious* Internally divided.   353 *priests* Religious dissension was a prominent feature of Milton's own time.   356–357 *they seize / The sceptre* The Maccabees, one of whom, Aristobulus I, was the first to style himself "king of the Jews."   358 *stranger* Antipater the Idumaean, father of Herod the Great, appointed procurator of Judea by Julius Caesar in 47 B.C.   359 *Anointed* Chosen, marked for kingship.   360 *Barr'd* Dispossessed.   362 *eastern sages* The Magi, or three wise men.   363 *incense, myrrh, and gold* The gifts offered by the Magi to the infant Christ in Matthew 2:11.

The power of the Most High; he shall ascend
370 The throne hereditary, and bound his reign
With earth's wide bounds, his glory with the heavens.

He cease'd, discerning Adam with such joy
373 Surcharg'd as had, like grief, been dew'd in tears,
Without the vent of words which these he breath'd.

375 O prophet of glad tidings, finisher
Of utmost hope: now clear I understand
What oft my steadiest thoughts have search'd in vain,
Why our great expectation should be call'd
The Seed of Woman. Virgin Mother, hail,
380 High in the love of Heaven, yet from my loins
Thou shalt proceed, and from thy womb the Son
382 Of God Most High; so God with man unites:
383 Needs must the serpent now his capital bruise
Expect with mortal pain: say where and when
385 Their fight, what stroke shall bruise the victor's heel?

386 To whom thus Michael: Dream not of their fight
387 As of a duel, or the local wounds
Of head or heel: not therefore joins the Son
Manhood to Godhead, with more strength to foil
390 Thy enemy; nor so is overcome
Satan, whose fall from heaven, a deadlier bruise,
392 Disabled not to give thee thy death's wound:
393 Which he, who comes thy Saviour, shall recure,
Not by destroying Satan, but his works
395 In thee and in thy seed. Nor can this be,
396 But by fulfilling that which thou didst want,

---

373 *Surcharg'd* Overwhelmed.　382 *God with man unites* In the figure of Christ.　383 *capital* Both "on the head" and "fatal."　386–387 *Dream not . . . duel* Michael warns Adam against a literalist interpretation.　387 *local* In a physical place.　392 *Disabled not to give* Did not prevent him from giving.　393 *recure* Cure a second time.　395 *Nor can this be* Fowler (pp. 664–665) comments that at this point "the abstract spirituality irrupts into Jewish history as if from another level of discourse."　396 *want* Lack.

The Prophecy of the Crucifixion

Obedience to the law of God, impos'd
On penalty of death, and suffering death,
The penalty to thy transgression due,
400 And due to theirs which out of thine will grow:
401 So only can high justice rest appaid.
The law of God exact he shall fulfil
Both by obedience and by love, though love
Alone fulfil the law: thy punishment
405 He shall endure by coming in the flesh
To a reproachful life and cursed death,
Proclaiming life to all who shall believe
In his redemption, and that his obedience
409 Imputed becomes theirs by faith, his merits
410 To save them, not their own, though legal works.
For this he shall live hated, be blasphem'd,
Seiz'd on by force, judg'd, and to death condemn'd
A shameful and accurs'd, nail'd to the cross
By his own nation, slain for bringing life;
415 But to the cross he nails thy enemies,
The law that is against thee, and the sins
Of all mankind, with him there crucified,
Never to hurt them more who rightly trust
419 In this his satisfaction; so he dies,
420 But soon revives; death over him no power
Shall long usurp; ere the third dawning light
Return, the stars of morn shall see him rise
Out of his grave, fresh as the dawning light,
Thy ransom paid, which man from death redeems,
425 His death for man, as many as offer'd life
Neglect not, and the benefit embrace
By faith not void of works. This godlike act
428 Annuls thy doom, the death thou shouldst have died,
In sin for ever lost from life; this act
430 Shall bruise the head of Satan, crush his strength

---

401 *appaid* Repaid.　409 *Imputed* Attributed vicariously.　419 *satisfaction* Payment.　428 *doom* Sentence.

Defeating Sin and Death, his two main arms,
And fix far deeper in his head their stings   432
Than temporal death shall bruise the victor's heel,   433
Or theirs whom he redeems, a death-like sleep,
A gentle wafting to immortal life.   435
Nor after resurrection shall he stay
Longer on earth than certain times to appear
To his disciples, men who in his life
Still follow'd him; to them shall leave in charge
To teach all nations what of him they learn'd   440
And his salvation, them who shall believe
Baptizing in the profluent stream, the sign   442
Of washing them from guilt of sin to life
Pure, and in mind prepar'd, if so befall,
For death, like that which the Redeemer died.   445
All nations they shall teach; for from that day
Not only to the sons of Abraham's loins
Salvation shall be preach'd, but to the sons
Of Abraham's faith wherever through the world;
So in his seed all nations shall be bless'd.   450
Then to the heaven of heavens shall he ascend
With victory, triumphing through the air
Over his foes and thine; there shall surprise
The serpent, prince of air, and drag in chains
Through all his realm, and there confounded leave;   455
Then enter into glory, and resume
His seat at God's right hand, exalted high.
Above all names in heaven; and thence shall come,
When this world's dissolution shall be ripe,
With glory and power to judge both quick and dead,   460
To judge th'unfaithful dead, but to reward
His faithful, and receive them into bliss,
Whether in heaven or earth, for then the earth   463

---

432 *in his head* As Sin sprang from Satan's head in book II.   433 *temporal* Both "temporary" and "in time."   442 *profluent* Flowing.   460 *quick* Living.

464 Shall all be Paradise, far happier place
465 Than this of Eden, and far happier days.

So spake the archangel Michael, then paus'd,
467 As at the world's great period; and our sire,
Replete with joy and wonder, thus replied:

469 O goodness infinite! goodness immense!
470 That all this good of evil shall produce,
And evil turn to good; more wonderful
Than that which by creation first brought forth
Light out of darkness! Full of doubt I stand,
Whether I should repent me now of sin
475 By me done and occasion'd, or rejoice
Much more, that much more good thereof shall spring,
To God more glory, more good will to men
From God, and over wrath grace shall abound.
But say, if our Deliverer up to heaven
480 Must re-ascend, what will betide the few
His faithful, left among th'unfaithful herd,
The enemies of truth? who then shall guide
His people, who defend? will they not deal
Worse with his followers than with him they dealt?

485 Be sure they will, said th'angel; but from heaven
486 He to his own a Comforter will send,
The promise of the Father, who shall dwell
His Spirit within them, and the law of faith
Working through love, upon their hearts shall write,
490 To guide them in all truth, and also arm
With spiritual armour, able to resist
Satan's assaults, and quench his fiery darts,

463–464 *the earth / Shall all be Paradise* After the apocalypse, Christ will reign on earth for one thousand years, before the Day of Judgment. 467 *sire* Father. 469 *immense* Immeasurable. 480 *betide* Become of. 486 *Comforter* An epithet ascribed to the Holy Spirit in John 15:26.

What man can do against them, not afraid,
Though to the death, against such cruelties
With inward consolations recompens'd,   495
And oft supported so as shall amaze
Their proudest persecutors: for the Spirit
Pour'd first on his Apostles, whom he sends
To evangelize the nations, then on all
Baptiz'd, shall them with wondrous gifts endue   500
To speak all tongues, and do all miracles,   501
As did their Lord before them. Thus they win
Great numbers of each nation to receive
With joy the tidings brought from heaven: at length
Their ministry perform'd, and race well run,   505
Their doctrine and their story written left,
They die; but in their room, as they forewarn,
Wolves shall succeed for teachers, grievous wolves,   508
Who all the sacred mysteries of heaven
To their own vile advantages shall turn   510
Of lucre³ and ambition, and the truth
With superstitions and traditions taint,   512
Left only in those written records pure,   513
Though not but by the Spirit understood.
Then shall they seek to avail themselves of names,   515
Places, and titles, and with these to join
Secular power, though feigning still to act   517
By spiritual, to themselves appropriating
The Spirit of God, promis'd alike and given
To all believers; and from that pretence,   520
Spiritual laws by carnal power shall force
On every conscience; laws which none shall find

---

501 *all tongues* In Acts 2:4–7 the Holy Spirit imbues the apostles with the ability to speak all languages, in an ironic recapitulation of the confusion at Babel. "Speaking in tongues" remains a common practice among Pentecostals.   508 *grievous wolves* Enemies of the church, who will devour the "sheep" of the congregation, quoting Paul's description in Acts 20:29; compare "Lycidas," 1.128.   512 *superstitions and traditions* The grounds on which the Catholic Church will rest its claim to spiritual authority.   513 *written records pure* The Bible.   517 *feigning* Pretending.

Left them enroll'd, or what the Spirit within
524 Shall on the heart engrave. What will they then
525 But force the Spirit of grace itself, and bind
His consort Liberty; What, but unbuild
His living temples, built by faith to stand,
Their own faith not another's: for on earth
Who against faith and conscience can be heard
530 Infallible? Yet many will presume:
Whence heavy persecution shall arise
On all who in the worship persevere
Of spirit and truth; the rest, far greater part,
Will deem in outward rites and spacious forms
535 Religion satisfied; truth shall retire
Bestruck with sland'rous darts, and works of faith
Rarely be found: so shall the world go on,
To good malignant, to bad men benign,
Under her own weight groaning, till the day
540 Appear of respiration to the just
And vengeance to the wicked, at return
Of him so lately promis'd to thy aid,
The Woman's Seed, obscurely then foretold,
Now amplier known thy Saviour and thy Lord;
545 Last in the clouds from heaven to be reveal'd
In glory of the Father, to dissolve
Satan with his perverted world, then raise
From the conflagrant mass, purg'd and refin'd,
549 New heavens, new earth, ages of endless date,
550 Founded in righteousness, and peace, and love,
To bring forth fruits, joy and eternal bliss.

He ended; and thus Adam last replied;
553 How soon hath thy prediction, seer bless'd,
Measur'd this transient world, the race of time,

---

524 *What will they* What will they do. 540 *respiration* Respite, breathing space. 549 *of endless date* Without end. 553 *seer* Prophet.

Till time stand fixt: beyond is all abyss,   555
Eternity, whose end no eye can reach.
Greatly instructed I shall hence depart,
Greatly in peace of thought, and have my fill
Of knowledge, what this vessel can contain   559
Beyond which was my folly to aspire.   560
Henceforth I learn, that to obey is best,
And love with fear the only God, to walk
As in his presence, ever to observe   563
His providence, and on him sole depend,   564
Merciful over all his works, with good   565
Still overcoming evil, and by small
Accomplishing great things, by things deem'd weak   567
Subverting worldly strong, and worldly wise   568
By simply meek: that suffering for truth's sake   569
Is fortitude to highest victory,   570
And to the faithful death the gate of life;
Taught this by his example, whom I now
Acknowledge my Redeemer ever bless'd.

To whom thus also th'angel last replied:
This having learn'd, thou hast attain'd the sum   575
Of wisdom; hope no higher, though all the stars
Thou knew'st by name, and all th'ethereal powers,
All secrets of the deep, all Nature's works,
Or works of God in heaven, air, earth, or sea,
And all the riches of this world enjoy'dst,   580
And all the rule, one empire; only add
Deeds to thy knowledge answerable, add faith,   582
Add virtue, patience, temperance, add love,

---

559 *vessel* Flannagan cites 2 Timothy 2:21: "If a man therefor purge himself from ["vessels of gold and silver"], he shall be a vessel unto honour, sanctified, and meet for the master's use. . . ." 563 *As* As if. 564.1 *providence* The mediated means by which God will reveal himself to fallen humanity; 564.2 *sole* Alone. 567–569 *by things . . . meek* Another prediction of the reversal of apparent oppositions, anticipating the Sermon on the Mount, when Jesus announces the coming dispensation in which "the weak shall be strong." 582 *answerable* Corresponding.

By name to come call'd charity, the soul
585 Of all the rest: then wilt thou not be loath
To leave this Paradise, but shalt possess
587 A Paradise within thee, happier far.
588 Let us descend now, therefore, from this top
589 Of speculation; for the hour precise
590 Exacts our parting hence; and see the guards,
By me encamp'd on yonder hill, expect
592 Their motion, at whose front a flaming sword,
593 In signal of remove, waves fiercely round:
We may no longer stay. Go, waken Eve;
595 Her also I with gentle dreams have calm'd,
Portending good, and all her spirits compos'd
To meek submission: thou at season fit
Let her with thee partake what thou hast heard,
Chiefly what may concern her faith to know,
600 The great deliverance by her seed to come,
(For by the Woman's Seed) on all mankind;
602 That ye may live, which may be many days,
Both in one faith unanimous though sad,
With cause, for evils past, yet much more cheer'd
605 With meditation on the happy end.

He ended, and they both descend the hill;
607 Descended, Adam to the bower where Eve
Lay sleeping ran before, but found her wak'd;
And thus with words not sad she him receiv'd:

610 Whence thou return'st; and whither went'st I know;
For God is also in sleep, and dreams advise
Which he hath sent propitious, some great good

---

585 *loath* Reluctant.   587 *A Paradise . . . far* Not a psychological paradise, which will be impossible in the fallen world, but the paradise that may be achieved by the soul after death.   588–589 *this top / Of speculation* In both the literal sense of the view from the top of the mountain, and the figurative sense of the apex of theological reasoning.   590 *Exacts* Demands.   592 *motion* Order to move.   593 *remove* Departure.   602 *many days* Adam lived to be 930 (Genesis 5;5).   607 *Descended* Having descended.

The Expulsion from Eden

Presaging, since with sorrow and heart's distress
Wearied I fell asleep: but now lead on;
615 In me is no delay; with thee to go
Is to stay here; without thee here to stay,
Is to go hence unwilling; thou to me
Art all things under heaven, all places thou,
Who for my wilful crime art banish'd hence.
620 This further consolation yet secure
I carry hence; though all by me is lost,
Such favour I unworthy am vouchsaf'd,
By me the promis'd Seed shall all restore.

So spake our mother Eve, and Adam heard
625 Well pleas'd but answer'd not; for now too nigh
Th'archangel stood, and from the other hill
To their fixt station, all in bright array,
The cherubim descended; on the ground
629 Gliding meteorous, as evening mist
630 Risen from a river o'er the marish glides,
631 And gathers ground fast at the labourer's heel
Homeward returning. High in front advanc'd
The brandish'd sword of God before them blaz'd
Fierce as a comet; which with torrid heat,
635 And vapour as the Libyan air adust,
Began to parch that temp'rate clime; whereat
In either hand the hast'ning angel caught
Our lingering parents, and to th'eastern gate
Led them direct, and down the cliff as fast
640 To the subjected plain; then disappear'd.
They, looking back, all th'eastern side beheld
642 Of Paradise, so late their happy seat,
Wav'd over by that flaming brand, the gate
With dreadful faces throng'd and fiery arms:

---

629 *meteorous* As high as meteors; the word is Milton's coinage. 630 *marish* Marsh. 631 *labourer's heel* The postlapsarian sons of Adam are laborers. 635 *adust* Burning. 640 *subjected* Lower. 642 *seat* Home.

Some natural tears they dropp'd, but wip'd them soon.　　645
The world was all before them, where to choose
Their place of rest, and Providence their guide.
They, hand in hand, with wand'ring steps and slow　　648
Through Eden took their solitary way.　　649

THE END

---

648 *wand'ring* With overtones of transgression, which will be the universal fate of humanity from now on.　649 *solitary* Without God's immediate presence; the human couple do, of course, still have each other.

Endnotes

1. (The Argument, p. 11) *the serpent, or rather Satan in the serpent:* The reference is to the Bible (King James Version), Revelation 12:9: "that old serpent, called the Devil, and Satan"; a similar passage appears in Revelation 20:2. Genesis does not refer to Satan by name, but only to a speaking serpent. Milton pointedly refers to the meaning of the serpent, not to the animal that bears its name. His aim is to establish the mediating function of signs by emphasizing that the animal is a symbol.

2. (Book I, ll. 17–22) *And chiefly thou O spirit . . . And mad'st it pregnant:* The Holy Spirit is deliberately differentiated from the "Muse" of line 6. In Genesis 1:2 the Spirit hovers over the abyss before the creation of the universe; in Acts 11:15 and 28:25 the Spirit is the power of God expressed in human language; in Luke 1:35 the Spirit makes Mary pregnant with the Son. For Protestants like Milton, the Holy Spirit was coterminous in human experience with the faculty of interpretation.

3. (Book I, l. 81) *arch-enemy:* In Hebrew "Satan" means "Adversary" or "Accuser"; the Bible frequently uses the word as a general noun, as in Job 1–2, where "the adversary" is found in Heaven consulting with God. The concept of Satan as an autonomous individual is a relatively late development. Even when personified, Satan is not truly independent of God because, as Milton often reminds us, he continues to serve God's purposes. The belief that Satan acts in opposition to God is the fundamental tenet of the Manichaean heresy, a dualistic belief system from early Christianity that contends there is a basic conflict between the good realm of light and the bad realm of darkness. Satan's basic error in *Paradise Lost* is acting in opposition to God.

4. (Book I, ll. 254–255) *The mind is its own place, and in itself / Can make a heaven of hell, a hell of heaven:* As throughout *Paradise Lost*, Satan confuses subjective experience with objective truth. The basic idea that psychological strength, or "virtue," enables its possessor to regard his

external circumstances, or "fortune," with indifference, is Stoic, but Hughes (p. 217) and Campbell (p. 156) (see "For Further Reading") note that a similar heresy to Satan's was expressed by Almaric of Bena, and condemned in 1204. Hughes also cites Jakob Boehme's doctrine that "we have heaven and hell in ourselves."

5. (Book I, ll. 371–373) *the image of a brute . . . And devils to adore for deities:* In other words, the demons will become the idols of the heathen. Milton viewed belief in the autonomous power of images as Satanic because it alienated devotion from the deity, bestowing it instead upon a symbol. The long catalogue of the gods worshiped by the ancient Israelites that follows this passage gives the impression of monotheism beleaguered and surrounded on all sides by heathen practices that constantly threaten to overwhelm it, either by force or by the subtle temptations to which several kings of Israel would succumb. The analogy with Milton's own predicament after the Restoration is clear.

6. (Book I, l. 386) *Jehovah:* The reference is to Yahweh, the God of Israel. The name literally means "I am who I am" (Exodus 3:14), indicating that God is pure subjectivity and pure self-consciousness. In the Hebrew, Genesis ascribes creation to *Elohim,* which is a plural and means "gods." As with Satan, it is only later that this force is personified.

7. (Book I, ll. 404–405) *The pleasant valley of Hinnom, Tophet thence / And black Gehenna called, the type of hell:* Tophet and Gehenna are biblical names for the Valley of Hinnom, sacred to Moloch, a divinity that idolatrous Israelites worshiped. The towns and topography of Palestine frequently play this role, as in Armageddon, Sodom, Jerusalem, and Mounts Sinai and Zion.

8. (Book I, ll. 412–414) *Peor his other name . . . wanton rites, which cost them woe:* En route to the Promised Land, the Israelites encamped at Sittim, where they "began to commit whoredom with the daughters of Moab" (Numbers 25:1), who enticed them to join in the sexualized worship of Baal-Peor; they were punished by God with a plague.

9. (Book I, l. 422) *Baalim, and Ashtaroth:* Baal ("Lord") was the most important Canaanite god, identified with the sun and closely associated with Ashtoreth (Astarte in Greek), goddess of the morning star as well as of war and sexual love; later they were known as Lucifer

and Venus. The plural forms of the names Milton uses here were employed as generic terms for heathen idols.

10. (Book I, ll. 423–431) *For spirits when they please / Can either sex assume, or both; . . . And works of love or enmity fulfil:* The passage is a topical description of the theory explaining that demons could take human form by manipulating and solidifying air. Witch trials of Milton's period abound with accounts of sexual encounter between human beings and demons in male or female form (incubi and succubi, respectively).

11. (Book I, l. 478) *Osiris, Isis, Orus:* The reference is to three Egyptian gods. Osiris, the sun-god, was chopped to pieces by Typhon; his wife, Isis, seeks the scattered pieces of his body throughout the world, and their son Orus eventually revenged his father's death. In *Areopagitica*, his pamphlet defending freedom of expression, Milton uses the myth as a figure for the crucifixion of Christ, and more generally for the dispersed form in which human beings encounter truth.

12. (Book I, ll. 503–505) *Witness the streets of Sodom . . . to avoid worse rape:* In Genesis 19, while Lot and his family are staying in Sodom, they are visited by two angels. The men of the town attempt to rape the angels, and Lot placates them by allowing them to rape his daughters instead. The Sodomites' inhospitable behavior provokes God to destroy their city; Lot and his family are allowed to escape, but his wife disobeys the command not to look back and is turned into a pillar of salt. Like the similar Greek myth of Orpheus and Eurydice, the story was interpreted to represent redemption, as Lot escaped from the city of destruction.

13. (Book I, l. 508) *Javan's issue:* The reference is to the Ionian Greeks, whose creation myth Milton is about to debunk as he shifts his focus from the bestial gods of the heathen tribes around Israel to the less reprehensible anthropomorphic deities of the classical pantheon. In Milton's view, these gods are not opposed to the Christian god but represent biblical truths in allegorical, mythological form. However, worshiping them, as the Greeks did, rather than interpreting them as signs of greater truths, involves literalism: mistaking the sign for the reality.

14. (Book I, l. 512) *Saturn:* In Greek and Roman mythology, Saturn is often equated with Cronus, one of the twelve Titans, the children of Heaven and Earth; he deposed and castrated Uranus, the

personification of Heaven, and was in his turn deposed by Zeus. Saturn's history of unsuccessful rebellion, as well as his name, associates him with Satan. Milton interpreted the war of the Titans against the Olympian gods led by Zeus as a mythological rendering of the fallen angels' rebellion against God.

BOOK II

1. (Book II, l. 59) *The prison of his tyranny:* Satan's basic, mistaken premise is that God is like him. A "tyrant" pursues his own ends rather than those of his subjects, as Satan does. God may appear to do this, but only from a perspective that assumes equality with Him. When God is understood not as a being with whom it is possible to compete, but as the omnipotent force that created and guides the universe, the conclusion that His ends are identical with our own is inescapable.

2. (Book II, l. 174) *His red right hand:* In Horace's *Odes* 1.2.1–4, Jupiter has a "red right hand" when he threatens to destroy Rome; Milton applies this image to the Christian God. The term "right hand" is often used for God in the Old Testament, where it designates God's effectual power, his practical impact on the world (see Exodus 15:6 and Isaiah 48:13). In Christian interpretations of the Bible such as *Paradise Lost*, the Son who sits at the Father's "right hand" (Matthew 22:44, Mark 16:19) also represents this power.

3. (Book II, ll. 650–658) *The one seem'd woman to the waist, and fair. . . . yet there still bark'd, and howl'd / Within, unseen:* Here, unlike in the biblical source (James 1:15), Sin and Death are presented allegorically, to show Milton's association of iconic representation with evil. For example, the "hell-hounds" to which Sin gives birth and which constantly consume her entrails represent the guilt that both causes and is caused by sin. Compare Edmund Spenser's portrayal of Error in *The Faerie Queene* (1590–1596): "Halfe like a serpent horribly displaide, / But th'other halfe did woman's shape retaine" (1.2.14). For Spenser and Milton, as for Plato, all sin was essentially error.

4. (Book II, ll. 664–666) *to dance / With Lapland witches, while the lab'ring moon / Eclipses at their charms:* Witches were thought to be able to influence the course of the moon. Milton's analogy between sin and witches concludes, and Death makes his entrance, at a significant line number: 666 is the "number of the Beast" in Revelation 13. It is not

necessary to excuse Milton's "belief" in witches. Such belief was universal in his lifetime, for the very good reason that witches certainly existed, as they do today. The questions at issue were whether they could truly perform the magical feats of which they boasted and, if so, how. Milton accepts the conventional opinion that they could, because they had made a pact with the devil. Witchcraft and ritual magic in general rest on the assumption that signs, words, and images can be efficacious or performative (that is, capable of having an effect by virtue of being uttered or displayed). For Milton and most of his contemporaries, this connected magic with idolatry, and thus with Satan.

5. (Book II, l. 895) *Chaos:* Milton's Chaos is the abyss of nonmeaning that results from a materialist conception of the universe; this is the worldview of the ancient philosophers Epicurus and Lucretius as well as the scientific thinking of Milton's time. In Ovid's *Metamorphoses* 1.5–20, the warring atoms of Chaos facilitate the monstrous transformations he describes.

6. (Book II, l. 910) *Chance governs all. Into this wild abyss:* The realm of Chaos consists of the materialist descriptions of the universe that were prevalent in Milton's time. Such a conception of creation replaces God's Providence with mere chance, thus producing an "abyss" (in Greek, "no bottom") of meaninglessness. Milton repeats the phrase "wild abyss" at line 917, and Flannagan suggests this may be an example of "Milton nodding" (p. 407). It is more likely, however, that the phrase is repeated for emphasis. In Genesis 1:2 (KJV), the Hebrew *tehom* ("the deep") is translated as "abyss." The English translations of Revelation 9:1-2 render "abyss" as "bottomless pit," and identify it with Hell. Milton does not agree; for him the "abyss" is purely the absence of significance.

7. (Book II, l. 988) *anarch:* This word, which means "chaos," is Milton's coinage. Compare the final lines of Alexander Pope's *The Dunciad* (1728): "Lo, they dread Empire, Chaos! Is restor'd / Light dies before thy uncreating word: / Thy hand, great Anarch, lets the curtain fall; / And Universal Darkness buries All" (4.663–666).

BOOK III

1. (Book III, l. 1) *offspring of heaven first-born:* The reference is to either the Son or the light created by the Son. In Genesis 1:3, light is

God's first creation, but clearly the passage from the poem cannot refer to the light of the sun; it is a pure emanation from God, and can thus be figuratively called the "Son." God's Son was frequently opposed to the material sun, which historically was the prime object of idolatrous veneration and so viewed as a false "son" of God and identified with Satan. Milton's Satan is naturally attracted to the sun, and so is the newly created Adam in book VIII.

2. (Book III, l. 6) *increate:* That is, created in God. Milton holds the heretical Arian opinion that the Son was created by the Father in time, rather than in eternity, as Origen held, and as was declared official doctrine by the fourth-century Council of Nicea. Enlightenment skeptics like Edward Gibbon (1737–1794) mocked the naivete of the early church for allowing such fine theological quibbles to cause war and revolution, but in fact the distinction is of vital importance. The Arian view suggests that the Son is in a relationship of likeness, or resemblance, to the Father—he is an "image"—while Origen's argument indicates that the Son is in a relationship of identity with the Father. The Arian opinion thus accords more closely with Milton's heavy emphasis on humanity's duty to discover the meanings behind images, rather than contemplating the images themselves. In John 5:18 the Jews charge that Jesus is "making himself equal with God," and in *Paradise Lost* Milton makes the desire to "equal" God the cause of Satan's Fall. He thus appears to suggest that the Jews, Satan, and Origen—and thus the entire post-Nicean Christian church—make the identical error of seeing the Son as identical with God, rather than as an image of Him.

3. (Book III, ll. 15–17) *while in my flight / Through utter and through middle darkness borne, / With other notes than to th'Orphean lyre:* One of the Orphic hymns is in praise of Night. The story of Orpheus was very important to Milton; this hero, who had extraordinary musical skills, appears in several of his works (including the poems "L'Allegro," "Il Penseroso," and "Lycidas"). A classical prototype of Christ, Orpheus traveled to Hades, where he played the lyre to induce Pluto to release his wife, Eurydice, but lost her again by disobeying the infernal deity's injunction not to look back at her. This myth is reprised in the biblical story of Lot's wife in Genesis 19. Flannagan finds the mention of

"other notes" to be "a rejection of the classical sources of inspiration, especially of the Muse who failed to save Orpheus" (p. 416).

4. (Book III, ll. 22–24) *but thou / Revisit'st not these eyes, that roll in vain . . . and find no dawn:* Milton had been completely blind since 1652, when he was forty-three. His enemies were quick to attribute his affliction to divine retribution, but in his political tracts and here, Milton defends himself by pointing to the tradition of blind "seers" whose prophetic gifts were the consequence of their lack of physical sight. His lifelong motto was "in weakness my strength is made perfect."

5. (Book III, l. 63) *The radiant image of his glory:* The Son is the image of the Father, but this does not imply inferiority, any more than does the later description of Eve as the "image" of Adam. Milton understood that otherness, or alterity, was necessary to the construction of identity. Satan does not understand this, and finds the suggestion that he was created by a power outside himself insulting.

6. (Book III, l. 189) *soften stony hearts:* The hardening of the heart, as with Pharaoh in the biblical book of Exodus, indicates an inability to interpret the signs sent by God, and was thus associated with literalism in interpretation; conversely, the softening of the heart suggests an openness to the messages of the deity.

7. (Book III, l. 195) *My umpire Conscience:* Right reason allows us to know good from evil, and conscience impels us to act on that knowledge. Hughes notes that conscience "is constantly equated with reason and individual judgment" in Milton's theological work, whereas Flannagan finds here "an emphasis on [conscience] as an allegorical entity or as a manifestation of God." Their views are not incompatible with Milton's syncretic perspective, which uses Plato's concept of the Absolute Idea, which, in turn, makes other ideas possible, to closely connect God and reason. Milton contrasts Conscience with Chaos, who is also described as an "umpire."

8. (Book III, l. 212) *The rigid satisfaction, death for death:* The word "satisfaction" is used in the sense of adequate recompense for a transgression, as in the challenge to a duel: "I demand satisfaction." The idea is that man's subjective choice of death over life requires an objective correlative in the literal death of the Son. The concept of "atonement," which means "making one" or "reconciliation," often

appears in the English Bible and is achieved by Jesus of Nazareth's unification of God and man.

9. (Book III, l. 235) *Indebted:* The financial metaphor of debt and redemption was frequently used to express the consequences of the Fall and the incarnation. This connection also formed the basis for the Aristotelian-scholastic "moral economy"—that is, an economy organized around ethical rather than pragmatic principles—that dominated European economic thought until Milton's time.

10. (Book III, ll. 358–359) *And where the river of bliss through midst of heaven / Rolls o'er Elysian flowers her amber stream:* The image conflates classical and Christian figures for the afterlife. Hughes (pp. 266–267) identifies Milton's river with St. John's vision of a "pure river of water of life, clear as crystal" in Revelation 22:1. But the concept of Elysium is pagan and could be thought of as a rival to the Christian Heaven. See Christopher Marlowe's *Doctor Faustus* (1604): "This word 'damnation' terrifies not me / For I confound Hell in Elysium / My ghost be with the old philosophers" (act 1, scene 3).

11. (Book III, ll. 455–457) *All th'unaccomplish'd works of nature's hand, / Abortive, monstrous, or unkindly mix'd, / Dissolv'd on earth:* Milton seems to hint at the extinction of species, and therefore at evolution. The theory of evolution is ancient, not modern: It was espoused by the Greek philosophers Empedocles and Aristotle. Darwin departed from them by arguing that the competitive adaptation of individual organisms to their environment was the *only* cause of evolution, while previous thinkers, including Milton, had concentrated instead on the intelligent design of a creator as the cause.

12. (Book III, ll. 523–525) *The stairs were then let down . . . His sad exclusion from the doors of bliss:* Satan interprets the stairs literally, and this mistake constitutes his alienation from God. In Silver's reading of this episode, Satan is excluded from Heaven because he does not understand that the staircase is "not an object but a meaning" (p. 262): ". . . it is only when he construes the ladder as proffering actual entry to the celestial fields he mourns, that it seems designed to spite him. For when the expressive or illustrative use of the ladder is ignored, when it is objectified and made instrumental in the physical sense, then it cannot but goad Satan to undertake the impossible yet once more" (p. 263). Milton thus delineates the "violence of magic" (p. 242) and the

"magical mentality in which we expect a correspondence between the nature of *invisibilia* and the things that represent them." To perceive a sign as efficacious—as is done in magic, idolatry, and commodity fetishism—is to forget that it is a sign. Such confusion about the mediating function of representation is for Milton the very definition of apostasy (abandonment of faith).

13. (Book III, ll. 572–575) *The golden sun . . . By centre or eccentric, hard to tell:* Hughes (p. 272) observes: "Editors surmise that Milton hesitates here between the Ptolemaic and Copernican views of the sun respectively as eccentric because not at the center of the universe, or at the *centre*" and Ricks, Campbell, and Flannagan agree. But a stylistic point is also being made: The ethical perversity of Satan's purpose is reflected by the syntactical convolutions that are necessary to describe it.

14. (Book III, ll. 598–605) *a stone besides . . . Drain'd through a limbec to his native form:* The reference is to the "philosophers' stone," "quintessence," or "elixir," which alchemists believed would act as a catalyst to bring the world to the condition of final perfection. Alchemical experiments involved calcifying, or "binding," mercury ("Hermes") and reducing all matter to its original, "native form" of "prime matter" in "limbecs," or test tubes.

BOOK IV

1. (Book IV, l. 37) *Oh sun, to tell thee how I hate thy beams:* Pagan idolatry leads to an adversarial relation to deity. Compare the narrator's preference for internal light at the beginning of book III, and also John 3:20: "Every one that doeth evil hateth the light." Note that Satan does not say he hates the sun itself, but the "beams" of light that emanate from it and remind him of his former state in Heaven.

2. (Book IV, l. 110) *Evil be thou my good:* Leonard cites Stephen Fallon, who notes that in *Leviathan* (1651), English philosopher Thomas Hobbes wrote, "These words of Good, Evil, and Contemptible, are ever used with relation to the person that useth them: There being nothing simply and absolutely so; nor any common Rule of Good and Evil to be taken from the nature of the objects themselves" (Leonard, p. 24). Hobbes connects this moral relativism with the growing power of money, or exchange value, which imposes an arbitrary significance

on, and so occludes, the essential natures of things, their use values or practical purposes.

3. (Book IV, ll. 168–171) *Than Asmodeus . . . there fast bound:* In Tobit 8:3 in the apocrypha of the Bible, the demon Asmodeus kills seven of Sarah's husbands on their wedding nights. Tobit's son, Tobias, is advised by the angel Raphael to burn a fish, and the incense ("fume") drives Asmodeus away to Egypt, where he is "bound."

4. (Book IV, l. 193) *lewd hirelings:* The reference is to unlearned priests who received wages for their labor. The commodification of priestly labor was a basic cause of the Protestant Reformation, and a violent objection to the idea that such labor can be sold informs much of Martin Luther's theology. In his pamphlet *The Likeliest Means to Remove Hirelings*, Milton argues that paying wages to priests inevitably leads to idolatry. See David Hawkes, "The Concept of the 'Hireling' in Milton's Theology," *Milton Studies* 43 (2003).

5. (Book IV, ll. 201–204) *So little knows . . . To worst abuse, or to their meanest use:* These lines are a succinct statement of the contradiction between the meanings, or values, of Heaven and those of earth. To "abuse" something was to wrest it away from its proper purpose, or "use." The word was very common in seventeenth-century religious discourse, and usually designated an idolatrous approach to creation: To "abuse" a religious icon was to worship it.

6. (Book IV, ll. 268–272) *Not that fair field . . . To seek her through the world:* In a tale from Greek mythology that Milton regarded as a prefiguration of the biblical story of Adam and Eve, Proserine (Persephone) was stolen away by Dis (Pluto) while she was gathering flowers near Enna, on what is now the island of Sicily. Her mother, Ceres, sought her release, but Proserine had to return to Hades for half of the year because she had eaten six seeds from the pomegranate of Jove. Renaissance scholars held that, along with the story of Orpheus and Eurydice, this myth anticipates the Christian understanding of sin and redemption.

7. (Book IV, ll. 275–279) *nor that Nyseian isle . . . where old Cham . . . Hid Amalthea, and her florid son, / Young Bacchus, from his stepdame Rhea's eye:* Cham (Ham), the son of Noah, was identified with the Egyptian god Ammon, or "Libyan Jove." Ammon was the father of Bacchus, whom he hid along with the boy's mother, Amalthea, on the

isle of Nysa, near modern Tunisia, to protect them from the vengeance of his wife, Rhea.

8. (Book IV, l. 472) *Whose image thou art:* Eve learns that her own identity is defined in relation to something beyond herself. She is the "image" of Adam in the same sense that Adam is the "image" of God, and the Son is the "image" of the Father. Satan will deny this relational concept of identity, claiming to be "self-begot," because he believes it involves a hierarchy and implies his subjection to a tyrannical other. But in Eden before the Fall, as in Heaven, the subordination of self-identity to an other does not produce relations of dominance and submission.

9. (Book IV, ll. 714–719) *More lovely than Pandora; . . . when to th'unwiser son / Of Japhet brought by Hermes, she insnar'd / Mankind . . . to be aveng'd / On him who had stole Jove's authentic fire:* In Greek mythology, Hermes brought Pandora to Epimetheus ("afterthought"), the "unwiser" brother of Prometheus ("forethought"), both of whom were identified by tradition as the offspring of Japhet, one of the sons Noah begets in the biblical book of Genesis. Milton suggests that the human use of technology (made possible by Prometheus' gift of fire) and the human fixation on physical beauty (Pandora "insnar'd mankind with her fair looks") are both consequences of original sin.

10. (Book IV, l. 750) *wedded love:* Adam and Eve, of course, are not married. Milton did not regard marriage as a sacrament, and in fact considered making a bigamous marriage while he was separated from his first wife, Mary. He believed that the only true marriage took place inside the minds of the couple, and it is in this sense that Adam and Eve are "wedded."

11. (Book IV, l. 767) *Casual fruition:* That is, confusing the Aristotelian model of causality, replacing the final cause, or "fruition," of spiritual love with the material cause of physical lust, and signaled by the reduction of sex to a financial transaction. As Flannagan observes, this "is surely one of the most telling phrases ever written to describe loveless copulation" (p. 466). Milton had a talent for such phrases.

BOOK V

1. (Book V, l. 43) *Shadowy sets off the face of things:* The moon's "shadowy" light seems to "set off," or improve, the world's "face," sug-

gesting the use of cosmetics. Face-painting was regularly castigated by Puritan pamphleteers as an imposition on the divine prerogative of creation, an obtruding of an idolatrous second nature, and as a form of witchcraft.

2. (Book V, ll. 272–274) *A phoenix, gaz'd by all, as that sole bird, / When to inshrine his reliques in the sun's / Bright temple, to Egyptian Thebes he flies:* The mythical phoenix's rebirth from its own ashes, supposed to take place at Thebes, made it a popular metaphor for the human soul ("sole") rising from death. But the facts that the bird is made a spectacle ("gaz'd by all") and that it makes an idolatrous "temple" of the sun give it more dubious connotations. Raphael remains an ambiguous figure.

3. (Book V, ll. 294–295) *For Nature here / Wanton'd as in her prime:* The word "wanton'd" has connotations of dubious sensuality, which the narrative voice ascribes to nature even before the fall. We gather that the narration is made from a postlapsarian perspective. Compare "On the Morning of Christ's Nativity": "It was no season then for her [that is, Nature] / To wanton with the sun, her lusty paramour."

4. (Book V, l. 440) *th'empiric alchemist:* Alchemists developed much of the methodology later used by empirical, Baconian scientists, but their enterprise presupposed nonempirical, ethical significances in the various forms of matter. The word "empiric" is thus derogatory when applied to alchemists.

5. (Book V, ll. 441–442) *holds it possible to turn, / Metals of drossiest ore to perfect gold:* Alchemists sought after gold as the perfect form or *telos* (the end or final cause) of matter. The "elixir" or "philosophers' stone" that would effect this transformation could be used to bring everything in the world to its perfect state, thus reversing the effects of the Fall. Alchemists who tried to make gold in order to become rich were viewed as perverters of the science, because they perceived in gold a quantitative, or financial, rather than a qualitative, or moral, significance.

6. (Book V, ll. 511–512) *In contemplation of created things, / By steps we may ascend to God:* This is an allusion to the idea of creation as a "book of the creatures," by studying which we can learn about the Creator. Once more, there is an unspoken comparison with Satan: Raphael means that we can ascend to *knowledge* of God, while Satan believes he can ascend to *equality* with Him.

7. (Book V, ll. 530–534) *such with him / Finds no acceptance . . . for how / Can hearts not free be tried . . . who will but what they must / By destiny, and can no other choose?:* Compare this passage with the following from Milton's pamphlet on the freedom of the press, *Areopagitica:* "We ourselves esteem not of that obedience, or love, or gift, which is of force. God therefore left free, set before him a provoking object, ever almost in his eyes; herein consisted his merit, herein the right of his reward, the praise of his abstinence" (1. 733). In both passages, Milton says that forced obedience is of no value.

8. (Book V, l. 665) *thought himself impair'd:* As Silver notes (p. 233), Satan's fall occurs when he rejects the idea that he was created a form, figure, or sign expressive of something unlike himself. He does not understand that all creation, himself included, is an image expressive of the divine will. The exaltation of the Son establishes that fact, but Satan feels himself damaged ("impair'd") by this revelation that creation is a sign that refers to something beyond itself. He cannot stomach the prospect of doing obeisance to both Father and Son, to both the Creator and His image in creation.

9. (Book V, l. 784) *To one, and to his image now proclaim'd?:* Satan cannot accept the mediating function of signs; he takes them as autonomous powers in their own right. As Silver puts it (p. 236), due to his idolatrous emphasis on the divine image as against the divine word, on sacramental sign over testamental promise in his very creation, Satan experiences only a further disproportioning, a veiling and removal of God from himself, the apostate's experience of mediation, since the Son now stands between Satan and God, obstructing what was notionally his free and rightful access.

10. (Book V, l. 805) *Abdiel, than whom none with more zeal ador'd:* In Hebrew, the name "Abdiel" means "Servant of God"; by using the word "zeal," Milton associates the character with the Puritans: "Zeal" was a term often used to mock Puritan zealots, such as Ben Jonson's "Rabbi Zeal-of-the-Land Busy" in *Bartholemew Fair* (1614). Since the Puritans had been defeated by the Restoration of King Charles II in 1660, Abdiel's insistence on speaking truth to Satan's power has a topical, as well as an archetypal, relevance. See also 6.147.

BOOK VI

1.　(Book VI, l. 101) *Idol of majesty divine:* The phrase concisely expresses Milton's conflation of images, kingship, and idolatry. Satan looks like the divine majesty, but he is worshiped as if he *were* the divine majesty. Milton thought that monarchy invited idolatry: Because the king's power *resembled* God's authority, people would be tempted to treat the monarch as if he *were* God.

2.　(Book VI, p. 181) *to thyself enthrall'd:* As in his political tracts, Milton argues that the first prerequisite for the exercise of power is interior freedom from vain and base desires. As Flannagan notes: "Satan's decision to commit himself to evil . . . enslave[s] him and anyone who listens to him. The liberty he vaguely brags of is licentiousness, which leads only to a state of slavery to one's own desires" (p. 513).

3.　(Book VI, ll. 291–292) *Or turn this heaven itself into the hell / Thou fablest:* Compare these lines from the passage in Christopher Marlowe's play *Doctor Faustus* (1604) in which the title character tells the devil Mephistopheles, "I think Hell's a fable." Mephistopheles' reply indicates that Faustus can only be convinced by empirical means: "Aye, think so still / Till experience change thy mind" (act 1, scene 5).

4.　(Book VI, ll. 297–301) *for who, though with the tongue / Of angels, can relate . . . Of godlike power?:* Raphael must find appropriate images to convey his meaning, and he takes care to remind Adam that his account must be understood as figural, not literal. His difficulty is expressed by T. S. Eliot in the poem "The Love Song of J. Alfred Prufrock" (1917): "It is impossible to say just what I mean / But as if a magic lantern threw the nerves in patterns on a screen."

5.　(Book VI, ll. 312–315) *Among the constellations war were sprung, . . . and their jarring spheres confound:* We now know that impacts between constellations do indeed exercise profound influence over life on earth. For instance, such collisions produced the meteorite that many scientists believe collided with earth and triggered the climatic changes that caused the extinction of the dinosaurs.

6.　(Book VI, l. 405) *By wound, tho' from their place by violence mov'd:* The angels are susceptible to physical violence, but this does not constitute a true "wound," because their virtue cannot be damaged by external force. Satan is unable to enter the human mind except by a conscious act of will on the part of the person; thus virtue lifts a human being above the reach of his power.

7. (Book VI, l. 568) *So scoffing in ambiguous words:* Ambiguity comes naturally to Satan, as one of his functions is to distort the proper meanings of words and things. God also deploys ambiguity, but the multiple meanings of his pronouncements reinforce each other (for example, 10.80), rather than ironically contradicting each other, as Satan's do here. Furthermore, the double or triple significances of God's sentences arise out of their grammatical construction, whereas Satan merely uses puns, a relatively facile type of ambiguity.

8. (Book VI, ll. 792–793) *Grieving to see his glory, at the sight / Took envy:* The fallen angels limit their understanding to the "sight" of the Son, not His significance. They do not understand that He is the expression of the divine will, and so they interpret the difference between themselves and Him as one of degree, rather than as one of kind. They therefore "envy" his exaltation.

BOOK VII

1. (Book VII, ll. 366–368) *And hence the morning planet gilds her horns; . . . they augment / Their small peculiar:* As Milton's hero Galileo had observed, the morning star, Lucifer, makes the "horns" of its crescent golden by reflecting the light of the sun, thus adding to the small amount of light it produces itself. The suggestion is that Satan merely borrows his glory from God, but there is a hint of complicity in the image, since God allows him to do so. The fact that the moon's light is in fact the reflection of the sun's has often been used for literary effect in the works of writers as far removed in time as William Shakespeare and Vladimir Nabokov.

2. (Book VII, ll. 599–600) *of incense clouds / Fuming from golden censers hid the mount:* Flannagan claims, "The fact that there is incense in Heaven does not mean necessarily that Milton would have approved of the Roman Catholic practice of using incense in church" (p. 557). But there is a notable aura of high church "smells and bells" about the heavenly liturgy, which contrasts strongly with Adam and Eve's spontaneous worship in Eden. Note also that the clouds of incense obscure the mount of God.

3. (Book VII, ll. 604–605) *greater now in thy return / Than from the*

giant angels: That is, from your victory in battle against Satan. As he does at 1.230–237 and 6.643–646, Milton again links the fallen angels to Hesiod's Titans, or Giants, who in Greek mythology fought against Zeus and the Olympian gods. Leonard claims that Milton "implies that the Greek myth is a garbled memory of the angels' rebellion" (p. 391).

BOOK VIII

1.   (Book VIII, ll. 91–97) *the earth / Though, in comparison of heaven, so small, . . . His beams, unactive else, their vigour find:* The earth is superior to the sun, because the purpose of the sun is to serve the earth. The external brightness of the sun should not be taken to indicate that it is valuable in itself; it has value only by virtue of its relation to the earth.

2.   (Book VIII, ll. 272–273) *My tongue obey'd, and readily could name / Whate'er I saw:* Flannagan notes, "The first thing Adam names is the sun, a symbol of creativity and divinity" (p. 569). There may be darker implications here, since the sun is also a favorite symbol for *false* divinity. The sun is the most immediately obvious, physical object to invite primitive idolatry, and we should note that Adam instinctively addresses it as "light," one of Milton's more prominent terms for the Son of God.

3.   (Book VIII, l. 317) *Author of all this thou seest:* This claim to authorship seems dubious. The true "author" of creation is the Son, but He never appears to human beings elsewhere in the poem, and Raphael has repeatedly remarked on the impossibility of representing Him accurately. Satan believes himself to be the rightful Son of God and has made false claims to creative power before.

4.   (Book VIII, ll. 406–407) *none I know / Second to me:* This goes beyond Arianism, apparently dismissing the Son completely, rather than merely denying him coeternal status with the Father. Hughes (p. 372) notes that the line alludes to classical, rather than Christian, conceptions of the unity of the supreme being, as in Horace's *Odes* 1.12.17–18 and Aristotle's *Nicomachean Ethics* 7.14.8.

BOOK IX

1.   (Book IX, ll. 16–17) *or rage / Of Turnus for Lavinia disespous'd:* In Roman mythology, King Turnus makes war on Troy when Lavinia is given in marriage to Aeneas instead of to him. Like the wrath of

Achilles, Turnus' rage is kindled by what he wrongly perceives as feminine infidelity, when in fact Lavinia has no choice. The word "disespous'd" is Milton's coinage and can be translated as "divorced."

2.   (Book IX, ll. 18–19) *Or Neptune's ire or Juno's, that so long / Perplex'd the Greek and Cytherea's son:* "The Greek" is *Odysseus*, who in Homer's Odyssey (9.526-535) angers Poseidon (Neptune) by blinding his son the Cyclops (to whom Milton was unkindly compared). "Cytherea's [Venus'] son" is Aeneas, whom Juno (Hera) hated because Paris had judged his mother, Venus, to be more beautiful.

3.   (Book IX, ll. 21–24) *Of my celestial patroness, who . . . inspires / Easy my unpremeditated verse:* Milton claims to be inspired while he sleeps, by a figure whose identity he keeps deliberately vague. The "celestial patroness" recalls the Holy Spirit, as well as Urania, a muse from Greek mythology, or even an incarnate Platonic Idea such as Dante's Beatrice, but Milton is still concentrating on "the meaning not the name" (see 7.5). He did in fact compose his verse immediately after waking.

4.   (Book IX, ll. 25–26) *this subject for heroic song / Pleas'd me, long choosing, and beginning late:* In these lines Milton is referring to his intention to write an epic while still in his teens. His notebooks show early drafts, but he was distracted from his task when called to the service of the revolution. He did not finish *Paradise Lost* until he was almost sixty.

5.   (Book IX, ll. 30–33) *fabled knights . . . and heroic martyrdom / Unsung:* The events of classical mythology, unlike those of the Bible, are "fabled" and "feigned" in the sense that they are not literally true, but more importantly in the sense that they present as external physical valor qualities that Milton believed were more truly manifested within the psyche.

6.   (Book IX, l. 101) *reforming what was old!:* This is one of several declarations in the poem that what is secondary, or reflected, is actually superior to what is primary, or original. The idea is deeply rooted in Christian thought: It forms the basis of Jesus' sermon on the mount (as told in the Bible, Matthew 5–7), and it was particularly appealing to Protestants, who held that their church was superior to Catholicism precisely because it was engaged in "reforming what was old."

7.   (Book IX, l. 214) *Let us divide our labours:* The growing division of labor was a perceptible phenomenon by the 1660s. Whereas in a

feudal, agricultural society, most people engage in all of the various tasks associated with small-scale farming, a society based on wage labor demands that people specialize in certain narrow areas of expertise. This "division of labor" is the prerequisite for its commodification, whereby people come to conceive of their activity as a thing—"labor"—that can be exchanged for money.

8. (Book IX, l. 440) *reviv'd Adonis:* In Greek mythology, Adonis was a beautiful youth who was killed by a wild boar but revived at the request of Aphrodite, with whom he was allowed to spend part of the year. Leonard notes that "since ancient times, small plots of fast-fading flowers had been called 'gardens of Adonis.' "

9. (Book IX, ll. 529–531) *with serpent tongue . . . His fraudulent temptation thus began:* Satan's habit of approaching women in animal form was well documented in witchcraft trials in Milton's time. The reference here is to Satan assuming the form of a serpent when he appeared to Eve and using the snake's tongue or compressing air sufficiently to make it "vocal" in order to communicate with her. Both fallen and unfallen angels were believed to assume physical form by either possessing a body or solidifying air and molding it into whatever shape they chose.

10. (Book IX, l. 670) *As when of old some orator renown'd:* Milton begins a passage in which he likens Satan to the practitioners of rhetoric in the ancient world, and especially to the Greek Sophists. They were opposed by Socrates because they believed that truth could be established rhetorically, not rationally, and because they sold their skills for money.

11. (Book IX, ll. 673–674) *while each part, / Motion, each act, won audience ere the tongue:* Even before he speaks, Satan wins his audience over with physical gestures. The use of visual techniques to win an argument was anathema to Milton: He would have regarded the advertising methods of modern political campaigns as fundamentally Satanic.

12. (Book IX, l. 924) *That sacred fruit, sacred to abstinence:* Flannagan points out that "Adam diminishes the value of the fruit while in the process of beginning to worship it" (p. 613). Milton regarded the abstinence of monks, nuns, and Catholic priests as an arrogant belief in the saving power of human deeds, or "works righteousness," so he seems to indicate here that Adam's consciousness is already susceptible to idolatry.

13. (Book IX, ll. 1092–1094) *What best may for the present serve to hide / The parts . . . unseemliest seen:* This is a reference to a passage from the Bible, Genesis 3:7, that reads, "And the eyes of both of them were opened, and they knew that they were naked." The Fall has instilled a sense of shame regarding the human body, hence a shame at being mortal and a desire to conceal the reproductive organs. Manichaean sects often discourage reproductive sex, since they believe that the world is evil, having been created by the devil.

BOOK X

1. (Book X, ll. 68–69) *Father Eternal, thine is to decree, / Mine both in heaven and earth to do thy will:* Compare the lines that follow with John 5:22: "The Father judgeth no man, but hath committed all judgment unto the Son." Milton's lines give a concise description of the relationship between Father and Son: The former wills what the latter performs; the Father is the referent, the Son is the sign; and faith consists in the ability to discern the referent in the sign. Satan reveals that he lacks this ability when he describes the Son as usurping his own rightful preeminence; Eve reveals that she lacks it when she fails to perceive Satan within the serpent. Fallen humanity reveals this incapacity every time we take a sign for reality; hence idolatry is the paradigmatic sin.

2. (Book X, ll. 82–84) *the third best absent is condemn'd . . . Conviction to the serpent none belongs:* Milton keeps us in suspense regarding the relation of Satan to the serpent, the referent to the sign. The "third" could refer to either Satan (in which case these lines would mean "Satan has fled from the serpent and can be condemned in his absence; the serpent, though present, is not guilty") or to the serpent (in which case they would mean "there is no need for me to convict the serpent; he has convicted himself by his flight and rebellion"). In 9.784–785, we have been informed that immediately after the Fall, "Back to the thicket slunk / The guilty serpent," but it is unclear whether this constitutes "flight" from an omniscient God (the same is of course true of Satan's "flight" back to Hell). Lines 83 and 84 can also mean "the convicted one (Satan) is no part of the serpent."

3. (Book X, ll. 90–91) *the speed of gods / Time counts not, tho' with swiftest minutes wing'd:* In these lines Milton is saying, "The motion of gods is unquantifiable, qualitatively different from time, even when it

expresses itself in time." He expresses the disjunction between Heaven and earth, and the strangeness of their union, by representing "minutes" as physical wings.

4. (Book X, ll. 129–132) *Whose failing . . . I should conceal, and not expose to blame / By my complaint; but strict necessity / Subdues me:* This performative contradiction expresses the new gap between conscience and action: Adam blames Eve in the act of saying that he should not blame her. Flannagan points out that necessity is described as "the tyrant's plea" at 4.394.

5. (Book X, ll. 164–169) *To judgment he proceeded on th'accurs'd / Serpent . . . justly then accurs'd, / As vitiated in nature:* As Hughes points out, "Satan is said to make a tool of the serpent applying it to a use which was not the *end* (object) of its creation" (p. 410). This would "vitiate" the serpent of its serpentine "nature," thus making God's curse "just" because He applies it not to the serpent but to Satan in the serpent. Compare 9.529–530.

6. (Book X, ll. 216–218) *he clad / Their nakedness with skins of beasts, or slain, / Or as the snake with youthful coat repaid:* The construction with the two "ors" means "either . . . or." The syntax suggests that some animals were "slain" for their coats, while others, such as the snake, were allowed to live and grow new ones. Fowler points out that this makes the Son "the immediate cause" of the first-ever death. He is also the final cause, since the animals' deaths form part of the divine plan, as well as the formal cause and, if He kills the animals Himself, the material cause.

7. (Book X, l. 219) *And thought not much to clothe his enemies:* The snake does not appreciate that Adam and Eve are its "enemies," and so does not mind clothing them. The line is ambiguous, since it indicates that the snake *qua* snake is innocent, while simultaneously reaffirming that it is indeed an enemy.

8. (Book X, ll. 246–249) *Or sympathy, or some connatural force . . . to unite / With secret amity things of like kind / By secretest conveyance:* Sin hints at a "secret" "force" that draws her nature ("kind") together with whatever is "connatural" with it. The repetition of the word "secret" in this passage suggests an occult magical power. Magic works by imposing an artificial unity on diverse phenomena by an idolatrous deployment of signs. For instance, sticking pins into an image of a man

is supposed to harm the man himself, because magic has replaced the referent with the sign.

9. (Book X, l. 251) *For Death from Sin no power can separate:* The proper end, or purpose, of human life is to serve the ends of the soul, which is immortal; but Sin consists in the perversion of human beings away from their proper end; therefore Sin will produce a life that does not serve the ends of the immortal soul; and therefore the soul will die (though it will not cease to exist).

10. (Book X, ll. 307–310) *Xerxes . . . Europe with Asia join'd:* King Xerxes of Persia left his palace at Susa, in what is today southwestern Iran, to invade Greece. He used a bridge of boats to transport his army across the Hellespont, which divides Europe from Asia, and lashed the waves when they destroyed his work. Like his contemporaries, Milton associated Greece with liberty and Persia with "Asiatic" despotism.

11. (Book X, l. 313) *Pontifical:* The word means, literally, "bridge-building," but here it carries an unmistakable suggestion of the Pope, or pontiff. Like most Protestants of his day, Milton regarded the Pope as Antichrist, the earthly or human manifestation of Satan's power, and thus as a kind of conduit between Satan and humanity.

12. (Book X, ll. 431–433) *As when the Tartar from his Russian foe / By Astracan over the snowy plains / Retires:* Ivan the Terrible of Russia, a Christian, took the city of Astracan from Moslem Tartars. Leonard notes: "The simile implies Satanic cunning, since Tartars were famous for shooting arrows to their rear while feigning retreat" (p. 845).

13. (Book X, ll. 433–436) *Bactrian Sophi from the horn / Of Turkish crescent, leaves all waste beyond / The realm of Aladule, in his retreat / To Tauris or Casbeen:* The reference is to Bactria (modern Afghanistan), whose ruler, the Sophi (Shah), was conquered by the Turks, whose emblem was the crescent. The "realm of Aladule" refers to Armenia before it was conquered by the Persians; Tauris and Casbeen were cities in Persia. Flannagan suggests that "Milton may have been naming cities along seventeenth-century trade routes" (p. 637).

14. (Book X, l. 516) *punish'd in the shape he sinn'd:* Since Satan only understands appearances, his punishment can be brought home to him only by means of a physical transformation: Whereas Satan had deceived Eve by falsely collapsing the image of the serpent with the reality of himself, now God ironically collapses sign and referent in re-

ality. The order of significance that Satan had supposed to apply is reversed so that, as Fowler puts is, "just when the devils seem about to become heroes in Satan's epic . . . they turn out instead to be monsters in God's" (p. 213).

15. (Book X, ll. 561–562) *The fruitage fair to sight, like that which grew / Near that bituminous lake where Sodom flam'd:* The Sodomites burned after God showered them with brimstone for their vices; the first-century Jewish historian Josephus reports that the area around the "bituminous lake" (the Dead Sea) where Sodom had been still produced fruit that dissolved into ashes when eaten (*Wars* 4.8.4).

16. (Book X, ll. 578–584) *However some tradition they dispers'd . . . ere yet Dictæan Jove was born:* These lines provide a clear description of Milton's understanding of mythology. The devils themselves "disperse" the heathen tradition that the Titan couple Orphion and Eurynome were expelled from Olympus by Saturn and Rhea (Ops), before Zeus (Jove) was born in Mount Dicte. The identification of Orphion with the serpent in Eden was ancient and traditional. "Eurynome" means "wide-encroaching," and Milton explicitly speculates that she was a mythical expression of the biblical Eve. He claims that the devils inculcate this version of events among the heathen because it robs the story of moral purport by omitting the fact that, unlike the Titans, Satan struggled against an omnipotent Being.

17. (Book X, ll. 668–672) *Some say . . . the sun / Was bid turn reins from th'equinoctial road:* Flannagan observes that the use of "some say" in line 668 and again in line 671 "indicates some lingering uncertainty between a heliocentric and a geocentric order in the universe. Either the earth was pushed off its axis more than twenty degrees, or the Sun's course shifted off the equator" (p. 644).

18. (Book X, ll. 743–744) *Did I request thee, Maker, from my clay / To mould me man?:* This is a reference to a passage from the Bible; Isaiah 45:9 uses the absurdity of the clay disputing with the potter to illustrate the folly of worshiping humanly created objects.

19. (Book X, ll. 746–752) *As my will / Concurr'd not to my being, . . . The good I sought not:* Adam now uses legalistic language to bargain with God, committing the idolatrous and Satanic mistake of questioning his Creator.

20. (Book X, ll. 884–886) *all but a rib . . . More to the part sinister,*

from me drawn: Adam runs through a catalogue of contemporary antifeminist arguments, including a reference to a "rib crooked by nature, bent," which alludes to the fact that Eve was created from Adam's rib, commonly thought to be from his left, or "sinister," side. The fact that he does so immediately after the Fall, while in the grip of passion and anger, can be taken to suggest that Milton considered such diatribes as misguided responses to temptation.

21. (Book X, l. 890) *spirits masculine:* Here, Adam assumes that angels are male, but in book I, lines 423–424 inform us that "spirits when they please / Can either sex assume, or both." Flannagan and Leonard cites this as proof that Adam is mistaken here, but the lines from book I are used in the context of describing the fallen angels who become the gods of the heathen. The fact that Raphael assures Adam that angels have gender does not, of course, preclude their all being male.

BOOK XI

1. (Book XI, l. 89) *Good by itself, and evil not at all:* This suggests a departure for the doctrine of *felix culpa,* the fortunate fall, that Milton appears to endorse elsewhere, and which suggests that, having been allowed by God, the fall must be a good thing. In *Areopagitica,* his pamphlet on freedom of the press, Milton argues that it is impossible for human beings to know good without also knowing evil, since the two concepts are mutually definitive.

2. (Book XI, l. 182) *Nature first gave signs:* Hughes claims that the animals begin to prey on each other as an indication of the Fall in nature; Fowler argues that such signs are portents of the expulsion from Eden. The two readings do not seem incompatible.

3. (Book XI, l. 389) *Temir's throne:* "Temir" is the fourteenth-century Tartar ruler "Timur the lame," otherwise known as Tamburlaine. He would have been familiar to Milton from Christopher Marlowe's play, *Tamburlaine the Great* (1587), in which he embodies worldly, atheistic ambition. His capital was at Samarkand, near the river Oxus, in modern Uzbekistan.

4. (Book XI, l. 622) *sons of God:* This is an allusion to Genesis 6:2: "The sons of God saw the daughters of men that they were fair; and they took them wives of all which they chose." As Leonard observes, Milton "here follows a patristic tradition identifying the sons

of God with Seth's descendants. Elsewhere [as in 5.446–450] he adopts a rival tradition that saw the sons of God as fallen angels" (p. 861).

5. (Book XI, ll. 797–801) *The conquer'd ... Against invaders:* Campbell notes that "Milton's description is designed to embrace the seventeenth century as well as the time of the flood." Hughes sees "an attack on time servers in [Milton's] own party." Leonard opines that Milton "is probably alluding to the backsliding Englishmen who had betrayed the English Commonwealth in 1660," while Flannagan claims that "Milton seems to be castigating his countrymen for lacking the courage of the religious convictions expressed during the Interregnum."

BOOK XII

1. (Book XII, l. 24) *till one shall rise:* The reference is to Nimrod (the name supposedly derives from the Hebrew for "rebel"), the archetypal tyrant who in Genesis 10:8–10 is described as "a mighty one in the earth." Nimrod was one of the descendants of Ham, and therefore cursed by God as a "servant of servants." Milton believed that tyrants were in fact slaves to their own desires.

2. (Book XII, l. 216) *not the readiest way:* This passage alludes to the title of Milton's final political tract, *The Readie and Easie Way to Establish a Free Comonwealth* (1660). The English people did not follow this pamphlet's directions to the political promised land, but preferred what Milton considered to be the Egyptian bondage of the restored monarchy.

3. (Book XII, l. 511) *lucre:* The word means "money." Milton opposed the commodification of priestly labor throughout his career, most notably in his pamphlet *Considerations of the Likeliest Means to Remove Hirelings* (1659). Flannagan is too mild when he describes this tract as directed against "prelates working only for the wages"; in fact, it opposes any and all remuneration of priests by wages, since the equation of priestly labor with a sum of money was in itself a form of idolatry.

Inspired by *Paradise Lost*

In addition to the watercolors of William Blake (1757–1827), which appear in this volume, many illustrators have taken *Paradise Lost* into the visual dimension. From Bernard Lens (1682–1740) to J. M. W. Turner (1775–1851), artists have created images inspired by Milton's epic. They bring a variety of styles to bear—sometimes Eve appears Rubenesque, sometimes the angels loom larger than the humans. Richard Westall (1765–1836) created engravings for two editions of *Paradise Lost* featuring dazzling angels and robust, well-muscled Eden-dwellers. In the paintings of Francis Hayman (1708–1776) the setting spills over with beasts: a dog, a lamb, a goat, a lion, and birds nesting in trees. The serpent of Edward Burney (1760–1848) probably qualifies as the most anthropomorphic, with his hair, ears, human-like eyes, lips that appear duplicitous, and a nearly upright posture. In the comparatively minimal illustrations of John B. Medina (1655–1710), figures traverse a mythological landscape filled with giant birds, walking skeletons, and cherub-like devils, while the *Paradise Lost* mezzotints of John Martin (1789–1854) portray a war between good and evil, light and dark, open skies and subterranean caves.

Swiss artist Henry Fuseli (1741–1825), who made his reputation with stunning illustrations of Shakespeare's work, brings to his *Paradise Lost* images a love of light, contrast, the supernatural, the classical human form, and man's darkest passions. The lack of color in Fuseli's engravings heightens the drama of the expulsions of Satan and of Adam and Eve, and the muscular energy in the two original human figures brilliantly conveys high drama, as well as their mutual devotion in the face of banishment. French illustrator Gustav Doré (1832–1883), famous for his biblical renderings, completed a series of fifty plates depicting *Paradise Lost* in 1865. The black-and-white engravings, typical of Doré's detailed and brooding style, are reminiscent of his illustrations for Dante's *Divine Comedy*. Doré imagines a darkly shaded, bat-winged Satan falling from the sky, a Heaven ringed by teams of impressive angels, and a windswept Moses clutching an upraised stone tablet.

As a sequel to his masterpiece, Milton wrote *Paradise Regained* (1671). *Paradise Lost* culminates with Satan's successful temptation of Adam and Eve, and *Paradise Regained* offers a New Testament–based resolution, in which Jesus is tempted in the wilderness but ultimately resists Satan. This four-book work, though ostensibly a sequel to the rich and sonorous *Paradise Lost*, unfolds in an unadorned, almost unpoetic style, and its action is more limited.

Milton's stature in the English poetic canon is nothing less than gigantic; his poetry—especially *Paradise Lost*—is second only to that of Shakespeare. Milton exerted great influence upon later poets. In 1667, the year *Paradise Lost* was published, John Dryden published *The State of Innocence, and Fall of Man*, a rhyming operatic adaptation of the epic. Throughout the eighteenth century, Milton's style was emulated by poets who sought to codify the sublime in their works. His influence even carried over to music; Franz Joseph Haydn based the German-language libretto for his oratorio *The Creation* (1798) on the book of Genesis and Milton's epic. The early English Romantic poets transferred Milton's notion of the sublime as reflected in the angels and their deeds to their own lives, a trend that reached its zenith with William Wordsworth's autobiographical epic *The Prelude* (1805).

Indeed, Milton's influence on the Romantics was unparalleled. For William Blake, Samuel Taylor Coleridge, John Keats, Lord Byron, and Percy Bysshe Shelley, *Paradise Lost* was as the Bible: sacred and known by rote. Shelley's greatest work, *Prometheus Unbound* (1820), is a poetic braiding of Aeschylus' *Prometheus Bound* with *Paradise Lost*, in particular Milton's character of Satan, whom Shelley considered the true hero of the drama. Shelley's wife Mary, in her first and greatest novel, *Frankenstein* (1818), draws on themes from *Paradise Lost* throughout. The novel's inscription is from the tenth book of Milton's poem:

> Did I request thee, Maker, from my clay
> To mould me man? Did I solicit thee
> From darkness to promote me? (10.743–745).

In 1897 English writer Thomas Hardy wrote one of his best-known poems—one that celebrates the geniuses of Edward Gibbon, author of *The History of the Decline and Fall of the Roman Empire* (1776–1788), and of Milton. In "Lausanne, In Gibbon's Old Garden: 11–12 P.M.," Hardy likens the fall of civilizations to man's fall from grace.

A spirit seems to pass,
Formal in pose, but grave and grand withal:
He contemplates a volume stout and tall,
And far lamps fleck him through the thin acacias.

Anon the book is closed,
With "It is finished!" And at the alley's end
He turns, and soon on me his glances bend,
As, as from earth, comes speech—small, muted, yet composed.

"How fares the Truth now?—Ill?
—Do pens but slily further her advance?
May one not speed her but in phrase askance?
Do scribes aver the Comic to be Reverend still?

"Still rule those minds on earth
At whom sage Milton's wormwood words were hurled:
'Truth like a bastard comes into the world
Never without ill-fame to him who gives her birth'?"

Comments & Questions

In this section, we aim to provide the reader with an array of perspectives on the text, as well as questions that challenge those perspectives. The commentary has been culled from sources as diverse as reviews contemporaneous with the work, letters written by the author, literary criticism of later generations, and appreciations written throughout the work's history. Following the commentary, a series of questions seeks to filter John Milton's Paradise Lost *through a variety of points of view and bring about a richer understanding of this enduring work.*

Comments

Thomas Gray

> Some village Hampden, that with dauntless breast
> The little tyrant of his fields withstood;
> Some mute inglorious Milton here may rest,
> Some Cromwell guiltless of his country's blood.
> —from *Elegy Written in a Country Churchyard* (1751)

William Blake

The reason Milton wrote in fetters when he wrote of Angels and God, and at liberty when of Devils and Hell, is because he was a true poet and of the Devil's party without knowing it.
> —from *The Marriage of Heaven and Hell* (1793)

William Wordsworth

> Milton! thou shouldst be living at this hour:
> England hath need of thee: she is a fen
> Of stagnant waters.
> —from "London, 1802" (1807)

Samuel Taylor Coleridge

While [Shakespeare] darts himself forth and passes into all the forms of human character and passion, the one Proteus of the fire and the flood, [Milton] attracts all forms and things to himself, into the unity of his own *Ideal*. All things and modes of action shape themselves anew in the being of Milton; while Shakespeare becomes all things, yet for ever remaining himself.

—from *Biographia Literaria* (1817)

Percy Bysshe Shelley

Nothing can exceed the energy and magnificence of the character of Satan as expressed in "Paradise Lost." It is a mistake to suppose that he could ever have been intended for the popular personification of evil. Implacable hate, patient cunning, and a sleepless refinement of device to inflict the extremist anguish on an enemy, these things are evil; and, although venial in a slave, are not to be forgiven in a tyrant; although redeemed by much that ennobles his defeat in one subdued, are marked by all that dishonors his conquest in the victor. Milton's Devil as a moral being is as far superior to his God as one who perseveres in some purpose which he has conceived to be excellent in spite of adversity and torture is to one who in the cold security of undoubted triumph inflicts the most horrible revenge upon his enemy, not from any mistaken notion of inducing him to repent of a perseverance in enmity, but with the alleged design of exasperating him to deserve new torments. Milton has so far violated the popular creed (if this shall be judged to be a violation) as to have alleged no superiority of moral virtue to his God over his Devil. And this bold neglect of a direct moral purpose is the most decisive proof of the supremacy of Milton's genius. He mingled as it were the elements of human nature as colors upon a single pallet, and arranged them in the composition of his great picture according to the laws of epic truth; that is, according to the laws of that principle by which a series of actions of the external universe and of intelligent and ethical beings is calculated to excite the sympathy of succeeding generations of mankind.

—from "A Defence of Poetry" (1821)

Thomas Carlyle

No great man ever felt so great a consciousness as Milton. That consciousness was the measure of his greatness; he was not one of those who reach into actual contact with the deep fountain of greatness. His "Paradise Lost" is not an epic in its composition as Shakespeare's utterances are epic. It does not come out of the heart of things; he hadn't it lying there to pour it out in one gush; it seems rather to have been welded together afterward. His sympathies with things are much narrower than Shakespeare's—too sectarian. In universality of mind there is no hatred; it doubtless rejects what is displeasing, but not in hatred for it. Everything has a right to exist. Shakespeare was not polemical: Milton was polemical altogether.

Milton's disquisitions on these subjects are quite wearisome to us now. "Paradise Lost" is a very ambitious poem, a great picture painted on huge canvas; but it is not so great a thing as to concentrate our minds upon the deep things within ourselves as Dante does, to show what a beautiful thing the life of man is; it is to travel with paved streets beside us rather than lakes of fire. This Dante has done, and Milton not. There is no life in Milton's characters. Adam and Eve are beautiful, graceful objects, but no one has breathed the Pygmalion life into them; they remain cold statues. Milton's sympathies were with things rather than with men, the scenery and phenomena of nature, the trim gardens, the burning lake; but as for the phenomena of the mind, he was not able to see them. He has no delineations of mind except Satan, of which we may say that Satan was his own character, the black side of it.

—from *Lectures on the History of Literature* (1892)

T. S. Eliot

In the seventeenth century a dissociation of sensibility set in, from which we have never recovered; and this dissociation, as is natural, was aggravated by the influence of the two most powerful poets of the century, Milton and Dryden.

—from *The Metaphysical Poets* (1921)

H. L. Mencken

There are no mute, inglorious Miltons, save in the hallucination of poets. The one sound test of a Milton is that he functions as a Milton.

—from *Prejudices, Third Series* (1922)

A. E. Housman

> Oh many a peer of England brews
> Livelier liquor than the Muse,
> And malt does more than Milton can
> To justify God's ways to man.

—from *Last Poems* (1922)

Questions

1. William Blake wrote that "the reason Milton wrote in fetters when he wrote of Angels and God, and at liberty when of Devils and Hell, is because he was a true poet and of the Devil's party without knowing it." There is an interesting argument here: (1) true poets are of the Devil's party; (2) Milton was a true poet; thus (3) Milton was of the devil's party. Are any of these three steps true?

2. Percy Bysshe Shelley wrote: "Milton's Devil as a moral being is as far superior to his God as one who perseveres in some purpose which he has conceived to be excellent in spite of perversity and torture is to one who in the cold security of undoubted triumph inflicts the most horrible revenge upon his enemy . . . with the alleged design of exasperating him to deserve new torments." Take the position of a defense lawyer or a prosecutor and argue for or against Shelley. Has he committed heresy by placing Milton's Devil above God?

3. According to Milton, all of humanity is to suffer because of Eve's initial act of disobedience. Is that fair? Remember that God, who is omniscient, knew in advance that Adam and Eve would fall. Why did he not prevent their fall and save us all a lot of misery?

4. Was Milton sexist? Does he treat Adam differently than Eve? What if it had been Adam who first ate the forbidden apple?

5. Just after he associates Satan with idolatry, materialism, and hedonism, David Hawkes writes: "There is a good case to be made that the power Milton calls 'Satan' has, in the twenty-first century, finally conquered the world. *Paradise Lost* is the prophetic story of how he has achieved his triumph. There could be no idea less 'dead' than that." Do you agree? Whether you agree or disagree, what are your evidence and your arguments? Do you have a better idea of who or what Satan is today?

For Further Reading

Biographies

Brown, Cedric C. *John Milton: A Literary Life.* New York: St. Martin's Press, 1995.

Hill, Christopher. *Milton and the English Revolution.* London: Faber and Faber, 1977.

Lewalski, Barbara. *The Life of John Milton: A Critical Biography.* Oxford and Malden, MA: Blackwell, 2000.

Parker, William Riley. *Milton: A Biography.* Second edition; revised version edited by Gordon Campbell. Oxford: Clarendon Press; New York: Oxford University Press, 1996.

Editions

Campbell, Gordon, ed. *John Milton: The Complete Poems.* New edition; text edited by B. A. Wright; introduction and notes by Gordon Campbell. Everyman's Library. London: J. M. Dent, 1980.

Flannagan, Roy, ed. *The Riverside Milton.* Boston: Houghton Mifflin, 1998.

Fowler, Alistair, ed. *Paradise Lost.* 1971. Second edition. London: Longman, 1998.

Hughes, Merritt Y., ed. *John Milton: Complete Poems and Major Prose.* New York: Odyssey Press, 1957.

Leonard, John, ed. *John Milton: The Complete Poems.* London and New York: Penguin, 1998.

Prince, F. T. *Paradise Lost Books I and II.* 1962. Oxford: Oxford University Press, 1997.

Ricks, Christopher, ed. *Paradise Lost and Paradise Regained.* New York: New American Library, 1968.

Shawcross, John T., ed. *The Complete Poetry of John Milton.* Garden City, NY: Anchor-Doubleday, 1971.

Collections of Essays

Benet, Diana, and Lieb, Michael, eds. *Literary Milton: Text, Pretext, Context.* Pittsburgh, PA: Duquesne University Press, 1994.

Bradford, Richard. *The Complete Critical Guide to John Milton.* London and New York: Routledge, 2001.

Corns, Thomas N., ed. *A Companion to Milton.* Oxford and Malden, MA: Blackwell, 2001.

Danielson, Dennis, ed. *The Cambridge Companion to Milton.* Second edition. Cambridge and New York: Cambridge University Press, 1999.

Dobranski, Stephen, and Rumrich, John, eds. *Milton and Heresy.* Cambridge and New York: Cambridge University Press, 1998.

Elledge, Scott. *Paradise Lost.* Second edition. New York: W. W. Norton, 1993.

Parry, Graham, and Raymond, Joad, eds. *Milton and the Terms of Liberty.* Cambridge and Rochester, NY: D. S. Brewer, 2002.

Rajan, Balachandra, and Sauer, Elizabeth, eds. *Milton and the Imperial Vision.* Pittsburgh, PA: Duquesne University Press, 1999.

Stanwood, P. G., ed. *Of Poetry and Politics: New Essays on Milton and His World.* Binghamton, NY: Medieval and Renaissance Texts and Studies, 1995.

Zunder, William, ed. *Paradise Lost: Contemporary Critical Essays.* New York: Palgrave, 1999.

Critical Monographs

Achinstein, Sharon. *Milton and the Revolutionary Reader.* Princeton, NJ: Princeton University Press, 1994.

Cable, Lana. *Carnal Rhetoric: Milton's Iconoclasm and the Poetics of Desire.* Durham, NC: Duke University Press, 1995.

Corns, Thomas. *Regaining Paradise Lost.* London and New York: Longman, 1994.

Empson, William. *Milton's God.* Cambridge and New York: Cambridge University Press, 1981.

Evans, J. Martin. *Milton's Imperial Epic: "Paradise Lost" and the Discourse of Colonialism.* Ithaca, NY: Cornell University Press, 1996.

Fallon, Robert Thomas. *Divided Empire: Milton's Political Imagery.* University Park, PA: Pennsylvania State University Press, 1995.

Fish, Stanley. *How Milton Works.* Cambridge, MA: Belknap Press, 2001.

Gregerson, Linda. *The Reformation of the Subject: Spenser, Milton, and the English Protestant Epic.* Cambridge and New York: Cambridge University Press, 1995.

Hardin, Richard F. *Civil Idolatry: Desacralizing and Monarchy in Spenser, Shakespeare, and Milton.* Newark: University of Delaware Press, 1992.

Haskin, Dayton. *Milton's Burden of Interpretation.* Philadelphia: University of Pennsylvania Press, 1994.

Hawkes, David. *Idols of the Marketplace: Idolatry and Commodity Fetishism in English Literature, 1580–1680.* New York: Palgrave, 2001.

Hoxby, Blair. *Mammon's Music: Literature and Economics in the Age of Milton.* New Haven, CT: Yale University Press, 2002.

Jordan, Matthew. *Milton and Modernity: Politics, Masculinity, and Paradise Lost.* New York: Palgrave, 2001.

King, John N. *Milton and Religious Controversy: Satire and Polemic in "Paradise Lost."* Cambridge and New York: Cambridge University Press, 2000.

Knoppers, Laura L. *Historicizing Milton: Spectacle, Power, and Poetry in Restoration England.* Athens: University of Georgia Press, 1994.

Kolbrener, William. *Milton's Warring Angels: A Study of Critical Engagements.* Cambridge and New York: Cambridge University Press, 1997.

Leonard, John. *Naming in Paradise: Milton and the Language of Adam and Eve.* Oxford: Clarendon Press, 1990.

Lieb, Michael. *Milton and the Culture of Violence.* Ithaca, NY: Cornell University Press, 1994.

Loewenstein, David. *Representing Revolution in Milton and His Contemporaries: Religion, Politics, and Polemics in Radical Puritanism.* Cambridge and New York: Cambridge University Press, 2001.

Norbrook, David. *Writing the English Republic: Poetry, Rhetoric, and Politics, 1627–1660.* Cambridge and New York: Cambridge University Press, 1999.

Rogers, John. *The Matter of Revolution: Science, Poetry, and Politics in the Age of Milton.* Ithaca, NY: Cornell University Press, 1996.

Rosenblatt, Jason P. *Torah and Law in "Paradise Lost."* Princeton, NJ: Princeton University Press, 1994.

Rumrich, John. *Milton Unbound: Controversy and Reinterpretation.* Cambridge and New York: Cambridge University Press, 1996.

Rushdy, A. H. A. *The Empty Garden: The Subject of Late Milton.* Pittsburgh, PA: University of Pittsburgh Press, 1992.

Schwartz, Regina. *Remembering and Repeating: On Milton's Theology and Politics.* Chicago: University of Chicago Press, 1993.

Shawcross, John T. *John Milton: The Self and the World.* Lexington: University Press of Kentucky, 1993.

Shifflett, Andrew Eric. *Stoicism, Politics, and Literature in the Age of Milton: War and Peace Reconciled.* Cambridge and New York: Cambridge University Press, 1998.

Shoulson, Jeffery S. *Milton and the Rabbis: Hebraism, Hellenism, and Christianity.* New York: Columbia University Press, 2001.

Silver, Victoria. *Imperfect Sense: The Predicament of Milton's Irony.* Princeton, NJ: Princeton University Press, 2001.

Smith, Nigel. *Literature and Revolution in England, 1640–1660.* New Haven, CT: Yale University Press, 1994.

Wittreich, Joseph. *Feminist Milton.* Ithaca, NY: Cornell University Press, 1987.

Zagorin, Perez. *Milton: Aristocrat and Rebel: The Poet and His Politics.* Rochester, NY: D. S. Brewer, 1992.

Look for the following titles, available now from
BARNES & NOBLE CLASSICS

Adventures of Huckleberry Finn	Mark Twain	1-59308-112-X	$6.95
The Adventures of Tom Sawyer	Mark Twain	1-59308-139-1	$6.95
The Aeneid	Vergil	1-59308-237-1	$7.95
Aesop's Fables		1-59308-062-X	$5.95
The Age of Innocence	Edith Wharton	1-59308-143-X	$5.95
Agnes Grey	Anne Brontë	1-59308-323-8	$5.95
Alice's Adventures in Wonderland and Through the Looking-Glass	Lewis Carroll	1-59308-015-8	$5.95
Anna Karenina	Leo Tolstoy	1-59308-027-1	$8.95
The Arabian Nights	Anonymous	1-59308-281-9	$9.95
The Art of War	Sun Tzu	1-59308-017-4	$7.95
The Autobiography of an Ex-Colored Man and Other Writings	James Weldon Johnson	1-59308-289-4	$5.95
The Awakening and Selected Short Fiction	Kate Chopin	1-59308-113-8	$6.95
Babbitt	Sinclair Lewis	1-59308-267-3	$7.95
The Beautiful and Damned	F. Scott Fitzgerald	1-59308-245-2	$7.95
Beowulf	Anonymous	1-59308-266-5	$4.95
Billy Budd and The Piazza Tales	Herman Melville	1-59308-253-3	$5.95
Bleak House	Charles Dickens	1-59308-311-4	$9.95
The Bostonians	Henry James	1-59308-297-5	$7.95
The Brothers Karamazov	Fyodor Dostoevsky	1-59308-045-X	$9.95
Bulfinch's Mythology	Thomas Bulfinch	1-59308-273-8	$12.95
The Call of the Wild and White Fang	Jack London	1-59308-200-2	$5.95
Candide	Voltaire	1-59308-028-X	$4.95
The Canterbury Tales	Geoffrey Chaucer	1-59308-080-8	$9.95
A Christmas Carol, The Chimes and The Cricket on the Hearth	Charles Dickens	1-59308-033-6	$5.95
The Collected Oscar Wilde		1-59308-310-6	$9.95
The Collected Poems of Emily Dickinson		1-59308-050-6	$5.95
Common Sense and Other Writings	Thomas Paine	1-59308-209-6	$6.95
The Communist Manifesto and Other Writings	Karl Marx and Friedrich Engels	1-59308-100-6	$5.95
The Complete Sherlock Holmes, Vol. I	Sir Arthur Conan Doyle	1-59308-034-4	$7.95
The Complete Sherlock Holmes, Vol. II	Sir Arthur Conan Doyle	1-59308-040-9	$7.95
Confessions	Saint Augustine	1-59308-259-2	$6.95
A Connecticut Yankee in King Arthur's Court	Mark Twain	1-59308-210-X	$7.95
The Count of Monte Cristo	Alexandre Dumas	1-59308-151-0	$7.95
The Country of the Pointed Firs and Selected Short Fiction	Sarah Orne Jewett	1-59308-262-2	$6.95
Crime and Punishment	Fyodor Dostoevsky	1-59308-081-6	$8.95
Daisy Miller and Washington Square	Henry James	1-59308-105-7	$4.95
Daniel Deronda	George Eliot	1-59308-290-8	$8.95
Dead Souls	Nikolai Gogol	1-59308-092-1	$7.95
The Deerslayer	James Fenimore Cooper	1-59308-211-8	$7.95

(continued)

Title	Author	ISBN	Price
Don Quixote	Miguel de Cervantes	1-59308-046-8	$9.95
Dracula	Bram Stoker	1-59308-114-6	$6.95
Emma	Jane Austen	1-59308-152-9	$6.95
Essays and Poems by Ralph Waldo Emerson		1-59308-076-X	$6.95
Essential Dialogues of Plato		1-59308-269-X	$9.95
The Essential Tales and Poems of Edgar Allan Poe		1-59308-064-6	$7.95
Ethan Frome and Selected Stories	Edith Wharton	1-59308-090-5	$5.95
Fairy Tales	Hans Christian Andersen	1-59308-260-6	$9.95
Far from the Madding Crowd	Thomas Hardy	1-59308-223-1	$7.95
The Federalist	Hamilton, Madison, Jay	1-59308-282-7	$7.95
Founding America: Documents from the Revolution to the Bill of Rights	Jefferson, et al.	1-59308-230-4	$9.95
Frankenstein	Mary Shelley	1-59308-115-4	$4.95
The Good Soldier	Ford Madox Ford	1-59308-268-1	$6.95
Great American Short Stories: From Hawthorne to Hemingway	Various	1-59308-086-7	$7.95
The Great Escapes: Four Slave Narratives	Various	1-59308-294-0	$6.95
Great Expectations	Charles Dickens	1-59308-116-2	$6.95
Grimm's Fairy Tales	Jacob and Wilhelm Grimm	1-59308-056-5	$7.95
Gulliver's Travels	Jonathan Swift	1-59308-132-4	$5.95
Hard Times	Charles Dickens	1-59308-156-1	$5.95
Heart of Darkness and Selected Short Fiction	Joseph Conrad	1-59308-123-5	$5.95
The History of the Peloponnesian War	Thucydides	1-59308-091-3	$9.95
The House of Mirth	Edith Wharton	1-59308-153-7	$6.95
The House of the Dead and Poor Folk	Fyodor Dostoevsky	1-59308-194-4	$7.95
The Idiot	Fyodor Dostoevsky	1-59308-058-1	$7.95
The Iliad	Homer	1-59308-232-0	$7.95
The Importance of Being Earnest and Four Other Plays	Oscar Wilde	1-59308-059-X	$6.95
Incidents in the Life of a Slave Girl	Harriet Jacobs	1-59308-283-5	$5.95
The Inferno	Dante Alighieri	1-59308-051-4	$6.95
The Interpretation of Dreams	Sigmund Freud	1-59308-298-3	$8.95
Ivanhoe	Sir Walter Scott	1-59308-246-0	$7.95
Jane Eyre	Charlotte Brontë	1-59308-117-0	$7.95
Journey to the Center of the Earth	Jules Verne	1-59308-252-5	$4.95
Jude the Obscure	Thomas Hardy	1-59308-035-2	$6.95
The Jungle Books	Rudyard Kipling	1-59308-109-X	$5.95
The Jungle	Upton Sinclair	1-59308-118-9	$6.95
King Solomon's Mines	H. Rider Haggard	1-59308-275-4	$4.95
Lady Chatterley's Lover	D. H. Lawrence	1-59308-239-8	$6.95
The Last of the Mohicans	James Fenimore Cooper	1-59308-137-5	$5.95
Leaves of Grass: First and "Death-bed" Editions	Walt Whitman	1-59308-083-2	$9.95
The Legend of Sleepy Hollow and Other Writings	Washington Irving	1-59308-225-8	$6.95
Les Misérables	Victor Hugo	1-59308-066-2	$9.95
Les Liaisons Dangereuses	Pierre Choderlos de Laclos	1-59308-240-1	$7.95
Little Women	Louisa May Alcott	1-59308-108-1	$6.95
Lost Illusions	Honoré de Balzac	1-59308-315-7	$9.95
Madame Bovary	Gustave Flaubert	1-59308-052-2	$6.95
Maggie: A Girl of the Streets and Other Writings about New York	Stephen Crane	1-59308-248-7	$6.95

The Magnificent Ambersons	Booth Tarkington	1-59308-263-0	$7.95
Main Street	Sinclair Lewis	1-59308-386-6	$7.95
Man and Superman and Three Other Plays	George Bernard Shaw	1-59308-067-0	$7.95
The Man in the Iron Mask	Alexandre Dumas	1-59308-233-9	$8.95
Mansfield Park	Jane Austen	1-59308-154-5	$5.95
The Mayor of Casterbridge	Thomas Hardy	1-59308-309-2	$5.95
The Metamorphoses	Ovid	1-59308-276-2	$7.95
The Metamorphosis and Other Stories	Franz Kafka	1-59308-029-8	$6.95
Moby-Dick	Herman Melville	1-59308-018-2	$9.95
Moll Flanders	Daniel Defoe	1-59308-216-9	$5.95
My Ántonia	Willa Cather	1-59308-202-9	$5.95
My Bondage and My Freedom	Frederick Douglass	1-59308-301-7	$6.95
Narrative of Sojourner Truth		1-59308-293-2	$6.95
Narrative of the Life of Frederick Douglass, an American Slave		1-59308-041-7	$4.95
Nicholas Nickleby	Charles Dickens	1-59308-300-9	$8.95
Night and Day	Virginia Woolf	1-59308-212-6	$7.95
Nostromo	Joseph Conrad	1-59308-193-6	$7.95
O Pioneers!	Willa Cather	1-59308-205-3	$5.95
The Odyssey	Homer	1-59308-009-3	$5.95
Oliver Twist	Charles Dickens	1-59308-206-1	$6.95
The Origin of Species	Charles Darwin	1-59308-077-8	$7.95
Paradise Lost	John Milton	1-59308-095-6	$7.95
The Paradiso	Dante Alighieri	1-59308-317-3	$7.95
Pere Goriot	Honoré de Balzac	1-59308-285-1	$7.95
Persuasion	Jane Austen	1-59308-130-8	$5.95
Peter Pan	J. M. Barrie	1-59308-213-4	$4.95
The Phantom of the Opera	Gaston Leroux	1-59308-249-5	$6.95
The Picture of Dorian Gray	Oscar Wilde	1-59308-025-5	$4.95
The Pilgrim's Progress	John Bunyan	1-59308-254-1	$7.95
A Portrait of the Artist as a Young Man and Dubliners	James Joyce	1-59308-031-X	$6.95
The Possessed	Fyodor Dostoevsky	1-59308-250-9	$9.95
Pride and Prejudice	Jane Austen	1-59308-201-0	$5.95
The Prince and Other Writings	Niccolò Machiavelli	1-59308-060-3	$5.95
The Prince and the Pauper	Mark Twain	1-59308-218-5	$4.95
Pudd'nhead Wilson and Those Extraordinary Twins	Mark Twain	1-59308-255-X	$5.95
The Purgatorio	Dante Alighieri	1-59308-219-3	$7.95
Pygmalion and Three Other Plays	George Bernard Shaw	1-59308-078-6	$7.95
The Red Badge of Courage and Selected Short Fiction	Stephen Crane	1-59308-119-7	$4.95
Republic	Plato	1-59308-097-2	$6.95
The Return of the Native	Thomas Hardy	1-59308-220-7	$7.95
Robinson Crusoe	Daniel Defoe	1-59308-360-2	$5.95
A Room with a View	E. M. Forster	1-59308-288-6	$5.95
Scaramouche	Rafael Sabatini	1-59308-242-8	$6.95
The Scarlet Letter	Nathaniel Hawthorne	1-59308-207-X	$5.95
The Scarlet Pimpernel	Baroness Orczy	1-59308-234-7	$5.95
The Secret Agent	Joseph Conrad	1-59308-305-X	$6.95
The Secret Garden	Frances Hodgson Burnett	1-59308-277-0	$5.95
Selected Stories of O. Henry		1-59308-042-5	$5.95
Sense and Sensibility	Jane Austen	1-59308-125-1	$5.95
Siddhartha	Hermann Hesse	1-59308-379-3	$5.95

(continued)

Silas Marner and Two Short Stories	George Eliot	1-59308-251-7	$6.95
Sister Carrie	Theodore Dreiser	1-59308-226-6	$7.95
The Souls of Black Folk	W. E. B. Du Bois	1-59308-014-X	$5.95
The Strange Case of Dr. Jekyll and Mr. Hyde and Other Stories	Robert Louis Stevenson	1-59308-131-6	$4.95
Swann's Way	Marcel Proust	1-59308-295-9	$8.95
A Tale of Two Cities	Charles Dickens	1-59308-138-3	$5.95
Tarzan of the Apes	Edgar Rice Burroughs	1-59308-227-4	$5.95
Tess of d'Urbervilles	Thomas Hardy	1-59308-228-2	$7.95
This Side of Paradise	F. Scott Fitzgerald	1-59308-243-6	$6.95
Three Theban Plays	Sophocles	1-59308-235-5	$6.95
Thus Spoke Zarathustra	Friedrich Nietzsche	1-59308-278-9	$7.95
The Time Machine and The Invisible Man	H. G. Wells	1-59308-388-2	$6.95
Tom Jones	Henry Fielding	1-59308-070-0	$8.95
Treasure Island	Robert Louis Stevenson	1-59308-247-9	$4.95
The Turn of the Screw, The Aspern Papers and Two Stories	Henry James	1-59308-043-3	$5.95
Twenty Thousand Leagues Under the Sea	Jules Verne	1-59308-302-5	$5.95
Uncle Tom's Cabin	Harriet Beecher Stowe	1-59308-121-9	$7.95
Vanity Fair	William Makepeace Thackeray	1-59308-071-9	$7.95
The Varieties of Religious Experience	William James	1-59308-072-7	$7.95
Villette	Charlotte Brontë	1-59308-316-5	$7.95
The Virginian	Owen Wister	1-59308-236-3	$7.95
Walden and Civil Disobedience	Henry David Thoreau	1-59308-208-8	$5.95
War and Peace	Leo Tolstoy	1-59308-073-5	$12.95
The War of the Worlds	H. G. Wells	1-59308-362-9	$5.95
Ward No. 6 and Other Stories	Anton Chekhov	1-59308-003-4	$7.95
The Waste Land and Other Poems	T. S. Eliot	1-59308-279-7	$4.95
The Way We Live Now	Anthony Trollope	1-59308-304-1	$9.95
The Wind in the Willows	Kenneth Grahame	1-59308-265-7	$4.95
The Wings of the Dove	Henry James	1-59308-296-7	$7.95
Wives and Daughters	Elizabeth Gaskell	1-59308-257-6	$7.95
The Woman in White	Wilkie Collins	1-59308-280-0	$7.95
Women in Love	D. H. Lawrence	1-59308-258-4	$8.95
The Wonderful Wizard of Oz	L. Frank Baum	1-59308-221-5	$6.95
Wuthering Heights	Emily Brontë	1-59308-128-6	$5.95

BARNES & NOBLE CLASSICS

If you are an educator and would like to receive an
Examination or Desk Copy of a Barnes & Noble Classics edition,
please refer to Academic Resources on our website at
WWW.BN.COM/CLASSICS
or contact us at
BNCLASSICS@BN.COM

All prices are subject to change.